# THE FOUR HEADLESS HORSEMEN OF THE APOCALYPSE APOLOGIZE

A novel by Theo Michelfeld

*****

The Problem We All Live With is a 1964 oil painting by
Norman Rockwell.

*****

ISBN: 9798730934689

# THE FOUR
# HEADLESS HORSEMEN
# OF THE APOCALYPSE
# APOLOGIZE

# TABLE OF CONTENTS

BOOK I. NIMROD.................................................................1

1. The Sky Ray .............................................................3
2. Junior ....................................................................8
3. The Piano................................................................12
4. The Third Thank You ...............................................15
5. Ix-nay on the An-may .............................................19
6. Baby Elephant Walk................................................23
7. The Wilson Rumors.................................................28
8. Insult Comedy ........................................................33
9. Grand Union...........................................................35
10. Pete Dawson's Basement .......................................41
11. The Black-and-White Dance....................................46
12. An Unsettled Mind ................................................48
13. Resentment Entirely...............................................50
14. Blue Dog...............................................................52
15. A Racist Joke.........................................................55
16. Aaron Law.............................................................58
17. The Church in Avaris .............................................63
18. The Nova...............................................................67
19. Self-Determination, or Whatever it Is .....................70
20. Water Land............................................................73
21. The Conversation King ..........................................76
22. The Retreat ........................................................... 88
23. The Compound......................................................93
24. That There is Cash Clarick ....................................103

BOOK II. THE SAW MILL ............................................. 123

25. Steeplejack.......................................................... 125
26. Nimrod & FuckFace .............................................. 129
27. Steam Donkey......................................................131
28. Nothing but Class ................................................134
29. The First Trip to Town ..........................................136
30. Couples Counseling with Cash Clarick...................141
31. Lou Gannon's Wife ............................................... 145
32. Couples Counseling: Second Session .................... 149
33. The Silo...............................................................151
34. Couples Counseling: Third Session ....................... 153
35. The Second or Third Trip to Town ......................... 155
36. Couples Counseling: Final Session........................ 156
37. The Third or Fourth Trip to Town ......................... 160
38. Sneaky Sonofabitch.............................................. 162
39. The Rite .............................................................. 165
40. Solstice ...............................................................171
41. Out of Them Ashes .............................................. 197
42. Sabotage! ........................................................... 202

43. Pole Position ........................................................ 206
44. Night Soil .......................................................... 221
45. The Heist ........................................................... 229

**BOOK III. THE CASTLE** ....................................... **241**

46. J.R. vs Dr. Arquimedes Arthur ................................. 243
47. The Auto Yard ...................................................... 258
48. The Watchtower .................................................... 268
49. Tyto the Owl ....................................................... 279
50. Lawn Billiards ..................................................... 284
51. The Feast .......................................................... 292
52. Haircut Day ........................................................ 308
53. The Nova Revisited ................................................ 314
54. The Star-Spangled Gremlin ........................................ 318
55. Live at Five ....................................................... 321
56. It's Called Poetry ................................................ 324
57. Origami ............................................................ 330
58. Power and Action .................................................. 343
59. Canada Geese ....................................................... 346
60. Love in the Belly of the Posse Umbellus ......................... 352
61. Chandelier Interlude .............................................. 356
62. Breakfast with Farrah ............................................. 370
63. The Bucket of Acid ................................................ 376

**BOOK IV: THE PROBLEM WE ALL LIVE WITH** .............**403**

64. The Ballad of Curtis Lemonhall ................................... 405
65. The Old Man's Valediction ......................................... 422
66. The Antique Naked-Lady Cigarette Case ............................ 438
67. Oklahoma City ...................................................... 471
68. Denver ............................................................. 476
69. Little Rock ........................................................ 478
70. Louisville ......................................................... 482
71. Cincinnati ......................................................... 486
72. Westsylvania ....................................................... 490
73. Richmond ........................................................... 495
74. Jersey ............................................................. 499
75. Blue Quarry ........................................................ 501
76. Florida ............................................................ 506
77. Pete Dawson's Basement Revisited ................................. 512
78. Malta Street ....................................................... 519

# DEDICATION

A few years ago, I had a steady gig as the guitarist for a local church. It was a modest paycheck, but a pious musician would have done the job for free.

Services took place in the gymnasium of a defunct elementary school that my mother fought for years to keep open. Her name was Kay, and she was the local school board president for a good portion of my youth. I could pay Kay Michelfeld no higher compliment than to call her a champion of public education, although she was many other things, with many other accomplishments to her name, and many other attributes as a person.

There is a plaque bearing her name, among other names, hanging in the hallway of the long-embattled school building. In my role as church guitarist, I would encounter this tribute to my mother's legacy on a weekly basis.

Services tended to leave me in a generous and loving spirit, and so I got the idea for a novel about school board intrigue, whose protagonist would be a fabled former school board president coming out of retirement to defend the public education system one last time.

Well, I couldn't make that novel work, odd as that may sound here in 2021. Instead, I wrote a subplot, a backstory, set in the 1980s, about a boy who dropped out of school, ran away from home, and got abducted by neo-Nazis.

My father's name was Ted Michelfeld. He was an educator, and a writer, and like my mother he has many accomplishments to his name, and many dimensions as a person. Among these, he moonlighted as a comp-lit professor of science fiction. He had a fascination for storytelling, particularly genre fiction, and as a boy I embraced this heritage with rather more enthusiasm than my mother's non-fictional volunteer work ever managed to inspire.

All these decades later, I know better than to elevate one legacy over the other, regardless of which comes naturally to me. With this novel I hope to honor both my mother's belief in the power of public education, and my father's belief in the power of storytelling. This book is for them, with gratitude, and faith in their wisdom.

# BOOK I. NIMROD

# 1. The Sky Ray

It was J.R.'s idea to transplant the '54 Skylark steering wheel onto the Sting-Ray bicycle. His father's response was predictable: "No, J.R. Dumb idea."

"It's just for fun, Dad... Daddio. Why aren't you fun anymore?"

His mother scolded him, "Junior!"

Janice came to his defense, "Don't call him that, Mom."

Jack Daddio ignored them all and returned to his newspaper.

Sunday mornings tended to lag into Sunday afternoons, which didn't usually bother J.R., since his father worked tirelessly to provide for his family, and such a man deserved his one morning off per week, even if he remained on call, always, for an emergency tow.

By comparison, his mother and sister were relentlessly irritating, with their stern disapproval of one thing, or cheerful contentment with another thing, or whatever girly impact they sought to contribute to the kitchen table and society at large here in the company of men who actually worked. At least Janice kept her mitts off the piano for a few exquisite hours of peace and let her father commune with his *New York Post*.

Meanwhile, the '54 Skylark steering wheel was down at the garage, mounted on the wall and collecting dust with a bunch of old license plates and road signs and other relics. Anyone could see it deserved better.

"You don't even remember where you got it."

Jack Daddio peered out from behind his newspaper. "That's because I'm not sentimental."

J.R.'s vision—the one he could not unsee—was of a bike he could call the *Sky Ray*. Unfortunately, this was too complex and refined a notion for certain zoo animals in present company. He had to stoop to their level, as usual, to explain things. "Come on, Dad. I don't care if it works. I just want to try it."

Jack Daddio shook his head. "Think about it, Junior. You won't have the range of motion steering."

"I'll steer like a bus driver. Hey, what are you calling me Junior for?"

Janice chimed in again, "Don't call him that, Dad."

"We're doing this," J.R. said.

His persistence would win the day. After brunch, he and his father took the Lemon Peeler Stingray down to the garage. They agreed that the gear lever would have to be repositioned, and the brake levers and cables would have to be freed from the handlebars and reaffixed to the steering wheel. J.R. measured out these modifications first, before taking action. Then, with his father's help, he taped down the cables and wrenched the brake levers into place upside down, not at 10-and-2 but at 8-and-4, where his hands would go.

When it was done, he climbed onto the banana seat and gripped the Buick steering wheel. Clutching up at the brake levers, he wobbled a couple of times, then got himself pedaling. However, he could not spin the wheel, and this was because of the brake cables. Exactly the problem his father had foreseen.

"This isn't over," he wheeled the *Sky Ray* back to Jack Daddio in waiting.

He needed coaster brakes and a replacement hub. *Wheelies!* in South Milford was already closed, so they drove up to *Cycle Forward* in Middletown.

"Kid, do me a favor and don't touch that," the clerk said. She was a lady wearing a blue bandana. Tough looking, weather beaten, leaning her hard elbow on the counter.

J.R. didn't like her tone. He said, "I came here to buy this, lady. I saved up for it."

"If you can pay for it, that's a different story."

"I saved up for it," he repeated. "And I can install it myself, too. Unlike you probably can."

"I've installed a million of those, young man. Listen, maybe *your father* would like to... umm..."

J.R. looked back over his shoulder.

Jack Daddio did a double take, looked back over his own shoulder, then back at the lady. "Father?" he feigned bewilderment. "Lady, that is not my kid."

J.R. played along, "Yeah, what makes you think that's my father, lady? I don't even know who that asshole is."

Everyone in the cycle store laughed at the lady clerk. J.R. tried for a ten percent discount but didn't get it. He had the part, though.

He met up with his father in the parking lot, and they exchanged no words or glances as they crossed to the car. Getting in from either side, they closed the doors in unison, and allowed another deadpan moment to pass in silence. Then they burst out laughing.

J.R. enjoyed the moment of levity with his father, but he also had something to say.

"See? Swearing doesn't always make you sound stupid."

"All right," Jack Daddio keyed the ignition. His laughter petered out.

Halfway home, he said, "I'm proud of you, son. Telling that lady off. I'll tell you. No brains and bad manners. You better hope there are some real women left in the world by the time you're old enough. It's your world to inherit, Junior. Don't forget that."

"Dad? What are you calling me Junior for?"

Jack Daddio turned and smiled. "What? You can call me asshole? But I can't call you Junior?"

J.R. laughed a little, got control of it. "Eyes on the road," he told his father.

Back home, parked in the driveway, Jack Daddio pointed a finger and said, "Listen. Do not tell your mother I let you get away with that mouth up at *Cycle Forward.*"

"OK. What about Janice? Can I tell Janice?"

"Only if you want to be dead," Jack Daddio raised an eyebrow and held it there. Like a real threat, as if.

The next morning, down at the garage, J.R. completed the bike modifications. If this worked, it would be a triumphant day. He wheeled the *Sky Ray* out into the parking lot and mounted. With the brake cables gone he could rotate the steering wheel, spinning it this way and that, underhand.

"Well done!" his father watched from the open bay.

"Backpedaling the brakes is easier too."

"That's right!"

J.R. wheeled in lowrider figure-8s around the lot, then levered the *Stik-Shift* and spun the bike onto Malta Street, where the strange and beautiful *Sky Ray* received attention immediately. A man and woman stopped holding hands and pointed in unison. A group of kids on the railroad tracks took notice, and one of them cried, "HEY, LOOK AT THAT THING!"

J.R. was victorious. He wheeled the bike back into Daddio's lot where his father waited. "Let's try a wheelie!" He grabbed the steering wheel overhand and raised the bike skyward on its heel. Backpedaling to brake, he bounced twice on the shock absorbers, then dropped the front wheel and pedaled away.

"I got work. See ya, J.R.!"

"SEE YA!" he pedaled off toward town. Crouching to reduce his drag, he turned the corner onto Spruce Street. A voice from a creeping station wagon shouted, "HEY, J.R.! COOL BIKE!" It was Mr. Carter's wife, leaning out the passenger's side window.

"THANKS!" he stopped, reached and popped a wheelie, watched her grin from her car window. He felt like a cowboy on a stallion. On his way, he was ecstatic almost to the point of delirium as sunshine flickered through the passing trees. It was possibly the greatest moment of his life. Another group of kids catching sight of him shouted gleefully. He waved back at them.

Where Spruce Street ascended, he reduced his speed and scaled to its apex. For a moment he paused, with the steering wheel cradled in his upturned hands. Levering the *Stik-Shift* he rolled the bike forward into the descent toward Main Street. He jumped up onto the sidewalk and landed where the paving stones buckled like a crooked staircase downward. It was strange and challenging work, wheeling underhand while pitching forward.

Spotting a group of girls playing Hopscotch, he abandoned his cautious descent, popped a wheelie on his rear tire and held it. Then, raised up precariously, he began to trundle down the paving stones, pedaling and backpedaling to maintain balance, just like he would with any other bike, except newly equipped with his vintage '54 Skylark steering wheel. Gradually, the course rose conquered behind him, and he crashed the front tire down in triumph. Then he coasted forward on his bizarre yellow bike with chrome fenders and front forks that gleamed in the sunshine.

The girls watched the *Sky Ray's* approach. Arriving before them, he hauled up the bike for another wheelie, and while the back tire danced on its shocks, he hooked the steering wheel by an index finger and spun the front tire gimballed like a gyroscope.

"Show off!" said the girl with the chalk.

That night, he lay on his bed with a tremendous sense of power flowing through his spirit. He was still just a kid, he knew that. And yet today he had caught a glimpse of the man he would become. Today he had foreseen his future.

The moonlit wall posters affirmed him by their company. The U.S. Presidents. The Viking warriors. An enormous, detailed map of the United States. Mickey Mantle, in pinstripes, swinging for the fences. In a solemn place where his dreams, inspiration and willpower comingled, he drifted off to sleep.

## 2. Junior

He was on the books, depositing paychecks instead of cash, so now the bank wouldn't accept his usual signature. A manager came out to explain it to him. Going forward, he would have to sign his name *Junior* instead of *J.R.*

It was no use arguing. The system, as always, was stacked against him. He marched out of the bank, mounted his bike and rode back to the garage.

"J.R., DO NOT EVER BITCH TO ME ABOUT YOUR NAME AGAIN!"

"But dad, you even said—"

"DO YOU HEAR ME?"

"You even said..." J.R. kept his own voice low, to demonstrate his comparative calmness. His father was always so coolheaded up in a deer stand, and yet so quick to boil over here in the real world. "You even said my coveralls would say J.R."

"I SWEAR TO GOD, I'M GOING TO PUT YOUR HEAD THROUGH THAT WALL!"

"Yeah right," J.R. let it go.

A week or so later, he took a different approach. "I need a checking account, dad."

"You should be saving your money."

"I am. But dad. They punish me for taking it out."

"Right. That's the idea."

They were seated in the office after work. Jack Daddio's coveralls bore the oval name patch *Jack,* stitched in cursive.

J.R. wore a plain T-shirt and blue jeans, like usual. The conversation was going as planned, more or less. J.R. leaned forward and said, "OK, well. But what if I want to upgrade my bike?"

His father shrugged. "Well, then, you come talk to me. I can always give you an advance out of petty cash."

"You want me taking hundreds of dollars out of petty cash?"

"Hundreds of dollars? No, J.R. Twenty dollars."

"OK. So what if something costs more than twenty dollars?"

"Well, then, you come talk to me."

"And what if something costs exactly twenty dollars, and I don't have your twenty dollars of petty cash on me?"

"Plan ahead better."

"You just want to control me."

"Stop it."

"You're just like mom."

"Hey!" Jack Daddio smacked his hand down on the desktop.

J.R. observed, for the millionth time, the depths of phony goodwill etched into his father's beleaguered face. *I'm going to inherit that face if I'm not careful,* he told himself.

He then observed the invoices and work-orders, the duplicates in yellow and pink and white, the catalogs opened and closed, all of which reminded him, *This crap is my birthright too.*

"You want a checking account?" His father broke the silence.

"Yes. Dad. What have I just been saying?"

"All right."

"Really?"

"Yes, really. We'll go tomorrow."

"OK. But dad. Daddio. There's one more thing."

Jack Daddio cocked his head, unsuspecting. This was the number one thing J.R. refused to inherit from his father. Never to be this gullible.

"My name."

"Goddammit."

"No wait."

"Goddammit, J.R."

"Think about it, dad. You even said. In fact, you *promised.* All I'm saying—"

"You faker," Jack Daddio muttered. He closed his fist and pressed his knuckle into his own eye socket. "You fucking faker..."

"My checking account!" J.R. protested. "It should be in the same name as my name patch! Think about it!"

"I am going to kill you!"

"That's all I'm saying. My savings account, too. I'll even pay for it."

"Get out of my office!"

"It was *your mistake,*" J.R. went back to the old refrain. "All you have to do is correct *your mistake!*"

"GET OUT OF MY GARAGE! GET OUT OF MY SIGHT!"

"Don't bother. I was just leaving."

Back at home, lying on his bed and repeatedly, rhythmically tossing a baseball up in the air to catch it, J.R. found himself considering his wall posters from a new perspective. The images were always available to him, ingrained in his imagination, so that he could visualize them without looking, or maybe especially without looking, with his hand-eye coordination otherwise occupied.

Tonight, a new and ominous quality emerged from the color they lent his daily disposition and worldview. The triumphant Mickey Mantle, number seven. The immortal United States Presidents arranged in thirty-nine oval frames. The fifty United States with their complex network of numerated highways and mythical cities. The pair of Viking warriors battling savage hordes in the snow. Only now could he see it. The Americana was nice. Sentimental. But the Viking poster was ten times more mature, more vital, more inspiring.

The bedroom door opened.

"Thanks for knocking," he maintained his rhythm with the pitch and catch.

"Listen. Son. Stop. Stop tossing that baseball."

He caught it, clutched it, looked over at his father in the doorway.

"Listen to me."

"I am listening."

"Let's say we do change your name. And then let's say there's an emergency. I'm talking about a medical emergency. And let's say there's some mix-up. All because of your name."

"Gimme a break."

"No. I'm your father. I'm responsible for you."

"That's the best you can do?"

10

"Listen—"

"Dad, that would that never happen."

"I knew you were going to say that. Because only a kid would say that."

J.R. waited, baseball in hand, trying to formulate a response. It was the system. It would always be the system. The system was stacked against him. And his father would always refuse to help.

"J.R., you're a twelve-year-old kid. I've got you driving around in my company truck." Jack Daddio loomed in silhouette. "I'm all in with you, man. A simple thank you will suffice."

J.R. stared at his father's shadow. There would be no thank you, simple or otherwise. Backing down would be concession enough.

"So I'm stuck with this name until I turn eighteen?"

"I'm sorry your life isn't perfect."

J.R. laughed a little, turned his gaze upward. "No, Daddio. It is. It's perfect."

"That's what I like to hear."

"All except my name."

"I'm sorry for yelling."

"Don't worry. We're still friends."

## 3. The Piano

He could have dropped out of school to work full time at the garage, but his father wouldn't let him.

For this argument, he waited, with perfect timing, for a family sit-down. The new piano they bought for Janice had arrived today. There was even a ceremony, of sorts, with musical arrangements by you-know-who, as the dumb old piano got carted out the door. Janice was eager to prove, over and over, that the so-called action and so-called pitch was a game changer. But J.R. knew afterwards what he already knew beforehand. That one piano was no different from the next. A massive box of clamor and whimsy and drama.

With his little sister's career all taken care of, he made his own case for dropping out of school. Predictably, his father said no.

"Listen, dad. You say it all the time. You said it just the other day. I would be a professional mechanic by now, if only the entire system wasn't stacked against me."

"I said rigged, not stacked. I know what I said. I wish you were allowed."

"Don't blame your father."

J.R. shot his mother a scowl. She lowered her eyes. The table fell silent.

In that space, Janice's always inane two cents found their inevitable self-expression. "I can't wait for school tomorrow!"

"I don't blame you, dad." J.R. pressed on. "I blame the State, and the Public Education System."

Jack Daddio smiled around at his family. "That sounds about right."

"OK. So why are you on their side?"

"Whoa."

"Face it."

"Watch your mouth."

"You're on their side. You're one of them."

Jack Daddio set down his steak knife and pointed his finger. "You want me pissed off? Now I'm pissed off."

"Jack!"

"What would you call that whole summer?" Jack Daddio turned to his wife, aiming his thumb over his shoulder. "Mary, what would you call that whole summer your kid spent doing?"

"Jack, please just watch your language."

"I would call it *learning a trade*. That's what I would call it."

J.R. sighed. "That's my whole point, dad."

"This one gets a piano," Jack Daddio jabbed his thumb sideways at Janice. Then he aimed his forefinger at his son. "This one gets a way of life!"

J.R. fell quiet. Another argument lost.

"Don't everybody thank me at once."

"Thank you for the piano, Daddy!"

"You're welcome, sweetheart," Jack Daddio smiled at his daughter. He winked at her, then heaved a sigh.

*"Ticked off,"* Mary Daddio advised. "Jack, you can say *ticked off* instead."

Her husband nodded wearily, forked in a bite of food. They all waited while he chewed. "Heck, Mary," he said, pausing to gulp from his glass of beer. "Last week, your kid did a complete repair on Mayor Moore's drive axle."

"Lefty Moore," J.R. said quietly.

"And it was a job well done, let me add that."

"Lefty Moore."

"Not to mention Dr. Daniels. You know Dr. Daniels, Mary—"

"Lefty Moore," J.R. repeated. "Lefty Moore. Dad, those are your exact words."

Janice said, "I don't know Dr. Daniels."

"Dr. Daniels," Jack Daddio turned to his daughter, "is a famous surgeon down in the city."

"He's not famous," J.R. could barely keep up with his father's lies.

"He told me personally how J.R. was very professional with the tow truck."

"He's not famous!"

"He's *renowned!*" Jack Daddio snapped. "Is that OK with you?"

J.R. shrugged.

"I thought you liked Dr. Daniels. What's wrong with you?"

"Nothing. I didn't say I don't like him. You said he was famous. But he's not famous."

Mary Daddio changed the subject, "Don't forget about Mike Aaron."

"That's right. Mike Aaron. Muffler job."

"Your father is making good points, J.R."

"What would you call that, Mary?"

"I would say we have two talented kids," she answered.

"I tell you what I would call it. I would call it a *paid apprenticeship.*"

"More like child exploitation," J.R. countered.

"That's not funny."

"It wasn't a joke."

"It better be a joke, Junior!"

The dinner table fell silent. Even Janice's prodigious bubble of blithe indifference evaporated. She sat wide-eyed and anxious over her dinner plate.

J.R. stared at the piano with its fallboard down. The amount his parents owed him was incalculable, but it would now include the weight, square footage and price tag of a brand-new piano. He broke his silence. "Why do I even bother? Janice gets a whole piano. I can't even have my own name."

"Oh, that reminds me. You can forget about your name patch."

"Oh, that reminds me. I already did."

## 4. The Third Thank You

The pistol shots from the junkyard did not go unnoticed by Erving's Finest. When the squad car rolled up, J.R. stood brandishing his father's Smith & Wesson, while several rats lay strewn around the outskirts, killed by gunfire. It was Officer Shields on patrol, offering a thumbs up, followed by a friendly wave before driving off.

J.R. was left to consider such local privileges and connections, and whether perhaps he should stick around. Currently, his plan was to leave Erving, New York the day he turned sixteen.

When he was done shooting rats, he pedaled for home into a bitter winter wind. At one point, Mayor Moore drove up alongside in his GMC Jimmy and called out the window, "Junior Daddio! Very cool bike!"

"Thank you," J.R. immediately regretted saying it. Mayor Moore, in addition to being a communist and a thief, knew better than to address Jack Daddio's kid as *Junior*. He muttered into the headwind, "I'll thank you for retiring. That's what I should have said."

The next day, after work, he confronted his father, "Why do you fraternize with the enemy, dad?"

"Who's that?"

"Lefty Moore."

"What? Mayor Moore?"

"That's right."

15

"What do you want me to do? Turn away customers over their politics?"

"He's taking money out of our pockets. That's a direct quote from you."

"OK, smart guy. What would you do? If you were in charge?"

"In charge of what?"

"Of Daddio's Garage?"

"What would I do?"

"That's right. Let's hear it."

"Are you serious?"

"Serious. Yes. Let's hear it."

J.R. sighed, relaxed, hung his hands on his hips. "Well..." He surveyed the area, peered back over his shoulder. "The first thing I would do is put a vending machine, or two, in the waiting area. But longer term, I'd be thinking about that deli..." he pointed out the window, "which is nothing more than a kiosk if you ask me. But it's soaking up a ton of our growth."

"No, J.R."

"Like a tick. Or a leach."

"I'm talking about the mayor. You're going to be in charge of this garage someday. What are you going to do about the mayor?"

"Dad, jeez."

"What?"

"I would probably just overbill him."

Jack Daddio lowered his head.

"As compensation. For picking my pocket."

"Wrong answer."

"Well, then. Don't put me in charge."

The next day, he pedaled back to the junkyard with the Smith & Wesson. He waited and waited, locked and loaded, but the rats had wised up, maybe.

Then the snow started falling. He was miles from home. He tucked away the revolver and scrambled the *Sky Ray* out onto Erving Turnpike.

The Buick steering wheel seemed to help, or promised to, here and there. However, in time he was forced to dismount and trundle the bike's useless carcass along Erving Turnpike's snow-battered shoulder. His sneakers and cuffs began to freeze his feet. At last, a car was coming. He looked back over his shoulder.

It was the mayor again, calling, "Junior Daddio! Good timing! Let's get you into town!"

The Blazer pulled over. The mayor got out. The two of them tossed the *Sky Ray's* mortal remains into the back. J.R. then climbed into the passenger seat for transport.

"Mayor Moore, thank you," he said. That was twice now, after being called *Junior* twice.

"You're welcome," the mayor said, climbing in from the other side.

"Let's go to my father's garage, instead of home."

"You got it."

"He probably needs my help."

"Roger that."

*Two times is too many. There will be no third thank you,* J.R. tried to come up with something to say. The loaded handgun in his possession was not something to disclose. He said, "You and my dad get along."

"Yeah, well," the mayor answered, "you and him, too."

The arrogance, the smugness, seemed so small. A certain satisfaction came over J.R. Daddio as he stared out the window at the falling snow.

In that silence, the mayor probed for information, "So let me ask you something."

"What?"

"Did that steering wheel help in the snow, or make it harder?"

He would have to stay sharp. The extent of his courtesy was exhausted, but he would refuse to spill anything personal. He said, "You mean the bike?"

"Yes."

"The bike is useless."

All he had to do was keep the mayor off balance between here and the garage.

"Well, I think your father raised a first-class prodigy."

J.R. shook his head gently.

"Not just because you fixed my car," Mayor Moore continued. "I mean. It's what you did with that bike—"

"The bike didn't work."

When they arrived at the garage the tow truck was absent, meaning Buddy was out rescuing somebody. Jack Daddio was alone in the bay to welcome the mayor and thank him for delivering young Junior Daddio and his useless *Sky Ray* bicycle back to civilization.

"I told him I think he's a prodigy," the mayor confessed.

Jack Daddio was smiling. "He'd better be."

"I need a car," J.R. said, to no one who would listen.

"Junior," his father delivered the final insult. "The mayor just called you a prodigy. That's a nice compliment."

With no better option, J.R. answered, "Yes."

"Yes?" his father wasn't happy about it.

Mayor Moore was easygoing, with a friendly smile for both of them as he left. "You're welcome, young man."

"What's wrong with you?" Jack Daddio pleaded.

"Nothing. I thanked him twice. That's all he gets."

"What?"

"Is he robbing from us or not?"

"J.R.?"

"Have you not said those exact words?"

"It's just..." Jack Daddio ceded the argument.

*That's because he knows I'm right,* J.R. told himself. He hauled his wretched *Sky Ray* into the bay, tucked the cold Smith & Wesson into the desk drawer, removed his wet socks from his bare feet, laced up his Red Wing boots, and congratulated himself that he had won. There had been no third thank you.

## 5. Ix-nay on the An-may

Winter was over, and the final year of middle school entered its home stretch. Sometimes, from the so-called playing field's muddy turf, he would stare up the hill at the high school, where supposed academic advancement awaited. He could see that it was not only the Federal Government and not only the State of New York and not only the Town of Erving and not only the Public Education System but the landscape itself... all tilted against him. Laid out that way on purpose, tempting him to gaze up from one prison and long for another.

On his thirteenth birthday, he went to school, endured all of that, went home for his bike, then pedaled down to the garage for work. Buddy had gone home so there was plenty to do. First, he would take care of Dr. Daniels, who had requested J.R.'s personal attention to his Olds Toronado.

When Dr. Daniels arrived, the garage was closed, so Jack Daddio let him in through the bay. J.R.'s *Sky Ray* was parked inside. Upon seeing it, the doctor remarked, "That bike. That thing is so nifty, J.R. Don't ever sell it."

"Oh," J.R. smiled politely at the doctor's bad advice. "OK."

Jack Daddio announced, "It's my son's birthday."

"Oh yeah? How old?"

"Jeez, dad. No one cares."

"Thirteen."

"Thirteen? When's the bar mitzvah?"

19

"I'm not..." J.R. started to say, but they were already laughing at him.

They were both Vietnam vets, an army doctor and a motor pool guy. Not that they ever served together. Even nowadays they didn't pal around, hardly ever. But they shared that bond, reserved only for those who had been there and lived to tell about it. J.R. was willing and able to understand this about his father, and about the previous generation in general. Just as long as they didn't dwell on it, and use it to exclude everybody.

"Don't worry," Dr. Daniels addressed J.R.'s near-confession. "Nobody's perfect. All I mean to say is *Mazel Tov.*"

J.R. summoned his bleakest smirk. "Thanks."

"Actually, I think a drink is called for."

"I don't drink."

"Not yesterday, you didn't. But today, you're a man."

Jack Daddio interjected, "Please."

"What?"

"He can have a drink," Jack Daddio agreed, and then drawing a fingernail across his own throat, he added, "but ix-nay on the an-may."

"I'm not saying he's bar mitzvah material," the doctor confirmed, removing a flask from his jacket pocket and raising an eyebrow. "But one schnapps..."

Jack Daddio turned to his son. "J.R. you can have one drink. One. And you're not allowed to like it."

"One schnapps," the doctor concluded.

There were only two chairs, so the doctor claimed a corner of the desk. J.R. had never tried alcohol before. He didn't even want to. But he wasn't about to admit it, or chicken out. They went with paper Dixie-cups from the water cooler.

"Straight down," his father advised. "Don't sip."

The doctor raised a forefinger, seemed intent to argue, then thought better of it. "If we had tumblers," he reasoned, "and ice... It would be different."

J.R. shot the schnapps down and waited a very short and clipped interim. His upper body convulsed. He gasped for air. He reeled in his chair, coughed, spasmed, lost control. It had no flavor. It was liquid fire. The men were laughing while his insides burned.

*Not much of a birthday present.* This and other nonsense spiraled up and down his brainstem.

Dr. Daniels was speaking. "It's really something, J.R. Just don't ever sell it. The bike. You understand?"

"What?"

"When you retire that bike, and you will, don't sell it. Put it in a museum or something."

"Museum? Museum of what?"

"The museum of nutty bikes," Jack Daddio chuckled.

"I'll tell you what..." His eyes were watering. His throat was seared.

"Be nice, J.R."

"I am..." he gasped, coughed.

"Be nice, for once."

"It's just... Hey, wait a minute. I am being nice."

"We're doing a second shot," Dr. Daniels announced.

"Not me," J.R. went for the water cooler. His father said, "Good."

"No, wait a minute?" the doctor objected.

"Are you kidding? Count me out. I did it. You saw me do it. I'm a man now. You said so yourself."

"Golly, he's right," the doctor turned to Jack Daddio. "On the ball, your kid."

Jack Daddio laughed without a trace of mirth. "I'm telling you. Don't encourage him."

After a second shot for the men, a new conversation began, this one intended to exclude J.R. but not excuse him. It was annoying. And yet, on his thirteenth birthday, in this cramped backroom office, with alcohol coursing through his bloodstream, he came to enjoy the new philosophical tone that was circulating, and he found himself listening intently.

Jack Daddio and Dr. Daniels were commiserating about their shared curse. How they had both tried to repair things, back then, instead of trying to destroy them. And how they were still trying to this day, while the world kept making such a mess of the difference.

"And for who?" Dr. Daniels awaited an answer.

J.R.'s imagination wandered, picturing the two of them back then, Vietnam altruists.

Jack Daddio offered only questions. "For Uncle Sam? Who screws you out of your benefits? And sends you home with nothing but paperwork?"

"Plus the twist ending," the doctor added, "where it turns out your whole country went leftist anyway."

"That is the sad truth."

"The sad truth followed by the bitter irony. That you were right all along. Fixing jeeps. Or in my case fixing bodies. I mean, what was it all for? Stop me when I'm off topic."

J.R. raised a toast with his Dixie-cup of water.

Dr. Daniels tilted his flask in return. "The whole point is to control you."

"It's like me," J.R. spoke at last, given the opportunity.

"Here we go," Jack Daddio warned, laced with just enough good humor.

J.R. ignored him. "Me?" he told Dr. Daniels. "I'm stuck with this name, Junior, until I turn eighteen."

"Also sad but true," the doctor agreed. "But look on the bright side, J.R. At least it's the perfect name for the jam you're in."

Afterwards, at home, tired and anxious from the alcohol and its diminishing effects, J.R. lay on his bed, surrounded by Mickey Mantle, Viking Warriors, and United States Presidents, trying in vain to unpeel the doctor's words, and whether they were meant as an insult, or just good advice.

## 6. Baby Elephant Walk

The Datsun wagon pulled into the garage, overheating. The owner went next door for a sandwich. J.R. popped the latch and sprung the cap. A spray of hot coolant shot off the hood and down his back. "GAH!" he cried.

"JUNIOR!"

"OH SHIT!"

He found himself hoping for some kind of permanent damage, but his father was spraying cold water on him, saying, "I gotcha..."

Seconds later, soaking wet, and having suffered no damage, he shouted, "I COULD HAVE OSHA CRACK DOWN ON THIS PLACE IN FIVE MINUTES!"

Jack Daddio began explaining, and J.R. knew, though he had momentarily forgotten, to squeeze the hose and test the pressure before springing it.

"You don't have to tell him that NOW," Buddy laughed.

"Buddy! When I want your advice, I'll ask for it! J.R. where are you going?"

J.R. mounted his bike.

"J.R.?" Buddy pleaded. "Are you for real? We need you, bub!"

He said nothing, tore off, never looked back.

The mistake with the coolant replayed in his head four or five times, until he forced it to stop. Along the way, he went to the bank, but they wouldn't let him in without a shirt.

Arriving at home to piano accompaniment—The Elephant Walk, or whatever Janice called it—he barged through the door and announced, "I'M GOING OUT TO SHOOT!"

"J.R?" his mother called from the kitchen.

The music stopped. Janice cried, "GROSS! WHAT HAPPENED TO YOUR SHIRT!"

Mary Daddio appeared, dishtowel in hand. "Junior!"

"No one wants to see your NIPPLES!"

"Where's your SHIRT?"

"It's at the GARAGE! In the TRASH! Covered with SLIME!"

"Go clean up—"

"What do you think I AM doing?!"

From upstairs, he could hear his mother lamenting to Janice, "He's always so *angry...*"

He took a shower. Instead of going out to shoot, he decided to run away from home. He finished showering, got dressed, and packed a backpack with a change of clothes, toothbrush and checkbook. He was ready. He was set. But he had nowhere to go.

At the dinner table, they all took their customary seats, with Jack Daddio ranting about J.R.'s unprofessional behavior at work. Meanwhile, the stereo was low, the same tape his mother always played during Janice's blessed downtime. "Lost in Love." "Pilot of the Airwaves." Songs like that. It was awful, but at least it wasn't Janice the pianist.

Listening to the so-called music, J.R. let his gaze find a comfortable respite, enjoying the couch and chair arrangement, the braided rug, the coffee table and table lamps, all of it hued in orange light and low angle shadows, although he knew he wouldn't miss this place, not really.

"If he got *burned*, though, Jack..." his mother protested.

Jack Daddio ignored her, pointed his fork again, "And don't give me that OSHA crap! No kid of mine cries to Uncle Sam about having to WORK!"

"I work," J.R. answered at last. "I got two bank accounts to prove it."

"And that's whether you work for me or ANYONE ELSE!"

Janice cheerfully sat up straight and announced, "I want you to know... that I have decided... that *Singin' in the Rain* is the best movie ever made!"

J.R. was not about to contemplate the workings of his sister's brain. Almost everyone else belonged to some species of barnyard animal, and yet Janice alone was some kind of all too human lunatic.

Jack Daddio was saying, "What do you think I do? When I get dinged at work? WALK HOME?" He turned to his wife. "What do you think I do, Mary? You think I close up shop? When I get a boo boo? And then what? Huh? Take us all to Burger King? Until we go broke? And lose the house? And live in a cardboard box? On the street? In an alley? In the rain? Like a litter of kittens? All because we didn't remember to check the stupid radiator hose? Before opening the stupid valve? That's just BRILLIANT!"

Mary Daddio smiled, beleaguered. "I think it would be nice if we didn't argue at the dinner table."

"This is a family!" Jack Daddio concluded, revealing his two empty hands. "That's exactly my point!"

J.R. watched his parents fluff their napkins almost simultaneously. The meal was standard. Chicken, spuds, peas and salad. Janice forked it down lazily, her eyes following her elders, her mind elsewhere.

Jack Daddio spoke, "So what you missed, J.R. And you should've been there..."

And then smiling, assuming all was well at his family communion, he began to recount his tale of the IBM computer salesman who had come by the shop at closing time to sell him a product he couldn't afford, just in case he wanted robots to infiltrate every aspect of his business, and take over his life, until ten years later, enslaved by robots, he would have no one to blame but himself.

"It's the future, Dad," J.R. told him. "You can't fight it. Believe me. The nerds in the computer room. At school. They're plotting to take over the whole effin' world."

He could see it now. His father was about to lose it.

"Oh, I love this song," Mary Daddio closed her eyes and lowered her head.

"Me too," Janice affirmed.

"*Effin'?*" Jack Daddio had chosen this one word, out of all the others, to fixate upon.

"*Love, so they say...*" Mary Daddio's singing voice began quavering along with the stereo. Janice began harmonizing, matching not only the intervals but the quavers.

J.R. tilted forward in his chair, while his mother and sister sang in his ear. "I'm just saying. If no one's gonna say it, I'll say it. We don't have to talk about it. Talk about whatever you want."

Jack Daddio withdrew. But the lid was just barely on.

*"Is a flower in the spring,"* the ladies sang in their female persuasion and lilting harmony. *"And a razor in the Autumn... By December you forgot him..."*

J.R. leaned back, smirking. "You don't know how to calm down, you know that, dad? Daddio? Not without a six point buck in front of you. Maybe if that computer salesman was a six point buck—"

"HEY!"

The ladies stopped singing.

"Come talk to me when you're a grown man, with a man's responsibilities. JESUS CHRIST!—"

"JACK!"

He threw down his napkin, stood up from the dinner table. "DON'T START WITH ME, MARY, HE'S YOUR KID TOO!"

She shook her head, bewildered. He went for the stereo, switched off the singer in mid heartbreak. The house was suddenly quiet. Into that void he shouted, "THANK YOU!"

He then returned to his seat, returned the napkin to his lap, sighed deeply. His family watched him. He picked up his fork and knife.

But instead of eating, he turned to J.R. and said, "Maybe if we could TALK at the dinner table instead of singing ROCK SONGS! Maybe if my own son would GROW UP for once in his life! Maybe if I wasn't raising a CRYBABY with no respect for ANYTHING! Maybe if my WIFE was more worried about THAT than my EFFIN' SWEARING! Maybe if I was raising a MAN instead of a JUVENILE EFFIN' DELINQUENT! To take over the EFFIN' FAMILY BUSINESS! That I BUILT with my own TWO EFFIN' HANDS! And maybe if AMERICA! Which was built by MEN! Men who WORKED! Wasn't getting DESTROYED! In ONE-ONE-HUNDREDTH the time! By EFFIN' CRYBABIES! Looking for EFFIN' HANDOUTS! And maybe if this whole country wasn't going straight to EFFIN' HELL—excuse my EFFIN' FRENCH—because no one takes responsibility for their EFFIN' ACTIONS! And everyone has a EFFIN' EXCUSE! Or a EFFIN' GRIEVANCE! Or some other EFFIN' REASON! To EFFIN' FREELOAD!"

They were all siting there stunned.

"And maybe if it didn't start with the GOVERNMENT!" he seemed to be winding down. "And spread down through the school... And infect every aspect of American life..."

"I never wanted any handouts," J.R. said quietly.

"We all love you, Daddy," Janice said. "We know you work hard."

"Well," he told them. "See that? At least I've got the piano player on my side." He lowered his eyes. His fork and knife still hovered over his chicken.

Janice said, "It's probably better with the music off."

"Probably... that's right... probably," Jack Daddio dug his utensils into his meal, forked some of it down.

J.R. hated sticking up for his sister, but he said it. "She actually likes you. And you can't even be nice to her."

Jack Daddio was chewing, chewing his meat. By the time he was done, the argument was over. He was defeated. He said no more. None of them did.

"I can't wait to leave," J.R. told them in the aftermath.

Mary Daddio lowered her head. Janice was chewing her food. Jack Daddio seemed adrift in some blissful state of rage.

"See?" J.R. said. "No one even cares."

"Don't leave, J.R.," Janice looked up at him earnestly.

He looked to his father. "Look at me, dad. Dad. Did you hear that? The piano player is on my side too."

But he knew otherwise.

Thinking it over, later that night, he came to understand that Janice was in on it with them. Maybe it wasn't her fault. Maybe she was just brainwashed like everybody else. She was probably sleeping peacefully in the other room, and would probably be the same happy, silly, well-behaved girl tomorrow morning, and for the rest of her life. She couldn't be trusted.

## 7. The Wilson Rumors

For one thing, auto shop was a joke. He was far more advanced than the so-called teacher, not to mention the idiots who actually had to take that class. After a week, he dropped it.

Even worse, the gym teacher was incompetent, corrupt, or likely both.

It made no difference on the first pitch of the game, which J.R. launched for a single into right.

It made no difference in the third inning either, when he tagged a 3-0 double through the gap, driving in a pair.

It was his next at bat. That's when the calls got shady.

The first pitch was close. "STRIKE! 0 and 1!"

He allowed it.

The next pitch curled well outside. "STRIKE TWO!"

He turned and faced his gym teacher. "Mr. Wilson, that pitch was ten feet outside!"

"0 and 2!"

"That ball was ten feet outside!"

The catcher threw the ball back to the mound. The so-called umpire said, "BATTER UP!"

"Batter up? I'm standing right here!"

*"Swing the bat, you pussy."* It was the catcher who said it. A split second later the ball struck his mitt.

"STRIKE THREE!"

"What?"

"YOU'RE OUTTA HERE!"

*"Sit down,"* it was the catcher again, squatting behind the plate, hidden behind his mask. This was one of the Wilson kids. Lane Wilson. Possibly Jordy Wilson. Possibly another Wilson. None of whom were related to the gym teacher, Mr. Wilson. The last name was just a coincidence, as far as he knew.

"Wait a minute..." he finally put it together.

"BATTER UP!" Mr. Wilson barked.

J.R. remained defiant at the plate. With the tip of his bat, he tapped the catcher's mitt. "Let me see the brand name on that glove."

"What? Why?" the Wilson kid was protesting even as he obediently turned it over to reveal the brand name. WILSON.

"THIS IS BULLSHIT!"

"YOU'RE OUTTA HERE!"

J.R. jabbed his bat at the tainted mitt, "I WANT AN INQUIRY!"

"SWEAR WORDS AREN'T ALLOWED!"

"I WANT AN INQUIRY!"

"THAT'S A 2:45 DETENTION! YOU WANT A 4:45? GO FOR IT!"

"HE SWORE FIRST!"

"4:45! SOLD TO THE HIGHEST BIDDER!"

J.R. flung down the bat, tore off his gear, ended his participation, proceeded to the locker room.

That night, he resolved to take down the Mickey Mantle poster. *The Mick,* curled eternally around that baggy pin-striped uniform, rendered in a kind of faded, yellowed, old-timey paint, and maybe aware or maybe not, to his dying day, that none of it ever mattered, slapping another easy home run for the sake of Polaroid Cameras and Valvoline Motor Oil, and rising player salaries, and counterculture ballplayers with left-ist leanings, which the boob tube in its eternal stupidity was all too happy to sell. For these reasons and more his father had vowed to stop watching professional baseball. And yet J.R. could hear it on the idiot box in the other room.

The next day, out in the courtyard, a short kid with a blonde mop of hair approached and asked, "Junior Daddio?"

"My name is J.R. Daddio."

The kid withdrew a notepad and pen from his back pocket and began scribbling.

"J dot, R dot. What are you doing?"

"I'm Eric August," the kid extended his puny hand. J.R. made sure not to break it when he shook it. He made sure to send the hand back un-mangled.

"I've been sent by *The Monitor,*" the kid explained. "Sports section."

"*The Monitor?* Sports section?"

"The school newspaper," Eric August explained.

"So you're in journalism class?"

"That's correct."

"Well you should say it like that."

The student journalist began scribbling again.

J.R. pointed to the kid's notepad and said, "Maybe if you're honest with people when you introduce yourself, they'll be more honest with you in an interview. And then you'll get better stories. And better grades. In journalism class."

It appeared Eric August was writing it all down.

J.R. was tall for his age, and he knew it. Just as he knew Eric August was short for his age. In fact, if Eric August proved to be a prankster from the middle school who had snuck up the hill to impersonate a high school reporter, it would not be surprising at all. On the other hand, the kid was so self-serious, with his notepad and pen, he had to be for real.

Looking up from his notes, Eric August continued, "A few people told me you were awesome yesterday. In gym class. I'm writing a story about it. And I wanted your input before I get started."

"You want to know if the rumors are true?"

"Which rumors?" Eric August had the pen set to paper. "The *Wilson* rumors?"

Reporters were notoriously mischievous little fuckers. J.R. folded his arms and studied Eric August further, as a nervousness began to creep into his stomach. Excitement too. To bully this kid. It was irresistible.

There were other kids present in the courtyard, following one path or another toward the nearest door. None of them were within earshot.

"Listen to me," he told the puny journalism student. "My name is J.R. Daddio. Not Junior Daddio. J.R. Daddio. If you print my name as Junior Daddio in the school newspaper, I am literally going to find you. And break your face."

Eric August held his pen still. He was staring up at J.R., wide-eyed, voiceless, mouth agape.

"Do you understand me?"

The kid's miniature Adam's apple visibly gulped. Gently, he pointed to his notepad and said, "That's what I wrote here."

"Fine. That's step one. Next step is to make sure your journalism teacher gets it right too. And your typesetter. And your editor."

"OK. I hear you."

"You don't think I know how it works?"

"I don't know how anything works."

"Good boy. So you'll probably be thanking me for the good advice someday."

Eric August inhaled through his translucent nostrils into his pint-sized lungs. He was a brave kid, on some maddening level. "So the rumors, J.R.?" he managed to ask. "Are they true?"

"How should I know? Rumors are your job."

"OK, I got it," Eric August lowered his eyes. He folded his notepad away.

"Did you get what you needed?"

"Yes," the kid spoke quietly. "Great stuff. Maybe even back page stuff."

J.R. cocked his head. "Are you being sarcastic with me?"

"No..." Eric August looked up, collecting his courage again. "Man, I know that crew of seniors that runs *The Monitor* are a bunch of sarcastic assholes."

This was news to J.R., but he allowed the journalist to continue spilling his guts.

"They think they're a bunch of satirists, or something. And granted, it's funny, sometimes. But it's not what I signed up for. I want to do actual journalism."

"OK," J.R. told him. "OK. That's good." The uneasiness for bullying the kid was beginning to twist his insides.

"I'm a freshman, like you," Eric August continued, brave and sincere beneath his blonde mop of hair. "It's not my fault things are the way they are."

"No, you're right."

"It's not my fault *The Monitor* is the way it is."

"You're right. That's right."

"So are you really going to break my face?"

"No..." J.R. was caught off guard even more so than before. Only now could he see how completely he had embarrassed himself.

"You're not going to break my face?"

"No. I'm sorry. That was—"

"I'm glad to hear it. Thank you for meeting with me."

J.R. was left standing alone in the courtyard.

Disgusted with himself, he could see that it was Jack Daddio's fault. This was what his father's refusal kept doing. The shame it kept bringing. The ways he had learned to predict it, but still never seemed to grasp how much more was due.

The system would not, must not, get the best of him. He would teach himself not to care. In five years' time, he would turn eighteen, and assume his own name, and put the resentment behind him.

Along the way, Janice started calling him Junior, which she never used to do, back when he cared. As if it had evolved, without his consent, into some term of endearment. She was no ally. Someday she would need his help, and he would refuse to be there for her, so that she could thank herself afterward.

# 8. Insult Comedy

Mr. Boaz brought his Impala wagon in for a transmission.

"Dad, this is Mr. Boaz," J.R. told his father, even though Mr. Boaz had just introduced himself. "He's from school. He's my teacher."

"Your math teacher," Jack Daddio said. "I got it."

"We'll take good care of your wagon," J.R. told his math teacher. "I'll see that it's done."

Mr. Boaz, with his circular glasses and bald head and thick black beard, offered a spare and expressionless, "Thank you. Thank you both."

After he was gone, Jack Daddio said, "Well done, J.R. You're starting to get it."

"Starting to get what?"

"Starting to get *it*. That this is your *community*."

"When did I not get *that?*"

Jack Daddio looked away and exhaled a long, loud sigh. "Never mind."

"Never mind what?"

"J.R., I don't have time... in my day... to make you accept a compliment."

But it wasn't a compliment. J.R. knew better. It was an insult. He wasn't *starting* to get it. Not *starting* to get it.

Mr. Boaz was ornery, and given to humiliating his students, which was one of the things J.R. liked about him.

One time, Michelle King raised her hand and asked, "Mr. Boaz, have you ever heard the expression, 'There are no such things as stupid questions?'"

To which Mr. Boaz replied, "There are stupid EXPRESSIONS though, and that's one of them."

Another time, Elaine Ross asked, "Can you run through that a little slower?"

To which Mr. Boaz replied, "I can WALK through it slower. But I can't RUN through it ANY slower."

No other teachers talked like that. J.R. laughed to himself about it.

He also liked the way Mr. Boaz looked, with his bald head, and his full black beard, and his fierce bespectacled eyes. And it was funny the way the chalk crumbled into white chunks when he jammed equations into the blackboard. He was more efficient, more uncompromising, and more dignified than Jack Daddio on his best day. This was obvious. Maybe the two of them were equally smart. But only one of them wasn't full of shit.

Night after night, J.R. weighed his options about taking over the family business. Along the way, he removed the thumbtacks and peeled down the obsolete U.S. Presidents poster. Number forty, Ronald Reagan, wasn't even on it.

## 9. Grand Union

He had come to see the waiting as precious seconds no one could ever give back. If it were the 1770's, he'd be winning musket battles, stabbing his enemy in the heart with a bayonet. If it were the Viking era, he'd be a stone-cold killer, with notches on his battle axe for every skull crushed. It kept him awake, night after night. The injustice of it all.

With the decision made, he reminded himself to calm down, to decrease his heart rate, and to breathe easy.

In short time, he managed something like relaxation, even as he rose up from his bed, electric with purpose, and crossed the bedroom to draw up the blinds and open the window. Climbing out into the night, he lowered himself to the ground.

Briefly, a pang of concern struck his heart. It was for his mother. She would worry to find him gone. But Jack Daddio was right about a few things, such as mothers and their worrying.

He left his window open just enough to get back in, then crossed to the maple tree, turning back for a glance at the house, with its front windows aglow by the light of the TV. This is how easy it would be to leave home and never come back.

And yet it would not be tonight. The neighboring houses in their eternal sequence framed his presence at this moonlit hour as an unfamiliar element. It was enjoyment enough, with more fun to be had in town. It would be a dry run, so to speak, in preparation for the inevitable escape. Rounding the corner up Pinnacle Place, he indulged the idea of his neighbors catching sight of his prowling figure and wondering... *Was that J.R. Daddio out there?* What his stalking shadow might portend had nothing to do, or very little, with his mother and father. It was more so created by his own will, his own choices, his own actions. A Viking warrior's conquering nature.

He turned onto Oxford Ave, followed downhill under the procession of streetlamps and maple trees, observed the familiar houses with their gables and dormers and parapets kissed by moonlight. The warm air caressed his arms and face and scalp. He strode past the bank, the funeral parlor, the Bucket o' Fries.

He found himself wishing a cop would pull over and recognize him, and say, "Oh, hey, J.R. Daddio!"

However, it wasn't the cops slowing down behind him, with the instantly recognizable, bullshit mournful, self-important cowboy rock blaring from the kickers. J.R. hated this song more than all other songs combined. And yet he knew it would still be playing, somehow, somewhere, in the irradiated aftermath of Armageddon.

He turned around. The headlights glared. He saw who it was. Jimmy Gates in his Chevette.

A couple of other morons were grinning from the back seat. "Hey, Daddio!" Curt Decker brayed, hanging his donkey face out the passenger side. "You forget to check your dipstick, bud?" The whole carload erupted with laughter. The Chevette roared off.

*Cowards...*

He wanted nothing more than to see them again tonight. He would require a weapon though.

He arrived under the streetlights at the intersection. Cars were parked up and down. Several public establishments were open for business. He chose Pitch N' Yaw.

The restaurant's foyer was congested, with one group arriving as another sought to leave. Bruce Springsteen groaned from the overhead speakers. J.R. made his way around the bottleneck of patrons only to encounter Mrs. Sellers, the hostess. "J.R. Daddio..." she looked surprised. "And how are you?" she asked.

"I just need to use the bathroom. Is that OK?"

"Sure, hon," she pointed and went back to work.

The crowd had spilled out of the bar into the restaurant. People would know him by sight here, if human beings had any situational awareness whatsoever, which they didn't. Officer Pierce, at the furthest barstool next to the clean silverware, could easily turn and see a steak knife get stolen from behind his back, but he wouldn't.

Following along the restaurant's bisecting partition, J.R. offered a friendly hello to Mr. and Mrs. Joyce. Also to Ellen from the bookstore, although he didn't go into bookstores anymore. At the partition's end, another group of patrons milled in close as he made his way through them for the bathroom door.

The urinal was occupied. The stall too. He went to the sink, ran the water, sized himself up in the mirror, and resolved, like he knew how, to collect the nerves. Everything follows from that. A few moments passed. He turned off the water.

On the way out, observing Officer Pierce's turned head, he grabbed a steak knife and tucked it into his back pocket. "Officer Pierce," he called out, but the restaurant was too loud. No one heard him. Officer Pierce carried on from his barstool none the wiser. J.R. paused to observe the whole lot of them making their senseless racket. Crows in a tree. Birds on a wire. Only Bruce Springsteen, groaning from the overhead speakers, sounded human. Not that this song was any good.

He was back out on Main Street with the steak knife tucked into his back pocket. He decided on the Grand Union parking lot, then made his way there to lie in wait.

The parking lot's stretch of floodlit concrete quartered a few dormant cars and wayward shopping carts. He crossed the black macadam to the market's brick wall, there to idle.

He would go for the tires only, unless someone drew a knife. Whatever happened, Jimmy Gates would not be driving his car home tonight.

He had never been in a fight. Never thrown or received a single punch. Tonight would change all that.

But now, instead of Jimmy Gates' Chevette, it was Pete Dawson's Duster turning into the Grand Union parking lot. J.R. had no beef with Pete Dawson. Hardly knew him. He hardly knew Audrey Buckhorn either, or Scotty Pomeroy, both of whom were in there with Pete, along with someone else, a girl. He couldn't see her face. The prowling Duster paused briefly, and all four of them laughed inside.

Suddenly the girls screamed with joy as the car accelerated, tires squealing, plowing forward, catching a stray shopping cart in its grill and propelling it on its rattling casters. Pete Dawson hit the brakes and sent the cart hurtling onward at runaway speed. It struck a parking chock, bucked skyward and crashed down on its side.

J.R. laughed. In the Duster they were laughing too. The car backed up, wheeled around niftily, curled up to meet him. Scotty Pomeroy leaned an elbow out the window. "You cool, Daddio?"

"Yeah, that was funny."

"What's up, J.R. Daddio?" Audrey Buckhorn taunted him from the backseat. It was Melissa Victoria in there with her, laughing. Melissa was Scotty Pomeroy's girlfriend. She leaned forward and cried, "GET UP ON THE HOOD!"

"Not the hood, the roof!" Audrey scolded her.

They were both out of control, laughing, flashing their teeth the way girls do, falling all over each other.

"These chicks are nuts," Scotty said with a sheepish smile.

"That's what I meant!" Melissa laughed. *The roof!*

"I'll get on the damn roof," J.R. said.

"Do it!" Pete Dawson grinned, revved the engine.

Remembering the steak knife in his back pocket, J.R. removed it and laid it on the brick window ledge along the store's façade.

Scotty scrutinized him. "What is that? A kitchen knife?"

"Yeah."

"What are you? Michael Myers?"

"I stole it from Pitch N' Yaw," J.R. approached the Duster's trunk.

"You did *what?*"

"Don't tell anyone."

"YAY!" Melissa cried, and the rest of them whooped and shouted as J.R. mounted from the trunk to spread his body atop the roof, grasping the Duster's moldings with his strong mechanic's hands. He could hear the girls going wild underneath him. The engine revved. The car began wheeling around the parking lot. J.R. clung like a panther up there. Scotty Pomeroy leaned out the window yelling, "YOU'RE NUTS!" Pete Dawson at the wheel cried, "WOOOOOOOOO!"

When the cops showed up, J.R. remained sprawled up on the rooftop.

"We came here for *Combos,*" Pete Dawson explained, sober, apologetic, respectful in the driver's seat. "But the store was closed," he shrugged.

Officer Powell in the prowler made a quizzical face. *"Combos?"*

J.R. had tuned up this exact squad car—car 207—not six months ago. Another time, he had fixed the radio in Powell's King Cobra Hatchback.

Officer Madison was in there next to Powell. Neither of them even bothered to get out. J.R. recalled the *Combos* TV ad, and in a humorless tone, to ape Pete Dawson's sincerity, he delivered the catchphrase from atop the Duster's roof, *"Cheeses Your Hunger Away."*

Powell reached an empty hand out the window. "For God's sake, J.R., get down from there! Can you get down from there now?"

They decided not to haul Jack Daddio's kid down to the station. They told everybody to go straight home.

"Everybody ride *inside* the car," Officer Powell ordered.

J.R. peered back at the knife where it lay on the brick window ledge. Neither of Erving's Finest had spotted it.

"Dude, we'll give you a ride," Scotty opened the door and pulled the seat forward. J.R. got in alongside Melissa Victoria and Audrey Buckhorn. "What's up, J.R.!" they welcomed him.

"Dude, you saved us," Scotty said.

Both girls were beautiful, but Melissa Victoria, with that body, seemingly every day in the tight jeans, was on a kind of unofficial, strictly imaginary list. Tucked up against her in the rear of the car, he tried to feel lucky. But Scotty Pomeroy was the luckiest sonofabitch in the world.

The cop car was still stationed behind them, waiting for them to leave.

"Well, they said to go home," Pete remarked, and he proceeded slowly, abidingly across the black expanse of parking lot toward the exit.

"Will your parents mind?" Scotty asked.

Pete shrugged, "Not if we're cool."

"J.R., you should be a stunt man," Audrey was leaning her face over Melissa Victoria's lap.

"I *am* a stunt man," he laughed at his own words, their validity. Everyone in the car started laughing.

"You wanna drink some beers in my parents' basement?" Pete Dawson asked.

"Yes," he peered back at the cops in the lot. He didn't like drinking beer, but he could hold one in his hand.

39

Pete Dawson clicked on the car stereo and cranked it. J.R. knew this song but didn't know, and didn't want to know, who the so-called artist was.

The girls were howling the lyrics. Audrey was playing air drums. J.R. tried to ignore the spectacle of it. He didn't want to think of Melissa Victoria this way.

A pair of headlights roared up behind them. Pete Dawson shielded his eyes from the mirror saying, "Who's this asshole?" The car swerved up. It was Vince Baldwin grinning from his Bonneville. Carolyn D'Amico was in his passenger seat.

"Vince!" Pete Dawson called, "we gotta..."

Slowing down the car, he lowered the music. The Bonneville sidled up until the two cars rolled to a standstill, side-by-side down the middle of North Street.

"We gotta go back to my place," Pete Dawson said.

"Whaddaya mean?"

"The cops busted us. They told us to go straight home."

"We'll meet you there. You're right down this street, right?"

"Yeah, dude... You can come over..." Pete hesitated, then added, "Just be cool with my parents, OK?"

"I'll be cool. Are they cool? I'll pick up beer. You got booze there?"

*"Jesus,"* Melissa said.

Vince heard her, leaned forward in the driver's seat and grinned, "What's up, Victoria?"

Pete Dawson repeated, "Be cool with my parents."

"We'll meet you there," Vince faced the road. Carolyn smiled and waved. The Bonneville roared off.

"Shit," Melissa said. "Why do we have to hang out with that idiot?"

"Good question," J.R. replied.

"He already graduated. What is he doing with her?"

"It's like you're reading my mind," he told her.

## 10. Pete Dawson's Basement

He did admit to liking the occasional song. For instance, *"I don't recognize my own wife!"* Or whatever the lyrics were.

"Now that's a good song," he announced, down in Pete Dawson's basement, as the turntable inevitably spun, every once in a while, in his favor. A few months had passed since the encounter in the Grand Union parking lot, and he was wasting time with this crew regularly now.

Pete's basement was basically finished, or half-finished, with heat pipes drawn around the ceiling and bisecting it diagonally above the teenagers where they gathered. Pete, Audrey and Carolyn had claimed the couch with its tie-dye slipcovers. Vince was hovering behind Carolyn holding a can of Schlitz. Melissa had taken a folding chair, one of a few arranged around the coffee table. Scotty Pomeroy lingered by the staircase, which was professionally built, but not yet treated. Two old oriental rugs warmed up the floor, with linoleum exposed only around the room's perimeter. A wood-stained bookshelf lined one wall with paperback fiction.

The song ended, and the next one was unbearable. This was a familiar racket. One song gets its hooks in, and then all the rest are crap. Watching the black circle spin, and suffering the sounds that throbbed anew from the basement's JBL's, J.R. was amazed to learn that for once in his life he wasn't alone in this world. It was Carolyn D'Amico agreeing with him, saying, "This music sucks!"

"Thank you," he told her.

"Put on *Bat Out of Hell,*" she said.

"Coming right up!" Pete Dawson answered cheerfully.

*Or we could have no music,* J.R. wanted to say. But there would be no point. Popular music had proven to him that he was some advanced form of life accidentally abandoned on a planet of morons. The code embedded in the lyrics was simple enough for a child to decipher. And yet they lapped it up. *"I need that feeling, or I'm gonna die!"* It wasn't even clever. It was weakness, packaged and sold by snake charmers. Somehow no one, or very few, could hear it.

Carolyn D'Amico set down her beer on an end table repurposed from a cable spool. She said, *"Bat Out of Hell* has more meaning today than it ever had in the seventies."

"Fucking WRONG!" Vince Baldwin hovered behind her. "That fucker is just ripping off The Boss."

"Excuse me," she looked up at him. "Does Phil Rizzuto guest star on *Nebraska?* I didn't think so."

Scotty Pomeroy asked, "Pete? Can I go upstairs and get a glass of water?"

Pete was busy changing the record and didn't answer him.

Melissa was visibly drunk. Quoting Meatloaf, something about werewolves and vampires and teeth.

Pete's Dawson's mom was on her way down the stairs with a laundry basket. She had an icy tumbler sloshing atop the heaped clothing. "What is that song?" she asked Melissa, "I know that song!"

"Pete?" Scotty said.

"I hate Meatloaf," J.R. told them.

Audrey Buckhorn gave him wry smirk. "I thought you knew how to party, J.R."

"I tell ya," Melissa said, "you took those words right out of my mouth."

Scotty Pomeroy turned to Pete's mother. "Mrs. Dawson, can I go upstairs and get a glass of water?"

"What's wrong with you?" J.R. asked him.

"Nothing, man. I gotta get up and run tomorrow, that's all. I gotta keep hydrated."

Scotty Pomeroy was on the cross-country team, so he spent all his free time, year-round, day or night, rain or shine, running around the back roads of Erving, New York. It wasn't crazy, J.R. figured. He got to fuck Melissa Victoria, for starters, so he was nobody's fool. But the running, the commitment to it, was annoying sometimes.

Carolyn said, "Angelico's Pizza. Growing up in Florida, there was always Meatloaf on the jukebox. But I never put it on. But now, when I go there, I put it on all the time. So I'm just saying. It has more meaning now."

"Angelico's water has sand in it," Scotty told them.

J.R. looked at him.

Carolyn continued, "I used to make fun of Meatloaf in the seventies. But now? Duh. Forget it."

Pete got the record spinning. The music began its testimony from the speakers.

J.R. glimpsed Pete Dawson's mom at her laundry station, with her icy beverage sweating atop the dryer. Her serene fascination with her son's friends was maddening.

Scotty was at the base of the stairs saying, "By the way, did you guys hear me? Angelico's water has *sand* in it. It has actual *sand* in it."

"So?" J.R. asked him. "Why do you go there?"

"I don't go there. The water has sand in it."

"By the way. It's not sand. It's silt."

"Silt?"

"Probably silt."

"Silt is *good?* It doesn't sound good. Or taste good."

J.R. shrugged. "It's minerals... you know. It gets in the pipes."

"Not in *these* pipes."

They all laughed, including Pete Dawson's mom. J.R. couldn't believe they thought Scotty had the upper hand in this argument. They couldn't possibly be that stupid.

He said, "So? What does *that* mean?" But he could hear his own voice rising, and he could feel his heart accelerating. He reminded himself to calm down. This was a fun time, or supposed to be, even if it required patience with his so-called peers.

Mrs. Dawson was watching him a bit more cautiously now.

"I'm just explaining," he told them. "Angelico's doesn't have sand in their water. It's silt."

"Whatever it is," Scotty answered him. "I've tasted it. There's fucking coral and seashells and shit. It's like, 'Welcome to Angelico's, here's a glass of beach water.' No thanks, I ain't drinking it."

Everybody laughed again.

Vince Baldwin said, "J.R., have you ever been punched in the face?"

"You mean by a douchebag? No."

The group of them laughed some more. For once they were on his side.

Vince stood there with that look on his face, the look he always wore, ready for a fight. He worked in the lumberyard, and he was probably eighty pounds bigger than J.R., so to engage him in combat was a guaranteed losing proposition, especially since J.R. had never thrown a single punch in his entire life.

"Fight it out!" Audrey said playfully.

"Pit fight!" Scotty agreed. "Right here! Right now! Arena fight!"

Everyone was laughing. Mrs. Dawson stepped in. "Pause! Timeout! I promise you boys, I will call the cops in two seconds flat if you start any rough stuff in my basement!"

Melissa said, "That's right, Mrs. Dawson! Get these boys under control!"

Mrs. Dawson sighed and threw her hip to one side. She plucked her glass from the dryer and raised it. "Boys will be boys. Just not in my basement! Am I right, ladies?"

Melissa shook her head, "I don't buy that 'boys will be boys' crap."

"Well, just wait till you have a couple of them."

Everyone laughed. Carolyn looked at Audrey, "Here she goes with the politics."

Mrs. Dawson said, "When you're raising two wild animals, there's no time for politics."

"I have something to say," J.R. spoke up. "That's not a boy, or a wild animal, Mrs. Dawson. That's your son, Pete."

Mrs. Dawson remained merry. "That's very insightful, Mr. Daddio. Your father knows you're here, right?

"My father knows everything."

Somehow, they took this the wrong way, all of them, and they groaned, in unison, like cattle. They thought he was bragging. That was how their minds worked. He shook his head in pity. *I'm going to leave this town,* he told himself.

"I'm going upstairs for water," Scotty announced.

"Why are you so obsessed with water?" J.R. asked him.

Scotty turned to Vince Baldwin, "Vince, did you say something about punching him in the face?"

"See what I mean?" Mrs. Dawson said. "Boys will be boys. Girls will be patient."

44

"Ha!" Melissa answered. "I can do anything the boys can do."

"That's the spirit," Mrs. Dawson said.

"It's not just the spirit. It's a fact."

"Well, the spirit is a lot more reliable than facts, honey pie, so don't knock it."

More laughter filled the room. Audrey was amazed. "Whoa!" she said. "Was that church or school, Mrs. Dawson?"

Melissa raised her head, "Women get oppressed by both."

Pete Dawson came to the rescue, "I gotta say, I think Missy's right."

"Oh, Petey!" Mrs. Dawson batted a hand at him.

Scotty was still halfway up the stairs, questioning his girlfriend, or advising her. "You know, you really make people uncomfortable when you do that."

"She's great, Scotty!" Pete told him.

"I know she's great. That's why we don't have to prove it every five seconds."

## 11. The Black-and-White Dance

The sophomores threw a black-and-white dance. J.R. resolved he would take a girl to it, and then try to get into her pants afterward. He didn't have his permit yet, but if he could get away with towing police cruisers, he could certainly take a girl to the black-and-white dance. All he had to do was find someone to go with him.

At first, the effort went so badly, and his mounting dismay became so overpowering, that it began to feel like stomach nausea all the way up in the chest. No less than five different girls said no in the span of an hour.

Finally, Nicole Van Buren said yes. Nicole Van Buren was pretty, but she was a completely random girl from school. He barely knew her. There was something embarrassing about the whole thing. For both of them.

He had a date, though. A pretty date. Holding the cradled handset in his parent's bedroom, with the phonebook in his lap, he began to wonder just how revolting he must be, that five different ones could say no before a single one said yes.

Also, what was wrong with Nicole Van Buren, that she couldn't see what the others were avoiding?

On the night of the dance, he drove over to Willow Lane to pick her up. She walked out the door wearing her black-and-white gown, and blurted, "Are you kidding me?" standing there in her parents' driveway, staring at the Daddio's tow truck.

At the dance, J.R. remained out of sight, against the wall, dressed all in black amidst the black-and-white cafeteria chairs and driftless black-and-white balloons.

The song went, *"Daddy, you're my number one. Mommy, the unlucky one. Cherry Bombs are so much fun. Fuh... fuh... fuh... fuh... fun."*

He listened with a degree of horror he had never experienced before, and absorbed the enlightenment into his system as he might absorb a snakebite.

Nicole Van Buren ended up making out with Todd Douglass at a party after the dance, while J.R. sat out on the back deck of Justine Smith's house, dangling his legs between the balusters, telling himself, "I need a car."

## 12. An Unsettled Mind

They took the tow truck out to Armitage Road, parked along the shoulder, proceeded into the woods on foot. J.R. listened to his father, though he knew the sermon well. To step quietly. To speak briefly, if at all. To keep the body still. The breathing even. The heartbeat changeless. Even an unsettled mind can spook a deer. J.R. knew this was true.

The peace and purpose of those long hours made his father's company more and more bearable lately. They communicated well, up in the deer stand, with hand gestures and expressive faces. At one point, without a word, they paused to wipe down their weapons for moisture. Later, again wordless, they shared a peanut butter sandwich.

After lunch the wind picked up, and they were freezing up in the tree stand, so they took it down and went exploring. The path they found was mostly buried under leaves and dead branches, but they traced it up the mountainside to a landing where an abandoned trailer sat in ruins up on cinderblocks. They found droppings and deer rub, and proceeded up the path to a fallen tree, where they set up a pit blind to lie in wait.

At one point, Jack Daddio removed a flask from his jacket and offered it. J.R. shook his head gently. His father nodded, twirled off the cap, took a shot.

Some stretch of time later, a buck strutted into view. J.R. raised his bolt action, but the animal skipped away.

*"Damn,"* he muttered.

*"Eh,"* his father said quietly. *"Easy come easy go."*

*"That was a perfect ten-point buck, dad."*

"Yep," Jack Daddio removed the flask again and hit it. When he spoke next, he didn't even bother to keep his voice down. "So, J.R., what kind of car are you thinking about?"

J.R.'s twisted his face into a wince and smirk both. "What do you mean? When I'm old enough?"

"Yes. That's what I mean."

"Dad."

"What?"

"I don't feel like dwelling on a car I can't buy. Did that ever occur to you?"

"Come on, J.R. Knock it off for once. What do you got in mind?"

*For once?* But J.R. didn't feel like arguing. After a long conciliatory sigh, he answered. "Chevy Nova."

"Chevy Nova?"

"What's wrong with that?"

"Nothing," his father was smiling. "Chevy Nova. I like it."

"Oh, that's a relief."

Jack Daddio gazed around at the forest, visibly pleased with himself. He said, "I'm glad we've been getting along better lately."

"Have we? I hadn't noticed."

## 13. Resentment Entirely

On his fifteenth birthday, he pedaled over to the garage after school, and received from his father, as a gift, a pair of Daddio's Garage coveralls. The garment was folded, but J.R. knew what was coming. The name patch would read J.R., not *Junior*.

Buddy was standing by, grinning, blameless.

J.R. unfurled the uniform, allowed the disappointment and satisfaction to comingle. "You can't be serious," he said.

"You don't like them?" his father asked.

"Why would I like them?"

*"Why would you like them?"*

J.R. shrugged. "This changes nothing. How stupid do you think I am?"

Jack Daddio lowered his head.

Buddy said, "I'm gonna bounce over to the kiosk for a sandwich."

Once Buddy was gone, Jack Daddio said, "J.R., this is your garage. You understand that, right?"

"Doesn't feel like it."

"Stop that. I'm talking about your future."

"What do you think I'm talking about?"

*Now he's going to blow his stack,* J.R. told himself. He could see it coming, just like he saw everything coming a mile away. The coveralls with the name. "Dad. Guess what. I don't even care about my name anymore."

"Since when?"

"Actually," J.R. continued. "I honestly think I have out-grown resentment entirely."

"You think so? *Resentment entirely?*"

"It's just that I'm not that stupid."

"You know what I think?"

"No, dad. What do you think?" He was about to suggest that his father try for a deep and meditative breath, to calm his heart rate, and soothe his nerve tendrils, and so on.

However, Jack Daddio was way ahead of him, for once, and maintained his composure. Perfectly calm, he answered his son, "I think I'm through with you."

"You wish."

"I don't have to wish. You'll be out of my hair soon enough."

"What's left of it."

"Soon enough."

"Sorry if I don't wear these," J.R. discarded the gift.

Later that night, lying awake in bed, he wasn't planning, exactly. Neither was he dreaming. Rather, he was using his imagination to make his future so, by promising himself that it would be, and believing hard enough that it could be. On the day he owned a car, he would drive away from Erving, New York and never look back.

The TV in the living room could be heard droning. The old bald guy lecturing again on PBS. As if once wasn't enough. His parents were talking to each other over the din of the tedium. She would say something. He would bark something back. It was undeserving of his attention. He went back to what he was doing.

Driving out of Erving. Making it so.

## 14. Blue Dog

Scotty was counting on a few scholarship possibilities, but they all fell through. Plan B was to save up for community college. Meanwhile, Melissa postponed enrollment in the U.S. Army and got a job at the Bucket o' Fries. A tension, more and more so, was growing between them.

J.R. tried not to smile. Not out loud, anyway. He liked Scotty. But he was jealous too. No matter the activity, no matter its importance, Melissa, the very thought of her, had become an ever-nagging distraction. She was the sexiest woman in all of Erving. And like J.R., she wanted out.

Pete Dawson came home for the Fourth of July. The plan was to go to the carnival on Friday night. "I'll pick you up," he offered.

"No need," J.R. said. "I'll ride my bike over to your place." He hung up the phone.

Then, out in the garage, he stood contemplating his *Sky Ray* bicycle anew. It was a toy. For a child. Who longed to be a man.

*I'm like the village idiot riding around on this thing,* he told himself.

"I need a car," he added, out loud.

He called Pete Dawson back. The words came out as one sentence, "I changed my mind come pick me up."

He rode shotgun over to the carnival. Scotty and Melissa were in attendance too. So was Carolyn D'Amico. There was no sign of Vince Baldwin, but Carolyn was done with Vince

Baldwin. She made that clear twice to anyone who would listen, as the group of friends roamed from tent to ride. She was smiling, wide-eyed, more than enough to get J.R.'s attention. Also leaning against his shoulder every time she laughed. They ended up pairing off together.

It was fun throwing baseballs at moving targets. He won Carolyn a big blue stuffed dog with floppy ears. She thanked him with a kiss on the cheek.

After the carnival, they all went back to Pete Dawson's house. Pete's parents were away, so they sat around the kitchen table. Pete had a bottle of Captain Morgan's rum, plus two cases of Miller Lite he had pilfered from a deli where he worked upstate. J.R. drank sparingly, watched Carolyn drink more freely. He knew the alcohol would make it a hundred times easier to get her clothes off.

And then downstairs, with no one else around except for the blue stuffed dog gaping joyously next to them on the couch, they started making out. He got his hands all over her, under her clothes, hardly believing it was finally happening, barely even conscious of it, with his heart racing, and his lungs surging.

But the kissing, which seemed to open her up so nicely at first, suddenly, unexpectedly, seemed to close her down. She was saying no, and then louder, "No! Stop! NO, J.R.! NO!" until he realized they could hear her upstairs, and he awoke from something, trying to remember what it was he had done.

"God..." she muttered.

"Whoa," he said. "I didn't..."

"When a girl says *stop...*"

"No," he corrected her. "It's like... just now... Carolyn... I can't explain... I'm sorry. I just... *came-to...* I'm sorry. I don't..."

"What? Oh, *gross!*"

"What?" he said. "No..."

Carolyn remained there on the couch. He fully expected her to flee up the untreated basement stairs and announce to everyone what a jerk J.R. Daddio turned out to be. Instead, she sat weeping into her hands under the basement drop ceiling with its exposed heat pipes.

Watching her response, he concluded that they could only be fake tears. She could not possibly be this passive. He had to say something. "Carolyn..." he began. But then he decided against it. He had already said he was sorry. If anything, the evening had been unfair to him.

*A kangaroo has more reasoning power,* he told himself.

He stared at the blue stuffed dog with its drooling tongue.

The next day, in the bathroom at the garage, he sat dwelling with mounting incredulity on the memory of what he had held in his hands. But the spell was broken when his father came jingling through the front door, yapping with a customer.

Gripped by a breathless pain, J.R. waited. The bathroom should not be right here in the office, this was obvious. Or "self-evident," as the Founding Fathers would have said. The bathroom should be in *the back* and *far away*. For everyone's sake. And since the garage was his birthright, he now enjoyed a brief resolution to install a properly situated bathroom someday, if he was still a resident of Erving, New York, which he would not be in a million years. *But I'll install it anyway,* he told himself, *just to make a point!*

## 15. A Racist Joke

He took a ride with Vince and Scotty and Melissa in Vince's Bonneville down to New York City, through the toll, over the bridge and into one, or more, or several black neighborhoods with numerical street names to differentiate them.

He had seen these neighborhoods on TV, despite every effort to avoid television, and from the Bonneville's backseat he now felt as if he were watching the local news and cop dramas and Sesame Street episodes and PBS documentaries all come to life.

"Look at the way that asshole is talking to her," Melissa said.

Scotty leaned back and said, "Let's not get out and teach them civics lessons."

"That's not the lesson I had in mind."

Vince grinned, gripping the wheel, "I'm in total agreement with Melissa."

"So am I, babe," Scotty faced forward.

J.R. watched Scotty's profile.

"Since when?" Melissa asked.

"Since when? Since ever. I don't treat you like that, do I?" Melissa gazed out the window.

"Let me tell you guys a racist joke," Vince interjected.

"Tell it, brother," Scotty said.

"Oh goody," Melissa said, all sarcasm. Scotty turned around to confront his girlfriend. "Will you stop?"

"It's a good joke," Vince said. "Why don't you stop acting so nervous?"

J.R. said, "Vince, you *are* a racist joke."

The others laughed. Vince released a sigh and sagged his shoulders, sitting at the wheel. The Bonneville idled at a red light several cars back at a busy intersection. The windows were rolled up and the doors were locked. A neighborhood filled with black people bustled all around them.

Vince said, "It's about the black guy who kept beating his wife—"

"No," J.R. said.

"What?"

He met Vince Baldwin's gaze in the rearview mirror and said, "Not funny, Vince."

"But it *is* funny."

"Yeah right. What's the punchline?"

"The punchline?"

"Yeah, what's the punchline? Of the joke?"

"What? Duh? I can't tell you the punchline first! It doesn't make any sense without a joke in front of it!"

"Tell me the punchline first, and then, if I think it's funny, I'll let you tell me the whole joke."

"What? Fuck you! You don't LET me do anything! I do whatever I WANT!"

"Will you just calm down and tell me the punchline?"

The light turned green. The Bonneville advanced slowly behind scattering vehicles through the busy city intersection and into another jam-packed corridor of vertical architecture in view of another red traffic light.

"What?"

"What what?"

"What is the punchline."

"Oh, fucking Abbott and Costello," Melissa balked.

"*What* is the punchline?" J.R. asked.

"Yes, are you happy? You spoiled the joke."

Melissa looked at him, "Nice going, J.R."

"OK, tell me the joke."

"No way," Vince told him. "You ruined it. You stupid asshole. Nobody likes you, you know that? You should look into that, J.R. Nobody likes you."

"Hey," Melissa protested, but then she just stared out the window.

Scotty said, "They shuffle so fast."

J.R. gazed wide eyed and fascinated and worried at the New York neighborhood outside.

Blacks. Abe Lincoln had freed them once. Dr. King freed them once again. Now only the liberals remained to keep them enslaved with their breadcrumbs and birdseed. He had heard this somewhere, and the words the guy used, the way he said it, made perfect sense. "I don't see anyone shuffling," he told Scotty.

"Two o'clock," Scotty pointed.

"Don't point!"

"Dude, relax!"

J.R. hated the word *dude.* "You're a fucking giraffe," he told Scotty.

"That guy," Scotty insisted, "that guy... under that lamp post. He's not even going anywhere. But look at him."

J.R. refused to stare, but still he could see, in several sideways glances, as the light turned green and the Bonneville rolled through the intersection, the skinny black man wearing a bucket hat, waiting nervously beneath a lamp post.

"So what's your point?" J.R. wanted to know, because even though Jack Daddio was a tedious fool, he was also infallibly right about one thing. Any one of these people could be your next customer.

"He's doin' a little dance the whole time," Scotty said.

J.R.'s frame of reference for dancing was MTV and high school auditoriums. He saw nothing of that sort taking place here. "I don't know anything about dancing," he said.

Vince in the driver's seat lamented, "It's a funny joke. Everyone keeps telling the guy to stop beating his wife. Except, come to find out... he's deaf."

## 16. Aaron Law

Jack Daddio had another big surprise in store.

"I've thought about it," he said, "and I *am* willing to legally change your name to J.R."

"Really?" J.R. fell for it. Just for a moment, he let himself believe it was all over.

Then his father added, "If you sign a contract with me. To inherit Daddio's Garage. And carry on its name in Erving. After I'm gone."

"Are you kidding me?"

"Do I look like I'm kidding?"

"I'll think about it."

"You take as long as you want."

"Tomorrow," he left it there.

That night, a noisy and crowded dream populated his sleep. When the buzzer sounded it was morning, and the memory was lost, though a distant racket still echoed.

He got dressed, ate breakfast. He said nothing to his mother, nothing to Janice.

He stood out on the street corner, waiting for the school bus, lost in reflection. Jack Daddio wanted to re-open a wound just so that he could heal it.

The school bus arrived. J.R. got on, and later debarked without remembering the journey. He sat through the tedious procession of classes and stalked through the scrambling in-between.

Along the way, it occurred to him that his former math teacher, Mr. Boaz, might have some useful advice.

"Mr. Boaz?" he found the teacher waiting in his empty classroom.

"Yes, J.R."

"Can I explain to you something?"

"I don't know. Can you?"

He approached the teacher's desk. "Everyone calls me J.R. Even my father calls me J.R. But my real name is Junior."

"The only reason I call you J.R. is that you asked me to."

"Right. And thank you. So we're on the same page. So what I want to know is... Does my legal name... Junior Daddio... legally *enforce* me to inherit my father's garage?"

Mr. Boaz appeared stunned by the question. His bespectacled eyes darted around. His eyebrows narrowed into the vertex of his circular eyeglasses. He was sizing up J.R. all over again. "Do you mean *entitle?* Or do you mean *force?*"

"Force."

"Force. OK. Did you sign a contract with your father?"

"No, not yet."

Mr. Boaz leaned back, taking it seriously, as predicted. "As long as you haven't signed a contract, you aren't bound by anything."

"OK. But what if I *do* sign it, under the name Junior, and then I change my name to J.R.?"

Once again, the schoolteacher was taken aback. Students were trickling in for class by now. Mr. Boaz glanced up at them, warily.

His eyes were stern and probing behind spectacles shot with fluorescent light. His bald skull gleamed, and his beard concealed his lips. Gravely, he whispered, *"Knowledge comes with a price, J.R. And my price is anonymity. So you didn't hear this from me. Because I will deny it."*

J.R. wanted to point out that Mr. Boaz drew a salary from the school, and so any conversation on school grounds was already paid for by his father's taxes. Instead, he responded, *"Of course."*

*"Especially your father."*

"What have I been TALKING ABOUT?"

*"Calm down, kid,"* Mr. Boaz leaned in. *"Listen. Here's what you do. You change your name to J dot R dot. Make sure your legal name includes the punctuation."*

J.R. was going to do that anyway, but he nodded along, and let his teacher continue.

*"See, that's what nobody will tell you. The more punctuation in your name, the better your odds. Especially with these new government databases. They can't process punctuation. Have you ever seen an IBM computer fry its circuit board? Well, I have. It's a thing of beauty. Or it was, before I put it down with a fire extinguisher. But never mind Man-Versus-Technology. Punctuation prevents the government from legally binding you to anything. Ever wonder why your junk mail comes addressed in all capital letters, with no punctuation? That's because they aren't legally responsible for anything they send you..."*

J.R. had never received junk mail, but it was a fascinating monologue. Meanwhile, students continued to arrive, and Mr. Boaz' suspicions visibly escalated with each new child at each remaining desk. Lowering his voice to within a tightening radius, he said, *"The only thing is, you have to have a lawyer. And I mean beforehand. Immediately. So that the minute you sign the contract, you're ready to file a lawsuit."*

*"Lawsuit? Really? I can't afford a lawyer—"*

Mr. Boaz shook his head, annoyed, *"Anyone can afford a lawyer. As long as they have a winning case. You have leverage as a citizen there. Keep that in mind."*

*"I know somebody,"* J.R. mused, with Mike Aaron in mind.

*"I just hope it's not too late for you,"* Mr. Boaz whispered. *"For me, it's too late. But you. If you start young enough. You might be able to live by the freedom that was promised to you. By the Founding Fathers. The freedom that American Flag stands for..."* he gestured his thumb over his shoulder at the Stars and Stripes.

J.R. was heartened by this reference to the Founding Fathers.

*"Listen to me, too,"* Mr. Boaz pointed up at the ceiling. *"About these fluorescent lights. They deliver a government issued phosphor-toxin designed to make us docile and obedient. It takes all my willpower just to fight it every day. But it's worth it... for me... if I can shape the mind of even one gifted child."*

His glasses were inscrutable white disks.

The bell rang.

"I'm not signing any hall pass," he straightened in his chair.

J.R. thanked Mr. Boaz, walked out into the hall, and got busted easily by Mrs. Sugarman with her notepad of detention slips. Now he had a time waster after school.

The fluorescent light tangent was weird, and disappointing. However, Mike Aaron was a good idea. He could still make it down to Aaron Law before five.

He waited in the detention room among an uncomfortable collection of slobs, including Curt Decker, who began snapping pennies through his fingers at the other kids. The first few pennies missed, pinging off a Formica desktop, a plastic chair, another chair's chrome leg. Then Wendy Wilcox got hit in the face and had to go down to the nurse. The detention monitor, Mrs. Carmody, took Wendy under her wing and out of the firing line. "Stop shooting pennies!" she begged on the way out. Curt Decker was left in charge of the room.

J.R. kept alert. Also tried to avoid eye contact. Although he had never been in a fight, he would expect himself, under normal circumstances, to get up and start throwing punches. However, today he had to see Mike Aaron down at Aaron Law before five o'clock.

Across the room, Curt Decker faked a couple of shots from his wrist, grinning each time. Finally, he let one fly into J.R.'s forearm.

"Motherfucker!"

"What are you gonna do, *hot shot?*"

The other kids were watching.

On the bus ride home, J.R. sat seething with rage for passing up the opportunity to fight Curt Decker. No one would understand if he explained to them. How it was his father's fault, for naming him Junior.

He got off the bus, went straight for the *Sky Ray,* wheeled it into action.

"I heard you had detention," Janice leaned out the back door.

"I heard you were dumb," he replied.

"You heard wrong," she went back inside.

He pedaled for Aaron Law.

Mike Aaron's law office offered a parking lot for cars, but no option to secure a bike. *And yet,* J.R. told himself, *if someone steals this stupid thing, they'll be doing me a favor.* He left it on its kickstand and went inside.

The receptionist was named Vanessa. J.R. didn't know her personally, but he knew her name, and he knew it was her Fiat parked outside. She asked him to wait on the bench, so he took a seat.

The minutes passed. Five o'clock came and went. Vanessa kept busy at her desk, and J.R.'s attention turned to the humming of the fluorescent lights overhead.

It was like he had heard them all along, heard them for the first time, and could never un-hear them again, all in the same awakening. He looked up at the ceiling panels. Mr. Boaz was right.

Mike Aaron came out of the office, accompanied by some clients, thanking them for coming by, seeing them off.

Vanessa said, "This young man is here to see you."

"Mr. Daddio?" Mike Aaron looked mildly surprised. "How can I help you?"

J.R. stood up from the bench, "I want to sue my father."

Mike Aaron sniffed once, raised his chin and scrutinized young J.R. Daddio through his spectacles. He briefly eyeballed his receptionist Vanessa, who shrugged in response. Then he peered again at his prospective client, a bit longer and harder. Finally, humorless, he responded, "How about you go home, kid. Before your father sues me."

J.R. said nothing. He wouldn't dignify it. He turned and exited the law office into the parking lot. The entire town was stacked against him.

The *Sky Ray* bike was waiting. He began to mount, then stopped and stood gripping its brilliant Buick steering wheel. He would sign no contract.

He swept up the kickstand and began wheeling the weird contraption through the shade up to the fence overlooking the creek and the plunge into it. Hauling up the bike with his two hands he slung it over and watched it crash down just short of the waterline. The sight of its upturned frame and spinning tires pleased him. He let the moment last.

The future had assumed its own gravitational pull. In a few months, he would turn sixteen. The wait would be over. He would drive out of Erving, New York. The affirmation had become almost superfluous, but he spoke it out loud anyway, "I need a car," as he turned away from the fence and started walking toward home, laughing to himself because of that word. *Home.*

## 17. The Church in Avaris

Scotty was calling from the payphone at The Millstone Inn. The Grand Am had sprung a leak, and he and Melissa were stranded out at the Church in Avaris.

"See, this is what I'm talking about," Jack Daddio complained.

"What's the matter, Daddio?"

"Now I don't have my guy or my truck."

J.R. shook his head. "Scotty can't keep his car running. What are you blaming me for?"

"Because he's your vagabond friend."

J.R. plucked the keys off the desktop. "You don't know what you're talking about. He works."

"Then why doesn't he pay me?"

"You know why," J.R. went out the front door, climbed into the tow truck and drove off.

Scotty worked. Evening shifts, three hours a night, loading trailers out at UPS. J.R. had stopped by just last week, to find Scotty in one of the sweltering trailers, dressed in a tank top and track shorts and Red Wings, loading packages from an unrelenting conveyor belt. "DUDE, WHAT'S UP?" he exclaimed.

J.R. waved and then watched. *This would be a good job,* he realized. The workouts in the high school weight room were nothing like this, nowhere near as intense.

Scotty never slowed down either, amazingly fit. And clever too, seeking out room and finding it for each uniquely useful puzzle-piece inside the jam-packed cargo hold.

It was understood there would be no break time. After a few minutes, J.R. left.

Melissa's job was quite the opposite. She was gaining weight and complaining about it, having advanced almost immediately into middle management at the Bucket o' Fries, the result being sexy and tragic all in one spectacularly diminishing half-life. J.R. tried not to think sarcastic thoughts about her.

He had last seen Melissa over the weekend when he got called out to the high school for a tow. There was a big track meet that day, and some lady and her sourpuss kid were trying to leave, but their Vega wagon wouldn't start. The car needed a jump and a new battery, but a tow wasn't in great need, so J.R. got the thing wound up and told the lady to drive straight for Daddio's Garage.

Then he went down the hill to the track where he had spotted Melissa Victoria among the parents and students and athletes and school alumni. He figured she was here with Scotty Pomeroy to cheer on the track team. However, Scotty was nowhere in sight. Melissa was alone, wearing her boyfriend's Minutemen windbreaker.

Sneaking up behind her, J.R. grabbed her by the shoulders and wailed a chorus of, *"BE... ALL THAT YOU CAN—"*

WHACK! she punched him in the face, dropped him to the ground.

The next thing he knew, she was speaking to him, saying, "Wait a minute..." and trying to hoist his dead weight up by his lifeless arm. He could see that they were surrounded by a small and startled crowd of hot dog holders and soda straw slurpers and ice cream sandwich clutchers while the greater multitude of high school track fanatics remained undistracted down the stretch of the race in progress, shouting along with the P.A.'s frantic gibberish until a referee's whistle pierced the air and the sky was shattered by shrieks of joy.

"Did you say, *Be All You Can Be?*" she asked him. "You fucking asshole!" She released him and he collapsed to the ground, laughing up at the sky. *She knocked me out!* he realized.

The encircling crowd was beseeching her, *"Hey, hey. Calm down, calm down."*

"Wait..." J.R. spoke at last, lying on his back, clutching his ringing cranium with all ten fingers. "You're not sorry? For punching me in the face?"

"Don't EVER grab me!" she told him. She told them all.

The day was bright over Melissa Victoria's towering silhouette. The sun-white sky was all encompassing. J.R. raised both hands to shield his eyes as he peered up at her. Without words, in the shade of his own interlaced fingers, he believed he saw the misunderstanding untangle. It was just an Erving track meet. And he was just her friend. And they were just surrounded by dozens of onlookers. There was no reason to punch anybody in the face. Finally, she extended her hand down to help him.

"No, I can stand up," he demonstrated, "all by myself."

It was amazing. He snapped-to, all at once, suddenly awake, wide awake. It was like a dream behind him, the knockout punch.

"Don't blame me," she told him. "Maybe you shouldn't grab people."

"'Nothing to see here, folks," he told the crowd. "Ouch!" he told her.

But she was pissed off. *"Be All You Can Be?* Fuck you, Junior."

She walked away in her overlong windbreaker, bearing her grudge. The longing he felt was terrible, watching Melissa Victoria disappear into that crowd of Minutemen track and field fans.

That was last weekend. The headache had persisted for a few days, but it was long over by now, as he drove past the Millstone Inn and approached the Church in Avaris. His friends were waiting for him under the willow tree in the parking lot, Melissa Victoria leaning against the disabled Grand Am while Scotty Pomeroy performed a walking handstand in the grass nearby.

The church was still called a church, even though services weren't held there anymore. It had become a community center, with A.A. meetings, crochet lessons... Today, a used book sale, as J.R. steered the truck around the willow tree in the driveway and observed the book-stacked and book-strewn card tables, and the book-stuffed cardboard boxes on display. A part of him longed to peruse those volumes for some rare and fortunate text about Andrew Jackson or Teddy Roosevelt, even though he knew that he had outgrown any interest in reading as an activity anymore.

Scotty's black Grand Am, with its coupe frame, its rally wheels, its V8 engine, and its catalytic converter, was a thing of beauty. Somehow Scotty Pomeroy, in his track shorts and racing flats, had acquired both the best-looking car and the best-looking girl in all of Erving. It was an embarrassment of riches, or could have been, if Scotty was capable of embarrassment.

J.R. stepped down from the cab, saying. "What's up, kids?"

Melissa, with her arms folded, freed up one hand to wave, "Hi."

It was a thermostat valve, contrary to Scotty's diagnosis over the phone about head gaskets. The car would have to be towed, so J.R. offered them a lift home.

Five minutes later, as he curled the truck out of the lot, with his friends at his side, he glanced back at the church, and said to no one in particular, "They're used books for a reason. Nobody wants them."

## 18. The Nova

A few weeks later, he turned sixteen. He had found a well-tuned '72 Nova two-door, with a 454 Big Block, and quarter panels that aimed down the chassis in perfectly straight lines. The snub-nosed frame was more aggressive than the Grand Am's profile, although the Nova's brown finish was nowhere near as dazzling as Scotty's black-on-black tuxedo shine. When Scotty's Grand Am was clean and waxed, you could see the world reflected in it. The blue sky. The white clouds. The scattering crows. The telephone wires. The drivers passing by, gawking. J.R. would never achieve any such result from the Nova's drab brown paintjob. Otherwise, the car was perfect. He bought it for a thousand bucks, cash.

He dropped out of school under the condition he would work full time at the garage until his eighteenth birthday. At that point, he would be the master of both his trade and his destiny, and he would be free to do as he wished, including change his legal name to J.R. Daddio.

"I'm proud of you," Jack Daddio told him.

J.R. gave his father a thumbs-up, then pointed with his index finger, "Thanks, Daddio."

Driving out to Garfield in the Nova with the windows open and the bucket seat beneath him and the gearshift levered at his caress, he was born anew, a free man at last. He had a trio of Sunpros down below the ashtray, a Pioneer stereo at his knee, and a dashboard speedometer spread left-to-right just aching to get pegged.

But Scotty and Melissa ruined the occasion. She had been fired from the Bucket o' Fries, and Scotty was yelling because he couldn't possibly carry both of them on his own. J.R. pieced it together from all the shouting. Melissa had been propositioned by her boss, Doug Donnelly, and when she rejected his advances, he fired her.

J.R. had no doubt Scotty would barge that very evening into the Bucket o' Fries to confront Melissa's former boss. But he allowed his friends to convince him otherwise. All he wanted to do was get away from them and their domestic drama. It was the best day of his life, and they were ruining it.

As witnesses described it, Scotty Pomeroy stalked past the counter into the kitchen with its protesting staff until he found the business office where Doug Donnelly was huddled inside.

*"Don't hurt me!"* they heard the boss beg.

They heard Scotty bellow, "I DON'T HURT PEOPLE, YOU IGNORANT MOTHERFUCK!"

This was followed by a weak protest and a crash of something large and complex to the floor. It was Doug Donnelly's IBM computer, as confirmed by the shocked and terrorized Bucket o' Fries staff, all of whom agreed that Scotty stormed out crying, "GET YOUR OWN WOMAN, YOU FUCKING SLEAZEBALL!"

By that hour, J.R. had staked out the restaurant twice, without incident. The third time, cruising by, he was relieved to find the commotion winding down, and Scotty in handcuffs. No ambulance. No serious calamity. He wheeled over to Fountain Street, parked the car, got out, locked it, and made a detour for the deli.

He bought two cartons of Tropicana orange juice, one for Scotty and one for the cops. He was about to do a very good deed for Melissa Victoria's boyfriend, and the pride he tasted was sweet. He wasn't about to show up at the police station with anything as worthless as water.

Scotty's actual cell time amounted to zero minutes. A good man having a bad day, is how J.R. explained it to Officer Powell, who agreed, and uncuffed Scotty Pomeroy from the desk.

"Nice car," Scotty said miserably, getting into the Nova, clutching his carton of Tropicana.

"Thanks, man," J.R. delivered him back to Melissa Victoria and her avenged honor.

Then he sped off, racing out to Erving Turnpike with the windows down, the engine roaring under the hood, and the wind rippling in his ears. It was the best night of his life, whether anyone ruined it or not.

The next day, Scotty told UPS the truth. They fired him for missing his shift. Now he and Melissa were both unemployed.

J.R. knew a lot of cops, but it wasn't enough to get Scotty off the hook for destroying Doug Donnelly's IBM computer. "Tell your friend he can probably expect a summons," Officer Powell explained it like that.

J.R. had promised himself he would leave Erving, New York when he turned sixteen. All he had been dying to do, for as long as he could remember, was drive away.

And yet the days kept advancing, and he kept going to work, kept fixing cars, kept acting like everything was normal.

It was all for Melissa. Scotty Pomeroy was his friend, and he had nothing against Scotty. He genuinely liked the guy. But maybe she would leave him. Maybe she wanted a guy with money in the bank, who could fix his own car. A guy who didn't want to spend his career in a UPS trailer. A guy who wanted the hell out of Erving just as much as she did.

It lasted maybe a week, that fantasy, before J.R. regained his senses. She was never going to leave him. She loved him. It was stupid to wait on her, even stupider to dwell on her. He was in the middle of a routine tire rotation when he came to understand. It was time to go.

## 19. Self-Determination, or Whatever it Is

Jack Daddio was beckoning from Mr. Woods' Volvo 240, "J.R., come over here. I got a trick I want to show you."

J.R. remained in place, squeezed off the rivet gun once—*rrrrrrrrow*. "What, dad?"

"You should know this," his father insisted.

He stopped what he was doing and trudged over. He didn't like the smell of Volvos. The smell of crayons. Swedish crayons. His father, under the hood, was replacing a spark plug with a length of five-eighths fuel hose instead of using a socket wrench like a normal person.

Buddy interjected, "Hey Daddio, why don't you let that kid out of here so he can lay his own fuel hose?"

"Shut your mouth, Buddy. Don't mess with father-son stuff."

"He's gonna have his whole life to install spark plugs."

"You'll understand, someday, when you're raising a son."

"I'm right here," J.R. reminded them.

"No, you're not," Buddy turned away with a smile.

"J.R., I'm explaining to you, but I'm also explaining to Buddy, because he should understand too."

"I'm working," J.R. said. "I'm right here. Let's hear it. Spark plugs."

Jack Daddio removed his ball cap, wiped his brow and stroked his thinning hair with a curled wrist. For a moment, he looked like he might pass out from exasperation. "You're both just kids," he muttered.

That's when Scotty Pomeroy drove up in the Grand Am with perfect timing.

"Dad, I'll be right back."

"Two minutes."

"Yeah, right," J.R. turned and trotted out to the parking lot.

Scotty's mirrored shades reflected the sunshine. Melissa and Vince were in the car with him. Scotty handed over a flyer and said, "We're going to this thing tonight."

"What thing?" J.R. plucked the flyer out of Scotty's hands and studied it. "A Confederate flag. Two bald eagles. Don't Tread on Me. Self-determination. Declare your individual sovereignty." He handed it back. "Bullshit. You can't be serious."

"Totally serious."

"How do you know it's bullshit?" Melissa asked from the passenger seat.

"At the Church in Avaris?" he asked.

"In the basement," Scotty answered.

Vince Baldwin in the back seat avoided eye contact and withheld comment.

"9 pm?" he asked.

"What?" Melissa teased him. "Oh yeah, I forgot. It's a school night."

*Actually, it's a work night,* he wanted to tell her. But he couldn't get mad at her. Not Melissa Victoria. He might never see her again. He said, "It's not a school night. I dropped out."

"I know."

"So then you're fucking with me," he said it pleasantly.

"I'm fucking with you because you like it, Junior."

"OHHHHH!" his friends began laughing inside the car. He told them, "My name's J.R.!"

But at that moment his father called out from the garage, "JUNIOR! LET'S GO!"

It compounded their laughter. Vince was gleeful. Scotty and Melissa weren't able to help it either.

J.R. jabbed his forefinger at Vince Baldwin's laughing face and said, "Vince, get out of that car so I can smash your melon head into that bread truck!"

"WHOA!" Scotty and Melissa cried.

Vince made to scramble out, but Scotty restrained him with an outstretched arm, pleading, "Dude! You promised!"

"He's starting shit!" Vince protested, whining like a five-year-old, with that perpetually stupid look on his face.

"JUNIOR!" Jack Daddio bellowed from the garage.

"I don't like belonging to stuff," J.R. told his friends. "If you belong to stuff, you lose your self-determination, or whatever it is."

Scotty grinned. "Suit yourself, big guy." He revved the engine and faced forward. "I think it sounds cool. Doesn't mean I belong to it."

"Fuck you, Junior!" Vince Baldwin hissed from the back seat.

"Bye," Melissa waved. She probably thought her smile was playful, even though she knew, they both knew, it was cruel. The Grand Am roared off.

## 20. Water Land

J.R. left his Nova at the garage that night and asked his father for a ride home.

He endured a few of Janice's piano tunes, the last few.

He sat through the family dinner, getting by, deadpan and passive, more or less without effort.

Before he left, he considered going for the Smith & Wesson. It was a nice thought, but it would cost him his head start.

Sneaking out the window was child's play. He made for the shop, looking back at the house only once, and only to see it receding away.

He maintained a jog, with the backpack over his shoulder, ducking out of sight when a pair of headlights came towards him. He proceeded up Pinnacle, down Oxford toward Malta. He could be in the city in no time. Not that he wanted to be in the city, but there was nowhere else to go.

He arrived at the garage, unlocked the Nova, got in, keyed the ignition, gunned the engine, yanked on the headlights. Then he sat there in the shadows, at the helm of his idling car, with a resolution in his heart, and the City of New York waiting just a few dark and lonely highways downstate. It was not what he wanted. He didn't know what he wanted, and this disappointed him in ways he couldn't, didn't want to, untangle.

"Time to drive," he told himself, snapping out of his thoughts. He clicked on the radio, switched to the ballgame. A talk show was on instead. He turned up the volume, pulled the car out of the lot and floored it onto Malta.

"*Can anyone tell me why there's an S in the word 'Island?'*" the radio host was asking.

There was a long pause. In that silence, J.R. found that both the voice and the question had captured his attention.

"*Ok, follow me, people. Island. There's no S in that word. Let me say it again. Loud and clear. ISLAND. No S. You can hear it with your own two ears. There is no letter S in that word.*"

J.R. reached down and turned up the volume.

"*In fact, only an insane person—and I say this with no disrespect to crazy people—but only an insane person would put the letter S in the word Island.*

"*In fact, the only reason the letter S is there... And think about this for a minute... please...*

"*The only reason the letter S is there... is to undermine your natural human instincts. It's there to tell you, hey. Plain-as-day is not so plain-as-day. It's there to tell you, hey. You're not smart. Not until WE say you're smart.*

"*And they do this all day long. Just by complicating a very simple everyday word like Island.*"

"Preach!" J.R. began to chuckle.

"*Society says there's an S in the word Island, so you go along with it. Even though EVERY FIBER OF YOUR INTELLIGENT BEING knows that, hey, there is no S in that word. If there was an S, folks, it would be 'Eyes Land.' Heck, doesn't anybody question this stuff? What are we? Livestock? Do we just eat it all up? And ask for seconds? Until we're tender for the slaughter?*"

Livestock! J.R. couldn't believe it. Someone else actually saw things the same way he did. He drove spellbound.

"*My point is this. This is what they call EDUCATION!*"

That's when J.R. remembered. The Church in Avaris. It was ten after nine. The meeting was underway. He didn't even have to turn around. He was halfway there.

"*It's a perfect encapsulation of the brainwashing they've been doing since the day you were born. That you need the government to tell you what you know and what you don't know. Whether it makes an iota of sense or not. Government creates an S in the word Island. They just conjure it out of thin air. And they do it just so they can categorize you. And put a label on you. And put the Educated into this box over*

74

here. *And put the Uneducated into that box over there. So that every time you spell 'Island' with an S... my friends... I'm sorry to break it to you... But THIS... Is how YOU... Are telling THEM... That YOU... Are STUPID ENOUGH... To believe what THEY... Are telling YOU!"*

"Ha!" J.R. punched the ceiling.

*"Educated? Into the box you go."*

"Who is this guy?"

*"And they do this in a million different ways. Believe me, my friends. To control us. And subdivide us. And subjugate us."*

Driving, entranced, he waited on every next word.

*"But every free man knows he wasn't designed for this kind of mindless dependence and subdivision by the state. Every free man knows. We know in our VERY BEING. We know that MAN... Is SOVEREIGN... Unto HIMSELF!"*

"SELF-DETERMINATION!" J.R. cried. "PREACH IT!"

The church was up ahead. Several cars were parked under the willow tree, including two unfamiliar, nearly identical Silverado pickup trucks.

*"And I have proof that the government is afraid of me,"* the radio host continued, as J.R. wedged the Nova in between somebody's Lincoln Continental and Denny Lowe's 1980 Starlet. *"...because they actually require me to bring someone into this broadcast booth to offer an opposing point of view to mine. This is a requirement BY LAW, mind you. And no, I am not joking about that. The government of these United States of America. All those fine elected officials. They are so afraid of what I'm saying to you right now, that they require me to invite someone in here to disagree with me. So think about that for a minute, while you consider your first amendment rights..."*

J.R. waited a moment longer.

*"And so now, without further suspense, let me introduce, courtesy of the United States Government, Dr. Miroslav Kozinski, professor of linguistics and etymology at Antioch College."*

## 21. The Conversation King

J.R. opened the church basement door. All eyes turned his way, maybe two dozen faces. Vince Baldwin, whom he ignored. Scotty and Melissa, whom he acknowledged with a low-key thumbs up. Denny Lowe, smiling. Mr. Sacks declining eye contact, facing forward in his chair. Many unknown faces too, a collection of men, including an elderly man in a denim vest seated hunched over in a church pew. J.R. closed the door behind him.

At the head of the congregation, the evening's Master of Ceremonies had paused in mid-sentence. J.R. had seen it, but only now came to believe it, the guy's haircut. It was jet black, hale and thick, Elvis on top, shaved clean down the sides, high-and-tight, a Mohawk pompadour. Having seen a million weird haircuts over the years, on music videos and in real life too, this one, and maybe this one alone, actually came across as cool.

The speaker was intimidating beneath his rockabilly crown. His eyes and nose were fierce, eagle-like. His face was expressionless, predatory. His frame was massive, and his blazer and necktie were tight and nearly bursting with male musculature.

The flag on the wall was a variation on the Gadsden Flag's *Don't Tread on Me* iconography, except that the traditional yellow and green color scheme was rendered in black and red, and the iconic rattlesnake was accompanied by the brand

76

name *POSSE SERPENS* in gothic lettering, suggesting knighthood, holy warfare, or some other Medieval reckoning.

Fluorescent lights hummed and flickered, casting the room's walls and plastic chairs and vinyl floor in an institutional hue. J.R. had been down here once before, as a kid, for an animated film. Except it wasn't animated. He remembered this only now. Standing in the church basement, it came back to him. It was a puppet movie, about puppet babies talking to each other.

"Sit down, Junior." Vince Baldwin told him.

"Don't tell me to sit down." J.R. took a seat and faced forward, waiting for the Posse Serpens to resume their meeting.

"Thank you for joining us," the host took over, addressing him directly. "My name is Glenn Disteek. As I was just telling the others, I am not the government assigned, publicly registered, straw man identity GLENN DISTEEK—"

He air-quoted his name here, drawing a quiet laugh from the assembled.

"—but rather a flesh and blood sovereign citizen on this land. A lifelong soldier of sovereign citizenship as established by centuries of common law. Human Rights Director for the Posse Serpens Northeast Chapter. And direct descendant of James Disteek of the Candlemaker Minutemen. I know who I am. Do you know who you are?"

J.R. raised an eyebrow. "Minutemen?"

There was a long moment as Glenn Disteek withheld any response.

Coffee and carrot cake and flyers occupied a folding table beside the church pew against the wall. The Old Man sighed heavily from that direction. J.R. glanced his way, but did not enjoy, and quickly vowed to avoid, the Old Man's glazed, yellow, sentient eyeballs.

He turned back to Glenn Disteek and explained, "Minutemen is our high school mascot." When no one said anything, he added, "My name's J.R."

"Your name's Junior," Vince Baldwin blurted.

J.R. shook his head. "Same difference, Vince."

"No!" Vince Baldwin pointed an accusing finger. "Not the same thing! Nobody says, *Who Shot Junior?*"

Both Scotty and Melissa chuckled at this television reference. Otherwise, no one seemed amused. Glenn Disteek, the rockabilly sovereign citizen, listened patiently as the locals bickered.

J.R. said, "I hate TV, Vince. Maybe you should settle down."

"I am settled down."

"And by the way. It's just society that tells you those two things are different."

"No, it isn't."

"Yes, it is. Society brainwashes you. And you go along with it. Instead of reading the English language. For yourself. Because otherwise you would know that J.R. and Junior are the exact same thing."

"Sounds like the man knows who he is," Disteek intervened at last. "And you? Your name is Vince, right?"

"Um," Vince Baldwin answered. "Yeah."

"So, we all know who we are. That's very good. We were discussing liberty, Mister J.R."

J.R. nodded his head.

"Liberty. Every man's birthright. The founding tenet of this great land. The guiding principle. Even before the United States established liberty as a fundamental right under the Constitution, it was liberty that guided us here to America. It is a straight line from that quest to this meeting we are having here tonight."

J.R. continued nodding along. He only wished Jack Daddio would barge in at this moment, outraged to find his son at a Posse Serpens meeting out at the Church in Avaris. He imagined that the irony would be inevitable, as Jack Daddio would probably end up buying into the entire Posse Serpens' bullshit premise, since it was just good enough to believe.

"So let's get back to the conversation we were having," Glenn Disteek carried on, square-shouldered in his blazer and tie, rebellious in his rockabilly Mohawk. "Let's talk about the difference between common law and penal law."

Melissa Victoria was resting against Scotty Pomeroy's shoulder, chewing gum, working her jawline. J.R. watched until he had to turn away. Mr. Lowe was smiling. J.R. acknowledged him at last, returning the smile, pained by the phony courtesy of it all. Meanwhile—with his attention divided, he didn't remember exactly when—but Glenn Disteek was beginning to make sense with his words, explaining that common law pertains to crimes against the individual, which makes them enforceable, whereas penal law pertains to crimes against the state, which makes them unenforceable.

"The state acting as both victim and prosecutor?" Disteek paused here. "Let that sink in. When the victim is also the prosecutor, your so-called day in court is NOT going to go your way."

J.R. began to wonder. Maybe these guys were onto something.

He studied the formidable Glenn Disteek all over again, looked directly into those hawklike eyes, so that for a split second, maybe longer, he spotted a flare of fear and hostility in return.

And yet the rockabilly orator never faltered, inscrutably professional, addressing all assembled with a natural sense of inclusiveness, "So let's talk about a little tactic I call *Flooding the U.S. Court System with Legal Grievances.*"

J.R. felt he knew this territory, so he raised his hand.

"Yes," Disteek paused. "You. J.R. You have a question?"

"Yes. What makes a contract with you any different from a contract with them?"

A murmur arose from the congregation. J.R. was happy to see Melissa Victoria smiling.

"Will you shut up, Junior?" Vince Baldwin pleaded.

"What's your problem, boy?" a new voice chimed in, and Vince Baldwin fell silent. J.R. was amazed to find that someone else in the world was on his side. Seated amongst the congregation, this guy was dressed, more so than most, for duck hunting, in camouflage pants and a mallard themed overshirt.

When no one said anything else, Glenn Disteek proceeded to respond, "I'm not here to give you orders, son. I'm here to give you information."

"OK. Well. Thank you."

Seated at his church pew, with his shoulders hunched forward and one leg crossed over the other, the Old Man sat coiled, watching. His head was lowered, so that to square his gaze he had to raise his eyebrows and roll his pupils upward, as a man might peer out from under a cowl. His jeans vest was patched with badges and insignia and flags, including the First Cavalry's horse and stripe in black and gold. Also, a red and white oval stitched in block capitals to read FOLLOW ME. Other patches bore unfamiliar iconography, including at least one umlaut-crowned foreign language logo.

"I like skepticism," the Old Man was speaking, in a dry, time ravaged voice, as J.R. realized the words were meant for him. "Shackles of the misfit. You trust knowledge too much. Reality not enough. What answer you looking for, son? Tell us true now."

Startled, J.R. had no answer.

The Old Man's hair was white and wispy and soft. He was the least intimidating person in the room, including Denny Lowe. And yet his glazed and yellow poached egg eyeballs bound a spell.

Unsure what to say, J.R. responded at last, "What answer?" And then, while the Old Man waited, he said, "The truthful one."

"Looking for the truth," the Old Man affirmed. "Meaning you ain't found it yet. That don't reflect well on you, son. But at least you're being forthright with us now."

J.R. sat there bewildered. His father had never talked to him this way.

Everyone awaited his response, many with amused faces. It was no surprise that Vince Baldwin and Melissa Victoria were enjoying themselves, but the happy look on Scotty's face was a new disappointment, especially out here at the Church in Avaris, where he couldn't even keep his own car running.

The front man Glenn Disteek continued with a new air of satisfaction as the assembly now gave him their full attention. He began explaining the Posse Serpens militia training, which was supposedly the appealing part, but J.R. could pay only partial mind, having been dismantled in a matter of seconds by an old hillbilly. He was trying to remember exactly how the exchange with the Old Man went, and when exactly his first misstep had occurred.

"It can be grueling," Disteek warned the congregation, "but if you stick with it, you will receive combat training to defend yourself, your family, and your country, from enemies within and without."

"Live ammo?" Vince Baldwin asked.

"You better believe it."

"Hand-to-hand combat?" someone asked.

"Long as you don't mind getting hurt," the Old Man muttered from his church pew.

J.R. peered again at the Old Man, only to turn away immediately.

"So I have a serious question," Melissa announced. She deferred briefly to her man for permission, but Scotty wasn't going to stop her. The room fell silent. Everyone waited. She went ahead.

"OK, here's my story. In a nutshell. I was going to sign up for the Army, but I had to wait. What I want is military training. And the Army doesn't care whether I'm a girl or not. They'll take me as I am. Is this like that? Does it matter if I'm a girl? Because if it does, I'm not interested. I want to fight."

The men murmured their collective approval, but J.R. heard the sarcasm in it, and he guessed Melissa did too.

"If you are admitted into the Posse Serpens," Glenn Disteek answered, "you are entering into a culture of freedom. In the Posse Serpens, we are enslaved by nothing, except maybe *Freedom Itself*. That fundamental tenet. Mankind's natural state. The militia training is always ongoing, and operations are conducted by the best prepared. Opportunities are available to everyone..."

Melissa was nodding her head. Others nodded along with her.

"But that being said," Disteek continued, "as with any culture, people tend to fall into roles best suited to their strengths. That means if you're a killer, you can come and be... *our killer.*"

This was met with laughter.

"On the other hand, if you happen to make a great pot roast. Or if you happen to know how to sew up a knife wound. Well... We need those roles filled too."

"No chance of a pot roast," Scotty grinned.

"You asshole," she elbowed him. Scotty hugged her. The group was laughing along.

Glenn Disteek maintained his smile. "However," he said, "before any of that, there is an initiation process. And initiation is one of the things I'm proudest of as a member of the Posse Serpens. Our program is no faceless institutionalized brainwashing factory. On the contrary, we tailor our program to the individual. To bring out their best."

"But there's military training, right?" Vince Baldwin was asking.

Disteek nodded. "I would call it paramilitary. I was in the military, son. And I'm proud to say, this ain't that."

Vince nodded. Some chuckled. Melissa was rapt.

"Come to the Compound with us tonight," Disteek advised. "That offer extends to everyone, of course."

"So if we pass initiation," Scotty asked, "does that mean we're in the Posse Serpens?"

J.R. wanted to ask what percentage of recruits had failed initiation, but considering that everyone in the world hated him, he saw no reason to help them out by thinking it through.

"If you pass initiation," Disteek said, "then you're one of us."

"And what does that mean?" Scotty wanted to know.

"How do you mean?"

"I mean... Is there work?"

"Ah," Disteek smiled. "The Posse Serpens is a self-sustaining community. There's work all right. Plenty of it. But not the way you mean it. There's no paycheck or taxes. It's a family. With a family's pride. But bills? Debts? You can leave all that behind you."

Scotty was nodding his head, intrigued.

"Look at it this way," Disteek told him. "The Pilgrims who crossed in the Mayflower and settled this country. Did they need any of that? No, they did not."

Abruptly, the duck hunter raised a new concern, "So what are *you* doing," he wanted to know, "up at the state capital?"

Other men began murmuring disapproval, as Glenn Disteek tried to get on top of it, "Yes, yes, that's right. I am frequently at the state capital—"

"Which makes you just another politician—"

"Lobbying for freedom on behalf of the Posse Serpens, and all Americans."

The duck hunter wasn't buying it, arms folded, shaking his head.

"You think they'll just hand it over?" Glenn Disteek asked him. He was confronting all of them. "You think they'll just hand over your freedom without a fight? This is a *fight*. In point of fact, it's the only fight there is. And it is taking place on many fronts. And I've devoted my life to this fight, including my activities in Albany. But let me be very clear. When push comes to shove, I am no politician. I am no different than any man here. My retribution is swift."

He paused and let them think about it for moment. When no one spoke, he continued, "Real change is taking place in Albany. A state assembly seat has been vacated by the untimely bankruptcy and soon to be incarceration of Marina Pillagret-Kincaid—"

"All right, wait a minute..." another heckler chimed in.

J.R. was vaguely aware of the Marina Pilligret-Kincaid scandal. Another corrupt politician wasn't exactly newsworthy, but it seemed a lot of people were particularly upset about this one.

The heckler demanded to know, "Wasn't it you who shut down the Anti Marina Pilligret-Kincaid campaign?"

"Shut it down? No."

"She's a crook!"

"They proved she stole!"

"She's a thief! They proved it! Why isn't she in jail?"

"Yes. Yes. YES! She's a crook!" Disteek held his empty hands up for all to see. "Yes, she stole! But guys, please! Anti Marina Pilligret-Kincaid T-shirts? You just have to trust me on this. That is not an idea whose time has come."

It settled them down. Disteek was wrapping it up anyway. "OK, so, if there are no further questions. Just to conclude, I leave you with this. You will hear the word rebel thrown around. And it's got a nice ring to it. From the Confederate Army to Star Wars, am I right? Everyone loves a rebel..."

"That's right," someone muttered.

"But maybe rebellion is a word, and a notion, for a bygone era. Maybe it's time to call The Truth what it is. It's not rebellion. It's survival."

He had their full attention once again.

"Survival," he continued, "in all its legal, social, political and military dimensions. Many of these angles are beyond a recruitment meeting like this. Suffice to say, the Posse Serpens will teach you more than just combat scenarios and weapons skills. You will learn how to declare your individual sovereignty as a free man on this land. And you will learn the truth about the United States of America. That it has, in fact, become a global corporate legalistic evil enterprise. And that you have, in fact, not entered into any legal contract with this entity. Thank you for your time. I'm available for questions afterwards, but we'll be travelling on within half-an-hour. If you want to learn more, follow us to the Compound after the meeting. Meanwhile, there's carrot cake and coffee on the side table. Also, please take a flyer."

Chairs scraped against the floor as men arose. J.R. remained seated, unsure what to do. Denny Lowe was approaching, saying, "J.R., tell your dad I said hello," but he would leave it to Mr. Lowe to tell his father about this roguish meeting in the basement of the Church of Avaris. Standing up and suffering through the handshake, he could only promise, "Your car is in good hands, Mr. Lowe."

Meanwhile, he watched the Old Man, who had risen from his church pew to approach the folding table and the mostly intact carrot cake. Obviously, the Old Man was smart. Not daring to chicken out, J.R. approached him, asking, "So how do you do it?"

"I'm Edward," the Old Man extended a hand. "How do I do what?"

J.R. shook hands. A long moment passed as Edward awaited his answer. The Old Man's grizzled speaking voice was intriguing, but it wasn't the voice. Something—J.R. couldn't quite name it—had put him in a daze. *This is what being dumb feels like,* he realized.

"I'm sorry," he finally confessed. "I can't seem to think."

"Don't be stupid," Edward set a slice of cake on a paper plate and handed it over with a plastic fork. "Why don't you come to the Compound tonight?"

J.R. looked down at the cake piped with orange frosting.

Scotty appeared at the table with Melissa at his side, saying, "Dude, I'm checking this thing out."

"Are you serious? It's an hour away."

"Oh please," Melissa said. "So's everything."

J.R. smiled. "Actually, that a very good point."

"Thank you," she could be brightly demure and not sincere about it at the same time. She looked gorgeous just then, the blonde hair, the white smile, the luminous skin. It would be worth it, if only to follow her there.

"Dude—"

"What?" he was exasperated with that word, *dude.*

"Are you going?" Scotty wanted an answer. "Let's go."

Edward stood patiently observing the three young locals.

Now Vince Baldwin joined in, saying, "C'mon, Junior, are you a crotch-sniffer or are you a man?"

"A display of dominance," Edward noted.

"Gross, Vince," Melissa said.

"What about you, Edward?" J.R. asked.

Edward eyeballed him, chewing his bite of cake, "What about me what?"

"Are you driving to this Compound tonight?"

84

"I'm travelling there, if that's what you mean."

"You're not from there?"

Edward shrugged, "I travel. It keeps me young."

They laughed at that.

J.R. said, "I don't like belonging to things."

"Yes," the Old Man pointed his plastic fork at J.R. "Your feelings. They must be known to others. That's important to you."

"How so?"

"Don't look at me, son."

Scotty, Melissa, even Vince stood enthralled.

J.R. knew he had put himself here on purpose, over-matched once again by the Old Man. "So what are you?" he countered "A guru or something?"

"A guru? Son, I am nowhere near that perfect."

J.R. didn't like being called *son*.

Edward continued, "What's the matter with you? Some-body ain't taking you seriously, boy? Is that your problem? Or is it something you done? Maybe the past catching up on you. Got you chewing over your memories, squaring 'em out. Mak-ing sure what you seen can't be un-seen. But maybe that's where a young man needs some instruction. Thinking any of it is worth carrying around. Let me ask you, son. You ever paid a nickel to un-see a damn thing?"

"That's what I mean!" J.R. cried. He looked around at his friends, then back at the Old Man, who seemed a power source unto a spectrum only visible to a chosen few. "How are you able to do that? I want to know how you're doing that!"

The Old Man chuckled. "Me? Doing something?" The others laughed nervously. The Old Man paused to calmly enjoy another forkful of cake.

"I don't mean any offense, Edward," J.R. persisted. "I'm just asking respectfully. How do you do that? With your words? They're like spells. Can you teach me?"

"Do what now?"

"I don't know," J.R. shook his head. "It's some kind of trick."

"Trick? Ain't no trick. Skeptics trick themselves, son. It's in your head I tricked you. Save yourself the trouble. Just trick yourself into thinking you tricked me. Same difference, except you're happy. But it don't cross your mind to just hold a conversation with me, do it?"

There was another pause while everyone tried to keep up.

"But what if we was at *war?*" the Old Man continued. "What if your life depended on a conversation with me? You think you could do it?"

"This is the CONVERSATION KING!" Scotty announced, grabbing J.R. by the shoulders, breaking the tension.

"See you there, losers," Vince told them.

Glenn Disteek and two men in camouflage had begun clearing the table of flyers and cake crumbs and paper products. Edward, old and bent, peered at J.R. through his eerie yellow eyeballs.

"All right," J.R. said, "All right. I'll go to this so-called Compound. But on one condition. You have to answer me one question honestly."

The Old Man obliged, with all the time in the world.

Again, J.R. had set himself up. He was lost for his one question. *I'm the barnyard animal!* he realized.

Edward was waiting. So were Scotty and Melissa. The panic mounted. He had to say something. He said, "I see what you're doing. You're just jamming me up with details. Like all those legal briefs Mr. Disteek was talking about. Throwing words at me. Jamming me up. And it's okay. I'm not mad or anything. I'm just asking you how you do it? I just want to know how you do it. That's all."

The Old Man laughed. "Y'all are a microbe. Calling the cure a detail."

It was disorienting. The brain just turned over, helplessly mired. *You finally meet someone you respect... and they don't respect you back? Not at all? Am I supposed to just kick this old man's ass?*

Edward continued, "Or a very cooperative alien species. Like that Martian feller on Bugs Bunny. With his helmet in his eyes."

"OK," J.R. raised up his hands and laughed. "Let's just go to New Jersey."

Scotty was visibly relieved. Melissa snapped her gum.

Out in the lot, when they made for the cars, Vince Baldwin was already leaning against the Bonneville, waiting for the exodus. J.R. got into his Nova and keyed the ignition. Then he sat there, with his heart racing, staring through the windshield into the illuminated cornfields behind the Church in Avaris.

His father had never, ever, talked to him like the Old Man had talked to him just now. He could only imagine being

86

raised by a man like that. That kind of power coming second nature. He dropped the Nova into drive, and pictured Jack Daddio, asleep in front of the boob tube, with no idea of the hiccup that awaited him tomorrow morning.

## 22. The Retreat

The Lincoln Continental and the twin Silverados belonged to Glenn Disteek and his two bodyguards. That trio led the way out of town, followed by a second trio, Vince Baldwin's Bonneville, Scotty Pomeroy's Grand Am, and the '72 Chevy Nova with J.R. Daddio at the helm.

Inside the car, the ballgame was ghostly and distant from the west coast, fading into static. J.R. switched it off and welcomed the silence, even if it allowed more headroom for paranoia. As the southbound miles curled and dipped, he began to drift further behind the convoy's snaking taillights, ready and waiting for a change of mind.

No such moment came. Up ahead, Disteek's craft floated off road and the others followed, hurtling into swirling dust clouds until the surrounding woods closed in. Tree trunks, branches and leaves fled incandescent out of the darkness. The cars lurched and buckled as the corridor floor deteriorated into lopsided undulations. Finally, the terrain settled into a path. When a wooden bridge met their cautious approach, they filed to a crawl over that trestlework.

Once across they advanced, column-like, out of the forest and into a clearing where a settlement of trailers and shanties lay in wait beneath the moonlit sky. The watchtower ignited its floodlight. Two seven-foot plaster-of-Paris eagles flanked either side of the open gateway, with standing flags to accompany each. Posse Serpens. Stars and Bars. Don't Tread on Me.

The guardsman below waited unalarmed, brandishing a rifle. As the line of vehicles poured through, J.R. rolled down his window and shared a nod of acknowledgment with the gateway's lonesome armed and expressionless sentry. Only now, having crossed the threshold, did he realize. He really should have called his father first.

The next day, over the satellite phone, he explained, "It's a *retreat,* Dad. Try to understand. It's not that I went on a retreat when I left the house. It's just... That's how it played out."

"A retreat?"

"I really just went for a drive. Which I have every right to do. And besides, no one ever noticed before. When I snuck out."

His father fell silent over the phone.

"Anyway, for me and for Scotty, also Melissa Victoria, and Vince Baldwin... What we did is... We met up with some people... And now we're on a retreat."

"Wait. What? Vince Baldwin? You're on a retreat with Vince Baldwin?"

"Jeez, Dad... It has nothing to do with Vince Baldwin."

"You can't go on a retreat. I need you here, son."

"You'll be all right."

"No I won't. Wait. What kind of retreat?"

"You know..."

"NO, I DON'T KNOW!"

J.R. held the phone away from his ear as his father began shouting.

The Posse Serpens' so-called business office was little more than a plywood shed elevated on cinder blocks, but it was cluttered with purpose. Flyers, flags, posters, charts, maps, and other documents covered the walls. An easel-hinged blackboard rested mute and smudged with recent erasures. The wall calendar was scrawled with notations. Spare fatigues sat stuffed inside an open bureau of square cubbies.

Meanwhile, seated in the doorframe, with the butt of an assault rifle pressed against his thigh, an enormous, red-haired, colorfully dressed Posse Serpens soldier listened in. He was called de Ram, with no first name. de Ram wore a tight yellow T-shirt that emphasized his beer belly and also lent his complexion a jaundiced quality, which mismatched his freckles and orange suspenders and backward-sprung orange hair

in a way that evoked, for J.R., something horrific, like a bar-
baric clown.

Not wanting to look at de Ram, or have de Ram look back
at him, J.R. returned the big plastic phone to his ear, and
quietly endured another barrage of Jack Daddio's ranting and
pleading.

Reduced to that passive state, his thoughts turned back to
the previous night's arrival. As it turned out, the so-called
Compound was a glorified trailer park, a horseshoe arrangement of RVs forming a perimeter, with a watchtower and a
few other structures erected within that encampment. From
his prowling Nova, he had spotted a sleeping vegetable garden, a line of skinned deer carcasses, and a single-propeller
Cessna parked under a plywood canopy. He also took note of
the central social area, strung with white Christmas lights,
where a handful of Posse Serpens soldiers stood encircling a
roaring firepit.

Following past that welcoming party, he proceeded to the
parking lot, where the Lincoln Continental and the two Silverados had taken open slots, while the Bonneville and Grand
Am filed in a few rows down. J.R. drove past all those dusty
maneuverings and took a space at the end, wheeling outward
and backing in, all the better to make his escape if the need
should arise. When he killed the ignition, he could hear the
rumbling of a generator.

He watched as Melissa exited the Grand Am's passenger
side and casually executed, with her hands over her own body,
something she would likely dismiss as "stretching." He
wanted to tell her not to do that, not here. But how could he?
It was up to Scotty to tell her stuff like that.

That's when the Old Man appeared in the Nova's open
window, startling him. "Remember, kid. Don't ever miss an
opportunity to keep your mouth shut."

"J.R.?"

"What?"

"Are you there?" His father's nerves sounded shot.

"It's like a wilderness group," J.R. explained into the
phone. "Survivalist stuff. They need a mechanic too, so I'm
getting paid."

It was a lie, a harmless one, intended only to rouse, or try
to rouse, some good humor from the watchful, enormous,
colorful soldier de Ram, who reclined in the doorway with a
rifle at rest against his warrior-sized thigh. de Ram had a bar-

barian quality—Viking or Visigoth, whatever the difference—that promised, for J.R., a culture of personal freedom that Glenn Disteek, the recruitment officer, had failed to quite fulfill.

The night before, as they were standing around the firepit, J.R. had become fascinated with de Ram's appearance. The massive, ogre-like frame drawn in bright solids and stripes, the yellow T-shirt and orange suspenders. The copper hair slicked back over his scalp in curly and dramatic abandon. The bent and downward sinking nose, baroque in shape and seemingly in texture. The head that seemed to cant lopsided and heavy upon the muscled fulcrum of its neck.

Vince Baldwin had asked, "So is it Glenn Disteek that's in charge?"

Fat Ransom answered, "No one's in charge, kid."

The Old Man chimed in, "No formal hierarchy."

That's when de Ram's long and deep speaking voice intoned, "On paper, I'm the Public Relations Director."

"No bureaucracy, no humiliation," the Old Man added.

*"Public Relations...?"* J.R. questioned.

He had said it out of sheer curiosity, even as he understood that it came across as skeptical. Once again, the Old Man's poached egg eyeballs held him paralyzed by their spooky omniscience. The displeasure was like a physical forcefield weighing down on him.

Meanwhile, de Ram had lowered his head so that his backward flung hair dawned in firelicked shocks over his massive cranium. His tight yellow shirt served to buttress his beer gut, but also vividly bind his freckle mottled arms. His great right biceps flexed as he considered the bottle in his grip. Embers swirled from below to scale his powerful frame. His combat boots planted in the ashes seemed to conjure up solace of some greater kind. When at last he raised his drowsy eyeballs, they were overlarge, even for his size.

He said, "That's right. Public Relations. You'll get it. There's an art to it. Which you'll get. Or come to get. Or not. But don't worry about me. I'm on the other side of your troubles."

That was last night. Meanwhile, Jack Daddio was lecturing over the phone about the difference between collecting a paycheck and running a business. He was going on and on, and J.R. tried to listen, but mostly just waited.

When at last his father was spent, he said, "I'm sorry, Dad. But I'm taking off. Don't worry too much, please. It's not forever. I'll be back. It's just a two-week initiation in Pennsylvania."

"What? Pennsylvania?"

"Yes. Pennsylvania."

"No! NO! You're my SON! You don't go to PENNSYLVANIA! You don't go to PENNSYLVANIA!"

"You're such a hypocrite."

"Wait. Wait a minute. J.R. *Where* in Pennsylvania? Wait! Slow down! Where are you right now?"

J.R. didn't know where he was. "You're always saying how—"

"Son, please. Tell me where you are—"

"I told you already—"

"You ran off to PENNSYLVANIA? Are you fucking kidding me? That is the stupidest thing I've ever heard!"

"Here we go."

"Grow up, for fuck sake! We are busy today! BUSY! DON'T YOU UNDERSTAND THAT? IT'S YOU AND ME, SON!"

Once again, he held the phone away and allowed his father's tirade to spill into the Posse Serpens Public Relations office.

de Ram scowled. J.R. returned the handset to his ear.

"IS THAT WHAT I'M ALWAYS SAYING? YOU GOD-DAMN SPOILED LITTLE BRAT!? IS THAT WHAT I'M ALWAYS SAYING!?—*Excuse me just a minute, Mrs. Harrison, I'll be right with you*—We have a deal, mister..." Jack Daddio was gasping, out of breath.

J.R. said nothing, with the plastic phone pressed into his ear.

"A man's word is his bond. Don't you know that?"

J.R. peered over at de Ram.

"You are my third mechanic!" Jack Daddio erupted again. "You are my tow truck guy! There are five guys! FIVE GUYS! There are FIVE GUYS I could name RIGHT NOW who would KILL for your job—"

"Thank you for making my point for me, Dad. You'll be fine. Five guys will fill in for me. I'll be back. I'll call you."

He hung up. *That was easy,* he told himself. His heart was racing.

"Your friend Vince needs that phone," de Ram advised.

92

## 23. The Compound

The Old Man Edward introduced them at the firepit the night before. "I call them the *Erving Confederacy*," he said, hunched over in his colorful, patch-bedecked jeans jacket, unfurling and extending his open hand.

Four Posse Serpens members were there to welcome the newcomers. This included the colorful ogre de Ram, also a slender dark haired woman named Ruth, also a sinewy, bare-chested, bearded weirdo named Lafayette, and an overweight character dressed in black fatigues who insisted they call him, "Fat Ransom."

"That's my name," he told them, shaking hands.

A dog sat nearby, a Rottweiler. It raised its head for the introductions, then flopped its face back down into the firelit dust.

The flames burned hot and bright in a pit contrived from a semi wheel and two steel dairy crates. Ashes and embers drifted in the shifting smoke. Whiskey and Rum and Schlitz made the rounds. Melissa accepted a bottle, followed by Scotty and Vince. When the booze came his way, J.R. declined.

"You kids hungry?" Fat Ransom asked. "We got some venison leftover."

"Fuck yeah," Vince Baldwin answered. "I could eat a horse."

"Well, all we got is venison."

93

Everyone chuckled. Even the Old Man snorted a laugh. Fat Ransom maintained a relaxed and amused presence. His chubby fingers swirled his Schlitz can by its rim until he looked at it, downed it, and flung it into a nearby bucket. He then stooped to grab a replacement from the cooler by his feet.

The Rottweiler raised its head once again to watch from outside the circle's glow, as de Ram raised a spit, skewered a glazed deer cutlet from an aluminum pan and handed it off to Vince Baldwin. "It's cooked already," he advised. "Just warm it up."

Lafayette rubbed his own distended moonlit belly and said, "No more for me," as his gaze wandered up to the night sky.

"Me neither," J.R. said.

Edward hissed at him, *"What did I tell you not to do?"*

J.R. could hear his own voice whining at high pitch like a child, *"I'm not hungry!"*

And now from some helpless sideline he watched himself fold, once again, to the Old Man's will.

"Don't cook it too much," Glenn Disteek was saying.

Melissa plunged her deer cutlet into the flames.

"Melissa, baby doll..." Scotty said.

"Buzz off," she elbowed him. "I want it charred."

"Carcinogens—"

"Oh, grow a pair." She received a hearty laugh.

"OK, eat your paint chips," he told her.

"Where's mine?" Fat Ransom asked.

"It's over here whenever you want it," de Ram answered.

Fat Ransom raised an eyebrow. "Ruth, babe," he said. "Get our guests some clean plates and napkins."

Ruth handed her bottle to Vince Baldwin, then spun and wove off in the direction of a nearby shed. Meanwhile, Fat Ransom girthed the firepit over to the meat tray, where he seized up a poker and speared his own slab. The Rottweiler was watching. Fat Ransom turned, skewer in hand, and orbited back around the circle's semi-circumference where he slung the cutlet down onto a sauce-slathered plate with a flick of the wrist. *"Cash Clarick Vittles* it ain't," he said. "But damn it's good."

"Whoa, Fatso," Glenn Disteek admonished him.

Fat Ransom dismissed him, "Relax, Rambo. It's a brand name. Or soon to be one."

Disteek wasn't happy about it. He turned to the Old Man and said, "Five minutes." Then he stalked off in the direction of the Public Relations office.

"I've been wondering," J.R. asked, "about our quarters?"

*"Quarters?"* It was the Old Man once again, with his yellow eyeballs and crooked frame, in his vestment of striped and colorful patches. J.R. couldn't look at him anymore. The initial intrigue he felt in the church basement had become a smothering, inescapable anxiety.

For a moment, his evening flashed back to him in sequence. The final family dinner. The easy sneaking out. The radio host and his infallible logic. Glenn Disteek's church basement sermon. The Old Man's command of wordplay. The thirst for wisdom that had led him out beyond Erving, New York, to a militia compound somewhere in the New Jersey woods.

The firepit crackled. The Rottweiler dog watched from the dancing shadows. The Old Man was speaking, and not just to J.R., but to all of them, "These next two weeks is about being awake. Not about shuteye. You understand that?"

Ruth returned to the firepit with paper plates and napkins to hand out. The meat cutlets glistened on their turning spits.

Scotty took up the conversation. "I'd like to know more about the work regimen."

"It'll put you through the ringer, son, don't worry about that," Lafayette's voice spoke from the heart of his chest-naked reverie.

"OK, but for instance," Scotty wanted to know, "how do you keep your recruits hydrated?"

Ruth tilted her head, "You mean *water?*"

"Son," Edward chimed in, "ain't no Goddamn *Gatorade* there."

"No," Scotty insisted. "Yes," he told Ruth, "water."

de Ram eyeballed Scotty askance.

Ruth kept it pleasant, laughing. "You bet there's water, soldier. We ain't sending you to your deaths. It's just boot camp is all. We all done it."

"Water covers 89 percent of the earth," the Old Man reminded them all.

"OK, that's good," Scotty acquiesced.

J.R. kept his mouth shut. He figured maybe the Old Man was right, somehow, about the 89 percent. It didn't sound right, though.

95

Glenn Disteek emerged from the business office wearing a black leather trench coat. His pompadour bobbed along with his purposeful stride. "We're on our way," he announced.

"Well then," the Old Man answered.

"What?" Vince Baldwin protested. "You guys are leaving? Where are you going?"

Disteek arrived at the fire pit. Ignoring Vince's question, he spoke to all of them.

"Remember that this is a movement. And especially remember to vote for me. Not you, J.R., you're not old enough. But Scotty, Melissa, and Vince. I'm asking you, straight forward, for your vote."

"I'll kill for you," Vince Baldwin told him.

"That's perfect. And appreciated. But vote. Understand? Vote."

Vince pointed to himself. "I will. I'll vote."

"J.R.?"

"Yes."

"Vote for me in two years."

"I'll be in Colorado in two years."

Disteek ignored him. He spoke to all of them, "In the next two weeks, you will come to understand the forces aligned against you and your own freedom. You will also come to understand how the Posse Serpens is preparing, by any means necessary, to take this land back from those forces. I'm explaining this to you now because initiation will not be easy..."

Lafayette chuckled. Fat Ransom covered his mouth with his napkin. The Old Man remained watchful.

Disteek's hawklike eyes blinked a few times. Otherwise, he remained unmoving, boots planted at the firepit's edge. He said, "You might even find yourself wondering: Can I make it to the other side of this thing? In those moments, I want you to remember one thing. It only gets harder. Because nothing in this life is harder than the truth. And the truth is, they are never, ever going to give it to you. If you want your freedom, you have to take it."

No one spoke. Fat Ransom downed another Schlitz. With a rhythm both clocklike and graceful he tossed the empty can away to drag a fresh one out of the ice.

"See you in two weeks," Disteek concluded.

He departed, side-by-side with the Old Man, the two figures in tandem, one broad shouldered and strong, the other frail and hunched over, both diminishing beyond the firepit's rippling heat. Making for the parking lot they were accompanied in time by the two bodyguards, who made for their twin Silverados. Soon the dust was alight with headlamps, Glenn Disteek's Lincoln Continental leading the way toward the makeshift gate out of the Compound. When at last they were gone, the Old Man's physical departure was like some desperate dose of oxygen. J.R. heaved a sigh of relief.

And yet the Rottweiler caught his attention. It had pushed itself up to stand, and turn, and pad over, closer, assuming the Old Man's place along the heat of the tire rim's fire. J.R. could see, as he peered into the dog's dark, glimmering eyes, that it was intelligent. It watched him too, before lowering its muscled sternum to the ground, and flopping down its jowls upon its paws.

After the entourage drove out, the rest of them stayed up another half-hour or so. Melissa had questions about a woman's role in the Posse Serpens. Ruth had answers, explaining how she herself was a fighting soldier in the militia, and how she favored her .38 Special, but how, for the most part, she did not go on maneuvers. This, she stressed, was by choice. Because being in the Posse Serpens means being realistic.

"Which is not to say us women cain't fight here," she clarified. "Ask any one of these here tough guys, I ain't no one to fuck with."

The handful of men laughed approvingly. Melissa laughed too. Goaded on, Ruth grinned. "Plus I know first aid, too. Better than most doctors."

"Who are we training to fight?" Scotty wanted to know.

Lafayette answered, "Don't matter. The Feds. The Commies."

"Here here," Vince raised a toast.

"The Russians. The Mexicans," Lafayette continued. "The Blacks. The Jews. We ain't prejudice."

Somebody's sly chuckle greeted this punchline. J.R. tried to imagine an army of blacks or Jews marching on the Compound, but he couldn't. Russians, maybe.

Later that night, he was awakened by the sound of gunfire—two quick pistol reports, like an execution.

"Whoa!" Scotty breathed. Vince Baldwin whispered, "What the fuck!"

The dog was barking in dots and dashes off the echoing hills.

*"Guys?!"* Melissa's asked.

"It's all right," J.R. told her.

The four of them were sitting up, waiting for lights, alarms, and shouting armies. No such cavalry came.

A wooden platform, under a canvas lean-to, served as their quarters. J.R. could hear, only now, that the generator was silent. The crickets and frogs and katydids thrummed indifferent to the gunshots and the barking dog.

"Should we go say something?" Scotty asked.

"No," J.R. rested back onto his folded arms. "These guys knew there was going to be shots fired. This was a test."

"A test?" Vince argued. "A test of what?"

"I don't know. But stumbling around in the dark is not the way to impress these guys. Trust me. We're supposed to lay low. I say play it cool."

Vince snorted. "Oh, you're cool now?"

"We'll find out tomorrow."

Melissa chuckled, briefly, quietly.

With that small measure of approval, J.R. was happy. Afterwards, he slept in peace.

Before dawn there was a shift change. Men's voices in the dark. Jocular, hushed and comforting. He awakened only briefly, then drifted back under. The chilly temperature was part of the sleeping, its depth.

He awoke as the Compound came alive with the rising sun. There was no bugle call, nor any chain of command. Men and women, self-motivated, simply busied themselves. The Posse Serpens flag hung halyard-to-floor behind the coffee urn. The long breakfast table under the canvas tent gradually came together with servings and place setting and utensils as the women and children worked. The dog padded around, attuned to the human activity.

As J.R. watched, he released a long breath. He observed his companions stirring beside him. Melissa had her face rolled into her forearm. Her blonde hair was unkempt. Her curves were beautiful. He had to look away.

*"Hey, darlin',"* Scotty whispered to her.

"Would you stop?" Vince intervened.

"Would you fuck off?" Scotty retorted.

"Off of what?"

"Vince Baldwin is going to ruin this whole thing," J.R. announced. "I can feel it."

"Fuck you, Junior. You're a fucking embarrassment, you little stain. I'm just glad I don't have to kick your ass anymore, now that I've got the Posse Serpens to do it for me."

"You couldn't kick your own ass without losing," J.R. told him.

The smell of bacon got Vince and the others moving, but J.R. remained seated, watching the smoking stove pipe atop the makeshift kitchen's plywood and Plexiglas frame. Other Compound structures were professionally built, notably the watchtower. Several of the trailers were topped with umbrellas and beach chairs, every one of those posts currently abandoned. The firewood was in abundance, harvested out of a clearing through the forest. In the light of day, it was clear the Cessna airplane had no room to take off, no matter how many trees got cut down.

Eggs and bread and bacon were served. About twenty-five men and women seated themselves at the breakfast table, including Ruth, Fat Ransom, de Ram, Lafayette, and a tableful of others, including a few fidgety but well-behaved children occupying place settings in their junior black fatigues.

As a group they paused to pray, with hands clasped over their food, and Fat Ransom leading them in unison, "Dear Jesus, by the strength of the cross shall the white race overcome. We ask that you bless this feast and those gathered for the grace of its bounty. Amen."

J.R. and Scotty exchanged a brief, troubled glance but said nothing.

One of the soldiers had a Swastika tattooed on his forearm, which J.R. found worrisome. Not that the symbol itself bothered him. He had always liked the look of the swastika. When he was younger, he would draw them, along with many other symbols, on his paper airplanes. However, he knew, even then, not to show them to anybody.

As introductions began, J.R. endured the ritual of saying hello and shaking hands with those next to and across from him. Ruth was among the women present, along with a couple of fierce looking older ladies, and a couple of other possible moms. *This is no place to meet a girlfriend,* he gathered.

As for the men, he did his best to inventory their names. Lafayette, he already knew. The guy with the swastika was called Derby. And so on around the table. A few were young, J.R.'s age or maybe more like Scotty's age. A few others were elders, semi-retired. Most were in their fighting prime, effi-

99

ciently deployed, battle hardened muscle. J.R. made up his mind that he would eat as much venison, and run as many obstacle courses, and shoot as many Russians as it took to become a warrior like that.

As for the rest of it, the white race and the swastikas, he would listen to what they had to say, and then choose his own path, which he knew, ahead of time, was the other direction.

de Ram was asking Ruth, "What's the latest on the sturgeon?"

Ruth started laughing. "That's right, the sturgeon," she said. She had Melissa's ear. "Inside joke. It means whichever way the state is fucking with us today. See, they don't like us cutting down these here trees," she waved her hand around. "They call it deforestation, even though it's our own Goddamn trees."

"Why sturgeon?" Melissa asked.

"Well, I'll tell you why. See, they will tell you how many sturgeons you can kill. But then some bridge needs to get built, and suddenly—*abracadabra*—they raise the number of sturgeons you can kill. See, they'll do it for a bridge. But if it's just little old you and me, that's all, trying to make a living? Well they use these regulations to come after us. Which ain't even constitutional."

"Who's they?"

"Well, that's the funny part. We ain't even talkin' about the Feds, or even the State of New Jersey. We're talking about the town! The fuckin' *town!* These idiots that walk among us! So anyway..." Ruth looked around at all of them, "it's not sturgeon this time around. It's wood. But we call it sturgeon anyway," she grinned and winked at J.R. "Sturgeon is like a code word."

"Nice!" Vince Baldwin grinned.

"We got 'em jammed up in court," Ruth concluded, addressing Melissa again, "with their so-called deforestation. I mean, we subsist on firewood, don't we? I mean, look at us here."

It was after breakfast when J.R. rang up his father from the satellite phone in de Ram's P.R. office. Vince made a call too. Scotty and Melissa decided not to make any calls. They had each other; this was their theme of the day. After Vince was off the phone, it was time to go.

"What about clothes?" Melissa asked. "Do we get the black uniforms?"

100

"Dues!" Fat Ransom brightened. "We'll get to the subject of dues later this afternoon."

"You wash your clothes in the trough," Ruth answered. She added, "You wash yourself in the trough, too."

"This is about survival, you understand?" de Ram told them.

"Still time to turn around," Vince taunted Melissa.

"Fuck you, Vince. They're training me to kill assholes like you."

"In your dreams, Victoria."

J.R. was distracted. In someone's tent, he had spotted a woman sewing an electronic device into a Kermit the Frog stuffed animal that had big friendly eyes and a gaping, joyous mouth.

"You enter *blindfold,*" Ruth said.

"We do *what?*" J.R. halted, and the whole procession came to a standstill.

"The exact location of the Saw Mill is known only to some," de Ram explained.

J.R. laughed. "No fucking way am I leaving my car here." He looked around to make sure he was telling everyone present.

"Me either," Vince Baldwin concurred.

Scotty joined in, "Yeah, me either."

"That there Chevy," Lafayette interjected, "is safer here than nowhere's else on earth."

J.R. laughed, "You fellas don't understand. That car. My Nova. She's like my wife."

"Shit," one of the older guys said. "I'd give my left nut for two weeks away from my wife." His wife elbowed him in the ribs while the others laughed.

"No problem," de Ram said. "We got a garage in Flintlock. Am I right, Fatso? Hayes Garage. J.R., your daddy probably knows Hayes Garage in Flintlock. Dogs, armed guards, eight-foot walls. Very secure. You leave 'em there, your hot rods. Fat Ransom takes you blindfold from there."

"Hayes Garage," Fat Ransom backed up the proposal. "That's a great idea. We'll leave the cars there."

de Ram continued, "Five miles. OK, cadet? Five miles from your wheels. All of us been there. You man up. You come back. You suit up. How does that sound? Don't you think we need a mechanic? You were saying so yourself just before, to your own dad."

101

J.R. hesitated.

"All right, then," de Ram clapped his big hands together.

"Just..." Fat Ransom paused, holding up a forefinger, "Once we get there, before exiting your vehicles, just wait for my signal. That's all I ask."

They looked around at each other. J.R. took note of Melissa's blue jeans and tasseled jacket. Of Scotty's shades and track shorts and South Milford Marathon T-shirt. Of Vince Baldwin's Jack Daniels tank top and stonewashed denim. It occurred to him that these would be their uniforms for the next two weeks. J.R. alone had brought a change of clothes, but it was just another T-shirt and blue jeans combo, the same he already had on.

"It's this or go home," Melissa said, in a tone so neutral the slightest breeze might have blown it either way.

"Home?" J.R. snorted a laugh. "That's not happening."

"Yeah, fuck that," Vince Baldwin agreed.

The procession was underway, moving toward the parking lot. Fat Ransom angled toward the Cutlass Supreme. Vince Baldwin made for his Bonneville.

Scotty left Melissa's side and jogged over to J.R.'s Nova for a brief huddle. "White race?" he asked.

J.R. shrugged and waved his friend away. "Why? What race are you?"

## 24. That There is Cash Clarick

The fleet of four cars set off for Pennsylvania, advancing through Hopatcong, Netcong, and further from Erving with every passing minute than J.R. Daddio had ever ventured before. He had spiraled all over town and the surrounding towns in the tow truck for years. He could perceive the hamlets and neighborhoods and the routes and short cuts in-between as networks in his head. And yet he was following past all of that now. The great blue sky and the green mountains opened ahead of him as the road beneath his wheels fled behind. Highway signs with their numbers and arrows became abundant. Pennsylvania loomed up ahead, the Delaware Water Gap. He remembered the alarm in his father's voice: PENN-SYLVANIA! as he watched for the border.

Fat Ransom's Cutlass Supreme led the convoy off the interstate and up a stretch of road alongside the woods. As J.R. followed, he began to wonder if they were still in New Jersey. Flintlock, de Ram had said. But maybe Flintlock was in Pennsylvania.

After a stretch, the Oldsmobile swung a steep hairpin turn uphill. Wheeling through dust clouds, the quartet of cars advanced, climbing up into the woods. Before long, up ahead on the right, Hayes Garage came into view. There was no signage, but the place was as described, surrounded by an eight-foot brick wall.

J.R. arrived at the open gate and followed into the concrete lot, to park alongside the others. Fat Ransom rocked his Oldsmobile chassis standing out of it. The two mechanics on duty approached. At the same time, two Rottweilers emerged from the shadows of the open bay to sit on guard, well-trained and perfectly calm. Hayes Garage had two bays and two lifts, just like Daddio's. It was nothing special, other than the fortress-like walls and Rottweilers and surrounding wilderness.

Fat Ransom made easy arrangements with the men, then turned and beckoned the visitors with an open hand.

Obeying, proceeding slowly, J.R. and his companions stepped out of their cars.

Fat Ransom waved around at brick walls and guard dogs. "It's a fortress here. Your Nova is safe and secure, kid. Yours-guys' cars too. Lock 'em up. No one's gonna fuck with 'em. From here on, you ride blindfold. I'll go get the van."

"Over the river?" J.R. asked.

"Blindfold, kid."

They rode blindfolded in the back of the van, jostling around, with the exhaust roaring loud beneath them. J.R. was trying to pay attention to the sound and feel of the terrain beneath the wheels, and to follow, somehow, where they might be going. He felt tarmac below, then gravel, then grass briefly as the vehicle tilted uphill and down and back onto asphalt. Images of his father, his house, his mother, his sister and the garage swept through his mind, distracting him from his calculations. He was very far from home. His breath was short, and his heart was pounding.

"This is bullshit," Vince Baldwin muttered.

"Whatsa matter?" Melissa said. "All of 'em been through it. Even the girls."

Vince started bickering at her. Melissa bickered back.

Ignoring their voices, J.R. listened instead for clues from the wheel well. The van was careening downhill, rocking along the terrain, perhaps even losing control, momentarily, until it slowed, turned, evened out, and turned once again, before plunging downhill some more.

His friends were still arguing. J.R.'s concentration lapsed. Suddenly the van was crawling to a stop. When the motor ceased, so did the arguing.

Fat Ransom could be heard exiting the cab. Moments later he yanked open the door. "All right, blindfolds off. Everybody out."

They debarked, removed their blindfolds and landed one by one at the dusty entrance to the Saw Mill. Fat Ransom waited, gripping the open door by its handle. Scotty plucked his shades up from his collar and slid them on. J.R. maintained his backpack, slung it over his shoulder. Melissa and Vince seemed to share in some co-equal or competitive eagerness.

The facility was elaborate but shoddily built, begotten over its heyday into a complex sprawl of slapdash barn-like afterthoughts. Most were long decayed by now, and stripped, here and there, of plank and shingle. Trestle-braced conveyor belts hung canted between this and that pair of decrepit barns. More than one catwalk spanned from one useless roof to another's useless spire. The great industrial necessity of it all, once carved out of the timberline and then into it, now stood encroached upon by it, the expansive spread of maple tree crowns and evergreen steeples tapering down the valley walls into the straw and weeds and vines that took hold of and laced into and flowered up the surrounding chain link fence.

Parallel barbed wire strands crowned the fence at eye level. Through them, framed by them, J.R. could see a man waiting on the Saw Mill loading dock attired in a jeans jacket, hunting fatigues and combat boots, and carrying a Remington bolt-action.

"That there is Cash Clarick," Fat Ransom told them, as he slammed the van door shut.

J.R. nodded and followed. He could see that his friends alongside him were affecting the same kind of useless caution he was. They were trapped—*I've been Kidnapped!* a voice told him.

But fear was exactly what he had to face down. He knew this even as he followed, trampling the dusty weeds through the open gate. Even that martini-sipping limey sleazeball James Bond got himself kidnapped once in a while. It was literally part of the job.

At the front and center of his makeshift stage, Cash Clarick stood watching and waiting, the rifle angled on his belt, a pistol holstered inside his jacket, a set of keys clipped to his hip pocket, a large canvas duffel bag curled at his feet. From the platform he grinned at last. "Welcome to the mill, *Grist!*"

Behind him and above, in complex dis-uniformity, peeling dormers aimed their stovepipes skyward.

"Y'all know why I'm the perfect person they put in charge?" he asked.

J.R. didn't wonder or dare to. He had made a huge mistake, he realized, given only a glimpse of his captor's small and cruel eyes. What a man lacked in bulk he could make up for in savagery. J.R. figured he knew this better than most people. And he could see that natural law not only embodied by Cash Clarick but honed down all the way to some terrible edge, from his stubble topped cranium to his sharp and remorseless nose to his mouth that sliced a straight line between glee and joylessness.

Arriving in the dust at this Saw Mill altar, J.R. and his Erving companions stood in a row, while Fat Ransom hovered off to the side, expressing, facially, a quiet and gratified amusement.

No one had answered Cash Clarick's question, so Clarick answered himself, "On a count of I don't LIKE nobody!"

"That's why we love him," Fat Ransom responded. "Let's take a tour."

"Tour, shit. Call it what it is. It's a damn audit."

Fat Ransom's entire presence seemed to deflate. He turned his head to address J.R. and his friends, "Mr. Clarick thinks it's funny to be annoying. Just remember, after I leave, that it was me who I told you so."

"Maybe it just annoys you that I'm funny," Cash Clarick countered.

The recruits shared a quiet chuckle at the ironical tautology.

Shaking his head pleasantly enough, Fat Ransom withdrew a bag of peanuts from his pocket. He tore off the top and let the plastic tendril fall to the weeds. "Anyone want a peanut?" he poured some into his own hand, then held out the bag.

Clarick dropped down from the platform, exclaiming, "PEANUTS ARE FOR ELEPHANTS!"

He approached Scotty first. "What are you all about, Shades? GIMME THEM FUCKIN' AVIATORS, BOY!"

Scotty was startled. He took a moment to look around through his sunglasses, as if saying goodbye to them. Then he removed them, and looked at them, but didn't give them over just yet.

*"Don't embarrass me!"* Vince Baldwin hissed.

Clarick wheeled to holler into Vince Baldwin's face, "I'M THE ONE THAT EMBARRASSES YOU, BOY, RIGHT NOW! WORSE THAN YOU EVER GOT EMBARRASSED IN YOUR LIFE! DO YOU UNDERSTAND ME, YOU DIPSHIT HILL-BILLY FUCKFACE? YOU BEST UN-FLAP THAT PIE-HOLE LICKETY SPLIT!"

Melissa let out a brief snort of laughter, then stifled it with her hand.

Clarick spun her way. "You think I'm funny, girly? I look like Uncle Floyd to you?"

"No," she said. "Sorry, it's just..." she aimed her thumb at Vince. "I don't like him."

Clarick looked her over, top to bottom and back again. "He ain't the one you don't like, Blondie, you got that?"

Melissa nodded.

"I'm the one you don't like."

She nodded some more.

"None of you got ANY problems. None except me. You got that, kiddos?" He spared each of them a look in turn. "And I got problems for you, you best believe it. I got a wheel of problems. And you? You're strapped to that wheel. So's we understand each other."

J.R. watched their acquiescent faces, even as he offered his own.

Clarick turned back to Scotty, affecting something like a magnanimous frown. Extending his hand for the sunglasses, he spoke quietly, "I'll stomp them shades into the dirt, boy, right now. With these here boots. And then I'll stomp you. Your head. Your skull. Your brain. All that matter. All into the same puddle. Think I care? Trust me, I don't. And I won't say a word, neither, while I'm doing it. That's my signature. I'm the one who talks non-stop. Right up until I'm putting an end to you. That's when I don't say nothin'. Not in words, no how. Or I can give you them sunglasses back after you graduate from this here academy and make the grade. So what'll it be, Shades?"

Scotty held the sunglasses forward. Clarick snatched them, "Gimme that shit." He held them up, examined them, put them on, looked around. "Never mind what I just said, asshole, I'm keeping these." He took them off, hooked them into his shirt collar. "Let's get on with it, Fatso."

"After you," Fat Ransom chewed his peanuts.

"All right," Clarick said. "Quarters first." He about-faced and advanced, trying to affect a drill sergeant's authority and efficiency, but repeatedly throwing glances back at the lagging Fat Ransom and the recruits who tended to lag behind with him.

Following that frustrated pace, the group entered the wide, dusty yard of the rambling, decrepit Saw Mill. Many of the structures were disfigured, with great sections of their walls or rooftops torn out.

"This here is my fifth derelict," Clarick advised. "This operation is a proven success, year after year. So my advice to you, and I'm sure Fatso will agree, is to do as you're told. That there—" he pointed to a half-demolished storehouse, "—is our current project. We're pulling this whole place down, piece by piece, and selling it for scrap."

Fat Ransom paused beneath an old crane for his eyes to follow up its latticed arm to its pulley. Vince stopped beside him and said, "I'll have a peanut." Ransom poured a few peanuts into his open hand.

J.R. noted the range targets, makeshift signboards painted with bullseyes, planted in uniform increments down the weed-choked yard. "So is today day one?" he asked, "Or is it tomorrow?"

"Duh," said Vince.

"Knock it off, Vince," Melissa pleaded.

"Day one?" Vince ignored her. "No. It's day zero. Moron. Don't worry, Mr. Clarick. We're not all as stupid as this one."

"Mr. Clarick," Melissa said. "Please train me to kill this asshole."

Clarick wheeled around. "Everybody shut up!"

They froze.

Fat Ransom casually dropped his empty peanut wrapper in the yard.

Clarick pointed his rifle barrel at Fat Ransom. "Him and me..." he explained to the others, "we're on one level."

Then he pointed the rifle barrel around at his four pupils.

"You? You all? You're on another, lower, shittier level. The shittiest level imaginable. So shut the fuck up. Unless spoken to. Understand?"

They nodded in meek agreement.

"You may speak. Tell me you understand?"

"Yessir!" they replied. Vince loudest.

"What a bunch of slobs. We'll straighten you out." Clarick's beady glare settled on Fat Ransom, and then on the breezeblown peanut wrapper flapping in the dust.

Their next stop was the bunkhouse. "There's no door. That's so I can sneak up on ya!" Clarick explained.

Inside, four scuzzy mattresses lay wedged around the floor. A gallon jug of water sat in the center. The module was tagged like a dead appendix onto the greater refinery or storehouse that had spawned it. The window once overlooking that production was boarded up now. The walls were barren, peeling blue paint. Clarick paused as if daring forth any complaints. None came.

Next, they set across the sun beaten yard towards the office. Clarick paused halfway there, pointing his rifle barrel up and around at the Saw Mill's industrial belvederes. Four in all overlooked the dusty yellow yard.

"Nighttime," he said, "when y'all are sleeping... I'll be up there. Could be any one of them nests, could be none of 'em. So catch your shuteye when I allow it. Deserters will be shot. Ain't that right, Fatso?"

Fat Ransom shrugged. "Don't run off," he advised.

The office was an aluminum sided observatory overlooking the yard. Its fishbowl windows revealed vertically hung flags within. The Posse Serpens. The Stars and Bars. Don't Tread on Me. A Nazi swastika.

They entered through the squeaky screen door and formed an awkward huddle inside that threshold. Fat Ransom squeezed around them and made immediately for the file cabinet in the opposite corner. An oblong bookshelf of volumes and manuals occupied that same corner's perpendicular wall. Clarick's neatly dressed cot suggested sleeplessness or extreme fastidiousness, or a blissful union of those two conditions. At the foot of the bed sat a padlocked trunk. A blue cooler sat beside it. A wall calendar hung tacked above the cot, as did several uniformly-spaced maps that drew J.R.'s eye, locations in Pennsylvania, New Jersey, New York, Ohio, and elsewhere, here and there sprung with curious black pins. On the adjacent wall, a war hammer hung at an angle, uncrisscrossed with another weapon currently absent. Beneath the unpaired war hammer, a steel desk sat uncluttered, save for a flat and vacant blotter, a tidy notepad and pen, and a pouch-holstered satellite phone. On the opposite wall, the colorful and provocative flags offered vivid drapery for the room's otherwise stark utility.

"This here is my accommodation," Clarick explained. "You walk through that door without my permission, and I'll murder ya. And it'll be a legal kill too. But I'll bury your dead body in the woods anyway—Fuck, hold your horses, Fatso."

He unhitched his keys from his belt and proceeded over to the file cabinet. With an effort to match Ransom's impatience, he unlocked the top drawer and withdrew a leather satchel. Ransom seized it. The exchange was hasty, a kind of distasteful ritual sped through. Holding the prize at last, Ransom enjoyed a satisfied smile. He turned to the four newcomers and said, "Mr. Clarick and I will take care of your dues before I go. Play your cards right, and someday it'll be *you* picking up one of these here."

"A bagman," Clarick told them. "Splendid. Two weeks with me and you'll be tar-and-feathering this fat fuck."

J.R. didn't know what to make of the discord, but Fat Ransom absorbed it casually, unbuckling the satchel and peering in, saying, "As Mr. Clarick mentioned, there's a labor element to the camp." He began probing his hand around inside the bag, saying, "Consider your work here an investment."

Clarick turned to them, "We're training you here to *fight* taxation—"

"Without representation... is the rest of that battle cry," Ransom argued. "But that doesn't apply here."

Clarick hissed, "I'm teaching these younglings how to *fight* oppression. You want to teach 'em how to *rule*. Those is two different things. And they still know it. Even if you don't."

"Oppression?" Fat Ransom laughed. "I'm just telling them the truth."

"The truth? You don't know nothing about the truth. The truth is what happens after you scurry out of here."

"My friends," Fat Ransom pleaded to the baffled Posse Serpens recruits, even as he continued to rummage through the satchel, "The Posse Serpens is looking forward to your contribution. The most important, patriotic work of your life awaits you. Me, I am not here to indoctrinate you. That work is Mr. Clarick's specialty. But I'm not here to lie to you, either. You've got two weeks with him; you've got the rest of your careers with me. So keep your minds open and your chins up. Me, I'll be leaving this funhouse just as soon as we complete

110

our tour..." he had discovered something missing from the satchel and had fallen more and more into that distraction while his words trailed off.

Clarick backed up a step and sat himself down in the creaking office chair, to gesture with an open hand at the satellite phone, "Let's make our call."

"You call her," Fat Ransom agreed.

"You call her," Clarick countered.

Fat Ransom sighed, patient and calm. Coming to a decision, he advanced to the cooler at the side of the cot.

"Aw, fuck you, you asshole," Clarick groaned. "I'm just gonna take that out of your *tithe* next time."

Ransom knelt to one knee, opened the cooler, and peered inside. He removed a twisted chunk of cured meat. Kneeling there, he wrenched off a bite with his teeth, and began nodding his head, chewing, saying, "You're a fucking genius, Cash Clarick."

He raised himself up to address the recruits, "I'm sorry, kids, but I guarantee you, this delicacy will not be available to you over the next two weeks."

"That's Goddamn right," Clarick told them. "Because you cain't afford it. Because you're gonna be cleaned out of dough in about ten minutes."

"What I'm trying to explain to you," Fat Ransom continued, "is that six months from now, or maybe a year from now, you're going to be seeing *Cash Clarick Vittles* on the counter at the deli. Like *Slim Jim* or something. A product at the store. And you're going to be saying to yourself, 'Hey, I know that guy, Cash Clarick.' But in your state of awe, don't forget to buy it, and taste it. Because this product absolutely slays those fools from *Slim Jim.*"

"Can I try it?" Vince Baldwin asked.

Fat Ransom ignored him. "Let's make that call to Farrah now, Mr. Clarick."

Vince Baldwin asked, "Farrah?"

Cash Clarick unsheathed the satellite phone and held it out to Fat Ransom. "Call your sister," he said.

*"Cash Clarick Vittles,"* Ransom spoke the brand name again, casually, with the bitten remains clutched in his fist. "So good." He made his way not so much gracefully as inexorably to the desk. With his free hand he snagged the phone away from Cash Clarick. Gripping the jerky, he dialed the keypad.

J.R. had allowed his gaze to wander out the fishbowl window. He had spotted, under a wooden outcropping, at the yard's T-shaped corner, a pastel green Land Rover, Series Two.

"I hear you fix cars," Clarick stood up from his chair.

J.R. turned around, "Yes, I can fix cars."

Clarick turned to Vince Baldwin, "And you're a lumberjack?"

Vince stood at attention. "Not exactly, sir! The last job I had was in a lumberyard—"

"You're a lumberjack!" Cash Clarick aimed his face up at Vince. "What do I need a LUMBERJACK for at a SAW MILL?"

"Yessir!" Vince agreed, facing forward.

"I can't even call you Lumberjack. That's because I already named me somebody else Lumberjack previously."

"Yessir!"

Fat Ransom interrupted from the desk, "Will you two keep it down?"

Clarick waved him away, addressed Vince Baldwin. "So I gotta give you a more personal name," he explained.

"Yessir."

"Do you swear allegiance to the White Race?"

"Fuck yeah, brother."

Clarick looked back over his shoulder at Fat Ransom and said, "This one's perfect."

Fat Ransom waved an impatient hand.

Clarick turned to Melissa and said, "This one's perfect too, by her looks. What about you, Blondie? Do you swear allegiance to the White Race?"

"I'm white, ain't I?" she answered.

"You sure look white to me, sister," he smiled.

Melissa rolled her eyes, with that bored superior face women make, like they've heard it all before. J.R. wanted to tell her not to make that face. Not here.

Fat Ransom had the phone to his ear. J.R. was trying to listen in, but Clarick was talking over him, saying, "We start taking our country back in just a few minutes, kiddos. Don't worry about it. Just as soon as this parasite gets lost..."

He pointed out the window to the portion of the yard where circular bullseyes receded by the imperial fifty. "We got that range yonder. Plus an indoors range, too."

"You wanna talk to him?" Ransom was saying into the satellite phone. "Be my guest. Yeah, No. I don't think it's

112

worth the trouble. But I'm only standing here in front of him, so what do I know?"

Clarick couldn't help listening in now, along with the rest of them.

"OK," Ransom concluded, louder into the receiver. "That's what you want me to tell him. OK. I'll be on the road in twenty minutes. OK, over and out." He hung up, looked at Cash Clarick.

"Tell him what? Let's hear it. Let's let these pups hear it too. We got no secrets here. It's a free country here at the Saw Mill, even if nowhere's else on earth."

Ransom paused, leaning his bulk against the desk, holding the savaged jerky in his fist, considering and sizing up the four recruits. At last, he said, "They won't believe me. I mean, you'll believe me. But they won't."

"What? Fuck them!" Clarick jabbed his thumb at the newcomers. "Who cares if they believe you?"

Fat Ransom shrugged. "She said, *Blah blah blah.*"

Clarick looked around at the four of them, then back at Fat Ransom. *"Blah blah blah?"* he said. "Heck, that's a free pass."

"YEEHAW!" Vince blurted.

Clarick wheeled on him. "Will you shut the fuck up? Ever? You are literally not going to survive this night!"

Vince Baldwin stood frozen.

"Six feet down! Six hours from now! That is your career trajectory in this organization! Do you understand?"

"Yessir!" Vince straightened himself.

"I don't think you do!"

"I understand, sir!"

"ARE YOU GOING TO PISS ME OFF? EVER AGAIN? ONE MORE TIME IN YOUR LIFE?"

"NO SIR!"

"JESUS CHRIST!" Cash Clarick seethed. "EVERYBODY GET THE FUCK OUT OF MY OFFICE!"

They moved on, proceeding back into the yard, forbidden to speak, clustered together, with Fat Ransom lumbering casually in their midst.

The shooting range occupied a greater stretch of the yard, its targets receding in precise vectors.

J.R. wanted to huddle with Scotty for a moment, but he could feel Ransom's planetary presence behind him.

"The indoor range is in here," Clarick pointed. J.R. craned his neck to peer inside the approaching storehouse through the remains of its front facing wall. Mounting a single porch step, the group entered into a cavernous, sun-shot industrial tomb. Pigeons and other birds flapped, disturbed. Paper targets rustled six-strong along the far wall.

From this module, they moved along the Saw Mill yard to yet another desolate workhouse. This one would serve as their classroom, with no chairs or desks but empty skids stacked at random heights. In a corner nook beneath the partially destroyed ceiling, bird shit had congealed. Along that collection point, atop an empty steel bookshelf, a device, homemade, a mechanical arm and spoon-like scoop, sat collecting the white accumulating scat into a spackle bucket.

*"Did you see that thing?"* J.R. whispered to Scotty after they followed back into the yard.

*"What's going on between those two?"* Scotty was talking about something else.

"Shut your traps!" Clarick hollered. "Goddammit! It's only gonna hurt you worse!"

As they followed along the next leg on the tour, J.R. understood that he may have been the only one to have spotted the spackle bucket birdshit harvester.

The dusty weed-choked yard turned right at the outcropping where the bug-eyed Land Rover lurked.

"Urban assault," Clarick unfurled his hand past the Land Rover into the yard's cul-de-sac where a pair of makeshift domiciles framed from upright freight pallets and tautly stretched GLAD Bags awaited entry.

*"That's* what I'm talkin' about," Melissa grinned.

Clarick wheeled on her.

"Sorry," she said, "I'm sorry." She covered her mouth with both hands.

"Sorry about what?!" he demanded.

She lowered her hands. "For talking."

"For talking about what?"

"For talking about..." she hesitated.

"For talking about what you were talking about?" he answered his own question.

"Yes."

"What does that sound like to you, Blondie?"

"Sounds like a mistake."

"Well lookie here!" he raised his grin for all to see. "There's hope yet for this one!"

Scotty was getting hot, poised in his track shorts and marathon T-shirt. Clarick must have felt it. His wiry frame seemed ready to pounce.

Fat Ransom stepped in, "If I may, Scotty... Scotty, son..."

Scotty turned to him.

"The U.S. Army. They don't allow this kind of co-ed training for couples. And you two, you and her, you're exactly the reason why." He raised his forefinger and waggled it.

"But this here," he continued, "this is NOT the U.S. Army, is it? This here is Freedom. Here, we fight *side-by-side* with our women. And that means keeping a cool head. Am I right? Even when the circumstances aren't so pretty?"

"Couldn't have said it better myself, but leave Shades here to me," Cash Clarick turned and proceeded across the yard.

Fat Ransom shrugged for Scotty and the others. "After you," he extended his hand.

"This here is the silo," Clarick pointed ahead with the rifle barrel.

J.R. had counted four silos of varying girth and height among the mill's ramshackle grandeur. Their destination silo was the one facing the yard, a towering cylindrical patchwork of rust-brown corrugated aluminum, with a convex door hinged at its base.

Arriving there, Clarick opened the door and led them inside. They followed and crowded into that chamber, with Fat Ransom last to enter. The air was pungent. The room was dark. J.R. began to feel intensely unsafe. The smell of old sawdust smothered his nostrils. Cash Clarick kindled a lantern. J.R. looked around and saw that the silo was empty and scraped clean right down to its every encircling edge.

"You'll be manacled in here while I conduct errands," Clarick pointed around at the cuffs and chains hanging from the silo walls. J.R. peered upward. The cylinder stretched into depthless shadow above.

"Don't worry," Fat Ransom reassured them, "If this lunatic goes out and gets himself killed, we'll hear about it, and we'll come and getcha."

"Shit, ain't no force on this earth can get me killed," Clarick responded. "That's the number one fact of life you kids would do best to remember. The difference between me and every other sonofabitch alive is... I cain't be killed."

Back in the sunlit yard, breathing oxygen again, J.R. looked back at the looming silo. He didn't want to be chained up in there, ever.

"The outhouse," Fat Ransom said, "and then I'll be on my way."

"Oh, don't worry about missin' that."

The stark white fiberglass utility stood science fiction-like beneath a solitary tree inside the Saw Mill's far gate. The shadows all gathered where the industrial corridor grew narrow and the forest awakened tall and dark and green behind it. One perfectly healthy old linden tree had been left to stand inside the property's fence as a trophy, or memorial, or thickened survivor, casting a great green spread of shade. The obelisk below seemed almost to glow beneath those wizened bows, its blue-hued, pearl-white exterior, portending a clean amenity, which J.R. appreciated but also understood would be his and his friends' to keep clean for two weeks. And there was something behind it, something like a shed, dark and angular, crouching in the shadows, slapped together out of plywood, housing something mechanical, with a silver smokeshaft angling up from the side like a Harley muffler.

"He thinks he's got a patent on his hands," Fat Ransom explained, "so he keeps it out of sight."

"Maybe I do."

"Because he didn't build it."

"It was my vision that built it. And my resources."

"So he has no idea how it works."

"Shit, Fatso, I'll know how it works when I feed you into it, eyeballs first."

The strange pipe-fitted cabinet was affixed to the lavatory's rear wall and embedded in the dirt, supported by 2X4 shims where the ground sloped away from the tree's distended root system.

Clarick began explaining the utility's schedule of use and maintenance. J.R. half listened, as he looked around at Scotty, Melissa, Vince, and Fat Ransom, and then over his shoulder at the sprawling, ravaged Saw Mill complex. The breeze blew chilly down through the yard into the sunless alcove. J.R. shivered. *I walked right into this,* he told himself. *The Old Man played me like a damn banjo.*

Turning back to Cash Clarick, who was gesturing now at the bizarre chimney-fitted lockbox at the latrine's rear panel, he could feel his heart begin to race. Something about this nook of the yard terrified him.

He tried to remain stoic, at least in appearance, while cold sweat poured over him, his arms, his sternum, his chest and everywhere. He wondered if Cash Clarick could smell it, the sweat, and a memory of his father came back to him now. It seemed ready to flood his eyes with tears, and he could feel himself holding back.

It was maybe six years ago, an exchange in the woods off Armitage Road, with hunting rifles, geared in camouflage and orange, hours into a day of quiet stealth, of whispered tactics and strategies, a sandwich shared wordlessly.

And then, finally, lining up the animal in his sights, with his father's hushed voice advising him to calm down his breathing and his heart rate because a buck can pick up on those things. And J.R. finding that it came easy, perhaps because his breath and heart rate had been calm all day, in the woods, alongside his father, keeping quiet.

And later when he cut his hand with his pocketknife and yowled at the blood before the pain even started to set in, Jack Daddio sternly hushed him, *"Don't fuckin' cry! Not MY kid!"*

J.R. winced and inhaled and tried to keep quiet, while Jack Daddio sterilized the wound, pouring alcohol over the searing streak. Bandaging it up, he said, "OK, we're done. Let's get you some stitches. We're going."

And then in the truck on the way out of the woods, as J.R. held his bandaged hand in his lap, Jack Daddio said, "I'm not mad, J.R. You know that, right? It's for your sake I'm firm with you."

"I know," he answered his father.

"You're my son, no matter what. I want you to know that. You're still a kid. And you're allowed to be a kid with me, with your dad. *But not with them,"* he pointed randomly at the world outside his hurtling truck.

J.R. was annoyed to be reminded he was a kid.

"Not with them, you understand? You don't show them any weakness. You don't show them any pain. Your mother thinks she understands. That's because she stood by me through it. But she'll never understand."

"I know, I get it," J.R. said.

"NO, YOU DON'T GET IT!" Jack Daddio snapped.

The hypocrisy was unbelievable. And yet J.R. was used to it.

117

At the time, he just held it, with all the other grudges to bury. Now the wisdom proved useful, here in Cash Clarick's company. *You keep calm. That's what I'm telling you. If you don't, they will smell it on you.* J.R. sought to focus on the words, the idea, even as his sternum and limbs were paralyzed with dread.

Cash Clarick was saying, "You know what this here night soil is? It's the only thing left they don't tax. And by the way, don't nobody open that there strongbox without my permission."

"My work is almost done here," Fat Ransom said, with the satchel under his arm. "Let's do wallets."

"Let's."

"Miss Melissa mentioned dues earlier."

"That there is Blondie!" Cash Clarick pointed his finger. "That ain't Melissa. Not for these two weeks, noways."

"In any case—"

"In any case, this here is the part where you empty your wallets," Cash Clarick told them. He stood Remington armed in the shadows of the Saw Mill's museum-like linden tree, whose trunk and roots comingled in the dirt with the white fiberglass obelisk, and also with the plywood, pipefitted contraption attached ticklike to its spine.

He collected their wallets, their watches too, also emptied J.R.'s backpack to find his checkbook, saying, "Fucking shit. They won't even cash a check after three o'clock." He rummaged through the clothes too. J.R., with his checkbook and clothes, had proven to be *The Stupid One.*

Fat Ransom announced, "I'll be on my way, Mr. Clarick. Try not to puncture any lungs this time. Kids, be enterprising. I'll be waiting on the other side of your ordeal."

Clarick spared Fat Ransom a dismissive smirk only. To his captives, he said, "Never mind him. For the next two weeks, y'all are my children."

Without another word, Fat Ransom left them there. They looked longingly after his diminishing presence. They also looked around at each other, forbidden to speak, helplessly blinking their eyes and waiting.

"Grab up your shit!" Cash Clarick barked. J.R. knelt in the dirt for his backpack and clothes.

Another stretch of silence followed. Cash Clarick kept watching back over his shoulder after Fat Ransom's slow, indefatigable departure.

"Look at that," he snarled. "How far from the edge of life do you have to fall to end up like that?"

J.R. reminded himself to plan for their escape. It was not too soon to start. Above Fat Ransom's van, the hillside ascended in a vaguely defined trail through the weeds, the brush, the boulders, and the thickening forest. Down that way they had come, blindfolded. It would be their most promising way out.

He watched Fat Ransom climb into the van's driver's seat and slam the door. He listened as the engine revved up. His heart sank further, knowing he could tighten up the exhaust on that van, if anything that simple was wanted from him. He tracked the vehicle's ascension out of there, clouds of dust in its wake.

"All right, giddyup, rabbits!"

They made their collective way back through the dusty yard, following Cash Clarick and eyeballing one another, seeking in their enforced silence some ongoing group affirmation.

As if reading their thoughts, Clarick advised, "Y'all ain't even been sweared-in yet. Hold your horses with the regret already."

J.R. glanced back at the tree-shrouded fiberglass utility.

They marched efficiently back through the tour they had taken, past the silo, the makeshift urban GLAD Bag death-traps, the green Land Rover under its spare awning. The indoor shooting range, Clarick's office, the barracks, and back to the stage-like platform where they were first introduced.

Ascending that stage, Cash Clarick advanced out onto it and up to its edge where the black duffel bag lay. At the same time, J.R. and his friends began lining up below to stand in waiting. Another gust of wind came sweeping down through the valley into the dusty yellow yard.

"All right, stand tall, Caucasians! Fatso's gone, so we're going to open us up a... whaddaya call it... dialogue. You are free to speak now. Over this here music."

He leaned down and unzipped the duffel bag, removing an enormous silver boom box with ten-inch speakers. He set it down on the platform and pressed play. Nightmarish Opera music struck the yard. Heavy cellos, horns, kettle drums. Gothic voices howling strange syllables in some jarring tongue. J.R. hated it. The worst music he had ever heard. It felt like knives into his thoughts.

Clarick stalked forward to the edge of the deck, demanding, "DO YOU SWEAR ALLEGIANCE TO THE WHITE RACE!"

"I swear allegiance to the White Race!" Vince Baldwin proclaimed.

"FUCK YOU DO!" Clarick told him. "FAR AS I CAN TELL, YOU'RE THE STUPIDEST SONOFABITCH I EVER SEEN IN MY LIFE! BUT THAT'S WHY I WAS PUT HERE ON THIS EARTH! TO DELIVER ONE SIMPLE MESSAGE YOU CAN UNDERSTAND!"

Vince gazed up and awaited the one simple message.

Clarick turned to address the group. "This here is WAR! And in WAR! Your ENEMIES! You slay them by your HAND! Do you UNDERSTAND? Do unto THEM before THEY do it unto YOU! It's simple as THAT!"

The cellos and demonic choral voices thundered from the speakers. Cash Clarick turned J.R.'s way to peer down the length of his knife-like nose from the stage. "You! You Ichabod Crane looking Nimrod string bean fuck! I asked you a question! DO YOU SWEAR ALLEGIANCE TO THE WHITE RACE? You will swear allegiance before me, Nimrod! Or I will put an END to you right NOW!"

J.R. held up his empty hands, "I swear, OK. I pledge allegiance. I mean it. I'm white as... a sheet, OK?"

"Aw, son, are you kidding me? That ain't no oath. Tell ya what," Cash Clarick leaned down, opened his duffel bag, pulled out a stump of wood and set it down on the stage like a chopping block. Next, he withdrew a perfectly white human skull, followed by an enormous battle axe with a leather-bound handle. He held the axe in one hand, the naked skull in the other. He nodded at the skull and spoke, while the Gothic Opera backed up his morbid grandiosity. "This here... is Marty... somebody. Fuck if I remember. Rhino, that's what I called him. I call 'em like I see 'em, kids. Just like I do with you all. That boy was Rhino, no two ways about it. Wasn't that long ago, neither. Standing there just like you all are right now. Thinking he knew shit about fuck. I tried explaining... Don't nobody know nothin' here at the Saw Mill except for yours truly. Well, long story short, I smote Rhino in battle. As I do all my enemies. Rookie and salty dog alike, it don't matter. Then I cut off Rhino's head, and boiled it down to this here," Clarick showed them Rhino's chalky white skull.

He set the skull down on the chopping block, raised up the battle axe in his two hands and brought it down, smashing the skull into brittle shards, and cleaving into the wood with the blade. Releasing his hands he held them outward, accepting some surge of invisible power back from the quivering handle.

"Look at me, boy!" he glared down at J.R. "Do I look like Fat Ransom to you? Sure as fuck I ain't no Glenn Disteek! I am your shield against the light! I am your sword against the darkness! I am the only true power in this world! Why do you think they don't hand you a set of black PJs for sniffin' around their little commune, huh? Hell, why do you think they hate my guts? I am the ugly fucking truth! That's why! Am I gettin' through to you, Nimrod?"

Vince Baldwin spoke up now, "Excuse me, Mr. Clarick..."

Clarick froze in place. "Excuse you for WHAT?"

"That there ain't Nimrod. That there is Junior. You wanna get under his skin? *Call him Junior.*"

J.R. was starting to pity Vince Baldwin. Scotty and Melissa seemed concerned as well, subtly leaning their bodies in their friend's general direction, as if to silence him by force of will.

Clarick bent down and turned off the music. For a scarce, dwindling moment, the afternoon quavered and thrummed with field insects and birdsong. The four recruits stood lined up waiting as Clarick dropped down from the stage and landed in front of them. He approached Scotty first, pointing his finger.

"Your name is Shades."

Scotty agreed with a nod.

Clarick turned to Melissa, pointed his finger, "Your name is Blondie."

"Yes sir!" she said.

Vince Baldwin was next. Clarick glared up at him. "You? I ain't decided yet. You cain't be Lumberjack. You're gonna need some tenderizing before I give you a name."

He paused a moment longer, then roundhoused Vince to the face.

The others gasped. Vince Baldwin's head rang helplessly on his spine. He was out cold on his feet. His legs swam beneath him. His body collapsed to the ground. He lay there, helpless, face up, hands and arms twitching, insentient.

Clarick turned to J.R. "And YOU!"

J.R. waited and watched as Clarick's beady eyes studied him. He also stole glances at Vince Baldwin's flattened husk

121

and concussed face. He allowed himself to wonder if his name, for these next two weeks, might actually end up being Junior.

"Nimrod," Clarick grinned. "That's you. Nimrod. How you like that name, boy?"

# BOOK II. THE SAW MILL

## 25. Steeplejack

"Don't be afraid," Steeplejack was seated on a stack of empty pallets inside the U-Haul truck. J.R. sat facing him from the opposite stack. A lantern glowed between them casting complex latticework shadows around the trailer's boxy hollow. J.R. held a Remington 12-gauge. Steeplejack held an M16. Both gunmen wore black leather gloves. Both kept black ski masks at hand.

"Say you do get caught," Steeplejack reasoned. "It's no big deal. You're just off to juvie. It's no felony. Keep your chin up. That's all I'm saying."

With a manner part libertine, part gecko, and with ice blue smirking eyeballs, and with a focus of attention that slithered always in-between curious and invasive, Steeplejack offered no comfort whatsoever. The walkie-talkie sputtered static where it lay on the skid beside him.

"No one's getting caught," J.R. muttered.

Steeplejack carried on, "Except, of course, if we kill somebody. In which case, you'll be on the hook with the rest of us."

"No killing."

"What? No killing? What do think these guns are for, friend?"

"I know what they're for."

"*Sheesh,*" Steeplejack dismissed him.

J.R. never would have believed, didn't want to believe, that he could ever hate anyone as much as he hated—still hated—Cash Clarick.

And yet here was Steeplejack, the cokehead Nazi pornographer, who seemed more distracted from his studio than relieved of it, but no less enthusiastic, perhaps never more so, for today's agenda of armed robbery and murder.

At least a dozen armed, able-bodied Nazis remained on hand back at the so-called Castle this afternoon. And yet inexplicably J.R., and equally inexplicably Vince Baldwin, had been selected for this five-man armored car heist, to finance the cause of the Posse Umbellus. The crew also included Crosby Shue and the wheelman, Lou Gannon. Vince was with those two, parked outside in Lou Gannon's '77 Firebird, which was Burt Reynolds all the way, V8 engine, rally wheels, gold Phoenix emblazoned on black.

The Posse Umbellus was the sworn enemy of the Posse Serpens, and J.R. had joined neither posse, not that it made any difference, or offered any solace, during these final few minutes of being alive, with Steeplejack for a final companion.

All the while, everyday sounds from the untroubled parking lot bled through the truck's steel panels.

At last, J.R. spoke. "Drop some Russians in here. I'll kill 'em for ya."

"Kid—"

"Dammit, I'm neck-deep in blood already, aren't I? Ain't I? I just don't get it. These guys. They're *Americans*. I never agreed to take down armored cars! And murder Brinks guards! Hardworking *Americans!* With *families!* Are you *kidding me?*"

"Kid," Steeplejack advised. "Kid, kid. Don't get twitchy— hey. Did someone say families? I got thirteen kids of my own. So don't talk to me about families."

Steeplejack was rumored to have thirteen children, although none of them lived at the so-called Castle.

"My advice," he continued, "is to do what I do. Kill or be killed. Fuck Glenn Disteek and his fucking Posse Serpens summer camp. We are the Posse Umbellus. We are defending our kind from tyranny. This is the only war there is. So get yourself straightened out."

J.R. lowered his head and stared down at the shotgun in his lap.

Steeplejack jabbed his thumb back at the muffled and humdrum sounds from the parking lot. "Those stupid assholes? They're part of the machine. They aren't even human beings. They're just cogs. They even know it, on some level. A lot of them do. They're literally just waiting to get killed. So, if it's between you and one of them, don't hesitate..."

J.R. had no response. It was all true, even though it was all wrong. *I'm about to die,* he told himself.

With that, Steeplejack seemed satisfied, leaning back and allowing his gaze to settle nowhere in particular.

The upturned walkie-talkie spat occasional white noise through its transistors. Crosby Shue would check in from time to time, in a brief transmission of innocuous code words. The Trans Am served as lookout and getaway car both.

*Kill or be killed,* Steeplejack had said it, and J.R. had a notion to kill right here in the back of this U-Haul truck and NOT be killed. It might truly be his best option at this point, even if it meant spending the rest of his life as a fugitive.

"You know," Steeplejack fixed him with spooky ice blue eyes. "I could jerk off right now. Right on the floor of this U-Haul truck. I mean, just the word *U-Haul.* It makes me want to... I don't know." He opened his empty palm. *"Splat...* right here on this deck."

J.R.'s sternum corkscrewed. His pulse surged. He could feel the heat from his own face. He was going to do it. He was going to unload the 12-gauge.

Until it occurred to him, as if from some lowlit but urgent brainwave, that firing a shotgun inside the hull of a U-Haul truck would leave him deaf. And he could not possibly escape this nightmare deaf.

"Don't worry, though," Steeplejack added. "I ain't gonna do it. Long as you're sittin' there." He smirked, adjusted his crotch, looked away. "Look on the bright side, soldier. At least I ain't no Cash Clarick." A bit of satisfied laughter spilled out of him.

J.R. felt his solar plexus collapse. His head swam with rage. The shotgun in his hands seemed to whisper. Again, he had to summon the willpower not to murder his captor point blank, destroy his own eardrums in the process, and stumble deaf outside into a hail of bullets. Sometimes he hated everybody so much, every single person he had ever known, and all the ones yet to meet, that he came to fathom a kind of Biblical, sourceless, directionless wrath.

Steeplejack's twinkling eyes held J.R.'s helpless glare. "Socially uncomfortable," he said, "is so much better than

127

physical penetration. Am I right?" He laughed again, not overloud, just gleeful.

"If I kill someone, I'm gonna mean it," J.R. told him.

Steeplejack's laughing face became impressed. "That's the spirit. You just remember that when Joe Brinks draws down on you."

"I'll remember it now and always."

"Clarick's dead, boy. I ain't your tormentor."

"The fuck you ain't."

With that, he and his accomplice returned to their silent waiting inside the lantern lit, unsprung jack-in-the-box.

## 26. Nimrod & FuckFace

J.R. had observed, on occasion, Vince Baldwin's exhibitions, demonstrations, and occasional flickerings of humanity, even as he watched Vince succumb to Cash Clarick's lesson plan and its long-reverberating symptoms.

On that first day at the Saw Mill, once Vince regained consciousness, Clarick told him, "Your name's FuckFace!" and then explained Vince's nickname to him, spelling it out literally until his other students just stood there mortified. At that moment, Vince Baldwin's singular stupid facial expression compounded by his standing-eight level of consciousness and the dread he almost didn't dare grasp stirred in J.R. an unwelcome pity.

As it turned out, Clarick was only speaking semi-metaphorically. Breaking down Vince Baldwin would prove to be a rudimentary if staggeringly disciplined process.

The program began with Cash Clarick checking his wristwatch. "OK, FuckFace, it's two o'clock. Starting at three, every hour, on the hour, day and night, 24-hours-a-day, for the next two weeks, I am going to slap you in the face."

Vince Baldwin wouldn't have understood his consignment under any circumstance. However, here and now, with his bell rung, he seemed to relax. He was content, apparently, with the safety and security of the next fifty-nine minutes.

Clarick then proceeded to do just as he'd promised. It was, on some demented level, an incredible feat of human will.

Cash Clarick had to be admired, if only for suffering along with Vince Baldwin through the living schedule he came to embody. He was always there to strike the hour, hard across Vince's face, always on the left side, and always leaving a red welt to linger, to swell, to bruise, those effects compounding hour after hour, at breakfast, during drills, throughout educational conditioning, and vocational and paramilitary training. Before lights-out and then like clockwork overnight, every hour on the hour, waking Vince for a slap in the face, and leaving him sobbing sometimes, voiceless other times, and complaining, through breakfast and throughout drills, or whatever time of day it was, of blinding headaches.

Vince even hid in the outhouse once, to no avail, and to his utter regret and shame, because Clarick could not work up a backswing, and so he dragged Vince out by the shirt collar, bare-assed, with his jeans around his ankles, and with extra backswing SLAP! struck him down, harder than ever, leaving him lying in the dirt with his pale dick drooping.

"J.R...?" Vince whispered, later that night, as they lay drawn around their barracks mattresses. This was maybe the third or fourth night at the Saw Mill, if J.R.'s memory served. Vince had been slapped half-an-hour ago, and was going to get slapped a half-an-hour from now.

"You OK, Vince?"

"I can't take it anymore."

"Neither can I," J.R. said it for all of them. Scotty and Melissa, too, either of whom, or both, might be awake and listening. He knew Vince Baldwin had it bad, broken down to a single hopeless repeated longing for cessation of pain. But he wasn't the only one. And they were all desperate for sleep.

"Do you want me to call you J.R. or Nimrod?"

"Better stick with Nimrod, FuckFace. While we're here."

"Right, OK, gotcha."

A terrible, wretched pity flooded the heart. J.R. gathered his senses and dismissed it.

## 27. Steam Donkey

For long stretches, the Saw Mill was simply a labor camp. Cash Clarick had purchased the derelict from an eager seller, and had taken up residence there, to rob the recruits who came through, even as he indentured their servitude, at gunpoint, for them to wearily deconstruct the property's industrial obsolescence down to its elements, its tin shingles, its ceiling joists of hemlock and box elder, its barn-red siding, its copper plumbing—all of it tossed into a trio of dump trailers.

On their first day, shortly after orientation, they were introduced to the Saw Mill's steam donkey, which was stashed inside an abandoned barn. The engine was an ingenious old thing. The boiler and clockwork of gears held for J.R. a mechanic's fascination. It was a shame to tear it apart.

"All right, boys!" Clarick announced. "We're tearing this thing apart!"

He pressed play on the boom box, blaring the seemingly eternal reel of demonic opera music.

And then, as the boys set about their task, Clarick held Melissa aside and told her, "You'll get the drift, Blondie."

The steam donkey was maybe a century old. Unbolting its components proved stubborn work. At times, the strength of three men, their combined force of torque, was required.

Meanwhile, Clarick was chatting with Melissa, and Scotty was starting to worry about it.

"What are they talking about? What could they be talking about? What could he be saying to her?" He could only re-phrase the question repeatedly under the music's cacopho-nous and torturous spell.

"I don't know," J.R. answered several times, with deliber-ate nonchalance. Scotty's potential for jealousy wasn't necessarily a cauldron to stir under the circumstances.

When the hour struck, Clarick rose to halt production, and ordered Vince Baldwin to approach for his slap to the face.

That night, as they lay around on their mattresses, Scotty asked his girlfriend, "What were you and Cash Clarick talking about?"

"Oh, please," Melissa answered him. "You've got to be kidding me."

"What?"

"You're *jealous?* Of *him?* Scotty, this is the wrong place and time."

"I'm not jealous, I just want to know what he was saying."

*"I'm* jealous, Scotty! *Me!* Not *you!* Got it? I didn't run off to Pennsylvania just to sit around and watch you guys work!"

"Don't I have a right to know what he said to you?"

*"Keep it down,"* J.R. hissed.

*"J.R.'s right,"* Vince whispered.

They stopped.

J.R. already felt a kind of shameful disgust for any hope the others kept, not to mention any hope of his own. He could see it as the refusal it was, even as he bullshitted his friends, knowing when he said it how stupid it sounded, "I'm impressed with the individual sovereignty aspect of it all."

"Plus, it's not the Army," Scotty told her.

"This mosquito keeps buzzing in my ear," she said.

"That could happen anywhere," he noted.

"I gave that psychopath forty-three bucks?" she protested, "Just to sit and watch you guys work? What the fuck is that?"

*"Keep it down,"* J.R. pleaded.

*"Oh, fuck him,"* she said, although she lowered her voice.

"Babe, you're safe, so far," Scotty said. "That's got to count for something."

Melissa didn't exactly laugh. It was more like her nostrils rejected it.

J.R. was already formulating an escape plan. It would involve Cash Clarick's Land Rover, and also involve tracking

132

Clarick's whereabouts. The plan would require stamina and patience. He didn't want to explain it to his companions, or turn it into a committee meeting, or have them nag him about it, or nit-pick at it. He didn't want Vince to run and tell the boss either, which was probably guaranteed.

"J.R.?" Scotty asked.

"Yes, what?"

Scotty laid it all at his feet. "What are we doing here? Did we make the right choice? What's going to happen to us? Did we just give all our money away so we could work for free?"

"Did you guys see those guys?" J.R. answered. "The Posse Serpens? And the girl, what's her name?"

"Who? Ruth?"

"Ruth. Did you see her? Those guys are warriors. This is the real thing. I mean, think about Pete Dawson, up at college, getting initiated into some *fraternity*. What the fuck? This isn't any bullshit like that. This is staking our claim in the world. So don't pussy out. Or pussy out if you want. Go back to the Bucket o' Fries. I don't care."

He waited for Melissa to take exception, but she said, "Damn straight."

He didn't mean any of it, but it worked.

Cash Clarick's footsteps came prowling up until he appeared in the doorway. They were looking up from their mattresses. He held his gear up for them to see. "I'm watchin' through these here night vision goggles, with this here bolt-action rifle. Got it? Go to sleep tight, please. Or make my night. One or the other."

Just as quickly, he was gone.

J.R. was up off his mattress.

"*J.R.!*" Scotty hissed. "*What are you doing?*"

"*Shhhh!*" J.R. poked his head outside. He watched as Cash Clarick marched away across the moonlit yard toward the fiberglass outhouse under its ghostly tree.

"J.R.," Vince Baldwin cautioned, "don't do that."

## 28. Nothing but Class

They sat pupil-like around the sunshot, half-deconstructed classroom, as Cash Clarick went on about the haven for the White Race the United States had ceased to be. He had taken to cataloguing the various threats, beginning with the non-white races and race-mixing, then moving on to non-Christian religions, and then following up with Communists, Socialists, and other leftists and lunatics.

Next, he began explaining the threat of IBM computers, a rant J.R. could have received at home from his own father without having to bathe in a trough or eat a bullet-torn squirrel for breakfast. Raising his hand and interrupting, he said, "The Old Man and Glenn Disteek promised we'd be learning how to become free men on the land."

Clarick took a deep breath and released it, tilted his head and stared down at his pupil.

"*J.R., don't do that!*" Vince Baldwin whispered.

Vince had been slapped in the face just before class. Melissa looked deliriously malnourished, having missed her target squirrel yet again this morning. Scotty was forbidden to share his own bullseyed squirrel, and so he had thrown it away, refusing to eat.

Clarick finally began to dignify J.R.'s question with an answer. He explained that a *Zionist-Jewish Plot to Control the World* was well underway before they had ever even been born. And how could they possibly hope to be free, much less

134

learn to be free, when they did not yet understand what was keeping them enslaved. He explained that it was all connected, but how it would be stupid and undisciplined to skip ahead just because one student got impatient and started asking questions. He went on to remind J.R. that Rome wasn't built in a day, and further explained how we should learn to crawl before walking, and then walk before taking off to run.

"How does that sound, Nimrod?" he asked, when he was done. "Are you satisfied with that?"

J.R. nodded with a best effort at indifference.

Cash Clarick continued with his syllabus, explaining that it was wasn't just IBM anymore, either.

J.R.'s attention wandered. He kept peering back into the corner, at the bizarre contraption atop its cobwebbed bookshelf. The miniature engine arm continuing its curious mechanical purpose, spooning another gob of pasty bird shit into a spackle bucket.

At some point he dozed off, snoring, or maybe mumbling, because his brain awoke to a sound he was making just a second before a murderously mad Cash Clarick was bellowing, "NIMROD, WHAT IN GOD'S NAME ARE YOU SAYING!?"

"Ah..." he managed to say. "It's nothing,"

"Well this isn't nothing! This is class! And we only have one hour for it!"

## 29. The First Trip to Town

After class, Clarick slapped Vince in the face. Then he said, "All right, kids, me and your friend Nimrod have an errand to run. Everybody into the silo! Let's go! You too, Nimrod, you'll be helping me chain 'em up!"

They were herded across the yard and corralled through the silo's steel door. The air inside was pungent with the ghostly residue of vintage sawdust. Cash Clarick handed J.R. the key on its chain, and the shackling began.

"Sorry guys," J.R. said, more than once, until Clarick corrected him, "Hey, asshole! You're not sorry! You're following orders!"

Following orders, and avoiding eye contact as much as possible, he continued chaining up his friends. When he was done, Clarick beckoned to him, "Come on, gimme them keys."

The manacle key was a bit more silver in color, and a bit smaller than the others on the chain. J.R. stood memorizing it by sight and feel.

Clarick snatched it away, clipped it to his belt. He advised his captives, "We'll be back in forty-five minutes, tops. Vince, don't worry, I'll be back by ten o'clock."

They left the prisoners chained in the silo and proceeded across the yard, around the range targets toward the Land Rover parked beneath the wooden outcropping.

"Mr. Clarick, if I may speak?"

"Yes. What? Jeez."

"Your Land Rover. With the bug-eyed headlamps. That thing is boss—"

"No. You're not gonna drive it. Stop asking me."

Observing the vehicle up close, J.R. confirmed for himself, as he had suspected previously, that he could get the hood open with a screwdriver, although the hood-mounted spare tire would make it a heavy lift. The three front seats had been re-upholstered in snakeskin, but the jump seats assumed no such ostentation, and the rest of the vehicle appeared to be un-modified.

As they drove out, he took note of the path by which he had arrived only days before, blindfolded then, but getting a good look now as it rambled and buckled uphill through the sunlit straw, ascending flanked by stone-strewn brush into the woods. He also observed Cash Clarick's body language behind the wheel, but decided to draw no firm conclusions, not yet, about his skill as a driver.

"So why a Saw Mill?" he asked. "Is that like the politicians in Washington put this place out of business, and now you're here as a daily reminder of their betrayal?"

Clarick gave no answer.

"Or did the blacks do something to you?"

"*Pffffff,*" Clarick answered. He steered the Land Rover out of the woods onto the main road. J.R. kept an eye out for road signs. As they drove in silence, winding through the forest, he confirmed for himself a long-held suspicion that a safari tire mounted on the hood wasn't the greatest idea in the history of horseless carriages.

Clarick answered at last, "That's a good point, Nimrod. Maybe you should look it up. The politics behind it. Maybe Glenn Disteek can make it part of his campaign, and draw all kinds of attention to us. Shit, he probably would. Hell, he probably has. Maybe you can get rich off that racket yourself. But not me. I gave up on politics before I ever got started. There ain't but one way to make money in politics, Nimrod, and no thank you. What I happen to be is a sole proprietor."

Siting there in the passenger seat with a moron at the wheel spouting bullshit, J.R. found himself missing Jack Daddio, an emotion both rare and useless.

"Now we're only taking out five hundred dollars, you understand? If you take it out all at once, it'll look like you been kidnapped. Which you ain't, trust me. This here is a pyramid scheme, Nimrod. Stick around and you'll get your five hundred bucks back, five hundred times over."

"Wait. What? A pyramid scheme? Why are you telling me this?"

Clarick made a baffled face. "Why am I telling you what? This here is boot camp. You wanna graduate or not?"

"OK, sorry, It's just—"

"Never mind, *sheesh*. I'll chain you up next time and bring one of the other morons to forge your signature."

"Not necessary." After that, J.R. kept silent.

They turned onto Pine Hollow, then onto Kiln. He resolved to pay attention to the map from now on, not to the idiot at the wheel. It was only a few miles into town. As they arrived, a painted road sign greeted them. Proverb, Pennsylvania Welcomes You.

At the Proverb Savings Bank, standing in line, Clarick struck up a conversation with the man behind them, pointing to his cap, saying, "Mike Schmidt, can you believe the guy?"

"Mike Schmidt? Hell, what I can't believe is Pete Rose."

"I can't believe any of it," Clarick responded, friendly enough, but terminating the banter.

The thought of Mike Schmidt and Pete Rose out there, somewhere, made J.R. sad on a level he didn't dare dwell upon. He could almost imagine himself crying, although tears were a distant memory.

He wrote out and signed and dated a five-hundred-dollar check for CASH. The block calendar at the teller's window read MAY 11, 1983.

Walking back through the parking lot in the afternoon sunshine, J.R. understood that house pets feel this way all the time. Tantalized by freedom.

"OK, we're making good time," Clarick said. "We got a one game window, let's go."

"One game of what?"

Clarick said nothing. They got into the Land Rover and drove down the street to Charlie's Deli.

Pushing through the dinging door, Clarick pointed to the man behind the counter and said, "That there is Charlie."

J.R. nodded, recognizing the man as one of the mechanics from Hayes Garage.

*Pole Position* was a good arcade game, Japanese-made, nothing like reality, but a more responsive driving simulator than pretty much anything else out there. Clarick plugged in his quarter and overcorrected his way through not one but two circuits, while J.R. bore witness. Even on this crude simulator, Cash Clarick's driving sucked.

"That there is 25 cents well spent," Clarick said, when they were back in the Land Rover.

Open stretches of rural Pennsylvania bid them home, fields of green or gold bisected by roads and crossroads, landmarked in sequence by an aging church, a graveyard, a farmhouse, a homestead. J.R. made note, again, of the road names.

Clarick became sullen at the wheel, his seatbelt unfastened at his side.

J.R. hadn't fastened his own seatbelt, for fear it would provoke a reaction, even as they turned off road, downshifted and plunged through the ferns and ivy and mugwort into that brief stretch of open trail before the steeper decline into the wooded valley. Blindfolded the first time, he had sought a feel for the terrain through the wheel well of Fat Ransom's van. This time, he saw it for the plunge it was.

He also observed Clarick's negotiation, riding the brakes, a poor driver.

A hemlock tree awaited at one catch-all curve, just daring them to smash into it. Clarick prowled slowly up to and around it, then turned back down into the valley. The path shimmied twice more through the thinning trees before the sky opened overhead for the final tumbling maneuver through the green brush and pale straw descending into the Saw Mill's entrance. They drifted up to the gate and then through it. Clarick nodded toward the waiting silo and said, "We're gonna make us some white babies, Nimrod, with yonder *pussy.*"

"Wait... *What?!*"

"All's I'm asking," Clarick clarified, "is if your friend Shades don't recognize the situation, you be ready to man up in his place."

Easing the Land Rover across the Saw Mill yard, he continued, "I'm beggin' you, Nimrod. No wait. No, I'm not. I'm not begging you. I'm tellin' you, is what I'm doin'. Because you, I trust. Them others? They're sheep. But you? You're the smart one."

"The smart what?"

"The smart... I don't know..." Clarick guided the Land Rover past the range targets and wheeled it into its parking space beneath the yard's outcropping. "Border collie," he answered, keying off the ignition. "You're a border collie, or something like that." He stared down at the steering wheel, paused for another moment's thought, then burst out laughing.

J.R. couldn't believe he had actually been to town, at a convenience store, standing witness to an arcade game, like a normal person who was free. A free man on the land, as had been promised.

"Relax, Nimrod," Clarick told him. "I'm not talking about this here training program. I'm talking about afterwards. After boot camp. Then comes the real world. And someone is going to make babies with that gal. Understand? And if it ain't your friend, I'm just hoping it's you. I'm just hoping you come to grips with your duty to your race, that's all."

At that moment, J.R.'s fear and regret became dimensions beyond any breathing technique or adrenaline burst that might have served his adventurous nature. Every jealous notion he had ever entertained came back to short out his synapses, with Cash Clarick's suggestion spoken out loud.

"OK, ten hut, Nimrod. Time to slap FuckFace in the face."

## 30. Couples Counseling with Cash Clarick

The strings carved a death march while the tympani boomed. The brass embraced and tightened some sonic tension that strangled J.R.'s sternum by way of his inner ear before surging free at last and receding into the dark and monk-like consonance of choral moans, these vivisected by choral wails and topped by one lonesome upper-register angel, weeping and falling in some deathless, spent, cascading non-trajectory. A great cacophonous drama howled from the boom box while the sun beat down upon the weary recruits as they picked like vultures at the carcass of a dead age. The big, twin-axle dump trailer was already overstuffed on its fat tires, and so they had begun a separate inventory of the iron and wood and tin and copper, row by row on the floor of the dusty Saw Mill yard.

Meanwhile, they had been promised combat training, and so they received it, for an hour or two a day, beginning with the indoor and outdoor shooting ranges, taking turns with a loaded bolt-action, while Cash Clarick watched over them with his wieldy bullpup.

They also took turns shooting small game with the Mossberg. The drill was maddeningly useful, as many of the drills were, except that everything had to be a regimen of abuse.

For instance, Melissa lagged behind the boys when it came to mealtime, and Clarick forbade any of them to assist her, or give her any food, so that she went hungry most mornings, while Scotty fumed and argued and refused to eat.

It was left to J.R. to whisper into Melissa's ear, *"Make sure not to miss."*

She hit her target with her very next shot, and then skinned and roasted the squirrel and consumed it like an animal herself.

J.R. felt something he didn't welcome. It was embarrassing, her hunger. He had to turn away. He picked up the rifle where she had left it, and sat there holding it in hand, unable to say a single useful thing.

Additionally, Clarick would make Melissa stand up on a chair, while her three male companions endured impossibly grueling calisthenics in the yard below.

Vince broke down first. It was a simple exercise, jumping jacks, only too many, after too much. He lay face down in the dirt, possibly unconscious.

His punishment was for Cash Clarick to summon Melissa down from her chair to center stage for a haircut. The scissors were a shocking surprise. Scotty lurched forward but ended up watching, half relieved, half destroyed, as the butchered blonde lock fell heavily to the slats.

The drills progressed over the hours and then over the succeeding days. Scotty and J.R. pushed each other beyond agony, so that it was Vince Baldwin, time and again, who failed.

Off came another random lock of Melissa's hair. Scotty was ready to pounce, time and again. Cash Clarick always said, "Cool it, Shades," or some such thing.

Eventually, he told Melissa to turn around on her chair. "This should provide your White Knights with some extra motivation," he said.

Scotty was up, leaping onto the platform.

Clarick, weaponless, faced him down.

Scotty hesitated, wild-eyed, pointing a finger. "I'LL KILL YOU TO KEEP HER SAFE! YOU AND WHOEVER ELSE! I'LL KILL ALL OF YOU FUCKERS WITH MY BARE HANDS!"

Utterly benumbed to stress and peril by now, J.R. prepared himself to jump in and help.

"Look at me, Shades!" Clarick was saying, pointing into his own beady-eyed and lipless face. "She was lookin' one way. Now she's lookin' the other way. It's just a different perspective is all. Not with words, but with eyeballs. That's because Cash Clarick don't just *tell* the truth. Cash Clarick *is* the truth. You understand?"

He pointed his thumb at Melissa and explained some more, "Your girlfriend there is what nobody else in this life will tell you. 'Cause tellin' it don't do it no justice. You got to know it, white man. You got to live it. And I know you have. So I know I don't even have to tell you. That that there gorgeous blonde Barbie doll piece of ass is practically the only thing on this planet this whole war is about. You think I'm gonna let any harm come to *her?* You're out of your Goddamn mind! I ain't layin' a finger on your goddamn *Holy Grail* this whole fortnight! She's the damn ends AND the damn means, combined! Not like most nobody else you'll ever meet in your lifetime!"

Melissa stood above them, her blonde hair a butchered mess.

Clarick chuckled, "Well, not *that* kind of finger, anyway. I don't see her haircut getting through this."

*"You son-of-a-bitch!"* she glared down at him, at all of them, tears welling in her eyes.

"What did I tell you all before?" Clarick made himself magnanimous somehow, a friend and mentor to all. "I am the ugly truth. You all can learn all this stuff when you're 80 years old and it's too late. Or you can learn it right here and right now, from me, while there's still time in your life to live, not to mention redeem your race."

He then turned to Melissa up on her chair and said, "You wanna run around like Batgirl, Blondie? Kicking your foes in the face? What do you think these boys are fighting for? What you think ALL our boys are fighting for? There ain't but one thing priceless in this life! There's your fucking truth! All of you!" He studied them all. "Soldiers and suckers and cowards and leaders and pinheads and women too! Don't matter! All of you! When the shit goes down, *this one,*" he pointed his thumb up at Melissa again, "don't get sent to the front lines!"

They were exhausted. Cash Clarick leaned down and turned on the tape player, blasting the deathly opera music once again.

Slowly, J.R. and his companions returned to their positions, the three of them facing the earth, their strength failing, countered relentlessly by gravity, while Clarick went back to pacing and soliloquizing. "I'm training you for what's coming, shitheads! Not for no Hollywood movie! And let me offer you some other advice! And don't say I never told you no favors! There's a boy out there named Steeplejack..."

He turned to observe Melissa standing about-faced on her chair, until she craned backwards to meet his gaze. Her glare was murderous.

He looked her up and down, addressed her almost compassionately. "Steeplejack ain't no saint like I am."

### 31. Lou Gannon's Wife

J.R. sat eyeballing Steeplejack inside the cell-like lantern-lit U-Haul caboose, while the Libertyville Mall parking lot waited outside.

Unprompted, Steeplejack said, "I make love to my women."

J.R. looked away while the oration continued.

"With the others, it ain't quote-unquote makin' love. It's just. I don't know. Gettin' the bugs out...

"By the way, you ever notice how many songs are about one of those two things? It's either about *Makin' Love,* or it's about *Gettin' the Bugs Out?* Am I right? Well, anyway, I'm just a believer in both things, is all. Love is purity of heart. Lust is purity of spirit. Who am I to say one should or shouldn't conquer the other? Who am I to say one is good, and the other is bad? That's like splittin' a difference no man was born to see. Least of all me. Same here as where you grew up, J.R. What do you think of Elsie, by the way?" Steeplejack was smiling like it was a meal on his plate.

Elsie was the wife of Lou Gannon, the getaway driver, who was waiting in the Trans Am outside.

J.R. had taken to liking maybe one person and one person only at the so-called Castle.

Clearly, Steeplejack had picked up on this, saying, "Your friend Vince is training to be a soldier, right? But what about you? What do you think you're training to be? Here with me? Inside this U-Haul truck?"

J.R. shrugged, "I don't care."

Steeplejack laughed at him. "Don't lie to yourself. We're above all of this, you and me. We both know it."

"You don't know—"

"I don't know what?"

"What I know," J.R. answered.

"She's worth fighting for, is all I'm saying. She's worth fighting for, J.R. Am I right?"

"That's Lou Gannon's *wife*," he countered. "Let's get this thing done."

"Precisely what I'm saying. Lou Gannon's wife." Steeplejack smirked and turned away.

Elsie Gannon was pretty, which J.R. had resolved not to appreciate, especially if it meant she was going to end up like Melissa Victoria.

It was more like some ghost of his former self would briefly visit and admire Elsie Gannon's good looks.

She had blonde hair, more gold than sunshine, heavy drapes cut short and bell-like off her shoulders. There was something about her, some kindness. She seemed always to smile, and to make the delicate best of every situation. J.R. came to wonder about himself, and whether he was capable of that same state of grace. Perhaps it was the key to getting out of here. Perhaps he would never grasp it. Perhaps Elsie was the only person left on earth who could teach it to him.

She was older, but not by much, and she had arrived with Lou Gannon all the way from West Lewiston, Illinois. A city overrun by blacks, he had heard her say. This kind of talk was routine at the Castle.

Presumably, Elsie had been through the Saw Mill too, but other than the racism, and the belief in a bearded man in the sky, she was pretty much better company than all the rest of the Nazi Posse Umbellus combined.

He first came to admire her when Chuck Zorn returned with his arm slashed from a knife fight in parking lot of Handy Dandy Dan's in West Susquehannock.

The Castle had an unofficial head nurse, the one they called Lazy Farrah, although never to her face, the consequences being famously dire.

Farrah could not have been named after Farrah Fawcett Majors, but she was surely cursed by that association now, her permanently hungry gap-toothed sneer exhaling cigarette smoke nearly constantly, dragon-like. Imperfect, un-pearly, and grinning.

Escorting Chuck Zorn into the mess hall and dragging on her Marlboro, Farrah sat her patient down on one of the picnic benches, poured a careless splash of gin over the wound, and slapped a bandage onto the slippery arm. Chuck Zorn cursed through the pain and his own clenched teeth. A collection of Posse Umbellus had gathered to watch. Duke Drummond came to hover over the injured soldier.

"You mad at me, boss?"

"No, son," Drummond gripped Chuck Zorn's shoulder. "If I start telling you who you can and can't get into knife fights with, hell... I might as well go join the other team."

They all enjoyed a laugh, Chuck Zorn included. Drummond released Chuck Zorn's shoulder. "Just don't go starting the revolution without me in the supply store parking lot, OK?"

The laughter multiplied, Steeplejack along with the rest of them. J.R. saw Elsie whisper to Lou, and Lou nod to his wife, and then turn and say, "Hey, boss. Elsie here wants to sew up that wound. Would that be all right with Farrah?"

Drummond raised his empty palms. "It not my decision. It's Farrah's."

Farrah snickered through nicotine swirls. "Sure thing, little sister. Better you than me."

The Posse Umbellus soldiers sat around the Mess Hall picnic tables watching the field surgery unfold. The operation was nothing new to any of them, but there was something angelic about Elsie's performance, the way she carried herself through it, smiling pleasantly, sewing elegantly, taking hold of Chuck Zorn's naked arm, glancing back at her husband Lou, whose rush of jealousy she may have preternaturally sensed ahead of time and prevented.

J.R. observed that Steeplejack was holding his breath as he eyeballed Elsie Gannon up and down.

Duke Drummond was more clinically detached, enthralled by the needlework. "Those are tidy stitches," he remarked. "Where'd you learn to do that, girlie?"

Elsie shrugged. "My mother used to sew up the blacks in West Lewiston."

"Well, God bless you, sister. You are doing the white man's work now."

"I'm doing God's work," she countered.

Drummond twitched.

Elsie remained disarming, serene, oblivious to her transgression, at least enough to cast doubt on it. "Long as I'm here," she caught J.R.'s eye, "I aim to make myself useful."

J.R. saw from the longing in Elsie Gannon's eyes that she was smart. He saw that she was trapped at the Castle, same as he was. He also saw that it didn't matter. Because he couldn't help Elsie Gannon. She was Lou Gannon's wife.

## 32. Couples Counseling: Second Session

Looking back on his stay at the Saw Mill, he had trouble, sometimes, placing events in the timeline. Several consecutive days seemed to blur together.

On one occasion it was pouring rain, and the three of them were lined up with their arms extended—J.R, Scotty and Vince—rotating at the shoulders until the pain was like crucifixion.

Cash Clarick stood above them on the platform, while Melissa stood above Cash Clarick on her chair, soaking wet in the downpour.

As usual, Scotty and J.R. suffered the drill competitively, waiting for Vince to fail, at which point they would be released, face down, guiltless on some desperately logical level.

Vince collapsed. Clarick said, "Well done, FuckFace!" and took another hank of Melissa's hair. Scotty had had enough for the millionth time.

"THIS AIN'T GONNA STOP!" Clarick shouted down at Scotty's rain-soaked, defiant face, "LESS'N FUCKFACE TOUGHENS UP!"

Vince moaned into the mud.

"Funny thing is," Clarick continued, "he's one of mine already. You? You're still hangin' onto somethin' that's gone. Because it weren't never there in the first place. But you'll get past it. Hell, the truth is, I like this'n here and this'n here. But you," he pointed his finger at Scotty, "you're just a pain in my ass. I might just skin you alive with the potato peeler in the mess yonder. That look I get from people's faces is all I look forward to anymore, sometimes."

*"I'm sorry, Shades!"* Vince moaned, face down. *"I'm sorry, Blondie!"*

"It's OK, Vince!" J.R. said.

Scotty shot him a glare.

The rain drummed down at them. "Who are you going to turn to in a bind, huh? Some rabbi? Some whatever the fuck? Some terrorist? Good luck, asshole! You turn to your own kind, that's who! The blood that flows in your veins! And by the way, maybe you boys ought to strangle ol' FuckFace to death, in case rescuing this here damsel becomes of interest. Don't you think you'll be the first to take such measures outside these here gates?"

Vince just lay there, drenched in the mud, probably hoping they would do it.

## 33. The Silo

Cash Clarick chained them up in the silo and left for town.

Strung up in the darkness, J.R. listened as the Land Rover drove away. He tried to breathe easy, but the smell was too close. Cricketsong echoed all around the cylindrical death-trap.

"It's that *white race* bullshit," Scotty lamented, his chains clanking off the silo wall. "Once I heard that, I should have run. I knew it in my gut, but I didn't listen."

Vince moaned, wordless but sonorous.

J.R. didn't want to say anything about the plan he'd been formulating. He ventured a cryptic message instead. "Clarick's Land Rover is a big part of his operation."

"I'm glad you're having a nice time," Scotty spat, "in the company car."

*My friends don't trust me,* J.R. understood. He exhaled his breath, tried to stay sharp. There was little oxygen, even less light. His arms hung restrained and aching. His mind was maybe not so tireless after all.

"J.R., what's he going into town for?" Melissa's voice echoed up into the empty tower. "Besides your five hundred bucks? Why isn't he taking that scrap metal to town?"

"Not enough time. He has to get back for... you know." J.R. nodded in the direction of Vince Baldwin.

"So what's he going into town for?"

"I don't know. Maybe he's making a deal to unload the next load of scrap. Or maybe he's just playing that arcade game at the deli. He's in love with that game. Or he thinks he is."

His friends left him alone after that, to hang in sightless audience to the cricket kingdom's hypnotic reverberating echo.

He chose not to tell them what he had seen the other night. Cash Clarick retrieving a weighty jerrycan from behind the moonlit fiberglass outhouse and its ramshackle plywood aft-appendage.

## 34. Couples Counseling: Third Session

Clarick was leaning down over Scotty, saying, "Seriously, Shades. Listen to me now. That boy Steeplejack is gonna *want* your Barbie Doll up there... if he gets his hands on her. You'll understand, when you meet him, the difference between him and me. And I ain't no liar, neither. Someday, you're gonna thank 'ol Cash Clarick and look back on him. Or not. Folks don't tend to thank the one that never lied to 'em. That's what I've come to find."

*"Water..."* Scotty gasped, semi-conscious, with his face sideways in the dirt.

Melissa Victoria implored Cash Clarick from atop her chair, "HE NEEDS WATER!"

"Oh, for Pete's sake!" Clarick was disgusted.

J.R. offered his own plea, "Scotty is a champion athlete, Mr. Clarick. He runs a 2:05 five hundred at will. The man can do anything. It's just that you have to keep him hydrated. With water."

"You're supposed to *frag* your friend, Nimrod. Not beg me for more rations!"

"You should listen to me," J.R. told him.

"Very well," Clarick relented. He handed the jug of water to Scotty. It seemed, for that moment, that a semblance of mercy had been achieved.

Thereafter the dunks began. Cash Clarick plunging Scotty's head into the trough and drowning him, until Scotty began to flail and splash for air. Only that first time did Melissa leap down from her chair, crying, "STOP IT! YOU'RE KILLING HIM!"

Clarick yanked Scotty out of the trough and flung his soaking wet track-athlete body to the ground. At the same time, with his right hand, he drew a pistol on Melissa Victoria. Fearlessly, she went to Scotty and knelt at his side.

"Just remember," Clarick told Scotty, "who loves you. It's her, Shades. It's Blondie. She saved you, with her love. No kidding, I mean it. You'd both be dead, if I wasn't so impressed. So don't get the idea that you didn't just fail. It was her who didn't fail."

Scotty lay in the wet dirt, coughing.

"Also," Clarick added, "Nimrod and FuckFace would have let you drown. So keep that in mind. You're welcome for the insight into your own friends."

It would be drowning three times a day, while the others watched. Clarick would bind Scotty's hands behind his back, lead him to the trough, kneel him down, and hold his head under water. He would wait until Scotty started to struggle and buck, while the others began their predictable screams for mercy. Then he'd release Scotty's wet head to gasp for air, although he waited just a bit longer each time.

No stopwatch demarked Scotty's every new threshold. No logbook recorded his progress. This bothered J.R. until he protested, "You have to keep a... What do you call it? ... A *Composition Book*... Or something."

"What? *A Composition Book?* What are you talking about?"

"To write it down. To write down Scotty's time."

"For what?"

"To track his progress."

"Look around, Nimrod. How many witnesses you need?

"But he's making progress. And no one will know it!"

"You stupid asshole! What do you want?... A scrapbook?... For this?"

J.R. was exhausted, unsure what he was saying.

Melissa, with her blonde hair hacked away, cried out, "What is wrong with you?! You are such a fucking asshole!"

"Who?" J.R. pleaded, "Me?"

"No, not you, *him!*"

## 35. The Second or Third Trip to Town

The next day, at a quarter past noon, J.R. wrote out another check. After the bank, they drove down the street to play *Pole Position* at Charlie's deli.

"Shit," Clarick said, steering with blistering incompetence through the never-changing racetrack. "I gotta go slap FuckFace in the face."

Back in the parking lot, they mounted into the Land Rover's cab. J.R. buckled his seatbelt. Clarick took notice. "What? You don't trust my driving?"

"No, I do."

"Well, what?"

"It's nothing. Believe me, I can spot a good driver. And you? *Pole Position* only proves it. But I figure... and correct me if I'm wrong. If we get into an accident. Could be a deer in the road or any such unforeseeable thing. And I get hurt? You're just gonna smother me with a pillow or something. So fuck that. I'm wearing my seatbelt."

"Pillow? There ain't but one pillow at the whole Saw Mill, boy, and that's the one I lay my weary head on in between your pesterin'. I wouldn't kill you with it, nor a spider neither. Gimme that fucking money!" He snatched the five hundred out of J.R.'s mitts.

## 36. Couples Counseling: Final Session

Scotty was given Command of Tactical Assault, just like he'd been given everything else in life.

*Drowning?* J.R. brooded. *Just drowning? Three times a day? Gets you Command of Tactical Assault?*

At the same time, he knew his companions had each been treated to their own personalized humiliation. Even Melissa, who hadn't been slapped in the face or held under water, but merely excused from the program she had signed up for, and paid for, while Cash Clarick hacked chunks of her hair away.

As they lay around on their mattresses in the middle of the night, delirious with exhaustion, awake with Vince, either just before Cash Clarick's hourly visit or just after it, Scotty would insist to Melissa that she could get her hair cut so that it looked good short once they graduated from the Saw Mill. Then, she would be free to grow it out as much she wanted to. Just like that lady Ruth back at the Compound.

"I don't give a fuck about my hair," she told him.

The next day, at last, she got to participate in one of the drills. She would be the kidnap victim, held captive somewhere within Clarick's GLAD Bag pseudo-urban deathtrap.

Scotty held his tactical assault team outside, to crouch behind shapeless obstacles nailed together from repurposed planks of wood.

Birds chirped in the tranquil, afternoon air.

*"Let's go!"* Scotty whispered, advancing.

156

He led the trio of rifle barrels pointing level and forward, albeit empty of bullets for simulation purposes. The walls that contained Melissa Victoria were sheathed in taut, black plastic, and braced with wooden pallets, so that Scotty could simulate backing himself up against the structure's south-facing wall, and sidling around its corner to its front-facing door.

Upon arriving there, he left J.R. and Vince behind and stormed in all alone.

"SCOTTY, LOOK OUT!" Melissa cried.

The trap was sprung. Scotty's murder was simulated with a can of blue paint.

Clarick began laughing from somewhere within the black partitions. "Now aren'tcha glad I'm holdin' your sunglasses?"

Scotty proceeded to rescue Melissa, although she wasn't restrained, so he simply explored until he found her, and then led her by the hand through the GLAD Bag corridors and out the front door.

Melissa was paint-speckled too. Hands, clothes, and sneakers. Clarick followed out after them, sidestepping the puddle of paint in the entrance. J.R. volunteered, "I'll take Command of Tactical Assault."

"Negative, Nimrod. You're recon."

"Why?"

"BECAUSE YOU'RE A SNEAKY SONOFABITCH!"

J.R. felt a bolt of panic. Had Clarick somehow spotted him out of his bunk at night?

Clarick offered no clues, turned his attention to Scotty and said, "Shades, your team always needs one skinny and expendable douchebag to scout what lies ahead. You want your logistics all figured out ahead of time, understand me? Not just space but time, too. Mapped out in advance, before show-time ever starts. Nimrod is your man for that. He's a sneaky sonofabitch. Understand?"

"Yes, sir!"

"So give him some damn orders next time!"

"Yes, sir!"

That evening, with the day's third drowning over and done with, Scotty was wet and unkempt, also flecked, splattered and crusted with blue paint. Deliriously, and in front of one and all, he told Cash Clarick, "I'm white. I confess to nothing and apologize for less. My conquering nature is my God-given gift. No man's blood is ever his choosing. Every man's blood calls him home to his destiny." He recited it just as he'd been taught.

"You know, Shades," Cash Clarick said, "I think you're Posse Serpens material after all. Honestly, I don't think there's a damn thing I got to fix about you."

A moment of peace fell over them, which J.R. didn't quite believe was happening, though he didn't dare take it away either.

They were all too pitiful for their own good. Scotty was smiling, validated. Melissa was smiling too, proud, at last, from up on her chair. Vince wore the vapid, merciless semi-grin he had settled into. Even J.R. broke into peaceful approval, without meaning to, or wanting to.

The sunset in the valley tipped the millscape's parapets in tangerine sunfire. Dragonflies rose and plunged and hovered within the sunbeams through the trees. Birdsong peppered the air; some were calling, some responding, some asserting isolation. Crickets ground their winged pulsations to sonorous heights.

"Except I don't fix things no how," Clarick said. "I fuck things up is what I do." He pressed play on the boom box. Operatic demonic monks began chanting down in slashing, malicious, reanimated tongues. "That's all I do. That's all I was put on this earth to do! So giddy the fuck up! I spent years of my life in prison, kids! So don't start whining at me about no two weeks!"

"YOU CAN DO IT, SCOTTY!" Melissa encouraged him.

"I love you, babe!"

"I love you too, babe!"

"Wait a minute!" J.R. offered an empty hand. "Scotty's already been drowned three times today!"

"Math?" Clarick spat. "You stupid asshole! All's you ever had to count to was one!"

"I can count all the way to five hundred!"

Clarick ignored him. Scotty's head went underwater. The music's dark complexity compressed J.R.'s brain. He felt elevated above himself. Clarick began hollering down at Scotty's submerged head, "YOU GOTTA FIND THIRTY MORE SECONDS, SHADES! AND YOU GOTTA DO IT WITH OR WITHOUT YOUR BARBIE DOLL IN THE CLUTCHES OF DICK DASTARDLY! AIN'T BUT ONE PERSON IN YOUR

LIFE! NOT IN HERS, NEITHER! YOU EVEN KNOW WHO
THAT PERSON IS? IT'S YOU, BOY! SO FOR YOU AND HER
BOTH, COME ON NOW!"

In that moment of blind and enlightened exhaustion, J.R.
felt an unearthly relief. It was between Melissa and Scotty.
None of this was his fault.

## 37. The Third or Fourth Trip to Town

As he was writing out another five-hundred-dollar check for CASH, it occurred to him to write S.O.S. on the memo line, but that was too dangerous. He made some small talk with the bank teller, accomplished nothing by it. Clarick wasn't happy about it either. Outside in the parking lot, beneath the open sky of freedom and normalcy, he was hissing at J.R.'s neck, "You don't make friends with no locals, you understand?"

Back in the Land Rover, handing over the wad of bills, J.R. said, "So this is my dues? Fair enough. But why are my dues higher than the other guys' dues?"

"Security deposit. Don't worry about it. You'll thank me, someday, with your money gotten back, several times over."

"So is it getting invested?"

"What did I just say?" Clarick keyed the ignition.

"It's just..." J.R. buckled his seatbelt. "If my money is getting invested... I'm not a fool... Let's make it work. My bank will get suspicious—"

"That's why it's five hundred at a time, Sherlock."

"I remember Mr. Taylor telling my dad that he would personally see to freezing the account if they noticed anything suspicious."

"Five hundred. Five hundred bucks at a time."

"...and investigate."

"Shut your mouth."

"On consecutive days... is all I'm saying."

"Every two days! Unbuckle that seatbelt."

"Every two days. Got it."

"Except... you know... weekends."

"Every two business days," J.R. affirmed.

"Every day is a business day," Clarick argued. J.R. didn't argue back. He understood the schedule.

## 38. Sneaky Sonofabitch

Daybreak broke with a slap to Vince Baldwin's face.

Then began their morning on the edge of the forest, shooting varmints for breakfast.

"What about this chipmunk?" Scotty asked, aiming down the Mossberg's sights. "Is it worth it? I'm sick of squirrel. But can a person eat a chipmunk?"

"Don't bother," Vince advised.

"Really?" J.R. asked him.

Vince nodded his head, convincingly, like he had eaten chipmunk once, and regretted it. "Trust me," he said.

Scotty shot a squirrel instead. Melissa bullseyed her own squirrel. Everybody had breakfast.

Scotty's first drowning of the day played out, followed by another slap to Vince Baldwin's face. An hour of so-called education followed in the so-called classroom, upon haphazard stacks of spiderweb bivouacked freight pallets, with Clarick advising them to come to terms with various apocalyptic scenarios, all of which were nigh-inevitable on their own, but even more so in mutual collision, all forming an undeniable truth you could see many miles away from many different directions, a collapse of civilization around every corner, with the white race prepared to inherit that scorched earth, born anew from that crucible, with their intellect, industry and ruthlessness eternal heralds of their God-ordained sovereignty.

Then another slap to Vince Baldwin's face.

Then the paramilitary training, with Melissa held out and standing on her chair.

Then another round at the water trough for Scotty, followed by hours of unpaid labor set to cacophonous and gothic opera music, disassembling the great and crumbling Saw Mill, with Melissa once again watching from her chair while the boys collected the wood and scrap metal.

Then the nighttime, at last.

J.R. lay awake on his mattress, his heartbeat throbbing in his eardrums.

The early hours grew longer as they passed, perhaps because he slept here and there, or semi-slept, listening for Cash Clarick, tracking his footsteps, waiting out each clockwork visitation, trying to maintain some measurement of the minutes in between, with no frame of reference beyond his own beating heart, understanding all too clearly that he was not conditioned for sixty minutes when there was nothing to tick through it, even when the top of the hour came around again, almost noiseless but not quite, startling Vince awake, Vince pleading in truncated animal terror and then collapsing mute afterward, shocked into stupor, savoring the relief, his next slap-to-the-face never further away than now, leaving the quiet cruel window of peace to shorten again in-between, while Cash Clarick slipped out into the night.

To compare Vince Baldwin's plight to his own? J.R. couldn't contemplate it.

However, he could sense each visit growing more perfunctory, more weary from the commitment. Unless perhaps Cash Clarick was inhuman, never sleeping a wink, never needing to. *"Sneaky Sonofabitch!"* is what he had called J.R. more than once, suggesting he knew everything.

Finally, in one dark and diminishing pre-dawn interstice, J.R. arose from his mattress and crept out of the barracks into the night.

The moon was bright in the windless yard. Above the treetops, the clouds lay perfectly still. He kept to the shadows. He knew Cash Clarick might well be stalking behind him with a hunting knife. Or nestled overhead, as promised, from one of the Saw Mill's crenellations, the rifle leveled down into the yard, the killshot coiled against his trigger finger, his one eye closed and unseeing, his other eye unblinking through the scope. Nevertheless, J.R. ventured ahead.

Creeping inside the pinnacled shadows of the Saw Mill's rooftops, he probed his hands cautiously forward, praying to a non-existent God not to spring a slapstick Wile E. Coyote garden rake to the face. He had never felt more mortal. And yet each passing moment became another deathtrap unsprung.

Where the silo's shadow cast a bridge over the yard, he crossed it. The katydids and crickets thrummed with presence and power, every one of them likely to outlive him, as they glorified their ongoing limitlessness, while J.R. understood a bullet to the brain and an end to everything lay only an instant away.

And yet no such end came.

He crossed the yard, approached the office peripherally, to squat beneath the dim glow of its fishbowl windows. He had no idea how much time he had left. Counting the minutes, he had lost them in the moments. It was somewhere past three, or four, or possibly five, with dawn yet to glimmer. He heard the office chair creak, and enjoyed, profoundly, for this moment anyway, knowing something Cash Clarick didn't.

Satisfied, he made his way back to his quarters, retracing the shadows with considerably increased confidence, arriving to take cover inside the doorframe and peer around the corner. In time, he saw Clarick emerge from the sleeping unit.

He retreated to his mattress, to splay himself out dramatically, in imitation of his enslaved, defeated companions. They had all been physically brutalized. He had merely been robbed in multiples of five hundred. A final shoe was yet to drop, and he knew it. With or without his friends, he would have to get out of here.

## 39. The Rite

The next night, after Cash Clarick slapped the sleeping Vince Baldwin's face, he bid J.R. back to his office.

Up on his feet and following through the night across the Saw Mill yard, J.R. found himself indulging some half-hearted, ridiculous hope that none of this was happening. It could only be an extremely plausible dream.

"This here is a job interview, Nimrod. You up for a job interview?" Clarick opened the business office screen door.

"A job interview?"

"Consider it that."

He went inside. A video camera on a tripod stood behind the desk, pointing at the cot in the corner.

"It ain't a court of law," Clarick said. "It's a job interview. You understand the difference?"

"OK, for what job?"

"That's what we're here to find out. You see that war hammer hanging on the wall?" Clarick pointed to the weapon crisscrossed in reverence with the battle axe over the room's tidy desk.

"Yeah," J.R. shrugged.

Proceeding to the desk and taking a seat behind it, Clarick directed his recruit to face the Betacam. Reaching up and pressing RECORD, he said, "Yeah? What does 'yeah' mean?"

"Yeah means yes."

"Yes, what? I asked you a question."

"Yes, I see that Viking war hammer on the wall."

"*Viking?* I never said *Viking*. The *Vikings* are a bunch of cavemen from Norway. That weapon was made in the U.S.A.!"

"I'm sorry, it's... yeah, *yes*... you're right. I'm sorry, I wasn't expecting this. I'm just really tired—"

"Tired? What about me? Do I look tired to you?"

"Yes, and you're not complaining. But I was. So point taken."

"Business," Clarick reminded him. "Mixing races. You say it's good for business. Well, business is my middle name, Nimrod. So let's hear all about it."

This was something J.R. had brought up several times before, including earlier that day, in a delirium that seemed admittedly defiant upon reflection. He shook his head now, confronted by it. "It's just... where I come from..."

"Where you come from is Daddio's Garage in Erving, New York. That's on the record."

"Yes, that's correct, on the record. Where I come from, we talk about this stuff. But I don't like where I come from. I never did. That's why I'm here. So it's my mistake. Let's move on."

"Come on now, son," Cash Clarick said. "How do you suppose I got where I got? I got a *radar* for money. So help me understand this angle of yours—"

"I really don't want to argue about it."

Clarick snickered. "I'm gonna let you in on a secret, Nimrod. Something these here Posse Serpens don't know, and the Posse Umbellus don't know neither. And they don't know 'cause they never cared, never bothered to figure it out. All's I want to do is to squeeze a extra dollar out of this here. You won't believe how they screwed me... if I told you."

J.R. kept looking back and forth between the Betamax camera and Cash Clarick, as if one or the other would suddenly reveal itself.

"I don't give a rat's ass about no so-called *racial superiority*," Clarick continued. He was confessing, his voice recorded for posterity on Betamax tape. "I mean, it's true and all. But lots of other bullshit is true, too. Ain't that right? You don't put no money down on no *Capital T Truth*. You put it down on... well... that's the magic question, ain't it? Where to place your chips? So tell me what you was sayin' before, Nimrod. I know I ain't gonna like it. I know I heard it all before, but maybe not so strongly yet, from such a newly minted believer. Strong men are known to keep after that darned old truth even after it hurts their darned old sensitive ears. So I'm strong, I reckon. So let's hear it."

"It's just," J.R. sought for words that could conceivably get him out of this room. "There's a lot of business out there... Blacks... Jews... believe me... all I'm saying is... you can't just put a sign out front saying you hate these people. They have wallets."

"Savages and Christkillers, yes, yes, go on..." Clarick nodded his head a couple of times. His pin eyes settled into the light of some hypnotic self-actualization. The Betacam on its tripod awaited more. "Nimrod," he said calmly, "I'm not just talking about fixing up cars, which you better snap to and do, if I ask it. I'm talking about fighting for what's *ours*. So don't lose sight of that, white man, if you want me to appreciate your so-called perspective."

J.R. shook his head, "OK, but..."

"But what?"

J.R. looked at the camera. "You said you wanted to know my angle."

"That's right, boy. And believe me, I heard it."

"No, you didn't. And it's on tape, too. For you to play back, if you want. You didn't hear me—"

"You ever been punched in the face?"

"Yes."

"How many times?"

"Thirty."

"Thirty?" Clarick looked surprised. "Thirty. So, this will be a breeze then."

The fear came in a sickening bolt. This was going to hurt, bad. And it would be on tape. J.R. had been knocked cold by Melissa Victoria once. Aside from that, he had never been punched in the face.

"What about sodomized?" Clarick said. "Ever been sodomized?"

Looking back, he could only imagine what his own stupefied expression might have said. His friends thought they had it so bad, and they did. But they were not right to envy him.

Clarick gestured back to the war hammer on the wall, elevating his open hand to the weapon on display.

"And how 'bout getting hit over the head with one of those?"

J.R. shook his head.

"I used to bring that on missions sometimes…" Clarick reached up for the war hammer and brought it down from its wall hanging. He cradled it, gripped the leather-bound handle in both fists. "But this monster is for executions only. It won't do in no raid."

"I bet it would do in a raid."

"Nope. Not practical under any circumstances." He set the weapon back upon the wall mount. "Another personal question, Nimrod, have you ever been poisoned?"

"This is still the job interview, right?"

"I ask. You answer. So."

"Ah," J.R. remembered when he was a kid. "Pizza from Mi Amore's, the whole family in the ER… food poisoning, long time ago."

"So, you're a mechanic. Can you fix a handmade, twin-engine vacuum pump?"

He was cautious here. He had already decided to keep Cash Clarick guessing. To be incompetent, falsely modest, and overconfident all at once. He answered, "My dad taught me some things."

"What else, besides fixing cars?"

J.R. shrugged. "I know pretty much everything in the world is bullshit—"

"No, I mean useful knowledge. What useful knowledge you got?"

J.R. shrugged again. "Just the Presidents."

"The Presidents? Like Dutch and Tricky Dick?"

"Yes."

"What about Polk?"

The answer came slowly, with caution. "Sure… President James K. Polk."

He hated Cash Clarick more than the totality of his whole life, the entire string of events that had brought him here, the episodes unfurling, beginning from his birth and continuing until now, with every family member, every customer, every neighbor, every friend, every adversary, every random acquaintance, all of them scrambling to keep atop their own teetering piles of bullshit, clinging desperately to their personas at the expense of any vision they had for their own selves, much less a vision for the humanity they shared. J.R. hated Cash Clarick more than all of them put together. And yet he would come to reflect upon this moment as perhaps his last of blissful innocence.

"They cain't hear us yonder," Clarick said. The chair's stem and casters squeaked as he stood from his desk. He reached into his pocket and began explaining to J.R. that his friends would resent him for the rest of his life if he was exempt from the conditioning they had endured beside him at the Saw Mill. In fact, logically speaking, exemption from punishment was the worst conceivable thing he could hope for. Blondie could cry all she wanted, and yet no one would hold it against her afterward. But not Nimrod. Nimrod's friends would never forgive him, never work with him, never trust him. Not unless he got broken like they did.

J.R. stood unrestrained. All he had to do was act.

"You're welcome, by the way, for not making your friends watch—"

The cloth was at his face—chloroform, ammonia, ether— whatever it was...

*"This here is sterilized..."* Clarick promised.

J.R. passed out.

The U-Haul was sweltering hot.

"Armed to the teeth," he lamented, "and no fucking water."

"Speak for yourself," Steeplejack told him. "I got a canteen right here in this satchel." He unzipped the bag. "Have a swig—"

"No... NO!... No thanks."

Steeplejack brought up the canteen and drank. "Ahhhhhh," he capped it. "Suit yourself, kid. Know what else I got in this knapsack?"

J.R. watched in horror as Steeplejack brought forth a Betacam.

"Are you kidding me?!"

"We gotta figure out a way to outfit these things, so we can film the job while it's going down."

"Sure, the cops won't even need surveillance."

"Ha, that's funny. But you know how much fucking money we could make with a tape of this job? Especially if someone gets blown away? That would be like... porn-times-twenty."

J.R. shook his head, closed his eyes, and tried to breathe, while Steeplejack went on about the money he and Clarick had made with sex tapes, and how the crazier ones made so much more, because that market may be one fifth the size, but it's twice as willing to pay ten times as much. And by the way, it's all a hundred times easier than dealing coke. Videotape was the future.

"Oh, wait a minute, I get it," Steeplejack said, finally recognizing the subject as touchy. "See that's what you don't get. I don't even think about it, J.R. It's you... *you're* the one that's obsessed with it. But you don't have to worry. No one's peddling your tape. Why on earth would we do that? When we got you on our side? Jeez, kid. Get over it."

J.R. awoke, groggy, face down on the cot. Clarick had waited, brandishing the turkey baster. One hand guided the shaft. The other cupped the bulb. "I ain't no Steeplejack," he was saying. "To tell you the truth, I don't want any part of what's about to unspool... But it's better if you're slightly awake, so I waited..."

Afterwards, he said, "It's the same as prison, Nimrod. You just get over it, both parties. I have no equal. Now, go on. Lie to your friends. And never mind that there videotape recorder."

J.R. left the office with no memory of restoring his jeans and belt buckle.

There was no oxygen that night, even as his lungs breathed in the air. Along his nerves, the tendrils received no feedback. His psyche was an encounter not yet comprehendible. The mattress seemed to float beneath him on its layer of stale volume. He lay witness, as if from above, to the geometry of his own imprisonment, arranged with his friends like pieces on the floor of something broken. Katydids and crickets sawed in hypnotic, symphonic normalcy outside the door.

"I can't take it anymore," Vince moaned.

"Me neither," J.R. said.

"Oh yeah?" Scotty growled. "Bad day, Nimrod?"

J.R. said nothing. He would kill Cash Clarick or go out trying. This was decided. He lay awake thinking about it, until he came to understand his advantage. Clarick was the only person left on earth who didn't hate him.

## 40. Solstice

The next night, after another hourly visitation upon Vince Baldwin's battered face, Clarick summoned J.R. up from his mattress and out the door and back across the yard to the office. Following most of the way, J.R. could feel himself succumbing, or awakening, to shell shock or something like it, until he snapped out of it, and paused where he stood, and said, "OK, go ahead and shoot me."

Clarick withdrew his .357 Colt long-barrel. "I ain't gonna shoot you, Nimrod. Look, I'm putting it away," and immediately he re-holstered the weapon. "Tonight's different," he explained, raising his empty palms. "Much different. I promise. It's the exact opposite of last night. I've got to tell you a story is all. Story time, no kidding. I swear. No camera. No nothin'. Don't forget, Nimrod. I ain't no liar. You got to admit that. So please, step on in. And hurry up. We've got to slap FuckFace's face again in T-minus." He turned and proceeded through the office door.

J.R. held his ground another moment. Death wasn't much of an option, but he resolved to keep it in mind. He followed Cash Clarick inside.

A pair of lanterns cast shadows over the wall maps and vertically hanging flags, while the gleaming silver melee weapons hung crisscrossed, wall mounted in shrine-like veneration. The Betacam stood idle on its tripod, facing the room's back corner like a punished child, where the filing cabinet, bookshelves, cooler and the locker occupied their familiar geometry opposite Cash Clarick's narrow and neatly kept cot.

"You can sit there," Clarick pointed, but J.R. wasn't interested in sitting anywhere, especially not the cot.

Clarick ignored his guest's defiance. He pointed to the silken Posse Serpens flag hanging on the wall and began explaining that the logo had been his design concept.

"The Posse Serpens trademarked that logo," he said, "without even obtaining yours truly's permission. Something I cain't even forgive myself for letting happen, much less forgive them for perpetrating. You're smart, Nimrod. Not like them others. I tell you. It's lonely out here at the Saw Mill, without a man of intelligence to parley with."

A knot of murderous violence gripped upward into J.R.'s chest. He didn't want to hear that word *lonely*.

Cash Clarick continued on, explaining how the Posse Serpens had prevented the merchandising of his logo. How the product had made it all the way to the silk-screening phase before Glenn Disteek, in his eternal wisdom or lack thereof, shut it down.

"Buttons, bumper stickers, T-shirts," Clarick lamented. "My design. "I repeat. *My design!*"

J.R. nodded his head, avoiding eye contact. He noticed the flip clock on the desk. It wasn't there the night before. A pale green bulb set its bold rectangular numerals aglow. 3:05.

"The siren call of *politics*," Clarick explained. "Glenn Disteek... Mister Cool... he felt it was too soon. The time for merchandising? It hadn't yet come. And it was always so convincing. Always the time, never the moment in it. Always that spin on it, his patented pontifications. Whatever it is you got on your mind, that boy is bound to convince you that its time ain't come yet.

"Well, you know what I say? I say mark my words. That boy will NEVER go to war. He just rattles his sabre. Fake balls, is what I say."

J.R. waited and found the nerve to speak. "So he's stealing from you by taxing you. I have to be honest with you. I understand that concept."

"Don't pretend you understand everything, OK, Nimrod? Thank you very much. Property tax, income tax, sales tax. Without the guts to call it what it is. See, fuck 'em. I'm putting something together. Something serious. Serious money. Porn. Cocaine. I dare you to name me a better windfall than them two windfalls. So's I can leave this here subsistence farming behind me. Understand? I know you don't like your mattress, Nimrod, but how do you think I like that there cot, in this here broken down old Saw Mill?"

*Porn?* J.R.'s brain had come grinding to a halt five seconds ago upon that word. He had barely heard the rest.

"Speaking of the cot, sit down already. So's I can tell you this here yarn."

He remained standing. *Porn.* They had him on tape. Death was no option. He had to get that tape.

"OK, well, stand there and listen," Clarick carried on, "The State, Nimrod. The Posse Serpens. The Posse Umbellus. All of 'em. All's they do is steal my money. Back then and now too. Pretending the bottom line don't exist right there in them ledgers. To the surprise of no one, least of all yours truly."

J.R. pointed to the idle video camera. "Is that tape still in there?"

"Jesus, Nimrod, trust me. Don't worry about that there Betacam. It's mine, for one thing. And for another thing, the thing you're worried about is the stupidest thing in the world I could possibly do. Just as long as you don't do the stupidest thing in the world you could possibly do. Get me? Tell you what. How about a peace offering? Something I ain't never done before in my life. I'm about to let you try some of my *Cash Clarick Vittles.*"

J.R. shook his head briefly, and then fell utterly still. Even his mind fell still, for him to observe in its blank state.

Meanwhile, Cash Clarick retrieved the cured meat from the blue cooler at the foot of the cot. "Believe me, Nimrod. Jesus H. For once, will ya? This here is *Cash Clarick Vittles.* It's got my name on it. Don't you know what that means? That means I stand by it. I aim to have a legitimate business someday, not that you asked, after porn and cocaine get me off the ground."

J.R. accepted the snack from Cash Clarick and lowered it to his side. It was poisoned. Had to be.

"Or don't believe me, I don't care. You think you know everything, but you don't even know what a shit attitude you have. You'll thank me someday for being the one that told you so. But let's change the subject. You can eat that there peace offering or don't. I don't give a hoot. But please. Have a seat."

Setting the example, Clarick seated himself in the squeaking office chair.

J.R. sat down too, at last, drawing both percussion and string music from the bedsprings.

"You don't trust nobody," Clarick observed. "That makes you about the smartest sonofabitch I ever seen come through this place. Problem is when nobody trusts you neither. But I know how to get to folks. And with a feller like you, it's funner than most. I been out at this here Saw Mill or at some other prior derelict, for forever, seems like. Classes come and gone. So has Glenn Disteek, Duke Drummond, Old Man Edward. Hell, even the amazing Harold Mariner, from time to time, though not no more, it should be said. Not to mention Fat Ransom, and pretty much everyone else. All except for Lazy Farrah, who ain't got the time nor the inclination to get down here and visit her old friend Cash Clarick. But besides her, every last one of 'em come popping up from time to time, to pay their old friend a visit. Maybe even more so nowadays, with Glenn Disteek actually running for state assembly on the Neo-Nazi ticket. And in so doing, trying to join forces with, and merge with, the *American Aryan Republic Institute*... or whatever mouthful of bullshit they call themselves these days. What the fuck? Posse Serpens is a brand! It's our brand, motherfucker! And we get sold out? To some institute of bullshit? All for Glenn Disteek, and his quest for so-called legitimacy? Not interested, in case you ain't guessed. Not that I'm actively endeavoring to sabotage that stupid fucking asshole's career neither. How would that do me no good? With this here needle I'm threadin'?"

"That's a good question," J.R. agreed.

"So this here is the tale of the Scions of Ichor, Nimrod. How we was born. The tale of Glenn Disteek. The tale of Duke Drummond. Maybe a tale or two you don't know about the Old Man. But first things first, you've got to acquaint yourself with the tale of Harold Mariner."

J.R. nodded his head, following along.

"Harold Mariner, Nimrod, that boy was a damn folk hero. Better than most folk heroes, too. He never went by no *Harry Mariner* neither. He didn't like the way that appellation rang, which you cain't blame him for. No, sir, he was Harold

Mariner. *The Irish Herald at Arms Extraordinary…* he would sometimes explain it that way. Like it was a poem or a spell, this being the old days, don't forget. We're talking early seventies, before no Posse Serpens and no Posse Umbellus, nor no rift in their betwixt.

"And by the way, that's right, I said *appellation* not *Appalachian*. I done two-years-plus at the University of Mississippi, Nimrod, back in the day. You can look it up, if you want. Plus all the learnin' I done on my own. So don't start thinking you peeled back this old onion even one skin deep, much less the rest of the skins deep, you fucking know-it-all prick.

"So once upon a time, we was as one. Me. Harold. Edward. Steeplejack. Arriving not quite yet, but early enough to call ourselves founding members. Except that Edward never was no member, not exactly. Just more of a fellow that found us actual members and united us. And Harold Mariner, he wasn't exactly no member, neither. He just lived on the road, traveling the continent on his bike. He couldn't be no member of nothing, just by his own sheer nature.

"But the rest of us, we was members. We're talking about seven years or so back, J.R., to be precise. I mean not the beginning but the end. Incidentally, seven years is a lifetime. You will come to understand this. Everyone will, I have no doubt of it. The beginning was closer to fourteen years back, and the ending was more like exactly seven. And pardon me if I call you J.R. once in a while by accident. I'm trying to tell you a story with a certain level of sincerity. So forgive me, Nimrod, pretty please, if I break character once in a while."

J.R. hadn't noticed. He was deliriously tired, but also frustrated that the story never seemed to get started. He glanced again at the flip clock on the desk.

"So this was before Glenn Disteek never heard no siren call of politics," Clarick continued. "Also before he was walking around with no damn Mohawk hairdo neither."

J.R. chuckled a bit, unable to prevent it.

"Also before Duke Drummond up and betrayed Glenn Disteek out of sheer spite neither," Clarick continued. "It was before a lot of stuff. Back then. You also had de Ram with his wife and kids as-yet unimmolated, and them fireworks many years yet to ignite. Plus him yet to rise from them ashes, so to speak, breathing fire. But I'll get to de Ram.

175

"Plus you had Steeplejack, who had but two abandoned kids back then, not no thirteen. And he wasn't making no living *off* no predilections neither. Not yet. He was just living *for* them predilections. So to speak.

"Likewise Fat Ransom. He was maybe two-fifty back then, not no three-fifty, or four-hundred-fifty pounds, or whatever he is now. I honestly have no idea.

"And Lazy Farrah—and by the way, don't NEVER tell her I uttered them words, Nimrod. Never mind taking it under advisement yourself. Do not NEVER call that woman *Lazy Farrah*."

J.R. looked down at the uneaten *Cash Clarick Vittles* in his fist.

"Get it?" Clarick was saying. "It's a play on words. I thought you were on the ball, Nimrod. Or maybe I was wrong."

"I get it. I'm listening. Tell your story."

"In any case, she's lazy too, so it's a two-part joke. Neither one of which is funny, in her opinion. That's the important thing to remember."

J.R. nodded along.

"But not only that," Clarick continued. "Don't never say it behind her back neither, like I just done. Lest you find yourself crippled for life from its very invocation. I'm telling you, it don't matter how many miles away from her ears the transgression occurs, you are always in the blast radius. I seen wounds that don't heal, Nimrod. OK? Trust me. And that's even before she got the notion she was the Nazi version of Jackie Onassis."

J.R. could only shake his head at this impossible association.

"Anyway, the Scions of Ichor was formulated on Reno Ransom's Farm. Twenty acres out in Tyler County. Horses galloping around, rescued from competition, or so we was told. As if competition ain't the Lord's Own Voice. A few rich lunatics going all-in for their precious horses while a bunch of cows are standing around at exactly the same rate. That's what I'm asking you to picture, J.R."

"I picture it just fine."

"OK, good for you. Anyway, turns out both Duke Drummond and Glenn Disteek was renting rooms from old Reno Ransom. They was both back from the war, just like yours truly, and they hit it off right quick, as you'd expect. I have imagined in my mind, in them moments we carve out for imagination, how that first handshake went.

"Meanwhile, Farrah and Fat Ransom, them two are Reno Ransom's children, him being their common forebear, with their mothers, both of them, whereabouts unknown. See, that's one thing I got, Nimrod, or don't got, to lose. I ain't got no mom and pop. Not no wife and kids neither.

"But look at de Ram. Tell me that son o' man ain't no cautionary tale. He had moved in up the road, him and his wife and kids. The way de Ram tells it in his own words, he spotted, through his rifle scope, the whole Reno Ransom clan having a picnic. And he decided it ain't no picnic without him and his kin showing up uninvited.

"So up they showed. Wife, kids and everybody. And funny thing, turns out they was welcome as could be. Next thing you know, the idea is very much on the tips of everybody's tongues, a feeling of best friends being made.

"Glory days they was, Nimrod. This being the seventies, mind you. Although this entire part of the story is all hearsay out of my lips, all of it having unfolded well before my arrival. On the day de Ram sealed all them little fates, I had yet to even join up. But I'm splitting hairs you ain't even grown yet."

"Would you stop? I can follow your story just fine."

"All right, settle down, Nimrod. You think I don't know what you follow and what you don't? See, you don't actually want no freedom, that's what you don't follow. There ain't no money in freedom. What you want is the fight *for* freedom. That's where the money is at. That's free tip number two, or three, or whatever the fuck. Since you're so smart, and you follow so well."

"This story sucks."

"No it doesn't. It's only your fault it sucks."

J.R. shook his head. "Just get on with it."

"Case in point, back then, it weren't even so much about being white, if we're being honest. Not to say none of us was ashamed of it. But in terms of philosophizing, it was *Living Outside the Government* that mattered.

"And yours... yours truly... came to understand this almost immediately upon arriving at Reno Ransom's Farm.

"Ideas was in the air back then, Nimrod, like blessings on the horizon. See, ideas don't never ruin nothing. And man don't tend to ruin nothing neither. It's only events that lay stuff to ruin. It's events, Nimrod, every time.

"Meanwhile, me and Steeplejack was already partners. In mayhem, not so much in crime, not yet. But me, I was just pissed off at life.

"And for good reason, I might add. Reason I still got, no matter how thin you slice it. But never mind that. I was twenty-two. Six years older than you right now, with a lot yet to learn. You'll understand someday if you don't already."

"Stop setting it up and get on with it."

"And Steeplejack," Cash Clarick continued. "That boy never had no age. Just like he never had no body hair. We didn't have no philosophy back then, nor belong to no outfit, is what I'm telling you. We was just vandalizing shit, and gettin' into bar fights. On my honor, that was my sole purpose in life back then. I was back from 'Nam, but 'Nam weren't no trauma for me, like it was for so many. Me, I was never nothin' more than no redneck outlaw killer all along. And Steeplejack, that boy is just exactly what he always was too, which is a stone cold pervert. Have a crime spree with a man, Nimrod. His true nature, not to mention your own, will be revealed.

"So me and Steeplejack... we was starting to get more ambitious, becoming less a pair of hooligans and more a pair of thieves. And I gotta pat my own self on the back for this, because it was me that woke up to it. All that time spent hellraisin' and dodgin' the Keystone Cops. Just to get the ya yas out for the million trillionth time. Fuck that, anymore. Stop jerking off.

"You probably think I'm just rambling about the old days here, Nimrod. But unbeknownst to you, I am offering up the shiniest chestnut of wisdom you'll ever see getting polished in front of your face in your entire lifetime. You'll come to know this in your soul someday or die without one. So get yourself a head start and believe me now when I tell you. You might as well get paid, son."

"No, I know that."

"No you don't. How many times we been to the bank this week? Listen to your elders, boy. I'm telling you a story. One I earned, while you was playing in your sandbox."

"I'm sorry."

"Sorry, *sheesh*. That's big of you. So like I was saying, me and Steeplejack, before long, we was taking down gas stations and liquor stores. Two men in masks, like you read about. Until... well...

"At last it was Graduation Day, so to speak. We hit a bank. 10 a.m. on a Tuesday morning. Bandanas, cowboy hats, pistols. Just like the Old West. Except this was up in Monroe, New York. And you know what? We got away with it. We fled ourselves back to the great state of P.A., bona fide bank robbers.

"But guess what never occurred to old Cash Clarick. Not back then. Not never once. Come on, go ahead and guess."

"I have no idea."

"Shit, Nimrod. You're supposed to be the smart one. Money laundering, boy! Fucking money laundering! I thought you knew everything! *Sheesh!* So here we was, walkin' around with five grand in cash, and no notion it might be poisoned, or radioactive, or otherwise traceable, all over our personages.

"But then along comes the most amazing stroke of good luck in the whole entire world. Me and Steeplejack, we was mouthing off in the pool hall about this score we just took, while all the while, standing against the wall, in his motorcycle gear, minding nobody's business but our own, you might say, stands this feller we never seen before. And three guesses who this feller is."

"Harold Mariner."

"Bingo. Harold Mariner. So picture him, nice as can be, as he starts to enlighten us two dummies that you got to launder this shit. Else you might as well put an ad in the paper saying *I'm the bank robber.*"

J.R. eyeballed the flip clock on Cash Clarick's desk. 3:17. Vince Baldwin's next visit was a ways off.

Clarick continued, "I admit, Nimrod, I wasn't too crazy about this notion at first, neither. In theory, it ain't about making no profit, you understand? Taking a loss is intrinsic. Name me a feller who seeks out such a course of action. Well, don't bother, neither can I. But that was before I met Edward."

"The Old Man."

"That's the one. So Harold Mariner introduces me and Steeplejack to Edward, the Old Man. And by the way, Edward was just as old back then as he is now, only more so. When they told me he was an antiques expert, I joked to myself that Edward was the antique, and I was the expert. But that just goes to show you. Bein' funny and bein' right ain't always the same thing.

"You gotta understand, Nimrod, these was strange times. Me, I was homeless, so to speak. But I never did sleep all that much. Never did need no amenities neither. The truth is, that's how come I came to live so much more of life than most other folks ever get to. It's because of all the time I don't spend sleeping.

"So there I was, living out of the Land Rover. Not this Land Rover, the previous one. And I was very happy about it, too. Sure, I wound up in a hotel room a couple of times, sleeping something off. But other than that, I never saw no point in layin' out no dollars for no quarters, if you catch my meaning."

J.R. acknowledged the play on words with a vague, impatient smile.

Clarick continued, "Meanwhile, Steeplejack? That boy was just as homeless as me. But never shy of no bed, that one. And Harold Mariner? He was just wandering the earth on his motorcycle. He never had no home to return to neither.

"So out of the four of us, it was Edward, the Old Man, who had an actual place to meet up in.

"So up we ended, convening in this old shed, in the middle of nowhere. Botley Down, it was called. Lantern-lit, austere. Neat, with a blanket, and a couple of books. And a pistol at the ready, for anyone to pick up, if taken by the urge. We held palaver long into the night. You could feel it in the air, the verge of something forming. We even made a joke, a play on words, a pun. Not forward. Not backward. Edward.

"So the next day we drove all the way to Bethlehem, and we spent maybe five minutes in this antique shop before I'm offering up the entire wad of stolen cash for a floor lamp. I repeat, five grand, in seventies money, for a floor lamp. That wasn't no easy wad to part with, Nimrod.

"And yet, at the same time, handing off them tainted bills was a massive relief, too.

"What I wasn't beknownst to, though, but soon would come to see, is that an hour later, over in King of Prussia, the Old Man would be selling that very same floor lamp for fifty-five hundred bucks. I tell you, this was the mother fucking age of enlightenment, Nimrod.

"It was Edward who planned the next two jobs. It was two jobs, before we settled out in Tyler County, on the Reno Ransom Farm.

"One of them jobs I will never forget. First, you got to picture Harold Mariner, in his biker gear, black leather, with red piping, and orange hair, like de Ram's hair in color, but thicker. A fucking Leprechaun. I don't mean that in no bad way neither. I respect that boy more than most other people combined. Him, he's Irish. Me, I'm straight off the Mayflower into the hills. You, you're Italian. No one gives a fuck. It's just funny is all, when you see a man's heritage so plainly reinforced, like a crown on his head. But the bike is what you shoulda seen, Nimrod. This 1950's Indian. You shoulda fucking believed it when you saw it, which you never will, because those fuckers destroyed it, along with Harold Mariner, and his ability to walk, talk, eat, shit and fuck. You won't never know Harold Mariner, though you might lay eyes on him yet. But that bike is something you won't never behold."

"What color?"

"Maroon, if I had to testify. Otherwise, fuckin' cherry. This was back when stuff was cool, Nimrod. Not that it cain't be cool still, but it was so easy back then. The Old Man drew up the heist. The train came through town like clockwork. The boxcars got surveilled ahead of time. With the getaway its own operation, we had us thirty extra seconds in the bank. This is what it means to squeeze a extra dollar out of every second, Nimrod. We had it all in one bag, and we stuffed the pistols in there too. And we completely trusted Harold Mariner, by the way. There wasn't no question about whether he was on board. Even so, we couldn't help but ask ourselves if he was up to this Evel Knievel shit.

"Well, you better believe he was up to it. All the rest of us did was believe up front, and then find out afterwards we was right.

"So out we was, in the parking lot. Harold Mariner was right on time too, speeding towards us. I hold up the bag. Out of the air he plucks it, racing by. Off he roars, down a side alley that will take him four blocks over and into the woods that stretch along the railroad tracks towards the Suburban Propane yard.

"Me and Steeplejack drove fast as we could out of there. Our job was done.

181

"Except fuck all that, we decided. We had to check out this stunt Harold Mariner was aiming to execute.

"So yes, Nimrod, my friend, it was stupid to stick around at the crime scene. But not as stupid as it would have been to miss that grand finale.

"So up I drive us to this rise overlooking the train station, and it's from there we watched Harold Mariner on his old Indian bike. And this bike is so old it looks like Buck Rogers or something. And by the way, this satchel over his shoulder is loaded with cash, plus the weight of the hot pistols. The point is this. No one on this earth knows how he reckoned all them angles and all that physics for that platform jump into that fleeing boxcar's open ingress on that antique motorbike under those criminal circumstances.

"So he launched through the air off the ramp we laid the night before, clearing the chain link fence easily in one miraculous descending pinpoint angle. I didn't so much see it, Nimrod, as hear it. The rear wheel against the empty floorboards peeling to a stop. And then experiencing a state of something like triumphant bliss as we watched the train bear the whole glorious caper away. We had us a team.

"It was Edward who knew Reno Ransom. So now it was us joining up with them, you understand? The Old Man making the introductions, explaining that this was the group we needed, and how together we would create a movement.

"By the way, a feller named Frank Brool showed up around this era too, courtin' Farrah Ransom. Frank Brool was on board, you have to understand, as far as creating a community was concerned. So, just keep that poor slob's name in mind, is all I'm reminding you to do, as you follow this here fable.

"So the bunch of us, we would pull off scores. But not often, and never with nothing desperate about it. Everything was always planned out. Stress free.

"It was eight of us. Heck, nine, if you included Harold Mariner. And Frank Brool too, once in a while, to make us ten.

"Elaborate planning, months in the making, Edward laying it all out, deploying us for recon, reconnaissance, choosing different operatives based on a particular talent and resource. Even old Reno Ransom getting in on the act at one point, in his straw hat and flip-flops. Undercover, so to speak, just loving the chance to stick it to the system. Remind me to tell you about them scores sometime, Nimrod. Especially the one with Reno Ransom in his flip-flops. It's a tale unto itself."

"OK, I'll remind you."

"What you have to understand. And this was Edward's genius, by the way. Edward was so selective, and so careful, and so precise in planning a job. And the windfall afterward was so serious as to border on the luxurious. That what ended up happening is we all had time on our hands. To delve into matters philosophical. Maybe even to pursue our dreams.

"There ain't no need to make a move right now, is how Edward would explain it to us. Let's everybody just cool our engines. We got everything we need right here, don't we? Ain't no need to screw up a good thing. Why not live a little? Enjoy what it is we've been fighting for. Come to understand its value...

"Do you hear what he was saying, Nimrod? How it differs from what I'm always saying? Well, maybe you hear it, and maybe you don't. But this here is what I've been trying to explain to you, that maybe you ain't been listenin' to.

"That Old Man? He may be the grandmaster of drawing up heists. And he may be the supreme being of eyeballing antiques. And he may be the final authority on a million trillion other things, too. But his idea to kick up the old boot heels? Bullshit, I say. Scions of nothin', I say. You've got to stay above the parasites. That's the one thing I say. You've got to squeeze a extra dollar out of every minute of every day, all the time. That's all that life actually is, Nimrod. It's your own self-worth ticking up or down, tick-tock, tick-tock, up-down, up-down, every second of every fraction of every moment of every single day. Not to say them days on the ranch wasn't downright Halcyonic, though. I tell ya. Bucolic as fuck, too. Paradise lost. That's what it honestly was. Something I won't never forget.

"You know what it was like? Picture one thing, upright and natural and true, moving unstoppably in one direction.

"Now picture another thing, and it's also upright and natural and true, and it's moving unstoppably in the oncoming direction.

"Now picture both of them things moving toward the same place at the same time, one from the left, one from the right. You can see that they are not just fated to collide but fated to part ways afterwards. You can see it before it even happens. And see the aftermath beforehand too. But being there when it actually occurs. That's the only thing worth waiting around to see.

"There is a place in time, and it's not no era—it's just a year, or maybe two, or maybe even three if you're lucky—but it's a place in time when them two forces are collided with each other.

"And maybe even for one shining split-second they are both in perfect harmony, not so much collided but in union, as one.

"That's what we was, Nimrod. The Scions of Ichor. Everyone on that same page we had arrived at, even though what brought us there was already tearing us back asunder. Like a solstice that comes around only once.

"So picture the Ransom Farm, the ranch house, the barn, the silo, the stables, the windmill, the gazebo. Don't forget the gazebo, sitting there like a public park or something.

"Picture them fences and fields stretching everywhere too, up and over the hills and down around not one but two ponds. Plus the crick, rambling through. An idyllic paradise, mostly. Notwithstanding the horses and cows that eyeball you with their spooky animal alarm every time you get near one of 'em.

"But imagine wanting for nothing. Not food, not shelter. Not companionship, not security neither. Every day, all in abundance. It was in this setting that Edward revealed it to us. This was the feeling of *No Racial Tension.*"

J.R. stole a glance at the clock. 3:29.

"Yes, I can see the time, Nimrod. We got a half-hour yet, before we slap FuckFace in the face. The more you pay attention, the more we can squeeze the rest of this here tale into this next half-hour. If you wouldn't mind."

"I'm paying attention."

"Yeah, and so am I. So getting back to what I was saying, there was no racial tension. It didn't even have to exist. Because everyone was with their own kind, and free at last of the whole conversation. *Free at last,* is one of the things Edward tended to say. He was saying it in fun. Mimicking MLK. This was the early seventies, mind you."

"I get it," J.R. answered.

"All right, all right, you get it, Nimrod. You think you're so worldly. That's maybe the funniest thing of all. The fact is, there ain't no arguing with Old Man Edward's logic. Never mind your Zionist fairly-tale, where you merrily mix races while the money trickles in. Me, I make twice as much money every time I tell Kareem Abdul-Jabbar to drive down the street for his fucking oil change. Get me?

"But at the same time, I was more mild mannered back then. I mean, just a little bit more so, is all. I bought into the Old Man's vision, like everybody else. Because, you know, he's the Old Man, and he knows his shit, mostly. Let's just say, the wisdom I carry to this day was forged, in part, in the kiln of that day. Which ain't nothin' for you to question really, since I was founding a white man's paradise while you was skinning your knees on the playground at Erving Elementary."

"I get it. You're not mild mannered anymore, like you used to be."

"So de Ram, on the other hand, is another story. He used to be downright jolly, Nimrod, if you could only imagine that, with that big brain of yours. You see, he had himself a brood back then...

"You had de Ram and his family, plus you had Steeplejack, with twenty acres to exploit, instead of his usual zero, with stables and lofts and woodsheds at his disposal too. Plus you had Farrah Ransom and Fat Ransom. And by the way, what you have to understand about the Ransom clan is that Farrah Ransom and Fat Ransom, they liked each other just fine. There wasn't never no family discord, this one jealous of that one, nothing like that. Not back then anyway.

"But funny thing is, along come Duke Drummond and Glenn Disteek, and for them two, old Reno Ransom was a father figure. And they both wanted to be his favorite. They wanted it bad, Nimrod. This stuff is kids' stuff, to me. I hate to say it. It's embarrassing, sometimes, to look at, or observe, or whatever. But back then, of course, it didn't turn into no kids' stuff.

"You see, back then, Reno Ransom was sovereign over twenty acres. Picture him out on his front porch, or better yet out on his gazebo. Savor that picture. Reno Ransom with his shotgun at his side, basking in the freedom of it all, with his bushy eyebrows and his big, gap toothed smile. I liked Reno just fine, by the way. I admired his will to stay out of old Uncle Sam's greedy, groping paws.

"But them two? Glenn and Duke? They was beyond liking him. They just worshipped him. That's because Reno knew the system, knew how to play it. And where he couldn't play it, he just up and defied it. The nonchalance was a whole part of it. You had to meet him to see it. And you cain't never meet him, so you're fucked.

"So picture this whole sense of community developing out at Reno Ransom's Farm, with everybody pitching in to create something sustainable, and secure, for when the entire system collapses, and the so-called Mighty Dollar becomes toilet paper, and all of mankind gets brought to its knees. Your basic apocalypse scenario.

"Glenn and Duke was like brothers about all that stuff, by the way, with everything they got in common, and everything they was working towards. But you will come to know, Nimrod, like I told you before. It's events that lay men to ruin, not ideas. Everything else comes in a distant third.

"Duke Drummond and Farrah is married nowadays, by the way, in case that weren't clear. And Fat Ransom, him and Farrah is still allied, somewhat, by blood, although split across their two different posses, as you have gathered."

"This posse and that posse."

"And us in the middle, ain't we?" Clarick smirked. "You get the picture. Duke Drummond, Nimrod. You ain't met him yet, but you'll cross his path in your lifetime, you can count on that. The more your lifetime keeps lasting, that is.

"Duke Drummond is a killer, same as Glenn Disteek. Just not as broad-shouldered and tall. More like yours truly, a mere mortal. Centered and steadied around the solar plexus. Closer to the ground, you might say.

"By the way, you ain't got that, Nimrod, sorry to tell you. Sure, you'll end up tall, with that vantage point in your favor. But it won't matter, lessen you got a center. People like you and me is stuck in-between, whether you got that or not. It was spiritually true long before it was empirically true."

"Elaborate on that."

"Well, for instance, Glenn Disteek may be a fool for vain-glory, but he's still a business partner, ain't he? Meanwhile, Duke Drummond and the Posse Umbellus, that gang is fundamentalists, hell bent on war. So here I am, stuck in the middle. How is old Cash Clarick supposed to side with one or the other faction? That Nazi flag behind me ain't no guarantee Duke Drummond won't come kicking in my door someday. Meanwhile, I don't want no Glenn Disteek sending no Fat Ransom around here with no tax bill neither."

"What would Harold Mariner say, if he could say something?"

"Harold Mariner? See that's where—and I mean no offense when I say this—but Harold, he don't get me. Harold is like the Old Man. He's got everything he needs, wherever he is. No concern for no money. Never lacking for nothing. No expenses, never, somehow. Just roaming the earth with a message. I mean... that's what Harold Mariner used to be.

"See, that's what's so enraging about seeing him lying in that coma, Nimrod. Because believe me, I get it. I ain't growin' no roots around here, no more than necessary. I got my own way to go, always have. But at the same time, I ain't got no secret stash of money neither, or whatever Harold Mariner was tappin' into. I got to keep some kind of racket going. I got to get paid for my time."

"I get that."

"I know you do. I knew you would."

"So what caused the falling out?"

"So what would happen, now and then, is that Harold Mariner would say his good-byes, and take off on his Indian. And then a week or so later, Old Man Edward would travel onwards too.

"It was always the same pattern, and always a power vacuum leftover, to refill itself, with Reno Ransom the patriarch, and Reno's kids, plus Duke and Glenn, plus de Ram, plus Steeplejack. Not to mention yours truly, not so much giving a fuck. I weren't no central player in the downfall. More of an unwitting puzzle piece.

"You see, what happened, Duke Drummond, being from New Jersey, decides that in honor of the Garden State he is going to plant a garden for the self-sustaining tribe. And then out of the earth he carved and planted and seeded and fenced in and patrolled, as promised, a garden, with lettuce, beets, beans, cabbage, and whatever else growing.

"The Scions of Ichor was a big family, and everyone at the picnic table was appreciative of the homegrown vegetable servings. Old Reno was proud of Duke Drummond, grateful for his labor and contribution and so on. So far, so good.

"But then one morning, Glenn Disteek stands up and announces that he's from the Bacon State, not no Garden State. And by the way, there ain't no such thing as no Bacon State, Nimrod."

187

"I know that."

"Hey! Don't get uppity, boy!"

"I'm not uppity. I know my shit, is all."

"You don't know shit."

"As if. Just tell your story."

Clarick tapped his finger ruminatively at his own nose. The flip clock's green numerals read 3:38. FuckFace would require another face spanking in 22 minutes.

"Disteek's idea was to raise pigs, chickens and cows for slaughter. Soon enough, he was herding the livestock around on his dirt bike, with the animal's bloody last rite the climax of the show. This is the same guy, by the way, who walks around in a Mohawk pompadour nowadays, and a blazer and tie, under a leather trench coat. Back then he was a dirt bike cowboy."

J.R. laughed.

"Meanwhile, before you finish laughing, picture Duke Drummond, in contrast, keeping watch over his rows and rows of inanimate vegetables. Suffice to say, it was as sad as it was funny to behold.

"Finally, one morning, in addition to them vegetables at the ritualistically crowded Reno Ransom picnic table, a bounty of fresh meats gets offered up for the hungry crew, including strips of bacon.

"So without really meaning to hurt poor old Duke Drummond's feelings, Reno Ransom did just that, at the head of the table, raving on about the bacon strips, with the veggies shoved off to the side, bitter, green and cold.

"Now I admit that I, myself, might have contributed personally to Duke Drummond's resentment, although it weren't on purpose, I promise you that. Any more than Reno Ransom did nothing on purpose his own self. Honest to Pete, Nimrod, I was just tryin' to help out. Why would I lie? Ask yourself that, and you'll find no answer. It was just an offer, a gesture. The garden and the toil was just appreciated, is all. But it got took the wrong way.

"See back then I was becoming very interested in making sure everything paid for itself. And I ain't never let go of that interest, neither. But back then, on the lookout for ideas of self-sufficiency, what I did—and again, it was only meant in good faith—but I went around with a bucket, and I collected up all the manure and pellets and scat from Glenn Disteek's livestock.

"And then, gentle as can be, I lugged that bucket over to Duke Drummond's garden and presented it, heavy by now, so that I was clenching it in both fists, as I started to explain how I had brought it over from Glenn Disteek's livestock, and how we could use it to fertilize the veggies.

"Well, next thing you know, that bucket is flying through the air, wrenched out of my hands, spilling three kinds of shit everywhere, while Duke Drummond is coming after yours truly, no kidding, and no exaggeration neither, with a pitchfork in hand.

"Picture me and Duke Drummond, Nimrod, though you met me yet but not him. Suffice to say we're about evenly matched.

"That is, except when I ain't holding no damn *trident!*

"So I went for his balls. Had to. I didn't get impaled that day, Nimrod. Picture that, is all's I'm asking you to picture.

"So me and Duke, we made amends afterward. It weren't no hill to die on, for neither of us. But didn't old Duke Drummond just let that old veggie garden go to hell after that?

"There was that and other augurs. You could see everything coming apart before it ever did. And maybe not exactly the way it would. But the end was within sight and closing distance.

"Especially that last job. Once again, it was planned out, to the second, by Edward, who was back from his travels.

"Harold Mariner would not be present for this one, set out once again on his eternal sojourn.

"And Frank Brool didn't want to lay witness to this one in particular, so that boy begged off.

"And so it was the seven of us. The Scions of Ichor. Deployed and set to our clockwork task.

"This was the Hoover Bank, over in Hoover. First Farrah faints on the floor on a hot day, and she is dressed to make an impression, so that everyone comes running, the bank manager, security, basically anyone who ain't a gal, plus maybe a couple of gals too.

"Meanwhile, de Ram and Steeplejack is already implanted within that bank lobby. And Farrah's brother, Fat Ransom, he's outside, fixing to block traffic in a strategic manner from his Cutlass Supreme.

"Me, I'm armed to the teeth, with Glenn Disteek and Duke Drummond, the three of us waiting to make our move.

"Suddenly, Duke Drummond says he's doing it this time.

"No you're not, Glenn Disteek tells him.

"I'm doing it. You can't stop me.

"Just watch me stop you.

"I swear, Nimrod, I had no idea, at that moment, what these two was bickering about. But there we was. 29 seconds from go time. And suddenly, somehow, in and amongst ourselves, we had us some kind of dealbreaker.

"28... 27... 26...

"Well, it turns out Duke Drummond wanted to leave a Nazi flag at the crime scene, to send a message. Mind you, I'm processing all this as the seconds are counting down. And Glenn Disteek is telling Duke Drummond the timing is all wrong.

"There ain't nothin' more powerful, he says, than an idea whose time has come. And this idea? Its time ain't come.

"Pride goeth before the shitstorm! quoth Duke Drummond.

"Haughty words, guttersnipe! came Glenn Disteek's retort.

"I was there, Nimrod. To this day, I cain't hardly believe what I heard. But it was those words exactly. I cain't believe what I seen take place neither. All of them seconds came and went, and no bank robbery unfolded, although many would call it a crime.

"The Old Man's plans came to naught. Farrah lay on the lobby floor, her reward a crowd of bewildered gawkers. Steeplejack and de Ram came ready for action and left deprived. Frank Brool back at the farm? He was none too happy neither, expecting a return on what he gave.

The Old Man looked us all over, long and hard, before going his own way. Times is getting worse, he explained, in a brief pep talk. It's self-evident, he added, before leaving.

"And yet, we was like a family, Nimrod. It weren't so easy as it sounds, now that you might suggest it, after the fact. Not so easy to split up.

"As it happened, fate would step in and do it for us. And don't worry, Nimrod, I see the clock. 3:45. We got ourselves fifteen minutes yet.

"So, for starters, de Ram stole some fireworks from a couple of teenagers. So factor that in, please. Poor old de Ram blames himself for what happened. You have to understand this to understand de Ram.

"But me? God forgive me, I egged him on. I got to fess up to my own part if I expect you to believe the rest. See de Ram is worried about telling Glenn and Duke about the fireworks in his possession, since by now they'll start a Goddamn Civil War over anything and everything.

"And he was right, by the way, for whatever that's worth.

"Glenn and Duke, them two, they will tell you till their bitter end that none of it was their fault. But they're just as full of shit as me and everybody else, with their power struggle infecting everything that took place. They know they caused it.

"So me, I told de Ram to keep it secret. That's all I did. Don't even tell your wife, I advised. And I ain't proud of it, Nimrod. To this day, that's the one thing I'm least proud of.

"But at the same time, I was just speaking the truth about the times we was living in. We didn't need no Glenn and Duke soap opera infecting every Goddamn decision we made. I convinced him of this. I swear to God, that's all I did.

"And so de Ram hid them bottle rockets and such in the shed. And now let me just repeat them words, for the record, in case you didn't hear me. It was *de Ram* who hid them bottle rockets in the shed.

"But now he's got to leave for some citation he got in town for hollering at some garbage picker in the park for being the Living Quintessence of Government Bloat, those being his exact words.

"Disturbance of the Peace, this was deemed, in the words of the Almighty State.

"Not that this was the worst experience old de Ram came to suffer that day, but he was due in town, that's how the story goes.

"Meanwhile, along comes Farrah, and de Ram knows his wife and kids is comin' down the hill for iced tea with Farrah later. And since Farrah and his wife is best of friends now, he asks Farrah to tell them not to go near the shed, hoping to avoid the exact catastrophe that ended up happening. *Sure,* Farrah tells him.

"See that's the thing. There are so many different ways it could have not happened. You can understand de Ram, Nimrod, if you can understand that. She forgot to tell them not to go near the shed, in case you ain't guessed.

"Meanwhile, Frank Brool was pivotal. He's been trying to quit smoking, 'cause he can sense that Farrah don't like it.

"Part of the grotesquery, or irony, or whatever you call it, is that Farrah smokes like a chimney nowadays. But back then, she was against it. And her husband, he did his best, most days, to read her, and obey.

"And yet, Fat Ransom is on Frank Brool's shoulder. Always talking about keepin' on keepin' on.

"Not that Fat Ransom smoked cigarettes neither. But that's only because he never got started. Try telling that boy to quit drinkin' beer, or eatin' sandwiches, or whatever... That boy don't want to hear nobody talk about quitting nothing.

"So Fat Ransom is asking Frank Brool what the point is. And he's asking Frank Brool what he's saving up for. Tomorrow ain't promised to none of us, he explains, to the nicotine starved and chemically twitching Frank Brool.

"It was all in good fun, no doubt, but with a layer of conviction just beneath the surface, which sent the poor old circumstances one way instead of the other. Frank Brool, goaded on, went behind the shed for a smoke.

"And for the final piece of the puzzle, you have Steeplejack, my old friend, in absolute uncontrollable lust for Farrah, and with literally nothing to offer Frank Brool except for sabotage of the poor bastard's marriage.

"Well aware that Frank Brool was behind the shed smoking a cigarette, and happening upon de Ram's wife and kids on their way down the road for iced tea with Farrah, and with every reason to believe the encounter coincidental and not pre-ordained, our man Steeplejack relayed something about Frank Brool that Farrah would surely want to know, those two women being friends and all, the message sure enough to get through.

"Except de Ram's wife and kids? They didn't go and tell Farrah. Oh, no. They owed Mr. Brool the benefit of the doubt. And so off they marched toward the shed in question, to see for themselves.

"Well, it all ends in a technicolor chain of whistles and kabooms, as you no doubt have gathered already.

"But out of that explosion, a fair number of epilogues come tumbling.

"First and foremost, you've got de Ram, whose world is forevermore destroyed. I'm not exaggerating when I say de Ram was on the verge of killing every last member of the Scions of Ichor in one sweeping rampage of blind vengeance.

"Instead, he went out and committed a series of random atrocities upon the general populace. Or so I have sleuthed out, in my spare time.

"Meanwhile, he finally did something just plain dumb and threw a teenager over a bridge into a crick in broad daylight. When asked why he did it, he stated, with psychopathic nonchalance, that the kid had been walking toward him on the bridge.

"Long story short, de Ram got himself a light sentence, on account of his circumstances, his loss and grief factoring in, which some protested as lenient sentencing, but at least the victim wasn't strung up in no hospital bed, not like some other people. Not like Harold Mariner. This kid was on his feet after a month or two. He got thrown off a bridge into a crick is all.

"As for de Ram, he spent six months in prison, with three years' probation, those years come and gone now, in case you're counting.

"Meanwhile, you still got Reno Ransom. The explosions and fatalities and stolen fireworks drew the cops and the FBI. Next thing you know the Feds are very interested in Reno's previous years of tax returns. Long story short, Reno Ransom and Uncle Sam was on a collision course. Drummond, Disteek and Steeplejack was armed to the teeth, and ready for the cause. But honestly, the rest of us was just kind of hoping it didn't come to no violent standoff.

"Well, it didn't. Old Reno Ransom dropped dead of a heart attack, right there on his gazebo, before the fighting ever got started.

"Can you imagine dropping dead of a heart attack? What it takes to bring such a thing on? It was the government, Nimrod. Our own government. They murdered old Reno Ransom, with the stress they put on him.

"In the end, the Feds seized the farm. As for Reno's kids, Farrah never had no interest in no farm no how. And Fat Ransom, I guess that boy opted for a low profile, instead of a lost cause.

"Meanwhile Frank Brool ends up losing his legs, but surviving. You can consider him excused from the remainder of this here yarn, though. What time is it?" Clarick leaned forward to peer at the desk clock.

"3:54."

"I can see that. Hour's nearly over, but we got a few minutes yet. So Farrah, in that moment, she leaned on Glenn Disteek. By the way, Duke Drummond is married to Farrah now, so you got yourself a head start on the conclusion of this here love triangle. But even though Drummond got what he wanted in the end, picture the guy who gets what he wants, and he's still bananas with jealousy. No kidding, Nimrod, a lunatic. Here we are, everything coming apart, and Duke Drummond and Glenn Disteek is ending their friendship over a woman, a.k.a. Farrah Brool, a.k.a. Farrah Ransom, a.k.a. Lazy Farrah, a.k.a. NOT Cleopatra.

"Not to mention, at the time, she was married to a whole other guy. Or, you know what I mean. Not a *whole* other guy. Don't make me say it, Nimrod. It ain't funny what happened to Frank Brool. Watch out for women, is my point."

"You don't have to tell me that."

"Well, I did. So get over it. So the final battle—the only battle, I should say—took place where we all ended up convening. It would have been better if it got to play out where it all began, on Reno Ransom's homestead, in the foreground of that gazebo. Instead, we had to scramble to, and arrive at, and briefly occupy, for one night, some state campground out towards Chadds Ford.

"We was all gathered under the moonlight, with these picnic tables all around us. And somethin' about them tables, how brand new they was. Also, somethin' about the neat, flat gravel plots them benches was embedded into. It was all so phony, is what I'm tryin' to express. It wasn't nothin' like the grand old dignity and the fearless timelessness of old Reno Ransom's place.

"So I'm disclosing that detail, Nimrod, so you'll know I was there. But I ain't telling you no more. Not the tale of Glenn Disteek and Duke Drummond in combat on that field of moonlit grass. Nor the tale of any of us that stood around watching, neither. That was the last time we was all together. The Scions of Ichor. It ain't nobody's business but our own."

"All right, good story."

"It ain't over, hold your horses."

J.R. glanced at the clock.

"Yeah, yeah, it's late. So, a couple of days later, with timing well-suited to himself, and perceived by all of us as something like a comet that orbits the Scions of Ichor in regularly startling intervals, Harold Mariner, on his 1950s Indian, comes sweeping in to seduce the quote-unquote grieving Farrah Brool, and then vanish with her on the back of his bike, when no one was looking.

"Now, mind you, Cash Clarick ain't no judge and jury. You think old Cash Clarick don't understand what old Harold did? Believe me, I do. Truth is, I aim to be fleet myself, someday, like Harold Mariner was on that day. Making to chase the great continental highways over the endless horizon, until you don't belong to nothing, nor answer to no one.

"But for now, I carry this here leviathan on my back, this Saw Mill, until every last chunk gets recouped. I ain't in no Posse Serpens, nor no Posse Umbellus neither. Remember that, for yourself, as you play your cards. Yours truly is more like the ilk of one Harold Mariner. Maybe more so than Harold Mariner himself, anymore."

Clarick hung his head for a silent moment.

"It's a disgrace," he continued. "Harold Mariner never deserved to be guinea pigged around by no Medical Community, soaking up blood money out of no taxpayers. It ain't nothing he'd ever abide, not never. If only he could wake up or die. If only it was anything but what it is. Duke Drummond left that boy a mockery of his own living self."

"For poaching?"

"That's a bullshit story. We all know why he did it. He did it over Farrah. For the time Harold seduced her. And took off on his bike. You think Duke Drummond ever forgave that? You don't know Duke Drummond if you think that."

"I don't know Duke Drummond."

"Well, like I said, he's in your future, to the extent you got one. You ain't even asked me about me, though. How did old Cash Clarick fare through all them shake ups? That thought never even crossed your mind, did it?"

"I'm listening."

"Don't bullshit me, boy. You're askin' all kinds of questions, except for questions about yours truly."

"Besides, I can see how you fared."

"Oh, you think so? You ain't even fathomed how you fared yourself, much less how I done. You don't know nothing. See, I got the misfortune of being a so-called artist. I got a quote-unquote gift. Don't ask me why, but suffice to say it ain't no way to scrounge up two nickels. It's more like losing them two nickels, every time."

The hour was over. It was Vince Baldwin's turn now.

"I finished the logo. Simple and cheap, incorporating that old *Don't Tread on Me* rattlesnake, that immortal defiance, but prefabricated, public domain, royalty-free. The design was yet to be silk-screened onto buttons, T-shirts, bumper stickers, in three colors. Which you probably didn't even know they can do nowadays, even though you see it all the time. In any case, there it is, on the flag, where it cain't earn no money. But the buttons, and T-shirts, and bumper stickers? Well... I told you already...

"I already knew Glenn Disteek got his nutsack gelded off by politics. But I didn't yet know to what extent it would fuck me over. Not until he cancelled that T-shirt order.

"Next thing you know, the Posse Serpens considered my design a quote-unquote group concept, not mine alone. So on top of everything else, they got the nerve to cut into six-sevenths of my Goddamn zero-dollar pie. You understand what I'm saying? This was *my move*. But it was more than that. I didn't just compromise. I compromised on the compromise. I did it for *them*. And in return they didn't just kill me. They aborted me. And gutted what was left. Back-stabbers, fuckers all—"

Clarick rose from his office chair. "Shit, Nimrod, look at the time. We got to slap FuckFace in the face. Ten-hut. I'll tell you the rest after."

## 41. Out of Them Ashes

They were up and out through the squeaking screen door
into the yard. Clarick proceeded under the moonlight. J.R.
followed, his instincts sharp, his eyes open, his ears attuned
to the night air. Insects thrummed, close, distant, sourceless,
omniscient.

"So after them fireworks," Clarick carried on, "Glenn
Disteek started to take himself a serious interest in politics,
getting more and more that way inclined. You see, with the
farm lost, and Reno Ransom in the ground, and de Ram's
brood gone from this earth, and de Ram himself an
inconsolable monster... and with Farrah up and betraying all
three men who loved her... and so on and so forth... it was out
of them ashes that a man could fly straight, so long as he knew
which way that was.

"That was Glenn Disteek, in that particular nutshell of
time. He would tell you he had found faith in the power of
ideas. But Duke Drummond, he would tell you that boy lost
faith in the power of men. *Shhh, no more talking now...*"

They slowed their approach. Clarick whispered, *"Be right
back."*

J.R. waited in a state of surreal impatience for the sound
of Vince Baldwin's clockwork face-slap.

Seconds later, Cash Clarick returned, whispering, *"This
way."*

Proceeding into the night, J.R. could sense it, maybe not so much the moment as the realization afterward that his eyesight had adjusted, watching the range targets emerge in procession out of the darkness. Halfway across the yard to the outhouse, Clarick switched on his flashlight, casting its probing beam over that pearlescent cocoon beneath the ghostly reach of the Saw Mill's lonesome orphaned tree.

"So nowadays, Glenn Disteek is a politician..." Clarick laughed a bit. "With Fat Ransom his highest-ranking official, that insatiable bloodsucker, doubling and tripling down into the coffers of yours truly. And with his own sister at the same time, fully embedded, as it were, into the opposing Posse. You see what I'm saying, Nimrod? How are you gonna believe any of these snakes? Even old Steeplejack. I've known him forever. But that just makes my point for me."

The outhouse glowed nearer within the flashlight's tremulous volley. J.R. felt a dread creeping under his skin, turning the nerve endings cold up the length of his arms. This abandoned linden tree, in this corner of the Saw Mill's reservoir of decay, with its creepy, unearthly fiberglass utility and its creepier plywood aft-appendix, was the last place on earth he wanted to be. The pearl white shell seemed a light source all its own as they arrived before its ghostly hue.

"And you also got Duke Drummond, who won't rest until old Glenn Disteek goes down in flames. I tell you, that boy never met a grudge he didn't hold. He became the political opposition to his former best pal.

"Mind you, the Posse Umbellus wasn't formed yet. This was a Duke Drummond solo act. More of a talker than Glenn Disteek. More of a performer than his rival. With better comedic timing. Saying how the White Race, in its perpetual war for survival, would persevere, until that day when nothing remained unbent to its conquering will. And how the nimble minded understand this, and how the government must be defied, not joined up with. And how this is non-negotiable, and always will be, despite the best and fanciful efforts of the hippies and dreamers and preachers and liberals and communists and rock bands and movie stars, and whatever other idiots you want to throw in, but don't forget to throw in Glenn Disteek and his Posse Serpens...

"Meanwhile, here I am, Nimrod, in my corner, with my hand raised, because I'm the one stupid idiot who knows the actual answer. Except no one is calling on old Cash Clarick. Because no one wants old Cash Clarick to know. Because no one wants to PAY old Cash Clarick to know. Because it's the *logo,* Nimrod. It's the Posse Serpens logo. That's the God-damn ticket. Glenn Disteek ain't goin' nowhere with no so-called *American Aryan Republic Institute.* Ergo, Duke Drummond's whole crusade is to stop a thing that cain't never happen. It's the logo, Nimrod. And they took it away from me."

"I get it. I'm sorry. It's just. It's always ten degrees colder here under this tree than anywhere else, isn't it?"

"What? No. Maybe in the daytime, under the shade. But how could it be colder by night? Shade don't make no thermal difference at night. The moon. She's all light, Nimrod, no heat."

"Sorry."

"Dammit, you stepped all over my punchline."

"Sorry."

"Sorry, well, that changes everything. May I finish? The press, they showed zero-to-no sympathy for Glenn Disteek after his campaign office got firebombed. That was Drummond for sure. But it wasn't just that. You see, out on the lawn, upon a flattened campaign sign, a token was left behind to cool down in the open air from its steaming and recently internal temperature...

"To take the time to defile the scene. As an animal would. It had to be Duke Drummond. Right, Nimrod? It had to be.

"And yet, Glenn Disteek, he rebuilt himself. As you have seen with your own two eyes. The clothes, the haircut. The Mohawk pompadour. But not just that. He got revenge, too.

"It seems old Glenn had foreseen Duke Drummond's betrayal far enough ahead of time to rummage through old Duke's footlocker and make away with a crinkled old black-and-white photograph. The Doc Drummond Bayou Band.

"You see Duke Drummond, maybe he was from New Jersey like he said he was. But maybe his kin was from Louisiana. And maybe... Well... Maybe he wasn't even white.

"Shhh. I'm whispering this so's you'll know how sorry I am to say it. Maybe that boy is Creole or something. That's how the *Brandywine Sentinel* explained it anyway, after Glenn Disteek mailed in that picture.

"Of course, it only made the quote-unquote news in the first place because of who Duke Drummond was. His political leanings. Never mind that old Duke never wanted no career in politics in the first place. His involvement was strictly for the purpose of sabotage, to upend old Glenn Disteek at every opportunity. Nevertheless, he had followers, as this here cause always draws.

"And now, through the eyes of them followers, picture this supposed white man, surrounded by black musicians, and holding out this squeezebox for the camera, like somehow it explains everything. *The Sentinel* didn't even verify whether the accordionist was Doc Drummond himself, or whether it was some other feller in the band. It may have been the drummer, for instance, in a feathered fedora, with a kick drum initialed DD."

"Is that the end of the story?"

"Oh good, you paid attention right up to the end. Yes, more or less, the end of the story. There ain't yet been a second dust-up between them two. But I reckon it's brewing."

"That was a good story. For real."

Clarick raised a skeptical eyebrow. "For real, huh? You know bein' for real ain't the blessing it sounds like, Nimrod. Nor does it make a man perfect. Nor does it make a man satisfied, neither."

J.R. nodded, shivering in the dark.

"So check this out," Clarick proceeded to unlock the plywood strongbox and shove open its slick moldy walls. The structure had begun to embed itself into the earth and visibly distress where the tree's rootways made gain into its foothold. Clarick shone the flashlight inside.

The contraption was fascinating, hideous, beautiful. J.R. understood it instinctively, even as he wondered at its slap-dash ingenuity. It was fashioned from an old beer keg, powered by a pair of five-horse motors bolted into a 2x4 along the barrel's topside. It seemed that every component contributed some unique disparity to the machine's overall patchwork continuity. The flywheels repurposed from mismatched table saws gave the gears some impractical but nifty menace. The bowing and curling tubing was black rubber here, copper there, grease-stained orange elsewhere. A coiled, mustard yellow accordion hose conjoined by a length of PVC pipe locked into the pump's shut-off valve. The yield emptied into a removable collection tank. The suction port was fastened into the stern of the outhouse. The wheels at the base of the compressor, along with the handlebar, suggested something to be trundled around like medical equipment. All of this J.R. gawked at and wondered upon in the split-second before Cash Clarick trained the flashlight back upon his own chin.

"This thing's running at half capacity. I reckon it's one of these here connections."

"What is that thing? I'm sorry. Never mind. I know what it is. You need me to fix it?"

"For the life of me, I cain't diagnose it."

"I'll get it running like a champion. All I need is a toolbox, some WD-40, and some daylight."

"The first two things you got. The last, you cain't have. That's why we're out here in the middle of the night, genius. Let's fix this beauty. The toolbox is over yonder by the Land Rover."

"Screwdriver," J.R. added. "I'll need a screwdriver too."

## 42. Sabotage!

The next night, after another day of trials, the four recruits lay around on their mattresses, marinating in sweat and filth.

"You guys should be ready for anything," J.R. whispered. "Keep your hopes up. You never know."

"Shit," Vince Baldwin whispered. "It's only a few more days till graduation."

"You have no idea what day it is, Vince."

"My name's FuckFace."

"Just be ready."

"Posse Serpens, motherfucker! We're almost there!"

Vince was going to be a problem. Clarick's slaps to the face had worked their magic, tenderizing whatever brains FuckFace had left to begin with. The only thing worse than bringing him along would be leaving him behind.

J.R. whispered, "Scotty?"

"I'm sorry you're having such a hard time," Scotty groaned.

Vince spat, "Nimrod's jealous of Blondie. Because she gets to stand on a chair."

"It's a pedestal, you stupid idiot," Melissa gave him her flattest deadpan tone.

J.R. snorted laughter, then silenced himself.

"I'm glad you think it's so funny," she hissed.

It wasn't funny, he wanted to tell her. It was what she said. The way she said it. But it was too much to explain, too complex a leap in human communication. "I don't think it's funny," he heard himself plead.

"Is that what you guys do in there?" she asked. "You laugh at the rest of us?"

*Don't say anything more,* he told himself.

Something like a sacred ember smoldered deeper into his solar plexus. *I'm all alone,* he understood. The others were losing their minds and could not be trusted. He would come back for them. And they would come back to him, in a moment of truth, even though they had turned against him now. Every decision was life and death. Every move was freighted with consequence. It was too much to carry, too much to believe in. He may have witnessed, if only for a moment, the shorting out of his trusty brain.

"J.R.," Scotty whispered, "you never liked me."

It was a nightmare. Silence was the only way through.

"Scotty, babe," Melissa said. "There's plenty of water here—"

"Oh, fuck off," he spat.

J.R. listened, paralyzed. Melissa's voice was choking up. Finally, she asked him, "How can you say that to me right now?"

"Babe, I'm sorry..."

They began consoling each other, both of them whimpering, weeping in remorse. "I'm just so tired, babe. I don't know what I'm saying. Come on, let's go to sleep."

"Wow," said Vince. "Some white man's army we're putting together here."

The gentle sobs, his and hers, ended. Soon they were all sound asleep. J.R. knew, by now, when they were.

He had fallen asleep, too. His mother was saying, "I'm sorry you don't like me, except I think you *do* like me," and he was repeating her verbiage back to her, not to prove her right or wrong, but just to annoy her. "I'm sorry you don't like me, except I think you *do* like me."

Scotty said, "J.R., shut up!"

He snorted. He had been dreaming about his mother. It was confusing, unwelcome. He had no time for her. He had to stay awake, had to will it so.

Clarick's stealth was impressive but audible, closing in. He was through the doorway. Vince cried, "NO!" Clarick descended with demonic efficiency. Vince blurted "GUH!"

Clarick's hand struck the hour. Vince groaned into his mattress. Clarick exited swift and silent.

It had to be now. J.R. was up.

He was just outside the barracks, back against the wall, peering around the corner. The moon was bright. Clarick was making his way across the yard. J.R. sprang.

Before he knew it, he was crossing catlike after the distant office window.

Where the building's sidewall provided cover, he coiled himself and watched Clarick's foreshortening promenade. He observed the arrival at the outhouse, not to go inside, but to hover nearby. *Just pissing,* J.R. surmised, knowing there was no way Cash Clarick had walked all that way just to piss into the grass. He had gone there to empty the tank.

In time, Clarick disappeared behind the outhouse. Shortly afterward, he fired up the compressor's motor. J.R. made his move, quietly manipulating the office door on its hinges to slither inside. He eased the door closed behind him.

The Nazi sanctum's soft lantern light drew his eye up to the silken backdrop of fascistic iconography, then to the battle axe and war hammer crisscrossed against the adjacent wall. The battle axe was one way to go, but he wasn't even sure he could wield it, what with his teenage build and lack of expertise. He made instead for the desk and opened the top drawer. The turkey baster lay stashed in there alone. He stole it, then swiftly and silently stole himself out the door.

Clarick was still running the vacuum. J.R. kept to the sprawling shadows of conveyors and ventilation shafts until he came to a safe vantage point behind a Saw Mill shed to wait, clutching the stolen implement down at his side.

In time, the vacuum ceased. Clarick began making his way back across the yard toward the office, to enter routinely, and remain within, behind the dimly glowing fishbowl windows.

The hour was running out of minutes. J.R. allowed at least five more to elapse. He had no idea what time it was.

At last, he made his way into the open yard. The remaining stretch to the Land Rover was flooded with moonlight. He scrambled across the makeshift-battlescape of range targets to the vehicle's sheltering overhang. Arriving, he caught sight of his own spindly shadow in black and fluid tandem with his own mischievous self.

The toolbox was stashed in the outcropping on a wooden shelf girded into the stable wall. It lay at arm's length from the vehicle, just where Clarick had revealed its presence the night before. He removed the five-eighths screwdriver. With near psychedelic noiselessness he knelt to the Land Rover's hood, pried under it, sought out and found its latch, and opened it up.

He listened as crickets and frogs and night owls—the entire biosphere outside his prison of happenstance sang. If the beasts had not heard him, neither had Cash Clarick.

On the other hand, he had no idea how much time he had left. With no sun in the sky, he could only guess. Discipline was the key to any moment, he knew. Also a deathly slog through any moment's post-mortem. Ideas tormented him. Cash Clarick's voice rang almost dreamlike in his head. Echoes about pre-planning, and how the Old Man was a mastermind of foreseeing and coordinating the dimensions of space and time beforehand.

But he was only scrambling in the present, taking his shot in the dark, draining the brake fluid, administering the stolen turkey baster, muttering to himself, "If it ain't broke, break it."

## 43. Pole Position

"Crash Clarick."

"What?"

"I'm sorry. I'm just. So tired. I mean. You are. Or I mean. This is. Really. If you think about it. This is a crash course in life, Mr. Clarick."

Climbing into the Land Rover, J.R. buckled his seatbelt. Clarick watched with open disgust and said nothing. He keyed the ignition and pulled out into the yard.

Peering back at the silo where his friends hung imprisoned, J.R. understood that if his plan didn't work, he would be leaving them to die. But it would work. He would make it work. He faced forward from the passenger seat's reptilian hide. They drove out.

Clarick's boot worked the gas pedal, braking very little, except at that series of plateaus where the path zig-zagged, including that tricky curl around the hemlock tree. The Land Rover accelerated onward, uphill, through the woods and out of them, lurching where the path bumped upward and the terrain leveled out. The engine revved as Clarick gunned it. The off-roads came to an end at last through the cross-hatched ferns and proliferating ivy. Clarick wheeled onto Pine Hollow, applying the brakes, which continued to respond from their doomed dregs of ability.

J.R. braced himself, and tried to urge, by sheer force of will, the brakes to fail. He realized he looked nervous.

"What's your problem?" Clarick snapped.

Clarick was sleep-deprived too, which could prove to be an advantage. It was best to keep the nonsense flowing.

"I need a *Chocodile*," J.R. answered.

"A what?"

He looked back. Dust fell away behind them at the trail's exit. "Or a *Sno Ball*," he mused.

He had mapped out the roads by now. Pine Hollow was tree-shrouded, with guard railings and road signs, houses and homesteads and telephone poles. Ahead came the right turn onto Kiln, where the forest halted and fields stretched in billowing gold on either side. Past those fields lay Deciduous Lane, its population of farmlands and perfectly square corn-fields a paradise beneath the open blue sky. Then right onto Baptist Church Road, where the households began to creep closer together, just past the old ramshackle graveyard. J.R. felt the magnetic draw of civilization, where he'd be less and less free to grab Cash Clarick's pistol and keys off his hapless corpse. At the same time, he was venturing only further by the second from his silo-shackled friends, whom he would have to retrieve one way or another, after the forthcoming and pre-sumably inevitable car accident. He began to realize that his plan was sure to fail, even if it did succeed.

"A *Chocodile* or a *Sno Ball*," he said. "But preferably a *Chocodile*."

The vehicle slowed down when they came to Grand Avenue. The speed limit dropped to thirty. Now the brakes would have to hold, and not give. J.R.'s nerves corkscrewed around some more. Clarick braked the pedal, slowed, stopped, and waited at the first light. Then he advanced, braked up to the second light, and stopped to idle.

The Proverb Saving Bank awaited them opposite the intersection. When the light turned green, the Land Rover proceeded.

Clarick at the wheel turned into the parking lot, braking, braking harder, and parking it, to pause, and kill the engine. "You can't be serious," he said. "You got a sweet tooth? I thought you were a man, Nimrod."

J.R. unbuckled his seatbelt. "I don't want it anymore."

"I don't ever want to hear the word *Chocodile* again."

"Jeez. What are you, my father? I came all the way out here to get away from that asshole—" J.R. recoiled, frozen, leaning back, eyes upward, observing the Land Rover's vinyl ceiling as perhaps his final backdrop, as Clarick pressed the unholstered Colt long barrel into his chin.

It was broad daylight, in the parking lot of the downtown bank, in Proverb, Pennsylvania. Everything was deliriously bright and fleeting. Something transcendent of fear and degradation transpired.

Cash Clarick was saying, "I'm going to murder you," pressing the barrel painfully into J.R.'s prideful chin, "with this pistol, if you ever say *Chocodile* again. Do you understand me?"

J.R. couldn't stop himself, "What about *Sno ball?*"

The gun barrel remained steady. He could smell Cash Clarick's breath and feel the heat from the surface of his face. Clarick began chuckling. "You know I want that five hundred bucks. *Look at me, boy!*"

J.R. rolled his gaze down from the vinyl ceiling to meet his captor's black and wounded eyes.

"You think you're so smart," Clarick plunged his handgun back into its jacket. "Well, I guess you are. Let's go. We got time for *Pole Position* yet."

Advancing across the blacktop toward the bank, J.R. glanced back at the parked Land Rover. This plan was poorly laid. What if the damn thing kept rootin' and tootin' all the way back to the Saw Mill? The next day, he would be chained up in the silo with the rest of them, with no one the wiser, as Clarick went off to play *Pole Position,* or sell cocaine and porn, or unload buckets of human fertilizer to the local pumpkin farmer, or whatever he went off to do, leaving them all to die of crucifixion, heatstroke, sawdust inhalation and claustrophobia, moaning to each other in their dying words how could they possibly have been this stupid, when only J.R. knew the answer. It was a disastrous plan.

He made no small talk with the bank teller, simply wrote out another check.

Back in the Land Rover, he handed over the money. "Are you going to shoot me now?"

"No, I'm going to buy you a fucking *Chocodile.*"

J.R. buckled up.

He had left it to chance to thread this needle. Somehow that was clear only now, after it was too late. Even to plow the Land Rover through the deli entrance, with Clarick nosediving through the windshield into the *Pole Position* console, and the cops descending moments afterwards, sirens blaring, to secure the area. And his friends released from the silo no more than thirty-minutes later. Even then, the result would not undo the damage. Because they had him on tape.

Only one option remained.

Clarick parked easily in the deli parking lot.

Inside, behind the counter, the deli man Charlie smiled. Clarick grabbed a *Chocodile* from the confection stand and tossed it onto the countertop. "This greasy teenager wants a *Chocodile*. How much?"

"19 cents."

Clarick paid with pocket change. The snack cake sat purchased on the laminated countertop. Clarick raised his fist and brought it down—SMASH—spewing the burst contents everywhere. He laughed, delighted. "You know what that is?" he asked Charlie.

"I reckon so, but lend me your perspective!"

"That's 19 cents well spent!"

Charlie laughed.

"I'll clean it up..." Clarick offered, but Charlie insisted he would take care of it. "Go on, Mr. Clarick. I know that *Pole Position* game is callin' out your name. I'll take care of this here demonstration."

Standing at the video game console, steering through its eternal loop, Clarick hissed to J.R., "You know, I reckon maybe I been too nice to you."

"Don't worry. You ain't been nice to me at all."

"Worry?" Clarick countered. "Funny you should mention worry, since it's the biggest thing you and me don't got in common."

"Break *before* entering the turn," J.R. pointed at the screen.

"Oh, I got plans for you," Clarick said. "You done crossed the line."

J.R. pointed again at the busy gamescreen. "It's you crossing the line. Look."

"What's this one's name?" Charlie asked from the deli counter.

"This one?" Clarick answered. "This one here is Nimrod."

"Ride the brakes," J.R. turned back to the arcade game, "like you do in real life."

Now he had Charlie to worry about too.

Back in the Land Rover, they wheeled out of the deli parking lot, pulled onto Grand Avenue and drove.

Lucky at the light, they accelerated up and out of town. The vehicle performed perfectly. Clarick was doing 45 in a 30, even past the police cruiser. J.R. understood how that worked. Now he had the police to worry about too.

They turned onto Baptist Church Road, with the houses flashing by, down to the fenced-in historical-looking grave-yard of crooked, pale, unsmooth headstones lurching defiant in rambling multitude.

Deciduous Lane followed, its estates of American fields tumbling or lying down for bisection with straight-shot fences in distinct quadrangles. One fence alongside the road was strangely and surpassingly creative, its squat concrete posts topped with rounded crowns and arranged in a row, like un-played chess pawns.

Next they peeled around the corner onto Kiln Road, traversing empty fields of breezeblown straw, braking at the end, curling hard onto Pine Hollow. Clarick was driving angry, pissed, determined. The woods closed in. J.R.'s entire consciousness had been reduced to a single, agonizing experience of anticipation. Clarick worked the brakes, swung wide into the oncoming lane, took the right at the dirt road, bearing forward and down through the jungle hill strewn with ivy and abundant ferns, to land at the brief stretch of weeds that followed a straight path for one blessed moment before descending into the woods again. The Land Rover was infuriatingly stout.

A certain unwelcome irony crept in upon J.R.'s so-called preparedness. His fate, at age sixteen, had come to depend upon a car superior to his own mechanical sabotage. His plan, conjured up out of everything he knew, had failed. And in some way, this befitted him. The limited options remaining were his due. Desperation was at hand. His only choice was to attack and choke to death Cash Clarick inside a moving and plummeting runaway vehicle as a final resort with no conceivable positive outcome in sight.

Except that now Cash Clarick's foot was braking, and braking, and braking to no avail, while the Land Rover accelerated mercilessly, and the rutted trail hurtled upwards. "WHAT THE...?"

Clarick bit his lip, pumped his boot frantically against the floor. "HANG ON, NIMROD!" Still one puzzle piece short.

Then he got it. And looked upon his passenger anew. "SONOFABITCH, WHAT DID YOU DO TO US?"

He reached and brought out the pistol. J.R. grabbed the wrist. The gun went off—BANG!—blasting through the roof. Clarick was too strong, leveraging him back. The hemlock tree flew up at them with split-second speed. J.R. popped Clarick in the face, but it was too weak. *I should have been angrier!* he realized, in a strange and timeless farewell to himself.

Sound and pain and violence came together as Cash Clarick went sideways into the steering column and J.R.'s body got wrenched around the cab by his own seatbelt.

Then it was over.

For some time, hissing sounds from mangled pipes and valves remained.

J.R.'s eyes were open. He was sure he had seen Cash Clarick's neck break, the head launched face sideways into the windshield, then caught by the chin coming back into the steering wheel. Dead for sure.

And now, having killed a man, he was struck numb. He felt no physical pain from the impact either. It occurred to him that he might be dead too, his spirit preparing to wink out into oblivion, after one last moment to savor. One last glimpse around.

Gradually nothing winked out. He was OK. *This is an amazing car,* he realized, laughing to himself. *What a shame,* he realized on top of that.

He looked at the pistol on the gator-skin seat amidst countless diamond-shots of shattered glass. He unbuckled himself, all his limbs and muscles in working order, no pain or feeling of any kind. He picked up the pistol, studied it in his hand. Another shot had gone off, he remembered. He had heard it go off. Two shots fired. Four rounds left.

He braced his left hand on the seat, and with the other hand cocked the gun and raised it to Cash Clarick's lolling head. It would be worth it. To make sure.

Except he had seen the neck broken, seen it snapped around at least once, maybe twice. Cash Clarick was dead.

To blow him away? To do that to someone's dead body? A voice inside told him it wasn't right. He listened.

The keys hung from the crumpled steering column. He wrenched them out. He kicked open the buckled door, exiting the wreck. Wasting no time, he began to jog forward down the mountain, brandishing the gun, making for his friends chained up in their dungeon, and for other matters that required his attention down at the Saw Mill.

As he jogged down the path, sweat began to pour out of him, and he began to feel his muscles laboring. Down the hill, out of the tall grass, he could hear the birds singing, sweetly oblivious to man and his evils. The mill stretched below. His vison swam. The sweat from his body suggested the exertion of a nine-inning baseball game.

*Water. I need water. I sound like Scotty!* he laughed to himself. *Otherwise, I'm keeping pace!*

Arriving down at the dusty landing above the Saw Mill entrance, and gazing over that sprawling plundered relic, he understood that his friends—Scotty, Melissa, and even Vince Baldwin, hopefully, with the promise of no more slaps to the face—would be priority number one. Once he had the tape.

He banged into Cash Clarick's office. Perhaps the accident had injured him, because the pain was rising, throbbing at every nerve ending, as he shoved those concerns aside and made for the desk where the satellite phone sat waiting. He opened each drawer until he found one locked. The keys. He had them. Sorting through them, a dozen or so, he found the one that looked right and unlocked the secrets it held. Scotty's shades, and a white binder. No tape.

The curiosity was insurmountable. Inside the binder, he found schematics, four pages, rough mechanical drawings of saw blades and pressure gauges, valves, tubing and tank. He closed it, dropped it back into the plundered desk drawer. No time for that bullshit.

He kicked over the boom box, made for the file cabinet. It was three drawers high. He fumbled for the plausible key, applied it. Top drawer first, then the next, then the next. No tape. Just files, one drawer devoted entirely to mechanical line drawings.

He had blood on his hand. He traced it to its source. Spots gathered on the floor. He looked around his own body for the wound, even as the pain struck from his shoulder. *I'm shot!* he realized.

Clutching at his right arm, his hand came away, bloody. Then pain throughout his body dawned. Adrenaline had been his willpower. Now it was gone. Every muscle was sore with strain. He was hot, sweating, and bleeding.

The cooler. He opened it, rifled through it. Water, deer jerky, a bottle of vodka. He came away with the water jug, drank from it, thirstily, then exhaled.

The footlocker was padlocked. He intuited the key from the collection, sweating and suffering, still well aware his friends were in need of rescue. Unlocking the trunk, opening it, he found tapes.

Bleeding into the locker, he sorted with his hands, violently, six or seven tapes, each labelled down its spine with a name—not a nickname, not a Posse Serpens name, but a real name, first and last. None were labelled Junior or J.R. Daddio.

He flung the bloody useless tapes around the plundered chest.

Wallets. His, theirs, he collected them for his friends. He then looked around the office, then up at the silken fascist flags, and then the war hammer crisscrossed with the battle axe. The notion came over him again, to declare one or both of those weapons, and tear this room apart until he found his tape. But he was bleeding freely and losing energy.

Vodka. He went to it, and began the agonizing, sweat drenched process of dousing the wound with alcohol. He found himself listening to his burning arm, more than feeling it. *There's no bullet in there,* he was sure of it.

Kneeling into the pooling bloody mercury-thick booze, dosages of pain bringing him back from something like death to something not quite like life, he knew he had to get Scotty and Melissa out of the silo. He had to forget about retrieving the tape. His mind was made up.

Then he saw the camcorder, tripod-craned, lurking in the opposite corner. He bled his way over to it, powered it on, or tried to, unable to reckon the controls. "FUCKING FUTURIS-TIC BULLSHIT!" he cried into the abandoned, flag festooned, fishbowl office.

He went back to the desk for the metal ruler he had spotted in the center drawer. He returned to the Betacam, jammed the jimmy down into the contraption and pried it open. The tape was unmarked. This was the one. It wasn't labeled because it wasn't finished.

He tucked the gun into his back pocket, looked again upon Cash Clarick's death dealing weaponry crisscrossed in domination over its altar. Smashing the tape, hacking it up with the axe, would be an option. But what if that didn't erase it?

He could just blast it with the pistol, too. But what if it wasn't that simple? This new technology. It was the spools inside that had to be wiped clean, the tape completely destroyed. Only a pit of fire or a vat of acid or some such measure would do.

Leaving the water jug and the satellite phone behind, he pushed through the door and carried the poisoned videotape into the dusty dilapidated haunted yard. Instinctively, he looked up the hill for Cash Clarick's zombie form to stumble down in pursuit. He raised the pistol in defense, but no one was coming. Cash Clarick was dead, neck snapped like a stick of celery. J.R. had seen it. The wind through the straw down the valley toward the entrance into the gauntlet blew a foreboding chill. The tape wouldn't fit into his back pocket, so he would carry it with him, double-fisted with the pistol.

*Shoot the thing! Drop it on the ground and shoot it!* Such thoughts tormented him, but he had to be smart. He would melt it, or burn it, something like that, first chance he had.

The silo loomed higher as he approached. He wrenched open the door.

"J.R!"

"We're outta here."

"Are you shot?"

"What did you do?"

"Fuck you, Vince. I'm saving your life."

"Is this for real?"

"You're Goddamn right it's for real."

"If you're fucking with me—"

"HE'S NOT FUCKING WITH US!" Melissa cried. "LOOK AT HIM!"

J.R. began setting them free of their shackles. "Jesus, J.R. you're all fucked up," Scotty rubbed alternately at each freed wrist. J.R began unlocking Melissa.

"Don't even think about unlocking me!" Vince told him.

"Vince," Scotty pleaded, "what are you talking about?"

"What is that?" said Vince. "That plastic thing?"

J.R. had the tape under his armpit. "What? You mean this thing I'm bleeding all over?"

Melissa was free. "Jesus, J.R. thank you!" she made to hug him, but he recoiled and winced, "I'm shot."

"Don't unlock me!" spat Vince. "Posse Serpens, mother-fucker. I'm staying!"

"Vince, you'll die in here!"

"Traitor! You're a traitor to your race!"

"Vince, we're getting out of here!"

"ARE YOU KIDDING?! LEAVE HIM!"

"J.R.! A CAR! A CAR IS COMING! FUCKING SHIT! THAT'S YOUR NOVA!"

Vince began laughing with maniacal glee, "THAT'S RIGHT, YOU STUPID ASSHOLES! WHO'S THE IDIOT NOW? I'M GONNA *LOVE* THIS..."

Vince Baldwin's arms pulled the chains taut as he leaned out from the wall, baring his teeth, drooling, sub-human and insane.

"J.R., THE PISTOL!" Scotty cried. "BRING THE PISTOL!"

"Where's the phone?" Melissa pleaded. "Was it still in the office?"

J.R. arrived at the doorway with the pistol.

Melissa displayed her upturned fists like she was curling a barbell. "J.R., where's the phone?"

"It's in the office."

"Jesus," she said. "What about the hunting rifle?"

Vince was listening in. J.R. said nothing. Brandishing the pistol and cradling the tape, he peered outside the open door. *Those fuckers have my Nova!* he seethed. He could see them parked on the rise above the gate, three of them. At least one had a rifle. They remained in the car, waiting.

"J.R.?" Vince Baldwin hissed from his shackles. "What is that? Some kind of videotape?"

"What about the shotgun?" Melissa's voice was rising with desperation. She was criticizing him. He couldn't imagine it, much less imagine a response.

"Listen to me," he said. "If any of us can get to the office, that's the place to be. Meanwhile, I've got the pistol—"

"YOU GUYS SHOULD BE ASKING WHAT'S ON THAT TAPE!" Vince Baldwin demanded.

"Look," J.R. gestured to the open doorframe. Scotty and Melissa obeyed. The three of them peered up at the Nova with

215

its armed occupants making their plans inside. "There's three of us, and three of them. We each pick a guy and track him..."

But even as he spoke, the passenger door swung open, and the front seat jerked forward to disgorge two racing Rottweilers courtesy of Hayes Garage. The dogs sped frothily into the yard. J.R. understood with dismay this meant four shots for five assailants, two presently bearing down out of the animal kingdom. The dogs would be easy pickings, but Cash Clarick's purpose would be served. With no margin for error he allowed the doomed beasts to draw furiously closer. Then BANG! BANG! he put their lights out.

He looked up at the Nova again, the dead animals serving notice along that distance of danger. They didn't know how many shots he had left. He turned to explain this to Scotty and Melissa, but Vince Baldwin was listening in, so he clammed up.

He turned again to the threat outside. His opponents had at least one rifle. But they were just sitting there. The time to act was now. He had to say something.

"OK, forget tracking them," he said. "Keep an eye on me AND keep an eye on them. Try to get to the office. If one of those guys is Cash Clarick, trust me, he's all fucked up. He can barely move. I'm not wasting a bullet on him. I'll finish him by hand, after I kill the other two. OK? Try to get to the office."

He turned and sprang from the door frame.

"J.R.!" Melissa called after him.

Dashing into the yard, he could see they had spotted him. The rifle barrel was aiming after him from the car window. He slid like a ballplayer safely behind the nearest range target, kicking up dust clouds. Gunshots rained down around him, two in the dirt, one into the bullseye. The developing smokescreen was not something he anticipated, but it was good enough to conceal his flight, hurtling straight ahead for the next obstacle, with gunshots zinging in late behind him as he slid in once again. It was exactly like stealing second and third on one pitch. He was that much closer, pistol in hand, waiting as the dust settled.

"J.R.!" Scotty was trying to keep his voice low despite the distance between them. *"Can you hit them from there?"*

*"Closer would be better,"* he rasped back.

*"OK, I'm gonna make a break across the yard—"*

"NO!" Melissa cried.

*"Keep your voice down—"*

"HEY," Vince called out from his loyal shackles. "THESE ASSHOLES ARE UNARMED!"

*"I'm going,"* Scotty told Melissa. *"This is what I'm good at."*

*"Scotty..."*

*"J.R.,"* Scotty croaked, as quietly as possible, *"when they aim at me, you get closer. I'm going... on the count of three."*

*"Scotty, are you sure?"*

*"This is what I'm good at. They'll never hit me in a million years, trust me. OK? On the count of three..."*

J.R. hunkered down with the pistol.

Scotty counted off, "One... Two... THREE!"

To wait that perfect split-second, allowing Scotty's sprinting figure in his track shorts and South Milford Marathon T-shirt to distract the rifleman. Then to bolt out from behind the range target.

The gunshots rang somewhere over J.R.'s head as he angled straight forward, no zig-zagging, arriving closer still, even as the shooter turned the rifle back in his direction. It was Charlie from the deli, within range. J.R. dropped to one knee, raised the pistol and BANG! dropped the deli-man back against the doorframe to fall forward out the car window. The rifle fell to the ground beneath the shooter's dangling rag doll arms. J.R. backed himself into the range target, one bullet left in the chamber.

"I'm going again!" Scotty called.

"Scotty, wait! Wait 'till those morons decide who's shooting at you!"

"YOU ASSHOLES!" Vince's cry could be heard from the derelict silo.

Melissa declared, "VINCE, I SWEAR TO GOD I'M GONNA KILL YOU WITH MY BARE HANDS."

"THOSE ARE FIGHTING WORDS, WOMAN!"

J.R. held focus on the Nova and its two remaining assailants. Amazingly, one of them, the driver, was getting out, making a stumbling break, in his Hayes Garage coveralls, around the front of the car for the fallen rifle. J.R. took aim and observed the very moment his prey understood, and even paused, exactly like a deer in a floodlight. BANG! The body fell dead without a twitch.

No more bullets. J.R. crouched, turned back toward the yard.

"Scotty!" he said. "Well done! Stop running now!"

Tucking himself into the target's wooden framework, he examined the pistol's chamber, just to be sure. Empty.

It occurred to him—this time with a skepticism more or less married to self-preservation—that he had just shot two men dead. To cross that threshold should mean something. Except that it had failed to mean anything already, spectacularly so, back when he had quote-unquote killed Cash Clarick half-an-hour ago, to no avail. An emotion and reflection he had entertained out of sheer melodrama and would never, ever, under any circumstances allow to occur again. A lesson well learned, like nothing they manufactured and peddled at Erving High School. Cash Clarick wasn't remotely dead, because killing him wasn't nearly enough.

"Are you kidding me, Nimrod?" Clarick's voice called out from the hijacked Nova. "You're actually running around with that *tape?*"

"No, I'm running around with this *pistol!*"

"HE'S OUT OF BULLETS!" Vince testified from the silo.

Clarick slithered out of the Nova's back seat, kicking his bloody boots viciously at the swinging door, emerging to stand. His neck appeared to be broken, so that he had to tilt forward and sideways to eyeball everything and take it all in. His right arm was dangling, lifeless. His left hand held a Ruger pistol, carelessly. Swooning, staggering, he advanced down through the dusty weed-strangled path toward the Saw Mill's open gateway. Behind him, the valley's folding and crisscrossing layers loomed at softening depths of misty green. Against the blue sky, the white clouds, hued in gold and pink, lay still.

"Ain'tcha gonna shoot me?" Clarick drew closer.

"THEY'RE UNARMED!" Vince Baldwin sang.

J.R. remained huddled behind the range target, gripping the empty six-shooter like something to curse. *What a stupid reason to die,* he told himself.

"CASH CLARICK!" hollered Scotty.

J.R. called out, "SCOTTY! HE'S ARMED!"

Scotty stepped into the yard out of the shadows. "I KNOW HE'S ARMED! THAT ASSHOLE CAN'T HIT ME! I'M TOO FAST!"

"SCOTTY, GET BACK!" Melissa shrieked from the silo.

Scotty ignored her. "CLARICK!" he raged. "YOU!"

"Shades to the rescue," Clarick raised the Ruger pistol.

"YOU!" Scotty advanced. "You're NOTHING! Not without the upper hand! NOTHING!"

"SCOTTY, NO!" Melissa was out the silo door. Watching her bolt into danger, J.R. cried, "MELISSA!"

"WHAT DID YOU PROVE? HUH?" Scotty demanded. "WHAT DID YOU PROVE? TO ME AND HER? AND THE REST OF US? AT FUCKING GUNPOINT?"

Clarick lowered the pistol. "You want a fight? Is that what you want?"

"I WANNA SEE THIS!" Vince complained from his dungeon chains. "UNLOCK ME!"

"YOU DON'T HAVE THE GUTS!" Scotty closed in.

Melissa was pleading, "SCOTTY, NO!"

Clarick dropped the Ruger into the dirt. "Look at me, I'm half-paralyzed. You think that'll make a man out of you? Finishing me off?"

"Excuses," Scotty spat. "I didn't make excuses when you were drowning me to death."

"Fair enough, tough guy. Want me to tie my other arm behind my back? To make it even?"

"You're not a man."

J.R. rose to restrain Melissa as Scotty met Cash Clarick in battle. Melissa resisted, crying, "GET OFF ME!" Then the two of them watched, clinging to each other, holding on.

There was a moment, or longer, when Scotty seemed to have a winning plan, darting in and out, circling around his grievously wounded enemy. He would strike with all the force he could, with Clarick whirling to defend himself, taunting his assailant, spitting, "You fucking *athletes!* You think you're *men!*"

"I WANNA SEE THIS!" Vince Baldwin's plea grew frantic from within the silo.

J.R. held Melissa Victoria in his arms at last, under these worst of circumstances, or maybe these most romantic, because she was holding him too, with everything she had. The longing was so inescapable, and yet so completely wrong.

"You!" Clarick swatted at Scotty's lightning shadow. "You fucking pretend to chase danger!" he swatted again. "You pretend you're putting something on the line! Catching a bunch of touchdowns! Or riding a fucking bicycle! Or whatever it is!

Running around with a *ball!*" he reached again for Scotty, this time catching him by his South Milford Marathon T-shirt and ending the contest.

"NO!" Melissa shrieked, bolting free of J.R.'s arms.

"Without a football!" Clarick taunted Scotty, dragging him to the ground. "Or a bicycle!" He had him pinned. "You're just running around!"

J.R. realized. *What did I do?*

Clarick killed Scotty one handed, involving the elbow, with the arms pinned by the knees, something J.R. instantly regretted seeing, having not turned his head in time. And yet he could no more turn his head now, from Melissa's response.

In her jeans and tasseled jacket, with her butchered mane of ransacked hair, and from her perfectly-judged angle, she leapt onto Clarick's shoulders, and with the murdering bastard howling in agony beneath her knees she rode his buckling body, raging down from above with furious hands. Clarick's forearm defended his eyes, which left an opening for his broken neck. She struck and J.R. wouldn't have guessed it either, but this was a mistake.

Clarick came alive from some unknowable realm of pain— like a cat struck by lightning—instantly seizing Melissa's entire body weight one-handed and spinning her out into the Saw Mill arena. He went for the gun where it lay. J.R. bolted out from cover but too late. Clarick raised the Ruger and shot Melissa dead. He then turned the weapon on J.R., who ducked behind the nearest range target, once again cornered.

"I think you dropped your tape?"

"What'd you think I was gonna do?"

"We got four dead bodies here, kid. Not to mention the dogs you shot, you sick fuck."

"What'd you think I was gonna do?"

"WHAT DID I MISS?" Vince sounded off from the silo.

"JESUS, VINCE! HE KILLED THEM! ARE YOU HAPPY NOW?"

"YES! WHAT ARE YOU NOW?"

"We got *a lot* of cleaning up to do," Clarick said.

## 44. Night Soil

Inside the U-Haul, J.R. dangled his legs from his stack of skids. The ski mask lay ready in his lap. The Remington lay at his side. The sounds of parking lot comings and goings through the trailer's steel walls provided an incessantly haunting reminder of the innocent lives in danger outside.

"I'd like to make Elsie Gannon famous," Steeplejack mused, his voice sonorous compared to those muffled and wandering musings delivered intermittently from without. "I wonder about Lou, though. Whether he's movie star material."

The walkie-talkie came to life. *"Visual on the armored car."*

"We're two minutes out," Steeplejack marked his watch. "Get that mask on and stay sharp."

"You keep tryin' to get me jealous," J.R. said, as casually as possible. "But it's not Elsie Gannon you want."

Steeplejack's ears perked up. He held his face mask in his hands, poised to lower. "Oh no?"

"No. Nope."

Steeplejack pulled his mask down, "Stay sharp, soldier. It's show time in T-minus."

"It's Farrah," J.R. said, pulling his own mask down. "It's Farrah you want. You've got it written all over you. Think about it. Duke Drummond. Glenn Disteek. Harold Mariner.

Hell, even poor old Frank Brool. They all had her. All except you."

"You don't know a thing about half of those people," Steeplejack's face was concealed by his knitted black ski mask. "Get your head into the game, rookie. We're about to spring a booby trap!"

"*de Ram...*" J.R. whispered.

"de Ram, what?"

"You make a call to de Ram. Send him after Duke Drummond. The wheels turn. The universe sets her free. She's yours to swoop in and rescue."

Steeplejack paused, inscrutable in masked contemplation. He looked at his watch. "45 seconds," he said. "We've been sitting here for two-and-a-half hours in this sweltering truck. And you schedule *now* for your plans of sedition?"

"I just thought of it. Wait. Sedition? No way. I said Farrah. I didn't say sedition."

Steeplejack looked at his watch. "35 seconds."

J.R. clutched his shotgun, watching his masked accomplice try to fit it all into the blender.

"Remember what I told you, J.R. Wait. Fuck. 25 seconds."

25 seconds wasn't much time. And yet it was all the time in the world. J.R. gripped his shotgun and faced the exit. His thoughts turned back to moments of greater desperation, from which he had emerged unkilled. He allowed himself to believe this would just be the next one of those. A growing string of jackpots that ended up accomplishments, with all of the adrenaline and burned bridges afterwards leaving him exponentially wiser.

His thoughts turned back to Vince Baldwin, in the escaping Nova, stuffed into the back seat with Cash Clarick's footlocker, and the Betacam, and the battle axe and the war hammer, asking, *"What about initiation?"*

"This is initiation you stupid asshole!" Clarick had barked, twisted into the passenger seat, hoarding the assault rifle, the bolt-action, the Mossberg, the bullpup and the Colt, even as he trained the Ruger on J.R. inside the highway-bound Nova.

"And quit yer questions, FuckFace. *Sheesh.* Shut your mouth for once. Or for the rest of eternity is fine too. How many million times you think I been through this here?"

J.R. had found hope for Vince Baldwin, who had briefly snapped out of it, back at the Saw Mill in the cold and tree-shrouded radius of the outhouse. It was not a moment to relive in his imagination, not ever. All except for the desperate and hopeful light bulb that seemed to fire off in Vince's diminished conscience. The look in his eyes, as he shared with J.R., at last, the awful truth. To arrive at this moment, this activity, something must have gone terribly wrong.

For J.R., the nightmare uncoiled at gunpoint, understood as his eternal punishment for leaving Cash Clarick's remains un-deceased inside the wreckage of that carefully and deliberately and painstakingly sabotaged Land Rover, after which, and after the gunfight, and the death match, and after loading the methodically collected assault rifle, hunting rifle, bullpup, armful of files, armful of *Cash Clarick Vittles,* and bloodied videotapes into the footlocker, and then making off with the Betacam, plus the battle axe and war hammer, plus a couple of long-handled shovels, and not forgetting the water jug, they packed it all into the Nova, ready to go, all but for the bodies, which outnumbered them four to three, not factoring in the two dogs whose departed souls no one would miss, and whose carcasses could simply be left to rot in the abandoned sunlight.

They piled Scotty and Melissa into the open trunk, along with Charlie from the deli, and the nameless Hayes Garage mechanic, allowing the tangled arms and legs to spill out over the sides. J.R. then wheeled the Nova slowly around the range targets toward the gleaming white fiberglass latrine under its canopy of haunted leaves. "Park it here," Clarick said, leveling the pistol.

J.R. felt a pang of newer and deeper regret. Unforgivable regret. It left his memory vague and dreamlike, all but the look on Vince Baldwin's face, who seemed to backpedal at last, and to register in his own eyes a slumbering humanity, as if some promise were kept after all, at that eagerly rampaged threshold, feeding the bodies in head first, after emptying the stinking hopper into the yard, its capacity in full need. Bumpily, noisily, the first two went through, Vince and J.R. angling their broad shoulders down through the doorframe first, feet last. The next two, Scotty and Melissa, were not so cooperative. The hopper was full, there was no spare tank, and it was time to go.

At Clarick's armed insistence, they gave it one last effort, succeeding only as far as the tops of their best friends' heads.

223

His first, then hers. Their personalities, memories and dreams sucked down into the kitty, leaving their scooped-out faces in ruin.

Dusk took hold as they departed for West Susquehannock, the trunk heavy with bodies, J.R. at the wheel, Clarick training the Ruger, muttering, *"Happy now?"* and other probing sarcasms.

Interstates connected left, then right. J.R. wove those turns, following little else over the endless dark westward roadways. Clarick sat tucked against the passenger door, his head corkscrewed to one side, his bloody face diamond-shot with glass. Gripping the pistol, he ordered, "Stay off the pike." They followed several local roads by.

Finally, at Clarick's direction, J.R. plowed the Chevy up a slick grass embankment. They arrived upon headlights in great number, bearing down—trucks, buses, cars. J.R. pulled out, accelerating, comingling with the headlong traffic, approaching the first tunnel with the name caught floodlit in memorial. Alongside the other travelers he followed that length at that depth and emerged outside, quickly to approach yet another tunnel. Open farmland stretched between those feats of engineering, busses and eighteen-wheelers everywhere, J.R. holding the speed limit, Clarick huddled against the passenger door, holding the pistol steady, instructing him to pull along the rumbling tar-laced weather-beaten shoulder and follow off road.

"Too bad we don't got the Land Rover for this maneuver," he complained.

The shortcut led to a brief stretch of wilderness, as Clarick's lamentations about the deceased Land Rover became decreasingly prescient with every patch of danger ground beneath the Nova's rolling wheels.

Finally, onto a paved road and out of the wild they emerged. Could it really be called Mill Road? It seemed to J.R. the very landmarks of his doom mocked him.

An oncoming road sign read Burnt Cabins. They turned left. J.R. kept track, or tried to, of highway numbers, the names of lefts and rights forming a desperate map in his head, although it came to feel more like his gut.

Clarick pointed, "Here it is, the old turnpike." His face was grey. Clarick was dead, clearly. And yet he was sweating, and speaking, and pointing a gun. His pistol hand repeatedly came to steady itself. "Turn here."

They were off the map, plunging straight ahead up the abandoned road overgrown with weeds. The Nova's tires and suspension rumbled over the terrain.

"Through this tunnel. And don't worry yourself, Nimrod."

On cue, out of the night, the first tunnel approached, much like those before, but this time unilluminated, abandoned, burrowing into the Pennsylvania Mountains. "What am I lookin' out for?"

"Rays Hill."

"Raise Hell?"

"Jesus, Nimrod... J.R... you moron. Rays Hill."

Vince Baldwin remained silent in the cluttered back seat, with the footlocker and melee weaponry, and other treasure salvaged from the Saw Mill. J.R. glanced at Vince's shadow only briefly in the rearview mirror, then trained his eyes ahead, with no idea what might be lurking inside this abandoned tunnel. Could be a shopping cart. Could be a crack party. Could be some sick bastard glued a steel bar across the middle at face-height. He would have to be ready for anything.

However, nothing lay ahead, only a long stretch of hollow darkness. They emerged from that underground onto another stretch of desolate, derelict highway.

"This here is the tricky part," Clarick said, broken-necked, sweating where he had nestled into the passenger seat, hovering somewhere just inside of, or maybe beyond, the realm of death. "See that? Through that opening in the trees."

J.R. plunged off road again, determined he could get through anything with the gas pedal. And now, with the headlights cast before him, the Nova bucked violently into a meadow, the dead bodies and other cargo comingling audibly from the trunk. He was able to steady the car, although the ground was so soft that he had to keep accelerating.

"Just keep right and watch for the next opening," Clarick said. "This'd be easier in the Land Rover," he added. "All we're doing is going around them barricades. In a pinch, you drive through." After a moment he added, "Jesus, who am I kidding this ain't no pinch?"

Ghostlike cattle appeared before them, standing around, too dumb to be frightened, just waiting for an end to their bovine misery. J.R. kept his foot on the gas, ranging through and around them.

"That opening there," Clarick said, and with the last cow standing watch behind them, J.R. plowed the Nova forward out of the grassland through a division of copse back onto the forsaken, weed choked roadway.

"Very good," Clarick muttered from his fevered state. Reflectors and rumble strips hurtled up from the abandoned roadside. Another dark tunnel loomed ahead. "Wait," Clarick ordered. "Are we here? We're finally here. You know what we're doing?"

"We're following orders," J.R. answered.

"Oh, you're so smart."

"At gunpoint."

"Sooooo smart. Got yer friends killed. That's how smart you are. Ain't that right, FuckFace?"

J.R. checked the rearview mirror. Vince was tucked away in the shadows, unresponsive.

"Wonder what FuckFace has to say about who was smart today," Clarick went on. "Don't go through the tunnel, Nimrod. There's a path comin' up. It's up there. We take that."

J.R. took the path to the right. They were off road again, with Clarick saying, "Sooooo smart. Trashing that Land Rover."

They ranged into a barely discernable opening in the mountainside and then cascaded down into it.

"This here is the shortcut to West Susquehannock. Just watch and see if any of them others ever tell you a thing about it. Mark my words. They won't. Not never. Twenty years from now? Just wait and see. They still won't be lettin' you in. But that's what I'm here for, Nimrod. Twenty years from now? Heck, make it fifty years from now. Someday. It's gonna be you sayin' Cash Clarick... that boy... he's the only one. The only that didn't never lie to me. Not once."

Plunging the stony crag down the mountainside, J.R. followed and believed. At last, he pulled the Nova into a glade at the foot of the mountain. The car felt beleaguered and wary as it slid to a stop in the clearing. Clarick, still holding the pistol, bid them out. He clicked on a flashlight. "Let's move fast now."

Soon they had the trunk open.

J.R. reached for Melissa, withdrew his hands, reached again.

"Get on, boy..."

He didn't want to hold her. And yet it couldn't be Vince. And couldn't be Cash Clarick either. He was her only remaining champion.

He reached again, took up her lifeless weight, perhaps as much in shock, if not more so, than he had been repeatedly all day.

Vince gathered Scotty's remains. The two of them bore the dead over to the gravesite. Clarick's voice sounded from the source of the flashlight's beam, "Both y'all come back for this hopper next. It weighs heavy."

They dug a careless mass grave, as Clarick muttered, *"Poaching, I'll show them fuckers poaching,"* and other vaguely coherent resentments, meaningless echoes as J.R. remembered them, though he couldn't remember the last words exactly. From out of nowhere a bullet dropped Cash Clarick dead. At that moment, J.R. lost any last clinging belief in himself.

It would have been, should have been, so easy, to achieve the same result, back in the steaming, demolished remains of the Land Rover, with the pistol to Cash Clarick's broken, helpless head.

For some reason, he couldn't do it. Couldn't pull the trigger. Couldn't so much as kill a dead guy. The mistake was unforgivable. Nightmare upon tragedy had followed. And now BANG! so simple. Cash Clarick's reign was over.

Six or seven flashlights emerged from the woods, interrogations bellowing down with the crossbeams, Vince Baldwin insisting he was Posse Serpens, J.R. unable to silence him in time, and warn him that this was not the Posse Serpens but the Posse Umbellus.

"ON THE LEFT. WHAT'S YOUR NAME, BOY? AND DON'T LIE TO ME! I'LL SMELL IT! I'LL SMELL IT FROM UP HERE, AND I'LL COME DOWN THERE AND CUT YOUR THROAT! WHAT'S YOUR NAME?"

J.R. didn't know how to answer. He was blind in the flashbeams. *What's my name? I'm going to die.*

"Oh, I don't like you!"

"Stand down," a voice sounded. Music to the ears. It was the Old Man, Edward.

"I don't like this one," Duke Drummond demanded. "Is this one of yours?"

The Old Man's time-ravaged voice answered, "This here is J.R. Daddio."

## 45. The Heist

"ACTION!" Steeplejack yanked up the U-Haul door.

J.R. winced. The parking lot was bright. The Brinks truck stood directly ahead. One guard, closing the rear doors, staggered emptyhanded, two bags of cash at his feet. Another guard, behind the wheel, had seen them, his face grim and lethal in the rearview mirror. Steeplejack pounced down to the pavement. J.R followed, landing, crouching, gripping the shotgun. Mall shoppers began shrieking and fleeing behind parked cars. J.R. kept his eyes on the Brinks driver, who was making to shoot, pistol drawn. Vince Baldwin and Crosby Shue in ski masks were prowling up nearby. Lou Gannon waited in the Trans Am, at its wheel. J.R. held the shotgun tight. The Brinks driver was going to shoot. J.R. could turn on his accomplices now, desperately—Steeplejack first, then the other two, then Lou Gannon—to rejoin civilization a hero. He raised the shotgun, not knowing, in that moment, who to kill. A barrage from Steeplejack's M16 drove the Brinks driver back, knees buckling, body collapsing amidst shattering glass and excessive bullet hail, riddling the truck's open steel-paneled door. The gunfire rang each time before it ceased and afterward. The other guard, with the moneybags at his feet and pistol holstered, retreated awkwardly. He had a look on his face as if Martians had landed. Steeplejack trained the gun on him. Crosby Shue arrived, saying, "Whoa, whoa, partner!"

Steeplejack shouldered his weapon. The baffled guard turned to receive the butt of Crosby Shue's gun—SMASH to the face. Police sirens were wailing.

"ALREADY?!"

"PLAN B!"

The Trans Am peeled out, screeching.

J.R looked around, surveyed the sparsely parked cars, the sunshot chrome, the mirrors glinting, here and there a shopper fleeing or a family ducking for cover, screaming. The lot stretched up to the highway. Sirens were keening, but no lights yet.

Crosby Shue had the moneybags, handed them off to Vince Baldwin, barking out of his knitted mouth hole, "GET THOSE INTO THE CAR!" He grabbed up the shotgun from the pavement.

Lou Gannon bore down in his Firebird. The bloodied guard lay out cold on the ground. "FUCK, I KNEW THIS WAS GONNA HAPPEN!" someone said. The Trans Am chirped to a stop. Lou Gannon behind the wheel was shouting, "LET'S VAMOOSE!"

In that moment, the rear doors opened to reveal a third Brinks guard, shotgun in hand. In one split-second the guard surveyed his options, sized up Lou Gannon behind the wheel, pointed the gun and blew him away.

"NO!" they cried in unison.

The guard was immediately battered by a volley from Steeplejack's assault rifle, hurtled back into the Brinks truck hollow.

Vince Baldwin flung open the Trans Am's passenger door, threw the moneybags into the backseat, then himself in front. He then began pushing Lou Gannon's fresh and hemorrhaging corpse out the driver's side door.

"No!" J.R. caught the body before it hit the pavement. He found himself cradling Lou Gannon, looking at him, pushing him back into the car. Then he shoved the carcass over the cockpit's interior into Vince Baldwin's lap. "WE DON'T LEAVE HIM HERE!"

Vince Baldwin's masked face said, "THIS ISN'T THE PLAN!"

"THE PLAN IS FUCKED!" J.R. took the wheel.

Police sirens were closing in. Steeplejack aimed his assault rifle at the last fallen guard who lay unconscious on the pavement.

"NOT NECESSARY! LET'S GO!" cried Crosby Shue.

Steeplejack considered it a moment. He shot the guard where he lay. Then he leapt up into the open vault for more cash.

Shue approached J.R. in the driver's seat. "J.R., shove over!"

"Get in, you fucking asshole! Both of you assholes! I'm driving this fucking mission, or you can kill me right now with the rest of these fucking chumps!"

"What? No, J.R.! You're not driving. I'm driving!"

"WHAT DID I JUST SAY!?" J.R. leaned forward for Crosby Shue. At the same time, he began bashing the shotgun barrel through the jagged hole in the front windshield.

"JESUS CHRIST!" Crosby Shue paused, then swept open the door and climbed in behind J.R.'s bucket seat. The front windshield peeled away in shattered sheaths. Steeplejack leapt out of the Brinks truck with a moneybag in each fist, the rifle and knapsack crisscrossed at his shoulders. "We should have taped this shit!"

"FUCK YOU!" J.R. revved the engine. "FUCK ALL OF YOU!"

Vince Baldwin asked, "Even me?"

The rally wheels scorched the pavement as klaxons wailed. Steeplejack, with the moneybags, flung it all, himself included, into the backseat crying, "GO!"

"YOU FUCKING NAZI ASSHOLES ARE GONNA GET WHAT YOU PAID FOR!" J.R. floored it.

Ducking his head to glance up and left from the open window, with flashing lights approaching and sirens growing louder by the second, he could see that the parking lot was too complex to risk. They'd be fish in a barrel. He peeled right, swerving outward, powering into it, straightening the car and screaming down the mall by its length.

"NOT THIS WAY!" Crosby Shue roared. "THE EXACT OPPOSITE WAY!"

"YOU BUNCH OF FUCKING AMATEURS!" J.R. spat through his teeth. He sped down the open lane, passing one and then another column of escape. "I HATE YOU FUCKING ASSHOLES TILL THE DAY I DIE!"

"J.R., what are you doing?!" Steeplejack demanded.

"I'll show you what I can do!"

Crosby Shue leaned forward, "Hey kid! Who do you think yer talkin' to?"

"You don't know what you got when you fucked with J.R. Daddio! You fucking kill my friends, and then you expect me to hang out with you?"

"Cash Clarick," Crosby Shue countered, "Cash Clarick killed your friends—"

"Oh please, like you don't throw in with him!"

"Just stay with us," Steeplejack gripped the bucket seat from the back.

The Trans Am barreled past a gallery of mall shoppers stupefied in the crossing lane. Swirling police lights cascaded, perhaps a dozen in number, into the lot behind them.

"Shit," J.R. muttered. "You sound like chickens... cluck cluckin'... How about everybody shut the fuck up while I drive your sorry asses home! Fucking CLOWN CAR! How did I get the FUCKING CLOWN CAR! And look at poor Lou Gannon! Get him back there where he can lay down! That's Elsie's husband! What the fuck is wrong with you guys?"

J.R.'s hands crisscrossed at the wheel. The ticket booth into the underground parking area with the terrified ticket man inside flashed past them as the Trans Am smashed through the splintering gate. One great shard of black and yellow wood rattled noisily around inside the cab, then billowed out behind them, clattering off the ceiling as they plunged underground into the lot beneath the Libertyville Mall.

"I know exactly how this ends," Crosby Shue muttered through his ski mask.

"QUIT YER GUM FLAPPIN!" J.R. snapped, wheeling them sideways. He could hear, in his own voice, the maddening cadence of Cash Clarick's tutelage as the Trans Am roared beneath the low and loud and cavernous ceiling, the V8 growling and the rally wheels peeling through the fluorescent expanse between the occasional parked car or stray shopper fleeing in terror.

"GET HIM BACK THERE IN THE BACK SEAT!" J.R. repeated the order, spinning the wheel, dodging his way over networks of painted parking lines to the back of the mall. At last, they did as he commanded—*Because I'm right!* He told himself—and gently relocated Elsie Gannon's husband's corpse to the back seat, into the tender arms of Steeplejack and Crosby Shue. Meanwhile, J.R. chased the narrow horizon toward daylight. Sirens echoed but so far none had submerged after them. They were almost across.

"Did he do it? Is he gonna do it? Did he get us through it?" Crosby Shue cradled Lou Gannon's body.

"We're gonna find out," said Steeplejack.

Ahead of them a forklift loading a colossal appliance crate out of a garage bay halted in its pickup zone. The lane between the forklift and its customer at his flatbed was painted with yellow diagonals. J.R. blared the horn, even knowing, because he had heard it before, out of Elsie Gannon's husband's car, that it would bring forth Dixie. Everybody froze. The Trans Am blazed noisily through, up the tunnel and into the plentiful sunshine at the back of the mall. The V8 revved. J.R. gripped the wheel, making his plans.

"Did it work?" Crosby Shue demanded to know.

"Jesus, J.R.," Vince Baldwin muttered.

Sirens and lights wailed after them. J.R. slammed his foot down. The Trans Am screamed ahead, scorching black parallel lines onto the parking lot toward the exit. Inside the cab, the wind struck his face like it hadn't since his *Sky Ray* days. Now and then he swerved, burning rubber to avoid a random parking chock or parked car.

The back road out of the mall curled away and upward. J.R. took it. He could see in the mirror that he hadn't lost them or even come close. An access road lay ahead. They would have to funnel in after him.

"Turnpike!" Steeplejack advised.

"Fuck, like I don't know that! Say something useful or SHUT THE FUCK UP!"

The sirens wailed from all directions. Strobing blue and red lights could be seen above. J.R. jammed his foot to the floor. The rubber was pungent. Everyone grabbed for purchase against the G-forces. The Firebird tore up the ramp to the intersection where swirling purple lights arrived just in time to cut off their escape. A sign over the gas station read *Sheetz*. J.R. spun the steering wheel after it, bucked and wove the Pontiac over the humps of that rolling clearing, pitched Dutch-angled around the signpost. The police, having just arrived, began spinning their wheels in reverse. All except one, a lone, straggling interceptor barreling down, a Plymouth Fury, '74, two swirling strobe lights on top. J.R. had heard of them but never seen one in action. What a shame. The deranged Smokey was aiming engine first. J.R. yanked the e-brake, spun the wheel, scorched the tarmac, let the attacker commit past him the wrong way. The collision behind him, noisy and violent, involving multiple vehicles, brought a cathartic cheer from the besieged Nazis in their getaway car.

"IS THIS KID FOR REAL?!" Crosby Shue's cry carried a new tone of adulation.

"J.R. can drive," Vince testified through his ski mask. "I never said that boy couldn't drive."

"We're twenty miles from home," Steeplejack reminded them.

"No we're not. You're wrong about that, too. You're wrong about everything." J.R. aimed into the Dairy Queen parking lot.

"J.R., do you see that up ahead?" Crosby Shue leaned forward and pointed.

Burger King. He saw it. On the other side of Dairy Queen. He drove off-road, bucking over the landscaping and the cement curb, chirping on the pavement into the lot, peeling forward. The police cars in pursuit paused at that moment of truth, deciding whether to follow or go around. Ahead, Burger King was bordered by a row of miserable shrubs. J.R. plowed the Trans Am through it. A hippie in a jeans jacket with a milk shake stumbled backward to safety. J.R. braked as they approached the next divider up to the turnpike. The cops were closing in again, some from behind, others swinging around as the roadways allowed. J.R. climbed the curb and wheeled up through black soil onto the highway. The turnpike stretched before them at last. He spun the Trans Am on its smoking, squealing tires, swinging the chassis around, leveling out into sudden highway traffic.

Sirens and swirling lights were everywhere. Speed was the only way through. He slammed down his foot again. His witnesses grabbed around at the Trans Am's interior. The car tore down the highway.

"WELL FUCKING DONE!" Crosby Shue sounded.

"THAT'S FUCKING CHILD'S PLAY! CHILD'S PLAY!"

"All right," Steeplejack said, "You made your point, J.R. That's enough now."

"No, it isn't. Nothing is enough. Nothing is ever enough. You're the fuckers who taught me that. You think I'm your soldier? I'm not your soldier! I'm the thing you fucking idiots unleashed!"

"J.R."

The cops were relentless after them, multiple cars, awash in strobe lights.

Vince Baldwin pointed straight ahead, "J.R.! THAT TRUCK!"

J.R. wove, barreling forward, side to side, the V8 roaring through the open windshield, swelling his eardrums.

Amazingly a bird found its way into the open cockpit, enveloped in. J.R. maneuvered through the pair of eighteen-wheelers. The amazing, small, frantic, agile creature was ducking and swooping and darting around inside the violent vortex of energy hell bent on escape until BANG! it was disintegrated from the back seat, feathers floating like mementos around the windblown cab with the pistol shot ringing. The Trans Am roared out from in-between the two hurtling trucks.

"522!"

"Don't yell 522 at me!" J.R. pulled off the road with the tar sketching snakelike patterns into the weeds. Behind them the wailing police would hesitate, guaranteed. The Trans Am plunged downward into the dale and then drifted almost to a stop at the highway below where a random traveler cut them off, some local in his Rabbit.

Screaming purple police lights amassed behind them and above. J.R. pulled out onto the road, red taillights ahead just beyond the road sign. He accelerated, laced the Firebird along curve after curve into the hamlet, sweeping around the causeless Rabbit at the intersection. The road dipped. They braked into the next turn. The cops maintained relentless pursuit.

"WAIT A MINUTE! NO! WRONG WAY!" Crosby Shue cried.

Steeplejack's voice hovered at J.R.'s ear, "J.R.?"

"I know a better way."

He drove, turning left, then right, then left along the backroads he had learned from Cash Clarick, the lights and sirens diminishing then gaining with each relentless angle. He had veered off the map, but they were still after him into the rippling weeds. The Trans Am's chassis and cradle seemed to hover on its shocks over the terrain onto the abandoned highway. In that moment of communion, he pitied the car and loved it only more.

"J.R.," Crosby Shue ventured from the back seat. "Don't tell me you're headed for the abandoned turnpike."

"Listen to me. I'm sorry about before. I was excited. But I'm better now. Now that we escaped from that FUCKED UP SHITSHOW! So I'll tone it down. But you have to get used to something. And shut the fuck up about it. This ain't the way home from Manns Choice or Defiance. This is a different way home. Understand? From a different place. So quit yer damn hen peckin'."

"*Sheesh,*" was all Crosby Shue could say.

"The Old Man found him," Steeplejack said, as if that explained everything.

"I found that fuckin' Old Man, he didn't find me," J.R. argued. "I followed the radio one night and found him. So get that straight when you're talking about me."

"J.R. can drive, that's all I know," Vince Baldwin offered.

They entered into the first tunnel, blazing down the escapeway, purple strobe lights in pursuit, sirens wailing without relent. The tunnel seemed to withhold itself overlong, with no end in sight, the engine roaring in ear popping union with the wind, until finally they were out of it into the light, with the next stretch of weed-choked pavement roadblocked ahead.

"J.R.," Crosby Shue advised, "you know what's next, right?"

"Steeplejack's right," J.R. said. "We should have this on videotape."

He wheeled off road between the opening in the trees. But at this crucial moment, he miscalculated, sending his paroxysmal state of grace into jeopardy. The Trans Am's rally wheels splashed into the marshy pit that flanked the cow pasture. He revved the engine, jockeyed the stick, spun the tires, stuck in the mud.

"ARE YOU KIDDING ME?" Crosby Shue turned to watch for lights and sirens behind them.

"GET OUT AND PUSH!"

"GODDAMMIT, J.R.!"

"OH THAT'S JUST GREAT!"

236

"VINCE!" J.R. turned to face Vince Baldwin, "GET OUT AND PUSH! GET OUT AND PUSH, FUCKFACE, OR WE'RE ALL GONNA DIE! YOU CAN BE PISSED AT ME LATER—"

Vince was out the door, convinced.

"Is that how they drive in Erving?"

J.R. grabbed up the shotgun and wheeled on Steeplejack.

"Whoa, Jesus!" Crosby Shue whimpered.

Steeplejack stared down both barrels, wide eyed.

"I will murder you," J.R. promised him.

"J.R!" Vince Baldwin called from outside the car. "I'M PUSHING! HIT THE GAS!"

"WILL YOU STUPID ASSHOLES GET OUT THERE AND HELP HIM? THE COPS ARE COMING!"

Steeplejack backhanded Crosby Shue, "Let's go." He opened the car door and began sliding out, before pausing to say, "J.R., don't ever point that gun at me again." With that, he exited along with Crosby Shue, and they both hurried around to help Vince Baldwin push.

J.R. floored it, spun the wheels free of the mud. Lou Gannon's remains lay silent and bloody and without company across the back seat. Sirens and lights were wailing closer out of the abandoned tunnel after them. Steeplejack and Crosby Shue and Vince Baldwin chased the rolling Trans Am and jumped inside, slamming the doors. The car accelerated, plowing and fishtailing into the cow pasture. With no momentum, J.R. churned into the soft grasslands, gaining traction gradually, muscling ahead. The cows loomed. Behind them, police cars came screeching sideways. J.R. slalomed forward, avoiding the conveniently listless animals. In the rearview mirror, he could see the remaining hellbent cruisers following off road, stirring careless pandemonium among the beasts. Briefly he glimpsed all he cared to of those horrifying, purple, strobelit collisions.

Back through hedges onto the abandoned road, he peeled onward. But it wasn't over yet. One stubborn squad car remained in pursuit.

"We can't let him see our next move. One of you guys, make yourself useful."

"My turn," Steeplejack offered, shoving Lou Gannon's dead body out of his lap.

"Vince, pull your seat forward," J.R. commanded. Vince obeyed. Steeplejack took up the assault rifle and aimed himself backward out the window. A bullet rang past his ear. "MOTHERFUCKER!" he ducked back inside.

"You hit?" J.R. asked.

"What are you, my dad?" Steeplejack gathered himself. He then coiled his body out the window again, taking aim with the M16. Two more pistol shots rang and missed him. Then he blasted away, destroying the prowler's front tire, upending it on flapping rubber, kicking it over onto its hood and then tumbling twice, three times, into a slide, wheels-up through the weeds along the roadside. Steeplejack levered himself back inside the cab and said, "GOT HIM!"

"NOT GOOD ENOUGH!" J.R. yanked up the e-brake, spun the Trans Am 180 degrees around. "We can't let him see our next maneuver, or we're all burnt!" Leveling the car, he rolled up cautiously to the overturned cruiser.

The officer inside hung upside-down. Unmoving, except for his mouth.

Steeplejack spoke not a word as he climbed out of the Firebird's open window and advanced upon the wreckage. He paused only long enough to catch the victim's attention. Then, crouching, aiming his weapon through the shattered window, he finished the assassination.

In that moment, J.R. agonized yet again over his decision to allow Cash Clarick's return from the dead. The regret would torment him forever. He would choke it down eternally. He revved the engine, urging Steeplejack back into the car.

Steeplejack closed the door behind him. "See that, J.R.? There are winners and there are losers in life." He shoved away the carcass of Lou Gannon. "That's the only thing we've been trying to say, all along. There's no second place. Not in real life."

J.R. turned them back toward the Castle. "That's what I can do," he muttered, while he watched up at the open sky. He believed he could feel, if not quite touch, the clouds.

"Steeps, if I may," Crosby Shue interjected. "You did good, J.R. That was good. So hopefully now you understand what the problem is. This entire world is pitted against us. We're talking about the people who walk among us. Practically all of them. Trying to deny the simplest truth in the world."

"The funny thing is," Steeplejack interjected, leaning forward from the back seat, "they'll defend Darwin—*Survival of the Fittest*—all day long. To their dying breath. And then they'll lie down in their grave with it carved into their headstone. That's the funny thing."

"Meanwhile, turn out the lights," Crosby Shue added, "just for one night. Give 'em one good look at Darwin—"

"Losers have numbers, J.R. That's all they've got. But us? We've got a thousand and one ways to destroy a populace."

J.R. kept allowing their bullshit to spew. The next tunnel was approaching. He could feel their absolute certainty that he would drive right through it. He broke into a smile as he curled the steering wheel and turned off road, plunging around the guard rail and down the mountainside's narrow crevasse.

"Whoa, what?"

"What?"

"Steeps? What is this?"

"Relax."

"Relax?"

"What'd I say about your bullshit?" J.R. barreled down the craggy path toward the clearing that led through the woods to West Susquehannock and the Castle. "Steeplejack knows this way already, I'm guessing. He just doesn't want you guys to know it. So who you gonna trust now?"

"J.R.," Steeplejack warned, "You think you're being cool right now, but you're not."

"You guys," Crosby Shue changed the subject. "Lou Gannon is dead."

"Poor Elsie."

"And we have money."

"So we're not coming home empty handed, that's important."

"But what should we tell Duke Drummond," Crosby Shue wondered, "about J.R. calling us Nazi assholes?"

J.R. snorted. "There's fifty swastikas hanging up down there. You wanna tell me you guys aren't Nazis?"

"Yeah, but, J.R. It's the way you say it. It's your tone."

"Or assholes? We just robbed a Brinks truck. You wanna tell me we're not assholes?"

"You did good," Steeplejack was bent on de-escalation. "Please, J.R. You have to calm down. You were amazing. Everyone in this car is in agreement on that. Isn't that so, guys? Aren't we in agreement?"

They voiced their agreement.

"J.R. Daddio can drive," Vince Baldwin added, with authority.

"And he's a lunatic," Steeplejack added. "So hooray for us. That was a fucking folk song. Am I right?"

They all laughed, Crosby Shue, Vince Baldwin, even J.R., despite himself, as he steered the Firebird down the trail.

"So please," Steeplejack continued. "Just put it behind you, J.R. And drive us home. That's all we want. We just want to go home."

"Home?" J.R. heard it in his own voice, the uncertainty. "Home?"

"The Castle," Steeplejack told him. "Home is the Castle. Let's go back to the Castle."

# BOOK III. THE CASTLE

## 46. J.R. vs Dr. Arquimedes Arthur

*"J.R., the baby's coming!"*

He stood frozen, holding the phone to his ear. Out in the bay, the radio was blasting "Stone in Love."

"Elsie," he said. "you're sure, right? Tell me you're sure."

*"Yes, J.R., my... my water broke..."*

He could hear that she was short of breath, even as she tried to keep calm. He glanced over his shoulder at the jeans and boots of Mr. Adams sticking out from underneath the Beetle he was working on. In the next bay, J.R.'s transmission job sat abandoned. Rain was pelting the roof, hard. The radio was too loud, too crisp. He turned away from the noise, faced into the dark and cluttered office, and cradled the receiver to his ear. "OK, I'll be right there, Elsie. Elsie, are you OK?"

*"I..."* she exhaled, and then she groaned a little.

"Elsie?"

*"I'm OK, J.R., I'm just... having a baby..."*

"Jesus Christ!"

*"Don't blaspheme."*

He lowered his voice, "Hang tight, babe. I'll be right there."

*"OK, but don't—"*

"I'm sorry, babe. I won't blaspheme. Breathe out. Breathe out, remember? But breathe in, too. I'll be right there. Hang up now," he hung up the phone.

He paused for a moment, gazing into the dank garage where Mr. Adams lay at work beneath the V-dub. Mr. Adams was a nice guy, but J.R. felt an intense absence of patience with him, powered by a strange and powerful resentment like something tight in his chest. He found it audible in his voice too, though he wished it weren't. "Mr. Adams?"

"Who was that on the phone?"

"My girlfriend."

Adams pedaled his boot heels and emerged from under the car. "Oh," he smiled broadly, "is it time?"

He was just trying to be nice, supportive, whatever, with his squiggles of black hair matted against his forehead. But this wasn't his business.

"J.R.?"

"Yessir," J.R. turned to the slop sink, ran the water, began rubbing his hands together under it.

"Yes?" Mr. Adams pressed on. "Yes, you mean she's in labor?"

"Yes, yes. Yes, that's right, she's in labor," he worked his hands under the water.

"Well, get going, boy! You're going to be a daddy, son! Get out of here!"

J.R. grabbed the filthy bottle of *GoJo* and applied the soap. Adams Garage in Fillmore was kempt, in his opinion, not particularly well. Nothing like Daddio's Garage in Erving. There was no sunlight, even when sheaths of rain weren't pouring down outside. The garage was embedded, partially, into a mound-like rising of moist dirt and moss, giving the workshop a subterranean atmosphere, and everything within it, from walls to tools to ballpoint pens, a coating, real or imagined, of creeping alchemic sludge, part axle grease, part black mold. He soaped his hands thoroughly in the slop sink. He was getting paid nowhere near his worth, but it was all under the table, so he couldn't complain. And Mr. Adams was a good enough guy, generally speaking. And yet to masquerade as some kind of surrogate Dad at this moment. To have that kind of nerve. It was pathetic and unforgivable.

He turned off the water. Elsie needed him. He had to keep his head, had to be nice. He grabbed an extravagant wad of paper towels and turned around, drying his hands. "I'm really sorry to run out like this, Mr. Adams. I'll call you tomorrow, and let you know what's what."

"Don't be sorry! Go, go!" Adams was grinning like some proud papa. J.R. couldn't look at him another second. He turned and grabbed his jacket off the hat rack. "Good luck!" Adams called after him.

244

He was out the door. Rain pelted down. He bolted for the Nova.

Inside the car, soaking wet, he keyed the ignition. He flipped on the wipers, the headlights. Gripping the wheel, he curled out of the lot. The downpour hammered the roof. Thunder struck and trembled. He wanted to gun it, but he could barely see, leaning forward as the wipers did their furious best. A car came down toward him, bleating its horn, as if the conditions were his fault. He blared his horn in return, mashing his palm into it.

He and Elsie had stayed all over the place. Ashtabula. Akron. A motel room in Marietta. But rented rooms in the boonies proved both cheaper and more private.

Their current rental was plain, grey and rectangular, lying on its side like a fallen monolith along County Route 23. Its two floors of residence were stacked and connected, hinge-like, by a wooden staircase. J.R. had been repairing and bolstering this staircase in his spare time, as a favor and gesture of appreciation to his landlord, which also kept the landlord from coming around so often, and also gave J.R. access to the shed. He pulled into the muddy parking lot.

There was no time to gather himself. He was out of the car, slamming the door behind him. He splashed through the blistering onslaught to the dilapidated shed in back. His wet fingers wheeled through the padlock's combo.

He opened the door into the familiar, cluttered, spider-webbed delinquency. As rain pounded the roof, he reached for the coffee can nestled up amongst the junk. *Chock Full o' Nuts.* He peeled off the lid. Inside, two thousand bucks. It was his own money, not blood money. He pocketed it. Then he took it out, halved it, tucked one grand into his left pocket, one into his right.

The rain was a slashing and blinding reminder of how fate can hurtle a man from one vortex to the next. Even so, the storm might prove an advantage today. No E.R. would turn them out into this weather.

He was climbing the stairs toward the moment they had prepared for, together, through their strength, and loyalty, and love for each other. He burst in, "Elsie!"

"J.R.!" she lay on the bed, sweating, her knees pointed upward, her belly distended. He was ready, no matter the circumstance. He told himself again that he would deliver this

245

child himself, if need be. Approaching the bed, he opened his arms to her, and apologized, "I'm all wet."

"Oh..." she gestured ironically at the bedspread.

"Elsie, I will deliver that baby myself if I have to. You don't have to worry about anything. I am on your side, no matter what."

"I know, J.R. I know, but..."

"But let's get you to the hospital."

"Yes, agreed."

"That's been our plan," he reminded her.

"Yes," she agreed some more. "The hospital, let's go."

They had already prepared an overnight bag. He seized it from the chair. She was up and waddling. He grabbed her coat off the hook and huddled her under it, and then they were out the door and easing down the staircase under the cacophonous deluge. Moments later he was helping her into the Nova's backseat. He slammed her in, then careened around the car to slam himself into the driver's side. He tossed the bag onto the passenger seat, started the engine. At last they were bound for Marietta.

"It's OK, J.R., slow down... *Ow!*"

"What, what?" he reached a hand back for her. "Are you OK?"

"Hands on the wheel."

He snapped his hands back, ten and two.

"J.R."

"Yes, babe."

"J.R."

"Yes, babe, I'm listening."

"I've decided what to name her."

"Oh, good. But... Elsie..."

"No, J.R.," she said. "It's a girl, I know it."

"OK, all right. I know. You're right. So, her name... what will it be?"

"Wrigley."

"Wrigley? You mean...?"

"RRRRRRRRRGH!" she cried.

He gripped the wheel two-handed. His shoulders and forehead leaned forward past his white knuckles, as if to extend his sentience one crucial millimeter beyond the Nova's rain pummeled headlights as they turned and curled and occasionally raced between the snaking white highway lines.

Elsie was exhaling, all those exercises she had learned, while J.R. kept busy reminding himself and making sure, from what the doctors had said, that he understood his role, his responsibility. It was something the Old Man had said too. He would be Elsie's single-minded champion today.

"Wrigley!" he answered. "Wrigley! The ballpark! The Cubs!"

"Oh, J.R..." she might have been weeping.

"Plus the wriggling... of the baby... in your tummy," he concluded. "Wrigley! What a perfect name! I love you, Elsie! I really love you!"

"Oh J.R., I love you too."

"Let's deliver Wrigley!"

"Oh, J.R.!"

By the time the car was splashing around the corner into the emergency room parking lot, Elsie's contractions were regular. Like she said, the baby was coming. J.R. got out, went around, started to help her out of the back seat. At the same time, a pair of nurses came to assist.

"She's in labor!" he told them.

"Bring her through here!" one of them shouted over the din of pelting rain. "You go through that door, please, sir, to check her in!"

"J.R.!" Elsie cried. He gripped her wet hand, then released it. "It's OK, we made it!" he told her. "I'll be right back!"

Another nurse arrived with a wheelchair.

"J.R.!" she called out. He watched as they wheeled her inside. She sought for his gaze. She was scared. That was rational. Elsie was a mostly rational person, thankfully. He went in through the business office entrance, as advised. A snack machine greeted him in the vestibule that opened into the waiting room. On the other side of the door, Elsie could be heard, crying in pain. *It's just labor pain,* he told himself. *I'm a man today,* he told himself.

"Mister?" the lady receptionist was asking him. Another nurse idled behind her. They'd been talking to each other.

"She's not my wife," he told them. "I'd prefer not to give my name. It's not anybody's business."

"Well, OK, then. Nice to meet you too, sir."

"It's not personal or anything. Come on, jeez... Let's keep it professional. I'm not the one who's at work right now, am I?"

"Did you get the lady's name?"

"Did I...? Yes, I got her name. It's... she said her name is Elsie."

"OK, sir, we'll need her insurance."

"She doesn't have insurance."

"Did she tell you that?"

"Yes."

"OK, but sir, if she's signed up for the ADC, maybe..."

"She's not. She told me those exact words."

"She told you those exact words? Pardon me, sir, but who are you? Who would you be, sir, that is?"

"I would be the guy who delivers the WOMAN-WITH-CHILD through HELL-AND-HIGH-WATER to the EMERGENCY ROOM for the sacred ritual of CHILDBIRTH in the POURING RAIN! And by the way, Elsie wouldn't want me to swear... so sorry for the... you know... Listen, I'm not a conversationalist. Cash answers a lot of questions, doesn't it?"

Upon producing the thousand-dollar wad from his pocket, he had their proper attention. He would wait. They would realize the proposal was fair, and they would accept it. The receptionist said she'd be right back. Her accomplice went with her. "I just want everybody to be happy," he told them as they vacated the booth.

He waited only briefly inside the cramped, fluorescent-lit public lobby with its molded plastic chairs and dog-eared magazines. There was no reason to remain confined here.

He pushed through the door and easily found Elsie lying on a gurney in a semi-private alcove enclosed by drapes.

"J.R.!" she beamed, breathing in and out. She was beautiful. Her heavy hair was plastered in wet blonde sheets. Her big, dark, wide-set eyes witnessed him, the very best of him, from twin black pools of steady but panicked intelligence. Her big front teeth coexisted with an underbite that evoked a bunny rabbit and salamander both. Her skin was alight and aglow with passion and warmth. The attraction he felt was something beyond his circumstances, beyond hers or theirs together. It was also beyond beauty. He fell in love with her even more now, in an intense and wordless exchange.

He said, "Elsie, you're being so calm through this. I was ready to be calm for the both of us, but you... you're the one... you're the one who ultimately holds the fort down for both of us."

248

"Oh, J.R., I'm only calm because you're here."

"I'm just proud of you, is all."

"J.R."

"No, listen. I'm... I want you to know. I admire you so much. I want to... to *be* like you... in a way. You understand? We've both been through a lot. But me... I'm so... *angry*. And you... you're so... you're so far above any anger... You're so focused on what's right and what's good. The way you are able to get along with people. It's something... Something that everyone gets... I don't know... *disarmed* by. It's in your energy. It can't be contained. But me, I'm the exact opposite. Everyone just... grates on me. And I always feel like... and I mean *always*... I'm using the word *always* on purpose. I just feel like everything is always so obvious. But it's all just such... I don't know... useless knowledge."

"J.R.?"

"Don't interrupt me. I mean..." he looked at her distended belly, "unless you're crowning or something."

"No, go ahead, babe, I'm listening," she clasped his wet hand. Their intertwined fingers were slick with rain and sweat.

"I just..." he continued. "You're the strongest person, and the most moral person, and good person, I've ever met. I want you to know that. I can't tell you how much I admire you, and how much I feel like I've learned from you. And when I say *learn*... it's not like some... *lesson*... that some *person*... is trying to *teach me*. It's just something that I... that I want to learn..."

"Oh!... Oh!" she grimaced, leaned back and gripped his hand tighter. It was a muscle contraction. "RRRRRRH!" she moaned. Sweat poured out of her. The spasm wracked her distended belly. She moaned, "HRMMMMMMMMM!" in a kind of ripple effect that J.R. received as accumulating humbleness before something beyond his own reckoning and senses. He cradled Elsie as her pain abated. The hospital was taking a long time deciding whether or not to accept his thousand bucks. It might be time to get out of here.

Then he spotted, through the window to the waiting room, a hippie entering the lobby. The hippie was soaking wet, but not in need of medical care. He was just here for the snack machine. Observing this effrontery of callousness, J.R. looked around, left and right, to ensure the coast was clear, which it

249

was. Through the window of the reception room door, he could see the hippie pondering his candy bar choices. Backpacker might be a better word than hippie. Either way, a gaunt, wet, hairy sugar junkie had brought his filthy clothes and smelly butt into this hospital emergency room to spread his disease over this sacred place where children were being born.

"I'll be right back," J.R. released Elsie's slippery hand. He exited the module, drew the curtain behind him, then opened the door to the reception area and stood in the doorway. "What are you doing?" he asked the hippie backpacker.

"What, what?"

"I said what are you doing?"

"Getting a snack, man."

"Go to the gas station, *dirtbag,*" he let the door fall shut behind him, closing himself inside the waiting area with the backpacking hippie and his deposited change. "People come here," he tried to explain. "They come here to this emergency room. To fight for their *lives!* Or maybe *get born!* Can you understand that? Maybe you can... if you stop to think about it... before coming here for a fucking *Twix* bar! A fucking *Twix* bar? Look at you! You're no mountain man! Look up Teddy Roosevelt, you little twerp!"

The kid rose up with his purchased *Twix* bar, "Whoa. Chill out, Nazi boy."

"Whoa! Nazi *what?*" J.R. spat out a genuine laugh, almost suppressing it instinctively for no reason, but then remembering that he was free now to let loose laughter. "You dipshit," he laughed. "If you only knew how wrong you are—"

"Oh yeah? You wanna know what I see, *Mr. Marietta?*" the hippie taunted him.

"Yeah, let's hear it, *backpacker.*"

"I see a stressed-out *townie* who's never been *anywhere.*"

J.R. burst into deeper, more satisfying laughter, satisfying on a level he had never felt before, as the kid spoke his stupid, uninformed truth and retreated, backpack first, with his *Twix* bar firmly in hand. The hippie briefly paused to wave his free hand up and around at the low, cramped fluorescent ceiling, and say, "Take a look *beyond* your little cage here," and then bolted off, best he could, under his soggy backpack into the rain. J.R. called after him, "GOD ISN'T HUNGRY! HE HAS PLENTEOUSNESS, AND HE DESIRES TO GIVE!"

250

"Pretty close!" Elsie smiled warmly as he re-entered the triage room.

"You heard that?" he asked.

"Yes. C.S. Lewis."

"Elsie, I learned that from you. That's a perfect example of what I mean. I just... I wish I could be more like you."

"J.R., stop it. Just be you, babe. I need you to be you," she was gripping his hands again, both of them, her fists drenched and clammy. "I can see it," she was telling him. "I can see it shining through you, J.R."

"Thank you, Elsie."

"I love you, J.R."

"You love me?"

"Yes."

"I love you, Elsie. We are going to have this baby. We're going to have Wrigley, and raise her strong and true and good."

"Amen."

The nurses were back, storming through the double doors to retrieve their patient from the triage room. Sensing Elsie's calm, drawing inspiration and strength from it, he told them, "I'm coming in there with her. It's only right."

"We'll be just on the other side of these doors, sir," one nurse spoke through her mask.

"She's in good hands," the other advised.

J.R. lowered his head, shoved his hands into his pockets and stood there, a thousand dollars lighter. They wheeled Elsie away through the double doors, beyond his supervision. He tolerated this arrangement for seconds that he actually began to count. Then Elsie screamed, *"J.R.! NOOOOOOO, PLEEEEEASE!"*

He froze, understanding all at once the trap he had fallen into. Elsie's scream, the recognition it portended. It could mean only one thing. It was Edward on the other side of those doors.

Somehow, the Old Man had tracked them all this way, all this time, and had waited for this precise moment to pounce. Perhaps even to claim the newborn child. The nightmare would never end. J.R. had planned for, and prepared for, and paid for, a life lived in vain. The fear and futility was on top of him now, and not for the first time, but for the fifth, or tenth.

He was right where they wanted him, weaponless, and without options.

Save for one final act. To kill the Old Man, with his bare hands if need be. Then to get Elsie and the baby away to safety. He would get them away from civilization entirely, if necessary. One final act.

Violently he burst through the double doors.

Then he stood there, with no words to utter, as the doors swung shut behind him. It wasn't Edward.

Elsie lay on a gurney, wrestling weakly with a nurse, while the doctor backed away from both of them. J.R. felt an exquisite sense of relief, followed by disorienting panic. "Everybody calm down!" he heard the commanding tone of his own voice. "Everybody!"

Elsie's reached out, "J.R.!"

"Can I please talk to her? Please? Just let me talk to her..." he addressed them all, the doctor, the nurse, anyone on staff who would listen. He turned his attention to Else. "Elsie, please. The baby's coming."

"Wheel me back!" she pleaded. "Wheel me back, babe! Please! Please, tell them to wheel me back!"

"Just give me a minute with her," he begged them. "Please, in private."

The doctor looked angry and weary in equal measure, standing there with his photo-ID on his scrubs. He was a black man—perhaps the one scenario J.R. hadn't anticipated. The doctor's big, round eyes conveyed an impatient intelligence and professionalism that J.R. received as condescension, typical of so-called adults, but particularly unhelpful under circumstances like this.

Elsie was scared. He knew he had to keep his head for everybody, Wrigley included. He remembered to breathe, to focus on the moment at hand. Also to focus upon slowing his heart rate. This doctor had been through medical school. J.R. was just a mechanic. All that mattered was Wrigley's best in-terests. "She's a good person," he could hear himself pleading to the doctor. "A good person. Just scared, just scared..."

"Scared is dumb," the doctor said, "if your dumb ass is sacred of me."

"Whoa, whoa," J.R. looked at him all over again. The doctor was calm. He had said it calmly, but that's what made it so rude. It was like some kind of diagnosis.

"She's not dumb," he said. "She's the smartest person I've ever met. She's just scared."

He peered forward to identify the doctor by his nametag. ARQUIMEDES ARTHUR, MD, if it was to be believed. "If you're calling her dumb," he told the doctor, "then you're contradicting yourself."

"I'm way too busy for your pretzel mind, kid. She's my patient. Her, I can handle. You? You don't even belong here. Please wait outside."

"Please," J.R. countered. "Just... give her a break. She's a good person, is all I'm saying. If I didn't think you were... up to this... we wouldn't be having this conversation, would we? Did that ever occur to you?"

He waited, but Dr. Arquimedes Arthur didn't dignify his question.

"Please, just lay off for a second," J.R. continued. "Just let me talk to her. I'm trying to make things better, OK? Not worse. Better—" he was out of breath. *"Jesus,"* he muttered.

Knees up on the gurney, Elsie reached out her hand, "J.R., don't blaspheme."

J.R. nodded reassuringly, forced a smile. Dr. Arthur rolled his eyes. J.R. raised both empty palms. "I don't understand why she's afraid either, doc. Please just let me talk to her for one minute, please, in private."

Dr. Arthur shook his head but yielded.

"I'll go check on the bug bite guy," the attending nurse said. The doctor nodded, and they went their separate ways.

J.R. approached Elsie and embraced her. The emergency room seemed to slow down now. Electronic and hydraulic machinations thrummed vaguely harmonious with the maddeningly casual crisis-benumbed voices of the tireless medical personnel. But now another background noise began to realize itself as a sourceless clamor, until J.R. understood, as he held Elsie, that her entire body, through and through, was trembling in his arms at a kind of frequency. He felt it as something they shared, as something he almost owed her in return, for expressing it in herself so helplessly. The trembling was uncontrollable, no matter the consolation he gave her. "It's OK," he kept telling her, as she responded beyond language or reasoning to the contrary. Clinging, she looked up at him, into his eyes, begging him, "J.R., you said you'd deliver this baby yourself."

"Elsie, I meant it too," he met her gaze. "I meant it. If that's what it came to. But it didn't come to that, babe. We made it here. We made it. I mean, is that what you really want? To turn around and get back in the car and have me deliver the baby under a tree somewhere, in the rain? Think about Wrigley. Is that what's best for Wrigley? We made it, babe. For God's sake, for Wrigley's sake, let's have the baby here at the hospital."

"I know..." she wept.

"Plus we agreed to it, back at the place."

She nodded into his armpit, sweat drenched and shivering.

He held her. "It's OK, babe... Elsie... it's OK. I'm a mechanic. OK? Half an hour ago, I was under somebody's Toyota Celica. OK? We're at the hospital now, having a baby. Don't ask me to do *that*. That man is a doctor. Not me. Let's have this baby."

She laughed a little.

"OK?" he asked, tilting her chin up, gazing into her depthless, tearful eyes.

"OK," she agreed, quietly.

"Babe," he said. "It's *OK* to be afraid. But that doesn't mean you *have* to be afraid. Am I right?"

She nodded, sniffling, looking up at him, blinking her eyes. "You're right," she said, almost apologetic now. She was no longer trembling. She was going to be OK.

"Plus," he added, "If you think about the way the whites have treated you... *They're* the ones you should be afraid of, if anything—"

She stiffened. Suddenly, she was glaring at him.

"Whoa," he recoiled, "Bad joke, hun... sorry..." his defense came reflexively, but then he hated himself for lying. It wasn't a joke, especially not a bad one. It was actually a very good point. But this was Elsie's day. "I'm sorry, Elsie. Please, babe, I'm doing my best here."

"It's OK," she buried her damp forelocks into his shoulder. "I just don't need you to bring that stuff up right now, OK?"

"I understand," he said. "I'm sorry. I don't know what I'm saying, sometimes."

"J.R., it's OK. You, of all people, should understand." She exhaled, closed her eyes. "J.R., you're so good, and so right. I'm just so... there's so much happening right now."

"I know, babe, you're being really brave."

She released another sigh. "I'm... I'm safe, right. Right, J.R.? That's what I need to know. That's *all* I need to know. That I'm safe. That Wrigley is safe..."

"You're safe, Elsie. You're safe. And Wrigley's safe too. I'm right here."

She breathed out long and hard, cradled in his arms.

"OK, whew," he said. He looked around for Dr. Arthur, who was nowhere in sight. "I mean who cares if he's black, am I right?"

"*SHE!*" Elsie released herself again from his embrace. "She's a *SHE!* And she's not *BLACK!*"

"WHAT?" He gawked at her. She had it all wrong. "No! Not the *baby!*" he waved both his empty hands to shush her, leaning forward to clarify. "The *doctor!*"

She collapsed down onto the gurney.

"I'm sorry, babe, I'm sorry..."

"I don't think I'm pregnant anymore."

"Oh, come on, that's not funny," he found it dispiriting.

"You all done, Prince Charming?" asked the nurse in her facemask, arriving at last to wheel Elsie away.

"Hey," he protested vaguely.

"*She'll* be fine. *You* can take a break from solving problems."

A smug nurse behind a smug mask. Several biting responses swam up shark-like in his imagination, but he voiced none of them. It was Elsie's day. He raised his empty innocent palms for all to see.

"You're a good kid," the other nurse assured him through her mask. "Let us take it from here."

"We've got mental health practitioners on staff, too," Dr. Arthur advised, walking past, pivoting backward in mid-stride. "Sir," he added with an ironic smile.

J.R. could only let it all roll off his back. It wasn't his day.

The doctor maintained his effortless backward-facing stride. "They'll probably take cash, too. White ones. Black ones. Whichever. *Do No Harm.* That's our motto." He spun away.

While Elsie gave birth to Wrigley, J.R. idled in the waiting area. Low and fiendishly bright fluorescent lights hummed overhead. Nearby, the candy machine remained unmolested by hippies for hours on end. Emergencies came regularly. At one point, a man bought a *Payday,* having just escorted his fever-stricken wife in for treatment. After that, two ambulances arrived to disgorge three car crash victims. The rain had abated for a spell that left the floodlit blacktop visibly steaming. The spell ended, and J.R. could hear it scything down again.

A few more patients came and went, with loved ones in attendance, to restlessly occupy the strangely cold, bright and stale antechamber. Some exchanged friendly words, but J.R. kept to himself, with thoughts that spun from one trouble to another. The fact that he and Elsie had raised their profile considerably felt like trouble. And though the Old Man had not, in fact, reared his grizzled head for the occasion of Wrigley's birth, his long shadow remained no less a source of unease.

As for the law and its long arm, J.R.'s explanation for the fate of his no-longer-missing but officially-pronounced-dead travelling companions was still only half concocted. He had to get every nuance of that fictitious exculpatory timeline set in stone before asking Elsie to rehearse it with him, and memorize it, and deliver it, so to speak, on that day when they would at last rejoin society, a family. J.R., Elsie and Wrigley Daddio.

He was going to be raising a child now too. This was, in fact, his first priority, or it ought to be.

But thoughts of parenting led to thoughts of Jack Daddio, and Daddio's Garage. When the time finally came for J.R. to legally change his name, and marry Elsie, and adopt Wrigley, and return to Erving, a family man, he would ask his father, in good faith, for a job. Amazingly, that reconciliation was more impossible to imagine than everything else combined. And so, unseen, it loomed.

The carousel of concerns included Elsie also. The depth of her trauma had caught him off guard today. In fact, he could firmly conclude that he did not understand her. However, he did believe she would get over it, and stop being so racist. She would have to, if he was going to be showing her off as his wife, and mother of his children.

He would talk her through it, somehow. Not a conversation to look forward to. He had esteemed Elsie as mostly rational—remarkably rational, especially for a woman—even including her religious notions, which were actually more like rational fables, as J.R. understood them. Fables by which she lived admirably, so that they were nothing to complain about.

There was a movie of her, out there, circulating from Thailand to Times Square, it was said. And yet somehow it was the color of the doctor's skin that put her over the edge. So perhaps she wasn't so rational after all. The thought was worrisome. Steeplejack had woven his Nazi voodoo, or whatever it was, to bring Elsie under his control almost immediately upon the return home in the battered Trans Am with Lou Gannon's remains. As J.R. overheard and understood it, only one of the movies had been disseminated to the public. He had already vowed to track down any and every reel to the ends of the earth. At times, he even fantasized about leaving bodies in his wake as he went about this quest, with perhaps one witness left alive to warn the others of the doom they had courted.

As for J.R.'s own tape, it had changed hands several times before sliding from his own open hand into the bucket of acid Tyto cooked up.

## 47. The Auto Yard

They arrived at last, in the mud splattered, oil thirsty Firebird, sixty thousand dollars richer. J.R. steered them along the sheer grey crag down the mountainside's hidden stone- and branch-strewn trail. The felonious getaway car, its front windshield absent but for the tooth-like bloody shards of its remains, rocked and reeled. Inside, the four returning thieves bore the dead body of their fallen getaway man.

Crosby Shue kept at the CB, leaning into the mic from the back seat. "Panzer to Homeland, come in, over..."

The terrain leveled out into a clearing where the Castle loomed in plain sight. Up in the watchtower, a sentry could be seen alerting the others. At the corner posts, each watchman shouldered a rifle. A leftover birdfeather traced windblown curlicues. J.R. brushed it away.

*"Panzer, this is Homeland. Any company? Please advise."*

Shue depressed the button, "Negative, Homeland."

J.R. rolled the overwrought Trans Am past the croquet pitch that lay beneath the stronghold's ten-foot sheet metal front wall. The gates opened to reveal the Nazi flag hanging red-white-and-black over the Mess Hall's outer deck. Several armed Posse Umbellus stood waiting in the yard, Duke Drummond chief among them. J.R. spotted Elsie Gannon outside the chapel as he brought the car to a crawling stop for Buchanan at the gatehouse.

"Wow!" Buchanan sized up the car.

258

J.R. leaned out the window and discretely advised, "We lost Lou Gannon." He then gestured with his eyes into the back seat.

Buchanan seemed annoyed. "What?" He pointed them through the gate.

In J.R.'s estimation, the so-called gatehouse was a pretend gatehouse, a mere stall they had slapped together out of plywood and Plexiglas, fortified with mismatched sheaths of soldered and bolted scrap metal. Behind him, the so-called Castle's front doors swung shut, ten feet of corrugated steel. He drove on.

It became a parade, of sorts, as Lovejoy and Grossmark and Sandra Pride followed down from the Mess Hall deck, while Tyto in his greasy coveralls and prescription goggles approached from the auto yard. Little Bella Shue appeared in her pint-sized fatigues, eager to greet her father. All the while, Duke Drummond cast a long, curious, unhappy gander at J.R. behind the wheel of Lou Gannon's bullet-riddled 1977 Burt Reynolds Firebird. Onlookers were all peering inside the vehicle. Snapper, Harding and Brock Fowler had joined from the Mess Hall, Fowler bearing an M16. Then the Posse seemed almost to part, as they turned in sequence from the sight of Lou Gannon's remains to the sight of his widow advancing, crossing the yard in a straight line from the chapel. Elsie stopped in her tracks, looked them all over, not quizzical, but knowing.

Grossmark hadn't seen the corpse yet. Now he did. "Oh, crap," he lowered his head and touched his temple.

"Let's bring 'er this way," Tyto was directing the Trans Am into the auto yard's crowded pit. To J.R.'s mind, many of the Castle's network of slapdash structures and utilities were haughtily named, none more so than the so-called auto yard, which was a mud pit with scattered tools and a work bench, an engine hoist, a welding rig, a solvent tank, spare parts and spare tires, and a few parked cars where room was available. Weathered canvas stretched awning-like over the squalid workstation, above which J.R. could see that Skinner was manning the wall today, a corner perch they called the eastern turret, though it was nothing more than a wooden platform, roofed-over and crenelated with scrap metal.

Drummond barked an order, "Grossmark, get a blanket from the laundry!"

Snapper leapt to it instead. "I got it, boss!"

J.R. eased the Trans Am into the space between Drummond's Club Cab and Tyto's Road Runner. He keyed it off. The traumatized car shuddered in relief. Over his shoulder, he could see that Lovejoy had gone to Elsie Gannon, to put a sympathetic arm around her. Lovejoy already had a girlfriend, so J.R. didn't like to see this.

Duke Drummond was approaching, stalking, as he tended to, with his arms curled like a prizefighter. J.R. stepped out of the car to face the so-called music. He avoided eye contact. Drummond wasn't smart, but he was smart enough to be unpredictable, and his face bore a wounded, uneasy darkness that emanated perpetually from his brow, while his pale grey eyes bore some equally eternal solace, evoking a vicious and vengeful clockwork bent toward Utopia one grievance at a time.

Crosby Shue scooped up his daughter to greet her. "Daddy!" Bella cried, throwing her arms around her father's neck and embracing him in his bloody black fatigues. "Hey, baby!" he greeted her. Bella's pint-sized woodland camouflage was bloody now, too. "Eww," she said.

"It'll wash out," her father smiled.

"Lovejoy, hold your position!" Drummond called back over his shoulder. "Elsie," he added, "wait there just one minute, girl."

Most of the others had paused outside the auto yard to spectate, but Brock Fowler, brandishing his M16, had followed Drummond into the huddle.

"OK, let Daddy speak with Mr. Drummond now," Crosby Shue cradled Bella easily on his hip. J.R. remained outside of this inner circle, in the company of Vince Baldwin.

Drummond's tight, thin, dry mouth looked like the very epicenter of his resolve, even as the words he spoke were easy and ironic. "What was the score?"

"Sixty-K," Steeplejack answered, "give or take."

"What about the cops?" Brock Fowler asked.

"A trail of dead ones," Crosby Shue answered. "Not local to here. Or who knows? Maybe some of them were. Plus the Brinks guards."

"Dead ones, Daddy?"

Shue lowered his forehead affectionately to touch his daughter's own. "Dead as doornails, sweetheart. But there's always more *live* ones to worry about."

Bella recoiled and made a dramatically worried face, as she might respond playfully to a Halloween mask.

"Libertyville cops?" Drummond asked, musing, gazing elsewhere.

"*Judgment Day,*" Brock Fowler gripped his rifle two-handed, adding, "Count me in."

"It will be here soon," Drummond agreed.

"Think so, boss?"

Silence fell over the group as they listened attentively to their surroundings. An assault by law enforcement was imminent, or could be. Birds and insects sent loops and patterns around the Castle walls as if conspiring to distract them. No sirens could be heard.

Steeplejack finally spoke up, "Even if they come after us, boss, they're gonna be *one-thousand-percent sure* we went through that old tunnel up there. They'll never find us down here."

Drummond eyeballed J.R. and said, "That used to be so."

"Is Mr. Gannon a dead one, Daddy?"

Tyto stepped forward now, tilting his goggles and grease-smeared grin to Bella's inquisitive face, "I could take Bella to the mess for a salt rind."

"You want to go to the mess for some salt rinds, honey?"

"Yuk," she turned away from Tyto. Then she viciously rocked her father's neck. "Why is it called a *mess,* Daddy?"

Crosby Shue laughed a little, and a few others contributed nervous chuckles. Behind them all, the Mess Hall's façade displayed its silken, rippling swastika, red-white-and-black, its four sharp elbows encircling like compass points. "No one knows, baby," Crosby Shue told his daughter. "There's no way to even look it up."

J.R. winced, then eyeballed Crosby Shue all over again, as if for the first time, suppressing every urge to correct the man in front of his own daughter. It was times like these that he truly understood. Even without the murder and torture and racism and porn, the Posse Umbellus just wasn't right for him.

He could feel himself snapping out of the spell, having made it home alive from another inescapable deathtrap. Even though this was not his first awakening from some life-preserving jolt of adrenaline, it was perhaps the perception of the Castle as "home" that made the victory so distant and hollow. It seemed there was no outer concentric ring to this nightmare.

And so, Jack Daddio might never know what his son had accomplished. The incredible getaway run. He might never know J.R.'s pride, either, for not letting that gaggle of idiots get him killed.

Even so, his self-possession seemed to reach a kind of unsafe pinnacle, as Duke Drummond, from overtop the Firebird's roof, continued to study him suspiciously. That's when Snapper returned with a blanket from the laundry room. "Got the blanket, boss."

J.R. looked away from Drummond, told himself to keep keeping it together. He held out the car keys to Tyto. "I think the oil pan's cracked," he advised. "The radiator is not loving life, either. The tires... the tires should be enshrined some-where—"

"J.R.," Tyto accepted the keys and then flung them over his shoulder into the mud. "Get real. We're gonna incinerate this thing, and pull it apart bolt by bolt." Tyto's prescription goggles were perfectly still, his eyeballs magnified within.

"The kid's a hot shot," Grossmark smirked cynically.

"How'd this kid end up at the wheel?" Drummond wanted to know.

"Wow, what a wheelman, boss!" Crosby Shue testified, dramatically nodding his head.

"A prodigy," Steeplejack agreed.

Vince spoke up too, "He saved everybody's ass, boss."

"Not everybody," Drummond looked into the back seat at the dead man.

Snapper laid the blanket down outside the Trans Am's door. J.R. ignored the compliments and went to help with the body. He and Snapper carefully took up Lou Gannon by either armpit and slid his dead weight down from the back seat into the trampled mud. After quickly spreading a top blanket over the corpse, they gazed down reverentially at their work.

Others were free now to enter the yard and pay their respects. Elsie released herself from Lovejoy's listless paws and made her way toward her husband's shrouded body.

Drummond said, "I'll hear a full report, inside. 1700 hours." He glanced at his wristwatch, glanced at J.R. "You," he said. "Come here."

J.R. obeyed, approached Duke Drummond, who was shorter by an inch but more massive, and nigh aglow, in black fatigues, with violent intent. Behind him, Steeplejack had vectored across the mud pit toward Elsie Gannon where she came to stoop down and remove the careless shroud from her husband's murdered face. Steeplejack crouched behind the widow and let his fingertips whisper over her clavicles. Sheer muscle exhaustion seemed to grip J.R. It was not unlike the last time, except forearms first, turning to jelly. He looked around at himself, his own digits and limbs and ribs, confirming he had not been shot. His skinny forearms shook. His fingertips tingled. All the while, Drummond was whispering to him, nodding over at the grieving widow and her fallen husband. *"Look at that. But pain isn't power, son. It acts like power. But it isn't. It's the exact opposite of power. So don't forget it. Especially when it comes to her."*

J.R. nodded and watched Elsie, unsure what to say. Then he looked into the pale elsewhere of Duke Drummond's distant gaze.

"All right, get away from me," Drummond spared him.

J.R. retreated. The boss didn't like him, clearly. Neither did Grossmark. Or Skinner, necessarily, watching down from his eastern turret. Brock Fowler seemed almost fearful… in a violent way, not cowering. Armed and murderous Nazis in black fatigues surrounded him. He could feel himself trying to breathe, even remembering to breathe, though remembering wasn't enough.

Unprompted, Tyto pointed his thumb sideways and said, "This kid J.R. belongs in the auto yard, that's what I say."

Tyto's magnified eyes blinked, half-concealed by smudgy goggles. "I mean when he's not being the getaway driver," he added.

"J.R.'s a sick mechanic," Vince Baldwin vouched. "I never said he wasn't."

Skinner saluted J.R. from atop his sentry post. Possibly sincere, possibly sarcastic.

"That skinny twerp isn't working on *my* car!" Grossmark spat.

"Hey!" Steeplejack spoke up, "that kid paid his dues today! He saved our asses!"

"HEADS UP!" one of the Van Werts called down from the watchtower.

The Posse Umbellus sprang into action. Harding barked, "SNAPPER, ARMORY!" and the two of them bee-lined for the row of tin roofed sheds along the Castle's front wall. Drummond held his Desert Eagle unholstered and attuned windward, same as his visage. Sandra Pride stood primed, with just one of her two handy hunting knives unsheathed and gleaming silver steel.

Crosby Shue caught his daughter's attention, "Get inside and find Rose Archer, honey!"

Bella obeyed and ran.

"And don't come out until I tell you!"

Tyto had retrieved a shotgun from under the workbench. Steeplejack knelt in the pit with an arm around Elsie where she crouched. In that moment, watching Elsie continue to pray over her dead husband as everyone else answered the call to violence, J.R. perceived in her some beautiful and tremendous power that no one else could see. It was his privilege alone to witness it.

As the seconds mounted and nothing happened, Brock Fowler turned his attention to J.R., his jawbone tight, his black eyes wild with fear. He leveled the M16 two-handed, "Did you bring the law here, hot shot?"

J.R. raised his empty palms, knowing he may unwittingly have done exactly that.

That's when the Van Wert twin called down from the tower, "FALSE ALARM! IT'S JUST A BEAR!"

A collective sigh of relief came over them, notwithstanding Brock Fowler, who seemed annoyed by the good news. The others relaxed and holstered their weapons. Harding and Snapper, hauling ass from the armory, cradling guns and grenade belts in both arms, performed a comical about face.

"Wow!" Buchanan blurted from the gatehouse.

"PARTRIDGE, WHAT ARE YOU DOING?" Drummond called up to the southern turret. They all turned to witness Partridge poised and carefully aiming his rifle into the wilderness.

"SHOOTING THE BEAR!" came the answer.

Skinner hollered at Partridge from the eastern turret, possibly to spare his boss the indignity. "STAND THE FUCK DOWN! JESUS CHRIST!"

J.R. turned to Elsie. Her head remained bowed. Her heavy blonde curtains of hair concealed her face mid-prayer. Steeplejack hovered behind her. His clutching at her shoulder blades seemed to have no effect on her.

Sandra Pride had taken note of Steeplejack too. She jerked her thumb over her shoulder and told him, "Give her some privacy, you snake!"

Fowler scowled at this, looked to Duke Drummond for the cue to get mad.

Drummond just shook his head, closed his eyes. *Not worth it,* his gesture implied.

Sandra Pride relaxed. Steeplejack backed away from Elsie Gannon. At last they were all at ease. Conversation began among the ranks, while the sunlight collected orange and low in the mountainside's misty glade.

Within the Castle's ten-foot corrugated steel walls, the Posse Umbellus had constructed modular utilities and common rooms along duckboard gangways in the dirt, as a kind of parasitic matrix around the Mess Hall's central and foundational presence. The Mess Hall was not of this or any other Posse's construction, but rather a relic discovered by the Old Man along his travels. If the stories were true.

Here, so it went, Edward had found, looming, and topped by its watchtower, and all but inaccessible from civilization, where some previous hard-asses from some surpassingly more patient and artisanal era had constructed it out of the clearing, a great and noble lodge of stone and timber.

They would tell of how the Old Man had found it in his travels. And then, with Duke Drummond's help, he had delivered the wandering Caucasian tribe to its wooded sanctuary. Together, they had seized the clearing back from the forest, and erected their scrap metal fortress around their claim, and planted the seeds of civilization within its walls. They had even caulked up the word-carving DEITSCHEREI over the stone fireplace, before painting over it POSSE UMBELLUS, the medieval logotype bookended by twin swastikas.

The Mess Hall porch created a kind of stage beneath its silken Nazi backdrop, where occasional rock concerts were held, always featuring some band of high-energy maniacs from out of nowhere and bound for the same. Around the corner from the stage stood the humble but clean laundry room, and the well-worn, well-loved barracks, and so on. The showers. The latrine. Each slipshod annex focused only more prestige upon the superior architects that had come before. There was even a slipshod chapel, to which J.R. would retreat now and then, disdaining the iconography at first but coming to sympathize with it very sincerely in time, stooped within that phonebooth sized sanctum, with permission to think and breathe, and no swastikas or rattlesnakes, only Christ on the cross to keep tabs on him.

Atop the Mess Hall's firm and fortified roof, the watchtower aspired, manned by one of the Van Wert twins today. J.R. hadn't been up there yet, but soon would be, and soon would know what his imagination suspected from down in the yard. That it was sturdy and secure and safe up there.

Rose Archer emerged from the Mess Hall with the two kids scattering before her, Bella Shue dashing again for her father, while little Wallace, in sky-blue long johns, began the cautious descent of two porch steps. "It's Virginia, Mr. Drummond. She's come down with it again."

Drummond sighed and nodded, woefully.

"If you want, I'll take her," Rose Archer offered, though it was perfunctory. Everyone knew that Farrah was napping, and that Virginia's allergies had developed into a fever, and that Duke Drummond would take his own daughter to the emergency room. Drummond pointed at the stolen loot, then up toward the Mess Hall's second story, for his best and most trusted, like Brock Fowler and Crosby Shue, to haul inside and sit on. "I'll be back ASAP," he advised.

"What about Farrah?" Steeplejack asked.

"Be a man and wake her up."

"We don't tell no lies around here," Tyto observed, mysteriously, to no one in particular. Only J.R. seemed to hear it. He stared, and Tyto grinned back, eyes warped and overlarge behind grease smudged googles.

Evening was coming down when Duke Drummond rolled his green Club Cab out of the auto yard pit and up to the mouth of the gatehouse, with his daughter on the front seat beside him. Only now did the Old Man appear, seemingly out of nowhere, to approach the driver's side window, and point to J.R. in the auto yard. "This one's a true believer," he said.

266

Drummond peered back at J.R., suspicious, unhappy, before he faced forward and hit the gas, leaving a gritty dusk-lit hue in his wake.

The Old Man chuckled, winked at J.R. through the swirling orange veils of dirt. Then he walked out the front gate, leaving the Posse Umbellus to rule over themselves.

## 48. The Watchtower

The rec room was of quality build, an original annex to the Mess Hall, notwithstanding its drab nylon carpet, which the Nazis must have installed after moving in.

"Why don't you quit your crying, winner?" Shanahan told Partridge.

"Winner?"

"I just mean that in general."

They were bantering over ping-pong while J.R. worked the triceps bar. J.R.'s arms and even his palms were sore from the car chase, but he was determined to work through the pain and reclaim the discipline of weightlifting. The rec room offered free weights, also a ping-pong table and a dart board, also a tape deck, which was blessedly silent at the moment. Also, some beer hawking pin-up girls to break up the familiar rebel iconography. Newly, someone had tacked up a black-felt wall poster, a coiled rattlesnake, hided thick and scaly and garish with the rebel Stars-and-Bars.

"I'm done," J.R. laid down his barbell.

"No one cares," Partridge hissed. "6-17," he told Shanahan.

"Hey, be nice," Shanahan corkscrewed an ace off the corner.

"FuckFace!" Partridge sprang after the amok ping-pong ball.

"FuckFace is Vince," J.R. told him.

"What?" Partridge vectored around in heavy boots.

"FuckFace is Vince?" J.R. repeated.

Shanahan, on the other side of the table, was curious too.

"FuckFace is Vince Baldwin," J.R. explained. "So Shanahan can't be FuckFace. It has to be a different insult."

"What is that? Trauma? From the Saw Mill? No one cares, you teenage twerp. Anyway, your name's Turkey Baster, if I heard right."

Shanahan burst out laughing, and J.R. turned immediately out the rec room door.

"Hey, J.R.," Shanahan called after him, "he's just breaking balls..."

No need to look back. No longer given to the heat of rage, J.R. tended to feel it freeze and stockpile like ice now.

Upon entering the Mess Hall, he caught sight of Cash Clarick's battle axe and war hammer, which Duke Drummond had mounted crisscrossed on the opposite wall, always seemingly farther away when the room was empty. The weapons hung to the right of the entrance, so that all who entered by those doors would see them first.

"I got something to cheer you up kid," Steeplejack said from above.

J.R. craned his attention up to the balcony where Steeplejack slouched over the railing.

"No, you don't."

"No, I do. I swear, J.R. I owe you... how many now?" he shook his head.

"None."

"Come upstairs. That's actually an order. But honestly, I don't mean it that way."

J.R. had devised a response for these circumstances. "Whatever you say."

He let the words signify an unspoken condition, even as he obediently ascended the sturdy staircase to the Mess Hall's mezzanine. To the credit of the Posse Umbellus, and unlike what they did with the rec room, they had not carpeted the floors and balconies and stairs of this mountain lodge with snot green nylon carpeting.

Steeplejack was hunched over, waiting, lingering outside the open door to his own quarters, or chambers, or studio, or whatever he called the operation that involved the famously heavy rotation of linens through the Castle's laundry room.

"Snapper screwed up," Steeplejack advised, "so you're assigned watchtower duty. That's the good news."

"What's the bad news?" J.R. asked.

"None whatsoever. The rest of the news is awesome. It's Elsie. Your woman. She's up there, waiting. What you did. For Lou. I was there. I told her about it. It got her attention."

J.R. shook his head. He couldn't express it in words, but he could see it. They were taking her away, not giving her away. All he could say was, "What?"

"J.R., there's no Betacam up there, I promise," Steeplejack was high on something. Coke, maybe. "How could I possibly look you in the eye and lie to you?" he asked, smirking, nodding.

J.R. said nothing. Words would only corner him further, he was sure of it.

"Look around, *mi amigo*," Steeplejack spread his hands wide, and even reached out with his open fingertips, as if to unfurl every crevasse of the Mess Hall's rustic grandeur from his belvedere of privilege. "The master's chamber across the way. The parlor. The conclave into the watchtower... or is it enclave? I forget the word. Anyway, the party is up here, my friend. That is my only point. Up here where the deer and the deer-antler chandelier play..."

Steeplejack pointed to the Mess Hall's elaborate and disused central light fixture, then vaguely back towards his own chambers, without pressing the matter. "You're one of us now, J.R., baby... *Es tuya... mi Cabaret, su Cabaret...* Got me? There's no camera up there, man. You have my word. OK? I mean, get yourself up there and look around for yourself. There's nowhere to even *hide* a camera. OK? Elsie is *waiting* for you, man. Go on up. Oh wait..." he fished a condom out of his pants pocket and tossed it.

J.R. caught it. *Ramses.*

"The only thing you have to remember, J.R., is one thing. You're on lookout duty, OK? It's *you*... on the hook... *not me.* So don't get too distracted. Got it? Have a good time, though. God knows, you've earned it. Just don't let some horde of marauding Jews in here either, to cut all our throats, while you're sneaking a peak at Betty Boop."

*Cocaine,* J.R. kept telling himself, although he knew nothing about cocaine. Also, Steeplejack seemed fairly relaxed, so it probably wasn't cocaine.

He could think up no response, no argument, no choice. He shoved and then pressed his hands into his pockets to conceal the intentions of his uncoiling and stiffening dick. "I'll need my 12-gauge," he said.

"What good is that gonna do ya up there?" Steeplejack smiled like a game show host.

J.R. tried imitating the way Reagan would inflect things, "Well... just give me a long gun, then."

"Just use what you're packing," Steeplejack laughed.

J.R. kept his hands in his pockets and followed, for the first time, the length of glossy cedar balustrade that sealed the upper story away from the first floor's majestic dining hall. His hard on was throbbing in his pants, but his fatigues were heavy canvas, and his hands in his pockets safeguarded him from walking pecker first into anything. He hunched past the sight of the Mess Hall's central deer antler chandelier, dusty and disused, leftover from the mysterious culture that had hung it there. The parlor door stood open too, upon the watchtower's open spire. The iron stairway spiraled upward. J.R. remembered to calm himself, but found it boring, for once—or boring at last. Excitement rose into his chest and throat.

The rest just happened, something to remember, or dwell upon, or count upon afterwards.

The twisting iron staircase led up to the watchtower's double doors, beyond which the sunlit and wide open bird's nest awaited.

Elsie lay reclined on the twin mattress beneath the sunny windowsill. Her gaze remained downward.

"Elsie."

"Hi, J.R."

"I'm supposed to keep watch up here."

"They told me."

He kept his hands in his pockets. "I guess... I guess maybe Snapper screwed up, so I'm replacing him."

"I won't bother you."

"No no. You're not bothering me. You're like... my favorite person here," he said it with a smile. "You're not bothering me."

She lowered her head, hid her face behind her hair.

"I mean that," he added. His love for Elsie had become a story as much as an emotion since then. But on that day, her spirit, her beauty, her company. It was all emotion, no story.

"I know," she told him.

"So, I'm gonna keep lookout," he told her. And then he made that very effort, turning away from her while stealing glimpses where she lay. The mattress was clean beneath the watchtower's circular battlement.

"Elsie, I just have to... you know... look around," he explained, and he turned, observing the evening-lit and butterfly-besieged woodlands beyond the Castle walls. He heard Elsie sigh. In his peripheral view, he could see her resting her chin thoughtfully on one cantilevered palm. The birds seemed to chirp differently up here, with a different insistence, like they were smart and proud both. J.R. could see everything. He saw the croquet match. He saw Lovejoy manning the eastern turret above the auto yard, while Tyto toiled at his workbench below. At the southern turret, Brock Fowler stood watch above the so-called barracks, which was just another shed of corrugated metal inside the so-called Castle's walls. Trauer was on shithouse duty above the shithouse, this turret commonly considered by the soldiers a quote-unquote design flaw. And at the northern turret, Chuck Zorn stood watch above the chapel, its minimal to nonexistent comings and goings. Meanwhile, the gatehouse was occupied by Rudy Van Wert, twin brother to Aesop, who was presently shouldering a sack of flour from the storehouse with Grant Archer at his side. In the clearing, just beyond the wall, the croquet match was well underway, featuring Duke Drummond and Skinner versus Sandra Pride and that asshole, Krabbe.

"I'm from Chicago," Elsie told J.R.

"I thought you said West Lewiston."

"Oh, you heard me say that?" she seemed pleased.

"Yeah," he said. "Yes. That time you sewed up Chuck Zorn... Chuck Zorn's arm. From his knife fight."

"Yes, that's right, I remember," she tilted her head. "You heard me right, J.R., that's where I'm from. West Lewiston, Illinois. I just tell people Chicago out of habit."

"I've never been to Chicago."

"Where are you from?"

"Erving, New York," he could hear his own voice, the wistfulness.

"You miss it?" she asked.

He shrugged. "I don't miss my father," he narrowed his eyes upon the horizon's complex and ragged edge.

"I don't miss West Lewiston," she said.

"Your mother... she's a nurse there?"

"She was. Lou got me out of there, after she died. Lou was fierce."

They fell quiet. The wind was calm with its whisperings.

J.R. could see and almost lament, from up here, how they could have formed a swastika's four pinwheeling right hooks out of their slapdash, effortful walkways below. Actually, they were halfway there by accident.

The croquet game in the clearing had fallen quiet. Duke Drummond was lining up a shot. He was taking his time, and J.R. found himself studying the treetops instead, the tip of orange they caught at this hour.

He spotted a doe, strolling slowly out of the forest, with a fawn trailing behind her. The fawn was limping, favoring its right front leg, doomed for the food chain.

At that moment, a cascade of blackbirds flocked noisily free of the tree line. Drummond balked in the pitch below. "GODDAMMIT!" His wayward ball went one way while his mallet spun off another. He drew his gleaming Desert Eagle, aimed it two-handed and fired four precision shots into the clouds. BANG! BANG! BANG! BANG! Shots that rang, even as he pointed up to Lovejoy in the eastern turret and barked, "DON'T LET THEM LEAVE!"

Lovejoy aimed at the birds with his long gun and BANG! dropped one. BANG! dropped another. At last, he was aiming uselessly after nothing. He lowered his head, lowered his rifle.

"GODDAMN BIRDS!" Drummond roared beneath the open sky.

Other soldiers had come hurtling into the yard from the barracks and the Mess Hall. Crosby Shue came stumbling out of the outhouse, pulling up his britches. Collectively, and rectangularly, the four Nazis at the four Castle turrets advised the scrambling militia personnel of the false alarm. "THE BOSS IS SHOOTING CROWS!" came the explanation. Quickly, the men offered groans of relief, then went back about their business, Crosby Shue not quite withstanding.

273

The Castle was well defended. J.R. resolved to give Elsie Gannon some actual attention, for a minute or two at least, though it was all he wanted to do for the rest of his life, even though this happenstance was all staged, which made it all so wrong. In any case, he turned away from the spectacle of the Posse Umbellus croquet match, and said, "I think these guys have it under control."

Elsie laughed a little.

"No, seriously," he argued. "That Lovejoy is a crack shot."

"Lovejoy is going to hell."

"Oh... yeah... well... I didn't mean to say he wasn't."

He waited for her to elaborate, then decided not to ask.

She followed up, "These people. They may think they fear God. But they sure don't fear Hell."

J.R. nodded, silent. The God thing would be a topic to avoid, he knew.

"Thank you for what you did for him," she said.

"Oh," he said. "For Lou?"

"That's how I know you're a good man," she said.

Thinking about what Elsie had been through, plus whatever else she might have been through, he felt an increasing anxiety about the sexual arrangement to it all. The mattress was not merely clean but apparently brand new, and two clean pillows had been left for their purposes. The watchtower was the Castle's highest vantage point, and thus, despite its 360-degree view of the walls and surrounding timberscape, a privacy beneath the windowsill prevailed from all but overflying airplanes, of which there were none.

He lowered himself beneath the waist-high rim, crouching out of sight. The chamber was not circular but ten sided. Not octagonal—the nomenclature escaped him. It was well built, of lacquered pine, and scattered with comforts beyond just the pillowed mattress and the spellbinding and grieving Elsie Gannon, whose eyes seemed to read him, maybe not his thoughts but his soul. There was a cubic refrigerator, a space heater, a lantern, and a transistor radio. He remembered the word now. Decagon. He rested his shoulders against the decagonal wall. There was something hooded and wounded and dark in Elsie Gannon's eyes that gave him the warmth he craved. "Were you at the Saw Mill?" he asked her.

"Yes."

274

Another silence followed. He had no idea how to initiate the prescribed sex.

"You mentioned your father before," she observed. "Don't you miss him?"

"I can't explain it," he said.

"Yes, you can."

He made an annoyed face, then quickly smiled to make up for it. "I can?" he asked, instead of getting mad. "How do you know I can? Anyway, what about you?" he asked.

"God is watching. Don't forget that, J.R. But I'll tell you something about me, I don't care."

"Great, OK, go ahead."

"No, I mean... after you go first," she said it playfully, which he didn't expect. It was her face. He loved her face. Her big dark intelligent eyes. Her square white teeth, the way they bit into her hungry lower lip. Her warm glow and benevolence framed by blonde hair so heavy and healthy it darkened to gold.

"It's nothing," he told her. "My father wanted me to... just... like... be the next version of him. Just a replacement. For after he was gone. Like I'm just some... *seed*. He even named me *Junior*. Although he called me *J.R.*, mostly. I have to give him credit for that. Except that he never bothered to correct the colossal mistake he made when I was born."

"What does he do?"

"He's a mechanic. Daddio's Garage in Erving, New York. That's him. I was practically raised in that place. I'm a better mechanic than Tyto, or anyone else in this so-called Castle. Although no offense to Tyto. He's not so bad, he's..."

Elsie frowned at the mention of Tyto.

"Never mind."

"What about your mother?" she asked him.

"What about her?"

"Was she hard on you or something?"

"No," he knew to say. He wasn't sure what to tell Elsie about his mother.

"Well?" she said.

"Well what?"

"I guess you held up your end of the bargain," she shrugged. Her fingers were interlaced where she rested her cheek.

"I did?"

"Yes, we don't have to talk about your mom."

"OK, well," he said, "she's just someone that's always trying to discipline you, instead of trying to teach you anything," he volunteered these observations. "At least my father taught me stuff. All my mother ever did was... I don't know... disapprove."

Elsie's face was warm-hearted. The way she took his words to heart enchanted him. When she spoke, her voice was dreamy and distant, spellbinding and spellbound both.

"The father builds his own business," she explained, "but no one appreciates it. Not even his own family. Even though it's all any woman should ever want or expect from a man. And all any community should ever expect from its leaders. The father stands up and delivers. Before God. His country. His community. His family. Even himself. But it's not good enough. Not for the wife. It all came at her expense, she wants you to know. And she spreads these ideas to her kids. And it becomes a plague across America."

He was staring at Elsie, dumbfounded.

"You should forgive your father, J.R., before it's too late. It's your mother. It's *Feminism* that spreads this poison."

"Whaaaaaa...?"

Crouching out of sight beneath the watchtower window-sill, his heart wasn't so much racing as filling up, alarmingly fast, with a newly discovered reservoir of power. He decided right then and there that he would marry this girl, with or without accomplishing his primary goal, which was to dissolve his own sex tape in a bucket of acid, and then escape from the Castle. He had met the perfect woman.

A vague panic set in. There was an expectation, from Steeplejack and the rest of them. It was too much to think about, and yet he knew he had to make every right move somehow in the exact right sequence.

He was also supposed to be keeping lookout, and he was delinquent from that explicitly imposed task.

First, he had to respond. It was too soon to propose marriage. He said, "Listen... I think I'm supposed to... have sex with you. But I don't know... I mean... What about Lou?"

"I know," she shook her head. Her face concealed itself behind her blonde drapes of hair.

"I mean..." he asked her, "Do you want me to have sex with you?"

"No," she shook her head, then raised her face to him, pulling her hair out of her eyes. Her sincerity broke his heart along a wide open spectrum of emotion.

"Oh," his voice fell away. "OK, so... I mean..."

Had he screwed up? He didn't know. But it wasn't good. He could at least make Drummond happy. "Excuse me," he told her. "Elsie, I promise, I'm not being rude. I better just... you know..." he pointed his index finger up at the windowsill.

*"Don't stand up,"* she whispered.

*"Really? OK,"* he loved her even more now, for keeping him down there with her, out of sight, in the privacy of the watchtower windowsill.

The expression she wore was one he had seen many times, but had never once believed, until now.

*"OK,"* he sought for the best response. *"But why not?"* he asked.

She gestured around at the decagonal confines, whispering, *"It's just..."*

He waited.

*"For starters,"* she said, *"I don't want to get pregnant."*

"Oh," J.R. course corrected. "Yes, right, that too..."

They were talking about two different things, he realized. He had to smarten up. He didn't know what to say now. But he knew enough to remain crouched down there with her, to make her happy, if he could. Steeplejack had provided a condom, and now would be the time to present it from his pocket, but he wouldn't. He remained out of sight with Elsie Gannon, listening to the birdsong and to the Posse Umbellus at work and leisure outside the tower.

An argument broke out among the men. Listening to it, Elsie mused, "They churn up indignation about every little thing around here." She didn't even have to whisper over the roiling in the yard below. "The world is just out to get them," she said out loud, "sure as the air they breathe. And they do it, constantly, for their false idol, while God watches. He watches them pretend everything is so bad all the time, which it isn't. It isn't any such thing."

"But it *is* bad!" J.R. blurted. He didn't want to contradict her. He loved her! But he had to say something. "They're..." he stopped himself.

"What?" she asked. "Go on, say it."

*"They're filming you, right?"* he whispered.

She shrugged, hid her face behind her falling hair. "I wake up each morning to a beautiful day," she said.

"You can't be serious."

She shrugged again, more elaborately, more assured. She parted her hair and looked him in the eyes.

Afterwards, he could not stop thinking about her. Out of all of them, ever, not just here at the Castle but back in the real world too, she was the smartest person he had ever met.

## 49. Tyto the Owl

Tyto tossed aside his oilrag and offered J.R. his grease blackened hand. Returning the grip, J.R. noted the hemi rocker heads on the workbench. "Is that from your car?"

"Nah," Tyto answered. "My car is all good. That's from the boss's."

Drummond's kept his Club Cab in the auto yard along with Tyto's pewter Road Runner and a third car, recently Lou Gannon's Firebird, now a vacancy to be filled. The waiting list was lined up outside along the Castle's northeast wall, with the Nova in that line. Out through that door, J.R. knew he would have access to his car, maybe not to drive away at last, but to repossess at least. He was now the Posse Umbellus' second mechanic.

"The boss wants it back under the hood before sundown," Tyto advised.

"Lapping in these valves manually?"

"Yep. And back under the hood. In one day."

"Oh."

"That's how I talked him into letting you work with me. No way I can do this job in one day. Or in any days, all by myself. I've never done this, dude. I've only ever seen it done."

J.R. chuckled a little.

Tyto grinned, "If you want to know the truth, I'm a C-tech, dude. Or B-minus, at best. But you. You're an Ace. That's your story, right?"

J.R. shrugged. "All right. Let's get to work."

"OK, where do we start? You're in charge."

"What?"

"I just told you. I've never done this before."

Skinner called down through the eastern turret's sun beaten tarp. "You've been promoted, Daddio!"

J.R. peered upward briefly, then back at Tyto, whose goggle-refracted eyeballs were unreadable. "Tyto? That name sounds like a Roman emperor or something."

"Tyto means Owl."

"Oh."

"Look at this here," Tyto pointed out the valve seats.

"It's sucking in oil."

*"Si, senor."*

"Who's speaking Spanish down there?" Skinner called from above.

Tyto craned his neck and grinned. "No one important, Skinner. Just your mother."

Skinner was silent for several seconds before responding, "Comedy... Comedy is the enemy of trust. You know that, right, Tyto?"

Tyto shook his head, annoyed. He called upward, "You're on look OUT duty, Skinner."

"I beg your pardon."

"Look OUT duty. Not look IN."

J.R. laughed along with their Nazi banter.

"Fucking lunatic," Tyto muttered.

Skinner heard him, "I heard that."

"You hear everything. You're like a creepy bat up there."

Later on, as their labors continued, J.R. asked Tyto, "New head gaskets, we got those?"

"They're in the back," Tyto advised. "The back of the Dodge."

J.R. went to get them. However, as he approached the Club Cab, the crisp *chick-chuck* of a bolt action froze him in his tracks. "Whoa!" he raised his hands.

"Whoa!" Tyto shouted. "Skinner! Relax! He's just going for head gaskets!"

"I know," Skinner called. "I can hear you boys just fine. And I trust you just fine, too. It's just I trust you a whole lot more when I'm holding THIS!"

"OK, but Skinner! He's doing what he's supposed to be doing!"

"Just as I am!"

Later that afternoon, as they were working under the hood, Tyto must have surmised that they were out of earshot, because he asked J.R., *"Are you into all this Nazi stuff?"*

Skinner's voice called down from the eastern turret, "I trust you're joking, Tyto!"

Tyto cringed beneath the truck's open hood. *Fuck!* he mouthed the word silently. His magnified eyes met J.R.'s gaze. He whispered, *"I'm a prisoner here too, dude!"* Then he called up to Skinner, "STOP BLOWIN' MY COVER, YOU MORON! YOU'RE MAKING A FOOL OUT OF BOTH OF US!"

It could all be a set-up, J.R. figured. But as far as he could tell, the only thing wrong with Tyto was his frequent use of the word *Dude*. And given the dearth of allies at the Castle, this shortcoming was forgivable.

"What's up, dudes?" Vince Baldwin joined them now.

"Jesus, Vince," J.R. moaned. "Can't I ever get away from you?"

Vince looked disappointed. "That was mean. Friends should be nice to each other."

"What the fuck, Vince? You get weirder and weirder, every day."

Vince offered a harmless smile. Tyto laughed nervously.

J.R. became briefly distracted then, as Rose Archer came chasing the two children Bella Shue and Wallace toward the edge of the auto yard pit. Each child scrambled headlong into the oncoming soldier Buchanan, who cried, "Hey!" and then "Hey!" with each impact at knee level. At the same time, J.R. spotted Elsie emerging from the Chapel and making her way toward the auto yard.

"Baldwin?" Skinner demanded from the turret overhead. "What are you doing?"

"It's my downtime," Vince complained up at him. "Why is everyone on my case?"

"Downtime?" Skinner taunted him. "What is this, nursery school?"

"NO, IT'S THE POSSE UMBELLUS, MOTHERFUCKER! I'M ON MY BREAK! FOR LIKE TWO SECONDS! JUST LET ME TALK TO MY FRIEND!"

"All right. Calm down, tough guy. This ain't New Jersey."

Vince brayed upward, "I'M FROM NEW YORK!"

"New York, New Jersey, same thing," Skinner concluded dismissively.

"Men, with their arguing and fighting," Elsie observed, arriving at the edge of the pit.

"And their fixing of cars," J.R. backhanded Tyto's shoulder. "Let's get this sucker put together before sundown." He winked at Elsie.

Tyto agreed, "That's a good point."

"It ain't me stopping you," Vince Baldwin whined. "I'm just trying to be friends."

Tyto ignored Vince, addressed Elsie instead, "Elsie, I'm not a fighter."

"That's for damn sure!" Skinner eavesdropped from his watchful turret. Vince Baldwin burst out laughing.

"I'm just a mechanic," Tyto continued, and he grinned, even as his goggles amplified his blinking, impassive sentience.

Elsie lowered her face. "Mr. Tyto, you answer to God, not to me."

Tyto shrugged. "Well, that's a slam dunk for me, then."

Vince laughed again.

Skinner hollered, "We don't need all these distractions! Vince! Elsie! Go find something to do!"

Vince complained, *"Aw!"*

J.R. smiled apologetically for Elsie. She returned his smile. He said, "Thanks for stopping by." She said, "See you around."

His self-restraint seemed to occupy the very space around her presence, like a plaster into which her beauty kept impressing itself. It was her jawline, her underbite, her Bugs Bunny teeth, her dark eyes cloaked behind sheaves of bell-shaped blonde hair. But more than that, it was her presence. A force that seemed to contain more reality than the backdrop of her imprisonment. He tried to comprehend the power in her beauty, but she'd been ordered to leave, and so was gone now. Probably for the best, because it was time to hustle, and get the engine back into the truck.

"Tyto, eyes on the prize," he said.

"My eyes are on everything," Tyto responded, peering around.

"That's my point. Eyes on the prize."

"Right," Tyto laughed.

"You think I'm lucky?"

Tyto was taken aback. He thought about it for a moment. "A little bit," he grinned.

J.R. laughed. They both did. But J.R. didn't want to hear from Skinner again. "Eyes on the prize," he said. "Let's do this."

They went back to work, and stayed at it, steadily, until much later, beneath sundown's last orange spillage of light, finally bolting the engine in.

## 50. Lawn Billiards

It was Tyto whispering, *"Wake up. You've been summoned by Duke Drummond."*

"What?" J.R. awoke from a dream that was immediately out of reach.

Scotty and Melissa were alive again, as they should be. The rest was too abstract, too impossible to retrieve.

"The boss wants you on the croquet pitch."

"Tyto, am I dreaming? Or am I awake?"

"Doesn't matter. Get up. That's all that matters."

"Both of you disposable assholes shut the fuck up!" Krabbe was snarling from another cot. A couple of other sleeping soldiers harrumphed along.

The barracks held two rows of six cots, plus a thirteenth at the end. J.R. sat up from his own. Compared to the Saw Mill, he got plenty of sleep here. But it wasn't enough, not today. Scotty and Melissa had found him in his dreams, and he wanted to go back to them.

Instead, he was awake, on his feet, following Tyto out the barracks door. It was midday, in midsummer, under a perfect blue sky. To waste this day on croquet was a shame. Even more so than wasting it on sleep.

He associated croquet with picnics and other such benign gatherings, and deemed it inferior to Frisbee, badminton, horseshoes, beanbags, lawn darts, bocce, shuffleboard, and pretty much any other asinine, arbitrary pastime. It was strange enough that his violent captors had made such a ritual out of it. But forcing him to participate was downright annoying.

Elsie Gannon had tried to explain the croquet culture the other day, during an impromptu stroll, after a chance encounter among the adjoining nexuses of Castle utilities and amenities.

J.R. was leaving the rec room as she was exiting the laundry room. Their eyes met across the wooden duckways embedded in the yard. Elsie was cradling a basket of linens. J.R. said, "Let me grab that for you," and crossed the boot trodden lawn to relieve her of the weight.

"Thank you, J.R. You're a gentleman."

He almost argued about the gentleman thing. But there was no upside to it. He simply offered a smile.

He walked beside her, bearing her linen basket as they approached the barracks door. The corrugated steel shanty awaited them, braced beneath the junkyard wall abutting the storehouse and armory.

"Pretty nice day," he said stupidly.

"See," she said playfully, "I told you it could be a nice day."

He followed her into the darkened barracks. Maybe a half dozen soldiers were chasing shuteye in there, snoring, honking and whistling in the dark. It was Shanahan, splayed out, deeply unconscious, making most of the noise. J.R. also identified Lovejoy, who seemed to yearn for something beyond language from his body curled up on the cot's rectangular surface.

Elsie made up one cot and then another, with J.R. helping her, the two of them efficient and quiet and cooperative in the dark. He made note of her professionalism. At one point, as they both reached for the same pillowcase, his hand brushed over hers, and he whispered, *"Sorry."*

She said nothing, lowered her eyes in the dark, even as the sleeping Nazi Krabbe hissed, *"SHHHH!"*

In short time, they were out of the barracks, back in the daylight, strolling along the plankways that ran in straight lines along the Castle's southwestern wall. Avoiding the outhouses beneath the western turret, they angled past the showers around the Mess Hall past the kitchen where feasts for two dozen hungry mouths routinely got prepared. "Gosh, look at all these," she spoke with a note of sorrow for the line of deer carcasses and smaller game that hung in dubious ceremony along the pathway toward the chapel.

He was thinking it would be good to get out of here with her, so they could go for a walk and have a normal conversation in the real world. Even so, he understood that their harmless small talk was made only more intimate, only more exciting, by the very surveillance he resented.

She stopped, having arrived, as if purified by gravity, at the chapel door. She invited him in, and he accepted.

Once inside that cramped wooden shed, she knelt. He knelt beside her. Side-by-side, they were not quite touching, although he could feel the warmth from the back of her hand against the cool back of his. They spoke no words, down on their knees, out of sight from the others. He found himself breathing easily, the way he preferred to.

Then Brock Fowler flung the door open. "GOTCHA!"

They looked back at him. Fowler stood visibly disappointed and yet unapologetic, and in no way embarrassed. He left the chapel door standing open and skulked off in his heavy boots.

J.R. and Elsie then abandoned the chamber's shattered peace.

As they proceeded in mutual silence toward the auto yard, he figured he ought to think of something to say. He asked her, "What's with the croquet around here?"

She explained to him that no one could beat Duke Drummond at croquet. The story went that Drummond had found the old croquet set upon arriving at the Castle. He had played croquet as a child, in his grandmother's backyard, and had demonstrated an aptitude even then, or so his Grammy had said.

"And his Grammy was no liar," Elsie commented with a whimsical raised eyebrow, although it turned out she wasn't kidding. She went on to explain that to this day Duke Drummond has only ever vindicated his Grammy, dragging every last Posse Umbellus soldier, stalwart, rookie, upstart, wannabe, proven killer and salty dog out on the pitch to prove it, with mallets.

"Really?" J.R. responded. And then fatefully, he added, "Not me, yet."

286

That was a few days ago. Now here he was, getting summoned out to the croquet pitch. *Summoned by Drummond,* as Tyto had put it.

He followed Tyto's lead, stepping down from the walkway onto the well-worn path that bypassed the laundry room through the dirt and grass trackways alongside the armory and storehouse's shanty-like double appendix.

"GOOD LUCK OUT THERE, BOYS!" Chuck Zorn called down from the southern turret.

At the gatehouse, Trauer bid them, soberly, and without a trace of sarcasm, nor a pinprick of light, "Good luck."

A collection of participants and spectators had gathered upon the well-manicured quarter of gamescape that lay beyond the Castle walls. To J.R.'s disappointment, Elsie was not among them, although Vince Baldwin was there like some ironic consolation prize. Snapper was present too, along with the Van Wert twins, Aesop and Rudolph, in their jackets and ties. The doubles match featured Duke Drummond and Sandra Pride versus Grossmark and Buchanan. The Pennsylvania mountainside offered a natural backdrop from one sideline. The Nazi fortress loomed behind the other, with Chuck Zorn and Harding watching from their turrets, and Crosby Shue hovering high up in the watchtower, half-concealed in shadow.

As Drummond strode in black fatigues and boots upon the wicket field, the mallet in his hand took on a lethal aspect. "You know," he said, "the bereaved widow isn't here, so I'm going to assume I can speak candidly on this subject matter without anyone breaking down in tears..."

He gazed downward and executed a few practice strokes.

*"You guys..."* he continued, raising his head, addressing J.R. and Vince. "You two guys, not Lou Gannon. *You* were supposed to be the... you know... cannon fodder."

Nervous snickers arose from the onlookers. Snapper seemed a bit awestruck by the boss's candor. Others, like Sandra Pride and the Van Wert twins, maintained quiet, vigilant faces.

Drummond shook his head, allowing them all to see his amused expression. Then, still addressing J.R. and Vince, he said, "But Lou Gannon is gone. And now I'm stuck with you two heroes. So, OK, then. Time you did as Romans do."

Vince Baldwin looked to J.R. for assistance.

"Don't look at your friend," Drummond snapped. "I'm talking directly to you."

"Yessir," Vince obeyed.

Along with Drummond, the other three contestants stood waiting in tableau beneath the vast mountainside, clutching their colored mallets. Here among these militant bank robbers, J.R. had somehow encountered croquet enthusiasts, to strike sporting poses in fatigues and combat boots, brandishing hickory hammers. It occurred to him that he should pay attention to where they stashed the sports equipment. In a pinch, a croquet mallet would make for a plausible melee weapon.

"Croquet is just a game," Drummond continued. "Not a sport. A game. Like chess. Either of you guys know the difference? The difference between a sport and a game?"

J.R. waited. He knew the difference. He just couldn't put it into words.

"Well, there's no risk," Drummond answered himself. "Everything we do, everything we don't do, everything we fail to do, carries a risk. Everything except for games. Like croquet."

Vince Baldwin chuckled a bit, with his mouth hanging open.

Drummond smiled. "You may think I'm saying that as an insult to the game of croquet, but I'm not. I'm saying it as the ultimate virtue. It's how and why a game can say so much about us."

*What a bunch of bullshit,* J.R. concluded. He had to say something. He said, "What about the physics and mathematics?"

"Oh, I'm about to show you those."

"I would prefer a lesson on those."

"You'll get a sermon on those."

"OK, I get you," he backed off.

"Sounds to me like you want to play."

"I'll hit the ball with the hammer, sure. Doesn't mean I want to."

Drummond gripped the black-stripped mallet by its handle. "I'm so glad to have your blessing."

Crosby Shue bellowed down from the watchtower, "HERE COMES SOMETHIN', BOSS!"

"I GOT HIM!" Chuck Zorn leveled his rifle from his own turret.

"I SEEN IT AND HEARD IT TOO!" another voice cried.

"LOCKED AND LOADED!" Harding called out with conviction that reverberated down the mountainside.

"It's just Partridge," Drummond shook his head, and began knocking his croquet mallet against the side of his boot.

He was right. J.R. knew it by the sound of the engine. Partridge's Z28 lurched into the clearing, while onlookers nodded along, pleased with the boss's divination. The blue Chevy wheeled past the field of wickets to park in the row that stretched along the Castle's northeast wall.

Duke Drummond turned away now, to face down the artful croquet shot at hand.

His audience watched, rapt.

Crouching over the lawn ball, lining up his attack, letting the pendulum swing between his boots, while no one dared to speak, he struck a shot that cracked over a cluster of colored balls to hit the ground and billiard off the red one through the desired wicket.

"Not bad at all, boss," Sandra Pride admitted.

"Damn," Buchanan added.

Partridge was approaching from the parking lot with a newspaper under his arm. In one hand he gripped a Styrofoam cup. With the other he raised in a lazy Nazi salute.

Drummond stood waiting amidst his croquet- and fascism-themed gallery of followers. "You know," he told them, "Partridge ends up in town more than any single one of us. He gets the paper every single day."

"Got your paper, boss!" Partridge held up today's edition of the *West Susquehannock Dispatch* as he arrived at the pitch. "Look at that headline," he said. "Our boy Snapper made the front page." He pointed above the fold, grinning.

Drummond drew his Desert Eagle.

"Whoa!" Partridge dropped the paper and coffee cup, raised his empty hands. "You're not gonna shoot the old messenger, are ya, boss?"

The silver pistol gleamed. "Maybe you linger a little too long in town."

"What? Whoa! Boss, you're scaring me! All's I do is go pick up the paper in the morning and bring it back—"

"All's you do."

"I'm NOT going out like this! I've been nothing but loyal to the end!"

"Not what Farrah tells me. You idiots think she's not paying attention? Do any of you fucking idiots *actually think* Farrah is not paying attention?"

They all began frantically shaking their heads.

"She followed you last night, Partridge. You fucking *mouse* of a human being! She saw you stick your little squirming snout where it didn't belong. So now, we're gonna be making some changes around here."

Partridge spun and fled top speed toward the forest line. Duke aimed his gleaming pistol two handed. J.R. saw the silver wicket in the grass. Partridge didn't, and fell forward, rolling, grasping his ankle, spewing profanity. Duke watched, annoyed. Partridge made to rise and limp off, hobbled. It was useless. Something was busted. He fell to his knees, sobbed and spat a verse of Pig Latin or Pidgin English into the void. Drummond shot him dead.

"Whoa!" Buchanan said.

"Uggh!" said Grossmark.

"Suck it up!" Duke Drummond commanded. "Who's on shovel duty? Grossmark?"

Grossmark pointed at J.R. and Vince. "These two."

"Sounds about right," Drummond allowed himself a snicker. "But we have one other order of business to address first." He holstered his sidearm. "Partridge tried to steal from us, so that's a death sentence. Everyone is in agreement on that, I can safely assume?"

They murmured in eager unison.

"But then there's just stupid shit," Drummond picked the newspaper up off the ground, "like Snapper here."

"Oh shit," Snapper said.

"What the fuck are you doing on the cover of the *West Susquehannock Dispatch?*"

"It was just some *Photographer on the Streets* thing. Interviewing people about how their summer is shaping up."

"I can see that."

"They didn't tell me it was for the cover... man... when they stopped me on the street. Please don't kill me, boss. I'm so into this here cause. Just let me go. Just let me do my thing. Just let me go out there and kill ten liberals for you. Please. Ten, guaranteed. I will bring you back their actual scalps. And then, if you still want to kill me after that, you can go ahead and kill me. I'll even help."

"I just said two seconds ago it's not a death sentence, Snapper, get it together."

"OK, will do, pronto."

Drummond raised the croquet mallet and bopped it gently against Snapper's forehead. Snapper laughed. Drummond barked, "Ace and Rudy!"

The Van Wert twins stepped forward.

"See this byline? Curtis Lemonhall. You go look into this prick tomorrow."

The Van Wert twins shared a smile. Aesop spoke for the both of them, "You got it, boss."

"As for tonight," Drummond explained to everyone present, "dinner in the Mess Hall is mandatory. I want all five lookout towers emptied out. I want all hands on deck."

## 51. The Feast

The war hammer and battle axe hung in symmetry like headless crossbones at the Mess Hall entrance, greeting all who entered through the double doors off the front porch. Most of the Posse Umbellus came filing in from that direction, although a few stragglers emerged from within. Notably, Steeplejack the pornographer was arriving in languorous descent from the balcony, escorting a pair of casually composed newcomers of the female persuasion. Also, beneath that same staircase, Grossmark and Trauer made their entrance from the rec room doorway, each discarding a ping-pong paddle. Krabbe was stationed behind the bar setting up pitchers of beer and mugs, while a collection of bottles glistened behind him. Rum, whiskey, vodka, gin. The Mess Hall was abuzz, as various parties at varying speeds, proximities and efficiencies remained unseated, holding conversations that swirled in eager energy-packed escalation.

On most nights, no more than two picnic tables were in need to serve dinner. However, for this occasion a third had been dragged in from the perimeter. Oblong, with attendant oblong benches, each picnic table occupied its triangular equidistance beneath the grand circumference of the Mess Hall's centrally hanging deer-antler chandelier.

Serving ladies Rose Archer, Sandra Pride and Elsie Gannon rotated in and out of the kitchen. They had already set the tables with dinner plates, white napkins, and clean silverware. Now they had returned with trays of carved venison and steaming casserole bowls to lay down in tantalizing aromatic rows. White starch, green mush, orange sludge, yellow pudding.

The child, Bella Shue, was running seemingly objectiveless among and around the collection of adults. Little Wallace spun his own toddling frame in blissful circles until he stopped, dizzy, and collapsed onto his rump. J.R. still didn't know whose kid Wallace was, although he wasn't Rose Archer's kid. She had made that clear, repeatedly, in noisy protest and pursuit of the child every day since J.R.'s arrival.

It was time to eat, time to occupy the triad of picnic tables with facing rectangular rows of Nazi butts. J.R. took a seat with the likes of Tyto and Grant Archer, choosing that company easily from his options. He eyeballed the serving trays and serving bowls. The vegetables were out of cans, as always. As per Duke Drummond's insistence, gardening was forbidden at the Castle.

Someone, an unseen shadow, lowered a needle onto a vinyl record. Crackles and pops sounded from the stereo's loudspeakers, and then brass horns began to rise, massive and bright and sonorous, as if from a musical realm compounding sound and light into one singular power. J.R. wondered briefly what, or who, the music was, even though he didn't want to distract himself with frivolities.

Skinner, Chuck Zorn, Brock Fowler, and Lovejoy—that whole crowd occupied one table to its capacity. The other table was managerial, with Farrah making an appearance tonight, vaguely corralling the eternally fussing baby Virginia in and around her lap. Crosby Shue had seated himself at that same power table, as had Steeplejack, in his own time, with his anonymous, half-bewildered half-sedated VIPs taking their seats at his either side. Duke Drummond remained standing, hovering in Farrah's vicinity. His unattended place setting— J.R. realized this curiously—traced a perfectly straight line to the vertex of the picnic tables' triangular arrangement.

As Drummond pumped his fist along with the turntable's orchestral percussion, J.R. endured a brief reminder of Cash Clarick's Saw Mill and its deathly opera soundtrack. He resolved even further to keep a low profile tonight. Duke Drummond ruled his dominion by sheer force of personality, in a way that his voice, his face, his figure, and his movements, served always to affirm. Even the Old Man himself sat deferential, in waiting, observing the busy banquet hall through his yellow, glistening eyeballs.

The serving ladies laid down the finishing touches. Krabbe had enlisted Shanahan to distribute the beer pitchers on teetering platters. The music got louder, even as the sense grew, among the assembled, that Duke Drummond would begin his speech any moment now.

The Castle's very ramparts had been emptied for this occasion, and so, under this rarest of circumstances, J.R. thought to count them all to the last head. Partridge was excluded, of course, having been buried earlier, with Vince's assistance, in an unmarked plot, at the same gravesite where Lou Gannon, Cash Clarick, Melissa Victoria, and Scotty Pomeroy lay. Not to mention Charlie the deli man, and the other liquefied Flintlock mechanic. The dead were inventoried, but more than that etched in J.R.'s memory. For the living, an inventory would suffice.

Farrah, at the power table, wore a gap-toothed smile that seemed to reveal, always, some gleeful but lightless and bitter spectrum of lethality. Her amusement with others, for their petty op- and co-operations, held no flickering candle to her own self delight, as every action, every movement, and every facial expression came affected with a fatalistic gravity that her humanity appeared only occasionally to express. Like an apparition, and only for the least fascinating of instinctive physical tasks, such as keeping her own squirming daughter within the vicinity of her own lap.

Even as J.R. watched her dump the child onto the bench, and then watched her pause to drag on her cigarette, he understood, for once, or maybe at last, that Farrah's piano key grin had an animalistic appeal, and that her blue-eyed blazing eyes were vacuous beyond the so-called company and so-called walls of everybody else's pretension. He could understand her charm, from a certain perspective. For instance, as witness to Steeplejack's agony. *I'm not in love with her,* he could assure himself. *It's just that I understand why HE'S is in love with her.*

"DINNER IS OFFICIALLY SERVED!" Rose Archer announced, at a proud volume, her stage voice instructing all who remained standing to sit, even though everyone had already done so, save for herself, Sandra Pride, Elsie Gannon, and the master of ceremonies, Duke Drummond.

"*J.R.?*" Tyto whispered from across the table.

J.R. turned, "What?"

"Nothing. Just making sure you're paying attention."

Tyto had come to the dinner table smudged nearly head to toe with machine oil, including his goggles, which were presumably his only pair, to manhandle as little as possible, given no hope, ever, of replacing them. The goggles amped up the volume on his eyeballs even as they housed that intensity within filthy telescopic cabinets. It was hard to read his face.

"I'm paying attention," J.R. assured him.

The music inside the Mess Hall's vaulted ceilings pulsated down from brass Wagnerian heavens, until Drummond made a face for Crosby Shue, who understood, and rose from his bench, and made for the sound system, and reached for the receiver's dial, competently, discreetly, to fade out the fanfare.

"OK, time for a few announcements."

J.R. had completed his inventory. He counted twenty-six present, not including himself and Elsie. Also not including Steeplejack's two temporary girlfriends, or Chuck Zorn's temporary girlfriend, or Lovejoy's. The girlfriends were not unfamiliar, but they were not fixtures either, and certainly not soldiers. Everyone else got counted though, including Tyto and Vince Baldwin. Even the kids, Bella Shue, little Wallace, and Virginia. If J.R. had it right, they totaled twenty-six. An easy number to remember. One for every letter of the alphabet.

"I wanted us all present for the next few announcements, and forthcoming promotions," Drummond told his seated militia, "as long as we are sitting here undefended from the Pennsylvania wilderness. So let's get on with it, so we can partake of this feast, and then go back to war."

"Gotcha, boss," someone answered, followed by compounding affirmative murmurs.

An enormous Nazi flag hung to the left of the fireplace. The rec room doorway was darksome and lonesome. The bar was deserted. All activity from the kitchen had ceased.

Farrah's cigarette smoke went raftering up into the Mess Hall's grand, neglected, deer-antler candelabrum, to swirl around its several dozen long-extinguished pikes. Looking back down from that fixture to observe Duke Drummond, and seeing him etched now at that diminished perspective, and seeing how the chandelier could drop at the exact moment some poor soul might happen to pass beneath it, and tracing that axis to the woodwork in the floor at the center of the room, which was currently triangulated in plain sight by the very three picnic tables that hosted this occasion, J.R. became certain that the loot from the heist was just beneath their feet.

"Men," Duke Drummond was saying, "I always say *Semper Paratus,* which is Greek to me. But in all seriousness, it means *Always Ready.*"

"Uh oh, it's gonna be a comedy act."

"What? No! Fuck you!" Drummond shot the comment down. It was Snapper. "Shut your MOUTH, Snapper!"

Even in anger, Drummond's self-satiated eyes beheld a realm of near-alien disassociation. "Or back me up, your choice. You told me earlier that you love this cause..." He vectored a finger after the croquet pitch outside the Castle walls, then pointed the same finger at Snapper's face. "So for the next couple of minutes, you either applaud what I say, or you shut that stupid hole in your pancake face! Got it?"

Snickers and snorts resounded. Ace Van Wert reached and playfully kneaded Snapper's peach fuzz head. Farrah rolled her eyes and slouched further, ragdoll-like, twisting her dead cigarette into her hexagonal ashtray.

"Not that I want to hear bullshit out of anybody else's mouth either," Drummond continued. "We're talking about American vigilance. So get your shit together, and show some respect! It's pronounced *Semper Paratus!*"

"*SEMPER PARATUS!*" some of them cried, while others were caught unsure whether the cry had been aroused.

Duke Drummond shook his head and paced a few feet in his boots.

"Fucking clowns. I'm embarrassed. Just ask George Washington. Just ask Paul Revere! Just ask patriots, and men of that ilk. Or just ask Dwight D. Eisenhower! Or Harry S. Truman! You get my point? You know who to ask, and who not to ask."

J.R.'s ears perked up. If these guys wanted to talk about those guys, he was ready to contribute. He knew his United States Presidents.

However, Duke Drummond had lost his audience, and quickly moved on to bread and butter subjects. "If you want an education," he said, "go find a government tit to suck on. Me, I'm here to destroy the government, not jack off about dead jackoffs!"

*"Keep your head down,"* someone whispered, an unidentified voice offering good advice, possibly Grant Archer.

J.R. knew better than to let himself become, as Snapper had become, part of the act. Meanwhile, he was only getting hungrier. His eyes kept returning to the serving trays and serving bowls laid out in variously stagnating and steam-vacated neglect.

"OK, first, an update on the activities of our very own personal Benedict Arnold, Glenn Disteek!"

Groans and boos and raspberries greeted the invocation of Glenn Disteek's name.

"Posse Serpens, how stupid a name is that?"

Laughter came tumbling in answer.

"My friends, I don't know where to start. So let me just wade in. This week, Glenn Disteek's efforts to destroy the white race by appeasing public outcry against racial pride and racial unity, and to quote-unquote *legitimize*—cough, excuse me? *Legitimize?* Did he actually say that? *Legitimize* his candidacy for the job vacated by the disgraced and ousted plutocrat, Marina Pillagret-Kincaid? Are you kidding...?

"Well, no. Not kidding. He lost in an avalanche to the worst candidate in the history of politics, not to mention humankind. Our guy sells us out. All of us, our entire white family, just so he can lose to a renowned lesbian pederast. My friends and fellow militia men, I can't eat or sleep until this villain is destroyed. Not the pederast... I'm talking about the loser... I'm talking about Glenn Disteek. Although he's probably a pederast too, with that fucking rockabilly pompadour on his head..."

Drummond's captive audience spewed guffaws.

"That fucking Cherokee... Elvis... pompadour... hairdo... Plus the leather trench coat..."

They howled, raising their beer steins, banging their fists on the table. The balustrades and balconies and deer antler chandelier seemed almost to shake. Chuck Zorn had begun stomping his feet on the floor in a spasm of joy. Bella Shue and Wallace had become overwhelmed, cowed, awestruck, until they were laughing along. Virginia squirmed, oblivious, spilling off her mother's lap again onto the pine bench.

"THERE CAN BE NO PRIDE WHEN YOU HAVE NO SHAME!" Drummond proclaimed, and the howls escalated as this remark, perhaps more than any other, stirred their passion. "GLENN DISTEEK IS TO BE VANQUISHED FROM THIS EARTH!"

They cheered and slammed together their steins, enjoying each other as much as Duke Drummond, while he applauded their applause, and let it draw out, until the cheers at last abated into mere zealous murmurings.

"So, moving on," he continued. "Our friend Mr. Partridge is no longer with us. OK, now go ahead and say your peace, Trauer."

Trauer looked around, taken by surprise. They were waiting for him to speak. He shrugged, shook his head. "No," he said. "It's just. It's just sad, is all. I just wanted to say that it's sad. I had mentioned that earlier. That is was sad."

"Well said, Trauer," Drummond picked it up from there. "Mr. Partridge is no more. I just voiced his name. Let it be for the last time it gets spoken. Anyone says his name from now on, and it's *your* name we stop saying next. That's the rules. You know it. We all know it. We all live with it. Some more than others."

Drummond paused to let them consider his words.

"Or..." he continued, "have yourself a fit. Go rogue. Set up your own operation. Seek vengeance. Get shot dead. And get buried in an unmarked grave. That's what Cash Clarick did. Remember, you can't say his name anymore either, even though I just did. Just to remind you he's a fucking traitor!"

No response, only silence. Drummond stood observing the intense, unspoken emotion that seemed to possess the soldiers, perhaps Steeplejack more than the rest.

"OK," Drummond said, "so maybe that's the so-called elephant in the room." He waggled his index finger upward. "Although that dumbass deer-antler chandelier would still get my vote."

Nervous chuckles met this comedic misdirection.

"Let's not kid ourselves, men. Everybody here has crossed paths with Cash Clarick. Heck, some of us still have the scars, am I right? I don't have to remind you about Cash Clarick. Remind you of what I remember. So go ahead and correct me if I'm wrong. But he believed in the ugliness of things. He believed *only* in the ugliness of things. And good for him. But that ugliness? It ain't the truth. And we all know it. We knew it then, and we know it now. To be around Cash Clarick was to *know* he was wrong. He was a fool. And now, finally, at last, you know it's true. Because he's dead, and you're not."

The room was silent, enraptured.

"Me, I believe in the beauty of things. I believe in the perfection of things. I believe that we are fated to chisel ourselves down, fact by fact, until only the Capital-T Truth remains. A perfect state of being. And I believe this is not only believable..."

"Here here!"

"And I believe it is not only achievable..."

"That's Goddamn right!"

"I believe it is inevitable!"

"Yowza! Hot Damn!"

"You! My friends! It's up to you. You either get out of the way, or you get the fuck on board. Only fools want to stay behind and worship their own afterbirth in a puddle of filth and ugliness. And by the way, you can argue with me all you want. But I'm still alive. And what's-his-name? Cash Clarick? He's dead."

They erupted in agreement, sought each other out for affirmation—*"Can't say it ain't true." "Can't argue with logic"*—a chain of sensible observations.

Notably, Steeplejack, wasn't celebrating along.

"As for Snapper here," Drummond went on, "appearing in the newspaper—"

"Snapper!" Steeplejack chimed in suddenly. "You stupid sonofabitch!"

"Hey!" Drummond snapped, "If I want a sidekick, I'll hire a midget!"

Laughter sputtered and chortled from the assembled. Drummond remained no less agitated. "All right, pipe down," he said.

Steeplejack sat quiet and still.

Drummond addressed him with all the civility of a heckled comedian, "What are you thinking? I talk, you listen. I talk, you laugh. I talk, you cheer. That's the way this goes. There's no... what do you call it? *Audience participation."*

Snorts burbled. Laughter spurted. Steeplejack smiled, desiring to play along, and saying so with his smile.

"And by the way," Drummond maintained the attack, "I asked, but you weren't quick enough to answer, so I rest my case. So why don't you shut the fuck up, and let me talk?"

Farrah grinned gargoyle-like within her husband's radius. She was wearing coveralls tonight, not unlike Tyto's, but considerably cleaner. She had a fresh cigarette lit, ready to ash it.

The food on the table could not be called hot anymore, but the meat still glistened with liquid fat, and the gravy looked savory, even in stagnation. The coagulating vegetable mush was another story, less appetizing with each diminishing second. More than a few of the soldiers had an eye on the forsaken feast by now.

"Democracy, Liberalism, Socialism, Communism. They all have one thing in common. They all arise from Envy. Envy of thy neighbor. Envy of who earned his Goddamned keep instead of crying about how no one handed it out to him. Envy. Anyone got an argument with that?"

"Aw, here we go!" someone hollered. The cheer arising was staggered, disjointed, but quickly unified in applause. Steeplejack would keep his arms folded. Drummond would maintain his placid and sagacious gaze until the audience calmed down again. "But we're all white here," he continued at last. "So let's have us a realistic conversation about that."

Applause burst forth a bit more, holding back at first, or trying to in vain, only to spasm out all the more so.

"Let's talk about the history of quote-unquote being nice. Let me explain something, folks. This is literally a quote-unquote true story. This is NOT... quote-unquote... BASED... on a true story. Or some bullshit like that. It's not based on anything. It's the ACTUAL TRUE STORY... Of being nice.

"Being nice. It begins like this: 'Hi, I'm nice. Who are you?' The answer comes." Drummond pantomimed a blow with his fist. "Smash, with a club, you're dead."

Laughter sputtered. Chuckles circulated. Amusement spread, almost rowdy.

"A couple of centuries, later: 'Hi, I'm nice. Who are you?' This time it's some Samurai. Or some Mongoloid with a sword, or whatever. Try making nice with one of those assholes. They'll cut you into little cubes of meat and eat you with chopsticks, you know what I'm saying?"

300

"Chop Suey!" someone cried. The laughter was contagious, from one face to the next. Even the children, Bella Shue and Wallace, were grinning, gazing around, amazed. *"Chop Suey!"* little Bella cried in triumphant mimicry. Farrah flashed her gap-toothed grin and extinguished another cancer stick.

Duke Drummond asked, "You know what they call themselves. They call themselves *progressives*, right? Hmm? Let's see. Nice thought. Except how can you *progress* two feet in front of your own *ass* when your entire philosophy of *life* is to ensure your own *natural selection for extinction?*"

Their laughter continued pouring forth. Drummond paused to enjoy the moment he had wangled.

"Literally, we are all, all of us, the ancestors... Or not the ancestors, but you know what I mean... We are the children, the descendants, the progeny... of cruelty, murder and war. I mean how much stupid bullshit can you take? If we're going to quote-unquote progress as a species, we've got to kick ass! Not stand around smelling each other's butts!"

Two of the soldiers dropped to the floor and began rolling in the aisles. It was Brock Fowler and Buchanan, collapsing down to the Mess Hall's floorboards, seized by laughter. Both Lovejoy and Crosby Shue dropped to a knee to help their fallen brothers upright. Laughing hysterically, they made a great show of it all, neo-Nazis un-splitting their sides, trying to spill back into their britches, and back onto their Mess Hall benches. Meanwhile, Trauer had produced a guitar from somewhere, or miniature guitar, or ukulele. The sonorous instrument thrashed out violent and dramatic acoustic chords from its curlicue soundbox.

"And so, a few centuries later..." Drummond continued, wry of tone, trailing off.

The guitar strings resolved into deconstructed minstrel pluckings. It was a mandolin, J.R. realized. Two strings sounding for every attack. Trauer was good at it too. The belly laughs from the assembled had reduced to coughs, a-hems, burbles, and belches.

Drummond continued, "A few centuries later, you're walking down the streets of Detroit, or Baltimore. Or maybe West Lewiston, Illinois, where our white sister Elsie hails from..."

All of them, it seemed, turned their attention to Elsie Gannon now. She lowered her eyes. She had served their meal, and then taken the nearest seat, musical chairs style, and perhaps regretfully, or perhaps wisely, because her husband's memory surely protected her at the table of soldiers that included Lovejoy, Brock Fowler, Chuck Zorn, Trauer, and others.

"Well..." Duke Drummond continued. "Does anyone feel like giving Elsie here a lecture about being nice?"

A hail of vague approval rang out. J.R. didn't like it. She *was* nice. Singling her out, Drummond had twisted the whole thing around.

Steeplejack was clapping, happy to see Drummond's attention deflected elsewhere.

But Farrah had let her own grin transmogrify into curdling malice. Seeing this, J.R. realized that the boss had put Elsie in danger.

"How stupid is it to be nice?" Drummond was saying, "How fucking stupid?"

Farrah's blue glare remained fixed on Elsie, who kept her own gaze lowered.

"I tell you, we... And let me repeat that ALL OF US! We are the descendants of intelligence. We are the descendants of survivors. Am I right, Old Man? Not idiots. This is a stone cold fact. And as a matter of fact, that's the whole *do-si-do* about so-called Darwin that our side never bothered to pick up on. Much less hit them back with...

"We didn't come crawling out of the muck, building and conquering and marching and stomping our war-forged avatar of enlightenment, tadpole to caveman to Viking to Adolf Hitler, all the way to this moment in the history of fate, just to give it all over to a bunch of sorry ass churchgoers, or chapelgoers, or whatever that plywood box is out there, where you-all go and hold hands, and play make believe, and try to sell us on a so-called afterlife, while you sit in judgment over our quest for survival? I may not know everything, but I surely know that. I'm sorry. I say this with all due respect to Lou Gannon, who gave his life for this cause. But the truth is, if he were here, he would be saying the same thing I'm saying."

Several Posse Umbellus soldiers seemed poised to spasm on cue into further jubilance beneath the Mess Hall's rafters, even as Drummond's words practically commanded them to de-escalate beyond silence into something like prayer.

302

Certain soldiers were visibly disappointed. Duke answered them too, the whole spectrum, "I know, I know... I know how the so-called story goes. But I also know the truth. And the truth is, there is no sin. There is only power. They've been arguing about the afterlife forever. So far, no one... NO ONE... has ever come back to vouch for it."

Many of them were nodding their heads.

"Except for you-know-who. Starts with a J. And I don't mean J.R. I mean the other guy who starts with a J."

Howls of approval and laughter erupted unbottled, raucous enough to overwhelm the few shrinking faces of dissent. J.R. tried to avoid attention. He stared at the food as it cooled. When he looked up, he could see Sandra Pride's exhausted dismay. He could see that Rose Archer was anxious, her eyes darting repeatedly to the un-plated helpings, even as she clapped her hands alongside her husband.

Perhaps Edward, the Old Man, could veto the remaining monologue and get the feast underway. But Edward had his eye on J.R., saying nothing.

"Speaking of J.R. Daddio!" Drummond said. "How about *this* hero, huh?"

The cheers compounded, startling J.R. away from Edward's gaze and around at the three table-loads of Posse Umbellus soldiers. He could sense their sarcasm. Maybe half of them, maybe less than half, were cheering sincerely. The rest were attuned to Duke Drummond's venom, as he smirked and looked away. *I'm part of the act,* J.R. lamented as his brain overheated, trying to sort out which of them, if any, were on his side.

"OK, so here is this hot shot from New York. Which explains everything about him if you ask me. Or maybe not everything about *him,* but everything about his attitude, is what I mean. But I'm not making fun of you, J.R., or pointing out your obvious weaknesses as a human being in front of everybody, J.R... J.R. Daddio... or Nimrod... or whatever the tape says... beyond your age, that is... I mean... Gosh, this is the worst toast I ever raised. But sincerely," Drummond raised his stein. "Cheers!"

A rapturous ovation erupted, a raising and meeting of sloshing, crisscrossed mugs. J.R. glanced again at the Old Man, whose poached egg eyeballs flashed a perpetually ironic twinkle.

"You know?" Drummond affixed J.R. with his cold, pale, future-informed gaze. "Every time I hurt you, it's your fault. You know that, right? I mean, *they?* They know it about *themselves,*" he turned to his audience. "Snapper, you know it, right?"

"Right, boss!" Snapper's face was red.

"You can put on that record now," Drummond said. Crosby Shue moved to obey. Drummond stopped him with a raised hand. Then, with the same hand, he pointed to Snapper.

Snapper looked around, set his beer mug down, and gestured to himself. "Beg pardon?"

The laughter in the room petered out.

"Attend to the record player, Snapper. Set the needle to vinyl."

They awaited Snapper's action. Snapper was on his feet. His footfalls echoed after him to the stereo. He looked back at his friends and career just once, wistfully.

"Screw up this cue and I'll murder you," Drummond told him. Laughter flickered, crackled, like distant lightning.

Snapper's trembling hand lifted the turntable's ready arm to lay its needle precisely onto the spinning black band. His fingers withdrew, open, free and clear, having dropped the stylus perfectly, to raise Valhallic pulsars, suspiring brass volumes inside the Mess Hall's bellows, warm tones up and around the balconies, harmonies throbbing in affinity with the furnace of burning firewood in the building's sturdy and vintage corner hearth. Snapper returned to his table from a job well done.

Drummond proceeded, "So, next announcement is this. They are literally coming to get us!"

This punchline was met with uneasy laughter. Many more of them were casting a hungry eye toward the forsaken food.

"It sounds like paranoia when I say it," Drummond explained above the commanding music, "but it's also the Capital-T Truth."

He paused to glance over their faces and offer his own grave countenance in reassurance.

"I shot a traitor today, as you know. I have no concrete reason to think anyone else is a traitor among us. But here is the truth. As of Libertyville, we have entered into a new reality."

Again, he sent his clement gaze above their heads.

"What do you mean, boss?" Lovejoy asked.

"I'll tell you what I mean. Promotions are merit based. Let's be clear about that. I trust you, because you've proven yourself, and earned it. If you weren't chosen, keep trying, is all I can say. Half of us are going to die before this is even over, so don't let yourself get discouraged..."

He paused to let them absorb his set up. J.R. studied their many watchful, hopeful faces. At this same moment, the brass and surging strings from the turntable settled into a march. Drummond had timed his oration perfectly with the music.

"AND SO, WITHOUT FURTHER INTRODUCTION, I HEREBY ANNOUNCE THE POSSE UMBELLUS' NEW ELITE SECURITY FORCE, WHICH SHALL BE CALLED, 'THE PRAETORIAN GUARD!'"

The Mess Hall broke out again in applause, men raising their mugs, hooting and whistling, responding favorably even as a few shared quizzical expressions.

"The Praetorian Guard will stand watch over *this building*," Drummond explained, pointing up and around at the room's geometry, also down and around at the floor. "Our future, and very likely the future of the white race.... For the time being, IT'S RIGHT HERE!"

"HEAR, HEAR!" Lovejoy raised his tankard.

"THAT'S WHY HENCEFORTH!" Drummond continued. "The eight Praetorian Guardsman will NOT be assigned to the corner turrets! And NOT to the watchtower either! You men are hereby assigned to THIS ROOM! This Mess Hall! In and around, at eight assigned stations!" He pointed, tracing a second-story octagon with his finger.

"Excuse me, boss," Snapper raised his hand.

Drummond shot him a look. "What is it?"

"What do you mean by promotion?"

"It means your life gets better."

"Oh," Snapper grinned. "Awesome."

"Awesome? Why is it awesome? Your life isn't getting better."

"Oh. I'm sorry."

"Don't say 'awesome.' You sound like a moron. Don't ever use that word again. Ever. For anything."

"Yes, boss."

"That's more like it."

"Yes, boss."

"Those of you who didn't make the cut, keep your chin up. If you're made of Praetorian stuff, you'll have your chance to prove it. Just stick with the program. In the meantime, we need longer shifts out of all of you, around the wall, and up in the tower. So man up for that..."

His eyes surveyed their faces, daring any questions. Then he continued, "As for the Praetorian Guardsmen, you can consider this promotion permanent. But rest assured, your assignment is only temporary. And yes, you'll be taking shifts. You'll get your precious shuteye, and precious food. And exercise and R&R, and all that bullshit. Just not as much. So don't worry. You get exactly what you've earned, which is trust, honor and respect."

He paused briefly, allowed the Praetorian Guardsmen to consider what they had won.

"But as of this moment, *this place?*" He pointed around at the Mess Hall's architecture. "This place is on lockdown."

They nodded their heads more and more as they came to understand and began to applaud.

"And you," he pointed around at the unnamed eight, but mostly in the direction of one table, the elite soldiers among all the other anxious, approving, enthusiastic faces. "You," he told them, "are the guardians of our future."

The response grew louder and more raucous, drowning out the fanfare from the record player, distending the moment with anticipation.

"AND SO, THE EIGHT PRAETORIAN GUARDS... PLEASE RISE AS I CALL YOUR NAME! LOVEJOY! SKINNER! BROCK FOWLER! BUCHANAN! TRAUER! GROSSMARK! CHUCK ZORN! AND CROSBY SHUE!"

Amidst adulation they arose, like a domino chain in reverse, most from the same picnic table, assembling in a wave, Crosby Shue at Drummond's table rising last in queue, smiling and clapping, even as his eyes shifted around skeptically. Lovejoy at the other table was laughing, thoroughly pleased. Chuck Zorn was smirking, affirmed. Buchanan looked surprised. Brock Fowler seemed vaguely worried.

"Praetorian?" Trauer could barely be heard, but his remark contained a question.

Crosby Shue ventured his own bold whiff of dissent. "Praetorian?" he asked. "Is that Italian, boss?"

"No, it's Roman," Drummond snapped.

"Wait," Buchanan hesitated.

The music marched on as the chatter petered out. The eight Praetorian Guardsmen remained standing, obedient. The awkward pause was painfully prolonged.

J.R. at last raised a forefinger, "Umm—"

"Why don't you shut up, squirt!" Farrah spat, grinning gap-toothed through nicotine swirls. Her blue eyes sparkled as they held J.R.'s gaze for one blistering split second before breaking contact altogether.

"OK, everybody dig in!" Drummond commanded.

His eight newly promoted soldiers sat down to eat, along with everybody else.

"Except," Drummond added, "there's going to be five of us who don't get to dig in. Like I said, we're in apocalyptic danger at every moment, so we need a few live bodies—five, although preferably more, but five will do this time—on lookout. We will send a plate up to you. Very soon, that's a guarantee. OK, grab a rifle and man your station when your name is called. Krabbe, eastern turret. Harding, northern turret. Sandra Pride, western turret. Grant Archer, southern turret."

The four soldiers stood from their benches and made obediently for the exit where the crisscrossed war hammer and battle axe hung in solemn remembrance. Sandra Pride glanced back regretfully at the uneaten feast. Harding did too.

"As for the watchtower, I changed my mind, two seconds ago, about who should go up there. Snapper, it's you in the watchtower tonight. Get on up there. I have to admit, Snapper. You've got heart."

"Yessir!" Snapper was up from his bench, crossing the hall to the staircase.

Drummond turned his attention to the rest of them, "Everybody else, soup's on!"

Farrah shook her head. "Umm, no," she had another cigarette lit, and her chicklet grin deployed veils of smoke. "Food's cold," she said, pointing around at the unserved trays and neglected serving bowls. Her blue eyes seemed to crackle.

Drummond looked up, sought out the serving ladies. Sandra Pride was already out the door. Rose Archer and Elsie Gannon remained. He pointed around at the un-served feast. "All right, girls," he said. "Let's warm this up."

## 52. Haircut Day

It was haircut day at the Castle, and assorted Posse Umbellus personnel, numbering well over a dozen, had come to the Mess Hall and assembled at the benches for Sandra Pride to artlessly shear their Nazi noggins all in a row. "You're done!" she told Trauer, rubbing his peach fuzz head vigorously and then shoving it away from her face.

Drummond and the Old Man were on hand too, although not for haircuts, rather to hold an informal meeting among the unit. After a noisy initial half-hour, the children had run off, and Grant Archer had gone about his dutiful way, and Steeplejack had retreated to his second-story bedchamber, so that the session had become more intimate and relaxed for the Praetorian to receive their haircuts and then venture back upstairs, one by one, to hang around the mezzanine like vampire bats. Finally, only two of the elite guardians remained in waiting, including Lovejoy seated on the bench alongside J.R., and Brock Fowler, who sat facing forward from the hot seat.

Sandra Pride tilted Brock Fowler's temples with the thumb and forefinger of either hand, then commenced to snip his lemony aftlocks. The Old Man watched the scissorwork through jaundiced but contented eyeballs. Lovejoy watched too, increasingly restive, as Fowler received intense attention from Sandra Pride's shears and fingertips.

J.R. was no less enraptured, watching Sandra's bare and sinewy arms work, her right-hand clipping, her left-hand tightly gripping the curls in question. Sandra Pride, in J.R.'s estimation, resembled, somewhat, and facially only, and only in some vague and bizarre aspect, a female version of Ron Reagan Jr., although her eyes were prettier and seemed to glitter. She was strangely attractive, but primarily a violent person through and through. Mean bones sculpted down to her frame by a ferocity that superseded even rage.

Preferring not to stare, J.R. looked away, looked around. Duke Drummond had all but announced, at the recent so-called feast, that the loot was here in the Mess Hall, and more than likely hidden beneath the very wisp-strewn floorboards at their feet. Taking note of the invisible bullseye where the money doubtlessly lay stashed, J.R. then cast his gaze up to the deer antler chandelier and its many upward facing pikes. The relic's pale and dusty frame was massive. As J.R. contemplated its lethal weight, and as Drummond and the Old Man held quiet palaver off to the side of its reach, Snapper came corkscrewing down the watchtower's spiral staircase, announcing, "THE VAN WERT TWINS RETURN!"

"WELL DONE, SNAPPER!" Drummond called up to him. "KEEP UP THE GOOD WORK!"

"WILL DO!" Snapper's boots bounded noisily back upward.

"I'M NOT SHINING YOU ON, SNAPPER!" Drummond called after him. "OR GIVING YOU LIP SERVICE!"

Snapper halted and turned. "I'M SORRY SIR?"

"THAT WILL BE ALL, SNAPPER! GO ON UPSTAIRS!"

"AYE AYE, SIR!" Snapper disappeared.

"Sandra, if you give that kid a pompadour, I swear I'll..."

Everybody else laughed, but Sandra allowed herself only a brief smirk, quickly negated by a shake of the head.

Drummond pointed to J.R. "Or this one."

J.R. said, "I don't want a pompadour."

"You know..." Drummond mused, leaning closer into the Old Man's confidence. "Correct me if I'm wrong, Edward. But with that black sweep of hair, J.R. almost has an Uncle Adolf thing going. I mean, slap a mustache on him and..." he backhanded the Old Man's arm.

J.R. raised his two empty hands lightheartedly, "Oh, please, no thanks."

The room fell silent. Sandra stopped snipping Brock Fowler's curls.

J.R. felt the blood in his veins go hot. He watched his own vision swim. He tried to keep cool. He had misplayed a card. It was nothing fatal.

"Whadayou mean?" Brock Fowler asked, seated, hovered over by Sandra Pride.

"A mustache," J.R. explained. "I'm too young... for a... a... a facial hair mustache," he fumbled the words instinctively, trying to sound as harmless as possible.

Drummond eyeballed J.R. but addressed the Old Man, "Edward."

"Duke."

"Please explain to me. Why did you tribulate me with this kid?"

"You tribulate yourself," the Old Man answered.

"That sounded dirty," Lovejoy observed.

At that moment, up in the balcony, Steeplejack opened his bedchamber door, stepping out casually in his bathrobe and slippers. Suddenly startled by Crosby Shue's Praetorian presence, he leapt sideways, crying, *"Jesus!"* Then, as he laughed about it, sharing the laughter with Crosby Shue and with all the other witnesses to his folly, he allowed his robe to fall open, so that his dick dangled for all to see, gently garlanded in bright Hawaiian colors, apparently, although J.R. averted his eyes so immediately as to leave himself only guessing at what on earth he had just beheld. Meanwhile, Drummond said, "Steeplejack, we're waging Civil War out here. Can you put your Johnson away?"

The Van Wert twins came banging through the front entrance. Rudy Van Wert announced, "We're back!"

"Oh, good!" Drummond wheeled to greet the new arrivals.

"And..." Ace Van Wert waved a manila envelope.

"...we do not come empty-handed!" Rudy finished.

"Hey," Aesop elbowed his brother, "we're in time for haircuts."

"OK, what are we looking at?" Drummond asked, and the twins approached.

"We're done here," Sandra Pride pushed Brock Fowler's head away. "Lovejoy, you're up."

Fowler rose and rubbed his hand through his freshly styled haircut.

"You asshole!" Sandra told him. "You just messed it up!"

"IT'S MY HAIR!" he barked at her. He grabbed his M16 from the picnic bench. Then, at his own pace, in his own time, he made for the staircase, to ascend and take his place among the Praetorian watchmen.

Meanwhile, Lovejoy took the empty seat beneath Sandra Pride's hands and scissors. The Van Wert twins, back from their reconnaissance mission, stood in Duke Drummond's favor, dressed plain and smart, as always, in jackets and ties, like detectives or salesmen.

"OK," Aesop began, "first of all, Curtis McKinley Lemonhall is black."

"Skip ahead," Drummond answered.

Rudolph said, "He's a quote-unquote investigative journalist from Philadelphia. He got fired from his job there, and landed here. At the *West Susquehannock Dispatch*. The *Photographer on the Streets* gig is well below his previous standards. We looked up his bylines from Philly—"

"Boss, we were looking at microfiche and shit. The evidence is there."

"Evidence of what?"

"He's hostile to whites."

"Imagine that," Drummond smirked. "You say quote-unquote? Who are you quote-unquoting?"

Rudolph pulled out a notepad. "Annotations are here, if you want 'em."

"I want 'em," Drummond beckoned with a finger.

Rudolph obeyed, then sheepishly pointed at the relinquished documents. "Burn after reading..."

Drummond frowned, tucked the notebook into his back pocket.

"There's more," Ace interjected. "Much more."

"Let's hear it."

"Lemonhall has a civil case against him in Cleveland. Some chick named Mercedes Jefferson. She claims he's the father of her kid. So we expensed a trip to Cleveland, boss, without asking."

"So this is good, then?"

"It's bad *and* good."

"What's bad?"

"Lemonhall..." Rudy Van Wert answered. "He's onto us. He's got pictures of our Castle and everything. He's been out here snooping around."

"WHAT? Pictures? Have you seen these pictures?"

"No. But get this. After Cleveland, we follow him back to Philly. And so while he's in Philly, he meets up with an old buddy, and pours back a few at the local watering hole. And starts flapping his gums about a story he's working on, and how he has to chase it in his spare time, because they won't let him do any real reporting at the *West Susquehannock Dispatch*. Except this story will be his ticket back to the big time—"

"And guess who the story's about, boss," the brother interjected. "It's about *us!* A group of free white Americans living by God's grace on the American land."

"That's not good," Drummond agreed. The twins nodded in tandem. "OK," Drummond clapped his hands together. "What's good?"

"I'll tell you what's good."

Aesop extended the manila envelope. "We've got pictures too."

Drummond took the envelope, tore it open, and removed and considered its first glossy 8x10. The room waited in silence.

Finally, he removed and examined the next picture. He put his hand over his mouth. Then he flipped back to the first picture.

The Old Man peered up from his chair. "You need a few minutes alone?" The others began to chuckle.

Drummond snapped, "HEY!" and they fell quiet. He then gestured to the photos. "This," he concluded, "is some disreputable shit."

"It's too insane for my tastes," Aesop confessed.

"My tastes are same as his," his brother confirmed.

"Don't let Steeplejack get his flippers on these," Drummond tucked the glossies back into the envelope. "OK, it's the best kind of simple. We destroy Curtis Lemonhall before he destroys us."

"Send me after him, boss!" Lovejoy's self-supplication came from the attention center of Sandra Pride's scissors. "I'll bring you his dog tags!"

Overhead, totem pole-like, Sandra Pride made a better offer. "I'll come back with his scalp!"

Drummond ignored them both, turned to Edward, "Old Man, did you see that *loco mamacita?*"

Edward shook his head. "She's mulatta, son. Not Latina."

Drummond became flushed. He barked, "She ain't white! That's all I know!" He turned his attention back to the twins, "We can't underestimate this guy. If Curtis Lemonhall can get a woman as beautiful as that—"

"A wha-what?" Aesop recoiled.

"Buh," Rudy stammered, "Buh... But... But but boss?"

Ace completed his brother's sentiment, "She's... She's black!"

"I know! Jesus Christ! But just *look* at her..." Drummond trailed off. "Actually..." he added.

They watched him, spellbound, slightly afraid, while he stroked his chin.

"That's perfect," he said at last. "We'll say she's white. It's obvious she's not, but what the hell? She's white enough. People will believe it. People just believe what they want to believe, don't they?"

The Old Man nodded to no one in particular, then chuckled to himself.

Drummond continued, "Meanwhile, all of the hubbub will throw attention on Lemonhall's legal problems. We'll follow up with something in the paper about how he's a deadbeat rapist, on top of all his other evils. Meanwhile, he'll be hell bent on trying to prove his girlfriend isn't white. That's just the icing on the cake."

"A delicious cake," the Old Man winked.

"That's why Duke's in charge," Sandra Pride affirmed.

"I don't know how you do it, boss," Lovejoy fawned.

## 53. The Nova Revisited

J.R. told Elsie about it later that day, seated with her inside the Nova. This was his first visit to his car now that he had his keys back, and he felt a strange and irrational guilt for bringing Elsie along for the reunion. After all, the car could not possibly be jealous, especially under these circumstances. Still, he felt bad for relishing a return to the driver's seat, if only to occupy it, with Elsie at his side, going nowhere.

First, he had to arrange it with Grant Archer up in the eastern turret. "I'm going out to start the engine," he advised, holding up the car keys and jingling them. "But I'm not driving away or anything."

"What? What are you saying?"

"Just to keep the battery from dying. We're NOT running away, or anything like that."

"OK, don't run away, or I'll shoot you down!"

"We're not running away!" J.R. assured the armed guard. "We're just hanging out in a *parked car!* But I'm going to *start* the engine of the parked car... Understand? So that the battery doesn't die. I work in the auto yard now, Grant. Mr. Archer. It's my job to start the engine of my car."

"You're on your own with that bullshit, kid."

"Just don't shoot me... Tell Snapper too."

"Snapper won't give a shit," Archer ended the conversation and turned away.

With the Pretorian Guardsmen now assigned to the Mess Hall, J.R. felt the outer turrets were manned with a notable absence of professionalism sometimes.

Outside the Castle walls, as he and Elsie approached the Nova in its line of parked cars, Snapper's figure was visible from the far turret, though whether he was standing down or gun-crazy, it wasn't clear.

Keeping his eye on that perch, J.R. led Elsie along the procession of vehicles that included, among others, Lovejoy's Cherokee Chief, Chuck Zorn's 4x4 Pickup, Partridge's widowed and as yet unclaimed Z28, and Krabbe's heavily modified Gremlin, which he kept under a tarp for the purposes of discretion. Krabbe's vehicle was deliberately conspicuous, as opposed to the twins' Buick Riviera, for instance, or most of the other vehicles parked along the Castle's southeast wall.

Arriving at the Nova, J.R. looked back at Elsie once, as if to assure her no love triangle was brewing between her and the car. He then turned his full attention to the beautiful machine. The lines and panels, eternally sleek and menacing, were made only more so by the vehicle's swamp brown paint job. Only now could he see it. The beauty of its coat.

Then he was back in the driver's seat, with Elsie beside him. For an alarmingly exciting moment it seemed a better fantasy than any actual one he had dared entertain since leaving home. He was at last inside his own muscular cockpit, amidst the leather and vinyl confines, relishing the beauty of a woman's eyes, mouth, jaw, neckline, hair. He tried to appreciate the moment, knowing there would be few as good, if ever again.

"I just want to get us out of here," he told her.

"Shhh."

"I wish we could..." he trailed off.

"We can hug," she told him. She was so nice, smiling with her big teeth, and with her raised eyebrows. He smiled in return, and they both laughed a little, an exchange witnessed only by the Pennsylvania pines, for all they knew. As the hug ensued, the bucket seats didn't so much ruin the moment as contort it. Elsie laughed. She found it funny. J.R. withdrew and smiled, knowing he had missed something, had spoiled it for himself, wishing for more. "I told them I'd start the engine," he said. "I should go ahead and do that."

She agreed, smiling. He keyed the Nova to life. The 454 growled. He looked up and back at one Castle turret, then the other. So far, the Posse Umbellus was keeping its cool. He glanced back at the auto yard door, where no one yet had come spilling out with guns blazing. He had earned this one outer ring of autonomy. He leaned his shoulders back in the leather seat and allowed himself the minor victory.

"So," she said.

"So."

"How was your day?"

That was when he told her about Duke Drummond's machinations against Curtis Lemonhall, the black reporter who'd been snooping around the Castle. In fact, for all they knew, Lemonhall might have a camera trained on them at this very moment, a telephoto lens to capture and publish their awkward embrace for the *West Susquehannock Dispatch's* front page.

Drummond's plan was to blackmail the reporter, with pictures of his girlfriend, who wasn't so much his girlfriend as someone who was suing him for paternity. J.R. went on to explain that from what he had heard, but not actually seen for himself, to call the leverage against Curtis Lemonhall "pictures" was an understatement.

At the same time, he didn't want to dwell on the subject. After all, he was, himself, a victim of "pictures." So was Elsie, though he had not yet returned to that conversation with her, and perhaps never would, since any other subject was preferable. He told her instead how Drummond was going to tell the newspaper Lemonhall's girlfriend was white, which wasn't even true, but wouldn't even matter, because that would be just one more thing the poor bastard was trying to disprove.

"People will believe what they want to believe," Elsie affirmed.

"That's exactly what they said."

She shrugged, and smiled a bit sagaciously, as if to say, *Welcome to Reality.*

"Elsie..."

"Shhh, better not to speak of this stuff. J.R. Please, I don't want you to get hurt. Not you."

"Maybe you're right."

"You wanted to know more about me," she reminded him.

"Yeah, yes," he was reminded, and she was right. "Yes, I do, Elsie."

"How I ended up here."

"Yes, why did you run away from home," he asked her.

"The whites..." she began.

He braced himself. He would hear her peace. Elsie's big dark eyes were trained on him, to see if he would stop her, though he wouldn't, and didn't, so she continued.

"We welcomed the blacks at first. And for a couple of years, everything went pretty smoothly. And maybe everyone got along, mostly. Until more and more blacks started moving into the neighborhood, looking for work, in the yards at first, but then coming in for the clubs, and the music, and the brothels, so that more and more whites felt like strangers in their own town, so that they started to leave, until the place was finally completely overrun, all except for my mom."

J.R. nodded and listened, uncomfortable, trying to be a good boyfriend.

"A saint, my mom," Elsie continued. "A nurse. A neighbor. The neighborhood loved her. I'm talking about the blacks too. They loved her. They treated her as one of their own. Church. Casseroles. A gaggle of friends..."

J.R. nodded. She met his gaze. He stopped nodding.

"But in the end," she continued, "it was the neighborhood that killed her, while she was walking home from the Community Center. They left her in a ditch, down in one of those lots below the flood line."

"Elsie, that's terrible. That's the most tragic thing I've ever heard. But that doesn't mean... You can't paint them all with that brush. I mean, your whole story illustrates my point."

"No, it illustrates mine," she said.

"But..." he paused.

There was no upside to confronting her, he knew this. But he had to say something. "You're *religious,*" he said.

"God gets me through it," she explained.

"But what I mean—"

"*J.R.,*" she hushed him. He waited for more. Her eyes darted around. *"What if they're listening?"*

She was right to be cautious. For all they knew, Brock Fowler was about to jack-in-the-box out of the trunk and apprehend them, mid-romance.

317

## 54. The Star-Spangled Gremlin

The next day, out on the croquet pitch, J.R. found himself purposed into a kind of handicap for Duke Drummond, whose desire was to vanquish Chuck Zorn and Skinner upon the Castle's sacrificial lawn billiard altar.

"With one hand tied behind my back," Drummond was saying, taunting his opponents, even as he held both hands behind his back, and let the mallet dangle lose from his grip, pendulum-like. Skinner was laughing. Chuck Zorn raised a battle cry, "You're on! Who's got some zip ties?"

"No," Drummond said. "I mean having J.R. on my team is the same thing as having one hand tied behind my back. Understand? No zip ties. I'll beat you. We'll beat you. Me and J.R. Right, J.R.?"

J.R. nodded just slightly.

"That's what I like to hear."

"You guys are dead!" Chuck Zorn pointed a finger.

"Hey, take it easy—" Skinner said.

"Hey, fuck you, Skinner! I didn't come out here to lose! And you better not either! Or I don't even know who you are!"

Drummond leaned into J.R. with mock confidentiality, and said, "These hot heads are gonna beat themselves. We don't even have to beat 'em."

"See what I mean?" Chuck Zorn admonished Skinner. "Did you hear what that asshole just said? Are you on my SIDE or NOT? Are we gonna BEAT THESE PRICKS OR NOT?!"

318

"ALL RIGHT!" Skinner fathomed it. "All right, all right. I see how it is!" He pointed an accusing finger at Duke Drummond. "You're going down, boss! I'm sorry, but Chuck Zorn is right! You have to go down!"

Both Skinner and Chuck Zorn were Praetorian Guardsmen, whose days and nights were newly spent overlooking the Mess Hall for hours on end in an octagon of boredom. Free now, and perhaps stir-crazy from that excruciating assignment, they were making the most of it, making a game of it, so that as the contest progressed, J.R. found himself recovering from a shot through the wrong hoop, and his team losing 16-14, and his turn coming around again, to whack like an idiot at the stupid, stationary ball.

The challenge of baseball is that the ball is *coming toward you*. That makes it a rational thing to swat. But with croquet, as with golf, the ball is just sitting there. Which is probably why Duke Drummond, and most of the others, preferred to swing the mallet back between their legs, which made them look like dogs taking a shit. Not J.R. though. He would continue to swing his mallet sideways, like a ballplayer.

That's when Harding hollered down from the eastern turret, "KRABBE AND SHANNAHAN, BOSS! ON THEIR WAY IN!"

J.R. relaxed his shoulders, let his mallet head hit the turf, and let the match come to a merciful halt.

Krabbe, it seemed to J.R., was always either watchfully asleep in the barracks or out on a mission in his lunatic battle car. Drummond often deployed him to harass Glenn Disteek's political pursuits, precisely because Krabbe's star-spangled Gremlin stirred up so much attention. J.R. would have identified the vehicle by the sound of its approach up the trail out of West Susquehannock. The Posse Umbellus had been anticipating its return all morning, which finally heralded up from the forest line, louder-and-louder upon the growls of its exposed and portentous engine, the car leveling out and tilting forward into the green clearing, bearing resources, reconnaissance, and maybe a thing or two else. It was half AMC/half dune buggy, painted Stars and Stripes all over, and roving on custom axles and oversized tires, with chrome exhaust pipes like war horns blaring down its sides. Mugwort peeled away from its grill as it curled to a stop along the playing field's perimeter.

Drummond was staring downward in bliss-neutral transcendence, observing the grass at his feet, awaiting the news.

Krabbe, exiting the Gremlin, looked anxious or pissed-off or bitter. Shanahan, emerging from the passenger seat, was more dutiful and mascot-like.

"What have you got there?" Drummond asked him.

Shanahan paused in his tracks, held up a gas mask.

"That's fantastic," Drummond said. "Where'd you get it?"

"Found it in one of the church basements."

"I want one."

"Lookee. Sticker's still even on it. Just two bucks. You want me to put it on?"

"I want to see us all wearing them. That's good recon, soldier."

"Check it out," Shanahan pulled on the mask. He looked around at them, snout-armored, like an alien from outer space.

Drummond nodded, "You're might just outlive us all, Shanahan."

Shanahan pulled off the mask and gasped a little. "Long as I keep this thing on," he said.

"We drove a stake into Glenn Disteek's heart," Krabbe reported.

"What'd you all do?"

"All's I did was watch," Krabbe advised. "It was Shanahan who dealt the death blow."

"And what death blow would that be?" Drummond wanted to know.

## 55. Live at Five

Later that night, J.R. was up in the watchtower with Elsie, the two of them alone together, arranged once again by Steeplejack's machinations, comfortable beneath the windowsill's sightline. They spoke intimately and commiseratively. He longed to kiss her mouth, though he didn't want to be a part of what they were doing to her, so he didn't attempt it. Nor would he, ever, so long as it was on Steeplejack's schedule.

He sat crosslegged against the decagonal wall, while Elsie lay on the mattress, raised up on one elbow and frequently cradling her chin, or cheek, in her palm. J.R. was explaining how Krabbe and Shanahan had probably destroyed Glenn Disteek's political career, or whatever was left of it. He told her how Glenn Disteek, reeling from his humiliating political defeat at the hands of some monstrously unspeakable candidate, and having contested the results and demanded a recount, and having done it all in vain, got reduced to making a show of his concession speech, a message for the future of the Posse Serpens, and its inevitable, unstoppable political movement. And how for this event Shanahan got the idea to hire a black guy to go up to the podium and punch Glenn Disteek in the face... right in the middle of his concession speech.

"No one will mind," Shanahan explained to the black guy, as he dealt out the five twenties. "It's a Nazi face you're punching. Everyone will love you for it. You'll be a damn cult hero. Plus, the money." Such was Shanahan's political genius.

But meanwhile, Krabbe thinks he knows better—he is confessing this to Duke Drummond, while they are all enjoying the story—that he told Shanahan at the time, "Nice idea, but it's a waste of money. No one cares about Glenn Disteek's concession speech."

Except Krabbe was wrong, albeit the first to tell you so now. Because as it turns out, Shanahan had got himself an additional notion, which was to call *Live at Five,* which is a TV News program of some renown over in New York, where all of this is taking place. His idea is to tip off *Live at Five* that a race war is about to break out at this Posse Serpens event.

But funny thing is, it's not so easy as it sounds. First, he tries calling Sue Simmons. She's a black lady, so he figures Sue Simmons—if no one else—will sound the alarm and send a camera crew out to cover the race war. But she does no such thing. She says she doesn't have time for prank callers, and she hangs up on him.

So next he calls Jack Cafferty. Jack Cafferty gives him a tip line to call. He calls the tip line, and some weird lady takes a message. So that's bullshit, he figures. So the plan is not working out so far.

So then he gets himself a third notion, which is the thrust of Krabbe's story, that Shanahan, with his creativity and notions, is the mastermind of this perfectly realized triumph. Shanahan makes a call to Frank Field, the weatherman, and says, "You guys are supposed to know which way the wind is blowin', right?" And Frank Field says, "Who *is* this?"

And from there Shanahan convinces *Live at Five* that he is not kidding around, not the slightest bit. There is going to be a race war at the Posse Serpens rally, which is actually more of a best-case scenario than an actual exaggeration.

In any case, they send a camera crew over to Glenn Disteek's concession speech in Rock Hill. And sure enough a Nazi gets punched in the face by a black guy on live TV. Everybody loves it. No one even bothers to chase the black guy down. Not even the Nazis. No one can identify the guy. No one even wants to. And Shanahan pulled the whole thing off himself. He's probably smarter than the rest of these idiots put together.

But Krabbe is maybe a bit too impressed with Shanahan's maneuvering. It's almost as if he's taunting Duke Drummond with his elation, delivering this punchline, "You should have seen it! *POW!* Right in the face! That fuckin' asshole. His career is OVER...!"

Such was J.R.'s recounting of the amazing yarn, which he finally wrapped up, saying, "For a second, I thought Drummond was going to shoot poor Krabbe, the proverbial messenger, for denying him the heads up, so that he could at least tune in and watch the *coup de grace* on TV. But he couldn't even vocalize a grievance. His employees had vanquished his enemy, and he could only praise them. Shanahan had probably single-handedly ended Glenn Disteek's career in politics."

Later, reflecting on it, and how it had centered around a moment caught on film, J.R. was left lying awake in the darkened barracks, regretting the callousness which bordered on glee with which he had expressed himself, when Elsie was just such a victim herself.

Not only that, they both were. They had it in common, though he had not told her, and never would, he had already decided.

He rose from his cot and walked out of the barracks into the blank, cool, eventless night. His tape was their leverage over him. Her movie was their merchandise. He couldn't lay down with either of these thoughts, much less sleep. He knew he could still escape. He didn't know whether she ever could. Staring up at the stars he entertained a brief fantasy that his father, at that very moment, was staring up at the same starry sky and wondering where he had gone wrong. If Jack Daddio was bewildered, it served him right.

## 56. It's Called Poetry

The next day in the rec room at the ping-pong table it was J.R. and Elsie versus Steeplejack and Sandra Pride, the four of them happily active and agile inside the beer stained, snot green carpeted, pin-up and rebel flag festooned Nazi arcade. Someone had tacked up a glossy 8x10 campaign photo of Glenn Disteek wearing his black leather trench coat and attention-grabbing rockabilly Mohawk. The picture was pierced with three darts and riddled with numerous previous punctures, all gleefully trending from every radial towards his face and balls.

Steeplejack had served up some soft rock from the boom box, maybe Steely Dan, maybe Elton John, whatever the difference was.

During doubles play, Elsie landed in J.R.'s outstretched arms more than once, and lingered just an extra second longer each time, before recovering and resuming the competition.

Steeplejack made similar clutching attempts at Sandra Pride. "GET OFF ME YOU FUCKING RINGWORM!" she lunged away from him and turned to let him know.

The ping-pong ball escaped with a ping-pong ball's particular liveliness into the Mess Hall, where the project underway, involving sardine sandwiches, caught J.R.'s attention. So too did the *Cash Clarick Vittles,* laid out like spoils of war on the picnic table.

As it happened, Grossmark had been summoned down from his Praetorian perch to craft a letter to the *West Susquehannock Dispatch* about Curtis Lemonhall's scandalous past in Philadelphia. Drummond was supervising the project, with Krabbe and Shanahan on hand, and the Old Man seated along the sidelines in his executive capacity. A pen and notepad lay ready but unclaimed upon the Mess Hall picnic table.

"Sandra Pride!" Drummond exclaimed, catching sight of her from the rec room's open doorway. "Perfect. Would you join us, please? We require your penmanship."

Sandra gripped her ping-pong paddle a moment longer before handing it over to Steeplejack. Then she joined Duke Drummond and the others, to take a seat and take up pen and paper on behalf of the Posse Umbellus.

J.R. turned to Elsie, "I want to see this."

"I have work to do," she shrugged easily.

"See you later," he said. "See you later, Steeplejack," he added, flinging his paddle back into the rec room. He made for the sandwiches.

At the same time, the Mess Hall's front door banged open just briefly as Bella Shue charged in, followed by little Wallace and Rose Archer. The trio circled once in madcap brevity and then went right back out the door, all in the span of a few rowdy seconds.

"Grossmark, it's your time to shine," Drummond said.

Grossmark cleared his throat, then began his dictation. "To whom this herewith enclosed letter concerns..."

"See?" Drummond nodded. "It already sounds super professional."

"That's right," Grossmark affirmed. He began pacing a short distance back and forth.

"Write it down," Drummond directed Sandra Pride.

"I wrote it down," she assured him. "What's next, genius?"

"Hey!" Grossmark snapped.

She slammed down the pen. "What?"

"Relax!" Drummond ordered them both.

They heaved their sighs almost in tandem, then returned to their assigned tasks in unspoken mutual hostility.

Grossmark resumed his pacing of the floor. "It has come to my attention..." he continued.

Sandra Pride wrote it down.

"That one Curtis McKinley Lemonhall..."

She wrote it down.

"Is in the current employ of your heretofore esteemed publication."

"I truly don't know how he does it," Drummond commented.

"No wait..." Grossmark stopped pacing. "Not publication. Make it *periodical.*"

"Jesus," Sandra complained.

"Just cross it out for now," Drummond told her. "We'll write it out later for real."

"Oh, great," she said.

"Sandra. Relax. Please."

"Can we engrave it in marble too?"

"Will you just try to be helpful? Please?"

She sighed, acquiesced, returned her pen to paper.

"Generally speaking..." Grossmark continued, "I am not one to stuffily besmirch herein the reputations and characters of such outsiders and newcomers to West Susquehannock's exquisite township and newcomership as one such Mr. Curtis McKinley Lemonhall would inhabit himself to be, despite said interlopers fleeing post haste from mulatto love-children of Cleveland prostitutes..."

"Grossmark, you are a genius of the highest order," Drummond meant it. The awe in his voice seemed magically to coincide with a surge of sunlight through the Mess Hall's windows.

"I relish the opportunity to express myself, boss," Grossmark responded.

"Carry on, good sir."

Grossmark's dictation continued, "But when the shadow of said *man-on-the-streets* casts itself over our very streets, our very yards, our very midsts..."

Sandra Pride's pen froze at attention. *"Midsts?"* she queried.

*"Midsts. Midsts.* Write it down."

Her pen hovered just above the stationery.

"Just write what I say."

*"Midsts?"*

"It's not a fucking term paper! It's war propaganda! You are a pest, woman! Do you know that?"

"Term paper?" she countered. "I am literally going kill you right now!"

"Will you stop it!?" Drummond pleaded to both of them. "Sandra, I know you're always angry, all the time. Heck, that's what I love about you. But I need you on my side, girl—"

"Girl?"

"Girl. Woman. Whatever the fuck! Jesus Christ! Will you knock it off? I'm going to demote you if you don't knock it off!"

"Demote me from what?"

Drummond quivered with frustration. "GODDAMMIT!"

"All right, calm down, Mr. Man," she told him. "I'll write your damn letter."

"PLEASE resume the dictation!" Drummond ordered Grossmark.

"...Collecting information and photographic evidence of intimate data," Grossmark continued as Sandra Pride took up the pen. "And finding his dark way out here for the sake of all that is holy we ought to write essays and diatribes and such to the very newspaper of our very locality, the *West Susquehannock Dispatch,* at the very least, if not much more so, and with more semblance of our actual townsfolk herewith represented..."

Sandra Pride paused again, raising pen from papyrus. "This sentence is too long."

"Boss, will you tell her again? For the zillionth time? To write down what I say?"

Sandra Pride exploded to her feet. "I WILL KILL YOU WITH JUST THIS PEN, GROSSMARK!"

The entire Posse Umbellus was on guard, Krabbe and Shanahan crouching with clenched fists while the Praetorian overhead racked their rifles and Grossmark unholstered his Walther pistol.

In response, Sandra slipped the pen behind her ear and unsheathed her twin hunting knives.

The men looked around at each other, then back to Sandra Pride, then back around at each other, seeming to agree, all at the same time, with the same face and body language, *Not worth it.*

Duke Drummond, perhaps alone on planet earth, had the ability to contain Sandra Pride's wrath. He did exactly that now, quietly pleading, "Sandra Pride, that's enough, stop it. We don't cast our lot with cynics, girl."

Maybe it worked like magic. Or maybe Sandra just didn't want to die. She stood her ground one stubborn moment longer, then exhaled, so that all in attendance could hear it. Backing down from her warrior's stance, she holstered her two knives.

"Would you please write down the letter for us?" Drummond asked her again.

She nodded.

"I'm counting on everyone, Sandra Pride, to work together here."

She sat down at the picnic bench, snatched the pen from behind her ear, and resumed her secretarial task.

"Go ahead, Shakespeare," she muttered. "Tell me about the *midsts.*"

"From our unsuspecting townsfolk..." Grossmark was dictating again with triumphant impatience. "I would expect no less," he continued, "from your venerated West Susquehannock institution—"

"Institution?" Drummond stopped him. "Wait a minute."

"What?"

"An institution is a place for crazy people."

Grossmark sighed. "Trust me, boss. It's the perfect word for this particular contextuality. Or contextualness. Trust me. It'll fuck 'em right up. That's the whole point... is the double meaning of it."

Drummond yielded. "OK. I trust you. Carry on."

Grossmark smiled.

"I'm counting on you here."

"It's called poetry."

"That's enough. Get on with it, before I change my mind."

"OK, sorry."

Sandra's head flopped down at the picnic table. Grossmark continued his dictation. Sandra straightened again, set pen to paper.

"...that you would on some fundamental, if not primal, if not primordial, if not legal level," Grossmark continued, "vet your mysterious employee. At least to the extent of preventing any of our own West Susquehannock flock. Or herd. Or congregation, as the case may be, from falling prey to Mr. Lemonhall's veritable crime spree of serial miscegenation."

"Cereal what...?" Drummond halted the letter.

"That's a fancy word for the idea you had, boss. About the mother being white."

"Mercedes Jefferson?"

328

"That's the one."

"What was the word?"

"Miscegenation."

"Miscegenation," Drummond mused over it.

"How's it spelled?" Sandra Pride asked, pen to paper.

"Doesn't matter," Drummond answered.

Grossmark countered, "All due respect, boss. This time it matters."

"No, I'm right," Drummond countered.

Grossmark argued, "To play this character—"

"No," Drummond shut Grossmark down. "This character should be trying to sound smart. But he should just be a regular Joe. Bad spelling will be part of his signature."

Grossmark yielded, humbled, "I don't know how you dig so deep into these things, boss. But that's why you're the boss."

"Spell shit wrong," Drummond advised Sandra Pride. "Especially what's it called?"

"Miscegenation."

"Miscegenation. Especially that. Only a fuckhead would spell that bullshit right. Grossmark, you will stand over Sandra Pride while she writes it out wrong. And make sure she does it WRONG AS FUCK! Be creative now!"

"You got it, boss," Grossmark answered.

"Jesus," Sandra responded. "Thanks a lot, boss. You think I can't misspell shit?"

"No questions," he told her. "Don't question me. Goddammit I thought we were done arguing! Do not go rogue on me, Sandra Pride!"

There followed a second letter, with Sandra Pride tasked again to take dictation, while Grossmark played the part from a fundamentally different state of grace. *"DEAR IDIOTS..."* the second letter began.

J.R. had lost interest in the drama by now, even when it stirred up an entire other knife standoff, which had begun to take on the quality of ritual, always to be quelled by Duke Drummond's soothing assurances.

## 57. Origami

Both letters were finalized and sealed to be mailed to the *West Susquehannock Dispatch*. With the task complete, and the creative fever broken for all involved, the room began to clear. J.R. turned toward the rec room, where the table tennis paddles lay abandoned. That's when Steeplejack spoke from overhead.

"J.R., come on up here."

He looked up, looked around for anybody who might protect him, which was nobody. Then he faced Steeplejack, and resolved not to speak, simply to ascend the staircase as called upon to do.

Steeplejack went back inside his bedchamber, where Vince Baldwin's protesting voice could be heard. Crosby Shue, who stood at his post to the right of Steeplejack's door, nodded in acknowledgment of J.R.'s arrival, but said nothing.

"Are you allowed to say hi?" J.R. asked him, with no sarcasm intended, though Crosby Shue responded, "Just be cool, hot shot."

At that moment, Vince Baldwin came storming out of Steeplejack's chamber door, brushing past J.R., almost knocking him over.

"Jeepers, Vince!"

"Fuck off, Junior!" Vince grabbed the banister, the newel post, the railing, then scrambled down the stairs.

330

Crosby Shue remained grim and tacit, slinging his M16 two-handed.

J.R. turned to face the threshold of Steeplejack's silken lair. Even as the barometer of his own culpability crept further by way of his nervous system into his spinal column, it was as if in slow motion, compared to his willpower, taking that fateful step, entering the room and shutting the door behind him.

"What's wrong with that asshole?" he asked Steeplejack.

"Who? Vinny B? What can I say?" Steeplejack shrugged and pointed vaguely around at the movie studio that occupied much of his workplace, a plush king-sized bed strewn with pillows and coverlets and stuffed animals and discarded garments, all of it attended by idle cameras and idle floodlights from surrounding tripods. "He doesn't have the talent for this kind of work. I told him he could be the bartender. He pouted and left."

J.R. shook his head, determined to keep his voice down. "You don't put Vince Baldwin on camera," he pleaded quietly. "Jesus Christ, he's a quote-unquote missing person, probably."

Steeplejack belted a loudmouthed laugh from his gleeful, gecko-like face. "We're all missing persons, son."

J.R. couldn't believe he had to explain it. "You don't want Vince Baldwin in the porn business," he spelled it out. "He's one of the four guys left alive..."

But now he trailed off.

Only a minute ago, out in the hallway, all four of them were rallied to one location—J.R., Steeplejack, Vince Baldwin, and Crosby Shue. Nothing had happened. But it could have. All at once. A single heavy strike. A rocket launcher, or pre-planted device.

He could see it now. The Brinks Job was never supposed to succeed. In fact, it was probably Drummond himself who had tipped off the police, to remove Steeplejack. Because of Farrah, most likely. Same for Crosby Shue, for whatever reason, maybe the same reason. But it made for a perfect hodgepodge of casualties. Management, middle management, the husband of Elsie Gannon, and the two new guys that nobody liked or trusted. A perfect crime, except that J.R. had screwed it up by driving them out of there, sixty thousand dollars richer.

331

"J.R.," Steeplejack assured him, "I don't want Vince Baldwin in the porn business."

"Not even as the bartender?"

"Don't take everything so literally, jeez."

J.R. sighed, collected himself, looked around, tried to focus on his surroundings instead of his woes. The production design also included a Universal Gym. Also a copper bathtub, presented on four baroque, curling feet. Otherwise, most of the room's textures were soft, curtains and linens and blankets and pillows in abundance, with a few stuffed animals strewn about. The wall mirrors multiplied the effect. And now, within those many dimensions of fabric, Steeplejack began to whisper of treason. "So, J.R. How about we summon de Ram like you said."

"Whoa!" J.R. said. "What? Wait a minute—"

"You," Steeplejack waggled a forefinger, elevating his hand so as to waggle from above. "It was your idea. You're the one who thought it up. Back when we were killing time inside the U-Haul. Except we weren't killing time anymore when you said it. We were 30 seconds from show time when you said it."

J.R. panicked. "I swear to God, that was the exact moment I thought it up!" His voice was loud, too loud. He could hear the loudness, even as his mouth spewed the words. He lowered the volume. *That was the adrenaline talking, man! We were all about to die, for all I knew!*

"All right, calm down."

His mind was racing. Steeplejack and Drummond were at war. Elsie was caught in the middle. Conspiring with the pornographer was almost as stupid as it was downright evil. And Vince Baldwin was a loose end, a force beyond containment, a perpetual liability. Also the tape. It was all too much to keep track of.

"Where's my tape?" he demanded.

"What?"

J.R. breathed out a sigh, lowered his voice again, leaned in, allowed his snout to reap Steeplejack's outer membrane of sleaze. *"If I'm collaborating with you on treason, I want my tape."*

"What tape?"

"You know what the fuck tape!"

"All right, settle down, calm down, easy does it, take it easy. You know Crosby Shue is stationed right outside that door, right? With nothing else to do but listen in on us?"

"Look around at this place," J.R. hissed. "This is a fucking Nazi Porn Studio. There is no conceivable privacy here. I want my tape."

"Hey, c'mon. We're the Posse Umbellus. We're not Nazis."

"I want it so I can *destroy* it—"

"The Nazis, they *lost*. We're not Nazis, J.R. We're *winners—*"

"With my own *two hands!*"

"That tape is just leverage, kid, to keep you in line."

"But now we're summoning de Ram. So there is no line to keep me in. So now I want my tape."

"All right, I get it. I got you. I understand. You're right. You are on point, my man. Relax. Let's send this note. I promise to get it into your hands. Pronto. OK? Consider it done. I completely get you."

"Good. That's what I want to hear. So you mean what, exactly, when you say *note?*"

Steeplejack explained what he meant. A note ostensibly penned by Duke Drummond, to be stashed in with de Ram's cocaine delivery.

J.R. said, "OK. So, before I write this down, I need to know Elsie is going to be safe. That's my primary concern."

"Elsie?" Steeplejack paused. The expression on his face revealed a genuine specter of sympathy.

"What?"

"You're kidding me. I figured you for a man already. Elsie is terrific, but this is not someone to get attached to, J.R. OK, never mind. I take it back. Say no more. I'm sorry."

"What do you mean?"

"Hey. You know what I mean. Man up."

The pen and paper lay upon the makeup table, arced over by a mirror frame of low-watt bulbs.

Reflecting upon Grossmark's so-called Shakespearean letter to the *West Susquehannock Dispatch,* J.R. resolved not to write anything anywhere near that stupid.

He took up the pen. "What's de Ram's first name?"

"He's just de Ram."

J.R. laid the pen to paper.

"That's it then," he said, two minutes later, applying the finishing touches. He handed it over for Steeplejack to read.

*Dear de Ram. I figured that by intercepting your nose candy, I'd get my memo into your filthy paws. Your wife was so passionate, is what I heard, out of her own mouth and lips, while you were playing around with your fireworks, in your Ronald McDonald clothes. I was so mad that you blew her to bits. I wasn't so upset about your little brats, though. P.S. Your boss got punched in the face on TV and took it like a pussy. Sincerely, Duke Drummond.*

"THIS IS TERRIBLE!" Steeplejack declared.

"As opposed to what?"

"You're a terrible person!"

"As opposed to who? What? Whom?"

"I thought you didn't want to do this—"

"I didn't, don't—"

"We can't send this—"

"That's exactly what I was saying two minutes ago! And I was an idiot back then! But now it's my fault? GODDAMMIT!"

Steeplejack sniffled and rubbed his nose.

J.R. pointed his finger, "You don't even know what the fuck you're doing. You're exactly as stupid as every other jerkoff in this place. Not to mention every other stupid jerkoff in this whole world. I truly hate you fucking fuckers. I hate you till the day I die. You're crazy. I'm sane. Fuck you!"

"No wait... all right... calm down... take a breath. J.R. Hold on. You didn't say you didn't want to do this. What you said is, 'Where's my tape?' Those were your words, am I right? 'Where's my tape?' Those were your exact tough guy words." He shook his head, sympathetic in a way that still seemed genuine, somehow. "Listen to me," he continued. "I get you. I got you. You'll get your tape. You've got it. You'll get it. But with this note, we split the difference. We write a more different note. A more softer note."

"Do you want to be nice?" J.R. asked him. "Or do you want what you want?"

Steeplejack cocked his head.

J.R. cocked his own head.

"All right," Steeplejack flung up his hands. "All right, all right. You're right. And when you're right, you're right. See, that's my boy. That's why everyone likes you, J.R. Even though nobody says they like you. Or some say they do. But most don't. Probably most of them don't say anything. Come on over here, J.R. One good line deserves another."

J.R. stood confused for a moment, then understood. "Wait," he said. "Wait... *What?*"

Steeplejack began to sing his words as he waggled his index finger and pinky in tandem, *"She's insane, she's insane, she's insane... Cocaine."*

"What the fuck? Are you out of your mind?"

"No! No way, man. I'm doing what Romans do. You would do what Romans do too, if you were you. Or maybe they don't do it. Romans, that is. Suit yourself. The way I see it, though, you're damned if you do and damned if you don't do. So do or don't do. Or my personal preference which is to do. That's what I do," Steeplejack chuckled as he scraped the razor against the mirrored plate.

Behind him, amidst the chamber's plush tapestries and curtains and pillows and duvets in its windowlit quadrant, the gym equipment sat idle under stark sunbeams of light. The apparatus wasn't so much shiny and new as frequently disinfected, offering a tactile alternative to the room's near fetishistic continuum of fabric, notwithstanding the pair of Betacams, plus the still camera. Also notwithstanding the copper bathtub that offered no faucets or spigots, only a contoured vessel for occupants to ladle in their own bathwater, or sheep's blood, or mother's milk, or tears of fools, or whatever other horrors went on in this sex chamber. It was painful to wonder what Elsie might have endured in this room.

Steeplejack snorted his line of cocaine, then pressed his knuckle into his right orbital. J.R. watched the molested nostril quiver.

Then came the monologue, while sun streaks beamed through the second story window where dust motes drifted around the gym equipment or disappeared into the den of fabric.

"See you think it's about Farrah... for me... because you think you know everything, at age fifteen, or sixteen, or whatever the fuck old you are. But it isn't, and you don't. I mean you're right in a way. But it's not a quote-unquote soft spot for me. This is the most obvious thing in the world, or in my life, if you have the courage to think about it. And not her, either, by the way. Are you kidding? Or crazy? It's Drummond, man. Looking down on me. Like I'm some kind of dirty secret.

335

All the while my networks of actual commerce actually fucking finance this place. So OK. Never mind that. So all of a sudden he gets his hands on some serious cash, courtesy of my other talents by the way, and yours too, more than a little bit, if everyone is being honest with themselves, in case you weren't noticing that they weren't, Mr. Trans Am driver. And suddenly this somehow means my services are not so much needed... or... is that the word? Needed? There's too many D's and E's in needed. Did you ever notice that, J.R.? Needed? Needed? It can't be spoken. Or I mean, I can say it, but it's too easy. It's too easy to say. It's too easy to say it's too easy, too. Have you ever noticed that either? How easy it is? I mean, seriously, how easy is it? Hold on a sec, J.R., I need to think..."

Steeplejack paused for several nanoseconds of near agonizing stupefaction, sorting it out.

"J.R. Daddio," he continued, "listen to my words, not my face, not my voice. My words. OK? Don't ever start snorting this shit. See, you? You're on the outside. And you can stay on the outside. Where you belong. But me? I'm on the inside. And that's the only way I can say it. But anyway..."

The pornographer sprang from the ottoman and seated himself at a dressing table before its mirrored and filament-lit arch.

With little choice but to press on, J.R. said, "It's not just that this is dangerous and maybe wrong, and bad..." striving to meet Steeplejack's stoned and wayward eyes. "If we send this note," he explained. "If we send this note, de Ram... de Ram is definitely going to come here and murder everybody. Do you understand that?"

"Not everybody. Do *you* understand *that?* But yes, that's the objective, more or less."

There would be no better scenario to wait for. "OK," J.R. said. "Let's get on with it."

"You wrote it perfectly already. It's perfect."

"We can do better."

"What do you mean?"

While Steeplejack hunkered in confidence on the nearby divan, J.R. took a seat at the makeup table and once again set the pen to its ruled tablet of notebook paper. First, he drew a ballpoint rectangle. Then the lines of the inner balcony. Then the bullseye. Then Cash Clarick's battle axe and war hammer, crudely demarked on the wall by the entrance. Then, with steely ballpoint conviction, J.R. superimposed the eight Praetorian guard posts, assigning each of the eight encircled initials, SK for Skinner, TR for Trauer, and so on around the horn, including CS for Crosby Shue. He also encircled the initials DD inside the master's chamber.

He thought of targeting LF as well, but his instincts stopped him. LF was Fat Ransom's sister. He left her out.

When he was done, he handed the map to Steeplejack and asked, "What are you going to do if he tries to kill *you?*"

"Are you kidding?" Steeplejack seized the offering. "The Posse Serpens is gonna love me. I've been in business with Fat Ransom for years. Plus, he's Farrah's brother. You'll see what I'm saying. We're running a business here, son. You'll catch on, after the dust settles." Finally peering down at the map, he gawked bug eyed at the crude geometric cartography. "Oh my God!" he said. "This is diabolical! You're a sick fuck!"

"What are you gonna do if he tries to kill *me?*"

"Just keep your head down, J.R. Watch your own ass. Instead of you-know-who's ass. I'll explain to the conquerors how you played a vital role in the overthrow, don't worry."

Casually, Steeplejack removed a black plastic 35-millimeter film canister from the vanity's desk drawer. He popped the cap with his thumb and forefinger, then extracted with his other thumb and forefinger a tightly wrapped baggie of white powder. Grinning, he displayed the baggie.

J.R. shrugged, "Is that a lot or a little? I don't know."

Steeplejack threw his head back and laughed. He waved a hand dismissively. "Bullshit!"

"What?"

"Sorry, son. You're flagged for that one."

"Son?" J.R. quarreled. He hated Steeplejack. It made his skin crawl to conspire with him here in this lair of vice.

But Steeplejack was done laughing, and had turned to face the make-up table, and to lay de Ram's letter down, along with the map, as flat as possible, one on top of the other. He then began to fold the aligned pages, first into rectangles, then into triangles.

J.R. watched with fascination. It was a more advanced note than any he had ever seen passed in high school. When it was done, Steeplejack presented the small, tri-cornered object for one last glimpse. Then he tucked it into the film canister with the drugs.

The cap was sealed. J.R. asked him, "What if Farrah opens it?"

"She won't. She doesn't care." Steeplejack selected one of the bureau's tinctures from its array, unscrewed its top and presented its slender and delicate paintbrush to inscribe the film canister in white nail polish upon the black cylinder's grey bottlecap.

A commotion sounded outside the chamber door. It was Snapper hollering from the watchtower, followed by Duke Drummond and many other shouting voices.

Steeplejack looked down at his wristwatch. "That's Fat Ransom. Damn, he's early. Come on. This'll be a hundred thousand times easier if we do some coke first—"

"You just told me not to do coke."

"That's because it's expensive. And I don't want to share it. But for this occasion, I'll make an exception."

"Maybe neither one of us should do coke."

Steeplejack scooped the powder up with a pinkynail and huffed it into his brain. He swiped his knuckles across his nose and blinked his eyes to open them wide. "Too late," he said.

Outside the door, Drummond was shouting to his Praetorian Guard, "BRACE FOR ANYTHING! WE DON'T KNOW IF HE'S ALONE!"

At that moment, Farrah opened the chamber door. "Steeps," she said, "my brother is here—Oh, Jeez! I hope I wasn't interrupting you two weirdos."

"Farrah!" he said. "We've got something. I mean. Sorry. I've got something. I've got something for you. To give to your brother."

Farrah's blue eyes blazed with a kind of demonic boredom, even as she broke into her gap-toothed grin. Her face was something J.R. longed to study more, even though he knew better than to gaze too long. She was wearing flip-flops again, he noticed, and then he noticed, and not for the first time, the way her naked toes and feet gripped the rubber thong of each sandal. Also the way her coveralls gathered tightly in a way one should avoid catching sight of helplessly, repeatedly, around her groin.

She remained holding the door open, still gripping its knob. She had taken notice of Steeplejack's contraband with something approaching curiosity.

Steeplejack beckoned to her, "Well, come on in. And close the door behind you."

She left the door standing open and approached.

He handed her the cylinder. She took it. Watching this exchange J.R. reminded himself that these two had known each other forever.

Drummond's voice could be heard outside, barking to his men. Farrah pointed to the cylinder's grey plastic cap. The name scrawled in white nail polish. "This says it's for de Ram."

"Right," Steeplejack twitched, sweating. "It's for your brother to give to de Ram."

J.R. felt his own temperature rising inside Steeplejack's suffocating paradise of sexual accommodation. Somehow, a plot to frame Duke Drummond, sealing J.R.'s very own culpability inside an implausibly dense triangular note stuffed into a film canister full of cocaine, had become a fateful bid for escape.

Drummond chose this moment to pop his head into the room, barking, "Wait in here until we secure the area!" and was gone just as suddenly.

Farrah sagged her shoulders. "Great."

Steeplejack pantomimed the unfurling of a red carpet for his guest. "Come on in. Have a seat."

"No thanks," she answered. "I'm not touching any surfaces in here."

She looked around incuriously, then back at the canister in her hand. She popped its top and peeked inside.

"Ah..." Steeplejack reached to stop her, withdrew his hands. He sent J.R. a panicked glance, just briefly. Then he went back to his solo fretting, massaging his nostrils with his thumb and forefinger.

Farrah tilted the cylinder around in her fingertips, as if an easier way might be found into it. Finally, she reached inside with her fingernails and plucked out the coke.

"Umm," J.R. said, "is she supposed to—?"

Farrah shot him a glare. Steeplejack's face was slick with sweat, his facial muscles visibly suffering from the strain of smiling. Farrah said, "What are you, nuts?" holding up the drugs while her other hand lowered the canister upside down. The note had slipped halfway out. "You're sending de Ram coke?"

"de Ram, yes, hey," Steeplejack explained, with decreasingly convincing nonchalance. "Hey, hey. Cash Clarick is gone, hun. Get it? We need a new go between—"

"*Shhh. You're not supposed to say Cash Clarick's name anymore.*"

"That's exactly my point—"

That's when a gunshot went off—BANG!—down in the Mess Hall. The three of them crouched instinctively. Steeplejack barked, "STAY DOWN!" and began sneaking toward the dressing table, and the shotgun stashed behind it.

Amidst all the shouting, a voice from the Mess Hall cried, "FALSE ALARM! FALSE ALARM!" followed by more shouting. "STAND DOWN! STAND DOWN!" Then, "JESUS CHRIST, CHUCK ZORN!"

Chuck Zorn could be heard apologizing only twice, "I'M SORRY! I'M SORRY!" Then, "GET OFF MY BACK ALREADY!"

Drummond hollered, "EVERYBODY CALM DOWN!"

Chuck Zorn made a point, "WHAT ARE YOU ALL? PERFECT?"

Drummond barked, "SHUT YOUR FUCKING FACE, CHUCK ZORN! THAT'S AN ORDER!"

From inside Steeplejack's chamber, Farrah demanded, "WHAT'S GOING ON OUT THERE!"

"CHUCK ZORN SHOT A HOLE IN THE CEILING!" came her husband's response. Followed by, "...AND HE WANTS YOU TO KNOW IT WAS AN ACCIDENT!"

The triangular note had fallen to the carpet. J.R. tried not to stare at it. There were two options, except there was only one. Because to spring after it was suicide.

Farrah hadn't noticed it yet. "Those idiots," she was saying, perhaps to herself.

Steeplejack had tipped the shotgun back behind the mirror. Now, as he drew closer to Farrah, he eyeballed the fallen note. It lay on the floor, a folded paper triangle. He moved to pick it up. Farrah saw it first. She stooped.

"Yeah," Steeplejack said. "That note is supposed to go in with the coke. Or not in *with* it, but you know... it goes *with* it... you know... *in*... you know..."

She said nothing, fascinated, holding the folded triangle.

"...the canister," Steeplejack finished. He watched her two hands.

340

She assessed, with her digits and fingernails, the folds of the sealed triangular document.

"Did I mention that's for de Ram?"

"Hey," she said. "Did you forget? Everything in this place is mine." She then looked at J.R., and with no apparent provocation, she said, "You got that, kid?"

J.R. mutely pointed to himself. He glanced at Steeplejack, whose face said, *We're dead.*

Farrah now stashed the empty cylinder and its cap and the baggie of coke into her coverall pockets so that she could attack the note with all ten of her meddlesome fingers.

J.R. was beginning to understand that he had made the wrong several choices several moves ago. Allowing Steeplejack to talk him into this deathtrap, so that he could finally actually get himself killed. It was nobody's fault but his own, for suggesting mutiny back in the U-Haul truck, before the heist, in that adrenaline spiked moment of panic, before he knew he would get out alive, a state not unlike this one, except that it was becoming more commonplace, so that he found himself angling subtly closer after Steeplejack's shotgun behind the bureau, just in case there might still be a chance for escape, even if it meant going headfirst out the window.

Except that Farrah couldn't figure out how to unfold the note, and she gave up almost immediately. The entire eternity of desperation was all in his head, lasting only a few seconds.

"Jeez," Farrah said, disappointed. "What do you call this? The way it's folded?"

She brought the disassembled film canister out of her pockets to restore the contraband, tucking the note and the drugs back inside and sealing the circular grey nail-polish painted cap.

"Origami," Steeplejack answered.

"You *would* call it that," she scrutinized him only briefly.

"I'm kidding," he said. "I don't know what it's called. I'll look into it for you. How does that sound?"

She shrugged, pocketed the cylinder. "What does the note say?" she asked.

That's when Drummond's voice from downstairs came commanding all to attention. "FAT RANSOM IS HERE! HE'S ALONE! AND HE'S WELCOME! YOU WILL WELCOME HIM! BUT YOU WILL STAY SHARP!"

"So long, creeps," Farrah told them.

341

"I'm going with you," Steeplejack said, making for the door.

J.R. was rid of them, finally, except that Steeplejack turned back to say, "You should get lost, J.R. Go fix a hubcap or something. Or go to church with your girlfriend."

## 58. Power and Action

Behind the Mess Hall, outside the kitchen, equidistant from either turret along the Castle's northwest wall, a semblance of privacy could sometimes be found at the right time of day along the path next to the strung-up deer carcasses. That's where J.R. whispered to Elsie of the mutiny he and Steeplejack had set in motion.

Elsie paused in her tracks, lowered her head.

*"Tell me..."* he was calm and dire, keeping his voice down. *"What choice do we have?"*

She raised her head, continued walking, without answering. He followed alongside her. Finally, with her stubborn and ominous sincerity, she responded, "It's God's choice what happens, J.R. Did you see the canister exchanging hands?"

"Yes, I did," he answered. "I didn't want to lurk around too much. But yes. I stuck around to witness the exchange. By the way, Steeplejack greeted Fat Ransom with a handshake and a clap on the shoulder, and then disappeared out the front door. So it was just the three of them. It was Farrah, Fat Ransom and Duke Drummond. And eventually the Old Man, who seemed to just... I don't know... materialize... from behind the bar. I was watching from the rec room. But I watched long enough to see Farrah give her brother the note."

Elsie stopped in her tracks. She looked worried.

"What is it?" he asked her.

That's when Vince Baldwin sprang out from behind a gutted, suspended deer carcass.

"JESUS, VINCE!"

*"Don't blaspheme!"* Elsie whispered.

"Hey, kids!" Vince greeted them with that recently acquired pretension of humility and benevolence that made J.R. want to strangle him to death along this very walkway and stash his corpse behind the deer meat.

"J.R., can I have a word with you in private?"

"Vince, I hate you. Get away from me?"

"I didn't mean to startle you. You either, Ms. Elsie."

"You jump out from behind a dead animal carcass?" J.R. balked. "But you didn't mean to startle us?"

Vince shrugged. "Point taken. Can I just talk to you in private, please? That's all I'm asking. C'mon. C'mon, man. J.R. Daddio. You talk to Elsie in private all the time. But you only just met her. Me, you've known for years."

"Now you're catching on."

"All I'm asking for is one minute."

J.R. sighed.

"I've got laundry," Elsie squeezed his hand briefly, warmly, and then left him to his Erving hometown intrigue, to stand conspiratorially in the alleyway behind the Mess Hall kitchen with the last person on earth he liked or trusted.

Vince Baldwin leaned in to whisper, *"Duke sends me around to spy on you, man. You're supposed to make a good impression on me, understand? I mean... Get it now? You've got to get with the program, idiot. I'm speaking to you as your friend. This is me being a double agent, literally. I'm trying to save you from yourself... from getting executed out on the croquet field."*

"Vince," J.R. responded, "you're a moron. I don't like you. I don't trust you. And I sure as hell don't listen to you. So why don't you run your game somewhere else?"

Vince shook his head. The look on his face, the despair, was almost convincing.

J.R. made to leave.

"Hold on," Vince grabbed his arm.

"Get off me."

"Listen."

"No, you listen, Vince. Murder is legal here. All I have to do is murder you."

"That's what I'm trying to tell you, you fucking know-it-all."

"What? What are you trying to tell me? What do you want?" J.R. shook his arm free.

They faced each other, along the boot trodden path, backdropped by the slain and trussed-up wildlife along the ten-foot corrugated steel wall.

Vince Baldwin leaned in further, with a quality suggesting faithful rehearsal, and whispered, *"Women..."* nodding his head for J.R. to see. *"They are temptresses. That's the role they play, to tempt you on toward destruction. Sex is Power and Action. Or it ought to be. Because if it isn't, then you're getting screwed..."*

Vince Baldwin had never talked this way in his whole life. Clearly, he had been coached, or brainwashed, whatever the difference. Either that or somehow, by some weird miracle, the language and the self-possession had been inside him all along, only to blossom now.

Vince walked away, mission accomplished.

J.R. remained alone, speechless, standing in the kitchen's back yard. He resolved to put the whole exchange out of mind, because if Vince Baldwin could get into his head, he was in more trouble than he thought.

## 59. Canada Geese

"Mr. J.R.!" Harding called down from the eastern turret. It was a friendly greeting, a grin and a salute.

J.R. saluted in return, without pausing for it.

The garage work was gratifying. Deconstructing a car to preserve the components for reuse or resale is such a cautious, precise undertaking. This was nothing like that, a much noisier and messier affair, since everything was getting scrapped afterwards. Partridge's Z28. The steel doors, the scooped hood, the side-skirts, the engine, the wheels, the seats, and so on, gradually pried apart and set aside for the pyre in waiting.

All the while, from the turret's eaves and through the sun-struck canvas awning, Harding engaged the two mechanics in steady conversation that turned, in time, to J.R.'s other wheelhouse of expertise, the succession of United States Presidents. Even so, Harding's querying voice from above and through the tarpaulin had taken on, for J.R., a relentless quality, like a hive insect buzzing.

"So what is it about the presidents, J.R., that you find so interesting?"

Prying weather stripping out of the Z28's doorframe, and growing increasingly annoyed, J.R. ventured a cagey response. "You really want me to bring up your cousin?"

"My cousin?"

"Your cousin. Warren G."

"I don't have a cousin Warren G."

Tyto magnified eyes remained expressionless, even as he struggled to untighten a hose clamp, leaning into it.

"OK, Harding," J.R. said, and then he paused to expound. "When I was a kid, some kids, they were interested in comic books, and superheroes, which I never understood at all. I liked baseball, and baseball players, which other kids did too. But even so, I never considered ballplayers to be heroes. You don't assign the title of hero that lightly. So, for me... Tarzan, Superman, Reggie Jackson, Bucky Dent... they were all the same bullshit. Because if you to want to talk about *actual* heroes, you've got to talk about George Washington, Thomas Jefferson, Andrew Jackson. Et cetera. Those were the guys who created our country, in real life.

"But guess what? Heroes in real life don't earn that kind of respect anymore. Not even Ronald Reagan, who is the actual current President of the United States. Everyone talks about Superman, or Reggie Jackson. Or some musician, like Bruce Springsteen. I'm sorry, no. I'll call Ronald Reagan a hero, if anyone, on this whole planet. And by the way, Ronald Reagan already did the movies, years ago, and he grew out of them."

"That kicks ass," Lovejoy interjected, appearing from the yard.

"I know it does."

"I'm on leave," Lovejoy told them all, "for half-an-hour, thirty minutes, from my post. Man, I'll tell you guys, I believe in this cause and all. But I think I'm going stir crazy up in that roost. My girlfriend can't even get this exact half-hour off, so this is my damn jerk off break too."

"You came to the wrong place for that," Tyto quipped.

Lovejoy ignored him. "OK, J.R.," he said. "So who's the best president?"

Under normal circumstances, the mention of Abraham Lincoln wouldn't be suicidal at all. "What'd I just say?"

"Reagan? Bah!" Lovejoy batted his hand. "He's just a watered-down Nixon, jacked up a few inches taller."

"I'm going to take a leak," Harding announced, laying his weapon against the turret's scrap-metal rim and beginning his backward descent of the ladder. "You guys, watch my gun."

"I'm out of here," Lovejoy told them. "This is my half-hour off. Washington is the best president." He left them there.

Very quickly, the auto yard had been left unsupervised.

Tyto laid the car battery onto the work bench.

J.R. whispered, *"Save that battery acid."*

Tyto's begoggled face, though somehow always blank, was somehow also quizzical now.

J.R. explained how he needed a bucket of acid to dissolve a certain videotape, which he would have in hand, soon enough.

"J.R.?" said Tyto.

"What?"

"Dude. You're sticking your neck out for this *Chiquita—*"

"Hey," J.R. squared up to him. "First of all, it's not about Elsie. Second of all, why is everyone warning me about her?"

Tyto shrugged. "Bad juju, man. Bad vibes."

"Don't tell me that. You're the only person here I like. Other than her."

"Oh, dude, I'm sorry. What do I know? I don't know anything."

"Why does everyone want me to not like her?"

"You can totally like her."

"Oh, really? Thank you."

"You're totally welcome. J.R., let me show you something."

"Show me what?"

Turning his back to the sight lines from the Mess Hall, Tyto produced a weapon from his grease stained coveralls. Not to brandish, but to reveal. Brass knuckles. Cast iron, in this case. Well-polished, and yet soiled with axle grease, blood, and whatever else. "This is all I've got left from California, man."

"Hey, look at those—"

Tyto pocketed the weapon just as quickly. *"Not only that,"* he whispered.

*"What?"*

*"I'm Mexican-American, dude."*

*"A Mexican Nazi?"*

*"Shhhh. I'm not a Nazi. That's what I'm saying."*

J.R. lowered his voice even further. *"Oh, I got you, Tyto. Me neither..."*

"I know, dude. Dude. My real name is Tito. Not Tyto. Tito. Tito Gomez. When they asked me my name, I couldn't say *Tito*. I was so scared, man. I swear to God, I couldn't think of what to say. So I said *Tyto*."

"I changed my name too!" J.R. laughed quietly at the coincidence.

"That's why we get along," Tyto affirmed. "So anyway, all this time, I've been telling these lunatics my name is Tyto. But the thing is, on that night, when they abducted me, I heard this voice telling me, *Tyto means Owl*.

"It was the Old Man's voice. Edward. Suddenly, he was standing there, out of nowhere. Out of the shadows, all hunched over, a hundred years old, eyeballs rolled up at me, yellow and murky, like a couple of egg yolks on the stove. *Tyto means Owl*.

"I looked at him, through my big ol' goggles, knowing how I look. And that was that. It was almost like a mirror I was gazing into. Like I owed him some kind of thanks for bailing me out. I mean, that was definitely going to be the end. You understand? Except that it wasn't. Because he believed in me. Man, I'm from California. I have no idea what I'm doing here."

"California..."

"What about it?"

"It's just... It sounds far away."

"Tell me about it," Tyto gazed up at the corrugated sheet-metal wall. "Coronado Island, my friend, is paradise on this earth."

"So how did you end up here?"

"A life of crime. I used to run drugs. Back and forth to San Diego. Then up and down the coast. West Coast, like I said. I was just a runner. I was a young man back then, although technically, I still am. And I was two or three whole guys—maybe twelve guys, who knows, I don't know—removed from the top guys. But my organization got super ambitious.

"So next thing I know, I'm on a damn twin-engine propeller plane, bound for some cornfield in upstate New York. And somehow a swarm of Canadian geese flies into one of the engines, which is not the usual thing that happens, even though it seems like it should happen every single time.

"So down we go, *Kablooey*... somewhere in the Pennsylvania wilderness. It was me and two other guys, crawling out alive. We get quote-unquote rescued by Neo-Nazis. We get sent to some labor camp, where everyone just gets killed. One guy gets fed to a pack of Rottweilers, that's not a joke. Another guy gets his throat cut, that's all, the lucky bastard. Me, I get

349

out alive. Next thing I know I'm in the Posse Serpens. You met those guys?"

"Yeah, I met those guys."

"So that's them. I helped them out with their cars, you know how that is. So then, maybe two months later, I'm on recon with a pair of Nazi SuperSpies, or whatever they are. It's like you got done, getting sent after that armored car, but different. Worse. I get captured by the motherfucking Posse Umbellus. Two more guys get killed. And yet, once again, here I am, still alive, and still breathing, somehow."

"You sound like me."

"That's what I'm saying, man. We're the same dude."

"OK, Tyto," J.R. chuckled, "You're cracking me up. I mean that sincerely. But I don't like that word *dude*. Why do we have to keep saying *dude?*"

Tyto ignored him. "So along the way, nobody questions this. That my name is Tyto. I mean, they question it, but they say things like, *What kind of name is Tyto?* And I say *Celtic Druid,* or stuff like that..."

J.R. laughed.

"Or *Greek Demigod*. Stuff like that. But meanwhile, the damn Old Man already told everybody what Tyto means. It means *Owl*. Except none of those stupid morons paid any attention when he said it. Only me.

"So I got smart. I started spinning stories about how my mom used to call me her *Little Owl*. And how I always felt destined to wear these goggles."

J.R. chuckled.

"Exactly so," Tyto answered with his own laughter, "except my mom knows nothing of owls, or Greek anything." He ventured a refracted and overlarge wink. He stared, wide-eyed, afterward.

Then he revealed the shotgun cradled under the work-bench, though J.R. had already seen it hidden there.

"So what have they got on you?" J.R. asked him.

"Nothing, man. Except that they'll kill me if I leave." Tyto jabbed his thumb over his shoulder at the Road Runner in its allotted parking space. "Look at that thing," he said.

The car was beautiful, J.R. knew this well.

Tyto continued to explain. "You think that thing fell out of the airplane with me into the woods? Nope. That was some other guy's car. A guy that tried to escape. When Drummond ordered the car destroyed, along with the dead guy's body, I objected, just briefly.

"*Aw, man,* I said. *Such a cool car.* Something like that. My exact words. A very much needless objection.

"So now here that car is. Mine. He gave it to me. In appreciation for all my hard work in the auto yard. He was daring me to drive off, understand?"

"I understand," J.R. told him.

## 60. Love in the Belly of the Posse Umbellus

Later that night, for the concert, the Posse Umbellus ordered a dozen kegs of beer. The Mess Hall's porch would serve as the stage, the Nazi standard as silken drapery behind the bandstand.

When the van arrived to unpack the cables and drums and monitors, it was five guys, four performers plus a sound guy, all of them aptly dressed in black boots, black fatigues and black T-shirts, notwithstanding the drummer who was already shirtless.

Observing the set-up, J.R. made ready to jump in and help. However, he never once found it necessary. The routine was clearly second nature for the band, the last thing on anyone's mind.

Silkscreened across the kick drum's front face stretched the upward slashing, underlined, umlaut-stricken logo STINKENHÖEMMER. The wiry shirtless guy was the drummer. The chubby bald guy and the lanky guy in a ball cap were the guitarists. Another guy without an instrument seemed pent up and moody. Their various roles became quickly understood once the show began, with an almost larva-to-butterfly quality. The bald guy was the bass player. The lanky guy was the guitar player, whose cap went flying off his head repeatedly, to be repeatedly retrieved. The moody guy was the singer, growling and snarling with a menace so unintelligible as to be, for all intents and purposes, not the English language.

Studying their effort, J.R. understood for the first time in his life that music was a process that human beings performed professionally. For the first time it was more than just dehumanizing poison oozing out of some moron's car stereo. Or worse yet, the demoralizing clanging of his sister's piano. It was, at last, a bunch of guys driving around, place to place, putting on amplified concerts for Nazi keg parties. As he watched the Posse Umbellus react, he saw them set free from their tedious vigilance, saw them wheeling and colliding into each other with a self-expression divulged shoulder first sometimes, boots foremost almost always.

He turned to Tyto, "IS THIS GOOD MUSIC?"

"NO," Tyto shook his head.

"I KNOW," J.R. agreed. "IT'S AWFUL." And yet a notion nagged at him, with no voice to speak it. He said, "I GUESS THEY COULDN'T AFFORD BRUCE SPRINGSTEEN."

"WHAT?" Tyto's floodlit lenses were white with scrutiny. "BRUCE SPRINGSTEEN? AND THE E STREET BAND? THOSE ARE NOT NAZIS, PALLY."

"NO, I KNOW... ALL I MEANT WAS... NEVER MIND," J.R. watched Stinkenhöemmer. Better to listen, not discuss.

It struck him as entirely possible that music had impressed him in earnest for the first time in his life. Even so, he knew his personal epiphany was spoiled by the most wretched circumstances imaginable.

Indifferent, the music raged, achieving hypnotic repetition, punctuated by a recurring and disturbing tone in the upper register, like some distress signal through the noise. *People don't ever stop to think about what they heard somebody say,* J.R. told himself, or reminded himself, with a measure of self-consolation.

"HEY AMIGO, IT'S TOO LOUD, EH?" Tyto was telling him, "TO HEAR ANYTHING? FROM EACH OTHER?"

J.R. smiled, mutely. He reached to shake hands and exchange goodnights.

The Praetorian Guard in their entirety had been loosed upon the celebration to slam into each other in heed of nothing but the band's torrential and dance-indifferent rhythm. At some point, Snapper jumped onto the stage and stumbled headlong into the singer. The bass player raised his boot and kicked him back into the crowd. The men caught him, amazed. Snapper bellowed something triumphant and primordial before they lifted him up and flung him into the dirt.

Duke Drummond had taken to the stage too, to watch the drummer up close, getting into it, playing violent air drums along with the band's girth of murk.

A firearm went off. J.R. ducked his head instinctively. Another gunshot followed, then another, both deliberate, both affirming the first. Little Wallace wasn't so much hit by a stray bullet as grazed across the cheek by it. The drama was unfortunate but brief, as Rose Archer whisked the face-bleeding toddler away.

Elsie was approaching. J.R. met her gaze. Lovejoy was approaching too, faster than Elsie, stumbling around the throng of pitmoshers, party cup in hand. "J.R., WHAT'S YOUR PROBLEM?"

"WHAT?"

"WHAT'S YOUR PROBLEM? STANDING AROUND LIKE A SOURPUSS?"

"I'M LISTENING!" J.R. explained.

At the same time, Brock Fowler came pinwheeling backwards against his own lost balance. A moment of sheer slapstick gave way to a graceful recovery as Fowler shoulder-rolled onto his feet in front of J.R. and Lovejoy. "J.R.?" he said, "WHAT'S YOUR PROBLEM, ASSHOLE?"

J.R. explained, "NO PROBLEM. I'M LISTENING."

They scattered as randomly as they had arrived. Elsie remained. She looked amused, though not self-amused. "IT'S LOUD!" she said.

J.R. reached and touched her shoulder. He led her away, out of the floodlights, back toward the chapel.

The northern turret was empty tonight. They could fold themselves discreetly around the corner and into the shadows beyond the Nazi jamboree. He could hear his own speaking voice in his own head, explaining to Elsie how music is a distraction from what's important, but how this music was better than most, because at least the guys with the instruments hated music too. "Elsie, you look miserable," he concluded.

"You don't actually like it?" she wanted to know.

"No, no way," he answered. *"Like?"* he questioned the very word. "Like isn't... No way... It's just..." he tried to explain.

It was always so exhausting to backtrack for people. But he would do it for her. Willingly. More than willingly. If he could figure out how.

"You never actually see how it gets made," he told her. "Not unless you go pay money to see it get made. And what idiot is gonna spend money on that? So, it's just... to see the actual noises get made... you start to root for the guys making the noises. Even though the music is trash. You understand? You can still root for them not to screw it up, even though it sucks. That's all I'm trying to say."

"Sounds like you're a fan."

"No, nope. Not a fan. Not of this. Not of any music. Never a fan of any music. Ever. Not ever."

"So what are you a fan of?"

"I'm a fan of you, Elsie."

"Really?"

"Yes, really."

She studied him with wily skepticism that infused the contours of her calculating and ruminating and infuriatingly sexy jawline. Her face was terrific, snake-like. "I don't lie," he told her, "like everyone else does."

"You're a fan of me?"

"You better believe I am. But more than that..."

"More?" she asked. "More meaning more?"

"Yes," he answered. "More meaning more."

She waited.

"I'm your biggest fan," he confessed.

She shook her head, lowered her face, let her hair fall around it, let her smile disclose itself. "And what does my biggest fan want of me?" she asked.

"I want your kiss."

"You want my kiss?"

"I answered your question."

"Well then."

"Well then, what?"

She waited. He waited. He waited no longer. "Give me what I want," he said.

"I'll give you what I want," she answered. She lunged. He lunged. With their mouths they began.

## 61. Chandelier Interlude

He was awakened by Tyto's hushed voice, *"J.R... we've been summoned by Duke Drummond."*

It was a dream about Melissa Victoria. No Scotty this time; Melissa was alone.

It was in no way disorienting to find her alive and well. But now he was awake, and Melissa was gone forever, and Tyto's shadow loomed anxiously over the cot. *"J.R.?"*

"What did I do?"

*"Shhhh,"* it was Krabbe hissing.

J.R. was on his feet and marching with Tyto along the wooden walkway toward the rec room door where a paper sign read CLOSED UNTIL DINNER. DO NOT ENTER OR YOU WILL BE SHOT.

"It's an engineering project," Tyto explained. He opened the door, held it for J.R., then closed it behind them.

They made their way through the vacant rec room to the Mess Hall with its sentried mezzanine, its high ceiling and its deer-antler chandelier. J.R. surveyed the Praetorian Guardsmen looming above. All were on hand, Skinner in the eastern corner, Trauer above the front entrance, Buchanan above the Nazi flag, and so on, including Chuck Zorn's assumed but unverifiable presence, tucked into the shadows behind the stonework chimney's vertical edge.

Drummond sat restlessly at one of the picnic benches, loomed over by Sandra Pride and Farrah, while the Old Man watched from the bench's other end, patient and amused.

Drummond sent Rose Archer away. "I'll grab Virginia on the way out of town, don't worry. But for now, I need you to skedaddle, OK? This Mess Hall is closed!"

"Yessir, boss."

"You too, Sandra Pride."

Sandra Pride got immediately annoyed. "Boss, I can help. Let me stay and help."

"No, Sandra. You don't have clearance for this mission. And I don't have time for a debate. And don't make your murder eyes at me, woman! If you want to be in charge of this militia, make your move! Otherwise, I give the orders! You want to live in a fucking hippie commune, move to Russia! Jeez, is everyone finished arguing with me now?!"

Rose Archer stopped lingering and left swiftly by the front door.

Sandra Pride still hadn't made up her mind. She maintained a warrior's stance, poised to unsheathe her knives.

From across the Mess Hall came the sound of a locked and loaded rifle getting racked.

Drummond glanced up and shook his head, gently. He turned his attention back to Sandra Pride. "Is there anything else I can do for you?" he asked.

She said no more, went out through the kitchen.

"All right," Duke Drummond commenced, "where's that idiot, Vince?"

Vince stumbled in through the front door right on cue, "I'm sorry I'm late boss. I was polishing the croquet mallets."

J.R. blurted, "What an ass kisser."

"Hey!" Drummond barked. He pointed back and forth between the two of them. "You two are going to get along this afternoon while I'm gone! This evening too! That's an order!"

Duke Drummond then explained that he and the Old Man were bound for a meeting in Kansas City. They'd be back tomorrow, and by that time they wanted the chandelier booby trapped to fall. "Look here..." Drummond said. He dropped to one knee. J.R. had spotted it already. Tyto remained expressionless. Vince was delighted to see it, the trap door opening to reveal the duffel bag stashed inside.

357

Drummond leaned in and unzipped the bag. He looked up at J.R. "This look familiar?"

"It's beautiful, boss," Vince was smiling, mouth agape.

Drummond retrieved two bundles of bills, tossed one to the Old Man, pocketed the other. He then zipped the duffel bag shut and closed the trap door.

"I'm leaving Farrah in charge," he said. "Try not to bother her. But if you need something, go to her. Knock on the door. If she doesn't answer, that means she's on her break, and you should come back later. Understand?"

J.R. glanced briefly at Farrah, who dragged casually on her cigarette. He turned back to Duke. "What about supplies? Blowtorch, trip wire...?"

"Oh yeah, I almost forgot. J.R., you're the smart one, so congratulations, you're in charge. Get what you need from the auto yard, the armory, the storehouse, the kitchen, wherever. The Praetorian are all in here with you, so nobody outranks you out there. That means no one should give you any shit. But if they do, you have Farrah's authority, OK?"

"OK."

"Just try not to *use* her authority. The less you use it, the less you look like a pussy."

Farrah glanced at her fingernails. J.R. dreaded the thought of asking her for help, knocking on her door. *Lou was fierce,* Elsie had told him, and he knew he would prove himself to Elsie, but if he could avoid Farrah entirely in the process, that would be preferable.

"And leave the Praetorian alone," Drummond ordered, making to leave. "Don't talk to them. Don't distract them. Don't ask for their help."

The Old Man was waiting, curled forward in his colorful denim vest. Drummond elbowed him, "We can't forget Virginia. Don't let me forget." And then the two of them departed, bound for Kansas City.

Soon afterward, J.R. and Vince and Tyto were up on ladders, extending their forearms, painfully at times, from three different vectors into the fixture's antler spanning radius. Fastening the chandelier with rope beforehand wasn't so hard. Cutting through its iron chain links with the oxyacetylene torch was like crucifixion on the wingbones. Even as he suffered, J.R. resolved never to share this crucifixion epiphany with Elsie, even in jest, though it was a comparison more apt than sacrilegious. At last, the iron link gave way, leaving the chandelier affixed to the ceiling medallion by a thick seaman's knot.

Meanwhile, the Praetorian stood dutifully observing this procedure from eight different angles, trying not to get distracted. "Buchanan, stay sharp!" Skinner barked. Buchanan looked surprised, said nothing, kept sharp.

Down on the first floor, directly beneath the newly reaffixed deer antler chandelier, Tyto volunteered to crawl under the Mess Hall floorboards to rig the trip wire to the trap door.

For this operation, the Praetorian Guardsmen came out of the shadows and up to the balustrade to hawkeye the duffel bag where it lay stashed below. Tyto paid them no mind, got to work. Occasionally he would pop his head out and request a screwdriver or a wire cutter.

J.R. and Vince stood by, waiting for Tyto to finish. Left to themselves, with unfortunate idle time, they struck up their banter.

"So, you were making out with Elsie pretty hard at that Stink Hammer concert the other night."

"That's not how it's pronounced."

"Whatever, twerp. You're finally getting laid. I'm happy for you."

J.R. hadn't finally gotten laid, but it was nobody's business. Holding the flathead in his hand, he twirled it and reversed it to bring downward, if necessary. "Vince, I'm going to jam this screwdriver into your eye."

"Shit," said Vince. "I'll break your arm like a wishbone."

"Not when you're lying on the floor with a slot drive in your brain."

"HEY!" Crosby Shue called down from overhead. "THE BOSS GAVE YOU GUYS ORDERS! YOU'RE SUPPOSED TO GET ALONG WHILE HE'S OUT OF TOWN!"

"Fuck that," Chuck Zorn muttered, leaning over on his elbows. "I want to see these two fight each other."

"Who do you think would win?" Grossmark wondered.

"Vince Baldwin," Brock Fowler's answered. "Hands down."

Lovejoy chimed in. "Nah! No way! My money's on J.R. Daddio."

J.R. looked around and above at the suddenly loquacious and taunting Praetorian Guardsmen. It occurred to him that this was likely Duke Drummond's plan all along, to gather the three of them—J.R., Tyto and Vince Baldwin—into the center of this Mess Hall, with the trap door open, and the money at their feet, with no witnesses on hand, fish in a barrel, for the Praetorian to massacre. Fear seized him in a cold sweat. The taunting continued.

"Buchanan, who you got?"

"Ha!"

"J.R., for sure," Skinner offered.

"Not so sure it matters," Grossmark postulated.

"It's always a shame," Trauer observed, "When someone gets stabbed in the brain with a screwdriver."

"You guys are crazy!" Chuck Zorn argued. "Vince would kick this skinny fuckhead's ass! Am I right, Fowler?"

"Goddamn right!"

"Come on, Buchanan. They're crazy, right? Are they crazy or what?"

"Nuts," Buchanan affirmed.

"Trust me," Skinner calmly advised, "conceivably, J.R. could win."

"You think it's hypothetical," ventured Crosby Shue, "but I've been to war with these two guys, don't forget. And personally speaking, I wouldn't even try to pick a winner."

Suddenly Sandra Pride emerged from the kitchen doorway brandishing a wine bottle.

"HOLD YOUR FIRE! STAND DOWN!" came the cries as numerous semi-automatic rifles aimed down from the surrounding rafters. Only one stray shot went off, and it was delayed by a second or two—BANG!—missing Sandra Pride's person and leaving a hot, smoking bullet hole in the floorboard behind her.

"JESUS CHRIST!" she bellowed. "YOU ASSHOLES ARE SHOOTING AT ME?!"

"Sandra!" Skinner called down to her. "You're not supposed to be in here!"

"Well, this bottle's empty," she said, "and I need something!"

"You're disobeying the boss's direct order! What are we supposed to tell him?"

"Tell him you're a pussy who couldn't pull the trigger," she made for the bar and went for the rum.

"We have orders!" Chuck Zorn protested. "It says so, right on the door! YOU WILL BE SHOT!" He aimed his AR-15.

She spun the cap off the Captain Morgan and flipped the bird up at Chuck Zorn all in the same swift gesture.

"THE BOSS WILL KILL US IF WE DON'T KILL HER!" Brock Fowler's cry was tremulous.

"STAND DOWN!" Crosby Shue pointed a finger around at them.

Sandra swigged from the rum bottle, then absconded with it, or made to, by the same way she had come. However, Farrah had emerged from the master's chamber door to call down from the balcony, "Sandra, what the fuck?"

"I could have helped!" she answered. "Look at those fuckheads!" she pointed at the workforce, and the three ladders, and the antler-spiked pendulum. "How many Nazis does it take to screw in a lightbulb? I could have climbed up there by the rafters and done that shit all by myself... in half the time... without a ladder."

"You defy my husband's orders?" Farrah spoke from above.

Sandra lowered the rum bottle. A dread came over her face.

J.R. was sure she was going to drop the bottle and unsheathe her knives, like she always did. And then die in a hail of bullets.

Instead, Sandra Pride strangled the rum bottle by its neck and slowly unsheathed only one blade with her free hand. "Everyone here knows," she said, pointing around with the dagger, "...including your husband... that they can come and kill *moi*, yours truly, Sandra Pride, any time they're feeling lucky."

"NOT WORTH IT! NOT WORTH IT!" Lovejoy pleaded to his fellow sentries.

"I got what I came for," she displayed the bottle for them. "Now if you'll excuse me..."

"When the cat's away..." Farrah called ominously down from overhead, before retreating to her own chambers.

J.R. sighed in relief. Vince did the same. However, among the Praetorian, a tension was maintained, grumbling about the breach of protocol and flagrant disregard for chain of command. Arguments and crosstalk began.

That's when, apparently at random, Steeplejack strolled sleepily out of his own upper story bedchamber, wearing his familiar bathrobe. He looked around at the lot of them, entirely disinterested, then went back inside. This cameo had an effect, however unintentional, of de-escalation, and was followed by Tyto's harmless emergence from the trap door asking, "What did I miss?"

When it came time to rig the explosives, J.R. went out to the armory, only to be halted in his tracks by Grant Archer. Although he explained that he was acting on Farrah's authority, Grant Archer said he would need to hear it from Farrah herself, or at least see a note.

"A note?"

Grant Archer pumped his shotgun and said no more. Behind him, from the southern turret, overlooking the exchange, Harding took notice and racked his own rifle.

J.R. went back to the Mess Hall. "I don't suppose either of you guys wants to go upstairs and get a note from Farrah?"

Tyto stared, unblinking.

Vince laughed, "Oh, I'm supposed to do you a favor now? Maybe if you were nice to me, ever, once in your life."

Tyto shook his head, pointed to the trap door from which he had just emerged. "I just volunteered for the last shitty thing," he pleaded.

J.R. shrugged and made for the staircase. Tyto whispered after him, *"Dude..."*

J.R. turned. "What?"

"Just don't—"

"I know, I know," J.R. brushed him off. *Don't call her Lazy Farrah.* He already knew that.

Cash Clarick's crisscrossed weaponry mounted on the wall caught his attention as the guards watched him ascend to the Mess Hall's second story. He knew about half of them didn't like him, and the other half saw him as some kind of curious gamepiece.

He nodded silently to Skinner, who stood sentry at the nearest darkened post. He then turned back toward the lodge's nearest corner, where Grossmark and Fowler waited on guard. He nodded to each of them in turn where they stood on either side of the master's chamber's door.

"You're sweating," Grossmark said, disgusted.

"I'm working," J.R. explained.

"Oh, and I'm not?"

"I didn't say that."

Striving to suppress all confrontational instincts here in this most hostile corner of the Mess Hall's mezzanine, J.R. simply knocked on Farrah's door, and then waited awkwardly in the Praetorian guardsmen's presence. During those seconds, it occurred to him that if they started shooting, his best chance would be to leap over the banister and dash for Cash Clarick's commemorative battle axe.

Farrah answered the door. He looked at her. Although people were always invariably grotesque on some level, with Farrah the grotesquery was magnetic, and never more so than now. "What?" she sighed. "Come in, jeez."

Thus invited, he entered.

She closed the door, looked him over. The intensity and depth from her blue gaze so starkly contrasted with the apathy dripping from her every other corporeal component that she seemed, at times, a sock puppet she dragged around by her own eyeballs. Even so, her coveralls hugged her body with an allure that corkscrewed J.R.'s spirit and intellect both, spiraling and spinning, imposing some repeating and maddening shape upon his grasp on life, and sense of self dominion.

"What do you need?" she asked, sincere only in her boredom.

"Ahh... a note?"

"A hall pass?"

"A what?"

"You need me to write you a permission slip?" she broke into a grin.

"Umm..." he faltered.

"Umm..." she mocked him. It was nectar-like, her disdain. Not an odor but a scent. "What do you need? From where?"

"We need explosives, from the armory."

"That wasn't so hard," she asked, "was it?"

She glanced at his crotch while he tried, and failed, to fight off an erection. "Oh," she said. "Poor choice of words, sorry."

His thoughts swam briefly but began to drown in mortification.

363

Mercifully, she released him from her gaze. She went to the bureau to write him a hall pass. Her yellow legal pad was ruled. Her black magic marker squeaked against the paper.

His gaze settled upon his surroundings, a large room, roughly the same size of Steeplejack's porn studio but not so plush, and much messier. Laundry was flung about. Books, newspapers and periodicals lay scattered amongst the scattered clothes. One of the paperbacks was *A Catcher in the Rye,* which J.R. had never read but knew about, or had heard about, and now wondered about, including wondering which one of them had discarded it, Duke or Farrah. Also, which of them had flung the cheaply bound manuscript, or screenplay, or manifesto to the floor. Whatever it was, it lay open, face downward. Tools lay scattered about too. A flat head screwdriver, a broken doorknob, a pair of rubber gripped wire strippers, a tire pressure gauge. It seemed several domestic, educational, creative and mechanical projects had been abandoned all at once in this bedroom. Farrah tore off the yellow note and gave it to him, folding it once before handing it over. He took it from her and unfolded it.

In block caps it read: GIVE J.R. WHATEVER THE FUCK HE WANTS. DON'T BOTHER ME AGAIN. FARRAH.

He looked up at her. "Thank you," he said.

"What's my name?" she said. She drew in closer and withheld herself at the same time, leaning back with her face even as her proximity increased. J.R. leaned away too.

"What?" he asked. "What? What's your *name?*"

"Don't be stupid. Answer my question."

"Farrah," he answered. "It's Farrah."

"Farrah the pin up girl?" she asked. "With the feathered, ashen hair?"

"No," he said. He didn't know if Farrah's last name was Drummond, or Ransom, or maybe it was still Brool. It was probably Drummond, he figured. But what if he was wrong?

She said, "My hair is honey, not ashen, wouldn't you agree? Honey blonde?"

"Your hair?"

"Like honey... not feathered... more like... dripping... out of a honeycomb."

"Jesus Christ!" he blasphemed.

364

She drew closer still, advancing nose-first. "It makes me weak in the knees," she breathed, "the smell of a nervous man."

"What? I'm not nervous."

She had something in her hand. Something she'd withdrawn from her pocket. He looked at it. It was an old-fashioned cigarette case. It was tin, and thin, and its lid was painted in full color with a nude woman, though nothing like a Playboy Centerfold or anything modern day. It was a vintage work of art. J.R. had never seen a painting rendered so small and exacting.

"I need your help, J.R."

"Oh."

"You see this here heirloom?"

"Yes," he looked at it again. The naked woman, painted. Finally, his gaze settled upon the inscription. Peering a bit closer he could see it in cursive.

*Rauchen von Zigaretten weiter, so dass wir all unser Geld verlieren kann.*

"What does that inscription mean?" he asked her.

"It means *This House We Built*," she told him. "It was Gramma Brool's. It's worth a fortune."

"It was? It is?"

"You think I'm lying? It's worth more than that sack of traceable bills under those floorboards, I can tell you that."

"That's amazing," he said.

"Yeah, yeah," she agreed. "So, J.R., are you going to booby trap this object for me or not? All this assignment is... It's just like the chandelier outside, only smaller, and inside. Probably take you two seconds."

"What?" he asked. "What kind of booby trap?"

"What are you asking me for? You're the smart one. You figure it out."

"Farrah," he pleaded, "Duke said—"

"I don't mean *now*. I mean *after*. After you're done with the chandelier, you come back up here and help me out with this here *hair*-loom. Tell you what, I'll even leave the door open. You won't even have to knock and wait outside."

He was paralyzed by her grin, her eyes.

"This..." she gestured down at it again. She was awaiting his answer. "J.R., snap out of it," she said suddenly. "You want your tape or not?"

365

"What? My tape?"

"Steeplejack told me you want your tape, and you won't take no for an answer. So? Do you want your tape? Or not?"

"Yes, yes, I do," he recovered his senses, thanks to the easiest question in the world. "I want my tape."

"Stammering fool. You're annoying. More than most. Get about your work. Complete your task. Do you have my note? Yes, you do. It's there in your pocket. I'll be here when you're done. My door will be open. No knocking. No waiting. Just enter, come in. Bring your tools."

When he was back out in the hallway, the eight Praetorian guardsmen were studying him more curiously than murderously this time.

He descended the stairs, once again taking notice of Cash Clarick's wall-mounted battle axe and war hammer.

Tyto and Vince were waiting. J.R. pulled the note out of his pocket and showed it to them. He marched past them with all the dignity he could summon, out the front door and down the steps to retrieve the explosives from the armory.

This time, Grant Archer stood aside.

Back up on the three ladders, J.R., Tyto and Vince Baldwin worked to rig the knotted rope to blow.

"J.R.?" Tyto asked, atop his ladder, as he wove plastic tendrils around the medallion's loop.

"What?"

"How was it in there?"

Up near the ceiling, the room's heat collected. The shadows of the Mess Hall balcony seemed both closer and hazier, as the Praetorian stood about in their watchful octagon. J.R. wasn't about to answer Tyto's question, not even cryptically. Instead, he told Vince, "Get your hands off that," and reached to seize the mechanism from Vince's thumbs and fingers.

"What, you don't trust me?"

"Will you stop?"

"Stop what?"

"You know what."

"No I don't."

J.R. felt some new and fantastic psychic stress come over him. He looked at Tyto. "Am I crazy?" he asked.

But Tyto's expressionless magnified eyeballs revealed mere sentience. "Dude," came his answer.

Of all the people Farrah could have enlisted to booby trap her antique cigarette case, J.R. had been called upon. When he was done with the chandelier, he bid farewell to Tyto, said goodbye to Vince Baldwin, and retained his canvas tool satchel. Thus equipped, he made his intrepid way back up the staircase to Farrah's bedchamber.

Arriving there, he found an open door as promised. She greeted him. He entered, and the door fell shut behind him.

"So..." he said, looking around at the ransacked bedroom. The laundry chute was perhaps out of order. If he were to booby trap an antique cigarette case for the boss's wife, a disused laundry chute seemed like just the place to do it.

"My first husband," she said, "this was his."

Again, she revealed to him the antique tin.

"The truth is," she continued, "he was just another asshole. But that don't mean I don't miss him, some nights. The thing is, this stupid naked lady cigarette case is worth a fortune. It's like a brick of gold. Except bricks of gold weigh something. So this is actually much, much better."

J.R. nodded.

"Duke, my current husband, he doesn't want to know about this here *hair*-loom. So I haven't told him. Nobody else knows about it either. I just figure you can tape it inside the laundry chute and rig it to mangle the motherfucker who sticks his hand in there, without hurting the actual *hair*-loom itself. But what do I know? You're the engineer. Just don't tell Duke. Or nobody else. That's the important thing."

J.R. was half repulsed, half aroused again. "I..." he said, trying to stand tall. "I would rather not be privy to this information."

"Too bad. You're privy. But there's a whole other booty in this here master's chamber. And you? You're useful, they say."

"What? What about Drummond?"

"Kid, don't even start to fuck with me. Every second of your life, I've got you by the scrotal sack with my overgrown claws here."

J.R. looked back and forth between the aforementioned and the bespoken.

"Whoa," she said, "Did you just proposition me again? That's twice."

"What? No. No, I hope not."

She looked again, shook her head, looked into his eyes. "Looks to me like you hope so. The first time I let it go. But now I think you're being aggressive."

He was sweating freely with shame. Also regret for this betrayal of Elsie. "I didn't mean anything offensive," he said desperately. "It's just... It's just... a bad idea... is all I mean."

"Bad Idea. That should have been your nickname. Instead of Nimrod. Do you even know who Nimrod is?"

"Nimrod is an insult. It's not me. That's all I know."

"Ha. You can't bother to know. So I can't bother to tell you."

"Tell me what?"

"Are you giving me orders now?"

"No..."

"Doofus. You just wish, don't you? You're just like all the rest. You don't even know. I probably saved your stupid life twelve times since you got here. Probably twelve. You're probably the twenty-zillionth stupidest asshole that ever lived."

"Well," he said.

"Well what?"

"The... umm..."

"The what?"

"The... you know... The cigarette case... That's what we're booby-trapping, right?"

He was right. She put it in his hands. He took it. Plans were laid.

He positioned the booby-trap inside the laundry chute, no hall pass required. It took some time. Night fell. In that interim, she retrieved his tape for him.

He said, "Thank you," and tucked the prize into his tool satchel. The chamber windows were open, and the air in the room was oxygen rich, though breezeless. Sounding in symphony outside, the crickets, frogs and katydids pulsated. He arose and stood. He let his satchel fall to the floor. He approached Farrah where she stood facing the moonlight.

"You see that?" she asked him.

"Yes," he said, "the moon."

"What are you looking at?"

"What?"

"Are you watching the clouds? Or the moon?"

368

He looked again, confused. "I'm watching the sky," he answered.

"Dumbass. That why you don't feel nothin'. Try watching one thing or the other. Maybe you'll take a stand someplace."

He had said moon the first time. She had him off balance, sounding like a child. He was sick of it.

He watched out the window. She watched too. The tractor beam of white moonlight drew their collective gaze. Above the dark tree line, the moonstruck clouds were still, utterly. He had his tape. He would destroy it.

Very little held him in check now, besides Vince Baldwin, who remained a nagging liability, having witnessed the Saw Mill, the Brinks Job, and the corpse-strewn getaway. Even though J.R. was still a minor, and had been kidnapped, and held at gunpoint through every crime, Vince could spill all those beans, not to mention whatever else he knew, or might know, depending on who had told him what. If anyone required murdering, it was Vince Baldwin from Erving, New York.

Farrah was speaking, "Don't you just want to say *fuck it all,* sometimes?"

"All of what?" he asked. He glanced at her. She was annoyed. He told her, "You're gonna tell Drummond I did this."

"Whoa," she leaned back. "Are you giving me orders again?"

"I have to tell Drummond I did this," he answered. "You understand that, right? This is some kind of test, right? It's a test. And there's only one right answer. Right?"

"Ha, good luck with that line," she laughed. She turned and abandoned the moonlit stretch of unkempt bedchamber to bid him out the door. He bent to collect his satchel of tools, allowing himself one last glance at her. Then quickly and clumsily he made his way out, saying, "Good night."

He stood inside the second-level Praetorian octagon only momentarily. Then he went downstairs and straight to the chapel, but Elsie wasn't there.

369

## 62. Breakfast with Farrah

The morning air was cool, its moisture dissipating only initially so far as the valley's risen sun began its daily surmounting of the Castle's corrugated wall. Breakfast would be held outside. The men had removed a pair of Mess Hall picnic tables to the front deck to accommodate the Posse Umbellus members in attendance. The likes of Tyto, Vince Baldwin, Harding and Krabbe answered a roll call largely non-managerial. Farrah was present, but Steeplejack wasn't up yet, Duke Drummond and the Old Man were still not back from Kansas City, and of the eight Praetorian, only Crosby Shue had descended from the rafters.

J.R. greeted Tyto and sat down. He said good morning to the others in his vicinity, Shanahan, Grant Archer, and so on around the horn. No one cared. Meanwhile, the din of the children began to eclipse the idle banter, as Bella Shue and Wallace refused to seat themselves. Loudly shrieking and laughing, and chasing after nothing in evidence, they plunged around, dancing, each in their own direction.

*"Guess what I got,"* J.R. whispered to Tyto.

Tyto was wide-eyed, expressionless. *"What?"*

J.R. smirked. *"Let's just say we're going to need that bucket of acid."*

*"Oh,"* Tyto smiled in return. *"There's good news about that too. I mean about the bucket of acid."*

*"Good. It's time for some good news."*

*"Seriously,"* Tyto said. *"Brace yourself. You're gonna be happy."*

After the women finished setting the tables, they came around with hot food—scrambled eggs, toast, venison strips. At one point, Elsie hovered close by J.R.'s side with a steaming coffee decanter. He kept more and more of an eye on her. He hadn't found her at all last night, after his misadventures in the Posse Umbellus master's chamber. Now, by the light of morning, he was searching her face for clues.

At the same time, he felt a maddening desire to snatch glimpses of Farrah where she sat bored and bright eyed at the other table. He'd been plagued by thoughts of her all night, of how it might have played out differently, if he had made different choices, said different things.

He knew it was not only wrong but unwise. For instance, he knew that Steeplejack, a drugged-out pornographer, had been tormented by Farrah for a decade or two, to the point of mutiny and beyond. This was no one to fixate upon. However, he also knew that any given day might be his last on this earth, and so he allowed himself a guilty moment of faithlessness, at least of heart, making up his mind, if only for this moment, that if one or the other, Elsie or Farrah, would just have sex with him, it would be so much easier to muster some devotion.

The meal was already underway when Snapper emerged from the barracks and made his way up to the makeshift grandstand. Arriving at the nearest table, he seated himself and said, "Rose, my dear. My dear and wonderful Rose. Would you fix me a plate, please?"

Rose began to rise, but Sandra Pride gripped her by the shoulder. "Get it yourself, Snapper. You're late."

"Whoa," Snapper smiled, showing his empty hands.

"The plates are right there, you lazy slob," Sandra continued. "Let Rose Archer eat her damn breakfast."

Amid heckling laughter, Snapper responded, "Oh my God," and laughed along. "I'm so embarrassed. I'll get it. I'll grab my own plate, for pity's sake. Whoa! These plates are even warm! That's so great! I love it here! I love warm plates!"

J.R. noted the absence of sarcasm and presence of humility. Snapper could not have been more sincere if he were saying a prayer on Thanksgiving Day.

Serving himself from the breakfast trays, Snapper continued to occupy everyone's attention. "The only reason

371

I'm late is that... well... I was writing a poem for you, Sandra Pride."

More smiles and laughter began breaking out among them. Finally, Harding asked, "A poem?"

"A love poem," Snapper answered.

*"Ah hah!"* Shanahan cried. "I knew it!"

Others shared in exclamations, murmurs, nods of approval.

Sandra Pride cut them off, "Poetry is for limp dicks."

Laughter struck the rest of them now, as if by a wave. Even Bella Shue and Wallace were stunned and awakened to the world of adults through the sheer force of laughter.

With his plate full, Snapper sat himself down again, entirely at ease with the atmosphere of mockery. When he spoke, he was addressing Sandra Pride in front of everybody. "Nothing you can say," he told her, "will make me love you any less."

"OHHHH!" the audience seemed to list the other way in his favor.

"Really?" Sandra Pride smirked. With that one word—its inflection—she turned the hecklers, most of them, back to her side.

Crosby Shue challenged Snapper, *"Nothing* she can say?"

Shanahan challenged Sandra Pride instead, "Come on, Sandra Pride, I bet you can think of something."

Snapper was not to be intimidated. "Hey," he told Sandra Pride, "I wrote you a poem." He looked around at the others, then back at her. "These guys? None of them ever wrote you a poem."

With that, self-contented, he forked down some scrambled eggs.

"You want a *poem?"* she asked him.

The assembly grew rowdier in their approval, everyone enjoying the moment. "YES!" they urged her on. "WE WANT A POEM, SANDRA PRIDE! WE WANT A POEM!"

She began, "Roses are dead."

"Oh, here we go."

"Violets are blind."

*"Violets are blind,"* one of them echoed.

They waited. She completed her stanza. "Snapper's a dick and cunt combined."

They burst into uproarious laughter, even Snapper, "Oh my God! Talk dirty to me!"

Rose Archer made vaguely helpless hand gestures at the kids, whose worldview inside their Posse Umbellus childhood had perhaps come to crisis at last, upon exposure to Sandra Pride's dirty talk. It was all comedic and light-hearted, until Harding got annoyed that his coffee wasn't hot, and held up his mug, barking, "SANDRA PRIDE! I DON'T WANT A POEM. I WANT HOT COFFEE!"

The laughter trailed off.

"I'll get it," Rose Archer offered.

Sandra halted Rose Archer once again with a stern hand.

Harding was at the other table. So were both coffee pots. So was Farrah, who had at least one of the vessels within arm's reach. J.R. became increasingly concerned that the only actual authority on hand was Lazy Farrah.

Vince Baldwin chuckled.

It seemed at first that Sandra had defused the moment, rising from her seat and making her way around to the coffee pot, saying, "I got a warmer for ya, Harding, take 'er easy."

But as she approached the next table, she locked eyes with Farrah and said, "They're so lazy, ain't they, Farrah? Every last one of them. All except you and me, that is."

Amidst nervous coughs and sputterings, J.R. felt an absolute certainty that violence would ensue, so prescient that only blissfully mundane details could capture his attention at this preciously dwindling moment of peace. He caught sight of Rose Archer grabbing a bite of meat from her husband's plate. He saw Brock Fowler emerge from the Mess Hall's sunlit door. He saw the Nazi standard billowing in a capricious and freshening breeze. It was inside these moments that Sandra Pride's impatient stride came to its unpreventable end, as Farrah grabbed up the coffee pot to deliver the punchline: "Lazy like this?" never leaving her seat, swinging the scalding glass weapon as far back as she could and then upward, unsprung, lightning fast into Sandra Pride's chin, shattering the decanter.

Sandra Pride screamed in rage and pain, reeling back, clutching her steaming, scalded face. "VILLAIN!" she cried.

Strong men bleated feeble syllables in shock and horror. Harding rose to his feet in mute protest of the violence he had set in motion. Elsie stood, too, or began to, until Rose Archer

373

held her back from interfering. Farrah was up on her feet, ready to fight, bare knuckled.

Sandra Pride became, in J.R.'s estimation, like a wild animal. He would never attest to having known her. However, he would have said, if he ever had to recount her presence, that she was like a mountain lion and viper rolled into one creature, and always had been, right up until that moment, reeling from Farrah's lethal cheap shot, in which she became more like a sand crab, bright red, advancing sideways, with eyes more implied than seen, drawing out two great knives to attack her foe by sheer animal sentience.

Farrah dodged, eyesight her great advantage.

"HOLY SHIT!" Crosby Shue blurted, "WHAT DO WE DO? DO WE TAKE HER TO A HOSPITAL?!"

J.R. watched Elsie struggle not to intervene. Rose Archer had probably saved her life, holding her back.

Farrah ducked yet another attack. "Are you guys just gonna let her kill me?" She put the question to all of them, a gallery of horrorstruck faces.

Sandra Pride's howls reached an ever more primordial pitch. Steam boiled from her bleeding, scalded face and shoulders. Wallace began to wail from a sheer living plane of human empathy. Brock Fowler exchanged a wordless glance with Crosby Shue, expressing, more than anything, a regret for having stumbled onto this dire moment. Seeing Fowler wasn't up to it, Crosby Shue rose from his picnic bench, drew his pistol, stepped forward and executed Sandra Pride with a bullet to the head.

Snapper watched with mouth agape. So did the kids. The wicked light was gone. Little Wallace's shrieks echoed in the yard. All others congregated in stunned silence. Bella Shue was mute.

J.R. caught Elsie's gaze. It was as if she knew—knew about Farrah, knew about everything—and would countenance him only now that he was shaken back to his senses, unenthralled.

An hour later, Sandra Pride's burial was complete down to its last shovelstamped scoop of dirt. J.R. and Vince Baldwin had been set to that solemn task, while Farrah, Crosby Shue and Brock Fowler watched over them.

Frequently, if not incessantly during his labor, J.R. stole glances at the weeds that grew over Scotty's and Melissa's unmarked plot. The rage he felt was too familiar. Vince

Baldwin just kept on living, while a trail of better souls got laid to an ugly rest.

When Drummond returned, holding Virginia in his arms, he said, "Jesus Christ!" in response to the news of Sandra Pride's poem, final stand, murder, and burial. "Sandra Pride's *dead?* Who gave the actual order?"

"Don't look at me," Farrah said.

"I shot her, sir," Crosby Shue confirmed. "It was a judgment call." He wore his regret for all to see.

"What the fuck?" Drummond asked them, all of them, from one face to the other, until his gaze settled back on Crosby Shue. "We're running out of guys!" he pleaded.

Farrah added, "Oh yeah, and no more speaking her name. That's the rules."

## 63. The Bucket of Acid

The bucket of acid was stashed under the workbench in the auto yard.

"Whoa!" J.R. said. "Where'd that come from?"

"We should avoid breathing it in," Tyto kept his voice down. "And definitely don't get any on your skin, or in your eyes."

"Yeah, of course."

"So, I was talking to Drummond the other night at the concert, you know... I told him how oil and petroleum can get brewed out of hydrofluoric acid and paving stones, and that we should give it a try here at the old Castle. So Krabbe, he was on one of his missions to terrorize Libertyville, in his Stars and Stripes mobile..."

Tyto paused and pointed over his shoulder at the Gremlin in the bay.

"By the way, we owe Krabbe a favor. So Drummond said what the fuck, why not try it? And so he told Krabbe to pick up some hydrofluoric acid and some paving stones down at Handy Dandy Dan's on the way back up here..."

Tyto nodded and pointed out the precisely unique grey quadrilaterals stacked in two jagged towers beside the white plastic bucket.

"You can do that?" J.R. asked. "Make gasoline? Out of hydrofluoric acid and paving stones?"

"I highly doubt it," Tyto grinned. "But you can try to do it."

They shared a quiet laugh.

J.R. had left the videotape in his tool bag. He glanced in that direction. He looked back up toward the canvas-obscured eastern turret, where Ace Van Wert stood guard above the splayed and tattered tarpaulin. The duffel bag lay in the watchful twin's line of sight. And yet it would hardly be suspicious for J.R. to retrieve his own tools for work. The time had come.

"Hydrofluoric acid?" he asked Tyto. "What is that? Water and flowers?"

"Sounds like it."

"It's just a guess."

"You're probably right."

"I may not be," J.R. admitted. "When it comes to public education, I was more inclined toward the Presidents of The United States."

"You've mentioned that—"

"More so than chemistry—"

"It's probably like..." Tyto touched his own nose. "You know dandelion wine?"

"Yes," J.R lied. He had never heard of dandelion wine, or had interest in wine of any kind.

"It's probably like dandelion wine," Tyto said, "only it's *dandelion acid.*"

"Right, exactly. Like I said, I need my tools."

J.R. made for the duffel bag. He would finally be free to escape the Posse Umbellus, even if de Ram never did answer the call to come murder everybody in a coke fueled rampage.

Returning with the satchel, he felt the occasion as momentous, and deserving of more ceremony. At the same time, he knew better than to break into so much as a smile.

"Don't breathe it in," Tyto advised.

"Gotcha," J.R. held a deep breath, then knelt. He leaned back from the powerful fumes and removed the object from the tool bag. He closed his eyes, allowed himself a single moment of reflection upon the evil omnipresence of things he didn't want to remember and would never have to think about again. Then he opened his eyes. With the departure from reality of this videotape, only Vince Baldwin would remain as a loose end.

Carefully and easily he deposited the evidence into the acid. Then he stood from the accomplished deed, releasing his breath and retreating from the odor that stung the air below. He looked at Tyto. As sincerely as he could into those monstrous refracted eyeballs, he said, "Tyto, I owe you one."

"I'm going with you," Tyto said.

J.R. was surprised. "Of course," he answered.

"I don't want to stay here."

"Neither do I."

"Dude."

Tyto had just done him the biggest favor in the history of life. And de Ram was coming to tear the place down. "Tyto," he said, "I have a feeling we're going to be getting out of here very soon. Trust me. OK? But please. Only the three of us. That's all I ask. Me, you and Elsie. That's it. OK? Please. I don't like anybody else here."

"Me neither."

"OK good."

"This stuff stinks."

J.R. nodded to the bucket at their feet, in which the leverage over his very soul dissolved. "Let's go do something else."

"We owe Krabbe a favor," Tyto nodded toward the mag wheeled, red-white-and-blue Gremlin in the bay.

"Cool, let's take care of that."

As they advanced toward the Gremlin, J.R. admitted, "I did sort of like Sandra Pride, though."

Tyto paused for only a moment. "She was a stone cold racist, amigo."

"Yeah, I know. Maybe like isn't the word," J.R. trailed off.

He would say no more about it. Today was a day of teamwork, of triumph, of freedom and rebellion. The last thing he wanted to do was to spoil it by arguing with the only human being on earth who had come through for him.

"Acid..." mused Tyto.

*"Hydrofluoric acid,"* J.R. mused along with him.

"What about acid?" Vince Baldwin asked.

"Jesus—" J.R. blurted, because Vince Baldwin had done it again. Appeared from out of nowhere. This time he had Shanahan with him, which J.R. counted as a strike against Shanahan's judgment.

Tyto's response was playful, "Acid, man... LSD. We're gonna trip out... at the next Stink Hammer show."

Shanahan chuckled. Vince said, "That's not funny."

Tyto shrugged, "Well I never said I was Groucho Marx."

Vince's self-vexation seemed his only consistent personality trait.

Tyto stood deadpan, googly eyed.

J.R. understood with an increasing desperation that Vince Baldwin would ruin everything, always. The tape was finally gone, and yet this one, deranged, cuckoo Erving parasite would haunt his life forever.

They all turned toward the Mess Hall now, distracted by the loud and playful Bella Shue scampering across the deck pursued by Wallace, with Rose Archer banging woefully and predictably after them. It didn't make for any kind of strange sight, even the day after witnessing the violent murder of a fellow soldier at the breakfast table, and so the quartet of men turned back to face each other again.

Vince's mouth hung open, suggesting to J.R. a crucial link between the septum and the intellect, though he could hardly stand to speculate anymore on Vince Baldwin's miserable idiocy. He looked away, observed Shanahan instead, whose intellect was considerably sharper, and who seemed amused, even as he fingered absent-mindedly at his Colt Python's holstered butt.

Vince Baldwin said, "I've known J.R. a lot longer than Tyto has, you know that, Shanahan?"

Shanahan shrugged, good natured. "You're jealous of Tyto. I get it."

"What? *Pssssh,*" Vince recoiled. "No I'm not!"

"Or not," Shanahan shrugged.

"Hey, Vince," Tyto said.

"What?"

"Vince," J.R. suggested, "why don't you stop ruining everything that ever happens."

"No wait, I have a serious question for Vince Baldwin," Tyto said.

"J.R., you should talk."

"Vince," said Tyto. "Vince. Vince Baldwin."

"What? What?"

"Answer me this."

"I'm not answering you anything."

"Which President of The United States was known for drinking dandelion wine?"

J.R. snorted laughter at Tyto's bizarre gambit.

379

Vince eyed the two of them, back and forth, suspiciously.

Shanahan said, "You guys are kids. I'll see you later."

J.R. felt stung by this rebuke.

Meanwhile, the happy and hysterical gibberish sounding from Bella Shue and Wallace spilled down the Mess Hall steps into the yard.

Over the shoulder of the departing Shanahan, Grant Archer could be seen opening the storehouse door, for the croquet set to spill out colorfully at his feet, hammers, wickets, balls and all. "Goddammit!" he cried.

Vince turned back to J.R. and sighed. "I don't know. J.R., do you know?"

"Do I know what?"

"Which president was famous for drinking dandelion wine?"

"Oh," J.R. said. He had to say something. "Are you kidding?" he answered. "Taft. President Taft. They made a movie about it."

"What? President Taft? Is that even real?"

"President Taft was real, yes."

"Wait. You're making fun of me. There's no President Taft!"

"Hey, idiot!" Aesop Van Wet called from the turret above.

Vince squinted upward. "Who, me?"

"President Taft was real! Jesus! Why don't you morons take your high school squabble somewhere else? I'm sick of listening to it!"

"Vince," J.R. said, "Go piss up a rope, would you please?"

"You've got a short memory, Nimrod—"

"I've got a perfect memory, FuckFace. You were hanging in your manacles, happy in your prison, begging to stay."

"I'm the only one here who knows who you are."

"Lucky for me you're the stupidest sonofabitch alive."

"Why don't you just let me *like* you?"

"HEY! WHAT DID I JUST TELL YOU GUYS TO DO!" Aesop Van Wert hollered. "KNOCK IT OFF!"

Almost simultaneously Bella Shue snatched up a stray croquet ball—the green one—and made off with it through the dust. Grant Archer roared, "GODDAMMIT, YOU MISERABLE BRAT, COME BACK HERE WITH THAT!"

Shouting followed from all around, from Ace Van Wert, from Rose Archer, from Grant Archer, and from the roving, reckless children. It was a passing moment J.R. misperceived but would reflect upon afterwards. The moment Vince Baldwin made up his mind, or whatever was left of it, while J.R. still believed, somehow, that it was not already a death match.

He would reflect upon how he could still be this dumb, even though he was the smartest person alive, and he trusted Vince Baldwin less than any other creature on earth, and never less so than at this very moment.

Perhaps it was because he caught sight of Skinner exiting the Mess Hall's sunlit door, presumably on his break, but bringing with him, presumably, his Praetorian authority, suggesting a measure of order and sanity over the yard's multiple conflicts.

In any case, he began to say, "Vince Baldwin, I was having a good day..." wasting those crucial milliseconds on banter while Vince Baldwin seized up the nineteen pound wrench from the worktable and granted J.R. one last glimpse of Tyto's wide-eyed, owl-like sentience before taking it away forever with a heavy THUNK!

"WHOA! WHOA!" someone cried out, followed by a chaos of protests, including Elsie's voice, which split the air, "TYTO!"

J.R. stared in mute regret as Tyto's ragdoll weight collapsed in the dirt.

"NOW you're paying attention!" Vince Baldwin heaved the weapon in his off hand while he pointed into J.R.'s face.

There was a moment for all present where the question needed answering. Elsie Gannon, best qualified, advanced without caution into the auto yard's battleground. J.R. was in love with her, never more so than now, witnessing her authority beyond courage or any other wavelength touched by fear.

Arriving at Tyto's fallen body, she reported him alive at first. "Alive...not dead... not dead... but..." She said no more. Her body language spoke plainly. She dropped his dead wrist.

Elsie had never much liked Tyto, J.R. knew this. However, her face was all regret now.

Meanwhile, she had also been drawn into harm's way. "Elsie," he said, "it's not safe for you here."

She believed him, and she retreated to the sidelines while he watched. It was Skinner, among the spectators, who gently assisted her when she stumbled those last five yards out of danger. Skinner never pawed at her once, or fawned, the way

381

Lovejoy would have. If the battle should be lost, perhaps Skinner would keep her safe. But probably not.

J.R. turned his attention to the murderous Vince Baldwin. He pointed his finger and said, "You killed Tyto! You're a plague on my life! You kill all my friends! And yet you still live! You have to die!"

"I didn't kill Scotty and Melissa!"

"You helped!"

"Oh, OK! What are you? Judge, jury and executioner?"

"Just executioner! You have to be put down!"

"Go for it, J.R.!" came Duke Drummond's voice.

Drummond had arrived outside the auto yard's muddy, deadly pit along with most everyone else. Snapper had vacated the watchtower's spire. Rudy Van Wert and Krabbe had both abandoned their turrets. The Praetorian octet had come spilling down out of the Mess Hall. J.R. could hear voices arguing and laying odds. If de Ram should arrive at this moment, in a cocaine fueled rampage, bent on revenge, it would not be miracle enough. The time had come to murder Vince Baldwin or die trying.

"You told me to keep an eye on him," Vince sniveled to Duke Drummond.

Drummond shook his head. "Listen to me, FuckFace. If you survive this arena fight, you and me are going to have a long talk, in front of everybody. So that there's no misunderstanding going forward."

"A talk?"

"Yes. A talk."

"All's I did—"

"All's you did was kill Tyto, you stupid asshole."

"Tyto was on *his side!*"

"I'm not betting my money on you," Drummond told the hapless Vince Baldwin. "Jesus Christ," he muttered to Farrah, "I'm down to my last mechanic."

Elsie held an impassive, watchful face. To her left and right money was brandished and laid on the line. The wagering steered momentarily in J.R.'s favor, but then others doubled down on Vince Baldwin.

Drummond urged the pit fighters, "Now please, for my sake, make it last."

"I HATE J.R. DADDIO!" Vince Baldwin squared his fist around the bloodstained wrench.

Suddenly, two loud and shouting Nazis came spilling into the auto yard's muddy amphitheater. It was Steeplejack and Harding, in a physical altercation, none of it going well for Harding, who was face down in the mud while Steeplejack landed on his kidneys. "OW! OW! OW!" cried Harding. There was no explanation for the violence, but J.R.'s fight with Vince Baldwin was momentarily derailed.

"STEEPLEJACK, WHAT THE FUCK?" Drummond bellowed.

Steeplejack arose from his work.

Drummond ordered him to the sidelines. He ordered all of them, "NO ONE IS TO INTERFERE! THIS IS AN ARENA FIGHT BETWEEN J.R. DADDIO AND VINCE BALDWIN!"

Harding lay sprawled face down in the mud. Trauer and Buchanan each grabbed a leg by its foot and dragged the wounded man out of the pit to drop along the crowded and noisy sideline.

Ace Van Wert had descended his turret's ladder just far enough to see what all might be decided beneath the auto yard's tattered tarpaulin. J.R. noted Aesop's apparent indifference, along with indifference on a few other faces here and there. However, most of the spectators had chosen a side, those for J.R. being Elsie, of course, and also the likes of Skinner and Crosby Shue. Those in Vince's corner included Grossmark and Chuck Zorn, screaming for blood. Meanwhile, Bella Shue and Wallace were watching, mesmerized, as Rose Archer hovered over the children, weary and sorrowful.

Krabbe cried, "I GOT FIVE BUCKS ON VINNY B!"

Lovejoy countered, "I'LL TAKE THAT ACTION!"

The whole gallery of faces had become a distraction. J.R.'s concentration came to center upon the pipe wrench in Vince Baldwin's clenched fist.

He would get out of this stupid Posse Umbellus Castle, and go on to live a productive, normal life in the land of opportunity. Duke Drummond, on the other hand, would perish, having invested his life, hopes and dreams into a lost cause.

J.R. would reflect upon it that way, when he and Elsie were living on the road, keeping a low profile.

As a minor, he had killed Cash Clarick's two henchmen in self-defense, those villains pureed afterwards, so that the crime was untraceable, even though it wasn't a crime, not J.R.'s anyway.

383

He had never been identified as the driver, either, in the Trans Am speed derby out of Libertyville that hurtled across the Pennsylvania countryside.

The Saw Mill video tape was gone too.

And though he had handwritten the note to de Ram, that note could have been written under duress, weeks or months beforehand. Not to say the note was ever even found.

Bodies had been incinerated or buried at gunpoint. There was a plausible tale to tell, back home, in Erving, with his wife Elsie and infant daughter Wrigley. Even J.R.'s actual killings—Snapper, Chuck Zorn, et cetera—those were untraceable crimes. The only part of it he and Elsie had to work on, to study, to memorize down to the last detail, was Vince Baldwin's demise, since the truth was so much more indelible than anything they could possibly dream up.

J.R. did receive an invitation from the Erving Police. The stationhouse was on Fountain Street, in one of Erving's old historical buildings. There was an open space in front, between a pair of cruisers. J.R. took it, killed the engine, looked at Elsie and said, "Ready?"

"I'm ready," she smiled, cradling Wrigley in a pink blanket.

"J.R., WOW!" Officer Pierce was descending the stone staircase.

"Officer Pierce!" J.R. stepped out of the Nova's driver seat.

Pierce shook his hand. "We were all so sorry about everything."

"Thanks, Officer Pierce. I really appreciate that."

"And your friends. Poor Melissa."

"Thank you."

"Anything you need..."

"Thank you, Officer Pierce."

"Please. Call me Nick."

"Nick, this is Elsie."

Officer Nick Pierce exchanged a brief and friendly hello with Elsie. Then he turned his attention to the baby in her mother's care. "Book this little girl for cuteness!" he joked, playfully reaching for his handcuffs.

They all laughed.

At the desk inside, Officer Shields stood to greet them, then to express his sympathies for J.R.'s compendium of loss. "We feared the worst when your friends were found. But we always held out hope for you, J.R. And sure enough, you proved us right, coming back. Isn't that right, Powell?"

"It's a miracle," Powell attested, standing behind his own desk. "I can't believe it."

It was Shields and Powell and Pierce on duty. Also a detective on hand, whom J.R. didn't know, and guessed wasn't local to Erving. The detective was in the interview room, along with a fresh pot of coffee. They invited in J.R. and his family.

"This is Detective DeForest," Shields explained. "The Chief is up in Albany today, J.R. I'm sitting in for him."

"Sure thing, Officer Shields."

"J.R., you can drop the formalities. Call me Blaine."

"Blaine, thank you."

Detective DeForest was old, world weary, with bushy eyebrows, a head slightly too oblong for his frame, and a loosened tie around an open collar. The interview began with an angle J.R. hadn't planned for. It was an explanation that the deceased children of Erving still have family and loved ones who want answers. It made him nervous.

Before offering his explanation, J.R. made it clear that he felt exactly the same way. He explained that he had joined a militia, and not as a group of Erving confederates, but as a decision very much in keeping with his own personality, out of curiosity, and admittedly, restlessness. It was a lark, the whole thing. The four of them spent the night at a trailer park they called The Compound. Then they began their training program at a weird Saw Mill labor camp. Melissa and Scotty decided to stay there for some kind of couples counseling. Vince Baldwin and J.R. advanced more quickly.

The two of them proceeded to the outpost they called 'The Castle,' where J.R. met Elsie, who had her own tale to tell, about where she was from and why she left it all behind. He fell in love with her. They both thought the Posse Umbellus was stupid. And crazy. So they drove off in J.R.'s Chevy Nova, and had a baby.

J.R. went on to explain that he wanted his baby girl to know her own father's name. And so he waited until he turned eighteen, changed his legal name from Junior to J.R., and got married, all before returning to Erving. He would come home a family man and a father, prepared to reconcile with his own father on his own terms.

The whole thing was a mistake he would never forgive himself for making. But in any case, he had no idea what happened to Scotty Pomeroy and Melissa Victoria, or how their bodies ended up at the so-called Castle's gravesite. He had no idea how Vince Baldwin met his end either.

Detective DeForest wanted names. J.R. reeled them off. Duke Drummond, Cash Clarick, Glenn Disteek, Crosby Shue. Some guy named Snapper. Another guy named Tyto. And so on.

"I need a *Snickers,*" he interrupted himself. "Can we take five? I just need a *Snickers,* or something from the snack machine."

First the wrench. The wrench posed grave danger in Vince Baldwin's clenched fist, windmilling down as J.R. ducked right, then left. It was heavy, J.R. knew this, so heavy as to be lethal from one pinpoint blow. However, the weapon's weight also slowed down its possessor, fatiguing Vince Baldwin just enough, costing him just enough balance, just a bit more each time, while J.R. gained an advantage with every retreat.

*Lou Gannon was fierce?* J.R. would show Elsie who was fierce. He would show them all. The crowd had turned against him. The boos and taunts mounting, led by Grossmark and Chuck Zorn. *Fuck them,* he told himself. *I'm putting Vince Baldwin away just by letting him be himself.*

The next time the wrench came down, Vince stumbled. J.R. kicked him in the ass, sent him plunging into the mud. The crowd loved it, tilting instantly back in J.R.'s favor. It was tempting to attack, but Vince was rising to his feet already. Better to let him cling to it, for as long as it lasted.

"DROP THAT STUPID THING!" came a coaching voice from the sidelines.

"IT'S AN ANCHOR, VINCE!"

"YOU CAN BEAT HIM TWICE AS FAST WITH YOUR FISTS!"

"TEN TIMES AS FAST!"

Vince looked down at the bloody wrench in his hand, considered it briefly, then flung it away BANG! into the corrugated metal wall.

The only trace of J.R.'s deception was a grainy, black-and-white photo in the *West Susquehannock Dispatch,* August 26th edition—inconclusive evidence that could be anybody of J.R.'s exact size, shape, features, and posture, stationed up in the watchtower, a figure clearly distracted from his lookout duties.

The matter never came up with Detective DeForest, but the FBI agents were more prepared, and more intimidating.

This was at the apartment in Blue Quarry. When the knock came at the door, Elsie looked at J.R. and wondered, "Your mother?"

He shrugged. *Not likely,* he knew.

The baby fussed dreamily in her crib. J.R. gathered himself to pounce, ready for anything. Elsie opened the door for a pair of plainly dressed men flashing badges from their suits. They introduced themselves as FBI Agents Epsom and Green. She asked, "Is that your real names?"

"Yes, ma'am, they are," came their answer in unison.

"You don't have to call me ma'am," she was pleasant. "You can call me miss." J.R. went to her side.

Agent Epsom removed a notepad from his breast pocket and flipped through it. "You would be Miss Elsie Ritzel, of West Lewiston, Illinois. Is that correct?"

"Ritzel is my maiden name," she answered. "I'm Miss Elsie Daddio now."

"Also known as Miss Elsie Gannon, is that right, miss?"

J.R. intervened. "What can I do for you, agents?"

"A cup of coffee would be great."

J.R. was stunned. The agents remained unfazed, waiting. "I thought I'd seen it all," he told them.

"I'll make you some coffee, agent," Elsie answered. J.R. allowed them to enter.

"Thank you, miss."

"I prefer tea, miss."

"You're in luck," Elsie said. "This place came with Lipton teabags." She glanced once at Wrigley in her cradle, then offered the intruders another polite smile before making for the kitchenette. J.R. admired her just then, as he did so often, all the time.

"So, Mr. Daddio, you've seen it all?"

"I thought I had," he answered, "until you asked my wife to make you coffee..."

"Mr. Daddio..."

"Perhaps we got off on the wrong foot, Mr. Daddio..."

"Excuse us, please, Mr. Daddio," Agent Green withdrew his notepad.

The agents politely asked him to go through the whole story again. But when he started to explain, they were quick to interject.

"Your fingerprints were found on the car antennae that tortured Vince Baldwin to death."

"I was their mechanic. Not that I wanted to be. Anyway, my fingerprints are all over the cars, all over the antennas..."

"You left the fort in West Susquehannock when?"

"*Fort,*" J.R. chuckled. "That's exactly what it was. Well said. Thank you. A fort. Not even a fortress. Just a fort. Those lunatics called it 'The Castle.' Thank you for putting it in the proper perspective."

"When exactly did you leave?"

"Exactly?" J.R. knew when it was, also knew the Feds were sneaky. "I don't know exactly."

"Mr. Daddio, did they have calendars at the fort? Everything was burned down, so one of the boxes we're looking to check off is whether or not there were wall calendars. Were there? On the walls? Any wall calendars?"

"How about the walls in the weight room? Maybe a calendar in there?"

"The weights were left standing in the aftermath—"

"One of the things left standing—"

"You look like you've been working out—"

"The hot water is almost done, detectives," Elsie said from the kitchenette doorway.

"We're agents, miss."

"Well don't that make you detectives too?" she asked.

"We're field agents, miss."

"Calendars?" J.R. pondered. "I mean... yeah... there were... they weren't... it's not like we were isolated... you know? Or like they were isolated, I should say. They had an agenda, politically. They needed to know what day it was."

"Nazi agenda?"

"Yeah. Hey. Don't give me that. Why do you think we left, huh? I just wanted to learn some survival skills, and get out of town, same as you did, probably, when you were younger, but without your advantages. It was the biggest mistake I ever made in my life, if you can understand that. But at the same time, give me some credit. The second I saw that swastika tattoo on that guy's hand, I was making plans to excuse myself, and say excuse me, politely, and leave."

"Which guy is this?"

"Forearm..." J.R. corrected himself. "Forearm, not the hand."

"Which guy?"

"No idea. None. I'm really sorry, detectives. The whole thing was so stupid. They were a bunch of cultists." J.R. remembered the guy's name as Derby, but had chosen that detail as something to deliberately forget, so as to acclimate himself to lying.

"Cultists? Or *Occultists?*"

"No... jeez... It was a cult. It was *a cult*. Not *occult*. Got it?"

"This kind of lexicological differentiation, is this a new interest of yours, Mr. Daddio?"

"You mean getting words right? No. That's just the man you're speaking to. And speaking of getting words right, it was *a* cult. So write it down that way, agent. Research these guys in the encyclopedia of cults, or whatever you guys do. You're the ones who know everything. I told Detective DeForest all the names. All the names from the Posse Umbellus. Every last one of them. But from the Posse Serpens, forget it. Sorry, I have no idea. It's like I told DeForest. There was Lafeyette. There was de Ram, no first name. There was Fat Ransom, possibly the poor slob's actual God-given name. And there was a lady named Ruth. But there were a bunch of other idiots, too. Like I told the police, I was there for twelve hours, tops. And half of that time I was just trying to sleep in the freezing cold."

"On a wooden platform... in the woods..." Agent Green flipped through his notes and found the passage.

"Agent, I met *my wife* on this adventure. She's making you coffee, as we speak. And tea, for your friend. I have my child, my family. If you want me to regret these developments in my life, and regret the decisions I've made in my life, including sleeping on a wooden platform in the woods, you can forget it. I already told you, I got the regrets I got. I mean no offense at all. I just want it on the record. So get out your tape recorder, so I can say my peace."

"What date was it, exactly, Mr. Daddio, when you and your wife escaped from the fort in the woods?"

"She wasn't my wife at the time. We got married afterwards."

"The date of your escape. Is what we want to know."

"We *left*. We didn't *escape*. Although it was a relief, I can tell you that."

"What was the date?"

"I'm sorry, but I don't remember, agent. It was survival. There were calendars, probably, yes. But why would I set my clock by their calendars? Huh? That's the exact opposite of the thing a person should do, under those circumstances. Which is something you probably don't know, but something I probably do. It was a cult, understand? They told constant lies, about everything. It wasn't even subtle. I didn't believe a word they said."

Elsie backed up her husband, "You don't know what it was like."

"I had to keep my own calendar. My own schedule. My own time," J.R. watched as both agents scratched their notepads. "Ever done that?" he added.

"The date?" said Green.

"It was late summer. But keep in mind it was Pennsylvania late summer, not New York late summer, whatever difference that makes, along meridians and airstreams and whatnot—"

"You mean late summer *August?* Or late summer *September?*"

J.R.'s punches to Vince Baldwin's face did no damage. Vince had been through too much, struck too many times. His face and brain were calloused over.

After landing several blows and ducking several counterblows, J.R. caught a moment's breath, stalking his opponent, while the crowd cheered greedily. He remembered something he had learned from a martial arts documentary, something on PBS, a karate expert explaining about aiming past the guy's face for the spot on the other side of it, and punching that.

Back then, as a kid, he was obsessed with baseball. And so he had incorporated the lesson into batting practice instead of fist fighting. To concentrate a whole symphony of force onto a single point just beyond the target's oncoming face.

It was the same thing now, only with his fists. The distant lesson rallied him. He summoned its wisdom. He used it to punch Vince Baldwin anew, just once, in the face and past it, with all his power. It had absolutely no effect.

Free of the weighty pipe wrench, Vince Baldwin began punching back, repeatedly, violently.

Dodging and blocking those blows, J.R. understood that he had followed Vince Baldwin's very same example of folly, spent his best effort in vain all at once. A sense of grave danger sounded through his body. He felt the dread of something beyond fatigue, something like doom, the plunging anvil wings of spent adrenaline.

The vat of acid under the workbench was an option. But there was no way he could get Vince's head into it without burning off his own hands. And yet, maybe if he shoved Vince Baldwin's snout nearer to it.

That's when the tide of battle turned entirely against him. As he hearkened to the bellowing syllables from Vince Baldwin's murderous face, and as the gallery of Posse Umbellus roared in cacophonous bloodlust, he found his very own fighting forearms seized by Vince Baldwin's grip, until he was wheeled and flung bodily backward into the face of Krabbe's red-white-and-blue Gremlin.

This time, it hurt. He panicked, trying to catch his breath, also trying to rise and square his feet as Vince Baldwin closed in for more violence. And yet, amazingly, at this turning point, Krabbe plunged into the arena, screaming after his damaged car.

"GET HIM OUT OF THERE!" Duke Drummond ordered.

Lovejoy was on it, grasping Krabbe by the shoulders, pulling him back toward the sidelines. Krabbe bellowed, "WHO'S GONNA FIX MY RIDE!"

J.R. bore hazy witness to this even as his head got slammed into the Gremlin's grill. Through pain-wracked delirium, he could still hear and even listen to the cheers and lamentations, and seek to know who was on his side and who wasn't, well after it stopped mattering. The lights were going out. He had been tossed like a slab of meat onto the star-spangled Gremlin's hood.

And yet he refused to die, reaching for the radio antennae, wrenching it free to brandish as a switch. Vince raised his fists over J.R.'s chest. J.R. slashed him across the face.

"GAHHHHHH!" roared Krabbe, breaking free from Lovejoy's grip and sprinting into the pit after his disfigured car. He leapt over the body of Tyto in his path.

Lovejoy gave chase, along with Brock Fowler and Chuck Zorn, everybody hollering.

"GAHHHHH!" Krabbe was closing in. Vince was crying out in pain, clutching his slashed and dribbling face. J.R. rose from the Gremlin's hood and attacked Vince's unprotected love handle once, then twice, drawing howls of animal sentience. He could hear his own unintelligible voice spewing nonsense, "DID THEY TEACH YOU THAT AT THE SAW MILL, FUCKFACE?"

Amazingly Krabbe was attacking. J.R. wheeled and slashed back and forth with the switch, facing two foes at once.

Drummond screamed, "KRABBE, GET THE FUCK OUT OF THERE! THERE'S FUCKING MONEY ON THIS, FOR FUCK'S SAKE! I'M GOING TO SHOOT YOU IF YOU DON'T GET OUT OF THERE!"

Krabbe looked insane, barking and snapping. J.R. beat him back with his own radio antennae. Lovejoy could not hold Krabbe. Krabbe spun and punched Lovejoy in the face. Brock Fowler and Chuck Zorn descended and started to beat the shit out of Krabbe. Vince was charging, trying to shield his face and body both. J.R. slashed him across the belly, let him wheel miserably and collapse onto the Gremlin's hood. The spectators were in love. Krabbe's beating at the hands of Fowler and Zorn spun into a kind of simultaneous undercard, while the bloody Vince Baldwin rolled off the bloody star-spangled Gremlin's hood to land in the bloody dirt. J.R. attacked again. Vince caught sight of the garbage can lid, snatched it up. Another swell of excitement erupted as Vince Baldwin raised the metal shield to desperately thwart the clanging and screeching switch. J.R. struck repeatedly, lashes repeatedly parried. Vince Baldwin was on his feet, shield in hand.

*Lou was fierce,* Elsie had told him. He caught sight of her. He could see he had won her over at last. He could see that she could see. That he was fierce, not Lou Gannon.

When he drove the Nova into Manhattan, it was his second visit to the island. The first time was an adventure. This time was a racket, paying as you go. Two bucks for the bridge. Total bullshit.

As he drove across the span it rained in red and grey and yellow emblazonry. His route was planned beforehand, to skip the Henry Hudson and cross town to the FDR for the sole purpose of driving upon a road named after old number thirty-two. The traffic was insane, and it was raining so hard that the city's snakes of access seemed ready to flood. J.R. felt for the holstered revolver inside his jacket pocket.

He made his way downtown. There was a space outside the theater, but he found a parking garage half a block away. The Nova had survived everything. It would survive New York City.

He parked in the garage. It was time to get Elsie's movie. He had planned it all out. Everything but an umbrella.

*"You want to buy umbrella?"* the parking garage attendant's voice sounded like Dracula. The man was pointing to a dozen or so umbrellas jabbed into a dust bin.

Walking beneath his newly purchased umbrella, J.R. observed the city's near impossible density of signage, from traffic signs to billboards to marquees to stickers to flyers. Some was neon-lit, some was old fashioned, some was half torn down. Selling anything from smutty movies to Coca-Cola to homemade cookies. All of it drenched in rain, and seemingly coated with grime, like the rain was the grime, not the washing away. He was not leaving this cesspool without Elsie's movie.

Inside the theater, a skinny, weasel faced guy in a leopard print sleeveless T-shirt waited at the ticket counter. J.R. checked his surroundings. No one else was on hand, besides a rickety old-timer smoking a cigarette and reading a racing form. The lobby was dim and tight through a haze of nicotine, with low ceilings and a couple of lewd posters on the walls. A purple curtain led to the back. A narrow staircase behind the ticket booth led upward. J.R. returned his attention to the counterman, who sported an earring and a lip sore. "I have an appointment with Mr. Bonehill."

"I'm Bonehill."

"You're Bonehill?" J.R. couldn't help it.

"Yeah, kid. You wanted to meet me, not my secretary, right? That's what you said on the phone."

"I'm not a kid."

"Hey, relax. We're all friends here. That's my secretary, by the way," Bonehill pointed to the old-timer in the folding chair. Both men snickered freely.

J.R. has seen this routine a thousand times before, a thousand times scarier.

"The office is upstairs," Bonehill said. "I meant it when I said I'm interested in your terms. Come on upstairs."

J.R. knew with complete certainty that his end would not come in this weasel's backroom staircase.

There would be no leaving without Elsie's movie, either. The old-timer snickered some more. J.R. went behind the counter, followed Bonehill upward. The pistol hung heavy, nudged rhythmically as he climbed. The back of Bonehill's sleeveless shirt was black, even though the front was leopard print, a shirt apparently sewn together from two different garments. At the top of the stairs, Bonehill opened his office door and went inside without waiting. If a gunfight was to occur, this would be the moment. However, as J.R. arrived at the threshold, his opponent was simply walking around his desk to take a seat.

The office was cramped but managed to include a couch. A few of the posters were framed, and a few dinky trophies sat atop the filing cabinet. A reel-to-reel film projector sat facing a blank white portion of the opposite wall. Two empty office chairs faced Bonehill behind his desk.

"Have a seat."

"I don't think so."

"Kid, gimme a break, huh? I ain't been nothing but nice to you. You don't want to sit down, that tells me you're nervous. And you bein' nervous makes me nervous. And why would you want me to be nervous? Huh?"

"I'm not nervous."

"You just don't want to get dirty, is that it?"

"I'm a mechanic," J.R. told him. "My hands haven't been clean since I was two years old. But whatever goes on in here... on that couch. That's not dirt, or grease. It's something else."

"All right, kid. You'd be surprised, but I'm duly impressed, OK?"

"I might stand on that chair in my boots..."

"I get it, I get it..."

"But not sit..."

"I get it, I got it. You're the mechanic, Charlie Bronson..."

J.R. must have made a face, because Bonehill was making a quizzical face in kind. "Charles Bronson? *The Mechanic?* You haven't seen that flick? I'll tell you, if I was a mechanic, that would be the absolute first movie I'd go and see. Just for the title."

"I hate movies."

"You hate movies? Well then, kid, we've got nothing in common."

"I'm not a kid."

"Excuse me. Man."

"I'm J.R. Daddio, Mr. Bonehill. Do you want this payday or not?"

"Yes, I do. I definitely want this payday, J.R. Daddio. I got to tell you, though, Mr. Daddio."

"What?"

"I'm assuming that's a made-up name."

"That's the name my father gave me," J.R. lied without hesitation.

"OK," Bonehill conceded. "I was gonna buy it off you for fifty bucks. But obviously I can't do that, if it's your real name. Man, I really thought this meeting was gonna go differently. Let's do some business, Mr. Daddio."

"OK, let's."

Bonehill reached to open his desk drawer. J.R. reached for his sidearm.

"Whoa!" Bonehill raised his hands.

J.R. kept his hand where it was.

*"Nervous..."* Bonehill warned, *"nervous..."*

"What's in the drawer? It better be the movie."

"That's exactly what it is. I'm gonna get the movie out now. Is that OK with you?"

"Yes. Slowly."

"And by the way, if you want to show me the cash, so I have any earthly reason to think this isn't a robbery, that would be a gesture I would appreciate—"

"The money's right next to my firearm, Mr. Bonehill. I've got my hand on both." As a general rule, J.R. preferred to tell the truth, but this was no such occasion.

Bonehill slowly removed the reel of film from his desk drawer and laid the silver hexagon on the desk. J.R. removed his empty hand from his jacket.

"Do you have what we agreed?"

"Yes," J.R. reached with his other hand into his opposite jacket pocket and removed the envelope full of Ben Franklins. He laid it on the desk and seized up the movie reel all in one gesture.

Bonehill was quick to snatch up the envelope and look through it. J.R. waited, watched him count. Bonehill peered up at last. "We can do business any time, Daddio."

"Good," J.R. said. "If you ever see this movie playing anywhere, or any other movie with this actress in it, you write to that P.O. Box on that envelope."

Bonehill looked again at the envelope, noted the typewritten address. "Daddio?" he said.

"What?"

"That's just a copy you're holding. You understand that, right?"

J.R. waited, allowed him to speak.

"I mean, it's the only copy I have. But it's not... you know... *the only copy in the world.*"

"What are you saying?"

"I'm telling you the truth, is all. I'm just giving you some advice, if you want to hear it. I mean... I'm starting to root for you, Daddio, in all honesty. So to actually destroy that movie..." he pointed to the reel in J.R.'s hand.

"Go on."

"You don't just show up here in Times Square where it's playing. Understand? You've got to find the *actual distributor.* And Daddio, I'm here to tell you. First hand. Those guys aren't nice. Not like I am."

"Yeah," J.R. nodded his head just once. "Someone already took care of the guys who aren't nice. I'm just cleaning up."

He would show her who was fierce. Lou wasn't fierce. Lou was dead. J.R. was fierce. There was only one allowable outcome to the death match. And yet the tables had turned once again. J.R. suddenly found himself in danger, in a headlock, with Vince Baldwin's knee lunging repeatedly up into his forward-pitched face. It was an amazing, almost surreal experience, because Vince's thrusting knee kept missing the mark, inexplicably, which J.R. registered as a fleeting miracle that simply could not and would not last, the upward-driving patella sure to strike paydirt any moment, if only by some sheer law of averages. It allowed him a moment to rally. There was no way in hell he was going to die at the hands of Vince Baldwin. He contorted his body under Vince's weight, to convert the balance in his own favor. Vince outweighed him—this was a given. But J.R.'s center of gravity beneath his opponent's off kilter dance-like violence created a suddenly overwhelming advantage, allowing him to drive his foe back toward the work bench and the bucket of acid, and to push Vince Baldwin's face down towards the chemical stench.

"AGH!" cried Vince.

J.R. shoved his opponent's face closer and closer to the noxious bucket's open maw. He wrenched his own face and nostrils free, which cost him some leverage, though he shoved downward twice as hard, crying, "SMELL IT! SMELL IT!"

"OH JESUS!" cried Vince, huffing, puffing, fighting back the toxins. "OH JESUS! IT BURNS!" The voice, its suffering, was sickening. Through intense concentration on survival, J.R. could hear the crowd drinking from the joy of it. "OH!" Vince was crying out. "OH, JESUS! OH JESUS!" the blasphemes compiling. J.R. caught sight of Elsie, saw that she loved him. He loved her too. Vince seized up a paving stone. J.R. got whacked in the face with it.

When at last he returned to West Susquehannock, he bypassed the green Appalachian ridges he had once called home, or never called home.

He plunged into the valley, his first visit into the town itself, and his last ever, if today's intentions were to bear out as planned.

A note he had handwritten had triggered a well-publicized massacre somewhere up above the Main Street he was currently driving down. He spotted the local hospital, surely the very same to which the chronically unwell Virginia Drummond had been ritualistically whisked by her father. He also spotted the newspaper headquarters, the *West Susquehannock Dispatch,* where Curtis Lemonhall had made his fateful stand.

He then found what he sought. The public library, on a day he had chosen for its liveliness. He observed the dozens of townsfolk milling about the library steps. With no room in the lot, he had to drive up another block, past a long line of cars, and park his Nova on the street.

It was a fundraiser, with an art auction inside, but much activity out on the sidewalk too. Three different folding tables offered baked goods, cold cuts, coffee, soft drinks. There was live music, a trio of kids, high school aged, dressed in black, two chubby boys and one skinny girl, all of them wearing broad, identical, red-and-white striped ties. The girl was on cello, the two boys on brass horns, the music coherent and slightly mournful. The adult conducting them was a sweaty, freckle-faced woman fully committed to the performance.

It was almost a toss-up, but J.R. decided it would do to be friendly. At the nearest table, the nearest lady looked friendly too, with a pale and pleasant countenance. "Hi," he said.

"Hi!" she greeted him. "Care for a blueberry muffin?"

"How much?"

"It's free. But we do ask for donations, whatever you can spare. You can do that here in this coffee can, or you can mail it in afterwards."

"Really? This blueberry muffin is free?" He reached for it, let his hand hover.

"Well," she smiled. "that's up to you."

Looking her over, he decided she was sincere. Some lady makes a tray of blueberry muffins for the local library, she doesn't exactly overextend herself. But he didn't want to be managing a blueberry muffin through this endeavor either, so he withdrew his hand. "Thank you," he said. "I just ate."

"There's an art exhibit inside," she told him. "And there's a movie at two o'clock. And a poetry reading at four, in the basement."

"What movie?"

"Umm. It's called *Free to Be You and Me.* I believe..." she shrugged a bit apologetically. "I guess it's for kids, more so."

"I don't like movies," he told her.

"OK, well, have a nice time," she said.

Unencumbered by free blueberry muffins, he went inside.

The art exhibit occupied easels by the dozens among the rows and rows of bookshelves. The presentation, offering simple watercolor landscapes at first, spoke less and less of accommodation as the tour of paintings darkened in smeared, bold, oil-based strokes for those visitors who ventured inside.

The library was crawling with patrons of every stripe. J.R. had come at the perfect time to blend in, even as he, and only he, had come to destroy evidence. He would require no assistance from the staff, remembering what they had taught him in elementary school about library research. For instance, in four stuffed file drawers he found the *West Susquehannock Dispatch*, issues dating back two years as promised, although it was more like four, he came to find.

The precise slice of microfiche was not so easily pinpointed, but he located the issue, and pocketed it, wearing a leisurely smile amidst the carefree and celebratory library atmosphere. *Lou Gannon was fierce,* Elsie had told him. Fierce nothing.

He dropped the August 26th edition of the paper in the trash with the candy wrappers, coffee cups, wax paper, vinegar, pickles, onions, and other garbage. The microfiche was snug with the Zippo he had purchased at a highway rest stop. Exiting the West Susquehannock Public Library, he paused to observe the plaque on the wall, its list of library sponsors, names that spoke of local power and influence. He wouldn't need this particular list for anything. But plaques could be handy for their names.

The shotgun was tucked beneath the work bench in the auto yard. Everyone knew this, and yet J.R. remembered it only now. Lying on his back, half alive and fully delirious from the paving stone to the temple, he spotted the game changing weapon where it hung stashed in waiting.

Vince rose to his knees, coughing and choking from the bucket of poison. J.R. tried to rise to his own knees, but he was badly hurt. The throbbing from his right temple registered only vaguely along a spectrum of pain. His thoughts and vision swam. The loud and crowded sidelines of bloodlusting spectators canted every last way but level. And yet, somehow, he rose not only to his knees but to his feet.

He looked down. Vince had him by the leg. Vince was possibly blind, red eyed, driving with a paving stone that missed by a centimeter. Kicking away the crude limestone cudgel, J.R. lost his own balance and fell backwards, whacking his head against an auto yard pit both hard and merciful.

A desperate, hallucinatory climb followed, though he knew he wasn't climbing but crawling through the dirt, with Vince Baldwin crawling and climbing over him, for J.R. to crawl and climb over in return, the two of them scaling each other as much as they scaled the distance that remained to the shotgun. It seemed to take forever. And yet when Vince arrived first, it was entirely too soon. Wresting the weapon out from the bench's underside, he held it up from the scrum. The cheering crowd fed off the gesture and sustained Vince Baldwin in return. He was still on his back, still chemically blinded as he pumped the shotgun and aimed. J.R. knocked the barrel away. The gun went off. Snapper fell, howling. Little Wallace was hit too, stunned, a bloody bolt across the wrist.

399

Elsie pushed through the wild throng to get to Snapper's hemorrhaging leg. Rose Archer whisked the wounded and shrieking Wallace out of harm's way.

Snapper's leg artery would bleed him out in real time over the remainder of the fight. J.R. would reflect upon this afterwards, that Snapper had fought for his own life during the death match, with Elsie's faith driven, unquestioning, non-judgmental assistance, and with everyone else's attention half divided. Elsie was a better person than every last one of them combined.

The tea drinking agent stirred his tea. The coffee drinking agent blew the steam off his coffee.

"You look familiar," one of them said to Elsie. "Have I seen you in the movies?"

"What?" J.R. turned his head. "What did you just say?" The tea was hot, steaming. "You would be Agent Epsom? Have I got that right?"

"I would be Agent Green, Mr. Daddio."

"Agent Green, we're not here to make your career, do you understand that?"

"Ah," Agent Green set his tea down on the coffee table.

"What are you doing?"

"Getting out my notepad."

"How about you put away your notepad and listen to me?"

"OK, Mr. Daddio," Green acquiesced.

"I'm not here to make your career," he told the agent, both agents, looking at each in turn.

"What are you here for?"

"Look for your victims somewhere else. I'm raising a family."

Agent Green took up his teacup once again and sipped from it, eyeballing his partner.

Agent Epsom, plucking up his own steaming beverage, said, "What about you, Mr. Daddio?"

"What about me what?"

"Have I seen *you* in the movies?"

J.R. knew the answer to that question. "I hate the movies."

The standoff lasted another fruitless twenty minutes, with no change of tenor before the agents were finally gone, their cups undrained.

"Please leave me alone for a second," he asked Elsie.

"J.R., I love you."

"I know you do. Will you give me a second?"

He was so angry, he couldn't look at her, or talk to her either. Wrigley was crying. Elsie went to comfort the baby. J.R. schemed.

In the end, he found his way to Tyto's dead body for the brass knuckles, and their fishing out, to slip on and raise. *Fierce,* she had called Lou Gannon. Now she would see who was fierce.

Afterward she was intense, inspired, from her own bloody watch over Snapper's corpse. She was in love with J.R., along with everyone else, cheering.

Maybe Tyto would have let him down too, in time, if allowed to live. It would never be known. But Tyto rescued him an entire second time, like nothing less than a guardian angel, provoking in J.R. a complex, quasi-religiosity of self-deification.

It came back to him, of course. The Saw Mill, and the routine slaps to Vince Baldwin's face. Clockwork, in every sense, and as bad as possible, even as Vince's facial and psychological calluses, seemingly beyond any further tenderization, gave way to bloody pulp beneath Tyto's brass knuckles.

Vince even awoke, finally, and much too late, fighting back in desperate earnest, shoulders and fists swinging, so that J.R. struck him where Cash Clarick never did. In the heart.

That's when Duke Drummond made his approach. J.R. saw everything. He saw what Duke Drummond wanted. Not in a million years. He slid the murder weapon into the bucket of acid. He saw the bodies, saw Snapper dead, saw Krabbe out cold, saw Harding on his feet and clutching his lower back. He saw money changing hands. And he saw Duke Drummond pause, and then keep coming, with applause bearing down all around him, saying, "They like you, J.R."

# BOOK IV: THE PROBLEM WE ALL LIVE WITH

## 64. The Ballad of Curtis Lemonhall

The Nova overheated somewhere along the desert highway from Albuquerque up to Santa Fe. "You're kidding me," J.R. muttered and flipped on the heat. Elsie recoiled, held her breath.

"Roll down your window," he told her. "All the way down. I'm looking for a place to pull over."

She rolled it down, then cradled the baby, who offered only a single cranky cry.

There was a rest area a few hundred yards up. J.R. parked there, got out, and advised Elsie to stay with the child. He opened the hood and left the radiator to cool. Wiping his brow, he wandered up to the guardrail to gaze off at the shrub-mottled, cactus-poxed, mustard yellow terrain beneath the great, cloud swept turquoise sky.

"J.R.?" Elsie asked from her open window.

"I'm waiting for it to cool down," he told her. "Can't open the radiator when it's hot, babe. That's a fact."

"Tell me again, why Santa Fe?"

He didn't want to lie to her, ever. He would lie to her as little as possible.

Despite everything he'd been through, he still wanted to believe in truth telling as some kind of good idea for most purposes. However, he had come up to Santa Fe to murder a man, something he shouldn't, and wouldn't, disclose to Elsie. So he told her again about work in Santa Fe, and she questioned him no further. Work was fickle to find, as it sometimes turned out, for a young man and his family far from home.

A hose was leaking. He topped off the radiator before turning the Nova back toward the gas station he had spotted previously.

Once there, parked alongside the building, he got to work on the repair. All the while, Elsie and the baby waited in the passenger seat with the windows down. Now and then, Wrigley would croak or squeak, but Elsie was adept at keeping the child content.

A Chrysler Imperial pulled into the dusty lot. The driver, an elderly man, went into the office. His elderly wife approached to fuss over the baby. "Oh, what's her name?"

"Wrigley," Elsie answered with a proud smile.

"Oh, Wrigley, look at *you!*" the woman shook her two fists over her mouth. "Oh, what a *dear!*"

The baby was blissed out.

The husband exited the office and sauntered up to say hello. "So. New York plates. What's brought you to town?" He seemed perfectly friendly.

"My man found work in Santa Fe," Elsie answered.

J.R. winced. This was an example of why he didn't want to lie to her. She might be willing to lie to the cops, if necessary. However, she would not want to lie to everyday people like these two. Elsie sometimes spoke of sin, and J.R. felt sometimes, for instance times like this, that he finally understood it on some rational level. It had nothing to do with a man in the sky throwing lightning bolts down. It was much more a feeling in the pit of the stomach.

"What line of work are you in, son?" the husband asked.

"This line," J.R. answered, from under the Nova's hood. He didn't like being called *son*. Not by anybody.

At last, they drove up to Santa Fe and checked into the air-conditioned Presidio Hotel. J.R. showered first thing. When he exited the bathroom, Elsie was breastfeeding the child in a plush armchair upholstered in jagged and colorful southwestern matrices. It was tempting to remain in these cool confines overnight, and acclimate to the thin air, before prowling off after his objective. However, that would involve deceiving Elsie for hours on end, which was not particularly practical, much less desirable, much less admirable. So he dressed himself, filled his canteen, slung it over his shoulder, said adios, kissed the baby on the forehead, kissed Elsie on the lips, and departed for the Santa Fe sidewalks, up toward the plaza, breathing hot gulps of high desert air, disoriented exponentially by the absence of oxygen even as he experienced its miraculous trickling out, clinging to an inner promise that he would escape from the Castle, and find and track down and kill the Old Man, and then swear off murder entirely, with that one final deed done, except that it made no sense, since he had not scaled this mountain to this high, hot spectrum of American terra firma for the purpose of killing the Old Man, but rather to kill... with a length of piano wire... to kill...

He was on the ground. Faces hovered overhead in a circle. They were difficult to define against the blue stratosphere, but he could sense their dynamic of genuine concern and blasé formality. "I passed out," he told them bluntly, from his back.

He rose to his feet. His audience dispersed. A few offered cautionary remarks and well wishes.

Collapsing in public was not part of the game plan. He was like a boiled frog up here, grasping much too late what he'd plunged into.

He sought and found a green tree in the emerald plaza's verdant shade. He leaned against the brown bark and remembered to breathe, and to drink cool water from his canteen. The shopfront architecture was more fortress-like than any of the bullshit they had slapped together out at the so-called Castle. This realization, more than anything, delivered J.R. shimmering back to the shores of consciousness beneath the shady tree. It wasn't the Old Man he had tracked down to Santa Fe, to kill.

Waiting beneath those boughs, he could almost feel, and maybe even see, the cool photosynthesis taking place. Meanwhile, clouds had gathered quickly overhead for a storm of portentous density. For a moment it got so dark that he stepped away from the tree, fearing imminent lightning. But in the end the storm clouds delivered only one single, fat raindrop. J.R. saw it fall to the sidewalk and evaporate. The foreboding dispersed as quickly as it had amassed, and left the sky roiled in blue and white and gold. In the aftermath, the high desert atmosphere seemed almost breathable. He was ready to proceed.

He couldn't help but smile at the street names—Washington, Lincoln. Names we all find in our pockets, rich or poor, bill or coin. Also, excellent American names like Old Santa Fe Trail and East San Francisco. The architecture, the fountain, even the stonework along the sidewalks, and many of the store fronts and galleries, and the plaza's pueblo church, which seemed gravitationally central, spoke of an effort blessed with creativity. *They're all starved for oxygen up here,* he gathered.

He drank from his canteen, tried to ration it, even though no amount of water could quench his thirst. He laughed to himself. *You don't track anyone down up here... only up. You only track them up.* Dizzy, getting dizzier, setting off from the plaza up a side street to climb steadily, hardly believing the terrain could ascend further, to arrive at last upon the sturdy and elegant Hotel Hidalgo which stretched an entire block opposite two art museums and an art supply store, he resolved that he would loiter, out of sight, pretty soon. First, however, he would scope out the hotel lobby, if only for a minute. He spotted a soda machine through the window. The plan would be to reacquaint his lungs with oxygen, buy a soda, and get a brief lay of the land. Then he would remove himself for a nearby stakeout.

The receptionist greeted him, a lovely girl who cast a spell of local flavor more immediately intoxicating than any he had ever encountered anywhere, from Ohio to Amarillo to anywhere else, Erving included.

As far as he knew, he had never met an actual Native American. She was beautiful, and approachable—he observed this right away. It was very plausible, he decided, that she was some kind of female shaman. He understood immediately that she could see right through him. Even so, he lied, "Hi, my wife doesn't like the hotel we're staying in, so I'm looking for a better place to stay."

"What doesn't she like?"

"Well, I don't know. I just need a soda, if you don't mind. This canteen isn't cutting it." Words that gave him the benefit of complete sincerity.

He went to the soda machine, bought a can of Coke that banged down and landed. He plucked it out. The can was cold. He held it against his forehead. The girl chuckled. He had patronized the hotel now, so perhaps she wouldn't ask so many questions. He cracked open the soda and chugged from it. It disappeared fast, almost gone. He wanted to save some. "This place is great," he said. "It's like some kind of fortress from the wild west."

She laughed.

"A real fortress," he clarified, "not an aluminum fortress."

"Please, sir, sit down," she pointed to one of the tan leather chairs on the zigzag sunset rug. "The climate can get to people, sir. Why don't you take a minute?"

"Thank you," he took the very cozy seat she pointed to.

"If you need anything, just let me know. My name's Juniper-Cloud."

"Really? Are you serious?"

"Yes," she laughed from her station behind the counter.

"That's a beautiful name."

"What's your name, sir?"

"J.R."

"J.R...," she mused. "So," she smiled, pointing back and forth between the two of them, "J.R. and J.C."

"Ha!" he enjoyed her company very much. A bit too much, he realized, because he should not have told her his real name. In fact, he could have said any other name. Tyto, Ben Franklin, Groucho Marx. Literally, any other name would have been smarter. Junior would have been smarter. Nimrod would have been smarter. Anything at all. To be this fatally stupid, after all of his efforts, blurting out information to total strangers. It was altitude sickness. He resolved to zip his lip.

Seated in his hotel lobby chair, he peered down the cloister-like hallway, its carpet of mustard, magenta and pale striations receding beneath a series of pueblo arches. He would focus on the thing he had resolved to do, had come all this way to do, all the way to Santa Fe and its air-conditioned fortresses and stretches of Martian aridity in between. Recovering his breath and draining what remained of his sweating soda and preparing himself for murder, he psyched himself up by conjuring memories of Vince Baldwin, and hovering over the auto yard battlefield, not unlike a shaman himself, observing his own as-yet unfallen mortal form, as Duke Drummond approached amidst the dead and injured, saying, "They like you, J.R.," and then pausing while the Posse Umbellus cheered. As money changed hands, J.R. saw that he had conquered the losers too.

Covered with the blood of his enemy, and delirious with adrenaline, he could feel his own words more than hear them, a bellows blast from the pit of his lungs—*Forget it! I'll bury any one of you Nazi fuckers! But not Vince Baldwin! I'll toss*

*Vince Baldwin into the fireplace! I'll feed him to the fucking coyotes! I'll throw him off a fucking cliff! But bury him? Fuck you! Forget it!*

Except none of it was real. He was only imagining it, jacked up on adrenaline, ready to kill, passing out, collapsing into the auto yard's bloody dirt.

When he awoke, Elsie was watching over him. He sighed in relief at the sight of her.

It was morning. He understood this from the angle of sunlight as it breathed through the doorframe. Other than the two of them, the Castle barracks was empty.

"Elsie," he croaked.

"Daddio," she had his hand. Her blonde hair hung over him. "How are you feeling? Does it hurt?"

"It feels great," he told her.

"You were amazing."

"What?" he asked. "Winning that fight?"

"Yes. I bandaged you up. I don't think anything's broken. You're all bruised and cut. But it's like you have bones made of iron."

"Water," he said.

She had a canteen ready. He drank from it. The feeling was vivid—more than any pain, the satisfaction of quenched thirst. He squeezed her hand. "What did I miss?"

"You missed a lot."

"Really, like what?"

She leaned down and kissed his lips and held it long and slow. He could feel her grace. He loved it. He loved the strength returning to his own spirit, where he had once conceived of, but only now achieved, replenishment. When it was done, she withdrew, smiling, biting her lower lip as if to taste it.

"I did miss that," he said.

"I miss it already."

"When are they coming to kill me?"

"They're not. But Drummond wants you back on your feet. I told him to give you a day, at least."

"Has it been a day?"

"It's been a little more than two days."

*"Eesh,"* he muttered. The more he came back to life, the more the pain intensified. His forehead was throbbing.

Elsie smiled for him, "How about breakfast?"

"Yes, food! Please! And coffee!"

"I'll be right back!" she stood, smoothed her sundress down over her thighs.

At one point, during one of their previous conversations, Elsie had explained that God put women on this earth to serve men. J.R. had always considered himself fifty-fifty on this notion. It was something he liked to hear, but on the other hand, the God stuff was useless.

Waiting for her to return, he may have blacked out. When she materialized, she was holding a breakfast tray. Her task involved helping him sit up on the cot, helping him steady the tray on his lap. The meal was scrambled eggs, bacon, buttered toast, coffee, and Hi-C. He dug in.

"Well," she said, "you want to know what else you missed?"

"Yes," he forked the eggs and bacon down his gullet. He might have faded in and out of consciousness along the initial threads of the story. However, shoveling in the food and pouring down the coffee, he began to regain the sentience of actual consciousness, and to listen as Elsie explained. Krabbe was dead. Snapper was dead. Harding was dead, which was a long story, involving Steeplejack. And the Van Wert twins were dead too.

"What?"

"Plus Tyto and Vince, of course."

J.R. didn't want to think about the death of Snapper, which he hadn't quite witnessed, but knew he had caused. "What happened to the Van Wert twins?" he asked.

"Well that's another long story. Do you want to hear it?"

"Yes, I want to hear it." He was tasting the bacon, the delectableness of which transcended anything imaginable, much less speakable.

"Well, it begins like this," Elsie said, and she began to tell the story about the owner of the *West Susquehannock Dispatch*—or the publisher, or whoever it was—asking Curtis Lemonhall, the so-called journalist he had hired, to step into his office for a discussion of the paternity suit filed by a female acquaintance in Cleveland.

Elsie's underbite and big, bunny rabbit choppers manifested as one impossibly sexy malocclusion. She was terribly beautiful. Sometimes J.R. felt this on an intense and downright painful level, but never more so than now.

411

Seated on the adjacent cot and helping him balance his tray of food, she continued to recount the story of Curtis Lemonhall, the so-called journalist, who had confessed his woes, and lamented them, to his only remaining friend in the world, over drinks, in public, all the while surveilled by the Van Wert twins. *The West Susquehannock Dispatch* wanted to know—and not only did they want to know, but they had asked him, point blank—whether or not the mother of his child was white.

"Which they have every right to know," Elsie editorialized, before continuing.

So Lemonhall got so indignant about this interrogation that he lied, and told them yes, the mother of his child was white. He said it out of sheer principle, even though Mercedes Jefferson was no such thing as white, and even though it might not even be his kid.

*I'm so angry...* This is one of the things Lemonhall was overheard saying, repeatedly. *I'm so fucking angry, I'm doing stupid shit like lying...*

"So now it's our fault he's a liar," Elsie framed the irony here.

There was no way the newspaper was going to publish the letters co-crafted by Grossmark and the dearly departed Sandra Pride and the mastermind Duke Drummond. Like pretty much any other newspaper in the country, they wouldn't have the guts. But that didn't mean the letter was useless. Drummond may have anticipated this, or he may have guessed at it, or he may have winged it entirely. In any case, Curtis Lemonhall brought the editor-in-chief his scoop about the Castle, and the editor-in-chief told him NO, they were NOT going to publish any such sensationalist nonsense in their newspaper. *The West Susquehannock Dispatch,* they reminded him, was founded over a century ago.

They were desperate for filler, though, so they would accept a human-interest piece about abandoned structures in Pennsylvania.

And so, with bills to pay, including lawyers' bills, Lemonhall agreed. He came back with a couple of other photos of abandoned buildings, along with a slapped-together puff piece, submitted under what remained of his byline. He explained to his friend that even including his *Photographer on the Streets* assignments, he had never experienced professional humiliation on any such level before, something Elsie found hard to believe, since on a level that was personally humiliating, he had just told a bar full of Philadelphia drunks about it.

So the twins, in their travels, had looked all around for, and found, an abandoned warehouse. It was the old County Line Brewery on the Schuylkill River. In fact, in a twist of serendipity, this particular abandoned warehouse came with its own ready-made drug den. Crack, or whatever it was, would serve its purpose. They made note of the place, jotted it down.

Returning to the bar, Aesop Van Wert called from a payphone outside and asked for Curtis Lemonhall. When a puzzled Lemonhall came to the phone, Aesop asked him, "Are you the one investigating abandoned buildings in Pennsylvania?"

"Who *is* this?" Lemonhall wanted to know.

"Never mind that," said Ace Van Wert. "We've got an abandoned building for you."

He then told the reporter about the abandoned County Line Brewery on the Schuylkill River, and gave him the address. And then, cryptically, before hanging up, he said, *"Maybe you'll find the pictures you're looking for, too."*

The plan was to send him there and then call the cops, and get Curtis Lemonhall busted, drunk, in a crack den. Nothing more, nothing less, in terms of ambition.

But funny thing, and amazing thing too, and the thing Elsie noted as bestowing upon the tale a quality of *Divine Intervention,* because we all know who's on whose side... Over the phone, in the noisy bar, Lemonhall had heard them say it was a Villanova sorority house on County Line Road.

Meanwhile, the twins went to stake out the dumb old County Line Brewery on the Schuykill, and wait there for the cops to show up, and bust the lawbreakers, and so on, all of which happened, but Lemonhall never showed, because he had chased his own drunkenly scribbled lead to the wrong doorstep, looking for pictures.

"Not much of a reporter," Elsie stopped to conclude, as J.R. swept his buttered toast into salted egg.

Lemonhall was arrested within minutes. His career was over. The Van Wert twins had accomplished their goal, half entirely by accident.

413

"So wait," J.R. asked, "how did that get them killed?" He found himself feeling better, just a bit, jolted awake by coffee, given new life by food.

"It didn't," Elsie answered. "What happened is, the twins gave Drummond the report. Edward, the Old Man, he was on hand too. And he was pleased with the outcome, you could tell by his expression. Everything was hunky dory. But then Aesop Van Wert noticed that Harding was missing. I don't know if you remember this, J.R., but as you smote Vince Baldwin in battle, there was a scuffle between Steeplejack and Harding, and Harding came out badly hurt."

"Yes, I caught sight of that. Steeplejack is a violent murderer, Elsie."

"He's a demon," Elsie affirmed.

"He's that too," J.R agreed. He liked the way Elsie challenged him. On a *hokum-pokum* level, demons and hell were as good a place as any to agree.

"Well, the beef between those two wasn't over," Elsie continued. "Obviously, I don't know the entirety of the politics of everything that goes on in this place, but Steeplejack smothered Harding to death with a pillow, and no one stopped him from doing it. Actually, it took place right here in these barracks, yesterday. You were out cold. Harding was right over there, getting killed. They asked me to leave for a few minutes, so I'm not an actual eyewitness. But that's what happened."

J.R. drained his coffee.

"I'll get you some more," she said.

"Wait," he grasped her wrist. She looked at him curiously. "I can't wait," he told her, "until we can have a normal conversation, in a normal place, in the real world."

She sighed. Her eyes suggested it would definitely come to pass. "Me too, J.R. I believe in you. I know for certain you're going to get us... you and me... out of here."

"I swear to do that," he held her hand. He savored the touch of her skin with his fingertips. He met her smart gaze with his eyes.

"Let me get you a refill."

"I don't need a refill, thanks. What happened to the Van Wert twins?"

She explained that the Van Wert twins found out that Steeplejack had smothered Harding with a pillow, and it set

414

them off. Both of them, both brothers. The outburst, she remarked, had a *final straw* quality to it, which was immediately apparent to everyone present.

This was in the Mess Hall, while the whole Praetorian guard watched from overhead. The Old Man was there, and Farrah. Everyone got an earful, as the twins, in their suits and ties, pointing and yelling, told Duke Drummond it was time to get rid of Steeplejack once and for all. Drummond used the F-word, and asked them who gave the orders around here? The Van Wert twins gave their ultimatum, announcing, more or less, *It's him or us.*

Drummond hesitated. For a moment, it seemed he might actually lean in the direction of the twins. Long enough so that he exchanged a glance with the Old Man. That's when Steeplejack executed the Van Werts—BANG! BANG!—with two rifle shots from his chamber door.

The Praetorian raised their own rifles, among them Crosby Shue stumbling away defensively, and Chuck Zorn crouching in the shadows of the Mess Hall's stone chimney.

Steeplejack, like some kind of deathless apparition, strode out onto the balcony in his bathrobe and slippers, brandishing his rifle, and standing there, judgmental over the lot of them. He was daring any one of them, or all of them, to take their shot. Crosby Shue put his rifle aside and raised his other hand, empty. The other guys lowered their weapons too. Drummond had waited too long. He couldn't order his men to stand down now. They already had. Meanwhile, Steeplejack turned and vanished back into his porn studio. Down in the Mess Hall, Rudolph and Aesop Van Wert lay dead, headshot, hemorrhaging all over the floor.

"They were dead," Elsie paused to reiterate for J.R. "They didn't need first aid."

"Wow," he said.

"Oh," Elsie said. "There's something else I've got to tell you."

"What's that?"

"Or maybe this isn't the time. I'm a healer, J.R. I don't want to make you feel worse, with my words. So maybe it can wait until you're back on your feet."

"I'm out of the woods, Elsie. What is it?"

She winced, "Well... the thing is..."

"What? Tell me."

"You made page 26 of the *West Susquehannock Dispatch*."

The photo in the paper was more an expression of posture, body language and attitude—the kind of thing a person would recognize only if they knew the subject beforehand. A character like John F. Kennedy or Muhammad Ali might ignite such recognition. But J.R. was no such personage.

Meanwhile, the article was Curtis Lemonhall's last, a mere blip on the entire breadth and depth of the recorded history of journalism. Upon the reporter's arrest for the harassment of Villanova sorority girls, his association with the Pennsylvania newspaper was terminated without complaint. And now J.R. Daddio had tracked Curtis Lemonhall's tailspin all the way up to the Hotel Hidalgo in the New Mexico mountains.

"J.R., can you watch the lobby for a minute?" Juniper-Cloud asked him.

"Yes," he said.

"Thanks! I'll be right back!"

"I'll keep watch," he told her.

"I gotta go pee!" she seemed almost to sing the words as she abandoned her desk and crossed the hotel lobby, disappearing down the hallway.

J.R. was left seated alone amidst the southwestern décor he had come to find pleasing. It would be so nice to stay and enjoy this setting, but he was playing with fire to loiter here. It wasn't likely Curtis Lemonhall would recognize him upon some chance encounter in this Santa Fe hotel lobby. Nevertheless, Lemonhall himself had snapped the incriminating picture. If the anguished reporter should come strolling along at this very moment, and recognize J.R. from whatever reservoir of attentiveness and journalistic professionalism he still possessed? And if he should further recognize that the hunter, so to speak, had become the hunted? To murder him then would become impossible.

Having regained his equilibrium, and having cooled his brow, and having guzzled his soda, and having cased out Lemonhall's Santa Fe headquarters, there was no earthly reason to hang around anymore, except that he had stuck his neck out for a lovely, delinquent Navajo receptionist. He would wait three minutes, he decided. Three minutes, tops, and no more.

In that cool and comfortable duration, with Curtis Lemonhall both occupying and eluding his thoughts, J.R. felt no hunger, and his seemingly interminable thirst was quenched.

Juniper-Cloud was back. "Thanks so much!" she said.

"You're welcome."

"No one came by, right?"

"Right," he said. After that, he didn't know what to say, because it was always so hard to be friendly, even when he only wanted to be friendly, which was almost never. In a moment of desperation, he added, "Just us chickens."

Juniper-Cloud grinned and began to sing something about "easy pickins" with jazzy angularity. Evidently there was a song about the conversation they were having.

He could only picture his own awkward smile. Had she just come on to him? Or had she just corrected him? Or had she done neither? Or had she done both? Generally speaking, ever since his escape from the Castle, the people he met in his travels proved only easier and easier to manage, pretty girls being no exception. And yet here, inside this random south-western hotel lobby, he had met a bedazzling exception.

They were interrupted. A noisy woman wearing a plastic pink sun visor entered the lobby, not so much spilling as careening through. "Goddammit!" she yelped as her shinbone struck a coffee table. Her husband or boyfriend arrived in her wake, comparatively steady on his feet, advising, "Be nice."

"Oh, hey," the woman said to Juniper-Cloud.

"Good afternoon."

"Can you please get on your staff about the towels?"

"How can we help with the towels?"

"Do you have a notepad or something there?"

"No."

"I beg your pardon."

"I don't have a note pad. But if you have a message, I can relay that for you."

"Oh. Well. Can you send up a smoke signal, or whatever you people do, and send us nine big towels and thirteen small towels. Nine and thirteen."

J.R. began glaring, freely.

"Nine big, thirteen small."

When the woman caught sight of J.R., her eyes beneath her pink visor zeroed in. She hissed, "What's your problem, sonny?"

"You suck," he told her.

"Please," Juniper-Cloud said.

"Hey now," the boyfriend intervened, leveling his steadiness at J.R. "There's no call for that."

"She's got it," J.R. said. "Nine and sixteen. She's got it."

"Well," the woman said.

"I'm sorry," Juniper-Cloud lowered her head.

"Is this man a guest here?"

"He's a guest here, yes," Juniper-Cloud stated without hesitation. "I'll have those towels sent up right away."

The woman seethed at J.R. He shrugged from his chair. After the couple made their way out, he said, "Wow."

"Yeah, wow."

"That was uncalled for. What she said."

"Hey," Juniper-Cloud shrugged, "Racism happens."

"Yeah," he said, "but that doesn't mean..."

She waited for him to continue.

"I have to confess," he confessed to Juniper-Cloud, "you might be the loveliest girl I've ever seen."

"Sorry, what?"

"You heard me."

"Sir, you have a wife."

"I'm not betraying my wife."

"Yes you are. I understand the climate can be a strain, sir."

"You're terrific. I'm really just being appreciative. It's not... You're right, I guess, Juniper-Cloud. But I'm right, too. I love my wife. I'm just... I might not know how to be appreciative, I guess."

"You're all right, J.R.," she said. "Don't be too hard on yourself."

"Thank you."

"But go back to your wife."

That's when the phone rang, and the cops arrived, all in one cacophonous shitstorm.

J.R. had no pistol, only the piano wire. But that was enough to suggest his intention. His goose was cooked. It was the fourth or fifth time now.

He allowed himself the doomful concession of failure, slipping up, after all he'd been through, all because of Juniper-

Cloud. All too predictable, all too perfect. Meeting his match, but remembering to breathe, as he had been taught long ago to do, so that as long as the air conditioning worked, he still had a chance of keeping his head.

Juniper-Cloud answered the phone. Two paramedics stormed in. "Yes," she said into the receiver. "Yes, they're here."

J.R. wasn't sure yet, but he was beginning to think the shitstorm had nothing to do with him. The police officers followed the paramedics.

Juniper-Cloud said, "Yes, sir, I'll let them in." She hung up the phone. "Room 118!" she said. "I'll let you in!" She dashed down the hallway with the uniformed men.

Several other guests opened their hallway doors, curious over the racket. 118 was Curtis Lemonhall's room. Just like that, it was both obvious and inevitable what had happened.

J.R. remained calm in his chair, calmer than before, because he had been all jazzed up to take a life, and now he didn't have to. He didn't quite know whether to feel relieved or frustrated, or even what the difference was. From a practical standpoint, he had been incredibly lucky. Or sort of lucky, because the Van Wert twins had set the outcome in motion on purpose, another lifetime ago. It was something like luck, but more like an advantage to cash in. He had planned a sendoff for Lemonhall, planned on tightening the piano wire and assuring his prey all at once that it had nothing whatsoever to do with race. But it was too late to convince him of that bullshit now.

J.R. came to smell himself, his own body odor, in the lobby chair. He wanted desperately to leave, but it was no option. Not until he was sure of the outcome.

In time, the paramedics wheeled the corpse out on a stretcher, the white sheet shrouding the face.

Juniper-Cloud returned to her desk, reeling with sorrow.

"Is he?" J.R. asked her.

"Dead, yes."

"Was it?"

"A suicide."

"Who was he?"

"Curtis Lemonhall, it says here. I wonder if he has family."

J.R. remained quiet for a few moments longer. "It was nice meeting you," he finally said. "I'm really sorry for what happened here today."

Frowning, she said, "Good luck, J.R."

As he crossed back down the canyon into the plaza, he found himself somewhat more acclimated, but still fundamentally uncomfortable on a respiratory level.

Re-entering his hotel room, he announced, "We're leaving, babe."

"You didn't get the job?"

"I'm sorry, babe."

"That's OK, babe. You don't have to be sorry."

"Thank you. That's encouraging, and I appreciate it. We're OK. We have money. There's nothing to worry about. But we have to get out of here. It's like we're in the stratosphere every living second. There's no oxygen. Let's go."

"It's all downhill from here," she said.

He erupted into laughter. She laughed too. He collected her and held her in his arms. The baby was laughing in her crib.

They checked out and left. Soon afterward, the Nova was snaking down the mountainside. J.R. could feel the altitude in Albuquerque this time, where he hadn't yet made its acquaintance on the way up, or so he had thought.

"We have to get out of here, too," he said, and down they went, further, out of state, into Texas, in the direction of Amarillo, not to stop there but to keep on driving into the night.

Occasionally, the baby would fuss. Elsie would awaken and rock the child or nurse her there in the passenger seat.

With Lemonhall out of the picture, it was time to return home. Not necessarily to stay, but J.R. wanted to introduce Elsie and the baby to his parents, and to Janice. He also wanted to let them know he was OK, assuming they cared. Also, to let them know he was a man now, probably more so than most.

He wouldn't ask for his job back at Daddio's Garage. However, when his father asked, he planned to say yes. The garage was his birthright. Certainly, he should always have a job there.

The trick, of course, would be showing his face back in Erving, since he was literally the last person to see Scotty

Pomeroy, Melissa Victoria and Vince Baldwin alive. He knew he had been through enough, and learned enough, to pull it off. The question was whether Elsie could, and would, hold up her end.

The Old Man was still out there somewhere too. J.R. knew he couldn't hide forever. But the time had come.

"We're going back home."

"Home?" said Elsie, drowsy in the passenger seat.

"My home. Erving, New York. It's time."

"Oh. When were you going to tell me?"

"I *am* telling you. *Now* is when."

"Oh, I guess you're right."

"We're not going now, babe. We have to wait until next May."

"Why?"

"Because first I have to turn eighteen. Then I have to change my name to J.R. Daddio. Then we can get married. And then we can go home."

"OK."

"So I am telling you. Many months ahead of time. In fact, I told you as soon as I decided. It's for your sake I don't tell you my decisions until I make up my mind."

"My sake?"

"Yes. Because, babe, I don't want you to have to memorize anything until I have it figured out."

"Memorize...?" she started to say. She shut her eyes and shook her head. "You want me to bear false witness."

"Don't be illogical, babe. Do you want to stay outlaws forever? Do you want Wrigley to grow up an outlaw?"

She said nothing. He drove them eastward through Texas. Along the way, he explained to her the story they would present to the police. Also the newspapers, the FBI, and everyone else.

She was unhappy, he could feel it. She and Mary Daddio would get along great, he realized.

*I might not know how to be appreciative,* he had heard himself confess, in the Hotel Hidalgo lobby. But it was highly doubtful he would ever run into Juniper-Cloud again.

421

## 65. The Old Man's Valediction

He awoke in his cot. He had no memory of drifting off, but at some point Elsie had left him there. She had brought him breakfast in bed, too, but it might have been yesterday. The barracks' sunshot crevasses suggested a midday hour. He rose to his feet, more hungry than anything. He could feel that his face was swollen from injury. He experienced his balance as tenuous. He staggered through the dark barracks and out into the overbright courtyard. Shielding his eyes with one hand, he made for the Mess Hall door.

"HEY, DADDIO!" a voice sounded from the southern turret. "THERE GOES J.R. DADDIO! WELCOME BACK TO LIFE, J.R.!"

It might have been Shanahan. J.R. waved carelessly.

Upon entering the rec room, he smelled the faint aroma. His quivering nostrils followed the sweet scent of food past the ping-pong table, the familiar wall posters, the weight bench, the Dodge wall calendar, and the dartboard where Glenn Disteek's disfigured campaign photo hung thrice pierced with feathered darts.

Inside the Mess Hall, the meeting encompassed Duke Drummond, Farrah, the Old Man, and Grossmark. Elsie was present also, busy with serving trays at the picnic table. It was Duke who spotted J.R. "Hey! Look who it is! Back from the dead!"

Farrah grinned, "J.R. Daddio!"

422

The Old Man chuckled. Grossmark sneered.

"J.R.," said Drummond. "I'm really glad you're up. We need you in the auto yard, pronto. We need every single car and truck road-ready in no less than 48 hours. It's a thousand-mile trek into the heartland."

"Can I eat a sandwich?"

Drummond sighed, sagged his shoulders.

"Thinks he's Oliver Twist," Farrah observed.

"Go ahead," Duke gestured toward the picnic table. Farrah dragged on her cigarette, grinned in smoky release.

J.R. didn't want to cast undue attention upon Elsie, so he nodded to her just once, politely, and then avoided further eye contact. At the table, a bowl of baked beans, a basket of steaming Pillsbury rolls and a grease splattered tray of spreadeagled quail torsos lay before him. He seized up a paper plate.

"Hey, why does this twerp get to eat before us?" Chuck Zorn protested from the eaves.

Duke Drummond sighed, shook his head, exasperated. It seemed for a moment he might say nothing.

Then he raised his weary head. "EVERYTHING IS ABOUT TO CHANGE! EVERYONE HAS TO QUIT THEIR CRYIN' AND MAN UP! IN TWENTY-FOUR TO FORTY-EIGHT HOURS WE ARE TAKING OUR GAME TO THE MAJOR LEAGUES! OK? SO YOUR SERVICE HAS NOT GONE UN-NOTICED! SO STAND YOUR POSTS AND STOP YOUR FUCKING WHINING!"

J.R. had two Pillsbury rolls topped with butter, a mound of baked beans, and a delectable bird on his plate. Listening and looking around, he registered only now that Steeplejack was absent from this most consequential of meetings. As if like-minded, Drummond returned his attention to the inner circle and said, "The biggest pain in the ass, far I can tell, is lugging that entire porn studio down from there and carting it a thousand miles across the country to Kansas City."

J.R. wrenched a bite of bread into his mouth, and so chewing, couldn't speak to ask. He began chewing as fast as he could.

Drummond mused, "I've got half a mind to burn it all down instead."

"Wait, what?" J.R. finally asked, through his bread stuffed, masticating face. "Kansas City?"

"Go fix a car."

423

"When? When are we leaving?"

"You're leaving... this room... right now. We're having a meeting."

"What about this food?"

"Make it to go, son."

J.R. didn't like being called *son*. Not by Duke Drummond. Not by anyone.

He did as he was asked, went out to the garage and tuned up the lot of cars for the impending exodus, those few inside the auto yard first, then those parked alongside the northeast wall, including the Van Wert's orphaned Riviera, Tyto's widowed Road Runner, and Krabbe's as-yet unpossessed Gremlin.

It was well after dark before he revisited his cot inside the barracks dormitory. Grant Archer had been singing earlier. The words of the song echoed back to him now, *"I'm a rodeo clown in El Segundo..."*

Hearing it from Grant Archer, J.R. understood, only today, and only now upon reflection, as if a light was suddenly shining on the melody, that it was country music.

Back then, on the transistor radio in Daddio's Garage, he had heard it differently, and hated it.

It was the same day the new mechanic showed up. Boyd.

Jack Daddio was in the office, chatting with the delivery guy. J.R. got bored and left his father's side, and wandered into the garage to hang out with the two mechanics. Buddy was under the hood of someone's Dodge Dart. The new guy, Boyd, had a Chrysler up on hydraulics. The bay doors were open onto a sunny day as Buddy and Boyd exchanged chatter in the presence of the boss' son. From the transistor radio, the song seemed almost taunting in tone, bothersome. *"Well, I came from Oklahoma with a banjo and a prayer... All the way out to Hollywood, but there ain't nobody there..."*

J.R. tended to look up to Buddy, whom he had known his whole life. But now he was beginning to look up to Boyd, whom he had known for only a few hours. It was something about the way Boyd carried himself, a confidence, a self-possession, something J.R. wished for himself.

He listened as Boyd and Buddy kept on about cars, until the banter became hard to follow. Except that Boyd was saying, "Shit. I open a comic book, and there's a black guy beating up a bunch of white guys. Then, I turn on the TV for a

James Bond movie, and everyone in it—everyone except for James Bond—is black. What the hell is going on anymore? Can't we have anything to ourselves anymore?"

"Jeez," Buddy responded, "Get over it, man. Or go be a golfer, or something, if you want racial purity."

"Shit," said Boyd. "I don't know."

"Racism is over, man. Civil Rights Act. 1964. Look it up. We're all equal now."

"Yeah, 'till you wake up and find out you're the slave and they're the master."

"What? What are you talking about? That would never happen. Plus, my girlfriend is black, partly. Plus, my other friend is black. You got something to say about my friends, and my girlfriend?"

"*Psssh.* Just you wait. Five or ten years from now, it won't just be your girlfriend, or your other friend. It'll be your police chief. Your kid's elementary teacher. Your boss..." Boyd smirked, nodding his head.

"So what?" Buddy argued. "That's my whole point. It doesn't matter, man."

"Sure it don't. So long as you're lying down with them."

Buddy straightened to face Boyd. "All right, that's not cool, man."

Boyd smiled easily, "Aw, come on, man. What's the big deal? I'm sorry if I caused offense."

Buddy stared a moment longer. The radio played, *"I'm a rodeo clown in El Segundo... A painted frown looks upside down from here..."* The two men went back to work.

Jack Daddio entered the garage from the office. "How's everybody doing in here?"

"Doing just fine, Mr. Daddio," answered Boyd.

"How's he doing, Buddy?"

"Jury's still out."

"Oh, *jury*, is it?" Boyd stood staring. He had a wrench in his hand, but he was a mechanic, so that wasn't threatening, necessarily.

The radio played, *"Aw, but that don't mean a man can't sing a tune though... So pour another round and hold my beer..."*

"I mean," Boyd followed up with Buddy, in front of the boss this time, "they have their own continent. How come they

425

get their own continent? But we can't even get our own garage? Huh? Ever wonder that?"

"Jack," Buddy pleaded to Jack Daddio, reaching out his hand. "This guy is actually the most ignorant person I've ever met in my life. I don't think I can work alongside this person."

"Mr. Daddio, I'm sorry," said Boyd. "Am I auditioning for *him?* I didn't know that."

"What *is* this?" Jack Daddio wanted to know.

J.R. watched spellbound.

Buddy said, "I'm sorry to tell you the truth, Jack, but this guy is basically a racist."

"Are you a racist?" Jack Daddio asked Boyd.

"No. No way, Mr. Daddio."

"There's no racism allowed here. I'm running a business. I have black customers."

"I understand."

"You better understand."

J.R. felt he was keeping up with the exchange. Boyd was wrong. But so was Jack Daddio. He lowered his head into his hands and tried to sort it out. He was just a kid. At this age, he could stand there pressing his fingertips into his forehead, and no one would care.

Jack Daddio tried to settle it. "Let's focus on that Chrysler's transmission, Boyd. Let's stop worrying so much about other continents."

"You got it, Mr. Daddio," Boyd agreed.

The song ended. Pat Saint John said, *"All right! That's right! He's a rodeo clown in El Segundo! That is the British Country Invasion right there! The inimitable Ringo Starr on vocals! We've got the Fab Four coming up this hour on WPLJ! And do NOT forget! Later tonight! THE KING BISCUIT FLOWER HOUR presents Bruce Springsteen LIVE from the STONE PONY! Sheer perfection. Do NOT miss it!"*

The two mechanics went back to their automotive projects. Buddy was sullen and wary. Boyd was trying to contain some visibly nervous and squirrel-like self-amusement. Jack Daddio's supervision was rapt and shaded with suspicion. J.R. was fully engrossed by the men at their work. One radio sponsor after another blathered nonsense. Inside the sunlit garage bay, and within those tenuous strands of equilibria, Boyd finally turned to Buddy, and in a tone not merely calm but dulcet, he said, "All I'm saying is... If I see a spider in my

426

house, I don't lie down with it. I smoosh it. That's all I'm saying. It's not hate. It's just so my house don't get overrun by spiders."

"WHAT DID YOU JUST SAY TO ME?" Buddy spoke, incredulous.

Jack Daddio stepped in, "What did he say?"

Boyd was grinning. As if the grin could somehow save his job.

"Get your tools and get out of here!" Jack Daddio delivered his ruling. "You're done!"

"Aw, that's just great! Are you kidding me! I only been here a couple of hours!"

"Which I am willing to write off! In fact, I'll round it up to the hour! Just get your bullshit and leave! Good bye!"

"OK, so, I guess it ain't a free country."

"No. It is very much a free country. And I am free to fire your ass!"

"Fucking communist bullshit!"

"What? What did you just call me, boy?"

"Fuck you!"

"I was fighting communists while you were shitting in your diapers!"

"Whoa, I'm sorry, gramps!"

"No, you're not. You're not sorry. Not yet. But you're going to be. Right here and right now. Right in the middle of that street..." Jack Daddio pointed beyond the open doors to Malta Street.

Boyd's face was flushed, embarrassed. He quickly collected his tools, made like a coward, and scurried off. Out of harm's way, he turned back and called, "THIS IS A FIRST AMENDMENT VIOLATION! I'M CALLING THE COPS!"

"DO IT! SAVE ME THE TROUBLE!"

Boyd lingered for a moment longer, almost crouching, not yet vanquished.

"HERE!" Jack Daddio dug into his pocket, produced a silver coin. "HERE'S A QUARTER!" He flung it, not with his wrist but overhand, a fastball. "FOR THE PAYPHONE!" Boyd was struck before he knew it. He fled.

Buddy stood watching at Jack Daddio's shoulder. "Man, Jack," he said. "Jack Daddio. That guy! He got me so mad! I'm so frickin' mad right now! I'm so MAD!"

427

"Don't tell me about mad," Jack Daddio began to wipe his hands with a rag.

"Thank you, Jack," Buddy said to his boss. "I appreciate you sticking up for what's right."

"I mean..." Jack Daddio paused to tell them, not just Buddy, but J.R. too. "What do you think would happen, all of a sudden—and let's face it, it's never all that much of a sudden—if Mrs. Coolidge should drop in here? Here's this racist villain on staff, under everyone's hood, including hers, not to mention hanging around my garage, saying racist bullshit, pardon my French. Tell me how that can possibly be a good thing."

"No, yes, no. Of course not. Yes. No. Thank you."

"Ignorance!" Jack Daddio sent the word out onto Malta street in case anyone out there was listening.

J.R. understood that the guy who had scurried out, stung by a well flung quarter, was not in the right.

Later, as his father was closing up the shop, he asked, "Are we white, Dad?"

Receiving only a brief, quizzical frown in return, he followed up with, "Dad?"

"Son," Jack Daddio answered. "What? What is your question?"

"Are we white?"

"That's a stupid question. What are you asking me?"

"What are we?"

"We're nice. And we're good."

J.R. liked to read about the presidents, so he had looked up the meaning of some big words by now. Smartly, he said, "Minus the platitudes."

"Minus the *what?*"

He knew to stand patiently.

Sure enough, his father answered, "It doesn't matter what we are, or what anybody is. How's that for a *platitude?*"

"But—"

"We're men. Men get along with each other. Best they can. One at a time."

"But..."

"Except, you're not a man. You're a boy."

"But we're Italian, right?"

His father chuckled. It carried a tone J.R. had never quite heard before. "J.R...." came the preface. He waited. The rest was somehow predictable. "Your mother is Irish. Me, I'm mostly Italian. None of it matters, son."

"Our heritage doesn't matter?"

"Our *heritage* matters. Yes. It matters. But how many times have you been to Italy? Or Ireland? Huh? This *garage* is your heritage, son. If your ancestors wanted to live in Italy or Ireland, they would have stayed there. But they didn't. They brought us here. We live in America."

That was three times now. J.R. didn't like to be called *son,* not even once.

Daddio continued, "I was born in America. This is where I learned that everyone is equal. I went to war for America. I built a business and raised a family in America. Your heritage, son? You are standing here, here with me, your father. You are receiving your heritage. Don't you see that?"

"You just don't want to lose any customers."

"And that makes me what? Besides smart?"

"What about wrong and right?"

"You think I don't know right from wrong? You little snot!"

"Dad! You should listen to me—"

"No, *you* listen to *me.* How you feel about people and how you treat people? Those are two completely different things. How you feel about people doesn't matter for shit. How you treat people matters more than anything else in the world."

J.R. threw up his hands, exasperated by the word play. It was useless.

"Some things aren't about right and wrong. Some things are about what's practical. What works. Treat people well. This is so obvious they gave it a name. The Golden Rule."

J.R. was just waiting for it to be over.

"Tell you what," his father was still annoyed, and getting more annoyed. "The day you walk in here and tell me you're the one who's a father, and it's you who's raising a family... That's the day I stand here and listen to my own son tell me about right and wrong. OK? How does that sound for a deal? Until then, how about you listen to me?"

J.R. just stood there. Just a kid. He could hardly argue, although he might have, at that age, if he could have articulated the notion, or at least traced its phantom shape, which he fully realized only now. If it's not about right and wrong, then what if it is practical?

At some point, he had drifted off. Now he awoke, with moonlight beaming through the dust shot slivers of shoddy misalignment. Two other soldiers were asleep on their cots, possibly Shanahan, possibly Trauer, he couldn't be sure. There was no point in lying around waiting. de Ram's cocaine-and-vengeance-fueled rampage wasn't coming to save the day. And now the Posse Umbellus was pulling up stakes and moving to Missouri. It was time to start thinking about a new escape plan.

He decided to get up and hit the free weights. The bigger and stronger he got, the better his chances for survival. At that hour, he had the rec room to himself, notwithstanding a brief visit from Rose Archer, who entered through the Mess Hall doorway with a laundry basket on her hip, offering one shy, unfriendly hello before exiting through the side door.

People began to stir upstairs. J.R. curled his dumbbells. The brief window of peace and normalcy was already closing. He gazed around at the pin-up girls, and the black velvet Confederate rattlesnake poster, and the transistor radio atop the ping-pong table, as he worked his biceps.

"Well, look whose eyes are open," the Old Man said.

A pain in J.R.'s right elbow flared. The weights dropped CLANG to the carpet.

The Old Man chuckled. "I tell you, J.R. Daddio, I really do like you."

J.R. rubbed at his elbow. The Old Man had come alone, apparently, and with impressive stealth, to stand smiling and hunched over in the Mess Hall doorway. "Pain?" he asked.

"It's nothing," J.R. lowered his arms to his sides.

"It's less than nothing. That's probably what you meant to say."

He would say no more. He could fool most everyone, although Duke Drummond only sometimes, and Farrah not at all. Elsie, he wasn't sure yet. In any case, there was no sense in lying to the Old Man. Not ever. The less said, the better.

"I'm not saying you have to enjoy killing, J.R. For goodness sake, please. I can only ask. But please don't enjoy it for my sake, or for anyone else's. Only your own. That's why you're afraid of yourself, son. You have to stop with that. It's no fun, murder, sure. But we might as well make the most of it. If God exists, it's because he's smart. It's because he needs me. Even the world's most peaceful man requires a blade, a sharp edge, from time to time. You know, J.R., they say the pain of having a baby is worse than any pain you'll find in the entire index of human injuries. Just keep that in mind, as you venture forward."

"How about the pain of pit battles?"

The Old Man sighed. "All I'm saying, son, is if you ever have the opportunity of becoming a father, you have to remember, on that day, whose job it is to bring life into this world, and whose job it is to help. It's her day, not yours. And she'll be in a lot of pain. So you just make like Joseph and deliver the mother and child. OK? Make it easier, not harder, for her. Do you think you can remember that?"

J.R. hadn't put a baby in Elsie, but it seemed like good advice, so there was no reason to argue.

The Old Man had drawn close—something like shuffling, but more fluid and graceful, all the while speaking, his yellow gelatinous eyeballs glistening. He was explaining how all the pain and suffering in the world could be collected into a bucket, and the worst pain and suffering you can possibly imagine would just be a drop in that bucket, and how there are worlds beyond this world, with pain and suffering on a dimension incomprehensible to the human mind, and how every effort to stem that tide of pain and suffering is literally the definition of stupidity, because mankind is engineered to endure and survive and prevail over pain. That this is the story of life, never mind its meaning. Compassion is a mental construct by which the weak reject pain. All the while, the strong, they *breathe in* pain. It's *pain* that makes them *real.*

J.R. had to admit it sounded like airtight logic.

It wasn't so much that he didn't trust the Old Man. He didn't trust himself. He didn't trust himself in the Old Man's presence.

"Mankind," Edward gave J.R. a smile so patient as to almost weep with sorrow, "was designed for murder. Killing, yes. But I'm not just talking about killing. I'm talking about murder. Murder over little things. Murder over grand things. Murder over money. Over jealousy. Over resources. Or just over hurt feelings. Pride, well... that's where it all begins. Or let's face it. Sometimes, it's just for fun."

"Murder..." J.R. mused, following along. So far, he hadn't murdered anyone, exactly. Certainly no one who wasn't worth murdering. Snapper's death would surely be considered man-

431

slaughter. Vince Baldwin was possibly murder, or probably murder, under the law, and also in spirit, because that asshole had to be put down. But as far as J.R. could tell, his biggest mistake in life was leaving Cash Clarick alive after the car wreck. His biggest mistake was a non-murder.

"People used to be so confused by it. Sport killings. Thrill killings. Serial killings. That's the new terminology. In the old days, they used to make up stories about werewolves and vampires, because they couldn't comprehend that a man, a man just like themselves, could leave such a hateful mess. But there's no such thing as werewolves and vampires, J.R. No such thing and never was."

J.R. shrugged at this insight. Not that the Old Man was wrong, but werewolves and vampires were kid's stuff.

"I assume you know all this. It's just a starting point, from which to build. All I really mean to say is don't be so worried about who it hurts, but rather think about how it feels. J.R., for goodness' sake, please. I can only ask. That's why you're afraid of yourself. You have to stop with that. It's no fun, let's face it. For every glimmer of hope, there's twenty glimmers of something else."

Edward shuffled easily over to the weight bench now, its hand wrought steel frame, its upholstered spine of red vinyl. He lay down, gripped the heavy barbell, raised it, executed a series of steady bench presses, returned the load to its cradle with a CLANG!

"Did you know?" he sat up, "that there is an entire religion, from an entire other side of this planet, beneath the rising sun of the IDL—which stands for Imaginary Date Line, no matter what anyone else tells you. And this religion devotes its entire self to the wanting of nothing, and to gathering in temples to pursue that lack of wanting. Like prawn, by the million, somewhere between the school and the net and the suffocation? Did you know that, J.R.? Have you ever heard of anything so precisely the opposite of intelligent in your whole life? I only ask that you meet me in the arena of belief that permits the sufferer to want something out of life. At least the wanting, J.R., even if the pursuit is just too greedy to admit to."

"You think I don't know what you're doing," J.R. told him, "but I do."

"Oh, do enlighten me. I hardly ever know what I'm doing." The Old Man arose from the weight bench. Hunched over and unwell, he was smarter than everybody else. J.R. understood that there was no right answer, no way forward. To speak even one more word would be foolish. The Old Man's very presence was quicksand.

"I'm leaving," Edward confided now. "I tell you I'm leaving, J.R. Daddio. I'm travelling onward."

"We're all leaving. For Kansas City."

"No, I mean, *I'm leaving*. In fifteen minutes. My work is done here. I just wanted to say toodles. And to thank you for your service to the white race."

J.R. said nothing. He might have said *you're welcome* but couldn't.

"And to wish you the best of luck…"

"The same to you," he managed to say.

"And to remind you of what you are. I saw that you see the difference. You are like me. And we are both going places, my friend."

Duke Drummond interjected, "OK, settle down, Old Man."

Drummond had arrived, apparition-like, from the rec room doorway. The Old Man greeted him with a playful smile. Suddenly it all seemed staged, which was flattering, in a way. At least the effort was there.

Drummond proceeded with a carefully prepared monologue about how we—The Human Race—had crawled up out of the muck and onto our feet so that we could see at last. How we are not sculpted from clay. How we are not manifested from some reptile in some fairy tale garden. How we are older than all of that bullshit combined.

"Can you imagine just pissing everywhere you want, just to establish dominance?" he asked, with his stand-up comic delivery. "Sorry, the world just doesn't work that way anymore. But it wasn't that long ago, J.R. And that is a stone cold fact…"

"That sounds about right," the Old Man affirmed.

"Thank you, Edward."

"Duke, I'm at your service."

"We level up, J.R. That's what mankind does."

"Even the religions are in agreement on this," Edward added.

"Leveling up is the name of the game."

433

"You'll find little to no argument, anywhere, in recorded history, from Plato to Aristotle to Arthur Clarke to the Posse Umbellus."

"We leveled up, thanks to you," Drummond advised J.R.

"What do you mean *thanks to me?*"

"You know what I mean. That getaway run in the Trans Am? Then you steal the show again, out in the auto yard. Shit. I got to admit, the first time I laid eyes on you, trespassing and disposing of bodies here outside the wall, I decided right then and there to put you down. But that's when the Old Man stepped in and vouched for you. And I heeded his words. And now look what you brought me. Don't you ever forget, J.R., and I won't either. Don't ever forget how wise that Old Man is."

"Not wise enough," the Old Man interjected, "or I'd be famous." He shared a laugh with Duke Drummond.

"I mean, you weren't born yet," Drummond told J.R., "or you were just getting born, maybe. But in any case, you weren't there to see it. Four hippie rapists out of England, on drugs, wearing marching band uniforms, come along to tell the human race we are all supposed to love each other, and pretend we're nice? Fuck that. We're not nice. That's what the white man knows, and what everyone else pretends isn't so. Everyone on this actual island paradise of a planet is descended from an intrepid, vigorous, ruthless survivor. The fucking weak are literally fucking extinct, thank you Mr. Darwin. We are *wicked,* son. Or just one generation, or maybe two, or maybe too many generations removed from that wickedness. Only phonies and hypocrites preach virtue. You have the solid rock of truth beneath you when you preach evil."

"Or the naïve," the Old Man added.

"Beg your pardon?"

"Phonies or hypocrites..."

"...or the naïve. Right, gotcha. All three. And that doubles back to what Edward here saw in you. That you weren't so naïve. Not too many illusions to lose in the first place. For you, it's much less a shock to the system to have the veil removed."

"Tell him about de Ram," the Old Man smiled.

"Oh, sure, de Ram," Drummond storied on. "You met de Ram, if I'm not mistaken, back in that trailer park they call the Posse Serpens?"

"Yes, de Ram, I met him. At the trailer park."

434

"Like an ogre got a job as a circus clown, and then got drunk."

"He's red-haired," J.R. affirmed. Back at the Compound, around the campfire, de Ram had arm wrestled Vince Baldwin by lifting him off the ground until his legs were dangling. Possibly the strongest man alive. It was funny at the time. Even Vince thought so, dangling off the ground, clutching at his opposite shoulder to keep it from separating.

"Beet red hair," the Old Man laughed easily.

"Face like a pot roast. And the suspenders," Drummond added. "And the bright colors. Meanwhile, here's the biggest, meanest, weirdest sonofabitch you ever saw in your life. You saw him with your own two eyes. You understand."

J.R. shrugged. It was impossible to argue with certain statements.

"What do you think made de Ram into what he is? Time ago, he was this gentle giant. A family man. I was there. I saw it, day in and day out. I am a living testament. The man wasn't ever angry once. Never cross. Never unkind. Never so much as distracted. And never once looking to bend the world, with all his strength, to appease his will. Such a cautionary tale. Almost hard to tell, it's so tragic."

"Not a phony," the Old Man added, "not a hypocrite."

"Naïve," Drummond affirmed. "Except not anymore. Nowadays, de Ram, what he does, when he does things, is he leaves a trail of destruction in his wake. His path is strewn with bodies, to let the enemy know his work. The idea is to terrorize them, on purpose, beforehand. But there is no such sign of any such wake of carnage approaching us here at the Castle."

The Old Man's smile became twisted and complete.

"You have to feel bad for the guy," Drummond went on. "To have so many illusions torn away, all at once. So painful. Look what it's turned him into, consigned to that motley crew."

"The Posse Serpens?" J.R. was trying to keep up.

"What's left of them."

"Why do you guys fight with each other?" J.R. asked them. "Wouldn't it make more sense to team up, and take care of the real problem?"

Both men laughed.

"What problem would that be?" the Old Man asked.

435

"You know..." J.R. said, weakly.

"Yeah, I know. But I want to know if *you* know."

Under the microscope, J.R. didn't quite know what to say. "The Leftists?" he ventured.

The Old Man chuckled, shook his head, lowered it, enjoyed the moment for himself. Drummond waited, not to intervene. The Old Man took his time but didn't waste it, raised his head and spoke, "Never mind no right wing and no left wing, kid. Both wings are useless."

"Fuck that," Drummond fired back.

"Don't listen to him, son. Listen to me. Drummond here? He thinks there's a war. But I say the war is already won. The left? They can't tell the difference between smart and clever. The right? They can't tell the difference between smart and cunning. Either way, left or right, clever or cunning, you just wander further and further from being smart. Wings are for butterflies. The war is already won. It's just the smartness that has to get taught, and spread, and cleaned-up after."

J.R. was nodding. He felt overcome by an emotion, almost like he wanted to cry, although there was no possibility of tears. But to have his suspicions affirmed so efficiently. It re-minded him why he had agreed, that night, however long ago it was, with Scotty and Melissa and Vince, to leave the Church of Avaris basement, and get into their cars, and escape from Erving, and chase after something that wasn't preordained. He gathered himself to speak, and found the words, "I've got to tell you. That's how I've actually felt my whole life."

"I know," Duke Drummond said. "Welcome, J.R. Wel-come to the Posse Umbellus." His smile was warm, genuine. His hand was open, extended.

J.R. snorted a single laugh, smiled. He reached and took and shook Duke Drummond's hand.

"Thank you, J.R.," the Old Man said. "I really have to go now. But I want to thank you for believing in me."

He was about to return the Old Man's thanks when Farrah appeared from the rec room's southwest shadows, lowering a Betacam to her side. She flashed her jack-o-lantern grin and said, "New tape."

"What? That's not..."

Drummond shook his head and laughed to himself.

"Take this thing," Farrah said, handing off the videotape to her husband. She set the empty camera down on the ping-pong table, and with both hands free she withdrew a cigarette to light it up. "You got to admit, J.R.," she said, exhaling a spectacular volume of swirling toxins. "This tape is a lot better than the other one."

She was signaling to him, conspiratorially. She wanted him to believe she had helped him out, in return for the effort he had made on her behalf behind Duke Drummond's back, since it was J.R.'s idea to replace the antique naked-lady cigarette case with a dummy pack of explosives, and it was her idea to use one of those sardine tins from the kitchen as the dummy.

"OK, work concluded, leaving now," the Old Man's gnarled voice seemed almost to chirp. His departure was merry, amidst polite farewells from the rec room, and then the same from the rafters of the Mess Hall's Praetorian balconies. At the same moment, Rose Archer hurried in and advised Duke Drummond that Virginia required a ride to the hospital again. The medical emergency was routine for the Posse Umbellus leader. Also for Rose Archer, whose offer was sincere but perfunctory, "I'll take her."

"No, no, I'll take her," Drummond fulfilled the ritual. "Would you excuse us for thirty seconds, Rose?"

"Yes, Mr. Drummond. I'll get her duffel bag."

"Thank you."

"Wait a minute," J.R. raced to comprehend what they had on him. He pointed to the videotape. "That's not even..." he said.

"It's like she said. Not as bad as the other one."

"Not turkey baster bad," Farrah affirmed with a merciless, smoky grin.

Drummond nodded. He handed he tape back to Farrah. "Exactly. And more than that, it's the truth. The truth is, you're Posse Umbellus, J.R. Remember? We all just said so. And shook over it. Welcome. Welcome to the Posse Umbellus. Now get out of here. Go fix a car."

## 66. The Antique Naked-Lady Cigarette Case

From the auto yard, J.R. glimpsed Elsie up in the watch-tower, a shadowy figure barely discernable against the blue darkness of the night sky. He wanted to go to her immediately, but he knew it would have to be a visit to Steeplejack first.

He had no more projects pending out here. All nine cars were tuned-up for the exodus. He had even swapped, in succession, outside the Castle's northeast wall, without asking anyone's permission, the Van Wert's Buick in favor of his own Chevy Nova.

Tyto's pewter Road Runner held the far end now, with Krabbe's star-spangled Gremlin next in line, followed by the twins' Riviera in its new company, then Skinner's Renault Alliance, and then Lovejoy's Cherokee Chief next to the Nova, which sat nearest the Castle door, primed for escape. Inside the auto yard walls, beneath the tarpaulin's V.I.P. overhang, three more rides sat clustered, Chuck Zorn's 4x4, Grossmark's Chevy Citation, and Duke Drummond's Club Cab painted green with white piping in nauseating shades of both colors. Within and without its walls, the Castle's highway armada was set for departure. Crickets chirped like useless heralds of eternity. There was nothing left to do out here.

Duke Drummond exited the Mess Hall, bearing the swaddled and colicky baby Virginia in his arms, while Rose Archer trailed after him bearing the ever-ready travel bag.

438

Drummond spotted J.R. and immediately barked, "Get to work! What are you doing?"

"These cars are ready, already," J.R. jabbed his thumb backward. "And those cars too, outside the wall."

"So what? Congratulations. Make yourself useful."

"I want to go up to the watchtower."

"I bet you do," Drummond halted. Rose Archer shuffled past him and opened the Club Cab's passenger side door. The door creaked very little anymore, though no one seemed to notice, least of all Duke. Rose flung the duffel bag onto the back floormat, then removed from Drummond's arms the squawking unwell baby to nestle into the vehicle's vinyl passenger side.

All the while, Duke Drummond held J.R.'s gaze. "We're packing up tomorrow morning. We're leaving tomorrow afternoon. Weapons. Food. Clothes. Not much else. If there's something you can't live without, pack it up. Otherwise, don't dwell on this place. They got their own auto yard where we're headed."

He left that truthful trail of words behind him as he made his way around to the driver's side and took hold of the steering wheel.

"You didn't say no," J.R. said.

"I'll be back ASAP," Drummond keyed the ignition, jerked on the headlights, and proceeded to roll the perfectly maintained Club Cab out of the auto yard, rounding to pause at the gatehouse for an acknowledgement from the vigilant Grant Archer.

Rose Archer retreated back to the Mess Hall without a word. The outer defenses were spare. Besides Grant Archer, only Shanahan in the southern turret watched over the Castle's four walls and corners. Neither of those guardsmen would complain, nor did they, as J.R. crossed the yard, wasting no time to the Mess Hall's front steps, mounting them to the deck, crossing that length of floorboards and bursting through the double doors.

"What's up, killer?" Grossmark called down from the Praetorian eaves.

"Every car out there is road ready," J.R. answered, making for the staircase across the room. No one could stop him from visiting Steeplejack, but some friendly banter wouldn't hurt

439

the situation either, so he called back over his shoulder, "Skinner, that Alliance is purring like a kitten!"

"Thank you!"

Grossmark wasn't satisfied. "So?"

"So? So what?" J.R. answered him. "I got shit to do. We're leaving tomorrow."

A few chuckles sounded. They gave him no more grief. He arrived at the staircase, vaulted assertively to the second level where he found Crosby Shue at his post and cradling his daughter Bella in his arms. J.R. cringed, offering the Praetorian dad an apologetic smile for the noisemaking.

Just then, Steeplejack's chamber door opened and two women lurched out, both robed in fur coats and teetering around on high heels. Chuck Zorn briefly leveled his rifle, then immediately stood down, by sheer force of competence. The women were blonde, one butter, one butterscotch, two heads of hair like cotton candy, somehow tousled and inflexible both. Steeplejack came stumbling out after them, barefoot, decked out in a kimono of vermillion and gold and black, barking his order to the eight Praetorian guardsmen around the mezzanine. "NOBODY BOTHER THEM! THE KITCHEN IS OPEN TO VISITORS! LET THEM THROUGH!—Oh, hey, J.R. Daddio."

*"Daddy?"* Bella Shue asked.

"It's OK, baby. Time to go. Daddy has to work."

"No, daddy."

"I love you, baby. But this is daddy's work."

Bella was set to her feet and sent to march past J.R. to the staircase and its railing. "Hi, J.R.," she said politely. "Hi," he answered, somewhat surprised that the child knew him by name. He watched only briefly as she gripped the railing to begin her careful descent. He imagined that her father had told her of tomorrow's departure, and that now she would make the rounds for one last goodbye to the Castle's spare wonders.

Meanwhile, up in the balcony, the two porn stars in their jackal pelt coats idled in a daze they seemed to share with each other at least, if not with Steeplejack also, all three of them wearing inscrutably needless faces. The women had removed and abandoned their high heels to proceed barefoot. Their kimono clad host stood outside his studio door on their same stupefied timetable.

440

"You all done in there?" J.R. asked.

"Yes, come on in," Steeplejack turned and went back inside.

J.R. reminded himself to breathe, to keep calm. The porn stars made their way past him, ignoring him completely and ignoring Crosby Shue and ignoring Crosby Shue's daughter, who was ahead of them down the stairs. J.R. watched as they began their barefoot descent in tandem, one at the near rail, one at the far. He then turned and advanced into Steeplejack's lair, closing the door behind him and standing in countenance of the film studio in all its tactile splendor, none of it packed up or even suggesting that future state. Steeplejack occupied the gaudy tableau unspeaking and unassuming, with manifest detachment and exponentially compounding expansiveness, out of his mind on drugs.

"Jesus Christ, Steeplejack."

"J.R.?"

"It didn't work! de Ram's not coming! And now you fuckers have got me on tape again!"

Steeplejack reeled on his feet, as if J.R.'s words had physical force. He found his way backward to the nearest divan and sat there, kimono clad, drowsy and edgeless. It wasn't coke, or maybe it was, mixed with something else. In any case, J.R. watched the pornographer swim after his own senses for an answer, finally to say, "J.R., I already got you your tape."

"No. I'm talking about the *new* tape. The *new* one, Steeps. The one they just made. The one Farrah just made. Just now. In the rec room. The videotape... of me..."

He trailed off. He couldn't say what he had done. The handshake with Duke Drummond. The accordance with the Old Man.

"Hey, like you said," Steeplejack answered, "de Ram's not coming. The writing's on the wall. The revolution? It failed. It's time to get with the program, bub. Time to live to fight another day—"

"What have they got on you?"

"What?"

"You're back on the team. I don't buy it. They've got leverage on you. What is it?"

"Hey, speak for yourself, Daddio. I was always on the team. The Posse Umbellus is moving to *K.C., Misery,* baby.

We got assimilated by the *American Aryan Republic Institute,* haven't you heard?"

"Yes, I heard. Putting that aside, Steeplejack... You just... you have to get me that tape, man..." J.R. paused just then, and added the word he hated most in the world, just for the purpose of getting through, "Dude..."

Steeplejack lowered his head, began to brood.

J.R. let the seconds pass before deploying the word again. "Dude..."

Steeplejack leveled his cosmic gaze. "Listen to me, Daddio. You got further in ten minutes than I ever got in ten years with Farrah, OK? So I am not your obstacle to happiness. You want your tape, go ask *her* for it. I'm not your bagman anymore, hero."

"I didn't..." J.R. started to say. But he had no idea what Farrah had told them, truth or lie, and how it might be helping or hurting him now. Unable to believe in escape any longer, he lowered his head into his two hands.

*"Sheesh,"* Steeplejack added.

J.R. straightened and collected himself. "Steeplejack, look at me. Look at me, please."

"I'm looking at you. I never had a problem looking at you, J.R."

"Never mind that. I want you to listen to me—"

"I always listen to you, J.R.—"

"No, shut the fuck up and listen to me—"

"J.R., don't be mean."

"Don't be *what?* Just listen to me, will you? I'm not being mean. I'm asking you to listen to me?"

"I'm listening."

"I could be dead... any second."

"Well, that's true of everyone."

J.R. pressed on. "If I die, there'll be no one to take care of Elsie... Do you understand me?"

Steeplejack nodded, and then his nonchalance apologized for itself, and he hung his head with pitiful sincerity. He understood perfectly, perhaps even more so in his current stupor, and so he took an extra moment to find and adopt a conciliatory air before confessing, "I put a baby in Elsie, J.R. She'll be safe. We're dropping her off in Indiana. There's a job for her there. It's all set up. She'll be all right. They don't stay, after I scatter my seed. They get sent off, although 'dropped

442

off" would be more like the situation in this instance, which is even nicer by comparison, you gotta admit. This'll be my four-teenth kid, J.R. Can you imagine if I kept them all around? And their mothers? Not a chance. You know how much it costs the Posse Umbellus every time Duke takes Virginia to the emergency room? Can you imagine if we had to support a whole Romper Room here? But I understand. Elsie is very likable. Hey, maybe if she was a doctor instead of a nurse... Hey, don't get dark on me, Daddio..."

Steeplejack kept talking, his mouth moving, but J.R. couldn't hear him anymore. They were taking her away from him, no matter how it played out. Maybe they would kill her. Maybe the baby, too. They weren't going to set her free, that much was certain. He hated Steeplejack more than all the rest of them combined. With his mind racing, he quickly lied, "I'm not attached to Elsie, man. But come on. Does she know, at least? At least tell me she knows."

"Does she know what? That's why we're dropping her off in Indiana?"

J.R. balked. "No," he clarified. "Does she know she's *pregnant?*" But then he perceived the answer, even prior to the careless laughter pouring out of Steeplejack's mouth, "J.R., who do you think told *me?*"

He felt his spirit, what remained of it, collapse.

*She doesn't love me,* he realized. *Doesn't trust me.* He still loved her, or insisted so, to himself, for a few seconds, even as he came to understand, in a way the Old Man could probably spell out in words but J.R. could only see. That so-called love was just some crippling, haymaking arm of stupidity.

Steeplejack turned away and stood for a moment in his ki-mono, then strode on his hairless legs to the window, to draw back the curtains and gaze upon his own serene reflection in the glass. He then reached for the hand lever and opened the window outward, to lean his head out into the night air and the inscrutable latitude and longitude he had, so far, refused to leave behind.

Meanwhile, J.R. sought to recalibrate his understanding of Elsie, and the expectations he had of her, and she of him. His would have to reconsider his own goodwill, his own pa-tience. Everything. He sagged in place a little more, paralyzed, with all his efforts seemingly ending here and now, whether his heart was broken or not.

Steeplejack spoke first, leaning back over his shoulder from the open window. "de Ram didn't show," he acknowledged. "You're right, J.R. The revolution? The damn thing ended before it ever got started..."

He turned his face, inhaled the night air.

J.R. could feel a hint of the breeze through the gently roiling curtains.

"Steeplejack."

"What?"

"Did you ever wonder why it was us Drummond sent to knock over that armored car?"

"It was you and me," Steeplejack agreed, "and Crosby Shue, and Lou Gannon, and Vince what's-his-name. We're not supposed to say a couple of those names. But that's who it was."

"But why was it *us?* Huh?"

Steeplejack had his head out the window, looking down.

"This place is packed with soldiers," J.R. pressed on. "Why did they send the five of *us?* On a suicide mission? And why did the cops—?"

"J.R., bring me that flashlight."

"What?"

"That flashlight."

"What flashlight?"

"In that drawer. Night table. Top drawer," Steeplejack had his head pointed down into the yard as he beckoned towards the night table with all five grasping fingers.

J.R. went over to it, opened the drawer, observed the flashlight rolling around inside with assorted fake dicks. "No way! Get your own flashlight."

"What?"

"I said get your own flashlight."

"Oh, for Christ's sake! OK, I get it, J.R. You've got your hang ups. Guess who doesn't care. But we can't lose sight of this thing in the yard. Come over here and watch it for me."

J.R. agreed and approached. Steeplejack was pointing down into the yard, saying, "Don't take your eyes off it, I'll be right back," until J.R. was staring down from the open window, and Steeplejack was confident to leave his side.

The object below lay discarded inside the simple boardwalk geometry between the barracks and the outhouse.

Vaguely, the Bunker Hill battle cry occurred to him. *Don't fire until you see the whites of their eyes!*

He got distracted by the rope ladder, which he had never noticed until now. It was folded up and tied at the window's ledge, ready to unfurl at a moment's notice. It was a fire escape, and not a vintage feature, but rather recently installed. The architects and carpenters and woodworkers and plumbers who had built this lodge had perhaps imagined its burning down, but never its abandonment.

Steeplejack arrived to aim his flashlight down into the yard. Shanahan began hollering incoherently from his turret, vectoring his floodlight upon the same spot, the bright beacon engulfing the flashlight's chaotically efficient beam.

"THERE IT IS!" Steeplejack called. "SHINE YOUR LIGHT ON THAT!"

The stuffed animal lay off to the side of the yard's T-squared elevations. Seeing it, J.R. understood in one exquisite combination of luck, brains and personal experience exactly what was about to happen.

"What is that?" Steeplejack asked, "Is that Kermit the Frog?"

"Kermit...?" J.R. echoed the Muppet's name once before answering, "It's a frog."

Steeplejack looked back into his pornography studio, the inventory of discarded stuffed animals strewn upon and fallen from the plush and messy bedspread. "Is that one of mine?" he wondered, turning back from the bedchamber to the deadpan glee of the visage in the yard below. "Who tossed that out there?"

J.R. didn't answer, didn't interfere.

"Hold this," Steeplejack extended the flashlight.

J.R. withdrew both hands, "No."

"You're a *baby.*"

"I'm a *man,*" J.R. retorted, adding, "That's the one thing you morons weren't counting on."

Steeplejack aimed the light downward. Then, casually, with his free hand, he untethered and unfurled the rope ladder from its window ledge. Only now did he say, "You're not a man, J.R. You're a teenager." He tossed the flashlight back into the bedchamber with a thump and added, "I've got mushroom patches growing on my ass that are older than you."

Then he swung one hairless leg over the windowsill, followed by the other, a scissor effect J.R. witnessed only peripherally, while his upper chest dropped into his abdomen, descending by some ancient machinery with every strategic non-spillage of truth. To warn Steeplejack? To give up the game in one disastrous moment? Or just to let him climb out the window on drugs in his kimono? He chose silence.

Steeplejack was halfway down the rope ladder, with the floodlight beaming up the Mess Hall's dark and weathered face to follow him. "NOT ON ME!" he called into the blinding light, pointing his finger, jabbing it downward. "ON IT! ON IT!" The beacon obeyed his command and waited upon the prize. Shanahan, the lone watchman, was following a chain of command he yet believed in. The walkway's illuminated corners framed the inert stuffed animal in the mud. Steeplejack landed on his bare feet and made for it. The frog's face gaped joyfully. Steeplejack picked it up. The puppet's nose began to blink on-and-off red.

KABOOM! Smithereens, a sonic bang, a flash of light so close J.R. saw few—but just enough—actual body parts.

Gunfire erupted. The floodlight turned wildly up and then down at the marauders, while the Castle's southern wall began to ripple severely, portending collapse.

"ELSIE!" he bolted out the door.

Across the balcony, Farrah was directing the Praetorian to stand their ground.

"FARRAH!" he called. They gawked at him. "I'M GETTING ELSIE! SHE'S UP IN THE WATCHTOWER!"

Explosions and gunfire thundered outside with renewed intensity, reverberating within the building's log cabin bones. Farrah's impossibly bright eyes glittered from across the way, even as she slouched, unsmiling.

"DON'T SHOOT!" he beseeched them all, eyeballing Crosby Shue personally but delivering the message to everyone. He then traversed in swift time that length of mezzanine toward the watchtower stairs. When he arrived, Farrah was waiting, passive, unimpressed.

"I have to get Elsie out of there!"

"What are you, her knight in shining armor?"

"You're Goddamn right!" he angled past her, making his way up.

Elsie was waiting, wide-eyed in the firelight. "Look at this," she told him.

He grabbed her by the waist and cast his gaze after hers over the watchtower's ledge and upon the siege. To hold her like that, like she belonged to him. He longed for it, even as she granted it, even knowing she didn't trust him, and never would. He watched her face glow from the sweeping fires of war. He felt his nostril muscles recoil in spasm at the fumes. In the past, he might have panicked and performed some desperate and useless breathing exercise, to see himself across another stretch of danger. Tonight, however, perhaps because of the three or four or five murders he had committed, or perhaps because he couldn't lose the woman he had already lost, or perhaps because his plan had worked after all, he found himself perfectly calm.

Shanahan was raining bullets into the mayhem from his mounted M60. Gunfire echoed down the mountainside. The floodlight exploded, followed by a second explosion, and then a moment later the entire southern turret was gone as Shanahan leapt down into the yard, alive, executing a shoulder roll, arriving on his feet, still wearing his gas mask. J.R. gripped Elsie tighter. Grant Archer, brandishing an AK-47, had vectored from his gatehouse post to meet the impervious Shanahan in the yard, and to stand beside him on that ground, and watch the blazing barracks collapse completely, while the corner of corrugated steel wall rippled in a cause and effect chain of ruination. The first ten-yard panel coughed forward, and through the smoke and flames marauders began pouring in, only to be mowed down by a twin barrage from the two surviving battlement sentries, the masked Shanahan and the hardy Grant Archer, sending body after body back the other way, ass over teakettle. "HEAVY CASUALTIES!" some desperate voice called out. Shanahan was hit with bullets instead of mustard gas and collapsed dead in the yard. Grant Archer dodged nimbly away from the same arc of fire.

Rose Archer came scrambling out of the laundry room with a shotgun, blasting two enemy soldiers dead—BLAM! BLAM!—then two more—BLAM! BLAM! The two children came trailing after her, little Bella shrieking and little Wallace shrieking too. Rose turned to them. "NO! BACK INSIDE!" Grant Archer was hit twice in the chest. "NO!" Rose Archer

447

spun and sent another volley into the flaming breach, dropping the crucial remaining attacker, but too late. The two children stood on the violent burning battle yard, crying, abandoned and terrified as Rose Archer went to her fallen husband to kneel and sob. The gunfire ceased. Rose Archer's grief sounded out, louder and louder, drowning even the children's wails of terror. The Castle's fallen bulkhead burned and belched black smoke. Although the attack had come from the Mess Hall's rec room side, Farrah could be heard barking, "WATCH THE FRONT DOOR! WATCH THE FRONT DOOR!" J.R. heard Crosby Shue's desperate voice, "I'M GOING DOWN THERE FOR MY DAUGHTER!" Farrah ordered, "STAND YOUR POST, CROSBY SHUE!" A long moment of cease fire followed.

J.R. then spotted, down in the battered, fireswept yard, the two bewildered porn stars wandering out from the auto yard's spare cover, clad in their fur coats, but without their shoes. At the same time, Elsie, at J.R.'s side, said, "Is it over?"

He answered, *"Shhhh... I doubt it,"* and watched the flames lick along the burning walkway toward the armory, which was sure to explode at any moment. The gatehouse would burn next, and then the auto yard, with the Nova parked just outside that quadrant's side door. Time was running out, and women and children were in danger below, not to mention the woman and child he had taken possession of tonight, up in this watchtower. He had no doubt a second wave was coming.

He watched as down in the yard Bella Shue held little Wallace in an embrace, even as she cried uncontrollably. At the same time, the two hapless actresses convened, one of them pointing and proposing an escape route. Their desperate faces recoiled in fear in one awfully bright split second before an earsplitting hail of machine gun fire mowed them down, mowed everyone down, all the women and children in the yard. J.R. gripped Elsie tighter, awaiting her prayer, or holy condemnation, something sure to follow from her lips, or from the spirit that made her so formidable, but she said nothing, merely watched at his side, which made sense, he came to see, as he held her, because what could a nurse do about any of this?

From the southern front, through the roiling combustion, he spotted the massacre's architect at last. It was, of course,

448

de Ram, brandishing an enormous belt fed M60 machine gun, much like the tripod-mounted weapon Shanahan had manned and then abandoned earlier, except de Ram had the weapon gripped in one hand and resting on one enormous thigh. Laying eyes upon him now, the agent of ruin he had purposefully taunted, a terrifying clown in a yellow T-shirt and overstressed suspenders, J.R. understood, finally, and much too late, that he had made a terrible mistake.

Hot flames crept closer toward the stout armory. de Ram strolled through the gaping wreckage into the cataclysm's battered and corpse-strewn heart, a man with many to blame and much to recoup. Behind him, out from the dancing shadows, the silhouettes of Fat Ransom and Glenn Disteek emerged, with no mistaking either, Fat Ransom's mobilized girth, Glenn Disteek's trench coat and rockabilly haircut. Assault rifles in hand, they completed de Ram's vanguard, and sized up the volume of destruction to be waged. J.R. could see, or was sure he could see, that if the armory should explode at this moment, it might be the best of all possible misfortunes.

A stratum of mustard yellow haze began to swell beneath the tendrils of orange fire. Black plumes billowed thicker. Particles of flickering ash drifted through the rippling heat. The armory ignited. The shed exploded in white and yellow light, sending a chain of sonic charges and pinwheels and plywood and sheet metal trash into the battlefield. Amidst a rippling mirage of heat, the three Posse Serpens invaders remained untouched, newly lit by brighter fire.

"J.R.?" Elsie pleaded.

"We're not gonna die," he promised her.

"Kiss me," she pressed into him.

He kissed her, felt her abandon, her longing, her strong tongue, her hungry jaws, her yielding lips, her unapologetic teeth. Steeplejack had taken it all away from him. He had stolen it from Elsie too, and much more.

"ALL RIGHT, COME ON DOWN NOW!" Farrah's voice called from below.

He released Elsie, as slowly as possible, first her lips from his mouth, then her waist from his grip, then her elbows, then her wrists, then her fingertips, releasing her at last from all but his gaze. He would save his grievances for later. He would protect her and her unborn baby—also himself, since none of it could conceivably be done without him. The decision was

449

made. He peered down the watchtower's spire and down the barrel of Farrah's Sig Sauer, or Beretta, or whatever it was she had pointed up at him. It was a Sig Sauer. Her one eye was squinted closed. Her other was saying goodbye, or preparing to, through the pistol's sights. "Don't make me ask twice," she told him.

He turned back to Elsie and gravely reassured her, "Follow me." Then he began his spiral descent while she followed behind him, and while Farrah maintained the weapon on both of them, backing away inside her chamber door. The Praetorian guards were paying all due attention, notably Brock Fowler and Grossmark in Farrah's immediate left and right radius, "EYES ON THE PRIZE, GUYS!" she snapped at them, and pointed her free hand down at the Mess Hall arena.

J.R. didn't want to try to guess whose side Lazy Farrah was on, what she wanted, or how he factored into her game plan. In that sense, he felt he understood her. Completing his descent from the watchtower, he showed her his empty hands. Grossmark on one flank wore a murderous glare. Brock Fowler on the other seemed ready to open fire, his blonde locks darkened by sweat, his eyeballs twitching back and forth between the threat of J.R.'s presence and the danger from the Mess Hall's front door below. Farrah backed further into her chamber, beckoning J.R. across that threshold. She beckoned Elsie too, who arrived down the ladder at the watchtower's base, while J.R. blocked her body with his own, shielding her belly foremost.

He said, "We're coming in there with you."

"Let's go," she ordered.

He kept Elsie behind him as he entered. He knew the master's chamber, its curious clutter, its open window onto the night, the explosive charge rigged inside the laundry chute, which he instinctively evinced no knowledge of, without a shred of guilt, since Elsie was keeping secrets from him too. He recognized himself very little, and Elsie even less, as he looked into her eyes and said, "Best we tell her."

Elsie was confused. He hesitated no further. "She's pregnant. And the father's dead. Whatever you do, none of this is her fault. And not the baby's either. So don't screw this up—"

450

"We're all going to live," Farrah countered, exasperated, also amused, adding, for Elsie's sake, "Your boyfriend's a moron."

J.R. studied Farrah for the ten thousandth time. She answered him now, "The only secrets in this room right now are between you and me. Maybe you should do a better job of leaving your girlfriend out of things, instead of doing such a bang-up job of getting her into things?"

"Umm," he said.

"Well," Farrah answered herself. "I guess it's too late for that."

"Never mind *me,*" he kept his body between the barrel of the Sig Sauer and Elsie's pregnant abdomen. "Just keep this unborn kid in mind."

"Don't give me that," Farrah said. 'We're all getting out of here. Just do what I say."

"I'll do what you say. But I'm smart too. You should listen to me."

"Shut up," she pointed. "Get that rifle. No one's smart. Don't forget that?"

"Which rifle?"

"That one."

The M14 rested by its barrel against a chest of drawers. J.R. grabbed it. He looked upon Elsie honestly enough to briefly glimpse his own desperation play a symphony over the passiveness she called Faith.

"It's loaded," Farrah said.

"I can feel that."

"Keep your pregnant girlfriend out of sight," she told him. "Kneel in the doorway. Keep the rifle steady. We've got one chance of getting out of here alive. If you want to live, and if you want your girlfriend to live, and if you want her baby to live, try doing what I say, for once. Otherwise, go ahead and take charge of things, Daddio. Tell me you believe one single person under this roof more than me. I want to hear it."

"Listen to me," he said. "This could be the end. Give me my tape."

Farrah laughed, half surprised, half amused. Before he could even protest, she answered, "It ain't even put it away yet," and reached into the back pocket of her coveralls to produce the black, plastic, ponderous prize. Her eyes twinkled. Always several steps ahead.

"Drop it on the floor," he said.

"You're gonna do what I say," she answered, taunting him with the tape in hand.

"Throw it on the floor," he said.

Grinning, she tossed it onto the rug. A pistol would have been easier, but a rifle was all he had. He eased Elsie aside to make way for his back shoulder as he leveled the weapon and aimed—BANG! BANG!—sending the target dancing, spewing black plastic chunks flying, disgorging black unspooling tape.

"FARRAH!" multiple voices cried from the balcony. Footsteps approached, charging. Farrah belted out, "GET BACK TO YOUR POSTS! CHRIST!" even as their faces briefly appeared in the doorway. Grossmark, Brock Fowler, vengeful, murderous. "YOU STUPID ASSHOLES!" she told them. They obeyed.

She turned back to J.R., "You got your tape. So now you're going to do what I say, so we can all get out of here."

"All right," he said. "All right, that's a deal. Elsie, you've got to hide—"

"No, J.R., I want to see this."

"What?"

Farrah laughed. "Oh, you're a hero all right."

He faced Elsie, stunned, speechless. She tucked herself into him, against him. "I'm staying here next to you," she said.

Farrah laughed some more. He had lost all control of the situation, and not for the first time in his life, although this time it was two women. He crouched down and faced the chamber doorway, rifle in hand. "OK," he said, "but stay behind me."

"Closer..." Farrah told him, "...to the edge. Up to the doorway. Me and Elsie are right behind you. Listen to me, J.R. Keep your head down. And keep your finger on that trigger. But don't fucking shoot until I tell you."

Below, the Mess Hall's front doors loudly crashed and buckled inward.

J.R. caressed the M14, willing himself to trust it. Farrah lit a cigarette behind him. *Do you understand me?* she hissed, and a cloying nicotine haze developed. *Don't shoot until I say.*

Grossmark and Skinner and Trauer took aim from their posts. Buchanan and Chuck Zorn and Crosby Shue. Lovejoy and Brock Fowler, all eight around the mezzanine.

"DON'T SHOOT UNTIL I TELL YOU!" Farrah snarled a third time, loud now, spitting in his ear.

The front doors banged and bent further inward. Gunshots sounded, earsplitting. Half a dozen from several directions. The doors had come almost entirely off their hinges. They held a stubborn moment longer by some freak of chaosphysics. They burst apart a second later, spinning opposite ways. A hail of bullets pelted the dead bodies of Shanahan and Grant Archer that de Ram wore over his shoulder as riddled and bloody shields of meat until he dropped them artfully and dove, shoulder rolling and landing just beneath the crisscrossed melee weapons upon the Mess Hall's entrance wall.

Trauer took aim from above the breached doorway but Glenn Disteek came blazing in next, firing into the balcony, drawing fire away from de Ram, who not only had the war hammer off the wall and in his hands but already had it swung around overhead whirligig style, purposed to smash the support post that held up the balcony and its Praetorian guardsmen twelve feet off the ground instead of faceplanted into it. The entire section of mezzanine outside Farrah's doorway collapsed. Brock Fowler scrambled and grabbed desperately for spilling floorboards while Grossmark got dumped straight to the floor, stunned, winded, raising his head, crawling desperately, releasing a scream as de Ram's war hammer landed.

"WILHELM!" Buchanan cried.

"YOU KILLED HIM!" Trauer howled.

"GET PAST IT!" Skinner barked, firing his assault rifle down at de Ram, who had already lifted a picnic table as a shield, the entire length gripped in one hand while his other gripped the war hammer.

J.R. edged closer to the doorway, better to see. He could feel the two women close behind him, peering out over his shoulder.

Disteek had taken cover outside the Mess Hall's battered doorway, and had taken to firing volleys into the rafters, then ducking back outside. Fat Ransom joined him, so now they both curled their weapons inside, sending bullets up at the sentries. Crosby Shue was first to leap down from that hail of lead for the safety of the bar. Chuck Zorn executed the same maneuver from the Mess Hall's chimney side, landing on his feet, gun in hand, which he fired repeatedly at his assailants as they ducked back out the door. He then sent a barrage after the roving picnic table as de Ram kept to the room's perimeter, shielding himself from the torrent.

Fowler still clung to the broken balcony's scaffold, crying, "GUYS! HELP!"

Lovejoy answered his call, "HANG IN THERE, FOWLER, WE GOTCHA!"

Chuck Zorn, down in the arena, stopped shooting, seeking his next angle of attack. He found it, shouted up to his companions, "THE DOOR! COVER ME, GUYS! THE FRONT DOOR! HIT IT WITH EVERYTHING YOU GOT!"

They responded, all four that remained, while Chuck Zorn stripped off his gun and sprinted top speed across the Mess Hall for Cash Clarick's orphaned battle axe.

At the same time, Crosby Shue jumped out from behind the bar to confront, alone, the charging de Ram, who flung the entire picnic table at him flush, flattening his face, chest and body, knocking him backward, dead at best, possibly still alive to receive de Ram's follow up, an unwound war hammer to the skull that smashed a good portion of the bar's countertop just as much apart or more so. The gunfire continued, ripping and spewing splinters into the front doorway. No voice protested Crosby Shue's demise. J.R might have witnessed it alone.

Fowler still dangled from his destroyed upper deck.

"DROP DOWN!" Lovejoy called to him.

"NO WAY!" Fowler's yellow locks were damp with sweat. His legs bicycle pedaled foolishly.

Below, Chuck Zorn had arrived at and claimed the battle axe from the front wall. He turned to face de Ram, but he was outside the combat radius.

de Ram reached back sideways with his enormous shoulders and muscled arms and with a flick of his massive wrists flung the war hammer just as Lovejoy from the balcony above made to rescue the hapless Brock Fowler. The bludgeon struck, missile-like, taking out another support beam, sending another long chunk of balcony collapsing, Lovejoy spilling with it, losing his weapon, although amazingly and cat-like he managed to land feet first, with teetering grace, upon the picnic table below. Overhead, Fowler still clung, isolated anew, while the remaining lengths of splintered floorboards continued to come detached from the wall by his own flailing weight and in desperate rhythm with his every panicked upward lunge.

Gripping the useless battle axe, Chuck Zorn remained in check, dodging volleys from the bullet torn doorway. Trauer and Skinner beat the assault back as best they could from their overhead angles. Lovejoy atop the debris-battered picnic table began to seek out his fallen weapon. de Ram seized two bottles from behind the bar, and in turn absorbed two gunshots, one winging his arm, the other grazing his side a bit more fleshily. It was Skinner shooting, as de Ram sent one bottle, then another, then another, each flung overhand, spinning, breaking against Skinner's weapon, his fortifications. J.D., Makers Mark—CRASH! CRASH!—shattering off the wall, knocking Skinner off balance. Absolut. Jameson. CRASH! Vectors not so much mathematical as straight. Skinner ducked repeatedly. His gun went silent. de Ram went for the defenseless Lovejoy.

Chuck Zorn charged along the perimeter, chased by volleys of gunfire from the front door that were beaten back from above.

At one point Buchanan reloaded, crying, "WHOA!" as de Ram angled after Lovejoy directly, launching himself forward, causing Lovejoy to duck his head and allow de Ram to clear the tabletop spread eagled, flying squirrel-like, to land precisely where his war hammer had fallen. Lovejoy spun. de Ram brought his reclaimed weapon down upon the tabletop, leveling one half of it down from its fulcrum, repurposing the other into a catapult and Lovejoy into a high diver over an empty pool. Just as Chuck Zorn arrived with his battle axe, pissed off, bloodthirsty, frothing at the mouth, and shielding the marauding de Ram from any further gunfire, Lovejoy smashed face first into the floor behind him.

"CEASE FIRE!" Skinner cried.

"CEASE FIRE? GOOD LUCK!" Disteek answered. A few more gunshots rattled off. Gunsmoke swirled around the grand hall.

de Ram and Chuck Zorn faced off with their melee weapons amidst the dead and dying soldiers inside the Mess Hall's bloody and hazy ruins. Chuck Zorn, bearing the sharper weapon, swung first, a great overhand would-be killshot, only to clang against the war hammer's hilt.

J.R.'s finger caressed the M14's trigger. Farrah whispered, *"Eyes on the prize. Aim for the chandelier. You know where. But I say when."*

*"Why don't I just shoot Chuck Zorn?"* he asked.

*"Are you kidding? Bullets are traceable, kid. Shoot the chandelier. Everything else falls into place."*

He leveled the rifle at the elaborate fixture's overhead stem, and the explosives he had been tasked to rig. He could hit it, no problem. But he couldn't help stealing glances, longer and longer, at the combat taking place in the Mess Hall's ruined pit.

*"If you screw this up,"* Farrah hissed in his ear, *"I'll kill Elsie."*

*"Shhh, please!"* He nudged her away, took aim again with the rifle. *"You want me to hit this thing or not? Don't tell me you'll kill Elsie!"*

de Ram had taken a slash to the forearm and responded by kicking Chuck Zorn back against one of the tables. Chuck Zorn was nimble, ferocious, back on his toes, charging again, weapon in hand.

"Now," Farrah said.

He took the shot, exploded the chandelier's ceiling plate, dropped its heavy matrix of piercing antlers perfectly timed onto Chuck Zorn's head.

Skinner saw everything from across the balcony. Farrah stood and pressed her Sig Sauer into J.R.'s skull. "I'VE GOT HIM, SKINNER! GET AFTER THE OGRE!"

Skinner turned his attention back on de Ram and howled, "OPEN FIRE!"

de Ram pounced away, took a glancing shot to the calf.

Brock Fowler cried out again, forlorn and dangling, pedaling his legs, going nowhere. From the doorway below, Fat Ransom took aim, but Glenn Disteek caught him by the arm and lowered it.

Skinner shouted, "SHUT UP, BROCK FOWLER! DROP DOWN OR SHUT UP!"

"WOW!" Buchanan said.

"WAIT A MINUTE! J.R. DADDIO KILLED CHUCK ZORN!" Trauer had seen it too.

"EVERYBODY HOLD YOUR POSITIONS!" Skinner ordered.

"WE"RE GETTING MASSACRED!" Trauer protested.
"WHO'S ON WHOSE SIDE HERE?" J.R. had lost sight of de Ram.

"GUYS?" Buchanan's voice was pitched with fear.

*"J.R., that was a good shot."*

It was Elsie whispering this time, very close to his ear with her lips. He turned to her and nodded, briefly. Better not to speak. The building had become deadly quiet.

Outside, a loud crash suggested another panel of Castle wall tumbling down.

de Ram howled, "DUKE!"

A smattering of wasted gunfire answered his war cry.

"DUUUUUUUKE! YOU BETTER COME OUT OR I'M COMING IN!" he was grunting and growling like a tiger set loose in their midst. Another barrage rang from Glenn Disteek at the front door, followed by another from Fat Ransom. They allowed Fowler to dangle, helpless to the very end, even as the wreckage finally came loose from the wall, carrying the lemon haired Praetorian guardsman howling in terror and slamming down to the floor, to lie in the aftermath, groaning, still alive, but not well. Lovejoy himself lay half dead in the same bloody, debris-strewn arena. Now another enormous section of woodwork collapsed to the floor around them, striking neither man with so much as a splinter, expressing for a moment the kind of slapstick blind luck that can only manifest out of actual calamity. However, the blind luck ended one second later when de Ram plunged out of the shadows with his war hammer and WHAM! and then WHAM! removed Brock Fowler and Lovejoy from the equation, *Whac-a-Mole*-style.

"RAAAAAAAAAAAAAAAAHHH!!!!" he roared, blood-stained, great and obscene, pitched heavenward, with blazing red curls sprung from his indomitable skull. He seemed almost to welcome the next rain of bullets—to linger and let a few more in—before ranging out of sight, trailing blood in thicker, darker pools.

"DUKE!" his human words resounded. "COME OUT, DUKE!" Gunfire followed the voice. Bullets lost him in countless number. The shooting stopped. The guardsmen reloaded. Gunsmoke and sawdust drifted up to the rafters.

Trying to infer de Ram's location, J.R. kept spying the bodies, including Chuck Zorn's twisted remains inside the clusters of bloody and broken deer antlers, but also the other

457

fallen Praetorian sentries strewn about the room, for all intents and purposes decapitated. He wondered if he was to blame, for Chuck Zorn especially, but for all of them equally. Or perhaps for none of them at all. He never wanted to get kidnapped, and blackmailed. Not to mention everything else they had done to him.

*"Mess hall,"* Farrah mused with a snicker, as she peered down at the gruesome battle torn arena.

A creaking sound of footsteps advanced. "ELEVEN... ELEVEN... ELEVEN O'CLOCK!" Skinner cried.

de Ram's yellow and blood-orange attacking figure plunged out of the shadows, bringing down the war hammer, shattering the deck, Trauer falling with it, crying out, "MY GUN!" and reaching back as it vanished beneath him with everything else, plummeting, then smacking into the floor. Gunfire rang up from the doorway, drawing fire from Skinner and Buchanan, while de Ram found Trauer helpless in the chaos, and with a downward stroke of the war hammer smote his brains all over the floor. Buchanan raged, "GAHHHH!" He and Skinner blasted away. de Ram was hit twice, perhaps vitally this time, the blood-soaked T-shirt and suspenders stretching tight over his perforated abdomen as he brought up the war hammer with both massive hands, torqued himself back and heaved the weapon overhand, missile-like. Buchanan had time enough to ask nothing before the impact through his face pinioned his remains to the wall.

Skinner held the remaining post and ceased fire. He had lost the target. Smoke billowed in from the rec room entrance. The Mess Hall was burning.

"FARRAH!" he called. "FARRAH, CAN YOU SEE HIM?" He peered across from his lonesome sentry post, met J.R.'s gaze instead. "J.R.!" he begged, "CAN YOU SEE HIM?"

*"This really worked out,"* Farrah whispered.

Down below, from the battered entrance, Glenn Disteek and Fat Ransom were both peering inside. To their left, de Ram was bleeding gravely as he prowled beneath Skinner's feet. The column of pine that held up the remaining lonesome slice of balcony looked more and more vulnerable the more and more attention he gave it.

"FARRAH?" Skinner kept calling out.

de Ram crashed shoulder first into the support post, snapping through it, sending Skinner spilling down amongst the planks and splinters with his rifle firing wildly, bullets that sent J.R. ducking behind the sawdust of the shattered doorframe and reaching behind him to shield Elsie and Farrah both. Skinner's gun became silent, as he began a desperate bargain from the ruin of his post, "WAIT, WAIT!"

J.R. peered down.

de Ram had seized his prey by the head in both hands and then, in an act to be heard more than witnessed, and with a stroke both improbably efficient and mercilessly non-instantaneous, the job was finished. When it was over, he emerged, wheezing, and bleeding freely, but covered even more so with the blood of his victims. "DUUUUUUKE!" he howled, one last time, as his voice gave way, followed by his body. He collapsed in a heap amongst the Mess Hall's near complete wreckage.

"FARRAH!" Fat Ransom called from the front door. "WE'RE COMING IN! DON'T SHOOT!"

"de RAM!" Glenn Disteek made for his fallen companion, who was both mortally wounded and dead.

Fat Ransom added, "J.R., WELL DONE!"

Upstairs, J.R. looked to Farrah.

She said, "Just keep your eyes open," and gestured for him to lower the gun.

"FARRAH! I'M COMING UP!" Glenn Disteek called to her.

She leaned out over the war-torn doorway's precipice to ask, "How?"

"This place is on fire!" Disteek answered. "We have to hurry!" He slung the rifle over his shoulder, went for the nearest picnic table, got his weight behind it and pushed it through the rubble into place beneath the second story's exposed doorway.

J.R. recalled Glenn Disteek from a lifetime ago, in the basement of the Church of Avaris. He had sized up the Old Man as formidable, but Glenn Disteek as something less, somehow. That was a mistake.

Reaching back for Elsie's hand he found it and gripped it. He turned to her and said, "All right. Let's go."

"Oh no you don't," Disteek's voice interrupted. J.R. backed away from the entrance. He kept Elsie safe behind him as he watched the Nazi marauder leap up to grasp the open doorframe's splintered edge. "No no no! I'm coming up there!"

"Glenn!" Farrah protested, "This is my bedroom!"

Disteek swung his great black boot up into that threshold, dug his heel in, then crowbarred the rest into view, cresting the doorframe with his Elvis-Mohawk first and his square shouldered bulk not far behind. Suddenly inside the room, he was stalking his way toward them in his black leather trench coat, saying, "I remember you."

"That's J.R.," Farrah explained.

"THAT'S J.R.!" Fat Ransom called from below.

"The runaway," Disteek knew exactly who J.R. was. "From Erving, New York. Nobody was looking for you, Junior."

"Who nobody?"

"The police. The FBI. So don't worry. You're not a cold case. You weren't even a case to begin with."

"What about my father?"

Disteek shrugged. "What about him?" He changed the subject to Elsie. "Who's *this?*"

Farrah started to answer, but Disteek interrupted her, "Oh wait. Never mind. I know this one. You're from the movie. By gosh. I should salute you."

"Whoa," J.R. said. "Wait a minute."

"For what? We don't have a minute."

"You don't make fun of her."

"I *saluted* her. Or didn't you hear me? Don't eyeball me, kid."

Farrah intervened, "Leave the kid alone."

"Don't tell me what to do—"

"I don't give a *shit* what you do."

"Where is it?" he wanted to know.

"You know where it is," she told him. "It's under the floorboards downstairs."

"No, no," he said, "No, no, no. I'm talking about the cigarette case."

"The what?"

"*The what?*" he mimicked her. "The cigarette case! The antique naked-lady cigarette case!"

"*Pshhh,*" she answered. "I sold that thing—"

"Bullshit—"

"Ages ago."

He called down over his shoulder to Fat Ransom. "FATSO! WILL YOU PLEASE TELL YOUR SISTER TO TELL THE TRUTH, PLEASE?"

"AHEM..." Fat Ransom prepared his speaking voice. "FARRAH!" he pleaded. "PLEASE TELL THE TRUTH, PLEASE!"

"And do it fast," Disteek added. "The place is burning down. Plus, the cops are coming, probably."

Farrah hollered out the doorframe at her brother, "I CAN'T BELIEVE YOU TOLD HIM ABOUT IT!"

"THIS WHOLE PLACE IS ON FIRE!" he answered.

She turned to Disteek. Even at her most deadpan, she could not suppress her mischief. "I sold it. A long time ago."

"GODAMMIT!" he erupted. He made for the nearest bureau, to desperately rummage through its drawers, flinging its contents out onto the floor, a rampage that further fulfilled the room's seemingly purposeful masterpiece of chaos.

"THIS PLACE!" he cried, overturning a dresser drawer, pitching a night table upside-down. "HOW DO YOU LIVE LIKE THIS?" he ransacked the next chest of drawers. Farrah crept incrementally closer to the laundry chute with every passing exposition of drama, but her proximity hadn't yet caught his attention.

Fat Ransom's voice could be heard protesting from the Mess Hall's burning ruination below, "WE GOTTA VA-MOOSE, PRONTO!"

"My husband..." Farrah started to say.

"Your husband isn't even here," Disteek unholstered a silver Beretta, leveled it at Elsie and said, "I'm shooting the porn star first."

"It's in the laundry chute!" J.R. pointed.

"That's called *Good Decision Making*," Disteek smiled. He turned his attention to the laundry chute, the trap door in the wall, approaching it, signaled to it.

Arriving, he pushed open the door to peer inside. It was Farrah who had sketched the forgery's colorful distraction, but it was J.R. who took up the brush in the end, when it was clear his finishing touch was needed. The booby-trapped sardine tin was then laid inside the chute, in a position J.R. calculated as tantalizingly unhidden, and yet just within one's grasp, if only one turned one's head away and reached all the way in, shoulder deep, and groped around blindly, and gripped the detonating explosive device.

BANG! The blast drew a stabbing shriek from Elsie. Farrah was decisive, turning her Sig Sauer on Glenn Disteek, who reeled, howling in agony from the post combustion cloud. She shot him for good measure, sent him down in a heap, with his mangled, hemorrhaging, formerly inquisitive appendage no longer an arm.

"FARRAH!" came her brother's cry.

"WE'RE ON OUR WAY DOWN!" she called. She made for the *Ivanhoe* hardcover where it lay strewn amidst the chaos.

It wasn't an actual hard cover book, but a hollowed-out strongbox. J.R. had seen her stash the treasure there, and now he watched her withdraw it.

He knew nothing useful about the antique cigarette case, except that it was worth at least sixty thousand dollars.

Farrah must have read his mind. "We're taking the sixty grand too," she said.

"Not advised," he said.

"Let's go," she waved her handgun. "Out the door. You first. Then help your pregnant girlfriend down after. And then come back for me, if you don't mind."

"All right, all right," he said.

She waved forward with the gun.

"FAT RANSOM!" he called down into the pit, advancing to the doorway's edge. "DON'T SHOOT!"

"WHY WOULD I SHOOT? LET'S GO!"

He gripped the perilous threshold, turned and dropped and allowed himself to dangle, release, and land, feet planted upon the tabletop.

He went back to assist Elsie, who let him take her by the waist and ease her down. Farrah was next, whose waist he greeted with his strong hands, wanting only to detest her, but desiring her helplessly as he helped her down, her coverall contoured body never less mysterious than in this crucial moment.

The Mess Hall was on fire. Sixty thousand dollars lay stashed beneath the floorboards. Some local bucket brigade and law enforcement contingent was almost certainly on the way, and though fire trucks would have no earthly means of reaching this plane of property, police cars would make it here, inevitably.

Farrah hugged Fat Ransom with a passing sincerity or semblance of it. She pointed at J.R. and said, "We don't kill this one."

"No, I get that," he let a smile cross his face, lit by the orange bonfires of calamity. With a comfortable, if not luxurious sense of impermeableness, he shook his head and said, "Hey, listen, sister. Just in case we all... you know... die right now... I just want you to know that I'm sorry for the way it turned out. I really am. I wish it was different. But the only difference between you and me, as we stand here today, is at least I got to eat."

Her smirk expanded with boredom. She said, "That must have been wonderful for you."

"Hey, I'm not you. Hey, come on. Don't be mean. Hey, what about Virginia? Where's my niece at?"

"She'll get along."

He tried for a moment to confront his sister with some pantomime of moral necessitude, but she read his mind instantly, and told him, "We're not picking her up at the hospital. Are you crazy? That's the exact way to get everybody killed."

"All right, all right," he agreed. "Money. Items of value. Let's collect it up."

She looked at J.R.

"What?" he asked her. "Where is it? Let's go! We have to get out of here!"

"You know where it is, killer. It's under Chuck Zorn and the deer antler chandelier."

J.R. dug into the bloody puzzle pieces, kicked away the broken antler clusters, and shoved Chuck Zorn's gory corpse aside. He opened the trap door and jumped down into the familiar cubbyhole. The satchel of marked bills lay where they had stashed it, but a new duffel bag had been added, a gym bag. He tossed up one bag, then the other. He pried himself up, saying, "Wait a minute, hold on. Is that a bag full of porn? Is Elsie's movie in there?"

"Will you stop?"

"No! Look at that bag! Look at how much stuff is in it! You don't need her movie! I do!"

"Fine, Romeo, take it."

He dove into the gym bag, found the reel of celluloid. It was a circular foot in diameter, labeled in black magic marker with Elsie's first name, plus another word.

"J.R.," Farrah said. "And Elsie, too, since it's your actual movie." She was leveling with them both. "You should know. You're wasting your time. It's been released to the public already."

"Released to the *what?*" he flung the reel Frisbee-like into the flames.

"It's playing in Times Square," Farrah told him. She turned to Elsie, pivoted back to J.R. "Maybe also in Thailand."

"That's not *released to the public,*" he argued.

"A porn theater in Times Square?"

"A porn theater in Times Square is not the public. It's a bunch of jerkoff winos. Plus, I'm going to put a stop to that too..."

"Oh, well excuse me for trying to help you," she told him. Fat Ransom smiled by the light of the blazing inferno, as he straddled the duffel bags of money and weapons and porn and contraband.

Elsie grabbed J.R. by his biceps.

"What?" he asked her. "What is it?"

"Thank you!" she dug her forehead into his armpit. He took her by the opposite elbow, folded her in, embraced her.

Farrah rolled her eyes. Fat Ransom intervened, "J.R., why don't you bring the car around?"

"What? Bring the car around? No. Are you crazy? I'm not driving my Nova into this inferno! We go out to the car!"

A section of ceiling broke free. Chunks of flaming wreckage collapsed to the Mess Hall floor. Clouds of smoke roiled and choked the air. "Let's go!" He rallied them. "I've got the duffel bags! Elsie, you carry the child! You two, try to keep up!"

"How far away is it?'

"It's right outside, come on!"

*Fat and Lazy,* he realized, as he led the charge. *Fat Ransom and Lazy Farrah. How did I get stuck with these two? How did this happen?*

"DROP YOUR WEAPONS!"

He spun. They all did. It was Glenn Disteek. J.R.'s heart collapsed. It was Cash Clarick all over again.

Back from the dead, Glenn Disteek's phantom animated corpse dropped down from the second story ruins of the Mess Hall onto the picnic table's tabletop. His right arm was mangled and squirting blood from crimson arteries. In his other hand he leveled his Beretta. His open jacket revealed slugs flattened into his bulletproof vest. Blood ran from the corner of his mouth, and his face beneath his oil black Elvis Mohawk was drenched with firelit beads of sweat. "DROP 'EM!" he repeated, and they obeyed. "OK, not the duffel bags! Grab those up! Let's go! All of you! Chop chop!"

"I got the duffel bags," J.R. said.

"I don't care who's fat, who's lazy, or who's pregnant!" Disteek added, needlessly, gleefully.

"I've got them," J.R held them up for all to see. "I've got the duffel bags."

But he had seen the murderous glitter in Farrah's eye, and he knew the inevitable had been set in motion.

"OK," Disteek sneered, coughing up some blood onto the tabletop between his planted boots. "Well then..." he waved the gun at the Ransom siblings. "I guess we don't need these two for anything..."

"Boss?" Fat Ransom protested.

Disteek, ghoulish in his sticky and bloody trench coat, limped down from the picnic table, approaching Farrah. She was readier to kill him than get killed by him, he must have seen this. "I'll take that naked lady cigarette case," he told her. She seemed to seethe in the hot firelight. Her blue eyes blazed with rage. Behind her, the stone fireplace remained untoppled as the Mess Hall's southern crook crumbled down into rubble and flame all around it. He said, "Don't look at me with your murder face, Farrah... *Lazy* Farrah... Everyone knows you're lazy..." He paused, gleefully, watching her consume so much intent so violently that almost immediately the inferno's heat no longer occupied or impregnated the elastic tension of the moment in time. It was only her rage. Only her rage drew power.

"I mean," he kept talking, "especially now, seeing as how I'm still alive and breathing—"

"No, you're not!" she lunged, nails first, eyes wide, teeth bared. Her brother, Fat Ransom, dove in to save her. BANG! the gun went off. The trio collapsed embattled to the floor amidst debris and hot cinders and deer antler shards and

465

thick, dark, sticky puddles of blood. Farrah emerged on top, straddling Glenn Disteek's chest, her two bare hands raised overhead to strike. BANG! the gun went off again, a head shot from below, fatal and messy, the end of Farrah. All the while, Fat Ransom had risen up to stumble backward, clutching his abdomen, to stagger briefly in the direction of the flames, to summon one last shriek of pain, one last jolt of adrenaline, to lurch away and collapse someplace that wasn't on fire. Disteek hobbled up to him and aimed his pistol. Fat Ransom sputtered upward through spittle and blood. Disteek answered with a headshot—BANG!—finishing what remained.

J.R. dropped the duffel bags. He used his body to shield Elsie as she huddled against him. He could feel her trembling. She gripped his hand, leaned into him. He kept his eyes on the mangled, one armed, wrathful and deathless Glenn Disteek, freshly splashed with blood and drenched with sweat, and aiming his pistol anew. "Let's go! Grab the duffel bags! Out the door!"

Staring at a wounded, weakened animal, J.R. knew he could still get it right. He could still get them out of this. He took up the loot. "It's going to be OK," he told Elsie.

"Yeah, yeah," Disteek barked. "Let's go!"

"The cigarette case," J.R. reminded him.

Hunched over in pain, and bleeding to death from his mangled arm, Disteek was beaten, and surely knew it.

"Want me to get it?"

"No, I got it!" he backtracked toward Farrah Ransom's unsightly corpse. He knelt, and fumbled for, and retrieved the prize from her coveralls.

J.R. said, "Elsie is a nurse." The heat from the fire seemed to create a slow rising delirium among the three of them. "You're going to bleed to death if we don't tie off that arm..."

"No," Disteek swam well enough to recover his balance. The silver Beretta reflected orange firelight. "Out the door, let's go!"

J.R. turned and led the way out of the furnace. Once into the yard and off the front deck, he spared a glimpse back at the silken, billowing, burning swastika overhanging the venue's makeshift stage. It burned and burned.

"J.R.," Disteek paused. "Do you see what happens when people underestimate me?"

466

J.R. understood that this was the end. He would face Glenn Disteek, here in this muddy yard. He would face down the barrel of a gun. Afterwards, he would face whatever, if anything, should follow.

But he was amazed to see Duke Drummond arriving, sprinting into view out of the bonfire's hazy and rippling yellow light with a croquet ball in hand, the green one. Disteek never saw it coming. The blow to his coiffured rockabilly skull left him dead in the dirt.

A long moment followed, though J.R. had lost all sense of moments and their length, while Duke Drummond stood over the bloody body, clutching the murder weapon. Once again there was no differentiation between the nightmare's end and its new beginning. However long it lasted, J.R. spoke first, "Duke?"

"Daddio."

"Is Virginia OK? It's a good thing she wasn't here."

"At the hospital," Drummond answered in a daze. He clutched the bloody, painted orb a moment longer. Then he let it roll out of his hand and fall to the ground. "Farrah?" he asked.

"She's gone."

Drummond lowered his head.

"They're all gone."

Drummond waited a moment longer, then looked up, with deadly sincerity. "Can you imagine, J.R., if you and me had teamed up? What we could have achieved. If we were on the same page?"

"Imagine?" J.R. balked.

"Yes. That's right. *Imagine.*"

"What are you, John Lennon?"

Another length of wall collapsed afire, followed by a new section of the Mess Hall tumbling down in noisy ruin.

"You know, J.R.," Drummond raised his head proudly. "You could have asked me along the way. You could have asked me about the game of... or sport of... I call it a game... of croquet. Or about this. Or about that. The Posse Serpens. The Scions of Ichor. Whatever it is Cash Clarick told you. About any of it. But you. You were too busy being a malcontent. Too busy being a hot shot. Too busy chasing this one's tail," he pointed at Elsie.

"I didn't want to ask you about any of those things."

467

"And then going to church with her afterwards. And then beating your high school friends to death—"

"*One friend,*" he protested, "not *friends.* Hey, wait a minute—"

"You never came around to talk to me about anything—"

"Vince was never my friend! I hated that prick!"

"Jesus, man! You even got a girlfriend out of this deal! But nothing was ever good enough for you! Nothing was good enough to make you happy!"

"Hey!" J.R. jabbed his finger into Duke Drummond's face. "Don't talk about Elsie that way!"

"You ungrateful bastard—"

KABOOM! an explosion from the Mess Hall sent a pinwheeling chunk of driftwood into Duke Drummond's head.

J.R. had grabbed Elsie. He was down on the ground, and she was down there with him, facing him. His ears rang. The air was filled with smoke. Briefly, he assured her she was OK, that they both were. Together they rose up. He took her by the elbow. She said, "We have to get out of here!" His ears were ringing, but he could hear her voice.

"We're going, I just need thirty seconds." He was looking around for Glenn Disteek's pistol. He found it among the debris. Disteek had been presumed dead once already tonight, and J.R. would never outlive the mistake of leaving Cash Clarick alive inside the wreckage of the nonfatal car crash. At this moment, executions were in order. Both Duke Drummond and Glenn Disteek lay dead and disfigured in close mutual proximity. J.R. leveled the pistol and started blasting away at them.

Elsie was horrified, "WHAT ARE YOU DOING?"

The clip was empty. He pitched the weapon into the inferno. "What I should have done all along," he answered. "Nazis are like zombies, babe. You gotta kill 'em twice."

"Sweet Jesus!"

"I'm not Jesus, Elsie," he was on his knee, going through Glenn Disteek's pockets. "I'm J.R. Daddio. I'm from *this* life."

He kept the antique naked-lady cigarette case and the dead man's billfold, then cast the duffel bags into the flames, one full of cash, the other full of porn. "Listen," he said. "No sirens yet... but wait, shit..."

"What?"

"It's starting to rain."

He found a can of gasoline in the auto yard and threw it into the flames. Exploding, it spewed hot fire.

"Oh, God!"

"Don't blaspheme," he told her.

"J.R.?" she said.

"Can I be in charge now?" he asked. "In fact," he added, "you blaspheme all you want. I'm in charge."

"Daddio?"

"You can even say fuck. Just let me be in charge now. OK, babe?"

He grabbed her by the hand, ushered her across the yard, out the side door and into the waiting Nova. The moment had finally come. He drove them out.

What remained was between him and the perfectly tuned car, scaling up the side of the mountain. It was the very same implausible way he had come down, once upon a time, at the wheel of Lou Gannon's Trans Am. The very same way he had come down previously, held at gunpoint, by Cash Clarick. The terrain was ragged going up, but he knew it, and found his way through its mud and rain-soaked rocky ascensions, leveling steadily off until he turned onto the weed choked macadam of the lonesome abandoned turnpike, far from anyone who could conceivably be in pursuit. He steered them out of there, undetected.

Somewhere along the way, in the dead of night, in the pouring rain, on that road to nowhere, it occurred to him that the whole thing had been his idea, and that it had worked perfectly. Asleep in the passenger's seat, Elsie woke up from a nightmare. She said they had to go to the cops. "Are you kidding?" he answered, gripping the wheel. "The only way out is through."

He turned on the radio, turned the dial, and amazingly found the same voice that had broadcast that fateful show on the night he left his hometown of Erving, New York. A funny bit about the word "Island," and the way it was spelled.

*"Nonsensical,"* the radio voice was saying this time. *"Think about this word for a minute. Nonsensical..."*

J.R. was certain it was the same voice. In any case, it was the same routine.

*"Nonsensical is a legal word. As of tonight, that is. Unless some midnight Star Chamber has just passed legislation*

*through Congress and The Supreme Court to outlaw the word Nonsensical... As far as I know, this is not on their docket tonight. As far as I know, Nonsensical is still a word they will allow you to use in the public lexicon... I repeat... The men who know. The men in charge. The men who run this country. The men who know what's best for you. They have all agreed and decreed that Nonsensical is a word, and that you are permitted to use this word. So in a certain sense, you may take solace in this blessing tonight..."*

"Who is this guy?" Elsie wondered.

*"But Sensical?"* the radio voice continued. *"Whatever happened to the word Sensical? Can anyone tell me? I mean... Is it just me? Has anybody seen, or heard, or even spoken the word out loud... Sensical?"* A dramatic stretch of dead air followed.

*"...or heard it spoken? Where is the so-called government? Where is the so-called public education system? Where is the so-called establishment? To come along and permit us to use the word Sensical. Oh no! On no, not THAT! Not SENSICAL! Not SENSICAL! Heaven forbid we use the word SENSICAL! Because, my friends, when something is so SENSICAL as to become SENSICAL, well... I'm sorry to tell you... It doesn't get to be a word—"*

"Shut the fuck up!" J.R. snapped off the radio.

"What?" she said.

"This guy is a used car salesman."

"J.R., what you did." She clung to him as he drove.

## 67. Oklahoma City

The Chevy Nova had been across half the United States, not to mention to hell and back, and yet it remained forever constant, perhaps the only thing unchanged from his previous life in Erving, New York. The cockpit, the steering wheel, the gearshift, the ratio of balance and power at his hands and feet, the 454 he knew just as well as any other engine on this earth but ten times more tenderheartedly. He had communed with countless vehicles in his lifetime. None compared to the Nova. It had become, for all intents and purposes, his home. The roof over his head. The bed he fell into. The pillow onto which he lay his weary head. He had dozed off at the wheel.

With his right hand, he slapped his own face to wake up. Then he slapped himself again in the same place.

He held the car steady, cranked down the window. Elsie and the baby remained undisturbed in the passenger seat. He had whisked them out of Santa Fe across Texas into Oklahoma City. Now the highway never ceased its elongation through the changeless plains. It was time to pull over and find a motel.

He took the next exit, found a place for the night. His face didn't hurt at all. His thoughts wandered back to Vince Baldwin's hourly Saw Mill regimen at the open hand of Cash Clarick, but he could quickly put such grim musings aside. Those days were over. This was no time to dwell on the past. The future would require his full attention.

The next morning, he went down the road for a newspaper and a coffee cake. When he asked the deli man about work, he learned of a local garage in need of an extra guy, because their guy had broken his tibia in a non-work-related accident. The garage was called Will Rogers Auto Repair. It sounded as good a place as any to bide one's time. He applied for the job and got it.

He and Elsie moved into a flat along the city's outskirts. Wrigley was sleeping through the night by now, or most of it. By day, Elsie took care of the baby while J.R. fixed cars. Money was tight, but freedom was good enough. He had abandoned his checking account. Cash Clarick had drained most of it anyway.

He and Elsie didn't need much in the way of leisure, other than an evening walk, or to stay indoors and watch TV. They also had sex, which he embraced with unflagging enthusiasm, an expanding repertoire, and every intention of making his own baby, though he had nothing against Steeplejack's baby. Fatherhood had come to feel like practice for him. He wanted the real thing.

Elsie followed the Cubs as they battled down the stretch of their pennant winning season. At night, over a hot cooked meal, or pizza, or TV dinner, she would catch him up. And he was genuinely interested, but also a little bit grateful, some nights, that they only got Rangers games on this TV.

Elsie was right about one thing. Ryne Sandberg. J.R. couldn't help rooting for the guy, if only because he was a second baseman in the tradition of certain legends by the name of Nap Lajoie, Rogers Hornsby and Joe Morgan.

And yet, at times, at certain hours, over long stretches, Elsie would draw connections and conclusions that seemed to border on the obsessional and absurd. For instance, the so-called "Sandberg Game," in which Ryne Sandberg performed mythical baseball feats. It occurred on June 23. Ryne Sandberg also happened to wear the number 23 on his uniform. The number 23 also had notable significance outside of the realm of baseball. Psalm 23, in case no one noticed. Elsie wanted J.R. to make note of this phenomenon.

"The number 23?"

"Don't ask me to explain it. Just look around. You'll see it."

She was also convinced that Major League Baseball was fixing the Cubs so that they would never reach the World

Series. That's because their ballpark, Wrigley Field, was the last major league stadium unequipped to broadcast night games. In this modern age of television, the league would never, ever, bow to such antiquity. They would fix the Cubs forever, or until they yielded.

"You need to get outside more, babe."

"You don't understand," she said.

"Baseball?" he argued. "Are you kidding me? I understand baseball. I *played* baseball—"

But then he backed off. It was a regional thing. He got it. Also, the baby's name was Wrigley. And Wrigley was Elsie's baby, not his, no matter how committed he was as the father. He would leave the matter alone. He would be proud to raise a child named after the famed, ivy-bedecked baseball citadel. To prove it, he went to Wrigley now and plucked her up from the crib, and cradled her gently, and rocked her in his arms.

On his next day off they went to the local ballpark. The 89ers' season was over, but their venue held other events, such as today's tractor convention.

J.R. wheeled though the city's efficient grid to the ball-park's accessible lot. The stadium had light stanchions three times higher than all else in sight. *Even this park has lights,* he wanted to rib Elsie, in jest, though it would probably sound mean. The parking lot was half full. The semi-circumference of the colosseum's single story was painted navy blue. The team's name 89ers was rendered in white-and-orange. The stadium was modestly beautiful and more authentic, in some ways, than most major league stadiums could ever hope to be. The gift shop was open. Ryne Sandberg's 1981 89ers baseball card was for sale at the counter.

"Are you *kidding* me?" Elsie took up the card in its plastic sheath. The store had two of his cards in stock. The other tipped forward in its cradle.

The clerk explained that Ryne Sandberg had come through these very parts back in 1981. Elsie could not quite contain her disbelief. Even J.R. had to marvel at the coincidence. He bought both cards.

"All two?" she asked him.

"Yours, we keep forever," he explained. "Mine, we sell in thirty years."

The clerk asked, "What's the baby's name?"

Elsie presented the child, "This is Wrigley!"

473

"Wrigley! What a great baseball name!"

Darkening clouds sent them retreating to the Nova and back home, but they were easily outpaced by the massive rainstorm. Peering through the furious wipers and buckets of rain, J.R. wondered if it might be a tornado after them.

Elsie asked, "Now do you believe in God?"

"What? Come on, Elsie, don't..."

"No, seriously."

"I believe in *you*, Elsie, OK? I believe in you. You believe in God. Therefore, I believe in God. How's that?"

"How do you think we ever got out of that place? If God wasn't watching out for us?"

"What place? That tractor show?"

"You know what place."

"Well, I would start by giving myself some credit."

She sighed, "That old chestnut."

It was no time to get angry. The rain was blinding.

"I *do* give you some credit," she said, with a strong hint of sorrow, after J.R. went silent. She added, "You can tell you have the spirit of The Lord, J.R., every time you feel it rise and fall."

They were almost home when the rain suddenly stopped. The wipers continued. J.R. shut them off. Wrigley pushed around in Elsie's arms, and made a gurgling and squeaking noise that sounded just a bit more like human language each time. J.R. caught sight of Elsie's raised eyebrow. Gently and liltingly, she sang to the baby. He kept his mouth shut. There was no arguing with certain statements. Or there was arguing, but only if he wanted an argument, which he didn't, hardly ever, including now.

Back home, the power was out, so they lit candles and waited. The subject of power and electricity led to Elsie's ninety-millionth foretelling of the Chicago Cubs' doom, which the league would conspire to cause, one way or another, because they wanted night games under stadium lights for a TV audience. J.R. listened for a few minutes more, before interrupting, "Elsie, babe, speaking of conspiracies..."

The regular season ended. The Cubs won the pennant. They went up two games to nothing over the Padres in Chicago. Then they lost three games straight out in California. All day games, stadium lights never factoring in. Elsie was satisfied she had seen it coming. And yet she had miraculously

474

come to own Ryne Sandberg's minor league card in mint condition. All things considered, everything was in order.

"The Padres should be called the *Priests*," she concluded. "We shouldn't have a foreign language World Series."

"Or *Fathers*," J.R. said.

"What?"

"*Priests* or *Fathers*," he said.

"*Priests* is better than *Fathers*," she said.

"Priests *are* better than Fathers," he said.

Elsie got annoyed. "That's not what I meant, J.R."

"I know, babe." His thoughts were preoccupied. He was going to be out of work when Will Rogers got their guy back with his healed tibia. It was time to sell the antique naked-lady cigarette case.

Coming home from his last day on the job, he entered the room prepared. Elsie greeted him. "I'm going to Denver," he told her.

"By yourself?" she asked.

"Yes."

"Why by yourself?"

"You know why?"

She sighed, shrugged her shoulders.

"I'll be back in 24 hours. It's 6:30 now. I'll be back by 6:30 tomorrow."

"The air there," she said.

"The altitude. I know. I'll know ahead of time."

## 68. Denver

He felt the distance to Colorado as a lonesome odyssey, and found himself longing for Elsie's presence, her companionship, her beauty, her touch. The Nova cradled him through it in some abstract dreamlike communion. A longing fulfilled, a motif of lessons learned, a parade of encroaching departed spirits. Still, he needed more, felt the absence as he needed it, his woman by his side.

Several antique shops occupied one grand, flat, open-skied avenue through Denver. He went first to Americana Unlimited. By its name it was perhaps the least likely place to successfully hawk a creepy German cigarette case. However, the appraiser, an intense hunchbacked man with a telescopic monocle and a Slavic accent, turned his every bit of attention to the item at hand. Remarking on the quality of the artwork, the craftsmanship of the tin, not to mention the pornographic aspect, not to mention the fantastically sarcastic inscription, he called it a box of questions, more than an artifact of answers. He cleared his throat, maintained his composure. His telescopic lens appraised J.R. now. A buyer was there in thirty minutes.

"I have to know how you came by this," the buyer asked, when the transaction was complete.

"I bought it down the street," J.R. smirked, "two hours ago."

The two men, to their credit, burst out laughing, although a suspension of all functionality presaged whatever catharsis of enjoyment they feigned. J.R. took the wad of money down the aforementioned street and spent it on a similarly expensive, pocketable prize. He sold that down the very same street a half an hour later. The Old Man would have turned a profit from this endeavor, but J.R. wasn't even eighteen years old. He would take a loss today.

He returned to Elsie, well inside the 24-hour time frame.

"We're wealthy now," he said. "Let's go."

"Hallelujah," she said.

## 69. Little Rock

Along the way, as she stared forward at the miles of oncoming highway, her approval turned to worry. "Is this where you ask me to bear false witness?" she said.

"No, Elsie. Come on. Why do you think I went alone? Give me some credit."

"I always give you some credit, J.R. How many times do I have to say it?"

He had no answer. Questions used to have answers. They didn't anymore, so much. Somehow everything became only more unknowable.

Elsie said, "God wants you to win, J.R., whether you want to admit it or not. How many times does He have to prove it to you?"

"OK, OK, I believe you, Elsie. I'm convinced. God wants us to win. So let's go over this story again. So we don't let Him down."

"Like I said," she answered, "I'm not going to bear false witness."

They stopped in the emergency room in Little Rock when the baby got sick with a stomach flu. J.R. paid cash. Over that long night of prayer and worry, his thoughts turned repeatedly to the 50-plus thousand dollars remaining where he had left it in the car. Three times he announced he was going out for air, and then went to prowl like an animal around the Nova's perimeter.

478

Back inside the E.R., the good news came at last. Wrigley would pull through. As he and Elsie shared a collective sigh, and he gripped her two hands in weary triumph, the doctor told them he could not discharge the child for another day, or possibly two. "We need to keep her hydrated," he explained.

It occurred to J.R. that this might be a kidnapping, since he was paying in cash, and they knew it. They figured they could keep his daughter just so long as the money flowed. He eyeballed the doctor, studied Elsie too.

"She's out of danger," the doctor assured them both, "so long as she's here under observation. Go home and get some sleep."

In the end, he could not take a chance with Wrigley's safety. Elsie remained at the hospital, while J.R. went looking for a place to stay.

Walking back to the Nova in the parking lot, his thoughts turned to little Victoria Drummond, whom Duke Drummond had dropped off night after night at the West Susquehannock E.R. The child would never see her mother or father again, and would perhaps be better off, though she could be worse off, too. In any case, J.R. was determined that Wrigley would suffer no such abandonment.

In two days' time, the child was released into her parents' loving care. The three of them went back to the hotel and took a nap. The next day, they went for a walk around Little Rock. Elsie explained to J.R. that she wanted to stay for a while.

He was biding his time anyway, until next May, when he would turn eighteen. Meanwhile, their finite sum of money had just become a chunk more finite. Perhaps he could find a job here in Little Rock, as he had in Oklahoma City.

Fall was in the air. The holidays were coming. Elsie pointed out that it would be Wrigley's first Thanksgiving and first Christmas. This was an opportunity to be a normal family, like they deserved to be. Like everybody deserved to be, if only for the holidays. J.R. agreed.

The next three months were postcard-like, in still frame, everything perfect. Along the way, Ronald Reagan won his second term in a landslide. J.R. and Elsie followed intently, glued to it.

He insisted on a nice restaurant for Thanksgiving dinner; he didn't want Elsie to cook and serve a meal on this special day.

Wrigley was in a highchair by now, so the three of them could hold hands. J.R. closed his eyes and listened as Elsie said grace. Her words and phrases came so easily, and seemed so inarguable when she spoke them, even though he could never imagine himself possessing such notions at the ready. Through the window, out in the parking lot, the Nova sat in plain view. He preferred to cast his faith there.

Over the three-course meal of salad, buttered bread rolls, turkey slices with mushroom-laced gravy, nutty stuffing, buttery lumps of mashed potatoes, breadcrumb sprinkled green beans, cold cranberries, and pumpkin pie and rhubarb pie for dessert, he turned his attention to the invincible Nova time and again, parked in relief against the shallow snowbank beneath the restaurant's modest flagpole that spired just one apex higher than its A-frame roof.

For the next holiday, he strung lights along the perimeter of the ceiling, bathing their room in a warm and random spectrum of light. A three-foot tree sat aglow upon the lamp table. Elsie found hymns and carols on the TV. Christmas morning arrived and the baby received numerous toys to chew on and throw gleefully to the floor.

Elsie insisted upon cooking dinner. At the table, J.R. made only one unfortunate joke. Otherwise, the day was perfect, absent of conflict. Wrigley, her innocence, her enthusiasm, and her eagerness to learn, and to know, served as a kind of guiding star on this day, just as it always seemed to do, so reliably. Steeplejack's contribution to this child's existence mattered as little to J.R as it did to Elsie, to Wrigley herself, or to anybody else in the world.

Their daily stroll led them to a church basement thrift shop, tightly packed with racks of clothes, shelves of toys, and rows of books and records. At some point, along the back wall, a framed painting caught Elsie's eye and held it, so that she became fixated upon it, until she was vibrating in fixation.

"J.R.?"

"Yes, babe."

"What do you make of this... hanging on the wall... in this church basement."

He approached and observed the painting. A little black girl. A tomato exploded against the wall behind her. Marching in profile, surrounded by faceless unknowable U.S. Marshalls that towered above her, marching in step, clenching their white, weaponless fists, the girl's own black weaponless fist mimicking her white protectors. J.R. could hardly believe his eyes. For one thing, the artist was clearly impersonating a classic American painter. For another, the picture, hanging for all to see, included the letters KKK scrawled upon the wall, while nearer the red tomato splatter, another word, the most racist of all, stretched over the child's head. The black girl carried herself forward, holding a level chin, and holding her schoolbook and ruler at her side.

"Do you see what that says?" Elsie asked him.

He saw what it said.

"Me? I'm not allowed to say it," she grieved. "But THEM... THEY... they get to say it all they want? In fact, they not only get to say it. They get to hang it up on the wall..." her eyes welled with tears for what she had lost. She whispered, *"Inside this church of God!"*

"It's a church basement, babe," he did his best to calm her down.

Leaning in closer, he saw that the painting was signed *Normal Rockwell*, although it was clearly some brazen act of satire. J.R. cared little for art, but enough so to recognize a fake.

"Just as long as they remember to escort *my* daughter to school," Elsie wept.

The holidays passed. The new year came. He and Elsie watched Times Square on TV as the countdown began, ticked away, and ended with a disco ball's careful, listless descent.

January was well underway, and still there was no work. Ronald Reagan got inaugurated. Little Rock would always be a memory to cherish. Once J.R. turned eighteen, and returned home, and went back to Daddio's Garage, he would no longer have to worry about employment. But here and now, it was time to go.

## 70. Louisville

In Louisville, they stopped at a Western Auto, which happened to sell Louisville Slugger baseball bats alongside tires and firearms. J.R. decided he could not pass through the city of Louisville without picking up a Louisville Slugger baseball bat.

Elsie nudged his arm.

"What?" he said.

"Let's stay for a few days."

"Elsie, babe..." he sighed.

He asked the cashier if there was any work for a mechanic. "Sure is!" the cashier grinned. Elsie nudged his arm again. He knew what she meant. It was God looking out for them again.

It was temporary work. They found a room to rent. The weather was bitter and cold for several days, and they were cooped up all over again with the TV, only in a different city.

Then one day the sun came out, and they went for a walk.

Down along the riverbank, J.R. became fascinated with the series of locks and dams and bifurcations, the sprawling but austere engineering feat that transformed the river's bend into navigable waters. Mother Nature's challenge met by Mankind's ingenuity.

The banks lay dry in great portions, exposed and traversable by foot; J.R. noted this from the safety of the path above. They would not be going down there, baby or no baby. Even if Elsie asked, he would say no. An apocalypse of fallen trees and green living crowns of their stout and sturdier undrowned neighbors wound along the river's margins among the boulders and smaller boulders, rocks and smaller rocks, into a treacherous, snaking gravel beach. The baby was fussing, and the wind was picking up. It was time to head back to the hotel.

A few days later they returned and met another couple walking along the riverbank. A greeting occurred, pleasant but brief in the cold afternoon before the two families went their separate ways. The other couple was older, mid-twenties, but untested, J.R. gathered this from their manner.

They were also impervious to the weather, and adventurous, making their way down to the waterline and the margin of wrecked trees, trash, cinder blocks and other debris from floodwaters past. At one point, the girl looked back and caught J.R.'s attention, and pointed to the lone fisherman standing surefooted in the falling waters from the slick limestone beneath the dam's concrete pilings, casting his line into the shallow pickings alongside the remains of an abandoned shopping cart.

Elsie nodded and smiled as she clutched the baby close against the wind. J.R. had not agreed to supervise these reckless strangers. He watched as they began their venture into the spillway, holding hands sometimes, letting go other times, clever and nimble, both of them, slipping occasionally in the riverbed but recovering every time, as they teetered farther into needless danger.

A panic began to take hold. It was irrational, J.R. told himself, even though it was completely rational. *Breathe,* he told himself.

"Babe, let's go," he said.

Elsie shot him a look. "What if they need help?"

"Exactly," he said.

Some nights he drove home from work through falling snow. Some nights there was no weather.

Elsie had taken a liking to the local radio station, country music, with a lot of busy banjo and jerkoff twang. She also had become more and more fixated on the TV. The World Series and then Reagan's re-election had left her craving more entertainment. *The Waltons. Get Smart. The Rockford Files. Hawaii Five-O.*

When J.R. came home from work, she would serially elucidate for him an ever complex web of malevolent signals coming over the American airwaves on an ever present, pulsating, almost inescapable frequency.

One night, after listening to yet another unchecked fairy tale, he confronted her.

"Elsie, babe, we're going home. Back to where I'm from. Erving, New York. In just a few months. Just around the corner. Very soon. Spring. We're going to be man and wife. With an infant child. We'd be crazy to do that and also admit to committing crimes."

"J.R., please don't call me crazy. I'm the least crazy person you'll ever meet."

"No, I know that. We agree on that, babe. But we have to get our story straight. We're both very sane. So the signals from the TV can wait, right? They can wait until after we get out of this mess. And land on our feet."

"You want me to bear false witness," she turned away from him.

"I didn't say that. I'm just saying, as far as conspiracies are concerned, we've got a very interesting one of our own. And don't tell me what's at stake. I'm telling you what's at stake. Elsie, please. This is me begging you. Please go over this with me."

"We'll pray over it, J.R. When you're ready."

"Babe, I'll go to church whenever you say."

She looked at the baby in the low and glowing yellow light. Then she looked back at him, her face never more lovely than inside this beautiful, soft spectrum of gold. "This is our church, J.R., until we settle down. Once we settle down, we'll find our church."

"Fine," he said. It was no use. He had other matters to ponder. "I'll be right back," he said.

He put on his coat and boots and went outside where the snowflakes drifted but had failed yet to stick. The Nova's windshield had just begun to seize with white fractals. He went to the car and started the engine, got out and started scraping. A stray cat was watching. Orange and white, skinny and wary, it stole away.

Not only his father in person but the Jack Daddio that occupied his encroaching memories awaited him every second he drew closer to home. The father he would return to, and face, at last, on a level playing field, after changing his name,

484

and getting married, and adopting the child Wrigley. Only some failure of vigilance could prevent this.

He went back inside and lay down beside Elsie. "You're cold!" she complained, half asleep, withdrawing her shoulders.

They left the next morning. Elsie wanted to see Cincinnati because she never had.

"Cincinnati?"

"Cincinnati," she explained. "The Reds. When are we ever coming back this way?"

It was the off season. "Fine with me," he told her. "Anywhere you want. Just not Pennsylvania."

## 71. Cincinnati

They hit a pothole. Wrigley got jostled in Elsie's arms and cried. No harm was done. However, J.R. understood it was time to buy a child safety seat.

He didn't care that she was Steeplejack's fourteenth kid, at least not in any way that felt like feelings. He was responsible for the child's safety, and they were on the road for hours. Wrigley should be as safe as possible. None of this was her fault.

"Wrigley should be in my arms," Elsie demonstrated, holding the child close.

"During the day," J.R. agreed. "But what about the middle of the night?" he argued. "When everyone's asleep in the car? And everybody is counting on me to get us where we're going?"

"God is watching over us, J.R. Isn't that obvious by now?"

"OK," he reasoned, "so that was a warning sign from God. That pothole."

"J.R., don't blaspheme."

"I'm not! I'm doing the exact opposite—"

"Dirty words are one thing. But making fun is really, really bad."

"I'm not making fun."

She looked at him sideways.

"We're getting a car seat," he said. "How's that? We're getting a car seat right now."

She shrugged and looked out the window at the flat, grey winter sky.

"And I wasn't making fun," he added. "I meant it."

"Bullshit," she said.

She swore. He noticed.

He peered her way briefly, thought better of it, then kept his eyes on the road, his hands at ten and two. She knew what she did. He didn't have to point it out.

They stopped at a shopping mall. It was half dead, or three quarters dead, with a scattering of cars in the parking lot and many of the stores out of business. They found and purchased a car safety seat for Wrigley. They also stopped for ice cream, the soft kind.

Out in the parking lot, high upon the flagpole, the Stars and Stripes rippled and snapped. J.R.'s hands were freezing cold. Thankfully, the car seat installation was almost finished. All the while, Elsie huddled in the passenger seat with the baby. She wanted to find a hotel first, but J.R. insisted on installing the car seat immediately, because how could they not?

"What would..." he started to ask her, but then he zipped his lip. He was about to ask her what God would think if Wrigley got hurt when they had a brand-new child safety seat in hand and then didn't bother to install it? He knew Elsie wouldn't allow such heresy. God was to obey, not to question. This would be her answer. They weren't on the same page yet, in terms of this particular metaphor, despite J.R.'s many efforts over many months to meet her halfway or three quarters, or even all the way, as long as their actions made strategic sense.

The child safety seat was well-made and easy to install. He was almost done when he paused for a moment. Although his hands and face were cold, he allowed himself to admire the American flag billowing in the snarling wind. He had seen enough other flags in his life. They all flew beneath this one, and maybe never more so than now, over this struggling but open for business shopping mall. With the job well done, he clasped his hands together for both warmth and self-congratulations.

"J.R.," Elsie's voice was uneasy.

He looked up. Two black youths were approaching out of the expansive parking lot. "It's OK," he assured her.

487

They might have been brothers. Possibly just friends. The older one wore a Tigers cap and a down coat. The younger one wore a Georgetown Hoyas jacket. They weren't dangerous, J.R. concluded this immediately, though he kept an eye on them all the same. When they passed by, the older one looked directly at him and said, "What's up, boss?"

"The name's Daddio."

It was the younger one who muttered, "No doubt," and avoided eye contact.

But the older one couldn't resist. "Daddio?" he paused and stood there, breaking into a smirk. He suppressed a chuckle with his hand, then lowered his Detroit Tiger's baseball cap to conceal his guffaw.

"Come on, Trey," the younger kid pleaded, tugging at his companion's coat.

Trey said, "What's up, Daddio? Boss not good enough for you?"

Elsie in the passenger seat said, "J.R., please, let's go!"

He could hear the terror in her voice. He had to protect his woman, and the child. The Louisville Slugger lay ready on the Nova's backseat floor. If need be. Which it wouldn't be. Because these were just two obnoxious kids, including one who wasn't even obnoxious.

Trey called back at them, "It's OK, nice white lady. We're just going to the mall. We're just going to the mall, nice white lady."

He had said it twice, J.R. noted. Two different ways. Why would he do that?

The younger kid, never looking back, said, "Come on, Trey. We're here for *Pole Position*. Come on!"

"Please, J.R.!" Elsie was trembling.

"Relax, babe."

"J.R. please. *Please,* can we get out of here?"

"Yes, we can, babe. Here, give me the baby. We have the new car seat."

"NO!" she gripped Wrigley tightly. *"Get in this car right now and drive us away!"*

He did what she asked, got in, and drove them out of the grey parking lot that matched the grey sky almost exactly in color and seemingly exactly in texture.

"No," she said. "Out of Cincinnati."

He did that too. Dusk fell as they drove all the way out of Cincinnati.

Along the way, he pondered how to soothe Elsie's nerves. He remembered the terror she had felt under Dr. Arthur's care back in the Marietta emergency room.

His thoughts then turned to *Pole Position*. The younger kid, in the Georgetown Hoyas jacket, who was probably nine years old, had just wanted his older brother Trey to stop making trouble so they could go play *Pole Position*. The idea that Cash Clarick and this nine-year-old black kid from Cincinnati shared that same passion for *Pole Position*. He had to laugh, although he couldn't laugh, and didn't.

"J.R., that car behind us," Elsie said inside the Nova's dark, dim, dashboard-lit cab. "It just stays and stays the same distance away. It never passes us or gets any closer."

The headlight beams in the rearview mirror were in no way alarming, only a bit blinding to keep peering up at.

"I think that might be a safe driver behind us, babe."

"It's *them*. They chased us."

"No, babe. Neither one of those kids is old enough to drive."

"That's not true, J.R., and you know it."

"Maybe the older one. Maybe."

"You've never been to where I'm from," she assured him.

"All right," he said, and with that he let the Nova off the chain, and left the conversation moot.

*What if it is practical?* Maybe his father would have an answer, now that he was old enough to pose the question.

## 72. Westsylvania

They crossed the Ohio River once again and drove on through the night.

Hours passed behind the wheel. Elsie had fallen sound asleep with the baby in her arms. The new child safety seat was installed in the back, not in use. The dashboard exhaled gentle heat. The windows were sealed. The radio was off. For a duration, everyone slept, J.R. included.

He awoke again, braking the car, easing it back across the center line. A landmark appeared up ahead. *The Westsylvania.* An abandoned hotel. He drove on.

As he began losing his way along the endless night roads, a song his mother used to sing came back to him. An annoying intrusion upon his thoughts. *Mama, West Virginia... They tried to name ya... Westsylvania... and take you on home.*

The way she would lean into those lyrics, *They tried to name ya...* It seemed like maybe she was making fun of his name. Or maybe she meant something else entirely. He didn't want to speculate. People should say how they feel, instead of paying some pot head to write a song about it, and then some other pot head to sing it, all so they can sing along with some hit record into somebody else's face.

He would be face to face with his mother soon. Just a few months from now. There would be fussing over the baby, of course. However, he hadn't really given thought to what she might confront him with. Not once.

With that realization, a panic began to grip his nerves. He had never cared what his mother had to say, but that wasn't good enough now. If he wanted to go home, he would have to start caring. The effort seemed impossible. Gripping the wheel, he found himself briefly struggling for air.

But then he remembered what Jack Daddio had taught him all those years ago, in the woods off Armitage Road. To gather the nerves, and to focus the attention on the heart rate and its slowing down. Also the breathing and its steadiness. Useful measures no longer in need, or so J.R. had concluded, wrongly, after all he had proven to himself and to Elsie, including all the murder, manslaughter, armed robbery and arson. He thought he would feel better, calmer, exhale more from his lungs, for a little bit longer. It alarmed him to be wrong.

A half hour later, once again over the Ohio River, the Nova crossed into West Virginia. Elsie and the child slept in the passenger seat, so J.R. remarked the achievement to himself, without a whisper.

The next thing he knew, he was in Maryland. Savage River Park. He had always been adept at navigating his way around, but he was tired, and continually falling asleep, slapping his own face to wake up. Elsie and the baby slept through all the slapping. There was nowhere safe to pull over.

He willed himself to remain awake but ended up in a gravel parking lot, coming-to amidst swirling dust clouds and the sight of another infuriatingly imprecise landmark. *Pennsyltucky's*. It was a roadhouse saloon, closed, in the middle of nowhere.

He steered the Nova back onto the empty highway and drove. It had become like a joke, only not funny. A joke on him. The Old Man had reared his head at last, replaced real road signs and landmarks with fake ones, to lure him and his woman and child into the American wilderness where no one would ever find them. Up ahead, the sign said Ray's Hill.

He had done it. The exact thing he had promised himself never to do again, not in this lifetime or the next, if Elsie was right about Heaven, which was no longer a joke he made to her, because she didn't think it was funny, which she always made known to him with an incredible knack for ominousness.

Now here he was, no doubt lured by the Old Man, not only back into the State of Pennsylvania but right back to the scene of the crime, or one of the scenes of one of the crimes, over the course of his juvenile spree of crimes, out of which he had not yet aged. He would not succumb to any such ambush. He would see Erving, New York and Daddio's Garage again. He pledged this to himself alone. The only way out was through.

He drove and drove into the night. Finally, he went off-roading, caught the steering wheel, slowed down to a crawl, rolled the family of three to safety alongside someone's winterswept field of desolation.

"J.R.?"

"We need sleep. We're safe just as long as we get some sleep. Right now. The only thing unsafe not to do is sleep."

"Get some sleep, babe."

Even so, he remained awake enough for one more stretch of eternity as he steered the Nova farther off into the empty field.

At last he slept, desperately, deeply, in the car's bucket seat. The baby awoke once. Elsie tended to her, their presence familiar to J.R. in his dream, which kept going, everything fitting plausibly and strangely both, which was the way dreams were now, so that he never questioned them. A parade of faces beginning to gather, familiar and haunting, not only the likes of de Ram, and Steeplejack, and Cash Clarick, and Lazy Farrah, and not only regular normal people like Tyto, and Vince Baldwin, and Scotty Pomeroy and Melissa Victoria, but also guys like Harding and Snapper and Trauer, and ladies like Sandra Pride and Rose Archer, and even little kids running around, oblivious to it all, like Bella Shue and little Wallace. The dream included those faces and many more. Men, women, children, monsters.

"Good morning, sir."

A man in a floppy hat was standing outside the car window. J.R. looked up at the upside-down face. He had slept with the baseball bat ready at his side. The man outside had seen it. J.R. gathered himself and sat up straight, tucking the weapon out of sight. Elsie stirred beside him. The baby stirred in turn. The man in the floppy hat was holding food in both hands. He had a boy at his side, bearing milk and water.

*Quakers,* J.R. surmised. *Or Amish. One or the other.* He rolled down the window.

"Forgive me, friend," the man in the floppy hat said, "but I can't abide your weapon on my property. Please take these blessings and be gone."

J.R. smiled, "That's a Louisville Slugger, friend. That's what Babe Ruth used to build Yankee Stadium. It's not a weapon."

"We brought bread and fruit. And water. And sheep's milk. Please take it and be on your way."

"Thank you," J.R. said. "Wow."

Elsie leaned forward from the passenger seat, waking up, pleased to say, "God bless you, sir. Thank you."

"God bless you, miss."

"One question," J.R. asked the generous stranger. "Are you Quakers or Amish?" He looked back and forth from the man to the son.

"We're all children of God."

"The Lord Jesus brought them to us," Elsie tried to explain.

"Amen, miss."

"So if you don't mind my asking," J.R. said, simply wanting to know, "Quaker? That means no weapons on the property? Or is that Amish? Or both?"

"This is my land, friend. I abide no weapons on my property."

"I understand. Thank you. That makes perfect sense. We're leaving. I apologize. It's just... you're very nice. Uncommonly nice."

The man in the floppy hat nodded in agreement, pleasant but increasingly grim in his demeanor.

"I just want to know who was so nice, so that I can know. I don't want to say to myself afterwards that the Amish are so nice. Or the Quakers are so nice. When I have no idea who was nice—"

"My name's Butler. Butler was nice."

"Butler, hello. I'm J.R. This is Elsie."

"Good morning, Butler."

"Good morning, miss."

"And this is Wrigley."

"It was nice meeting you folks. Please take these blessings and be on your way."

"Bless you," Elsie told him.

"God bless your child, miss."

She beamed at Butler. The morning sunlight illuminated her beautiful face and blonde hair an ungraspable hue of gold.

After they left Pennsylvania, never to return, in perfect safety, with food and blessings, under the clear blue sky, Elsie said nothing about it, although she could have. She could have said, *See what I mean?* and much more than that. And still, he would have known what she meant, but not seen it.

She switched on the radio. "Oh," she said, and she started to sing along. *"Mama, Westsylvania... It could have been ya ...'stead of West Virginia... Down that rock n roll road."*

## 73. Richmond

Fate had tested him, and he had come through. Elsie had one way of looking at things, which involved the intervention of a *Man in the Sky*. But J.R. saw it correctly, that it involved himself, his own willpower, his own foresight, his own grit, and his own half dozen other self-proven self-amazements and self-actualizations.

He next found work in Richmond, Virginia, once again filling in temporarily for a man on leave. However, in this case the man was a girl on maternity leave, which J.R. had never heard of before. He had heard of girl mechanics, just not maternity leave for them. In any case, he was glad for the work.

He and Elsie found a room to rent. As winter cycled into spring, they would sometimes take a stroll, as a family, along the promenade of Monument Avenue, with its long mall of barren but awakening sun tipped trees, and its statues on pedestals in the roundabouts above the traffic. Jefferson Davis, Robert E. Lee, and others.

It was another city, and another strange garage. At Gordie's, J.R. tried to keep to himself, and not get chatty. However, one day, out of sheer boredom, he couldn't help but ask Gordie whether he considered Richmond the north or the south.

"Are you kidding?" Gordie answered. "You're in the south when you're in Richmond, Daddio."

"That's what I figured."

"Bill Faulkner himself used to live right up the road in Charlottesville."

"OK, gotcha," J.R. had no idea who Bill Faulkner was.

"Of course, Faulkner lived in Hollywood too," Gordie added, "so there's that."

"That's another good point," J.R. went along politely with the conversation. He knew nothing about Hollywood movie stars. He wouldn't piss on a Hollywood movie star if he found one on fire in the middle of the street. But he wasn't about to say so out loud to his employer.

A few days later he quit and walked out of Gordie's. In that sense, it was true that he got fired, which is what he told Elsie when he came home.

"What happened?" she asked.

"Mrs. Ichiharo," he explained.

"Oh, babe."

Mrs. Ichiharo was demanding. This was known to everyone already. Mrs. Ichiharo believed only one person should ever work on her precious silver Jaguar XJ, that being the incredible and irreplaceable mechanic, Dana. But Mrs. Ichiharo was out of luck, because Dana got knocked up, so J.R. would have to do.

"Lady, I'm a better mechanic than Dana what's-her-name on her best day, not to mention anybody else around here." That's what he had said during the episode.

Mrs. Ichiharo bristled. *"Lady?"*

"J.R.!" Gordie cried.

He didn't tell Elsie that he dropped what he was doing that very moment and walked out. He didn't tell her that he drove the Nova around for a while. That he wound up coasting down the city's promenade of military monuments before coming home.

"See what I mean?" Elsie concluded.

"What?" he asked her.

She said nothing.

"Don't worry," he told her.

"I'm not worried about anything," she said.

She was worrying over nothing.

They had a lot of money. Spring was almost here. They were almost home. He was almost eighteen. They were almost married. He would take care of everything. She knew all this. She was worrying over nothing.

He lay in the motel bed with Elsie and the baby. The shades were drawn and the room was dark. Wrigley lay tucked in between the mother and father. The baseball bat leaned against the night table at J.R.'s side. Quietly, he lifted it. He found, at times, that it helped him focus his resolve upon his family's safety and prosperous future. It helped him focus his wits upon the story to get straight. This would all work out, he knew, if Elsie would simply agree to go along. To *bear false witness,* as she insisted upon calling it, the simple effortless wonderfulness of her purpose in service of that goal. They had no choice, she understood this. She didn't even have to come around to it. She was already there. He could feel his will-power in the presence of the weapon that wasn't so much a weapon as it was an All-American home run hitter in his grasp as he lay in the bed in watch over his family, at once vigilant and far beyond vigilant. He imagined that Elsie could only have felt the very same comfort and resolve he did, as she lay beside him, with the child in between. He had waited and waited for the discussion to open up. For the two of them to confront everything realistically and return to society. He loved her. She loved him. They would be a family returning home. They just had to get it right.

He initiated the conversation once again. She answered him, "J.R., you're worried too much about me."

"I'm not worried—"

"You shouldn't worry about me," she said. "Or Wrigley. We're both with you. We both believe in you. One hundred percent. We believe in you with all our hearts. More than you can possibly imagine."

He paused.

"Do you understand me?" she said. "I'm devoted to you."

"I understand," he said.

She started to cry.

"Elsie, I'm devoted to you, too. And to Wrigley."

"I love you, J.R."

"I love you, Elsie."

"J.R. listen," she was crying in the dark. She pressed her fingertips, and then the palm of her hand to his face. "J.R., I'm pregnant. It's your baby. He's a boy. He's *your* boy."

"What? You are? He is? What?"

497

"Yes," she laughed, with tears and sniffles.

He laughed too. "How? How do you know it's a boy?"

"I'm his mother."

"Oh."

"J.R.," she asked him, "what will his name be?"

Spring bloomed. The story for the cops preoccupied his mind. Getting Elsie on board was no easy task. At the same time, J.R.'s capacity for foresight also required a plan for reconciliation with his father, and reinstatement to Daddio's Garage. For one thing, he would show Jack Daddio his net worth, and make it clear that this was not about money. For another, Jack Daddio was going to be a grandpa.

It was time to move back to New York, though not yet back to Erving. He needed an outpost within distance and yet far enough away to retreat.

Elsie wanted to see the D.C. cherry blossoms. He had to tell her, "No way, babe."

"Why not?"

"The entire FBI is there."

He watched her shoulders sag, watched her face drop in disappointment.

"What?" he said. "Come on, now—"

"The FBI isn't looking for us in the cherry blossoms," she told him.

"We'll come back next year. I promise. After we get everything else right. Let's get everything right this year. And in this order. Then we come back next year and visit the cherry blossoms. A family of four. That's a promise. How about that?"

## 74. Jersey

They skipped D.C., stopped in Jersey along the way for cheeseburgers and sodas at the A&W. Out in the parking lot, three locals were idling around a blue Camaro. Inside the restaurant, over the course of the meal, J.R. welcomed the nourishment, and listened to Elsie, and shared in her attention to the baby. Every baby deserved attention, no matter who the father was. This was unquestionably true.

At the same time, the three rednecks in the parking lot drew the majority of his attention. It should have been the responsibility of local law enforcement, or at least restaurant ownership, but only J.R. Daddio was on hand to keep tabs on the local riff raff.

He assigned names to them for his purpose. The one in the red T-shirt was Red. The one in the floppy brown hat was Hat. The one with the overgrown hair was Wings.

After the meal, he exited the restaurant with his family and proceeded to the Nova, which sat eagerly waiting to bear them away.

"Hey, are you married to her?" Red was asking.

"Pretty," said Hat, addressing Elsie.

J.R. kept his eye on all three of them. He unlocked the Nova's passenger door and opened it for Elsie and the baby. All the while, he studied his foes.

Hat wore a heavy metal T-shirt. Red's blonde hair was short on the sides and long in back. Wings had a mustache

499

darker than his hair but half-hearted, or quarter-hearted, in volume. J.R. closed Elsie's passenger side door. He circled the Nova's front face to its driver's side. He didn't get in or pretend to. He reached into the back seat and emerged with the Louisville Slugger.

"Whoa, we were just being friendly, friend..." it was Wings retreating.

It was Hat who got vociferous, "Oh, I'm supposed to be scared of... you know... that baseball bat?"

"No, that's not what," J.R. answered. The dialogue ended. They didn't know quite how to disperse. He would leave it for them to sort out.

He got behind the wheel and drove his family out of there. Up the road, he turned his attention to Elsie at last. "You OK?"

She didn't answer. She spoke instead to the baby in her arms, also to her own pregnant belly. Both babies, comforting both, gently, joyfully, *"He is worthy... He is worthy..."*

## 75. Blue Quarry

They settled in Blue Quarry about a half an hour upstate from Erving, there to count down the remaining weeks until J.R.'s eighteenth birthday.

On the big day, Elsie baked a cake, which was sweet and sufferable in small bites. Together they delighted in Wrigley's gleeful destruction of it, eating it, spitting it out, mashing it with her baby hands.

Recently, J.R. was allowing the moment to unfold in his imagination. The return to Daddio's Garage. To simply walk through the open bay doors like he belonged there. He could picture the array of equipment, the die grinder, the machine press and so on, also the cluttered wooden counter it had once taken years to see overtop of. He envisioned the cement floor's indelible cartography of oil stains, and the arrangement of license plates and hubcaps and tin signage and personalized wall clutter. It gave him pangs of longing to belong once again to the childhood and family and birthright he had left behind. Only the looming reconciliation interfered with this daydream.

First thing first, he changed his name. Junior Daddio was no more. J.R. Daddio was his name, and no one could tell him otherwise. Even more importantly, Jack Daddio had just lost eighteen years' worth of leverage.

On his wedding day, J.R. was intensely proud of himself and could not stop smiling. For one thing, Elsie Daddio was the most beautiful woman in the world. For another, he had rescued her and her baby Wrigley from hell on earth. Most of all, he had taken control of his own life, with nobody's help but his own. He could even be wearing a suit and tie now, and shiny cobalt blue dress shoes, standing before a priest inside a chapel just as Elsie had insisted upon, in a ceremony that included a wedding photographer and an American flag just as J.R. had insisted upon. It was a private, joyful ceremony, and he had pictures to prove it.

They had just spent a year on honeymoon, so they didn't need another one. J.R. submitted the papers to adopt Wrigley. With licenses, paperwork and legalese, many dreams became realized in rapid order. There was no longer any reason to avoid going home. He could not have been prouder of himself. And yet an edge of panic was creeping in closer.

He tried to imagine Jack Daddio coming to grips with the fact that his son was a man now, with his own name and his own family. Jack Daddio finally admitting, and finally acknowledging, and finally moving on. However, despite all the experience and leverage and legitimacy of adulthood J.R. had amassed, he had no idea what his father might say.

And now it was time to call home.

Elsie sat on the bed at his side. He held the phone in his lap. It was just a phone call. He breathed in deep, almost routinely, and dialed his home number. The line was disconnected. He tried again. Again, disconnected.

He dialed the garage, then immediately slammed the receiver down. "Elsie, babe. I need you."

"I'm sitting right here, babe."

"I need you to call the garage. Just ask normal questions. You're new to the area. You've heard good things about Daddio's Garage. You just want to know. Can you get your car inspected there? No big deal. Stuff like that. But tell me exactly what they say."

She tilted her head.

"None of those statements is a lie," he argued.

She heaved a patient, exasperated sigh. "OK," she said.

"But let's wait a half an hour," he strategized.

And then his breathing technique came in handy for more than one length of that thirty-minute span.

She called. She said she was new to the area, and that she had heard good things about Daddio's Garage. She heard they were "fair and personable." Elsie added this verbiage herself, and J.R. responded with a thumb's up. She returned the gesture.

Elsie then grew serious, gripping the phone to her ear with both hands. She released one hand to bid J.R. caution with a forefinger.

He made no sound. She listened at the receiver. She nodded.

"And you say you're the new owner, sir?" She eyeballed J.R. sympathetically. "Thank you, Mr. O'Shea."

He watched her against the sunlit window. The Stars and Stripes rippled outside from the front porch above the Nova in the gravel driveway. Elsie hung up the phone.

"He's dead," J.R. confirmed.

"Not just that," she answered.

"What else?"

"The new guy," she said. "He's black."

"What did you say, babe?"

She looked at him.

"How can you tell that from a phone call?" he asked.

She tilted her head. "Are you kidding?"

"I'm not kidding about anything. Never mind. What about my father?"

"I said what you said to say."

Elsie could get under his skin, and not just because she was quote-unquote right sometimes, but because of the fine and raw nerve ending he came to share with her daily. He didn't ask for much. Somehow, she always seemed to ask for less. It made her religiousness an annoying force of constant self-reflection. But he couldn't even complain about it. Because she hadn't even brought up God in several days.

He explained that he had to go out to the Nova. He went out and checked under the hood, found nothing amiss, then kicked the perfectly balanced tires.

The Blue Quarry apartment was the lower floor of someone's house in the woods. The upstairs tenants were rarely home, if ever. The gravel driveway was surrounded by weeds and tall grass that teemed with mayflies, dragonflies and house flies, especially at this hour. At one point an oxfly the size of a hummingbird landed on the Nova's windshield. J.R. stared at it, watched it crawl and pivot around. He wondered at how, after surviving multiple armies of Nazis, a man could still be brought to such crippling vexation by his own wife.

The front porch displayed the American flag, which was always a welcome sight. The flag also reminded him of the wedding photo in his wallet, which he removed, and held, and reflected upon now. The family of three united by a priest under a golden cross, with the Stars and Stripes as their enduring backdrop. He began to feel his temper collect itself. He put the photo away. He held his hand to the dashboard. The Nova's cockpit would always be his home.

He exited the car, crossed to the front door, went inside and told his wife, "I'm sending you on recon, babe."

"Recon? I'm pregnant with your baby."

"Pregnant is good," he said. "Actually, pregnant is too subtle. Bring Wrigley with you."

Elsie protested at first, but eventually grasped the plan. She even tweaked it, insisting upon taking a cab. She could get out of a cab and do this, she explained, but not out of J.R.'s Nova. She wasn't going to lie to Mr. O'Shea, or anybody else.

"I know, I get it," he said. He found a cab company in the yellow pages.

She set off with Wrigley in her arms. He waited. He expected his wife to be on his side, but he also knew she was going above and beyond that expectation here.

It wasn't so much fear as anticipation, to receive confirmation of what he knew. He sat in an easy chair and understood and told himself to accept it. His father was dead. Daddio's Garage had been sold to a newcomer, a black man named O'Shea. Erving's lost children Vince Baldwin, Scotty Pomeroy and Melissa Victoria had been recovered and exhumed and returned home for burial. It would not be easy.

Elsie bore all this certainty back to the Blue Quarry hideout a few hours later. Returning pregnant, weary and sweaty, she embraced J.R. as he greeted her, so that they stood cradling the newborn baby and the unborn baby and each other in the doorway. He felt the warmth of Elsie's loving arms as she whispered to him that his father was dead. Cancer. He had fought hard. But now he was with God.

J.R. was certain, but not quite ready. After all the death he had caused, or merely witnessed, this one was different. This one was frustrating. This one was unfinished business.

Elsie held him a moment longer and then handed off the baby and went for the fridge to guzzle desperately from the Tropicana carton.

She went on to confirm the rest. It was exactly as J.R. had surmised. It also occurred to him that cancer treatment was very costly.

"What about the house?" he asked.

"Babe, I didn't get that far into it."

"You did great, babe. I really appreciate it."

"I never signed up to be Jim Rockford, babe."

"No. I know."

"Are you OK?"

"Yeah. Yes. I'm just so mad."

"About your father?"

He was mad about his father, yes. "This whole person standing in your way," he tried to put it into words for her, but it was like a stack of follies he couldn't quite dignify. "And then suddenly, just like that, this person is gone, forever. It's like they never existed at all. And you're left behind. And you never got the chance to even... the chance to even..." his words trailed off, uselessly.

"J.R., pray with me. Hold my hand."

He held her hand, and closed his eyes, and listened while she went about pleading their case to no one at all.

They arranged and accepted the meeting with the Erving Police Department and Detective DeForest. Elsie held up her end of the bargain and bore false witness. As it happened, that process went even better than hoped for. Elsie played her part perfectly, and J.R. suffered very few spells.

Officer Pierce explained about the house. It was as feared. The hospital bills had consumed not only Jack Daddio's Garage but his home as well. In the aftermath, Mary Daddio, along with J.R.'s sister Janice, had moved into a walk-up along Route 94 in Florida.

"I think your mother would like to hear from you," Pierce was wearing a warm smile. Officers Powell and Shields stood by in warm agreement. Panic was creeping in closer.

He asked them to call her. He would be there in two hours. He would let them explain that he was home.

## 76. Florida

He promised Elsie he would introduce her to his mother next time. *If there is a next time,* he wanted to say.

This time, he had enough to worry about, and didn't want to worry about Elsie too. Or Wrigley for that matter. *I don't want to be surrounded by women!* he wanted to say. But it wasn't necessary, because she understood immediately, and agreed not to go. She understood him. She was the perfect woman.

He dropped them off at the apartment in Blue Quarry, then turned back toward Florida. He could strategize now. He wouldn't take any shit, that was the first thing he planned not to do. Beyond that, he was starting from scratch.

All those well laid plans of self-defense in preparation of his own acquittal before Jack Daddio and the Erving Police had not prepared him for his mother's judgment at all. When he got to confront his father, and call him a hypocrite, and when Jack Daddio would say, "What? Wait! Hypocrite? Fuck you! You little snot! Hypocrite?" and when he got to retort, "Dad, I'm right. I'm not a hypocrite..." None of that was going to happen now. His father was dead.

It was Jack Daddio who said, *How you feel about people and how you treat people are two different things. How you feel about people doesn't matter for anything. How you treat people matters more than anything else.* Those were his exact words.

506

But it wasn't Jack Daddio waiting for him now. It was his mother.

Parked in her driveway, looking up through his windshield, he reminded himself not to take any shit. This was nothing to worry about. After everything he'd been through, this was barely even an occasion to rise to.

He would not be in need of any breathing technique either. Not today. Not for this. His adrenaline was stashed away, buried. He exited the car, proceeded upstairs, and knocked.

Janice opened the door. She was crying already. She shoved him by the shoulders, then gripped him by the shirt collar with her two hands, then threw a hug around him, which he suffered through and willed to cease, while she stubbornly clung, until nothing was left, and she let him go.

His mother was waiting inside on the couch, frowning, her face swollen with tears. She was much older than he remembered.

"Are you happy now?" she asked him.

"Happy when?"

"Hey, wait a minute!" Janice interjected, standing her ground. She sniffled, wiping away her tears. "Happy? We're supposed to be happy! J.R.'s alive! And he's home!"

Mary Daddio ignored her, addressed J.R., "Your father is dead."

"And whose fault is that?"

"Oh, good man! You win! Another argument in your pocket! That's all anything is about... is how smart you are... and how stupid we are!"

"Sounds right."

"Wait! Wait a minute!" Janice raised her hands and waved her desperate piano ticklers. "We are NOT doing this!"

Mary Daddio ignored her daughter, addressed her son, "You don't even like me."

"What are you, kidding?" he answered. "All you ever did was not like me."

She shook her head. "Don't you dare," she said. "Don't you dare blame me..." but her energy dwindled down to nothing.

Janice lowered her hands.

The apartment was nicer than a lot of places, J.R. noted. The furniture was all very familiar. He listened to his mother.

507

"I gave you everything I had, Junior. Everything I could. More than I ever thought possible, sometimes. But you never cared. Never cared about me at all."

"Don't give me that."

"Did you know?" she said. "Did you know that it was only after you left. Only then that I finally saw?" she paused and sniffled, wiping her nose.

*Saw what?* he waited, let her gather herself.

"Before you left," she continued, "it hurt my heart so much all the time. How much you didn't care. I was so sad. So sad that I lost you. So sad that I failed you. So sad all the time. But then it freed my heart so much to be rid of you. That's something I know that you'll never know, no matter how smart you think you are."

"She loves you," Janice assured him.

He shot his sister a glare. "What are you, her interpreter?"

"Maybe I am." She had her hands on her hips.

Janice thought she was so right about everything. But she had no idea. J.R. looked around the apartment again, all the transplanted furniture that could fit. "There's no piano," he noted, and his laughter came easily.

"Look how cruel you are to your sister, even though she's still so patient with you."

Janice jabbed her finger into his face. "I'M GONNA BE THE BEST PIANO PLAYER WHO EVER LIVED!"

He recoiled.

"YOU'RE JUST GONNA BE AN ANGRY BOY WHO LEFT HIS FAMILY! YOU COULD HAVE BEEN SO COOL!"

With that, she fled the apartment, slamming the door and pounding down the staircase.

"I guess she's not so patient after all," he noted.

"J.R., what do you want?"

"I don't want anything. I want you to know I'm home. Isn't that something?"

"I was sure you were dead."

"You were happy I was dead."

"Do I look happy?"

"No. Come on. Do I have to say it? You're not happy. That's because I'm not dead."

He didn't want to say it, but he had completely won this argument. For her part, his mother resigned, sighed and frowned. She stared at her hand where it lay on the armrest of the couch that occupied this new layout comfortably, with more window light than before, here in this upper story.

"I want you to know that I'm home," he said. "I want you to meet my wife, Elsie. And my baby girl, Wrigley."

"Wrigley?"

"Wrigley. Like Wrigley Field in Chicago. Elsie, my wife, she's a Cubs fan."

"I have a granddaughter?" her eyes welled with tears. J.R. lowered his head. He couldn't bear to watch. After hardening herself so admirably for her son's return, she was coming apart after all, all for Steeplejack's fourteenth baby.

*I'm the one who's angry,* he reminded himself. *Not her. It's me.*

But the voice in his head had no breath. His skin was cold. His stomach sank. The dread he felt was both familiar and new, a shape coming into focus. He was raising Wrigley as his own, so now Wrigley had a grandmother.

"Yes, I want to meet her," Mary Daddio was saying. He watched his mother manage a smile. "I want to meet my granddaughter," she said.

He could only agree. He said, "I'll bring her and Elsie over tomorrow."

"Good," she sniffled.

*I have to get out of here,* he told himself.

"Do you even want to know what happened?" she asked him.

He knew not to succumb to waves of fear, manipulation, or guilt.

She sniffled and cleared her throat, ready to confront him.

His panic surged. He spoke at last. "He died of cancer... A man named O'Shea bought the garage... Obviously, the house got sold."

*...to pay the medical expenses,* he couldn't say the last part.

She might have waited a full minute. Finally, she said, "Sounds like you know everything."

"I know all I need to know."

"Oh yeah? What does that mean?"

"You'll see."

"Oh, there's an encore? I can hardly wait."

"You won't have to wait."

"J.R.?" she said.

509

"Yes, what?" he looked at her.

"Just tell me. Just look me in the eyes and tell me you didn't kill those kids."

*"Kids?!"* It startled him. *What kids?* he wanted to say. He was in no way responsible for what happened to Bella Shue, or little Wallace, or even Virginia Drummond, who was probably alive and well. In any case, his mother couldn't possibly know about any of them.

"Your friends," she answered him.

"Oh, well..." he said, and he recalibrated. She meant Scotty and Melissa and Vince Baldwin. She was so old, she thought of them as kids.

"They're not kids," he twisted up his face.

"Not anymore," she said.

He didn't have to stand here. He could leave at any time.

"Look me in the eyes," she said.

He had killed only one of them. And Vince Baldwin wasn't a friend at all. Much less a kid. He looked her in the eyes.

At last he was outside, down the stairway, climbing into the Nova.

From the driveway, he could see the neon sign along Route 94. ANGELICO'S.

He wouldn't go back to Blue Quarry just yet.

Inside the restaurant, the jukebox was loud. He knew this song from way back. "Peach Tree Fiddler," or whatever it was called. A fiddle duel between the devil and a musical rival. The so-called devil doesn't even try to win. Instead, he lets his band do all the heavy lifting, and then lets the other guy win by simply trying. A fraudulent song, back then and now too. J.R. was sick of everybody's bullshit.

He walked up to the counter and ordered two slices and a Coke.

"We don't have *Coke*. We have *R.C.*"

"OK, *7-Up*. And a glass of water."

They gave him the glass of water while he waited.

He drank from it. The water had sand in it. It came back to him now, what Scotty Pomeroy used to say about the water at Angelico's, that it had sand in it. He had argued with Scotty that it was silt, and Scotty had argued that it was beach water, full of coral and seashells. The memory brought a laugh out of him, internal and unexpressed, with no reason to laugh out loud, or even crack a smile in public.

510

"Can I get a glass of water without sand in it?" he asked.

"We don't carry bottled water, sir. But here's your *7-Up*."

"All right," he muttered, pushing aside the waterglass. He peered into the *7-Up* before drinking it.

If he had gone to Scotty and Melissa first. At the Saw Mill, after the jeep wreck, after plunging down the hill on foot, bleeding from a bullet wound. Instead of going for the tape, if he had gone for his friends. How it might all be different. If only he had trusted them. If only that tape had never been made.

The pizza was fine. On the way out, he ran into Pete Dawson, who was leaving the adjacent liquor store with a woman on one elbow and a bottle in the other elbow's crook.

"Pete Dawson?"

Pete looked at him. "What the...? J.R.? Wow! I can't believe my eyes!"

Pete's girlfriend stood curious and eager by his side. Pete looked at her, then back at J.R. "I'm sorry, J.R.," he lowered his gaze. "I'm home for the weekend from college, man. Last I heard, you were..." he turned to his girlfriend, turned back to J.R. "I'm sorry, man. First thing's first. J.R. Daddio, this is Rosalie. Rosalie, this is J.R. Daddio."

"Oh, my God, J.R. Daddio, it is so nice to meet you!" Rosalie was enthusiastic, extending her hand. He took it cordially, "Nice to meet you, Rosalie."

"J.R., I'm so happy to see you, man," Pete Dawson said. "I'm just... I'm so sorry I'm not more current on current events. Your father..."

"Pete, you are a sight for sore eyes, if I can be honest."

"You are too, man. You too. You should come over."

"To your basement?"

"Yes, I mean, I guess... Where are you staying?"

"Just come over," Rosalie interjected.

"I'm staying in Blue Quarry. I'm married. I have a kid, and another one on the way."

"Married! Wife! Kids! Wow! Congrats! Yes, everyone is welcome! We must hang out in my parents' basement, just like the old days. We'll put on music and drink wine. My mom will probably be happy to see you, too, J.R."

511

## 77. Pete Dawson's Basement Revisited

They brought Wrigley and a bottle of wine. Mr. and Mrs. Dawson were highballing it in the TV room. Astonished at J.R.'s return, they insisted that the three of them stay for the night. They also conveyed that they were so sorry about J.R.'s father. He appreciated the invitation, and accepted it, though he wasn't so sure about staying. He would make up his mind when the time came. It was a brief and awkward reception, and then Pete Dawson led the way through the house toward the back hallway.

Downstairs in the basement, Pete lit a candle and put on a record. Rosalie opened the first bottle of wine and poured. J.R. had a few sips from his glass, but he didn't care for wine. The music was exceptionally awful. He kept tilting his head away from the speakers. Elsie had the baby nestled in one arm, as she sipped from her wine glass politely. They had agreed beforehand she would go easy on it, with the second baby in the oven.

Earlier, at Angelico's, Pete had sounded so excited about J.R.'s wife and family. Now, all he wanted to talk about was death and tragedy. And his girlfriend Rosalie kept saying things like, "I just can't believe all you've been through," and shaking her head and staring.

It was only natural that the conversation should center around J.R.'s father, and his house, and his garage, not to mention Scotty Pomeroy, and Melissa Victoria, and Vince

Baldwin. But he got sick of hearing it, and finally he said, "You know what? This is also how I met my wife, Elsie, and why I have a family now."

"Oh," Pete agreed immediately to this perspective, "that's totally so true."

"That *is* true," Rosalie tilted her head and smiled at Elsie and the baby.

Elsie began to tell them the story about the Ryne Sandberg baseball card. J.R. excused himself to go to the bathroom.

The upstairs hallway was dark, but he knew it, remembered it.

When he was done in the bathroom, he flipped off the light and turned toward the basement. Mrs. Dawson intercepted him, smelling of booze, grabbing him by the collar and pushing him into the wall.

"Whoa!" he said.

Her face was in his face, breathing on him. *"You better not get my son killed, so help me God..."*

*"Mrs. Dawson!"* he whispered.

She drew in closer, smelling him, swooning from it, her nostrils twitching. "Say, J.R.," she asked, "can you recommend a good mechanic?"

Many different answers came to mind simultaneously, all of which he abandoned, dismissed, suppressed. His mouth briefly opened and closed, wordless. Mrs. Dawson had a kind of raspy and rogue assertiveness, and friendliness, those two things combined, so that suddenly he couldn't feel his feet. She was so warm, and so close. He was paralyzed with fear. Her face tilted up at him. Her voice was smart, "You remember my Jetta?"

"Yes..."

She pressed herself against his erection, which wasn't paralyzed at all. He could hear the drunken husband laughing in the TV room. "Can I bring it to you?" she pouted. Two disasters were happening at the same time. He wanted to grab her by the hips so badly it seemed impossible not to. "Mrs. Dawson," he managed to say. "I'm a family man..."

She shrugged, sighed, withdrew from him, released his shirt collar from her clutches, pressed those same fingertips into his cotton folds to smooth them. If she was disappointed, she wasn't the least bit embarrassed. "Sure thing, Daddio." At last, she left him there.

*I don't know anything,* he panicked. But it wasn't true. He knew everything, or more than most.

He waited in the dark hallway, willing his temperature to drop, his blood to abate, his thoughts to clear. He caught his breath at some point too, without remembering it. He couldn't go downstairs just yet. He waited some more.

Back in the basement, they had opened the second bottle of wine. Pete Dawson's girlfriend Rosalie was good looking, but Elsie was better looking. J.R. concluded this immediately upon returning to their company.

They got to talking about Pete's experience at college, and Rosalie's, but J.R. couldn't concentrate on the words they were saying. He felt bad about it, because Pete Dawson was a perfectly nice guy, and there was no cause to offend him. Or Rosalie either, for that matter. He decided to blame the music.

"This music is really distracting."

"What?" Pete raised an eyebrow. "What, really? This is The Grateful Dead, my man."

"The who what? I don't like heavy metal."

Pete looked at him curiously, pointed at the record player. "J.R., this isn't heavy metal."

"No, I know. It's like... a country band submerged underwater."

Rosalie and Elsie burst out laughing. Even baby Wrigley chuckled along.

"Come on, man," Pete Dawson pleaded.

"Oh my God, so funny, right?" Rosalie commented.

J.R. continued, jabbed his thumb at the record player, "Just tell me one thing. Is that record playing at the right speed?"

They all agreed on Springsteen. J.R. hated Bruce Springsteen, but at least Bruce Springsteen wasn't all that other stuff. At least it made sense.

Diagonal heat pipes bisected the basement's low ceiling. The lone candle glowed and flickered on the familiar end table repurposed from a cable spool. Rosalie, who was from Palo Alto and didn't know anyone in Erving other than Pete Dawson, insisted upon a remembrance of lost friends. Elsie voiced ready approval, and then went further, submitting that they should take a moment to pray. They all agreed. Even baby Wrigley was with them.

The prayer ended, and then they went about their candlelit conversation, with Bruce Springsteen moaning and groaning unflagging from the JBLs, until the song was finally fading out.

The basement's handmade bookshelves offered the very same stash of paperback fiction from two years prior. The oriental rugs remained unchanged from that same lifetime ago. The couch, with its same tie-dye slipcover, was a foldout, theirs for the night. Elsie settled into napping with Wrigley in her lap. Finally, Pete Dawson got around to saying it, trying not to grimace so hard that he grimaced all the more so, "So, J.R., tell us about the *Nazis?*"

"You must have been freaking out," Rosalie added, with intense and sympathetic interest.

J.R. had endured more than enough sips of wine.

"I understand," he said, "that you want to know about the Nazis. But please try to understand. Elsie has already shown enough courage. Please don't ask her to re-live it."

"Oh, I completely understand," they stumbled all over each other apologizing.

Elsie was roused awake.

"Go to sleep, babe. I've got her. I'm done drinking for the night."

"J.R., I'm dozing off. But keep talking. I'm paying attention."

He took the baby and cradled her. Wrigley complained briefly, then relaxed. With everyone else getting sloppy, including the so-called Mom upstairs, someone would have to stay sober. J.R. was perfectly suited for the role.

Rosalie turned to Pete, "Oh my God, Pete. Next time I'm stressing out about... anything... please remind me that I haven't been abducted by *Nazis*. I mean, at least not yet. Right? I mean, talk about putting things in perspective."

"I will definitely remind you," Pete promised his girlfriend.

The room grew quiet. The candlelight flickered. Bruce Springsteen advanced a new rock 'n roll narrative. The conversation grew low key and intense.

"What about the garage, J.R.?"

"What about it?"

"Are you going to go back to it?"

515

Rosalie elbowed him, "Pete, he just found out his father's dead."

Pete corrected himself, "J.R., I'm so sorry about your dad."

"I know it, Pete. It's OK. You said so before."

"So what about the garage?"

"Well..." a long moment followed in the flickering candlelight. "I'm not the current owner of the garage."

"And who owns it again? I'm sorry, J.R."

"A man named O'Shea."

"Reminds me of a painting I saw in Little Rock," Elsie spoke up suddenly.

J.R. turned to his wife. "Baby, *please!*"

"Please what?" she said. Her eyes were closed, but in her wine induced delirium she smiled. "Women bring things to life with their words," she told them. "Men kill things with their silence."

They sat there stunned. Elsie seemed to drift back to sleep.

J.R. said, "That's getting carried away, I think."

"No, I like it," Rosalie said. "She's great, J.R."

"I think she's great too," Pete Dawson added.

J.R. looked at his wife, the face he could never fall out of love with in a million years, no matter what. "She certainly is that," he answered. "She certainly is great."

*What if it is practical?* He could pose the question right now if he wanted to. Instead, he held it close for the zillionth time.

He and Elsie and baby Wrigley spent the night on the pullout couch. A nightlight remained aglow upstairs. Its faint arc sliced down the staircase.

"Did you think she was pretty?" Elsie asked him.

"No way," he said. "You're pretty."

He tried to have sex with her, but they hadn't presumed to bring the crib, and with the Moses Basket carefully set beside them on the foldout couch, Elsie just couldn't do it. For his own part, he couldn't either.

He lay awake by the light from upstairs, bitterly self-amused that he would never, ever, have sex in Pete Dawson's basement, no matter who it was or wasn't with, not even his own wife.

In time, he found himself inside one of those dreams he'd been having, with characters from his past, some confirmed dead, others presumably alive, the likes of Mr. Boaz and Mr.

Adams, and Gordie from Gordie's garage in Richmond, but inevitably dead Nazis too, like Snapper and Sandra Pride and Crosby Shue. Also dead normal people like Tyto, whose blank, begoggled face was the sincerest expression of goodwill J.R. could sense from any spirit among them, even as they kept appearing, or reappearing, as it came to feel like a march of sorts, a parade, a committed unspooling of memories, a continuum drawn from the very Erving, New York basement he now occupied, the likes of Audrey Buckhorn, Carolyn D'Amico, Nicole Van Buren, and Melissa Victoria, but also reaching back to high school tormenters such as Curt Decker and Jimmy Gates, and certainly Vince Baldwin. Also Mrs. Dawson, then and now. Also friends like Scotty Pomeroy, and children, adventuresome and baffled, like Bella Shue and little Wallace. Also his own piano playing sister Janice. And his mother Mary, of course. And his father Jack Daddio. Buddy too. Mike Aaron from Aaron Law. The Erving cops, Officers Blaine Shields and Nick Pierce and all the others in uniform. Agent Epsom and Agent Green. Also customers like Mr. Carter's wife, and Mrs. Harrison, and Mrs. Ichiharo. Also customers like Denny Lowe and Mr. Sacks. Also the young couple that ventured out into the falls in Louisville. Also the two black kids from the mall in Cincinnati. Dr. Arquimedes Arthur of Marietta. And Butler, the Quaker and/or Amish sentry. Also Juniper-Cloud. Also Boyd the bigot. Also Rudolph and Aesop, the Van Wert twins. Also Eric August. The ghosts of Shanahan, Harding, and Partridge. Cash Clarick, and his cohorts from town, the deli owner and the car thieving mechanic. Their pair of doomed Rottweilers. The Old Man, still out there somewhere. Glenn Disteek, dead. de Ram, dead. Fat Ransom, dead. And so on, joining in the parade. Steeplejack. Duke Drummond. Lazy Farrah. Even the lonesome motorcyclist Harold Mariner, whom J.R. had never met, nor laid eyes upon, but somehow knew by sight from Cash Clarick's worshipsome folk tales. Likewise Curtis Lemonhall, mysterious and mythical. Co-mingling with the memories of Lovejoy, Skinner, Brock Fowler, Buchanan, Trauer, Grossmark, Chuck Zorn, Grant Archer and Rose Archer. They all arrived advancing in a strange dream logic, which J.R. helplessly struggled to cling to after he woke up and remembered taking them in groups on cab rides through Manhattan, sometimes driving, but increasingly a passenger in the back seat, as gradually a faceless stranger took the wheel. Along for the ride, Scotty, Melissa, Vince Baldwin and Tyto. Duke Drummond, and many others stole moments in time, even as a dance routine broke out, all of them gathered in lockstep. Not goose stepping like Nazis. Not high stepping like showgirls. Merely dancing freely in the streets, on top of idling taxis and other vehicles at random New York City intersections, obligatory steam rising from crucial gutters, like some kind of Broadway musical, except there was no soundtrack, no orchestra, no music playing. Only the stomping of feet.

Awake now, he found himself reflecting in the dark upon his life. Less a timeline of events, more a choreography of concepts. It was the kind of thing he would never get to discuss with his father. He was on his own now. He wanted back into the dream somehow, but it was over. In those small, pre-dawn hours he decided upon its meaning. He had to get control over all the people that occupied his life. All of them.

It seemed to him he had done just that so far. He had left home a boy and returned a man. His adversaries had fallen before him, with the sole exception of Edward, the Old Man, who might be out there somewhere, or might not, anymore.

In fact, his only current adversary, who countermanded him regularly, was his own wife.

Except that now he would have his mother to answer to. Not to mention Janice the pianist. Not to mention, possibly, suddenly, and inexplicably, Mrs. Dawson, although hopefully not, for instance if she was a black-out drunk who forgot hallway incidents in their entirety.

They all had one thing in common, J.R. did not fail to recognize it. His breathing was calm. He had, in fact, conquered his own life, at age eighteen. All except for the women. Once he got the women under control, there was no obstacle in sight.

Elsie stirred beside him.

He had promised her a garage.

As sunlight dawned through the basement window, he woke her up as gently as possible, whispering, *"Let's get out of here, babe. Before they ask us to stay for breakfast."*

## 78. Malta Street

They decided to check out the deli in the brand-new strip mall on Malta Street. Elsie went inside to order breakfast while J.R. idled on the hood of the car. He had Wrigley set beside him, dozing under the canopy of her bassinet. In terms of parental lingo, J.R. preferred *bassinet* to *carry cot,* while his wife preferred to call the accessory a *Moses Basket.*

Although the property across the street was still the same brickface storefront and macadam lot where J.R. had spent his youth and cut his teeth, the new signage O'SHEA'S GAR-AGE gave the intimately familiar setting a new alien quality. Otherwise, for all appearances, it was business as usual. The side lot was packed with cars, and a trio of mechanics was busy in the open bays, with Buddy notably absent. Meanwhile, the formerly neighboring deli, which J.R. used to disparage as a "kiosk," had been repurposed into an actual kiosk for the Erving Chamber of Commerce. Two years' time had changed Malta Street completely, and the new strip mall promised only more prosperity.

Growing up, he had seen it coming, this kind of growth, while his father never had such foresight, such vision. The arguments this engendered and the contempt it bred, those conflicts would remain unresolved forever now. It was too late anymore, to prove Jack Daddio right or wrong. And yet the garage was still out there, still a possibility. *What if it is practical?* the question nagged at him, and he would pose it

519

now, today, finally, eagerly, if only his father were alive to receive it.

In terms of resentment, entitlement, or any kind of actual racial animus, he didn't care that O'Shea was black. It's just that the opportunity was so perfectly tailored to the training he had received. The Posse Serpens. The Posse Umbellus. Cash Clarick. Duke Drummond. Steeplejack. Grossmark. The Van Wert twins, maybe those two most of all. They had taught him all he needed to know. How to take back what he had squandered.

Elsie returned with warm egg sandwiches from the deli. He unwrapped his sandwich and took a bite.

"So what's your plan?" she asked, seating herself beside him on the hood of the car.

"What?" he said with his mouth full.

She looked down and began unwrapping her own breakfast sandwich. "What's your plan?" she repeated.

He pointed around in a vague rectangle. "This strip mall," he said, still chewing, "it only raises the value."

She sagged her shoulders, then raised her eyes, then raised her entire face heavenward, praying for strength.

"Look at that," J.R. pointed across the street. "They actually situated the Chamber of Commerce right next to the place."

"You're actually thinking of paying him off?"

"Paying him off?" he protested her choice of words, even though he knew what she meant. He watched as she gazed down at the egg sandwich in her lap. "Buying it back," he corrected her. "That's what I would call it."

"J.R.," she said, "the man just bought the place. Why on earth would he sell it back?"

"Exactly," he said. "That's why it's not a good plan."

At last, without looking up, Elsie bit into her own egg sandwich. Now she and J.R. chewed together in silence. When baby Wrigley squawked, they turned to gaze lovingly at the child and then back at each other in some shared melancholy. Then back to their messy breakfast sandwiches.

Elsie said, "Remember that black reporter? What was his name? Lemonhall."

J.R. shook his head gently. "Elsie—"

"I mean, come on, man. Didn't you learn anything there?"

"Yes," he let out a short burst of laughter.

"What's so funny?"

"Did I learn anything? Are you kidding me? How about murder? How about armed robbery? How about blackmail, pornography, brainwashing—"

"J.R.—"

"Racism, libel, character assassination—"

"Don't mess with me—"

"And croquet."

"Come on, Daddio," she began pointing her finger in small jabbing gestures. "I've made phone calls. I've done pregnant recon. I've done a lot for us. It's time for you to be a man."

He turned his face away.

His egg sandwich was runny. So was hers. He maintained his. She threw hers against the deli's glass door front. "THIS THING'S FUCKING DISGUSTING!"

The doors were streaked with egg yolk. The workers inside stared frightfully at the remains of the product they had made, sold, and had flung back at them. Elsie's profanity echoed in the stillness of the early hour. Her transgression was followed by a demonstration of her cooling down.

He said nothing. His wife was a very different person when not imprisoned in a Nazi watchtower.

He finished off his egg sandwich. It was gross, but it was food.

"I threw mine back," she told him.

"I watched you do that. Heard it, too."

"You want to go in there and apologize for your wife's behavior?"

"You know," he said, "you're the best looking woman in the world."

"Go ahead," she said. "Go in there and apologize."

"You know I love you, Elsie. No matter what."

"I know a lot more than that."

With his paper napkin he wiped the grease and salt from his lips.

She knew a lot, mostly first-hand, but some gossip too. Even so, there was plenty she didn't know. Plenty he hadn't told her. Perhaps, someday, if she would trust him that much, he would trust her that much in return. Otherwise, he would just as easily bury those secrets forever.

Trust and love. Two different things. His trust was bruised, but his love was unbroken. He loved Elsie more than anything. Also liked her, more than anyone. Also needed her, the sum of proverbially weaker parts. Also, most days, he admired her.

He loved Wrigley, too. And his own unborn baby growing in Elsie's belly. He loved them all, his family. Just as she did, he knew. He could feel that this was how to get through to her. To appeal to this part of her, the best part. The nurse who loved children and prayed to God. Appeal to her heart.

"I remember Doctor Arquimedes Arthur," he said at last.

"Who? What? That black doctor?"

"Who delivered our baby girl. While you were begging me to do it instead. To drive us out into a hurricane. And bring our daughter into this world under a tree in the rain..."

He watched his wife's exquisitely symmetrical face go from hot to boiling mad. "He was completely rude to you!"

"I'm just reminding you of the end result, babe," he pointed over at Wrigley's healthy and blissful presence.

"That's not fair!" she countered. "You're not fighting fair!"

"Elsie, I'm not fighting at all."

"Like hell, you're not!"

"I never even wanted that garage in the first place," he confessed.

She went silent and stared at him. He watched her jawline twitch. A small shuddering negation of credulity. She pointed between herself and the baby. "You promised me!" she cried. "You promised us!"

"It's just—"

"J.R., it's your *birthright!* That's what you always *told* us!"

"Yeah, but I lost it, babe."

"You lost it?"

"Before I even met you."

She turned to conceal her face behind her golden drapery of hair. "So, it's you," she muttered. "You're the false witness."

"What?"

She could make it feel so physical. Like a punch to the stomach.

"To think, all this time," she reminded him, "I was worried it would be me."

A one-two combo. Some portion of his spirit reeled, winded, in pain, while his presence held fast atop the hood of the Nova.

"I'm no false witness," he answered.

Elsie spat her plosive laughter.

J.R. swallowed his anger and let the heat between them dissipate.

No one came out to clean up her sandwich. Likely, the deli staff was waiting for her to leave. Meanwhile, a customer approached from the parking lot and paused briefly outside the door to consider the mess that lay smattered there.

J.R. cast his attention across the street where they were rotating cars in the parking lot, including a couple of familiar favorites. Observing the routine, it occurred to him that he had always enjoyed the task of stacking cars, given his raw aptitude for spatial relations.

"We've got money," he said.

"I know that."

"And we can go wherever we want. That's the beauty of it, Mrs. Daddio. We live in a free country. The best country in the world. So why would I stick around Erving just to pick a fight with a stranger?"

She leveled her finger across the street. "Because he stole your father's garage!"

"Elsie, he didn't steal it. He bought it. Come on now, babe. Who's the false witness?"

"Oh, nice!"

"I swear I will show you," he pledged. "This whole thing is no big deal. I mean the whole thing. Come on. Let's just. Can we just get out of here?"

"I guess you must hate me too—" her voice broke.

He shook his head in pity. "Disapproval, my darling. It's not the same thing as hate."

"Oh, what a relief. Disapproval."

"Come on now, babe."

"When did you get so mean-hearted?"

"I don't disapprove of *you*, Elsie, baby doll. Matter of fact, I approve of you with all I've got. I just disapprove of this one particular thing you're saying."

She heaved a sigh and held it.

"It's tricky to put into words sometimes," he explained.

"Oh, and for me it isn't?"

The balancing act it required. The heart and soul and mind and spirit. Not to mention the flesh. He hoped to explain it someday, if only to his wife and no one else.

Meanwhile, he couldn't even explain it to himself. Not quite. Not today. Not yet.

"It's not about money," he tried anyway, if only for his own sake. "It can't be about money."

"What are you talking about?"

"I'm talking about the garage."

"I didn't say *money,*" she countered. "I said *birthright.* You're trying to shame me—"

He raised his index finger. "No, I'm not. This isn't about you. I'm talking about something else."

"Why am I so insulted, then?"

"I don't know. Just hear me out. And then I'll hear you out. I promise."

"OK, fine." She didn't mean it.

"To be good," he explained. "And to do good. You know. Just. Not that it's easy. But Elsie, by the way, you know more about it than I do. Because I learned it from you. Just from watching you. That compassion. That peace. And that calm. Like when I see you tending to a wounded guy. Or when I see you with the baby. The way you know what's right. The way you keep that solace, and that respect, for the beauty and truth of what's right. To do that. For people. For all people. You're the one who taught me how good it is to be good."

"That is an awful lot of butter, hun."

"What? No, wait. Hear me out. What I'm saying is. When it becomes about money. About making money, yes, but also about not losing money. Like for instance to keep from losing customers at your father's garage. That's not goodness. It's just some... some pantomime of goodness. It's just quote-unquote good behavior. I mean that's what they give you time off in prison for, right? Good behavior. That's not the same thing as goodness. It's just an illusion. A veil. It will disappear at any time."

"That's exactly right."

"Because what if it is practical? What if it does pay?"

"Well it doesn't, though, does it? It burns to the ground. And then their eternal souls burn in hell forever."

"Well... yes... that's true... but actually... it does pay... prior to the burning in hell. What I'm saying is... I think maybe I'm starting to get it. I mean, you? You have this unflagging faith in God. And me? All this time, I keep arguing against God. But

524

maybe it's just goodness all along. Maybe it's just Right-versus-Wrong. Maybe. Maybe I do believe after all."

"Wait a minute," she stopped him. "What is this? Are you bargaining with me? Since when do *you* believe in God?"

"What? No, not bargaining. I'm being serious. Come on, now, Elsie. We escaped from that place. We burned it to the ground. It's over now. That kind of paranoia."

"I know that."

"Plus, they were wrong. They were wrong about everything."

"Mostly. But come on. This is real life."

"You remember that Old Man?" he asked her. "Something he said to me once."

He raised his open face to receive the expansive morning sky.

"He was talking about the whole entire Human Race. He was saying how we're not nice. How it's not in our nature to be nice. How we're only authentic and virtuous and effective when we're vicious and cruel and cunning and lethal. At least in terms of survival as human beings is concerned. Survival of the fittest."

Elsie gathered herself, sniffling, preparing to dismount the car.

"But he was wrong," J.R. continued. "Or half-wrong at best. That Old Man. In terms of human history. Take the United States as a perfect example. There's more bloodshed and human bondage and corruption and evil than you can ever count. But that's not *how* we survived. It's *what* we survived. How we survived was all the tact and courage and diplomacy and knowledge and stuff like that. You name it. The good stuff. The benevolence. The good will. The charity. The generosity. The self-sacrifice. The open mindedness. The truth. The recorded history..." he trailed off, briefly, lost in thought, adding, "Preservation of knowledge, that's important, too."

Elsie eased her sneakered feet to the pavement and stood, squaring herself to face him. *"That's* the history of the United States?" she raised a skeptical eyebrow.

"It's the history of the *goodness,*" he explained. "We're here for the *goodness,* too. Am I right? Maybe most of all, the goodness."

She flung her empty hands up and dropped them, slapped her own thighs. "Swell," she said.

"We're in a good position," he ventured a smile.

Her demeanor was that of a losing chess player more so than a changed mind. Peacefully and gracefully but without mirth she plucked up baby Wrigley from her hood-top Moses Basket and proceeded to gently and carefully fasten the miraculous creature into the Nova's backseat safety harness. J.R. utilized this same interval to stow the empty bassinet in the trunk.

"We have to stop at my mother's before we go," he was climbing in behind the wheel, yanking the door shut. "I should tell her, this time, that I'm leaving. But I also want her to meet you. Also, Wrigley too."

"Oh, OK," Elsie eased herself into the passenger seat and pulled the door closed.

"Also, my sister Janice," he added. "I probably owe her an apology too."

"What did your mother say?" Elsie locked her door and fastened her seat belt. "About the garage?"

He shrugged, keyed the ignition. "She told me she doesn't want an encore."

"Oh, that's nice," she folded her arms and gazed out the front windshield.

"Nice is good for a change."

"And what about your wife, Daddio? What if your wife wants an encore?"

"That was it, babe. That was the encore."

THE END

Made in the USA
Middletown, DE
28 November 2021